James Bickford

James Bickford

An Autobiography of Christian Labour

James Bickford

James Bickford
An Autobiography of Christian Labour

ISBN/EAN: 9783337117993

Printed in Europe, USA, Canada, Australia, Japan

Cover: Foto ©Raphael Reischuk / pixelio.de

More available books at www.**hansebooks.com**

OF

Christian Labour

IN THE

WEST INDIES, DEMERARA, VICTORIA, NEW SOUTH WALES, AND SOUTH AUSTRALIA.

1838—1888.

"*In Journeyings often:*" "*In Perils of the Sea:*" "*In Deaths oft.*"

LONDON:

CHARLES H. KELLY, 2, Castle St., City Road, E.C.,

AND 66, PATERNOSTER ROW, E.C.

SOLD IN ADELAIDE, MELBOURNE, SYDNEY, BRISBANE, PERTH, AUCKLAND, AND HOBART.

1890.

Printed by Hazell, Watson, & Viney, Ld., London and Aylesbury.

PREFACE.

IN the year 1878, being then in London, and having leisure for so doing, I prepared a work, entitled : " Christian Work in Australasia," as a help to those of my fellow-countrymen who were anxious to try their fortunes in the Southern World. But no sooner was it in circulation, than I heard of a feeling of disappointment among many valued friends, because there was so little of the personal narrative in the publication. I could only reply that my object was not so restricted; but that a statement of a more comprehensive kind was specially intended, touching the evangelistic work of all Churches of Christ in Australia and Polynesia. It was, indeed, little more than a 'Handbook ;' but, judging from the favourable notices it received in the English Press, and the grateful references made to the work by hundreds of correspondents, I think I may conclude that my exact purpose was fairly accomplished. But I did resolve that, at some advanced period of my life, I would, if I were able, prepare an autobiographical sketch of my life-work ; and now, after nearly two years of application, I am able to announce the completion of my attempt. I have made no effort at the romantic in my description of men and things ; but have striven to give as simple a narrative as the knowledge of my mother tongue has enabled me to write. I cannot but regard it as a special mercy of God's Providence, that, on the very day that I reach my seventy-fourth year, I put in the last sentence of my tale. I may, in all candour, ask the lenient consideration of those who may honour me with notices of this, my latest—yea, probably, my last—effort of the kind, to remember that my public life has not been spent in 'learned leisure,' but in the active pursuits of the Methodist Itinerancy; and in lands, where new and startling problems of a social, political, and ecclesiastical nature have had to be faced by those who inherited the necessary instinct for so doing. Among that number of earnest and far-seeing men, not by my own choice, but by an 'election of grace,' my lot has been cast.

CONTENTS.

———◆———

INTRODUCTION.

THE subject of this sketch, James Bickford, came from an ancient yeoman stock in the South Hams of Devon. John Bickford, his father, for many years was tenant of the Venerable Archdeacon Froude, of Dartington, near Totnes, and farmed under him Edmeston Barton (Sax. Bere-ton—Barleytown), in the parish of Modbury. His grandfather, also John Bickford, farmed Rake, near Loddiswell, Devon.

Behind the homestead rose a high precipitous, overhanging rock, visible for miles distant. This notable rock served as a rendezvous for the peasant classes amidst the troubles arising from scarcity of provisions, want of employment, and a starvation wage. I remember hearing my father speak of one of those gatherings when he was a young man, from which several hundreds of day labourers marched throughout the neighbouring parishes to lay their grievances before the 'Squires,' and to tell those of the farmers, who were using threshing-machines for removing the corn from the ear instead of the flail, that if such operations were continued, both machines and buildings would be fired. Unfortunate labourers! With the exception of the harvest season, which lasted only for a month, when the men would feed at the farmers' tables, their fare was scant indeed. Barley-bread and water for breakfast; barley-bread and cider for dinner; and potatoes, with a sprinkle of salt, and a little fat, for the evening meal; who can wonder at peasant combinations for securing a just wage and a right to live, not simply to exist?

It is true there was the poorhouse in each parish for the peasant aged couple when they could no longer work, and a pauper's grave ready open for their worn-out bodies, provided out of parish rates. But this was not all. The vicar, or his curate, would appear on the scene, and, in solemn accents, but with a grim appropriateness, read a prayer in which he would say: 'We give Thee hearty

1

thanks, for that it hath pleased Thee to deliver this our brother out of the miseries of this sinful world.' Yes: too true; for it would be better to be dead than alive, for there would be rest in the grave from the hard lot of unrequited toil, and from the gnawing pains of hunger. And as for the soul, it may be hoped, in all charity and faith, that a 'RIGHTEOUS GOD' would make some reimbursement to the chafed spirit in the contentment and peacefulness of the future state for the unmerited disabilities the peasant classes a hundred years ago endured.

I return from this digression. On the maternal side I had much to be thankful for. My mother's maiden name was Whiteway, and was born, I believe, in the parish of Harburtonford. The Whiteways were a family of repute in the parish. This may be gathered from the sympathy of the clergyman, who took a great interest in my mother as an orphan, and saw to her education. As an evidence of my mother's sense of gratitude, I have heard her refer to the clergyman's kindnesses more than eighty years after their occurrence.

My grandfather Whiteway had a competency, and lived an easy, self-satisfied life. My mother used to speak of her father having a family 'coat-of-arms,' which was framed and suspended from the wall in his bedroom. She remembered but little of her mother, who was delicate in health, and died when she was about four years of age. My uncle, John Whiteway, was a fine, gentlemanly man, and died in Plymouth about fifty years ago. But there were two other uncles, George and Thomas, and two aunts, Lowman and Hine, all of whom are dead.

My grandmother's maiden name, on my father's side, was Gill, of Totnes. The only remembrance I have of her is, that my father took me to see her, when she had come to live with my uncle, James Bickford,—at that time a bachelor-farmer at Lincombe. I have a distinct recollection of her fine person. She was, although over eighty years of age, tall, erect, and well-proportioned; the expression of her countenance was benevolent; she spoke in the lower tones of voice, characteristic of her refined nature; and her whole demeanour was that of the higher grade of yeoman life. At the time of this visit, I could not have been more than seven years of age, for I rode on the same horse with my father, I sitting before him on a pillow. My grandmother took to me very much, and when I left with my father in the evening

EDMESTON FARM HOUSE, MODBURY, DEVON : THE BIRTHPLACE OF REV. JAMES BICKFORD.

she put a half-crown in my hand. Her venerable and beautiful figure is still with me. I have never lost her true ideal from that day when I first saw her to even now, which is not far from seventy years ago. My grandfather and father were practical farmers, and both died at advanced ages—it may almost be said with the reaphook in their hands. Both, like Boaz, of Jewish renown, had been in the field with the 'reapers;' when, from exhaustion, they retired, and went into their homes to die. It seems appropriate that it was so. It is the glory of a soldier to die on the field of battle; of a minister to die in the pulpit; and it should be equally the glory of a yeoman to die in, or from, the field.

Of my childhood I have not much to say. We were nine brothers and sisters. I was the fifth born of my mother on May 6th, 1816. I have understood that I was healthy from my birth, but my anxious mother had a strong desire to make me still more vigorous if possible. I have a vivid recollection of her taking me into the back yard, nude and shivering, to be put under the shute for a stream of cold water to fall upon the spine. I thus learned to 'obey' my mother even under the force and pressure of the stream. I had, nevertheless, a severe fever in my boyhood, and I well recollect Doctor William Langworthy's efforts to save my young life. My mother's tenderness also in personally carrying me from the large cold room I and my brothers occupied to the fireside in the little parlour, and taking me up again when the cold of the evening came on, I well remember. This was the routine task of each day's nursing, until, at length, I made my escape from the bed of sickness, and I seemed to jump back into life once more.

On our farm were two cottages originally built for the convenience of the men who worked at the Estate's lime-kiln. But the husband in one of the cottages died, whilst the widow and her grown-up son and daughters still occupied the tenement. This widow (Granny Gill, as we used to call her), kept a dame's school, and I and two of my sisters were sent to it. I soon learnt what of reading and spelling were set me; but, as something besides was required for filling up the time, we were told off to learn hymns. This was our *régime* of religious instruction. Widow Gill was a dear, good Methodist soul; and, although my father was a staunch Tory Churchman, strange to say, he had no objection to Granny Gill teaching our young ideas how to shoot. The first I learnt was the 43rd, in Wesley's hymns, beginning with the solemn inquiry:

> ' And am I only born to die—
> To lay this body down ?'

and so to the end. What we thus learnt in the day we repeated in the evening at home, my parents appearing satisfied that we were learning something that was good. And so we were as far as it went.

My next teacher was a Mr. Wreford, an extremely prim gentleman, a bachelor, and a sturdy Churchman. He had, however, rooms in the house of a Mr. and Mrs. Roberts, the founders, I think, of the Methodist Church in Modbury. Mr. Wreford held his school in the vestries of the parish church, because of their central position. The sons of the farmers attended Mr. Wreford's, whilst the sons of the tradespeople attended Mr. Peter's, school. In practice it was the germ of many a conflict since enacted: it was ' Country *v.* Town.' Each had its nickname; and nearly every day on the ' Green ' small battles were fought. The Bickford boys had rather more than their share ; my eldest brother and I, in particular. But I never liked it: I thought it a brutal sport, whilst wrestling, football, bat and ball, I much enjoyed as exercises strictly allowable and to be recommended.

My next school was at Ugborough (*alias* ' Ubber '), kept by a Mr. Nicholas Webb, a retired Lieutenant of the Royal Navy. This was about three miles from Edmeston. The main characteristics of the school were ' law and order ; ' and woe betide the boy who was caught transgressing our more than Spartan regulations ! In Mr. Webb's estimation the greatest crime in a boy was to tell a lie ; and punishment, swift and sure, and in full tale, always followed this offence. But every case of accusation had to be tried by a bar of bogus law officials and a jury of senior boys. If found guilty, there was no commutation of the sentence. We had not the cat-o'-nine-tails, but we had the rod, which Mr. Webb could lay on when he liked with much severity. But I am happy to know that I never was personally subjected to the indignity of this punishment.

My cousin, Mr. Robert Philips Moysey, having set up an academy at Ivybridge, I was removed thither ; the last and best of all the schools that I attended. Mr. Moysey was an enthusiast in his vocation, a good Latin and Greek scholar, and a master in the use of Saxon-English. There was a sprinkling in this school of a higher class of boys than I had hitherto been associated with. I can truly say that at this seminary I intensely desired to learn all that could be learnt, save going into the classics; of which, at that time, I did not see any immediate use. But, in every branch of what is known as a solid English education, I was the rightful dux of the school.

I sat at the upper end of the 'Latin desk' for two years, but I made no attempt at proficiency in Latin. When I saw the so-called classic boys so neglectful of their English studies, and in competition with the other boys so far behind, I stuck to the useful, leaving the ornamental to 'a more convenient season.' But I might, and could, with tolerable ease, have done both, and that I did not do it I have always regretted. Mr. Moysey, however, did not lose his interest in me; for he subsequently prepared a written copy of the Greek alphabet, and advised me to pursue the study of that divinely used language. But would that I had done it before!

When nearing my fourteenth year, it became a question with my parents as to whether their five sons should be brought up on the farm, or strike out in some other way of life. My eldest brother, John, was my father's right hand, and could not be spared. My other brothers, Edmund, George, and Nicholas, were younger than I, and had not finished their education. So that, if a rent was to be made in our home circle it must be by myself; and, in a sense, show my younger brothers the way.

I had become of great use to my father on the farm, for there was not a single branch of agricultural industry that I did not understand; and, up to the measure of my strength, was not able to do. But the prospects of 'renting' farmers were anything but cheering. There was looming in the near distance the inevitable 'Repeal of the Corn Laws,' which would seriously affect the tenant farmers then under leases to their landlords, who would probably make no abatement in their rents. Besides, there was in many a tenant-farmer's home a galling sense of vassalage to the owner of the soil, which the independent, native-born-yeoman-spirit, could ill bear. Altogether, therefore, it seemed better to be free than to remain in such conditions. Accordingly, and with the full consent of my parents, I 'went out' from 'my father's house,' and spent in business the next seven or eight years, in the beautiful little town of Kingsbridge, situate at the head of the Salcombe estuary, and the key to the South Hams of Devon.

The environment of my life now was totally different from what it had been up to that time. I itinerated throughout the South Hams on the business of the 'firm' as occasions required, and learnt much of the manners and intelligence of the local gentry, the better style of farmers, of tradespeople and operatives of all classes. I was recognised everywhere as no mean sprig of an ancient yeoman tree, and was treated with all respect. Mr. Quarm, whom I gratefully mention as a second father, was always kind to me, and I can say that I made his business as much my own as I had in previous years made my father's mine own. There was a mercifulness of providence in this change of my life.

I was free now to choose for myself in the matter of conscience and religion, i.e. from all outside interference or coercion. I was awakened to a sense of my lost condition when alone on a dark night in a bye lane near my Uncle Taylor's farm, Sherford Down, in the parish of Sherford. And on that very hour my mind was decided on the vital question of religion. I joined the Methodist Church in Kingsbridge, under the superintendency of the venerable Rev. James Odgers, and my 'ticket on trial,' which he gave me, is dated 'March 1832.' My first and only leader was 'Henry Popplestone,' to whose tender, yet, faithful guidance, I owe, under God, much of the stability of my early religious life. Mr. Odgers was a powerful original thinker, and was great in polemical theology. No man ever understood our doctrine better than he; and I greatly profited by his ministry.

My intellect at that time betrayed a power of receptivity which was somewhat extraordinary. I became both a reader and a thinker upon my conversion at the age of sixteen. It was no ordinary privilege to sit under the ministry of Mr. Odgers. In dealing with the Calvinian controversy, he was indeed 'a master in (our) Israel.' He was a veritable 'Greatheart' (à la Bunyan) for helping young theologians, for he scarcely ever preached a sermon in the Kingsbridge pulpit but he sharpened our weapons. Upon the 'Five points,' as they used to be called, he spoke ex cathedrâ, and no one doubted his views or challenged their scripturalness. The Evangelical Arminianism of Wesley, Clarke, Benson, and Watson gradually came into my intellectual being, agreeing with the instincts of my newborn life. I tried to get a grip of it by the most assiduous attention to the expositions of Mr. Odgers, and by reading controversial authors, until I became myself, in the judgment of my friends, a very David in the warfare we waged against the 'Goliath' of Antinomianism. I accepted also the political creed of my spiritual father. He was a Liberal of the most pronounced type. I became one, too; and I did not hide my 'light under a bushel.' Arminianism and Liberalism were the two beliefs which impressed their 'broad-arrow' upon my whole nature, and winged my soul for flight into any project for securing to my countrymen the possession of a generous creed of religious ethics and social improvement; religious equality, and the God-given right to the tenant-farmers, mechanics, traders, and peasant classes, to live happy and contented lives.

The introduction of Methodism into the southern part of Devonshire may be briefly noticed. In the Minutes of the English Conference, 1810, the words occur :—'*South Devon Mission:* Nicholas Sibley, John W. Cloak.' But the honour of first preaching Methodist doctrines in Kingsbridge belongs to the Rev. John Jordan, who, in 1806, was the superintendent of the Ashburton circuit, and who came over to Kingsbridge on a visit of observation as to the spiritual wants of the people. There was one Methodist family there; perhaps, only one. In the afternoon of the memorable day when Mr. Jordan came, a novel sight was seen in the streets of Kingsbridge and Dodbrook. The town-crier—an important public officer in those days—was found parading through the quiet streets, capped with headgear which made him very singular if not dignified, and bell in hand, which he swung to and fro with great vigour. He would then pause to attract attention; this being done, he lifted up his voice, and cried—

'This evening, in Mr. Parker's schoolroom, off Fore Street, at seven o'clock, the Rev. John Jordan, Methodist preacher from Ashburton, will hold a religious service. PUBLIC INVITED.'

As the result, many of the townspeople came and heard the words of eternal life. South Hams that evening heard through Mr. Jordan's voice the words of the great Prophet-Preacher: 'Arise, shine; for thy light is come, and the glory of the Lord is risen upon thee.'

The first money spent for Methodism in the South Hams was by Mrs. Tapp, the mother of my late dear wife, Fanny Bickford, who was of Methodist ancestry, being born and reared in Camelford, Cornwall, under the adopting kindness of the Lobb family; whose hospitable and happy home was a favourite resort in their rounds of such men as Adam Clarke, R. Treffy, F. Truscott, W. P. Burgess, and other able ministers of those days. It was but a solitary sixpence for the town-crier; but it told of her love to Methodism, and of her adherence to the religious principles in which the donor had been trained.

Methodism in the South Hams has not risen in numerical importance as might have been hoped. But it is easily explained. There has not been in the last sixty or seventy years any encouragement to the rising yeomanry to try their fortunes under the tenant and landlord system; or, in the town, for the young mechanics and tradespeople to compete for a position and a respectable living. Hence it has been a kind of breeding ground for America, and, in later years, for Australia and New Zealand. In London, Lincoln, Exeter, and Plymouth they are also found. And the adventurous spirit which the environment necessarily creates in the South Hammers has always kept down the statistical strength of the Methodist Church; but, then, there is this compensation, other countries and 'lands remote' are all the better for their advent into them as Christian citizens and fellow workers.

When I was eighteen years of age I was brought on the Plan by the Rev. William Blundell as an exhorter on trial. This was in 1835. The Rev. Thomas White Smith was appointed to the Kingsbridge Circuit by the Conference of 1836, and entered upon his charge in September of that year. As in duty bound, I called at the Parsonage to pay my respects to the new minister, when, to my surprise and relief, he asked me if I had ever thought of going as a missionary to the heathen. I replied, that I had thought about it until my soul was nearly dissolved with grief, but no encouragement had been given me. He then handed to me a Bible, and asked me to read from the prophecies of Isaiah, which I readily did. From that hour, humanly speaking, my destiny was fixed. I was to be a missionary, and the good minister began to regard me with more than common interest. He set me reading, directed my studies, passed me, after a searching examination at the Local Preachers'

Meeting, into "Full Plan,", and, in 1838, he nominated me in the March Quarterly Meeting for the missionary work. But I must also mention another minister, the Rev. P. C. Turner, of Devonport, who invited me to his circuit, and to go with him to some appointments. This I did, and derived much assistance and comfort in preparing for the work. In due course I was examined before the Devonport District Meeting by the Chairman, the Rev. W. P. Burgess, passed to the satisfaction of the brethren, and was recommended to the Conference for the foreign work. With what success that work has been done for fifty years, the records which follow will humbly show.

THE WEST INDIES.

1786—1838.

FIRST PART.

FIFTY years ago—August 1st, 1838—the black and coloured population of the British West Indies saw the end of the 'Apprenticeship System' and received unconditional freedom. About 800,000 persons were on that ever-memorable day fully 'redeemed' from the cruel bondage in which they had so long been held. But not without a heavy price! The English Parliament had voted twenty millions of the nation's revenue for this object, so as to indemnify the 'legal' owners of the slaves against any supposed loss. But it was well that it was done! A strange perversion of the meaning of a very plain word is noticeable in this great national transaction. It was called 'compensation' money! But to whom? Not to the negroes who had been robbed of the just reward of their own labours; but, to their so-called OWNERS, as if they had been victimised on the altars of national justice. However, the money was paid and freedom came.

Conscience, when roused, is a quick and powerful mentor of nations as well as of individuals. England's conscience spoke out in unmistakable language, and the Parliament felt compelled to bow to the nation's will. Wilberforce, now 'in feebleness extreme,' was struggling through his last illness when a friend informed him that the Bill for the 'Abolition of Slavery' had passed its second reading in the House of Commons; 'Thank God,' said he, 'that I should have lived to witness a day in which England is willing to give twenty millions sterling for the Abolition of Slavery.'

History is the memory of the world. But a century back from the present time, or a few years more, will be ample for us without further extending our notices into the dark and dismal part of the Western Antilles. About one hundred years ago Wesleyan

Missionaries were sent to these lands by the English Conference, subject to the general superintendence of the Rev. Thomas Coke, LL.D., an Anglican clergyman, who had joined Wesley in his great work of evangelising whom he could of mankind without regard to creed, complexion, or nationality.

In 1786, Coke visited Antigua and the Windward Islands, and in 1789 the island of Jamaica. On his return to England that same year he sent the Rev. William Warrener to take care of the work which he had begun. In less than fifty years from this auspicious period the Mission Churches had so grown that seventy-one ordained missionaries, not including catechists or other subordinate agents, were employed, having the spiritual care of nearly thirty-two thousand persons, of whom twenty-two thousand were slaves. This number was exclusive of the children of our people, and of a very large number of persons of all colours, who attended the public ministry of the missionaries, but who were not recognised as members of the Society.

It is not to be supposed that such glorious results were accomplished in the absence of opposition and even bitter persecution. The fact is, that both the slave-owners and the active abettors of slavery always cherished a latent hatred to the Missionaries, as the men who would before long bring about the destruction of their favourite institution. They clearly saw that slavery and Christianity could not co-exist in the same social body. The missionaries had difficulties enough to contend with in prosecuting their Godlike enterprise from the terrible disadvantages under which lay the coloured population; but, as if these were not enough, applications were made by the Plantocracy for restrictive measures, under Legislative sanction, for preventing the slaves attending the ministrations of the men who were their only friends and spiritual guides.

Jamaica appears to have taken the lead in this cruel policy. In 1807, the Lieutenant-Governor, Council and Assembly passed 'An Ordinance,' from which we make two extracts :—

(1) 'That from and after the commencement of this Act, all masters and mistresses, owners, or, in their absence, overseers of slaves, shall, as much as in them lies, endeavour the instruction of their slaves in the principles of the Christian religion, whereby to facilitate their conversion; and shall do their utmost endeavours to fit them for baptism, and, as soon as conveniently they can, cause to be baptized all such as they can make sensible of a Deity and the

Christian faith.   (2) Provided, nevertheless, that the instruction of such slaves shall be confined to the doctrines of the Established Church in this island ; and that no Methodist Missionary, or other sectary, or preacher, shall presume to instruct our slaves, or to receive them into their houses, chapels, or conventicles, of any description, under the penalty of twenty pounds for every slave proved to have been there, and to be recovered in a summary manner before any three justices of the peace ; who, or the majority of whom, are hereby authorized and empowered to issue their warrant for recovery of the same ; and on refusal of payment, to commit the offender, or offenders, to the county gaol until the payment of the said fine or fines ; which shall be paid over to the church-wardens of the parish where the offence shall be committed, for the benefit of the poor of such parish.'

The mockery of the first clause and the brutality of the second will be obvious to every intelligent reader.   The missionaries and their sable flocks suffered terribly under this enactment.   Some of them were thrown into gaol, the sanctuaries of God were violently closed, and the congregations were scattered.   We painfully hear the wail of one, amongst the many, coming down to us even after the lapse of eighty years.   The Rev. William Gilgrass says :—

'When I came out of prison, I found the chapel shut up, which almost broke my heart.   But, at the price of my liberty, which I had regained, and in the faces of my avowed enemies, I ventured to open the chapel, appointing door-keepers to ascertain the slaves as accurately as possible.   Thus I continued preaching for a fortnight, to the restoration of many of the people who were daily falling into sin.'

We can even now hear the negroes' lament : ' Massa, me no go to heaven now.'   ' White man keep black man from serving God.' ' Black man got no soul.'   ' Nobody teach black man now.'   In about two years after this, King George III. disallowed this nefarious piece of planter legislation.   The reader of English history in Charles II.'s time will readily recognise in the barbarous ' Conventicle Act ' and the ' Five Mile Act ' the same spirit of persecution as that resurrected in the Jamaica Ordinance.   The brutal system had not died out with the collapse of the Stuart dynasty ; but re-appeared in every form of diabolic hate, for the annihilation of the missionaries and their blood-bought flocks in that island.

The same dastardly spirit appeared in the lovely little island of St. Vincent's, in the Windward group.   The object was to prevent the missionaries preaching to the negroes.   An enactment of course was necessary.   But it had to be smuggled through the House of Assembly when most of the members had left. It was worthy of a Caligula or a Domitian. There were three stages; it began with oppression, and ended in murder. For preaching to the negroes the first punishment was a fine of eighteen pounds, or imprisonment, for not more than ninety days, nor less than thirty. For a second offence, such corporal punishment as the court should think proper to inflict, and banishment. And lastly, to return from banishment, DEATH. Thus religious persecution was established by law. The Rev. Matthew Lumb was thrown into gaol for breaking, in obedience to his conscience, this vile law. But this Act also good King George annulled.

The years between 1786 and 1834 may be characterised as the 'wilderness state' of the West Indian mission churches. It was a period of 'great tribulation' to them. The Israelites endured cruel bondage under the Pharaohs, and the unfortunate Jews in Babylonian captivity; but these were light when compared to the heartless, unmanly, un-English, and anti-Christian wrongs which were inflicted upon the slave and creole races in the outlying Western Antilles. These islands were an integral part of our own great, proud Empire, subject to the laws of England, and under the protection of the Crown. And yet these wrongs were permitted to be done as if there were neither justice nor mercy for the unoffending missionaries and their attached followers. We do not over-state the case: 'What I saw in the days of slavery, and in which I was compelled to take part,' said a penitent planter to the writer, 'can never be told. It could not be written. It is too bad to be put into human phrase and be published for the public ear.' *

But to return to the case of the missionaries. Were they good men or bad men? safe or dangerous men? Let an impartial Chief Justice in one of the islands answer for the many hundreds who would bear a similar testimony :—

'During nearly forty years' residence in the West Indies. I have been observant of the conduct of Wesleyan missionaries; and, although I have heard of their being discountenanced, and even abused and illtreated, I have

---

* Dr. Samuel Johnston thus speaks of Jamaica in those dark days : 'A place of great wealth and dreadful wickedness : a den of tyrants and a dungeon of slaves.'

never known them to deserve it ; but, on the contrary, all those whose deport-
ment has come under my observation have appeared to be men of exemplary
lives, and more useful among the lower orders of society than those of any
other denomination.   Let it, therefore, be earnestly recommended to the
Wesleyan minister here, to use his utmost endeavours to induce the Parent
Society in England to afford us more missionary labour.   I do not profess to
belong to this society, as a member, and therefore I am not biassed by its
particular interests ; yet, in the true spirit of toleration and Christian charity,
I am happy in contributing to its support.'

Such a testimony from the head of a judicial establishment in
one of the islands is of the highest value.   But we append another
from an influential merchant, a gentleman of colour, and a member
of the Legislative Council by appointment from the Crown, who
said :—

'I have had the honour of having had extensive transactions with the
Wesleyan missionaries for a number of years, and I have always found them
to be men of integrity and honesty.   I never knew one of them to leave our
island without paying his debts, which is more than I can say for the ministers
of my own Church.'

Then, why were the missionaries reviled, persecuted, imprisoned,
and, in one lamentable instance, killed ? The answer is at hand.
The missionaries were the friends of the oppressed coloured classes,
and of the unfortunate slaves. 'Banish the missionaries,' said the
Plantocracy, 'and we shall hold our prey.'   But God in heaven heard
the cry of His faithful servants, and of His sable children, and HE
'came down to deliver them.'   August 1st, 1834, saw the end in all
our West Indian Possessions of negro slavery.

The letters of the missionaries written at this time are little
known.   We may, therefore, allowably give from the correspondence
a few quotations, setting forth some of the scenes and experiences
of the never-to-be-forgotten ABOLITION DAY.   The Rev. Edward
Fraser, himself a coloured man, and once a slave, thus wrote from
Tortola :—

' That ever memorable and glorious day was passed by us in a religious and
most happy manner.   Our chapels were opened, and the human beings who
had that morning, for the first time, breathed the air of freedom—of freedom
at least from absolute bondage—assembled in cheerful crowds to praise and
worship Him who "looseth the prisoners."   Great was our rejoicing ;—the
more so because many had foreboded soreness and discontent.   As I came
out of our town chapel, a man from a group accosted me with, "Sir, we could

wish a petition to return thanks to the King." I replied, "No doubt the King will be greatly pleased when he hears of your thankfulness and orderly behaviour."'

The Rev. Matthew Banks wrote :—

'On Thursday evening, July 31st, I preached from 1 Cor. vi. 19, 20. The congregation was very large. About two minutes before twelve o'clock, I desired all the negroes and the friends of freedom to kneel down, the first to receive their liberty at the hands of God, and the latter to take from Him the consummation they had so devoutly wished. When the clock struck twelve, I announced that the 1st of August had arrived, and exclaimed, " You are all free!" Then the voice of their weeping was more distinctly heard, and it became general, and mingled with, " Glory be to God !" " Praise the Lord !" etc. Prayer was offered for our Gracious Sovereign, the Royal Family, the British Parliament, and British Christians generally, by whom, under God, the great boon is conferred. All the freed people seemed to acknowledge that it is the Lord's doing, and marvellous in their eyes.'

The Rev. William Box gives an interesting account of the preliminary services, and adds :—

' It being then within a few minutes of twelve o'clock, I stated the propriety of their receiving the inestimable boon upon their knees, and requested them to silently lift up their hearts to God, until I should announce to them that slavery was no more, by a hymn of praise to God ; but such was their joyous feeling, and so loud their prayers, that it was with difficulty I could raise my voice so high as to be heard. We sang, " Praise God from whom all blessings flow." This being sung, they rose from their knees, when I congratulated them upon their new state and relationship, so unexpectedly, so astonishingly brought about ; and while setting forth the demands which were now made upon them, not only of devotedness to God, but of loyalty to their beloved Sovereign, with an enthusiasm I never before witnessed in a West Indian assembly, they one and all shouted, "God save the King ! Long live King William the Fourth ! God save the King !" O how did my heart thrill with ecstasy, while hundreds upon hundreds just delivered "from the house of bondage," made the place ring again with the voice of joy and thanksgiving ! It was like Israel in the time of David and Solomon, when " all the congregation blessed the Lord God of their fathers, and bowed their heads, and worshipped the Lord and the King."'

But there was the holiday of jubilee to follow the night of their departure from this 'land of Egypt.' Two grand Sabbath services were held, and at the close of the second a fine burst of decision for God was heard. 'Who then is willing,' cried the missionary, 'to consecrate his service this day unto the Lord?' Several rose, and lifting up their hands, exclaimed, 'I will!' 'I will!' 'I will!' 'I will!' "I am!' 'I am!' 'I am!'—while the whole body simultaneously joined in the declaration.   Upon pressing the subject by asking, 'Are you decided?' nothing was to be heard scarcely, but 'Yes, Massa!' 'Yes, Massa!' while tears trickled down their sable cheeks, and heavenly joy sparkled in every countenance.   The Sunday school was then visited, and an infant negro child was baptized.

This was a very Pentecost—the inauguration of a new era in the civil and religious life of these emancipated and happy flocks of the missionaries' fold.   White and black, and coloured, by this merciful Act of SLAVE-Abolition, entered upon new and high responsibilities, which God in his providential arrangements had cast upon them. The whites, under governors appointed by the Crown, and subject to legislative bodies of diverse materials and functions, had now a favourable opportunity of making some amends for their past cruel and licentious misdoings ; whilst the blacks were prepared to conform to the requirements of the new 'apprenticeship *régime,*' which, in the nature of things, would be to them irksome, hard to bear, and savouring of a purgatory.   Fair treatment and a fair wage, just and equitable laws, political rights, and the 'rest of the Sabbath,' they asked, and were determined to have.

The creole increment of the population occupied a middle relation to both.   Descended at first, on the father's side, from the whites and on the mother's side from the blacks, they had inherited a superiority to the maternal stock ; and, in many notable instances, were not a whit inferior to the paternal.   Then, again, these creoles, or mixed persons, intermarried with each other, and from them sprang a numerous progeny which have pushed their way into the learned professions, the Christian ministry, and mercantile life ; they have become proprietors and managers of sugar and cotton plan-tations, and entered into the highest Governmental service.   An adjustment of relations as between two of these classes, say, between the whites and blacks, would have been comparatively easy ; but the existence of a third element made a difficulty.   This was the problem to be solved on well understood lines of political fairness, social justice, and Christian forbearance.   But the experiment of an interim apprenticeship proved a dead failure, and precipitated the alternative of complete emancipation on August 1st, 1838.

The ever watchful London Committee did not fail to anticipate the still greater social change about to take place throughout the

West India Islands. Under date, April 14th, 1838, the General Secretaries despatched a circular upon this subject to the Wesleyan Missionaries, containing wholesome and broad-hearted counsels, for the guidance of their whole conduct under the new and trying conditions in which they would soon be. The Secretaries say:—

'As the liberation of a portion of the apprenticed negroes in August next may probably have an unsettling effect upon those who are appointed by the Abolition Act to remain in the condition of apprentices for two years longer, and as the efforts which have been made to procure an immediate and universal extinction of the apprenticeship system may also tend to produce still greater excitement, we deem it proper to give you a word of advice upon the subject. On the question of the immediate and forcible termination of the apprenticeship system by the Imperial Parliament, it is foreign to our purpose to enlarge : our object is to enjoin you to use your influence to allay any excitement which may exist among the negroes, and to inculcate upon them the duty of a quiet and peaceable submission to their circumstances. The contrary conduct could only prove injurious to themselves ;—it would probably be made the occasion for imposing upon them new restrictions ;—and it would tend to check any disposition on the part of the local legislatures, or of individual planters, to introduce them to the enjoyment of entire freedom before the period fixed for the termination of the apprenticeship by the Abolition Act.

' We have good ground for hope that a satisfactory settlement of the important Negro Marriage Question will speedily take place. We have been alive to this subject ; and finding that a protective measure was likely to be adopted by the Imperial Parliament for the benefit of the apprentices, we respectfully urged upon the Right Honourable Lord Glenelg to insert, in his Bill, a clause recognising the validity of the past marriages which you have solemnized, and empowering you legally to solemnize marriage for the future. Such a result cannot fail to have a most important bearing upon the cause of religion and public morals, and will powerfully tend to promote the comfort and welfare of the negroes and their children.'

The document from which the above extracts are taken is very lengthy, dealing with the question in every possible aspect, and bears the signatures of the Rev. Edmund Grindrod, President of the Conference ; and of the Revs. Jabez Bunting, D.D., John Beecham, D.D., Robert Alder, D.D., and Elijah Hoole, D.D., General Secretaries.

The Plantocracy had evidently had enough of the 'Apprenticeship' system, which was simply one of semi-slavery, as all admitted. The meddling policy of the Imperial Parliament in granting only a half-measure of relief embittered both parties, and rendered every plantation a focus of discontent and alarm. The coloured population at this time were mostly in the towns. They were not unnaturally in a state of frenzied excitement, and were so far an element of danger

2

to the peace of the general social body. The time, therefore, had surely arrived when the necessary relief must come from the local parliaments themselves. Antigua, to its great praise, had shown a good example by giving unconditional freedom to its slave population in 1834. This action was right; and, as experience showed, the safest thing to do. Besides, it was just. For it may be asked, how could the slave-owners with any sense of righteousness hold the apprentices in bondage, and extract out of their sweat and blood gratuitous services, when they had previously received their share of so-called 'compensation' money out of the coffers of the English Exchequer.

Between the months of May and August the island legislatures reluctantly opened their eyes to the unsafe condition of things, and, in rapid succession, passed such measures as brought this desperate iniquity to an end. The letters of the grateful missionaries are of much interest and feeling. We may quote from one of these as a sample of the rest. The Rev. John Lee, writing from Calder, St. Vincent's, begins with a note of grandest jubilation :—

'"Hallelujah! The Lord God omnipotent reigneth!" and we are breathing a free atmosphere. Yesterday, the glorious first of August, the apprenticeship of this island was abrogated, and the long-enslaved population became fully free. The day came, and with it the rejoicing of ten thousands in these islands. Long before the time for service the chapel was crowded to excess. Knowing that the eyes of many were upon us, I previously requested the attendance of the proprietors, attorneys, managers, etc., to witness the behaviour of the people, and also to hear the whole of the advices we had to give: two magistrates and several white people came, who all heard the Word attentively. After singing that beautiful hymn, "For the Heathen," page 417, in which the congregation heartily joined, we engaged in solemn thanksgiving to our merciful Benefactor, for all the favours bestowed upon us, but especially for that which had brought us together that day. It was evident that the Lord was in the midst of us; for, O Sirs! it would have done your hearts good to have witnessed their devotion, and to have heard their responses; and, when thanks were returned for the successful termination of the long protracted struggle to obtain their freedom, and blessings were invoked upon the heads of their benefactors, then to have heard the burst of grateful feeling which flowed from their full hearts would have made British Christians rejoice. I proceeded to address them from 1 Peter ii. 13-19; after which I gave them some general advice respecting their future conduct as free labourers; on the nature of their agreement; the attention due to their children's education and subsequent employment; the best way of conducting themselves during their present cessation from labour; the necessity of all resuming their employment next Monday morning, etc. We then sung the doxology, and concluded with prayer one of the most interesting services I ever witnessed.'

Thus, by Heaven's decree, this cruel and hellish system of slavery came to an end. Nothing could have been more demoralising than was this nefarious traffic. The island plantations were, in many instances, managed by 'Legrees;'—who, in every phase of moral turpitude, equalled their famous prototype as drawn by Mrs. Harriet Beecher Stowe in 'Uncle Tom's Cabin.' Sir John Hawkins in 1556 acquired the distinction of being the father of this dreadful traffic in slaves for the West Indies. The account is that he sailed with two ships to Cape de Verde, where he sent eighty men on shore to catch negroes. But the natives flying, they fell farther down the coast; till, having taken enough, they proceeded to the West Indies and sold them. For 282 years the original Africans, with their children and children's children were enslaved; to which were added, as necessity arose for labour for carrying on the sugar and cotton cultivation, other cargoes of captured negroes.

By the Act of Emancipation, eight hundred thousand of freed negroes were put into possession of the priceless privileges of civil and religious liberty. These privileges are thus defined by Wesley in his scathing tract, entitled 'Thoughts upon Slavery,' as follows:—

'Liberty is the right of every human creature, as soon as he breathes the vital air; and no human law can deprive him of that right which he derives from the law of nature.'

And again:—

'Religious liberty is a liberty to choose our own religion; to worship God according to our own conscience. Every man living has a right to this, as he is a rational character. The Creator gave him this right when He endowed him with understanding; and every man must judge for himself, because every man must give an account of himself to God. Consequently, this is an inalienable right t is inseparable from humanity; and God did never give authority to any man, or number of men, to deprive any child of man thereof, under any colour or pretence whatever.'

This liberty is now the Magna Charta of every subject of our Queen throughout her great empire; but the history of the struggle for its acquirement, 'at home and abroad,' is a monitory illustration of the maxim—

> 'Who would be free,
> Himself should strike the blow.'

This ought not to have been required.

PERSONAL HISTORY.

1838—1853.

SECOND PART.

MY engagement by the Missionary Committee in London, acting for the English Conference, dates from August 1838, and the ending of Negro Apprenticeship in the West Indies occurred in the same month and year. By this action, new openings presented themselves to the London Committee, and the whole Methodist Church in Great Britain sprang to the evangelistic enterprise. 'More missionaries' had been once more the plea heard from across the waters of the Atlantic, and I was one among ten others who were chosen for the work.

The official education of young missionaries begins in London. Fifty years ago, soon after the holding of the Conference, they were examined by a Committee, and, if approved, they were billeted for a short time with the London Ministers. My good fortune, in the first instance, was to be told off for Westmoreland Place, the home of the Rev. President Thomas Jackson, whose fatherly bearing to me I can never forget. The President at that time was writing his Centenary Memorial volume. From day to day, when he came down to dinner, he would tell us of the progress he was making. Rev. B. B. Waddy, who that year was the President's assistant, had most of the remarks addressed to him. 'Did you ever preach,' said the President to Mr. Waddy, 'on St. Paul's visit to Troas?' 'No, sir,' was the reply. 'But if you were to do so,' rejoined the President; 'how would you treat that subject?' 'Well, sir, I hardly know, but I suppose I would make a point of the importance of wakefulness in hearing the Word of God.' 'But there is a great deal more than that in the narrative,' said the President; 'there is in fact a complete body of divinity in it. Only see ! we have—

(1) the recognition of the Sabbath institution—"the first day of the week;" (2) the conduct of the Apostolic Churches on that day —"the disciples came together;" (3) the observance of the Lord's Supper—"broke bread;" (4) the institution of the Christian ministry—"Paul preached unto them."' Then the President expressed his sympathy with the young man, Eutychus, suggesting as an excuse for his having fallen into a 'deep sleep,' that probably he was generally employed in the field, or in some department of active daily life, and was not therefore able to resist the drowsiness that attacked him. The miracle of his restoration to full strength, at the instance of Paul, was also noticed, and—(5) the result of a well-spent Sabbath—'They were not a little comforted.' This was good expository teaching for us young men, for two of us were the merest novitiates in the work.

The President always offered prayer at family worship in the morning. These exercises were of a highly spiritual character. The nation, the church, the missions, the family, the young men, the sick and distressed, came in for special notice and earnest supplication. One morning after prayer, in which the President had been praying for favourable weather for the ingathering of the crops in the north of England and Scotland, Mr. Waddy rather archly inquired 'if the President was aware that the harvest was over in every part of the country?' 'No, no, Mr. Waddy,' said the devout man; 'not yet. In the north of England and in many parts of Scotland there are hundreds of acres of ungathered grain, and if the Lord does not favour us for some time longer with suitable weather much of it will be spoiled; bread will be dear, then what will the poor people do?' I was much struck with the reply, as showing how much the President's heart had imbibed the spirit of his Master, whose special characteristic was His loving consideration for the poor.

My next move was to 77, Hatton Garden, the residence of the Rev. Dr. and Mrs Alder. Here I met several young men, who were, like myself, waiting for 'sailing orders' to proceed to our allotted work 'far hence among the Gentiles.' The two temporary homes I had in London, at this time, stand out in sharp contrast to each other. Westmoreland Place was much like a quiet, dignified Yorkshire home; whilst Hatton Garden was official, restrained, and everything was done to order. The first was an easy break from one's quiet home life in Devonshire; the other was a rather unwelcome discipline to fit one for the higher courtesies of society and diplomatic intercourse with governors and leading officials in colonial life. Long experience has confirmed me in the opinion that both the English President and the Missionary Secretary were right. Dr. Alder's *régime* was a kind of breaking in, of which, I am sure, that no young man capable of judging the doctor's motives would condemn as too severe.

A few details may be given. The young missionary at '77' soon learnt that he had to 'walk by rule.' On entering the house from the street a neatly clad and somewhat stiffish *femme* would conduct the stranger to a back parlour, and take her departure. The furniture was scant and plain. There was no sofa, nor couch, nor easy chair, for the comfort of the 'young man from the country.' There were a few books, and all of a certain kind. 'Butler's Analogy,' 'Pearson on the Creed,' 'Wesley's Sermons,' and 'Watson's Institute,' were among the more prominent and thumbed. On the wall over the mantelpiece was hung a copy of the rules to be read and observed. The bell would ring for breakfast at fifteen minutes or so before you were expected to make your appearance. Seated, with the 'Boss' at the head, and his amiable better half at the other end of the table, the ordinary formalities of breaking-fast commenced. Each one was expected to be prepared with a passage of Scripture for recital, the lady of the house leading the way. Next to her sat a nervous young woman, the wife of one of the missionaries about to sail for Africa, whose surprise and hesitancy were so great that she could not produce a single word from the grand old book she loved so well. The round came to me on the left, next the 'Boss,' and I did my best in giving the last text I had used before leaving Devonshire. Then the reading of the Scriptures followed, and prayer was offered. A funny incident occurred one morning. A small boy —a shoeblack and errand boy (whom we may fitly call 'Toby')—was sitting in a corner of the room waiting his turn at recitation after the rest of us had gone through our facings. He (Toby), it was said, had been misbehaving in some matter, and was under a threat of dismissal. Poor lad! What could he do? Nothing that he might say from his own mind could avert the trouble which now hung over him. So the arch little fellow chose a passage of Scripture which perchance might soften the ire of his master. His turn was the last of the lot—his only chance. But he came out with his selected passage, full-mouthed and emphasized, with painful emotion : ' And, ye masters, do the same things unto them, forbearing threatening, knowing that your Master also is in heaven ; neither is there respect of persons with Him.' The stroke was felt at both ends of the table ; the shaft went home. Not a word was said, but smiles were exchanged ; and for Toby's sake we may hope there was an end of the affair.

As may be expected, this *régime* appeared to some of our party as savouring too much of being at school. Be it so, it was none the worse for that. The diet itself was according to the ' Rule of Three,' —breakfast, dinner and tea, and no fourth meal. These were frugal enough, except the dinner, which was substantial and good. Breakfast ! yes, stale bread, cut about three-quarters of an inch thick, with a slight ' scrape of butter' to make it slide more easily, and one or two cups of coffee as we might choose. The tea had toast sometimes in addition, but not too much of that. The subscribers to the funds of the Wesleyan Missionary Society may take my word for it that, at that time, there was no waste of any kind, no superfluity whatsoever, at 77, Hatton Garden.

This was capital discipline doubtless for the young men, whether married or single. I felt the change very much from my freer former life in Devon, but I did not complain. Good for us perhaps that it was so, as a preparation for self-denial and unknown experiences which were awaiting us in distant parts. Fifty years have passed since then, and Dr. and Mrs. Alder have gone from among us ; yet their memories and many generous acts are not, and never can be, forgotten by me.

The year 1838 may be thought of by the English Methodists as one marked with strong faith in God, and of noble daring in missionary enterprises. The income of the Society was £73,875, and the expenditure had greatly exceeded that amount. There was, unhappily, a debt, including the deficiency of this former year, of some thousands of pounds. But, notwithstanding this painful fact, the Committee could not stand still when the West Indies, India, Australia, Polynesia, and North America were plaintively crying, ' Come over and help us.' There must have been deep anxiety in the councils of the General Committee for the salvation of the heathen, to have warranted the forward action so strikingly shown.

Australia and New Zealand were generously provided for, and so were the Canadas.

I was present in September, in London, at an Ordination Service, when Messrs. Warren, Ironside, Creed, De Wolfe, Lauton, Barratt, and Marshall were, by the 'imposition of hands and prayers' solemnly 'set apart' for the work abroad. I well remember also that never-to-be-forgotten Valedictory service held in City Road on the departure of the Revs. John Waterhouse, J. H. Bumby, John Egglestone, John Warren, Samuel Ironside, Charles Creed, and Peter Jones (the converted Indian chief) for Australia and Canada. Great men were on the platform—The President, Thomas Jackson, Dr. Hannah, Dr. Bunting, Richard Treffry (senior), Edmund Grindrod, John Beecham, Robert Alder, and Elijah Hoole. The President conducted the meeting with the impressive dignity of a true '*O pruestos*, and Dr. Bunting closed the service with a prayer, the remembrance of which has been cherished as an instance of impassioned pleading with the God of missions never before heard within the consecrated walls of Wesley's own church. But these were not all of the noble men sent out that year. There were, besides, Messrs. Moss, Edwards, Hetherington, Lauton, Parkinson, Burrows, Impey, Fleet, together with the following missionaries: Messrs. Railton, Davis, Bell, Whitehead, Hurd, and Bickford. It was a year of Pentecostal Baptism for missionary enlargement, for the 'Lord of the harvest' had heard the cry of His servants for more labourers, and the Conference authorities found them, and sent them out 'far hence among the Gentiles,' east, west, north, and south.

Voyage to the West Indies.

It was on November 2nd that the Rev. Henry Hurd and I were accompanied by Dr. Alder to London Bridge, to go by a small steamboat to Gravesend, where the *Berkely* was anchored ready for sea. We soon got 'under weigh' and made for the 'Downs,' where we remained until the 11th. After morning service fair wind sprang up, and we were speedily shaping for 'down' channel, some two hundred vessels starting at the same time. Among them were the *Fame*, bound for the Gambia, having Mr. and Mrs. Parkinson as passengers; the *Jamaica*, bound for Antigua, with Messrs. Fraser, Bell, and Railton; the *Houghton-le-Spring*, bound for Jamaica, with

Messrs. Burrows, Davis, Redfern, and Whitehead; and the *Vixen*, bound for South Africa, with Messrs. Richards and Impey. Fifty years ago the missionaries had to encounter the discomforts and dangers of sailing to distant parts in small and ill-equipped trading vessels; but now they are able to travel in monster steamships to every part of the world, with the enjoyment of 'pleasure trips.'

Nothing remarkable occurred during the voyage. We were thirty-eight days from the 'Downs' to the island of St. Vincent's. We had the customary storms, contrary winds, and heavy seas, with other disagreeablenesses, but, upon the whole, for that season of the year, it was a fair voyage. Our worst weather was in the Bay of Biscay, where the sea was lashed into fury by the north-west gales, threatening our immediate destruction. A short vessel, like the *Berkely*, was ill-prepared for easily riding over such yawning depths as ever and anon we descended into. One of these in particular can never be forgotten. The captain, Mr. Mann, and the chief mate, Mr. Frost, were standing on the larboard side of the quarter-deck watching with intensest apprehension the approach of a mountain of water. Its height was above the highest yard of our struggling, trembling ship, and we appeared to be within a measurable distance of engulphment in the appalling waves. But, as it approached, within a few yards of our 'bows,' it broke and disappeared below our quivering vessel, and left us unharmed. We then rose upon the crest of another sea, and finally escaped the further terrors of this fearfully dangerous bay. We caught the 'trades' on December 3rd. some two hundred miles west of the Canary Isles, from which time we had pleasant sailing until we sighted Barbados.

Life for land-lubbers on shipboard is a curious phenomenon. A Mr. Cockran, a sugar planter, and a really good-natured son of Erin, was then one of our fellow-voyagers. He quite took to me; and why should he not? Is there no affinity between Saxon and Celtic blood? He always addressed me as 'The Bishop,'—I presume of the saloon. One day he said to me, with affectionate simplicity, 'Bishop, if you will come to see me on my plantation in Grenada, I shall be so pleased that I will kill a sheep for you.' His 'bulls' were frequent and amusing. We were sailing close-hauled to the wind,—it was some days before we fell in with the 'trades;' but, it so happened, that whilst we were below dining, the chief mate had 'put the ship about' so that we were on another tack, when he came again on

deck. Said he to Mr. Frost, 'What have you been doing? Why,
you have put the wind on the other side of the ship.' But he was
tender and sensible to every little act of kindness from us. I liked
him very much. Our passengers were Grenadians by birth or
choice, and were wholly free from those complexional prejudices
which have so much disturbed and even embittered the social life of
Jamaicans and Barbadians. A missionary on board ship, provided
he act wisely, cautiously, and be tolerably reticent, may wield a
powerful influence as a general peacemaker and friend. Mr. Hurd
and I, in these respects, did our best, and succeeded. Dr. Alder's
many counsels stood us in good turn now that we were thrown upon
our own resources in our ship-life for the first time.

On December 18th we sighted Barbados, and at 9 a.m. were off
Carlisle Bay. We stood away at once for St. Vincent's, some ninety
miles to the west. We reached the island at daylight, and early in
the forenoon we landed at Cropper's Wharf, Kingstown Harbour.
An interesting young gentleman—a Mr. Rapier, slightly coloured
—addressed to us the inquiry, 'Whether we were Wesleyan missionaries just arrived from England?' We said, 'Yes.' He then
politely offered to conduct us to the mission house in the next street.

The Rev. R. H. Crane, a Nova Scotian by birth, was the resident
missionary. He was a fine, well-proportioned man, with a benignant
countenance, who received us with courtesy and smiles. We next
saw his wife, Mrs. Crane, formerly a Miss Black, daughter of the
Rev. William Black, of Huddersfield, Yorkshire, who had emigrated
to Nova Scotia with his parents when he was quite young. Mr.
Hurd and I were much shocked when we first saw her attenuated
frame, deadly white complexion, and, as we inferred, ill state of
health. But the climate had done it all; a common penalty, which
English ladies have to pay as the price for residing within the
tropics.

Whilst looking about the hall we heard the pattering of the
negroes' naked feet as they entered the mission yard, with our
heavy luggage on their heads. They, in much good nature, without
fee or reward, placed all our belongings carefully against the outer
wall of the strangers' receiving-room, and, scraping the right foot on
the ground as their expressive token of respect for 'Buckra,' they took
their departure. The reason of their kindness is not far to seek.
' Dem missionary imported for ä wee,' was the grateful idea which

underlay their action. Being glad to see us, they were willing to serve us as they had ability.

The island of St. Vincent's, situate in 13° N. latitude and 61° W. longitude, is regarded as the queen of the Antilles. Some travellers have appropriately called it a West Indian Switzerland. Indeed, the four leading characteristics of that famous country are here found in miniature. The Alpine, the mountainous, the hilly, and the plain are seen to great advantage as we approach the Carib country from the sea; also the peak-shaped mountains, and extensive, broken ranges of high hills, and clean-cut precipices, as seen at the back of Kingstown and at Fort St. George. There is, perhaps, no portion of our Colonial empire that abounds more in interesting physical phenomena, and rugged scenery, than this grandly outlined island. In some localities to the leeward there are numerous traces of the igneous character of their origin. The magnificent Cumberland valley, for example, is the resort of the scientific and the curious, because of its immense basaltic rocks, which, rising hard by the river's side, stand straight up in columnar order, whilst their surface, pavement-like, is laid in polygonal pieces, fitted most mechanically into each other. The Greathead valley is celebrated for its spa, or mineral springs, which are so valuable in fever cases. And the CARIB country to the windward is famous for its dry river. Before the dreadful eruption of the Souffrière mountain, in 1813, its bed was the natural floor of one of the most valuable streams that ever watered a plantation, or blessed a home.

From the time of our landing to that of holding the Annual District Meeting was about two months. I shall never forget the first evening spent in Kingstown. Mr. Crane asked me to preach, which I did as well as I could after the dissipation of a sea voyage. My subject was 'Wrestling Jacob,' and some seven hundred persons were present. A large choir, drawn up in a semi-circular form, was led by a coloured lady possessing a strong, full, and well-trained contralto voice. The first tune was 'Segina,' a grand and appropriate one for rendering with effect C. Wesley's greatest hymn—'Come, O Thou Traveller unknown!' The bass was given by a Mr. Clark, a white man, who had bought his discharge from the army. He sang with marvellous power. The motley appearance of the congregation: diversity of complexional shades, naked feet of the blacks, red cotton tied headgear, fantastic hats, with and without brims, together with a few of the whites and better-to-do coloured of the congregation dressed up in beautiful muslin or very light silks, presented the most curious audience I ever expected to see even in the West Indies themselves.

My first Sunday was spent at Calliaqua, a small village, surrounded except seaward, by populous sugar plantations. We had from six to eight hundred persons present. After the morning service, the classes were met by several leaders as arranged for them in every part of the building, which was probably fifty feet square, much after the manner in which modern Sunday schools are distributed. At the close of the fellowship by singing and prayer, the officiating minister had to call out, one by one, the names of all the members on the roll, who would answer ' one,' ' two,' ' three,' ' four,' meaning penny, or pence, as the case might be, and the leader would place the contribution in the numbered bag to be handed to the missionary, to be counted and entered in the Society book on the Monday morning. I thought 'This looks very much like business,' and suggesting the idea of ' paying as you go.' Two children had to be baptized ; a love-feast had to be held in the afternoon, and a preaching service in the evening. Not a lazy, or bad day's work for a ' new chum' (Austral), who had just come from the stormy coasts of South Devon, and exposed for the first time to the scorching and exhaustless rays of a vertical sun.

Dec. 25th.—Divine services were held as in the old country. The Kingstown Chapel was full of worshippers at four o'clock in the morning. This has always been a great day with our people in the West Indies. It is to them a day to be ushered in by ' songs in the night,' as well as in early morn, by a ' rejoicing with great joy.' The Rev. R. H. Crane preached at 5 a.m., and it fell to me to officiate at 10.30 a.m., and at 7 p.m. My thoughts travelled homeward, and I acutely felt the distance which then intervened between the sunny isle of St. Vincent's and Edmeston Barton, in the parish of Modbury, Devon, where twelve months ago we gathered around the parental hearth, rejoicing with our father and mother and nine brothers and sisters, whose happy and healthy circle up to that time had been unbroken. The thought would arise, ' When shall we meet again ? ' ' Never more ' in this world, was the stern reply.

Dec. 28th.—I was on the 'wings of the wind.' The Rev. John Mann, our missionary in the Carib country, had come into Kingstown on the preceding day to take me back with him for several services at his station. 'John Mann' was a *man* for the occasion. He feared neither sun nor rain. A salamander for heat and a duck for water;—two important qualifications for the kind of work he had been doing previously in Trinidad and Tobago, and was then doing in the windward district of St. Vincent's. Once mounted on our mettled steeds, off we went at a canter through the town long before the creoles had rubbed their eyes, or the blacks oiled their ebony. We ascended Dorsetshire Hill to the flagstaff, descended into Greathead valley, crossed the rushing river, proceeded at full speed over the flatter country, passed through Calliaqua, and then skirted the sea for some miles. But why all this haste? Why? Because old Sol was rising, and the Englishmen must avoid the exhaustion and danger of his fierce rays, not only by an early journey, but by losing no time by the way. Calder, the head-quarters of the Hon. Hay McDowall Grant, the just and good attorney of the Trust Estates, soon appeared in view. We were quickly at the humble, quiet cottage of the Rev. John Lee, before whose door we pulled up—

> " The wingèd courser, like a generous horse,
> Shows most true mettle when you check its course."

Riders and steeds seemed equally glad of shelter and repose.

Mrs. Lee—dear good soul—had for us a fine breakfast of salt-fish, roast yams, plantains, and exquisite coffee. Didn't we eat, and drink, too, after that ride? The best sauce for an Englishman in the tropics is a gallop of a dozen miles, now and then, before breakfast. Our kind host and hostess were not at all surprised at the devouring powers we put forth. The morning hymn, the reading of God's Word, and a short extempore prayer, concluded the repast. The negroes of the plantation came around the house to have a peep at the new Buckra (white stranger) and offer him a welcome.

At midday Mr. Mann and I remounted our horses, and off we went for the Biabou mission station, where resided the Rev. John Cullingford, the Chairman of the District. We had brought copies of the *Watchman* with us containing the accounts of the great meeting which had been held at Manchester in initiating the movement for celebrating the Centenary festival.   Mrs. Cullingford entertained us most hospitably.   Refreshed and comforted we proceeded on our way at 4 p.m., so as to have the cool of the evening for the remainder of our journey.   Romantic and precipitous cliffs, hills and valleys, narrow riding paths, and rushing rivers mark the way from Biabou to Georgetown, the station and home of Mr. Mann. Ordinarily, a few days' rest would have been wise after such a journey, but this was not to be.   The 'next day was the Sabbath,' and I had to do the best I could.   But there was such encouragement in the crowds that came for the worship that all previous fatigue was forgotten.   Hundreds upon hundreds could not get inside the building, but had to come within earshot on the outside, and get as much religious instruction as was possible under the circumstances. Such 'hunger' for the Word of God I had never seen before in England or elsewhere.   Speaking for the honoured pioneer of this great work, Mr. Mann, it seemed to me that no words could be more appropriate for the utterances of his soul than are the following lines :—

> ' Who, I ask in amaze, hath begotten me these ?
> And inquire from what quarter they came ;
> My full heart it replies, They are born from the skies,
> And gives glory to God and the Lamb.'

Two incidents occurred, of great interest to me, during this my first visit to the Carib country :—

(*a*) My being present at the class meeting of newly con rted negroes.   Mr. Mann was the leader.   His bearing was very tender and considerate of the feelings of these ' babes in Christ,' who were seeking for guidance and help in their spiritual life.   The meeting had the true ring.   The fellowship was genuinely good all through. The enquiries of the leader dealt alone with spiritual experiences and the trials of the daily life of the members.   Such replies as the following indicate the gist of the whole exercise : (1) ' Me have no friend but Jesus.   Me love my Jesus for what He done for me.'   (2) ' My Jesus give me faith : me want more faith.'   (3) ' Me be determined to live better this year ; me will ask more—love more— pray more—and be better Christian.'   To my own soul it was a precious season of peace and blessing.

(*b*) I had heard of a miserable remnant of the red Carib race located at Grand Sable, lying to the north of the Georgetown mission station, and I expressed a wish to Mr. Mann to visit them in their own settlement. We accordingly mounted our horses early one morning, and found them in due course as we expected. They—about fifty perhaps—were the sole survivors of a once powerful race, the original owners of the land, and masters of the seas which washed the shores of their beautiful islands. Being introduced to the old chief, it was easy to see from his bearing that we were not wanted, and that our presence even was irksome to the tribe. Physically, they are of a low stature, and bear a strong resemblance to the group of copper-coloured Indians seen in the Crystal Palace, Sydenham, London. Their look was strongly suspicious of the presence of strangers. Their eyes appeared contracted, and the unmistakable expression of the countenance was not only forbidding but revengeful. Some fifty years before the time of our visit, under the direction of the Rev. Dr. Coke, an attempt was made to civilize these people by establishing a school for the children. A Mr. and Mrs. Joice were sent out from London to conduct it. But the project failed through the severe illnesses of Mrs. Joice, and both had to leave.

The next attempt was made by the appointment of the Rev. Mr. Baxter, of Antigua, as a missionary to reside in the Carib country, near the river Byera, which separated the English territory from the Indian settlement. Two years of trial were given to this experiment; when, having no encouragement whatsoever from the Caribs, old or young, the mission was reluctantly withdrawn, and to all human appearance the 'day of grace' closed. It is said that Mrs. Baxter, on taking 'leave, wept at their rejection of the Gospel, and earnestly prayed that they might have another " call," before the things which made for their everlasting peace were for ever hidden from their eyes. At the same time, she earnestly besought God, that when another call should reach them, they might not reject it, as they had hitherto slighted the overtures of salvation which had been made to them.'

Half a century has elapsed since the visit of Mr. Mann and myself to the Grand Sable Settlement. But the impression made upon me as I gazed at this remnant of a once numerous race, and called to mind the cruel methods by which it had been almost destroyed 'from off the face of the earth,' created an agony of regretful sorrow and shame which has never wholly left me since. They were dejected, sulky, and apparently so much under the influence of an ungratified revengefulness of feeling, that it was almost an unbearable burden to see them. We had intruded into their secrecy, and were standing face to face with the unfortunate survivors of an ancestry whom our countrymen had so cruelly spoliated and killed. What could we say? What could we do? Such wrongs could not be condoned by anything that we might proffer. We stood self-convicted for our country's villanies to an innocent and helpless race. As we came, so we departed, from a scene so full of mournful antecedents, feeling that our absence would be a sensible relief to those whose 'hiding-place' we had so sacrilegiously invaded.

Jan. 5th, 1839.—My visit to the 'Windward' now closed, and I returned to Kingstown, drawing bridle only at Biabou. On entering the mission house our Father Crane, as he was affectionately called, met me with a benignant smile and greeting: 'Welcome back again,' said he: 'how are you? I am glad to see you.' I felt much at home with this common-sense, happy, dignified family. The true affinity of Methodist mission life was a realistic fact in St. Vincent's. The Calder, Biabou, and Georgetown Homes were occupied by generous inmates, who were pleased, on every proper occasion, 'to entertain strangers' without ostentation, fuss, or niggardliness. The mission house at Kingstown, the centre of population and head-quarters of our ecclesiastical establishment, was, by general consent and understanding, 'a house of call:' a place of refreshment and rest for the brother- and sister-hoods of mission families throughout the island. And nothing could exceed the generosity and affection of the Reverend 'Gaius,' 'our host,' and that of his excellent wife, Mrs. Crane, whose full-orbed and intelligent countenance was itself a welcome to the obligated visitor.

A halting stage, but not a place of rest, was Kingstown to be to me at this time. By water to 'Leeward,' under the watchful 'steer' of the Rev. Joseph A. Marsden, our indefatigable missionary at Princes' Town, Barronallie, was the course laid out for me. At 5 p.m., we were in our canoe with four black men 'laying to the oars' with all their strength, pulling us with rapid speed to the place of our destination. We glided pleasantly over the green, pellucid waters of the bay, and rounded, without a 'baptism' from Neptune, the 'Old Woman's Point,' where the rush and roar of the converging waves are sometimes appalling. We hugged the coast-line as much as possible, keeping clear of the rocks and backwash of the sea as we cleared the boldly jutting promontories, which mark the romantic outline of land and cliffs, and arrived at length at the mission place of disembarking, safe and sound. This was my first experience in canoeing, but I took to it as if 'to the manner born,' and soon learnt to steer over any kind of wave or sea without fear or trepidation. Indeed, my nautical daring for seven years on the Kingsbridge river, Devon, now stood me in good stead in piloting our cockle-shell canoes in these West India waters. Mrs. Marsden's reception of me was most kind, and quite in keeping with the unobtrusive, warm hospitality for which the Yorkshire Methodist homes, from one of which she came, are beautiful examples.

My first Sunday at the Leeward was a busy day. Early in the morning I rode some seven miles or so to Layon, where we had an old rickety chapel full of people waiting for my arrival. I preached and held a Love-feast. The Missionary Marsden was a true Yorkshireman for feeding and drawing out the unsophisticated nature of these negro Christians. The mother of the Society, as she was filially called, was a coloured elderly lady—a Mrs. Gardner—a woman of rare piety, gifts, and commanding influence. She rose and gave her testimony to the work of the Holy Spirit in her soul with modesty and hopefulness. Others also, in rapid succession, gave witness with tearful joy to the comfort with which the religion brought by the missionaries had invested them. At 10.30 a.m., I remounted my steed and hastened back to Barronallie, and commenced a second service. The chapel, to use an Irishism, without I hope offence, was filled inside and out. The Renewal of Covenant Service followed, and the Lord's Supper was administered. In the evening I once more preached to a full house, and thus concluded the laborious exercises of this hallowed day.

Alas for me! before I had time to recoup my used-up strength, Mr. Marsden summoned me for a trip farther to the Leeward. We were this time to go to Chateaubellair, about twelve to fifteen miles distant, bearing to the north-west of the island. Our first adventure was at the 'Bottle and Glass,' so called because, to the poetic fancies of the natives, this reef of dangerous rocks resembled near its outer point a bacchanalian party convivially employed. Such was the rush of the turbulent, boiling sea at the outermost point that no canoe could live in it except in very calm weather, so that to shoot our little Niagara was the alternative to progress. Our 'skipper'

3

(Mr. Marsden) gave orders to pull straight for the opening and take advantage of the swell and rush of the wave to get through to the other side. Stealthily coming up within a few feet of the edge of the opening our men 'lay on their oars.' Counting each wave as it dashed over, the fifth, which was always of greater volume than were the ordinary ones, the stroke oarsman, John B., cried, '*now*'—'*now*'—'NOW,' with tremendous emphasis, and away we went on the crest of the swelling, rushing sea, clean over the sharp pointed rocks, and the danger was passed. Many a canoe has come to grief, and many lives have been lost, at the 'Bottle and Glass;' but, strange as it may appear, we became so accustomed to the romance and danger of the 'pass,' as even to like it. In after years, when stationed to the 'Leeward,' the 'Old Woman's Point' and the 'Bottle and Glass,' were an inspiration to me. I liked the peril, and gloried in facing it.

But we were not to reach Chateaubellair on this occasion. A strong north-wester had been blowing all the previous night, causing a terrific sea all along the coast, and making it dangerous for us to proceed. Mr. Marsden, therefore, ordered the men to pull into a small bay, where we landed. We spent the day with a Mr. Beilby, the hospitable manager of the plantation, and in the cool of the evening we walked over the intervening hills back to Barrouallie.

A new experience was now awaiting me. The next morning, just as the day began to break, I was awoke from a sound sleep by a kind of subterranean wave of jerky and undulating motion. It seemed to come from seaward, passed up under the house and shook it most violently. What is this? thought I. Before I had time to pick myself up, Brother Marsden, whose room was on the other side of the hall, called out, 'Don't be afraid; it is only an earthquake; it will soon be over.' But, if not afraid, I was concerned for my personal safety, and wondered whether I would not be better off outside the building than inside of it. Jumping out of bed and throwing open the shutters, I could see how matters were looking in the yard. The female servant was all astir, and rushed towards the kitchen to the man-servant for protection. 'Budde Cudgo,' said she, 'do hear de ground shake? I did tink the house wid fall.' But it did not fall. For, being built of wood, it caught the sweep and jump of the commotion underneath and escaped unhurt. But Mr. Marsden that morning at the family altar did not forget to recognise the presence of the Fatherly hand which had protected us from harm and death.

I remained at the Leeward over the Sabbath, and returned to Kingstown on the Monday morning. I found Mr. Marsden engaged in raising subscriptions for the remnant of a shipwrecked crew of English sailors who had landed on the previous Sabbath day. Charity, like religion, seems to know no fatigue. Here was this indefatigable missionary—a man whose height was six feet at least, and weight perhaps fifteen stone—trudging about under the fierce rays of a vertical sun, begging from all classes of the people money for purchasing clothes for these unfortunate men, and to send them on their way.

The case was this. On December 6th they had sailed from Sierra Leone bound for London. On the eighth day after their departure the ship was struck on the weather quarter by a heavy sea, and she began to fill very fast. Two boats were launched and victualled, the captain and thirteen men manned the long boat, and the chief mate and seven men the other. The first attempt was to reach Cape de Verde, and for eight long days this course was tried without success. The second boat in the meantime had disappeared. The captain then steered for Barbadoes, which was some three thousand miles distant. For thirty-two days there on the Atlantic they had to subsist on the scantiest supply of food, whilst, during the last fortnight, they had to subsist on two wine-glasses of water and a small bit of biscuit per man *per diem.* Arriving off Barbadoes, the men had not sufficient strength to pull into Carlisle Bay, and so they had to drift to leeward in the hope of catching St. Vincent's and anchoring in Kingstown harbour. Poor fellows, ' when the eye saw them it pitied them,' and 'the blessing of them that were ready to perish came upon' the good missionary and his sympathising friends.

Jan. 20th.—I preached at Kingstown, and received six candidates for 'membership. I laid down for them only two conditions: (1) That they would, by the grace of God, abandon all sinful ways and practices. (2) They were to resolve, by the same help, to be good members. And were not these sufficient? So I believed, and so I said. The pledge on their part was: 'We are tired of sin and are ashamed of ourselves. We pray God may forgive us.' I entered their names in the Candidates' book to be read at the first Leaders' meeting thereafter, when, if no objection was raised, the names would be entered on the class-books for further instruction. Up to that point the pastor's action was scripturally complete.

I went a second time to the Windward, and spent nine days with Mr. and Mrs. Lee and Mr. Parsons, their adopted son, at Calder. During this time we went to Georgetown to the laying of the foundation stone of a new mission church for the accommodation of the numerous families who had been brought into church relations with us through the untiring labours of the Rev. John Mann. The Christian negroes as a thankoffering to God placed seventy-nine dollars on the stone. The next day I returned to Kingstown to attend the District meeting.

A sad event has now to be noticed. The Rev. Mr. Crane on the 30th was seized with malignant fever. In the hope that a change of air might be helpful to him, he was removed to the hills about three miles from Kingstown, where I went to see him. Everything that medical skill could do for him was promptly done, but without avail. On the fourth day of his illness he died. His last words were : 'I am on the rock. I am safe—all is well.'

Feb. 4th.—The District Meeting was commenced under the able presidency of the Rev. John Cullingford, besides whom there were present the Revs. George Beard, John Wood, William Moister, George Ranyell, John Mann, John Blackwell, Joseph A. Marsden, John Lee, William Bannister, James Bickford, and Henry Hurd. The last three had just joined the district, and were affectionately received. The usual annual letter from the London Committee was read by Mr. Moister, the District Secretary. This was a comprehensive and valuable document, in which the financial and spiritual condition of each circuit, as shown in the reports and accounts of the preceding year, were reviewed. There was, I thought, an air of sharp business in the whole of the proceedings. The grant for the year, for example, was apportioned, after a full discussion, to the respective circuits, according to their wants. With this assistance all deficiencies were to be met, as the London Committee would not admit any supplementary claim. Special cases of affliction, medical and funeral expenses, were, however, not included in the ordinary expenditure. The education grant was divided according to the number and classification of the schools in each of the islands. The District Treasurer was an important functionary. He had to receive from the brethren their dues to the 'Old Preachers' Fund,'

Yours affectionately

Wm H Moister

WOODBURYPRINT, WATERLOW & SONS LIMITED.

From a Negative by **BRUNSKILL,** *Windermere.*

the Connexional Education Fund, the Foreign Missions' Contributions made in the circuits, the annual subscription to the *Watchman* and John Mason's account. This was to be a yearly settling up ; hard lines for some, but safe lines for all.

Feb. 13*th.*—The District meeting closed, having been in session nine days. I was appointed as colleague to the Rev. William Moister, in Trinidad.

Feb. 15*th.*—Messrs. Beard, Wood, Moister and I, went on board a small American schooner, and sailed for our destinations. As the time for ' turning in ' came round, I enquired of my superintendent, Mr. Moister, what were the arrangements for our sleeping. His look, rather than words, was an answer ; looking down upon me, for he was a tall man, he seemed to say with that expressive eye of his, ' Inexperienced youth, you will soon find out for yourself.' Then looking upon the cleanly swept quarter-deck, he audibly said, ' Well, as for me, I shall take the softest plank, and I recommend my brethren to follow my example.' The fact is, that we had neither mattresses nor pillows ; and so, making the best of it, clad in my outfit cloak and travelling cap, I stretched myself, for the first time in my life, upon a plank bed, and quietly went to sleep. The sky was clear and the wind fair ; we soon passed under Bequia, hugged the Grenadines, and at dawn of day we stood across the channel and sheltered under the lee of Grenada. Mr. Moister, our ' captain of the mess,' was on the look-out for a good breakfast for us, of which we all partook with hearty relish. With the forenoon we had nearly a dead calm, and not till the evening had we the usual land breeze to enable us to enter the Caunage at St. George's the next morning.

At 10 a.m. I went on shore and called on my fellow-passengers per *Berkely*, and found them very glad to see me. At 3 p.m. I went on board the schooner and found Mr. Moister displeased that I had remained so long on shore. I had learnt, when a Sunday-school teacher in Kingsbridge, that ' a soft answer turneth away wrath,' and so I thought I had better begin the practice at once. It answered admirably. Mr. Moister was placated, and I had shown no unworthy temper. Good for both of us.

We had a fine run across the ninety miles' stretch of sea lying between Grenada and Trinidad. We made the north coast of the island, which is bold and sharply cut, behind which, and rising in some instances over two thousand feet above the sea-level, there is a chain of mountains truly South American. As we reached the Bocäs (Sp. mouths), we had hoped to pass quickly through one of them into the Gulf of Paria, but we were cruelly disappointed through the failure of the wind. Our little vessel rolled and tossed on the unbroken, heavy swell of the sea all that day and the next, which was the Sabbath. Sometimes we were so near the rocky cliffs and headlands that we could touch them with a long pole ; and then the relentless current, rushing from the Gulf, would sweep us far back into the ocean outside. The fierce rays of Sol fell upon the deck during those two terrible days in such a degree that loco-motion was impossible, and our faces and hands were sorely blistered. At 10 p.m. on the second day a light wind sprang up from the north-west, and gently wafted us beyond the inner line of the sweeping currents.

Feb. 18th.—We reached the ' Five Islands,' when we were again becalmed. We waited for four long hours for a favouring breeze, when the good captain, out of sheer pity for us, manned a boat and sent us on to Port of Spain, the capital of the island.

TRINIDAD, 1839.

We were soon at the mission house, and Mrs. Moister did all that lay in her power to refresh and comfort us after the blistering and the exhausting ordeal through which we had passed. The ordinary heat of Trinidad is as much as most white men can bear ; but the additional blaze and fire of the sun we had outside the Bocäs and in the Gulf were enough to half kill the bravest of men. This was to me a terrible ' baptism of fire,' the effect of which I felt for long. Mr. Moister, however, after such experience he had had in Western Africa and Demerara, very soon recovered. Of course, I was not to go to Couva, situate about halfway on the eastern side of the gulf, between Port of Spain and San Fernando, until I had spent a Sabbath in this queen of tropical cities, and had called upon the Kennedys, the Cleavers, the Beilbys, the Brodies, and other friends. By invitation I preached in the morning in the Presbyterian Church, and in the evening in the Wesleyan. Several of the ' Lady Mico Charity ' day-school teachers, just come from England, were present at the evening service.

The time had come for me to go to Couva, the station to which I had been appointed by the District Meeting. Mr. Moister went with me to lay in such provisions as I should require when 'down coast.' Mr. Gould, a respectable coloured merchant, attended to my wants. A good Yorkshire ham, a half-firkin of Cork butter, two hampers of American potatoes, a small bag of flour, with tea, coffee, and cocoa, were recommended as essentials for my daily consumption. Drinkables, in small quantities, were also put in. In those dark days—now fifty years ago—it was thought that without alcoholic stimulants no Englishman, nor Scotchman either, for that matter, could live and labour in the exhausting climate of Trinidad. But this dream, like many others, equally foolish and pernicious, has been dispelled by the larger experiences of Europeans and better modes of living. My kind superintendent accompanied me to Couva, to see for himself that all proper arrangements had been made for my comfort, and in the evening returned by the local steamer to Port of Spain.

And now I was 'left alone:' a kind of missionary Crusoe, 'the monarch of all I surveyed.' But I had a man 'Friday,' in the person of Alfred, who was to be my cook, butler, groom, housemaid, church-keeper, gardener, errand-man, and companion, all rolled into one. 'A faithful man' was Alfre' (Nig.), 'and feared God above many.' Said he to me one day: 'Minister, I want you to let me get married!' 'Indeed,' I replied, 'to whom?' Said he, 'Sister Phillis!' 'What,' I rejoined, 'marry your sister?' 'Minister no understand,' said he naïvely; 'is she not a member of the Church? Is she not a sister then?' 'Yes, yes,' I replied; 'Alfre', fix the day, and I will tie the knot.' They were married in due course before quite a select company of 'brothers and sisters' in the mission church, and a happier couple never lived on the premises than were they. One day I sent him to the bay for a hamper of potatoes. He put his naked feet into the stirrups, except the great toes of the right and left feet, which he wisely kept outside the rim with which to hold on. By-and-by, hearing some one riding up to the gate, I looked from my study window to see what possible magnate (planter or doctor, perhaps) might be coming. To my surprise it was Alfre', but I never saw him look so tall before. As he neared the house, I perceived that he had hoisted the hamper upon the top of his head, thereby keeping his hands free for other purposes.

'Hallo, Alfre', what is up, eh?' 'Ah,' said he, 'metink he be easy for de horse for me carry him so.' 'Well done, Alfre',' said I; 'a righteous man regardeth the life of his beast,' the good Book has said.

I shall never forget this kind-hearted fellow. When I had my seasoning fever, he offered to cure me better than the doctor (Graham). So he set to work. He collected and boiled up together some new rum, just from the still; a quantity of lime-juice, Irish butter, and a handful of sweating herbs, and made of them a drink, certainly, such as for noxiousness, I had never tasted before. I went to bed, and then Alfre' administered his nostrum, and almost smothered me with sheets and blankets. That was a night to be remembered. The fever was not sweated out, but my poor life was almost perspired away. Poor, disappointed Alfre'! But he did his best: it was a perilous best for me. Fortunately, a Mr. William Cleaver, then a student for our work, came to my relief; and, at Mr. Moister's request, I immediately left for Port of Spain. By the blessing of God, under the skilful treatment of Dr. Murray, the affectionate care of Mrs. Moister, and the nursing night and day, without intermission for nearly a fortnight, by Polly Philips, one of our church sisters, I got rid of my fever, and was able to return to my much-loved work at Couva.

My work at this station lay mostly among the sugar plantations. The principal services during my first year, on the Sabbath, were at Couva and San Fernando alternately. On week evenings I preached at Felicity Hall, Milton, Carolina, Cedar Hill, and Palmiste plantations. I occasionally visited Camben, Exchange, Providence, Claxton Bay, and Cedar Grove, in the Naparimas. My hands were full, every minute of my time was employed, and all the planters received me with confidence, and all the people with gratitude. The Rev. Mr. Hurd was appointed our missionary at San Fernando in my second year, which relieved me from the longer journeys and exposure to heavy rains and scorching heat. The new church at San Fernando was built in Mr. Hurd's first year; the parsonage also. At the time of the consecration of the church, Mr. Hurd was ill with fever in Port of Spain, and Mr. Moister and I conducted the opening services. To Mr. Moister's great personal influence with the Government, and attorneys of the sugar plantations, is our church mainly indebted for the initiation and completion of this commanding establishment in the very heart of this the second town of the colony.

San Fernando was the natural key to the sugar-producing district of Naparima, and upon several of the plantations were located many of our best informed and loyal adherents.

My two years at Couva passed very rapidly. My health had so much broken, and my sense of solitude had so depressed my soul, that I found it indispensable to seek a removal to St. Vincent's as the most likely part of the district in which I might be set up again for the work of my life. My lot at Couva had been one of ever-recurring fever; my nervous energy had collapsed; I was no longer the same man. It was difficult to believe that my strong constitution could have been so wrecked in two short years. The official parting took place early in January 1841, after the morning service at Couva, amid much hand-squeezing, fervent prayers, and many tears. Mr. Hurd had come over from San Fernando, and in the evening we rode over to Felicity Hall plantation, and held another service. We slept that night in Brother Samuel Kennedy's house ('hut,' Nig.), so as to be ready at daylight to go to the landing place for embarkation. Nearly all the adult people marched with us in procession, and when we reached the bank of the Paria, there and then, under the branches of a lofty cocoa-nut tree, we sang the Hymn 534 (Wesley), followed by prayer and consecration. I sprang into the boat, for my heart was breaking, and begged to be at once put on board the sloop lying at anchor some distance from the shore. Such is the history of my first experiences on a mission station in the West Indies.

The District Meeting of 1841 was held in Tobago. We called at Grenada on our way, and were joined by the Rev. John and Mrs. Wood. We took a whole week to beat from St. George's, *via* the windward of Tobago, round to Scarborough, the port and capital of the island. We had to record the retirement of the Rev. Joseph A. Marsden, who, solely on account of health, had early in the preceding year, with Mrs. Marsden, returned home. Mr. Marsden's possibilities were undoubtedly great; but his build and bulk unfitted him for our West India work. The Revs. John Mann and John and Mrs. Wood had also gone to England; add to which the unexpected deaths of the Rev. John and Mrs. Lee, after a few days of fever, at Calliaqua, diminished our staff, and rendered the supplying

of the circuits a great difficulty. For the first time we received a
white canditate, a Mr. William Cleaver, who was born in Trinidad.
He was much help to us in our dire extremity.

St. Vincent's, 1841.

By the District Meeting I was appointed to labour in St. Vincent's,
and entered upon my work on the 10th of February. The congregations of my pastoral charge were those of Calliaqua and Calder,
numbering about fifteen hundred souls. The Marriqua valley had
to be missioned by me besides. In this romantic valley there resided
many families of freeholders, who were mostly engaged in growing
and preparing arrowroot for exportation to England; the cocoa-
berry also, which was a valuable article of export. The scenery,
with its majestic stream flowing through its centre, was mountainous
and grand. It was a place much to be desired, and here the people
lived in quietude, each family pursuing the cultivation of the rich
soil, and doing their very best for both worlds.

On 23rd of April, I received from Dr. Alder an interesting
communication. It was to the effect that the London Committee
had decided on sending the Revs. W. Limmex and S. Durrie to our
help, together with Mrs. Limmex and the Misses Tapp and Silifant.
Mr. Hurd and I were requested to be in Barbadoes on the arrival
of the ship *Mercy* to meet our friends. Accordingly, I left Kingstown
on the following morning in the sloop *Mary* for that island. After
beating up the Becqui channel from 6 a.m. to 1 p.m. without much
success, the captain resolved to proceed under the lee of St. Vincent
away to the northward, and when he had made a good 'offing' stand
direct for Barbadoes. In the middle of the next day, to my great
pleasure, I saw the Royal Mail steamer *Tartarus*, from Jamaica,
steering straight for Castries, the harbour of St. Lucia. I immediately asked the captain to follow in her wake and put me on board.
Having cleared the island, we made direct for Barbadoes, and when,
next day, we were about midway on our voyage, our attention was
called to a dismasted emigrant ship on our lee with the usual flag of
distress flying. We made towards her, and our captain offered help.
A hawser was soon attached, and we had the gratification to tow her
in safety to Carlisle Bay.

Whilst breakfasting, on the 5th of May, one of our friendly

'watchers' announced that the good ship *Mercy* had hove in sight. My generous host, the Rev. Alexander Mausie, and I soon started for the wharf, secured a boat, and boarded the ship just as the anchor was dropped. All the members of the mission party were well and delighted at the termination of their voyage. As soon as possible we went on shore, when a hospitable and loving welcome was accorded to the party by Mr. and Mrs. Mausie. The next day, the 6th, Miss Tapp and I were married in the James Street Church by Mr. Mausie, in the presence of a large number of friends and well-wishers for our happiness. It would be impossible to forget the generous kindness of Dr. and Mrs. King, Mr. and Mrs. Walsh, Mr. and Mrs. Austin, Mr. and Mrs. Hamilton, the Gills and Hynes, and other friends.

On the 14th the party sailed for St. Vincent's in the brig *Helen*, and anchored the next day in Kingstown Harbour. Mrs. Bickford and I proceeded at once to Calliaqua, and took possession of our humble home the same evening.

The month of August in St. Vincent's is the most sickly of the year. I did not escape the endemic visitation. On the fourth or fifth day after my attack I had to be carried from my bed to the hall and laid upon the sofa for the benefit of cooler air. The leaders and some other members of our church surrounded the house and watched for the final event. In the merciful providence of God, Brother Parsons called to make enquiry for me, who, seeing the prostrate and dangerous condition I was in, he remounted his horse and hastened to the Prospect plantation, and asked the Hon. and Rev. Nathaniel Struth to send his carriage instanter to convoy me to the healthier locality of Calder Ridge, one of the Trust estates, of which he was the manager. In the course of a couple of hours Mrs. Bickford and I were on our way, and the cool air much revived me. But the crisis—the ninth day—was not yet passed. It came, however, and Dr. Choppin privately told my friend, Mr. Parsons, that if the vomiting returned during the night, I would die before the morning.

Two black women, Mrs. Ovid and Mrs. Harvey, who were in attendance night and day upon me, asked the doctor's permission to try what they could do. 'Oh, yes,' said he, with an ominous shake of the head; 'you may try!' Without the loss of five minutes these Christian nurses prepared a quantity of lime-juice and the coldest water that could be got for sopping the skin all over the body, and an admixture for internal use, of nauseous ingredients, to be swallowed without challenge or questioning. And so they went to work. For fully six hours they ceased not their efforts, when, at 2 a.m., they had the satisfaction of observing a change for the better. God be praised! The fever was broken, and the perspiration streamed from every pore. I shall never forget the 'sweet rest in sleep' which followed for several hours. Dr. Choppin came earlier than was usual for him, and learnt from Mr. Parsons the altered condition of things. Coming into the room, with an evident intensity of satisfaction, he addressed words of comfort to us, saying, 'The danger is over and gone.'

TOBAGO, 1842.

By the English Conference I was appointed superintendent of our mission in the island of Tobago. The Rev. S. H. Durrie was to be my colleague, and to reside at Mount St. George. After the District Meeting, January 1842, we prepared for our voyage. To go direct, as well as to save time and expense, I chartered the *William McCaul,* a sloop of thirty-five tons burthen, to convey us thither. Starting from the port of Calliaqua with a strong north-west wind we cleared Mustique, the most easterly of the Grenadines, and shaped our course for Tobago. But, making no allowance for the strong current to the windward at that season of the year, we were too high by a full point.

The voyage, under ordinary circumstances, should be made in twenty-four to thirty hours; but on our seeing no land after four days' sailing I became anxious, knowing that we must have overshot the island. To our dismay, I found that Captain Brown had neither chart nor quadrant, so that it was impossible for our real position to be fixed. Besides which, we had passed beyond the deep blue water, and were rushing along in the pale green, which I knew to be somewhere opposite the Oronooko, whose freshlets pale the sea for a hundred miles from the coast. After consulting with Mr. Durrie I insisted that the vessel should be put about, keeping down a point or two below north-west, so that, perchance, on our way back we might make land somewhere. Missing Tobago, I contended that we should be brought up at the Grenadines, or, possibly, at St. Vincent's itself. We had two captains; the responsible in Mr. Brown, and a consultative in Mr. ——. But they did not agree, so I had to assume the direction myself. ''Bout ship,' I cried. Brown dissented, but I was inexorable. 'Steer as I tell you, and we will find out in time where we are.' After proceeding about sixty hours in a north-west by west course, a man at the bows sang out, 'Land ahead!' I immediately called the two captains to tell us what land it was, but neither knew. 'Then lay off and on until daylight, when we shall be able to decide where we are, and in the meantime I will "turn in."' But, as soon as I left the deck, the captains resolved for another departure, and in a totally contrary direction. At 5 a.m. I was awakened by an alarm on the deck, and the cry, 'The boat, the boat!' I climbed up the 'companion ladder' and found that our craft had heeled over amid furious waves; one of which had 'come on board' and taken our cockleshell boat over the bulwarks into the raging sea. An attempt was made to get hold of the boat, but without success. 'Let her go,' said I, 'or presently we shall lose the vessel also.' Another grumble from the captains, and the recovery of the boat was given up. 'And now, Captain Brown,' I enquired, 'where is the land we saw last night?' 'I don't know,' he replied. 'Well, then, put the vessel before the wind, and we will go where God's good providence may take us. We shall fall in with land somewhere.' We thus sailed the whole day, when, to our great joy, we saw looming in the distance three sharply pointed mountainous formations. 'There are the "sugar-loaves" of St. Lucia,' I said; but the captains were so confused that they could not even recognise them. ·The island of St. Vincent,' I said, 'lies somewhere over there; shape your course in that direction, and we shall be all right in the morning.'

By the mercy of God we came to anchor in the Calliaqua harbour a little before break of day, and re-entered the mission house which we had vacated some ten days previously.

I duly reported our failure to reach Tobago to the Rev. John Cullingford, the District Chairman, and early in the following week we made a second start in the *William McCaul*, but with a new captain. This time we were successful. Our arrival at Scarborough was an immense relief to those of our friends who had learnt of our previous departure from St. Vincent's and were at a loss to know what had become of us. Mr. Durrie and I entered upon our work in good spirits and were determined to extend the mission to the

Windward as far as Man of War bay, and on the northern side as far as Englishman's bay. By God's favour, the good cause advanced by 'leaps and bounds;' and much jealousy in some quarters was felt at our great success. It was even averred that the whole island would become Methodist unless some check was administered. A rumour was accordingly started damaging to my colleague's ministry, which led to an interview between Governor Darling and myself, when I took the liberty of assuring His Excellency of my colleague's faith and of the prudence of his public utterances. And I published a somewhat smart and defiant letter in the press upon the difference we make between character and persons,—the former being within our rights; the latter we left alone. The most cutting thing I said was, that as ministers of Christ, we would do our best to meet the public demand made upon us as expositors of the Scriptures; but that we had come under no obligation to supply to an indiscriminate public a faculty for understanding what we said relating thereto.

In the month of December a great affliction came upon one of our best families in the death of Mr. Bovell, a respectable merchant, local preacher, and trustee of our church. Mrs. Bovell, his wife, was an eminently holy and useful woman. By the sudden removal of her husband, she was left with a large family of girls to be educated and fitted for the positions in life they were entitled to. And the widow's God helped her to do this. Mr. Bovell's dying testimony was highly satisfactory: 'I am a man,' he said, 'of few words, but I can say that ever since I was sixteen years of age, the good hand of God has been with me. I have never lost the peace of God. I have always had the evidence of my acceptance; and, at times, I have enjoyed the blessing of sanctification. I have no doubt on this subject; but my mind is not stayed upon HIM as I wish.' To Mr. Robert George Ross, a dear brother in the Lord, also a local preacher and leader, he said, 'Christ is precious to my soul. I am on the rock: all is right.' The day of interment was one of great sorrow to the inhabitants. It was felt by all that a good citizen and servant of God 'was not;' and the Church and community had suffered a great loss.

The commendable interest still felt in England by eminent philanthropists was practically evinced this year by the arrival of Messrs. Edwin Tregelles and James Jessop, from the Society of

Friends, that they might make personal enquiry into the condition of the emancipated classes. These excellent men made themselves quite at home at the mission house and we felt greatly honoured at having them as our temporary guests. They addressed the people in our churches as they had opportunity, and were well received. But the sight of two men sitting with their hats on in the pulpit, waiting to be 'moved by the Spirit' before they rose to speak, was a little too much for the risible faculties of the black and coloured people. When, however, Mr. Tregelles rose there was perfect silence; they seemed at once subdued and listened with rapt attention. Mr. Jessop followed in homely and touching words, and much feeling was evinced. These good men had been travelling all over the island in visiting the sugar plantations and free settlements, and were much satisfied with what they had seen and heard.

We ushered in the new year (1844) in a novel manner. We invited the teachers and scholars from Mason Hall, Mount St. George, and Plymouth to unite with the Scarborough school in a grand festival. We commenced with singing and prayer in the church, and then the Rev. William English and I examined the scholars in the catechisms and scriptural knowledge. We then marched in order through the town and formed a square in the market-place, which was admirably adapted for such a gathering. Immediately in front of the court-house the ministers and leading friends stood, delivered addresses, and sang 'God save the Queen.' We then returned to the church and regaled five hundred and forty children with tea, cakes, and many kinds of fruit. All our friends said the whole demonstration was grand and beautiful! This was our answer to those jealous co-religionists who had maligned us. Was 'there not a cause?'

It was a great sorrow to us to remove from Tobago at the end of two years. Our membership, during our incumbency, had sprung from about five hundred to twelve hundred and fifteen. The circuit income had correspondingly increased and was sufficient for the support of two married missionaries, besides which there had been contributed for foreign missions over three hundred pounds, for 1843, which I paid to the District Treasurer for transmission to the parent society in London. But a change, nevertheless, appeared indispensable for our health's sake, which had been much weakened during the year by severe attacks of fever. By the Grenada District

Meeting, I was removed to Chateaubellair, in St. Vincent's, in the hope that its better climate would contribute to the restoration of our strength. Still the inconvenience and hardships of such a wandering and unsettled life, in a tropical climate, affected our spirits and tried us greatly. And no wonder; because, in it all, there was the conscious fact of an undersapping of our originally fine constitution, which, sooner or later, would inevitably collapse.

Our voyage from Tobago to Grenada, a distance of perhaps one hundred and twenty miles, was very trying. Lying almost directly to leeward, we expected an easy run of some thirty hours or so. The Rev. William English and Mrs. English, Mrs. Bickford and I, were the only passengers. We had no sooner cleared the land and shaped our course than the wind utterly failed us, and for the next six days we drifted about as if upon ' a sea of glass.' The only breezes we could get at all were in the night. We at length got to St. George's harbour 'more dead than alive.' Ill in body and mind, I was completely unfitted for the business of the District Meeting, and it was a merciful relief to me when its sessions closed.

St. Vincent's, 1844.

I opened my mission at Chateaubellair on the 18th of January by preaching twice to our people. We had a few whites and about fifty coloured; the remainder being mostly labourers from the neighbouring plantations. The Rev. George Ranyell, the Rev. S. H. Durrie, and I were the circuit ministers this year. I had charge of Chateaubellair and the surrounding district, being twenty-five to thirty-five miles from Kingstown, where the superintendent resided. On the second Sabbath, the 25th, I preached twice in Kingstown to large congregations. This building will accommodate easily fifteen hundred persons, not including the children attending the Sunday school. It is a lasting monument of the foresight and zeal of the Rev. John Cullingford, who designed and superintended the erection of this noble structure.

It was our happiness once more to entertain Messrs. Tregelles and Jessop in our humble home at this station. They visited the plantations that they might see for themselves the condition of the field labourers. I accompanied these worthy men to the black

KINGSTOWN, ST. VINCENT'S.

Carib settlement along the sea coast about seven miles from Chateaubellair. Purposely, we passed through Fitzhugher, Richmond, and two other plantations on our way thither, that our friends might watch the process of cutting, carting, and crushing the sugar canes at the mills. The crop season is one of a cheerful character to whites and blacks alike. Extempore songs in the cane fields and willing co-operation at the works mark the recurrence of every day's engagements. At that time, so well did the planters and labourers understand each other that a large return was a mutual satisfaction. ' Plenty of sugar good for Buckra and Neger too,' was the expressed belief of employers and *employés* equally.

Arriving at the fort of Morne Ronde (Fr.) the head man, John Lewis, met us and conducted us up along the rocky steeps to the solitary and mountainous home of these sons of the forest. The shell was blown, and the people came from their hiding places to the house of prayer. Mr. Tregelles conducted the service. Every word he uttered was full of dignified courtesy; whilst his references to the terrible struggles of their forefathers with those Europeans who had reduced their once powerful tribe to a mere remnant of humanity were cautious and pathetic. The prayers offered by these Christian Englishmen, before parting, were such as could only be uttered by men accustomed to ponder over the misfortunes of aboriginal races with tearful regrets and burning shame.

St. Vincent's was the land of earthquakes. About 3 a.m. on *August* 31*st*, I was awoke from a sound sleep by an unearthly sound, as if ten thousand horses were trampling heavily on the ground. It appeared as if coming from the sea, making its way through the township into the valley which terminated in the mountainous range farther up. Mrs. Bickford tremblingly reached her hand to me, and asked, ' What is it ? ' I told her that it was an earthquake of a severe kind, ' but let us put our trust in God.' I got out of bed to draw a match, but could not move across the room to do it. When the shock really passed underneath the house it seemed as if we were being tossed up and down, to and fro, by some terrible monster, as easily as a child would jump and toss a doll. My poor wife in this extremity exclaimed, ' The Lord have mercy upon us ; ' and I fell upon my knees and joined in the appeal to Heaven for protection and deliverance. It certainly seemed as if the ' day of doom ' had come !

4

I transcribe from my journal the following record under date, *December 11th*, 1844 :—

'Six years ago this day Mr. Hurd and I landed from the ship *Berkely* in Kingstown. I have spent two years in Trinidad, two in Tobago, and the remainder in St. Vincent's. I have had four severe attacks of fever, and have been frequently exposed to imminent peril, both by sea and land. I have seen some souls converted to God, who will be my joy and crown of rejoicing. I have many dear and valued friends, and I believe no human foes. Praise the Lord, O my soul ! Let my life be wholly Thine ! '

1845.

My colleagues this year were the Revs. W. Bannister, J. F. Browne, W. Heath, and D. Barley. I gratefully record the fact that Mr. Barley's coming into the circuit was a great blessing to me. His earnest spirituality, untiring zeal and ability as a preacher, were a stimulus to me, from which period I date a new spring and force in my ministry. Under such conditions the year passed rapidly away, and the hand of the Lord was upon us for good.

'*April 25th.*—This day the Rev. G. T. Connell, Anglican minister, Mrs. Bickford, and I visited the Souffrière. We were well repaid for the fatigue we underwent in ascending the mountain. Mrs. Bickford rode a mule all the way up to the old crater, notwithstanding the furrowed and broken condition of the earth which had been deeply ploughed by descending lava. On the south side we found an extensive basin, 450 feet deep, nearly round, about four furlongs in width. In the centre rose to the height of 240 feet a miniature hill, which was full of rocky fissures, and covered, in many of its parts, with evergreens and shrubs. This huge crater has long been in a peaceful condition, and a small canoe is now floating upon its waters. Curious visitors sometimes row round this extensive lake for the purpose of sounding its depth. Proceeding up the north line from the eastern side, we came, after a most perilous and fatiguing walk of a mile or more, to the edge of the new crater. Here, on every hand, were marks of past violent eruptions, fearful to behold. There was a dense fog, which hid from our vision the terrible phenomena surrounding us ; but, after waiting for some time, it cleared away and the gulf below revealed itself in all its horridness. It reminded one of hell itself. The old crater charmed but the new one appalled us. We returned to Chateaubellair in the evening impressed with the almightiness of creation's God.'

It was during one of Mr. Barley's visits to Chateaubellair that I arranged for a second visit to the Souffrière, taking with us as our guide our faithful brother and missionaries' friend, Mr. Job Adams. Borrowing, because of their strength and surefootedness, a couple of mules, we made a start after an early breakfast. The first halting place was the 'Halfway Tree.' Here we paused and

were interested in reading the distinguished names which had been
cut into the trunk and branches of this time-honoured tree. We
also cut in our initials. We then proceeded up the side of the
mountain, threading our way on the narrow ridges of the paths
down which the destroying lava had rushed in 1813. Arriving at
the summit, we lost no time in making for the new crater, which was
the special object of our adventure. This dreadful abyss was
covered in by the densest fog I ever witnessed. When it cleared
we found that we were standing on the very edge of the abysmal
pit.

We determined that we would descend to the bottom of this
crater, and we requested Mr. Adams to lead the way. Down we
went over immense boulders, sliding over surfaces, or springing over
the spaces lying between, in a way not to be described. In twenty
minutes we reached the bottom, and we stood alarmed at the rashness
we had shown. Mr. Barley and I wandered all over the cindered
'floor,' tested the sulphureous water, which had gathered in a hollow
of whose depth we could not even form a guess. Job Adams squatted
upon his haunches not twenty feet away from the spot where we
first landed. He was evidently afraid, and some old tradition of the
supernatural must have possessed him. His happiest moment
evidently was when he heard us say, 'Come, it is time for us to get
to the top,' and he briskly led the way. I had never heard of any
white man trying this feat before, and assuredly I would never
dream of repeating it. It took us forty minutes to accomplish our
ascent, and it was the hardest ordeal of physical exertion I had ever
tried. We were so exhausted when we reached our more sensible,
restful mules, that, instead of at once making tracks homeward,
we had to recoup by refreshment, and rest on the ground. Upon
reflection, I am bound to say that it was a piece of foolhardiness,
and should not be ventured upon by English travellers.

1846.

The District Meeting was held in February, in Barbadoes, when
the Rev. John Cullingford presided for the last time over his
brethren. It was very touching to us to see him assisted from day
to day to and from the parsonage to the church in which the
meeting was held. He continued, notwithstanding his weakness,
to guide the deliberations until, within two days of the close of the

session, the minutes were finalized in his chamber, and he affixed his signature in our presence. He died on March 4th, and entered into rest.

My appointment was now, for the second time, Calliaqua, in the Biabou Circuit. But, in consequence of the lamented death of the Chairman, I was removed before the end of the year. The letter relating to this unexpected change is the following :—

'LONDON, June 1st, 1846.

'DEAR BROTHER,—

'The affairs of your district have cost us much anxious thought and deliberation. Such conclusions as have been already come to, we make known to you and the other brethren, by the packet now about to sail.

'In the first place, I have to inform you officially that the Rev. William Bannister is appointed as Chairman of the St. Vincent's District, and he is instructed immediately to enter upon his functions. The Committee are fully persuaded that yourself and other brethren will render him your affectionate and efficient support.

'In the next place, the arrangement decided upon for the Barbadoes Circuit will affect yourself. Mr. Ranyell is directed to proceed at once to Barbadoes, and you are appointed to go immediately to Grenada, instead of waiting until the end of the year. We are very reluctant to disturb a missionary in his appointment before the regular time of removal, but the sudden emergencies which sometimes take place render it indispensably necessary. The case of Barbadoes is one of those emergencies which must be promptly met, and after very anxious consideration of every possible plan, it was agreed that the one which I now announce is the best, and will be most easily effected. Your Superintendent and Chairman are both officially informed, and desired to facilitate your removal at the earliest convenient opportunity.

'Wishing you every needful blessing, I remain, dear brother,

'Yours very affectionately,
'JOHN BEECHAM.

'The Rev. J. Bickford,
    'St. Vincent's, West Indies.'

The application of the itinerant principle in the Wesleyan Methodist Church is sometimes one of great difficulty. Dr. Beecham recognises this fact in the brotherly and wise letter above given. In my case, I had only been a few months in my new station, and yet, without any reference to my people, or to my own sense of duty, I was told to proceed at once to Grenada and take charge of our mission in that island. But the Methodist itinerancy, in some of its aspects, is analogous to the Queen's service. It admits of no challenge ; it demands ungrudging obedience. 'Will you reverently obey your chief ministers, unto whom is committed the charge and government over you; following with a glad mind and with their godly admonitions, and submitting yourselves to their godly judgments?' This was one of the questions put to me by the English President in 1838, at my ordination! In the presence of many witnesses, I honestly said, 'I will.' This was the first time this test in its acutest form came home to me. But I had accepted it with all its consequences. In point of practice, as it then shaped, disobedience would have meant discontinuance in the Ministry—a dropping out of the brotherhood. In the Providence of God I accepted the call, and had the approval of my conscience in so doing.

Action could not be delayed, as my arrival in Grenada was necessary to the departure of the Rev. G. Ranyell. Without, therefore, waiting for the next mail steamer from England, I engaged, in the following week, a small sloop to take us thither. We left Calliaqua in the forenoon of *July 6th*, and anchored at 2.30 p.m., the next day, in the Carenage, St. George's, and were welcomed by Mr. Richard Walker, one of our pious coloured brethren, who kindly conducted Mrs. Bickford to the parsonage, far up in the town.

St. Vincent's has been called the Switzerland, but Grenada may, with equal correctness, be called the Italy, of the West Indies. Its clear, bright atmosphere, tempered by the trade-winds, the hospitality and friendliness of its inhabitants, and complete freedom of caste, make it one of the most inviting places of residence in any part of the Antilles. At that time, too, it was the central depot for coaling the royal mail steamers, and for despatching mails southward to Trinidad, Tobago, and British Guiana; westward to Jamaica, and northward to the Bahamas, including in their respective routes all intermediate places. By this arrangement large numbers of visitors from Europe from the east, and America from the west, were often at St. George's, which helped much to break the monotony of tropical life, and kept us in touch with the outside world.

I commenced my ministry in St. George's on *July 12th*, taking as my texts St. John xvi. 23, and Deut. viii. 2. Later on in the week, I rode across the island to La Baye and preached on the Sabbath morning, returning in time to take the service at St. George's in the evening. I was kindly entertained by Mr. and Mrs. Welch on their plantation, about three miles beyond La Baye, and by Mr. and Mrs. Rapier on my return journey to the capital. Being anxious before casting my plans for working the circuit proper to see what I had to do, I made a visit to Cariacou, an island lying about half-way between Grenada and St. Vincent's. We had two influential families there, Dr. and Mrs. Blair, and Dr. and Mrs. Proudfoot, who were most kind to me. I preached twice in the principal town, met the members for the renewal of their ticket of membership, and administered the Lord's Supper. After a week-evening service, I went on board the sloop *Dædalus*, and arrived in St. George's on the following day.

To show the routine of my work, and the number of visitors who came by the mail steamers, I may give a few extracts from my Diary :—

'*Aug. 25th.*—We were gratified on entertaining for a few hours the Rev. Mr. Burrell from Richmond College, who had been appointed by the English Conference as missionary at Montego Bay, in Jamaica. And by the same steamer, the Rev. Dr. Kalley and Mrs. Kalley came from Madeira. Accompanied by a Portuguese Christian, they had fled for their lives, which were in imminent peril. Dr. Kalley had raised a small Presbyterian congregation, which had set the priests so much against him, that he and his family would have been murdered had they not succeeded, with the help of the few converted Madeirans, in escaping on board the English mail steamer.'

'*Sept. 9th.*—The Rev. T. Haymouth came per mail from England, and preached an excellent sermon to our people, to whom I had sent round and invited to come to the service. It was a famous manifesto of the doctrines we most assuredly believe.'

'*Nov. 20th.*—The Rev. John and Mrs. Mortier came from St. Kitts, on their way to Demerara, to open Trinity Church, which the Rev. W. Hudson had been instrumental in erecting.'

1847.

'*Feb. 6th.*—Returned in the *Reindeer* mail steamer this morning from Demerara, where I had been for the District Meeting. The Revs. W. Fidler, F. Whitehead, W. L. Binks, and Mrs. Bickford came also. The Rev. W. Bannister presided for the first time, and with much ability.'

'*April 11th.*—The Rev. Joseph and Mrs. Webster, also Rev. Mr. Collier, called on their way to Honduras. We had a good time with them.'

'*April 16th.*—This has been a red-letter day with us in St. George's. Governor Hamilton and lady visited and examined our day school. They expressed the pleasure they felt at witnessing the proficiency and good order of the school. Mr. Campbell, the father of the Rev. John Allan Campbell, was our Head Master. His son, John, was a scholar in his father's school at the time the Governor visited it.'

'*June 15th.*—A mournful day for us. The *Great Western* mail ship came in and brought the distressing intelligence of the death of Mrs. Bickford's mother. Her last words were, 'O! blessed Jesus, into Thy hands I commend my spirit.' She had been from childhood a member of our church at Camelford; after her marriage she came to Kingsbridge to live, still maintaining her connection with God's people up to the period of her death. This was the first breach death had made in our family circle during the time we had been away from England. It was hard to say, 'Thy will be done;' for we had wished to see her again, if permitted to return home.'

'*June* 30*th*.—At 5 p.m., I received 'a message from the Government House that His Excellency, Mrs. Hamilton, and Miss Yeo would attend our church that evening. I did the best I could, preaching from Rev. vii. 14. The message was solely for the purpose of our securing for the Viceregal party the necessary accommodation, as our church on Sunday evenings was generally crowded.'

'*Oct.* 22*nd*.—A land of earthquakes, fevers, and hurricanes, is the West Indies. This morning I received a letter from the Rev. Joseph Biggs, Tobago, informing me of the devastating hurricane, which, on the night of the 11th inst., had swept over that island. There were destroyed 30 managers' houses, and 31 much injured. The sugar works of 26 plantations were destroyed, and 33 rendered unfit for use. The homes of 456 small freeholders were thrown down, and 176 rendered uninhabitable. Seventeen persons were killed, and a vast number were more or less injured. In some localities our mission properties had been wrecked. The total loss to the Society would be probably from £1,500 to £1,800. The noise of falling houses in Scarborough, the loud and continued moans of the dying, the danger to life and limb all through that terrible night, mark this visitation of Providence as the most disastrous ever known, or even heard of, by the oldest of the inhabitants.'

'The visitors, who still came as each steamer arrived, were Peter Borthwick, Esq., M.P., whose object was to ascertain by personal enquiry the exact condition of the agricultural and commercial interests in the West Indies; Captain Peel, son of the late Sir Robert Peel, who was passing through to join his ship, I believe, in the Gulf of Mexico; the Rev. David Barley, to preach on behalf of our Foreign Missions, and to address public meetings with the same view. In *November*, I was laid aside by a severe attack of fever, which brought me once more to the very gates of death. Dr. Belfon treated my case with much skill and untiring perseverance; and, in about a week or so, I was able to resume my beloved work, but very feebly.'

1848.

'*Jan.* 27*th*.—The *Everretta* arrived from London, bringing as passengers the Rev. Richard and Mrs. Wrench, the Rev. Thomas H. and Mrs. Butcher, and Miss Howse.—The Rev. W. L. Binks arrived on *February* 4*th*, and, on the next day, the party sailed for St. Vincent's, except Mr. and Mrs. Wrench, who were instructed to proceed to Trinidad. The Revs. W. Hudson, J. Banfield, Henry Pargham, and W. Cleaver called, on their way to the St. Vincent's District Meeting I went with them; Mrs. Bickford also, for the benefit of a change of air and scene.'

The year 1848 was spent 'in labours more abundant.' What with quarterly visits to Cariacou and La Baye, a visit to Gonave, where I preached in the court-house to a large congregation, and the routine work of the churches at St. George's, Woburn, and Constantine, the whole of my time was taken up, and all my energies were severely taxed. But I was happy in my work and in my 'helpers,' who willingly stood by me in all my responsibilities. It sustained me also to know that my character and labours were held in high esteem by the official and leading gentlemen of the colony. At the last public day-school examination in St. George's, we were honoured with the presence of His Excellency Governor Hamilton and Mrs. Hamilton, His Honour Chief Justice Davis, the Hon. the Attorney General, William Snagg, Esq., and many other influential friends. It went off admirably well.

The Sugar Duties Act of 1846, which admitted the produce of slave-countries to competition in the English markets on the same terms as sugar that came from the free (British) colonies, had wrought havoc in every part of our West India Possessions. Grenada was collapsed, and our wise-hearted Governor set apart a day for general humiliation and prayer. The English Government in their fiscal legislation did us a great wrong.

1849.

Feb. 7th.—The Rev. Messrs. Bannister, Corlett, Ranyell, Limmex, Hurd, Cleaver, Biggs, Hudson, Heath, Whitehead, and Barley arrived to attend the District Meeting. No brother had died during the year, and every one seemed in good heart. This District Meeting had a novel service connected therewith. Hitherto the English missionaries had been 'ordained' before they were sent to us; but now there was to be a departure from this custom, and it was determined that the probationers should pass through their usual examinations, and, if approved, be ordained at their respective District Meetings. Messrs. Barley and Binks, whilom students at Richmond College, London, were thus accepted and received by our unanimous vote into 'full connexion.' The charge was given by the Rev. John Corlett, and was eloquent, impressive, and appropriate. It was a time of much spiritual power; and to our people, who witnessed such a service for the first time, it was a deeply suggestive and important spectacle. With the holding of this District Meeting my connection with the work in Grenada closed. On the 24th I preached for the last time to my much-attached and loving congregations. A number of Episcopalians joined in the evening service, and thereby evinced their respect for me as the retiring minister of the Methodist Church.

March 1st.—I find in my journal the following entry :—

'A day never to be forgotten. The mail steamer *Conway* came in with the English mails, and her arrival was the signal for our departure. I pass over all the distressing scenes connected with the tearing of ourselves away from this affectionate and pious people. "If I forget thee, let my right hand forget its cunning." We sailed from the Carenage at 4 p.m., called at Trinidad and Tobago to land the mails, and reached Georgetown, Demerara, at 7 p.m., on Sunday, *March 4th*. Mr. Biggs, one of my colleagues, was preaching, and, at the close of the public service, I joined him in the administration of the Lord's Supper.'

Our appointment to British Guiana, of which Demerara was the central province, was more formidable than welcome. Still, as a matter of stern duty, it had to be undertaken. There were elements in the political, social, and religious life of the people which were unknown in the quieter islands away to the north. For example, at the very time of our arrival there was a deadlock in legislation, to remove which Sir Henry Barkly, afterwards Governor of Victoria, was sent by Earl Grey, Secretary for the Colonies. For a considerable time it was impossible for the Court of Policy to get a ' Ways and Means ' Bill passed for raising the general revenue. What were called ' Imperial ' taxes could alone be collected, which were utterly incommensurate for meeting the public wants. Perhaps a whole year elapsed before this sad condition of things was overcome. When the *crux* really came, the Hon. Bruce Ferguson, a merchant of high character and just ideas, gave his vote with the Government and ended the crisis. The contention secured the Civil List for the Crown ; and for the Plantocracy, coolie immigration, at the expense of the State. The ordinary routine of legislation was revived, and all necessary revenue was collected for the purposes of governmental administration. Governor Barkly was too wise a man to occasion hitches between his official members in the Court of Policy, or of the Combined Court, during the whole time of his stay in the colony. His reign was one of reasonable conciliation, and the peace and prosperity of the three provinces were thereby secured.

It always appeared to me a curious circumstance that so many educated and well-to-do English and Scotch settlers so contentedly put up with the form of Government as that which obtained in British Guiana. It was a Dutch inheritance, and could not at all be called a Parliamentary Government; and yet the merchants and planters quietly endured it.

There were the College of Keizers, the Court of Policy, and the Combined Court, as forms of public life quite unknown previously to the gentlemen who had now to take prominent and responsible positions in regard to them. The Keizers (electors, *English*,) dating, we suppose, from 1803, when British Guiana became an English colony, were seven in number; and, in the first instance, it may be presumed, were chosen by the Crown for life. They were colonists of the old type, were connected with the propertied classes, and out of all sympathy with the general community. The Court of Policy was the sole legislative authority, composed of the Governor as president, eight high officials, and of four gentlemen, who were chosen by the College of Keizers. This court had the power of self-creation and of self-perpetuation. On any vacancy occurring, the remaining members would nominate two, from whom the College of Keizers would select one, who would, in due form, be gazetted by the authority of the Governor. Thus this court was always packed; but, it must be admitted, it was quite in accordance with the *modus vivendi* of the constitution of the colony. The only 'set-off' to the great powers of this singular court was the presence therein of the Governor and his officers of state, who would, on occasion, checkmate the lay-members, but not always with success. It was a perilous game to play. The Combined Court was composed of the members of the Court of Policy and six financial representatives, elected by the provincial districts, whose powers were, however, limited to raising colony taxes, and in auditing the public accounts. When the court, thus constituted, did its business, the financial members withdrew, and the Court of Policy, with the Governor as president, took the necessary action for giving the recommendations of the Combined Court the force of law.

There was, as might well be expected, a feeling of disquietude among the emancipated classes. Within the memory of many of these, the former cruelties of many of the Whites towards their class were still treasured. They could not be forgotten, but rankled in their minds. And the utter absence of all popular electoral rights, enabling them to exert an influence favourable to their class, was a cause of much discontent. Governor Barkly was conscious of this, and did his best for its removal. At a large meeting held in the city of Georgetown for establishing a court of registration of the emancipated freeholders, he took the chair, and gave an admirable speech, which was instinct with justice and high consideration for the aggrieved.

But there was one more difficulty induced by the existence of 'State aid to religion,' which was recognised by the Government, and accepted by some of the denominations. The leaders in opposition to this branch of public policy were the missionaries of the London Missionary Society and the Rev. Joseph Ketley, an eminent Congregational minister in the city of Georgetown. These honoured men were not to be hastily blamed for their conduct, for they were the lineal successors to the Old Independents, who had suffered so much for their principles of religious freedom and equality in the Mother Country. The recipients of State aid, not for the White increment of the population, but as helpful in supplying the means of religion and of education to the recently emancipated classes, were the Anglicans, Roman Catholics, Presbyterians, and Wesleyans; the latter in an extremely modified degree. Against one of my predecessors, the Rev. William Hudson, the displeasure of the Independents was specially directed. But Mr. Hudson was, in many respects, a strong man, who could hold his own without even once entering into the arena of conflict with his co-religionists. In this particular instance, the passive power was the stronger, so that when I entered upon my mission in 1849, it had eventuated in something like a drawn game. Of course I was under no obligation to unsheath the sword, but let it remain in its 'scabbard' there to rust. Upon one point, however, my mind was made up, viz. that as long as the principle of concurrent endowment lasted—purely for the spiritual benefit of the black and coloured people—this assistance should be taken. But I also resolved, that for myself personally not one dollar should be accepted. I thus 'cut the Gordian knot,' and left myself free to act in the future as circumstances might require.

March 11th.—I opened my mission in Trinity Church, Georgetown, by preaching from Deut. viii. 2, to a large congregation. At the close I met six classes for the renewal of tickets of membership, which was always to me an exhaustive labour. In the evening I walked to the eastern extremity of the city, at Kingston, and preached from St. John xvi. 23. The first Sabbath in a new circuit is generally a time of much anxiety to the missionary

itinerant.   I found it to be particularly so in my case that day.
But my trust was in God.

The responsible work of my mission was scarcely begun when I
found that there was deepest crime to be contended with ; to correct
which, all the energy God had given me to do my part would be
needed.   A melancholy instance of awful turpitude had just occurred,
and a public execution followed.   The incident is thus noticed, under
date March 17th :—

'This has been a melancholy day.   At twenty minutes past eleven this
morning, Pompey Face, the murderer, expiated his offence on the scaffold
in front of the court-house.   To the last he asserted his innocence of the
crime for which he had been condemned.   But he confessed, I was informed,
to his having committed a murder before the transpiration of this one.   He
was impenitent to the last ; and not until he was pinioned and was conducted
to the upper platform did he evince any emotion.   Then his bosom hove
convulsively ; indeed, almost to suffocation, but not a word escaped his lips.
He was a married man, and died in his sin, it may be feared, even as he had
lived.   I drove through the city late in the evening. and there I saw the dead
body of the unfortunate man still suspended, which I could not but regard as
a grim mockery of the boasted dignity of man.   My whole soul revolted, too,
at the public character of the execution and unnecessary exposure of the
hideous spectacle for so many hours in the face of the multitude.   The effect
on the excitable natives, I am sure, would be anything but salutary, and in
dead opposition to that the officers of the law desired.'

In consequence of the settlement in Berbice, the southern province
of British Guiana, of many Methodist families from the Virgin
Islands, the Revs. W. Hudson and W. L. Binks paid a visit to
New Amsterdam, the capital.   A Miss Dow, a coloured lady from
Tortola, had been holding prayer-meetings—first, in her father's
house at the hour of morning family worship, and, afterwards, at
the east end of the town, where large numbers of the people
attended.   In the course of a few months nearly a hundred
members were gathered into church-fellowship ; added to which,
the Dutch Reformed Church was without a pastor, and a beautiful
sanctuary and commodious manse were unoccupied.   To meet this
double need a correspondence had been opened up with Mr. Hudson :
it was the Macedonian appeal once more heard—'Come over and
help us,' to which this honoured servant of God was bound to
respond.   Mr. Hudson recognised that 'a great and effectual door'
was there presented to our Church, and it was agreed that Mr. Binks
should remain for a while to 'shepherd the souls' already gathered

in, and to make any practical arrangements with the committee of the Dutch Reformed Church for public services and the occupancy of the manse.

In connection with my advent into Demerara—acting under instructions from our Committee in London—I hastened to visit Berbice. I was told at once to close up our mission and retire from the province. The ostensible reason was that there were no available funds for the commencement of a new mission in Berbice; the real reason was the unexpected and unjustifiable opposition of the agents of the London Missionary Society, who had made such representations to their directors in London, as led to the incorporation in the official letter of the instructions before referred to. But it was an easy duty for me respectfully to show our Committee that the brethren of the London Missionary Society had no justification for their unwise interference, and our good work in Berbice has remained intact to this day.

My jotting of this visit is as follows :—

' *April 3rd.*—On Monday morning last I left Georgetown for the country of Berbice by the English mail conveyance, and, after passing over shocking roads for twelve hours, I arrived at the Berbice river. I crossed over in the ferry-boat, and proceeded along the western part of New Amsterdam until I came to the mission house, consisting of two hired rooms. I remained in the town and country eight days, "preaching the kingdom of God, and testifying of the things concerning the Lord Jesus Christ, with all confidence, no man forbidding me." The Dutch Church is lent us for holding Divine worship, and our way is plain and cleared for future evangelising efforts. I left at half-past 2 on Monday, and arrived in Georgetown at 1 p.m. the following day. Never, never shall I forget the Lord's goodness to me in this visit to Berbice and return to Demerara.'

The best devised arrangements for working our mission circuits are liable, from want of unexpected circumstances, to serious disturbances. On the 15th of May the sad intelligence reached us of the deaths of the Rev. F. Whitehead and Mrs. Whitehead, in Tobago, within two days of each other, leaving behind them a daughter child. By the same mail I received a letter from the Rev. William Bannister, the Chairman of the District, directing me to send the Rev. David Barley, my colleague, to take charge of the bereaved circuit. I thus lost the society and willing help of one of the best of colleagues I ever had. Mr. Barley's departure from us, under such painful circumstances, seemed like a being ' baptized for the dead;' his parting words were, ' Brethren, pray for Tobago.'

Is it true that the English emigrant 'carries the soil of his native land at the soles of his feet' into whatsoever country he may wander? It may be so, or it may not be. But this is certain—the Christian Englishman, when he emigrates, carries in his heart a profound respect for the free institutions of the dear old land from which he hails. And even those of that honoured class whose lot has been cast in the 'swamps of Demerara' cannot separate themselves altogether from even the ecclesiastical contests of the Mother Country. As an example, the dispute between the Rev. James Shore, of Totnes, and Bishop Phillpotts, of Exeter, on the question of 'Baptismal Regeneration,' was as fiercely discussed in Georgetown as it probably was in the ancient, radical borough itself. And, as far as Demerara was concerned, it was not a profitless discussion, for there were those who showed substantial sympathy with the persecuted clergyman. I was honoured as the medium of sending a draft for the amount subscribed to Mr. Shore, and in due course received a letter of acknowledgment and thanks.

A few extracts from my journal will show how many were the incidents and how continuous were the labours of which my daily life were now made up.

'*June 15th.*—To-day the Rev. William Cleaver, Mrs. Cleaver, and Mr. Robert George Ross, a lay minister, arrived in the mail steamer,—Mr. Cleaver to assist me in the city during the absence of Mr. Barley, and Mr. Ross to labour in New Amsterdam.'

'*June 20th.*—This morning I sailed for New Amsterdam, Berbice, a distance of ninety miles up the east coast, with Mr. Ross, to introduce him to our friends and to the work in this part of the Georgetown Circuit.'

'*June 21st.*—Arrived safely this evening, after having contended with many inconveniences during the voyage. Preached in the church, and found it good again to meet my friends.'

'*June 24th.*—Preached twice to-day, administered the Sacrament, and met the Society. We had Lutheran and Methodist Christians at the Lord's Table; the former stood to receive the elements, and the latter knelt, each party following the custom of their own churches. This was Christian liberty.'

'*June 26th.*—Sailed last evening from Berbice, and safely arrived this morning in Georgetown. Found my dear wife pretty well, but I was suffering severely from headache occasioned by the sickening smell of the bilge-water on board the sloop.'

My next trip was to the Abram Tuil Station, some forty miles westward on the Essequibo coast. When I took charge of the Georgetown Circuit proper, I found that by previous arrangement this dependent out-station had been attached to it. This action brought a serious monetary charge upon our funds, and threw additional responsibility and labour upon the Superintendent. My first visit was to preach on the 22nd of July, in the Lorg, Abram Tail, and Queenstown Churches. It was a laborious day, but I got through with Divine help. I went on board a sloop the next day, which was lying in the Lorg Creek, and at three o'clock in the morning of the day following I landed once more in Georgetown.

1850.

'*Jan. 1st.*—Praised and blessed be God for having brought me and mine through another year. It has been a year of incessant labour and unremitting anxieties, but God has crowned it with loving-kindness and tender mercies. The " Watch-night Service " was a solemn time. Trinity Church was crowded with a serious and attentive congregation. Lord, help me this year in the work of this mission ! '

Feb. 24th.—The offering of praise is my grateful duty. The Revs. Limmex, Heath, Biggs, and I have been to the District Meeting in St. Vincent's. Mesdames Limmex and Bickford accompanied us. We sailed in the *Agnes*, a small brigantine, and took a whole week in going. The wind being northerly we were driven off our course, and the first land we saw was Point Galileo, on the south-east side of Trinidad. But the wind changing to the south enabled us to stand up for Tobago, to which island we were purposed to go to take up the brethren, Messrs. Barley and Elliott. Mr. Biggs and I only went on shore, as the vessel was anchored far out near the ' Red Rock.' It was a great pleasure to me to see again my old and dear friends, the Hon. J. Keens and Mrs. Keens, Mr. Joseph Commissiong, and Mr. Angus Melville, whose dear wives, since my departure, had gone to be 'for ever with the Lord.' I saw also Mrs. (Widow) Bovell, Mrs. Howieson, Miss McKenzie, the Wilcoxes, Mrs. Owen, and other friends. We sailed the same day at 5 p.m., and the next day we made the Grenadines, passed under their lee, and at 7 p.m. stood across the ' Bequi ' Channel for Kingstown Harbour. The night was so dark and windy that we were in imminent peril sometimes in tacking to and fro in the channel. The longest night I ever knew at length passed away, and we put forth new energies to beat up from the leeward for the harbour. The wind was of hurricane force, and by the time, at midday, we came to anchor we were in a shattered condition.

We remained in St. Vincent's eleven days, attending the session of the District Meeting. The business was most harmoniously gone through, and we could rejoice in the prosperity of the missions. We again embarked for Demerara, and in due course we reached our homes and circuits for the happy toil of another year.

The Foreign Missions of our Church have a grand record of successes among the Europeans as they have among the native-born in the West Indies. British Guiana is no exception to this remark. I had, for example, in Georgetown, Messrs. Retemeyer and Obermüller (Dutch), Messrs. Ross and Cameron (Scotch), Messrs. Davis, Spooner, Watson (English), not to speak of many others. The man, among these, who held the largest space in the public eye, was Meinhaard Johannes Retemeyer, Her Majesty's Receiver-General for British Guiana. Mr. Retemeyer sprang from a wealthy family in Holland, whose interests in sugar and cotton plantations he came to Demerara to watch over and to promote. Mrs. Retemeyer was a high-born lady, and in every way suitable to adorn the circle which her husband commanded in the city. But the climate forbade her residence in Demerara, so that she settled in Holland. Mr. Retemeyer was induced by a confidential housekeeper to attend the ministry of the Rev. William Hudson, who, under God, was the means of leading him to the Saviour 'in whom he trusted.' Mr. Retemeyer's subsequent Christian life was 'full of good works which he did.' He was a devout worshipper of God. The Holy Communion Sabbath was to him a day of deep humiliation and prayerful consecration. He never forgot the poor. He was a true friend to ministers. He promoted education among the emancipated classes. At his sole expense was published a monthly religious serial for gratuitous circulation. He gave largely to the cause of God. He was not encumbered in his last affliction with sordid wealth. I well remember him saying, after confiding to my discretion a hundred dollars' note for his 'friends,' meaning the Lord's poor—

'What should I do now if I had allowed the tens of thousands of dollars that for so many years have come into my hands to have accumulated as some do? Why, I would be so distracted and weighted that I would not be able to attend to my soul. No, thank God, I have no trouble of that kind to contend with.'

His character stood so high, that he was not expected to put in an appearance at the balls and great dinners at Government House as officials generally are expected to do. It was quite understood that

Meinhaard Retemeyer was as loyal to the Queen as was the dancing, flippant courtier, who never missed the golden opportunity of basking in Viceregal smiles on these exclusive occasions. To my great sorrow, I lost the presence and help of this rare Christian gentleman in the second year of my incumbency in the Demerara Mission. I lovingly attended him all through his last illness, and I was with him when he died. I may appropriately supplement from my journal the short sketch just given :—

'*March* 14*th*.—This has been a day of mourning and deep distress to us. Mr. Retemeyer, the old and valued friend of Methodism, died this day at 3 p.m. He had been ill for some months, but bore his sickness with much resignation to the will of God. He died in the Lord. "Come, Lord Jesus !" "Come"— "Come," he often said. I saw him die ; and from my heart I can say, "Let me die the death of the righteous ; and let my last end be like his."'

'*March* 15*th*.—This day I committed to the grave the remains of dear Mr. Retemeyer. It was an affecting time and touching spectacle. Eight black men from the Herstelling plantation, as directed in his will, carried him to his grave. His corpse was followed by the highest dignitaries, public officers, and merchants, and by thousands of the citizens. Oh, may his death make a lasting impression upon the community !'

'*March* 24*th*.—This day I have endeavoured to improve the death of our late dear friend, Mr. J. Retemeyer. My text was taken from 1 Thess. iv. 13, 14. It has been a trying time. Trinity Church was filled to overflowing, with friends and hundreds of others, who were anxious so show their respect to the memory of one of the best of men. Mr. Retemeyer's death has created a sensation in the community which I hope may ripen in the conversion of hundreds of souls. I have lost a father—a friend—a counsellor. Lord God of my fathers, raise up others, I beseech Thee : let the mantle fall in mercy and in grace !'

The taking on the mission in Berbice entailed upon me much harassment and additional work, so much so that in three days after passing through the exciting scenes of dear Mr. Retemeyer's last affliction and funeral sermon, I was again upon the sea on a visit to that country. This time I went in the schooner *Clyde*, and arrived on the 27th after a fair passage from port to port. I had as a fellow-passenger a Mr. Hollingsworth, a white Barbadian, who had a strong prejudice against our mission in Berbice. Of course, I had it out with him. How strange are the coincidences of thought! Why, a man of the same name had a hand in the demolition of our mission premises in the island of Barbadoes many years ago. The question crossed my mind, Is hatred to Methodism hereditary in some families ? Was some grandfather of my fellow-passenger one of the historic crew who sought to kill Methodism in Barbadoes ? If

5

so, we shall hear something more of this name farther on in our narrative.

April 1st.—I had a most agreeable interview with the Rev. John Dalgliesh, the resident London missionary. He is a man of fine spirit, and was glad to recognise us as fellow-labourers in New Amsterdam. The next day I returned to Demerara in the *Henry Trew*, and found all well.

May 16th.—A strange experience awaited me. I was sent for to visit W. F——, Esq., ex-Attorney-General, who was dangerously ill with the prevailing fever. I had not been more than two or three minutes in waiting, when two legal gentlemen came out of the sick man's room and addressed me. 'They hoped,' they said, 'that I would not say anything to Mr. F—— of a frightening character, but persuade him that he is not so bad but that he may soon be well again.' 'Gentlemen,' I replied, 'you have performed a duty of friendship, and I thank you. But I have to perform a duty of religion. I hope, by this time, I know how to speak to a sick man, no matter who he is.' With these words, I went into the room, and addressed my friend. This, under great pressure of conscience, I had done before, and nothing but family pride and caste prevented him from following my faithful counsel. But now that course of reparation to one who deserved it from him was impracticable; and I could only exhort him to cast his soul upon God's infinite mercy in Christ for forgiveness. I then proposed to offer prayer for him. But the offer was rejected, and I could only say in sorrowful tones, 'I will pray for you at home.' After I was gone, and several times during the night, he expressed his deep regret that he had treated me as he had, and asked whether I might not be asked to come to him in the morning, that he might apologise to me and still have the aid of my prayers. But it was too late. Nevertheless—

> 'When the wicked man
> Turns from his sins to Thee ;
> His late repentance is not vain,
> He shall accepted be.'

In the mercy of God, may we not hope that this now repentant sinner found salvation? Three days after my visit, W. F—— was buried. Members of the bar, the judges, and other high officials followed him to his last resting-place.

July 18th.—I was no sooner, as I supposed, settled down once more for my beloved work in Georgetown than I was called away to Berbice to befriend our lay-minister, Mr. Robert G. Ross, Miss Dow, the leader, and the members in New Amsterdam. These good Christian people had been informed against by the Mr. Hollingsworth before named, as a nuisance, 'for praying and singing Psalms,' somewhere in his neighbourhood, which greatly disturbed him. But this was not the worst; by his wily misrepresentations, he had even induced Mr. Sheriff Daly to threaten to send them to prison if the practice were continued. With letter in hand, I went over to the public buildings to see the Governor about it. The surprise of his Excellency was very great, and he promised me a letter to Mr. Daly, which I might send to him after my arrival in Berbice. So armed, I again sailed from Georgetown, having as my fellow-passenger the Rev. Mr. Bolinder, an Anglican (ritualistic) minister. He seemed somewhat stiff at first, and I thought he would be anything but an agreeable companion. However, in beating down the river, by some mischance the boom swung over to where we were standing, and both had to drop instanter inside the stern lee-bulwarks to avoid losing our heads. Thus a threatened danger made us speak to each other, and so we became friends. Mr. Bolinder proved to be an agreeable and an intellectual conversationalist, and I enjoyed him very much. We dropped anchor at 10 p.m. the next day in the port of New Amsterdam : the Methodist presbyter and the Anglican priest all the better and happier for 'the talk by the way.'

And now I had to deal with Mr. Sheriff Daly. By a policeman I sent Sir H. Barkly's letter to him. But he had been prepared for it by the news of my arrival on the previous night with a philippic from the Governor. I have often thought how he must have felt as he read this communication. Quoting now from memory, I may venture to say that His Excellency told him of the right of all classes of Her Majesty's subjects to worship their God as they pleased, and according to their own convictions ; that how much better it was the persons complained of so to engage themselves at the close of each day, than to be found in associations and practices of immoral and dangerous tendencies ; how that gentlemen holding good positions under the Government should encourage all those habitudes among the people which were promotive of sanctity of life and good order. He concluded by saying that he would as soon think of complaining of the services in the Cathedral

Church, in Georgetown, where he worshipped, as to complain of the innocent psalm-singing of the Methodist Christians in Berbice, and more of the same kind. The effect was immediate and sure in the interests of religious freedom and the equality of status of all Christian persons before their Creator. I remained over for the Sabbath, and visited the new station at Cumberland, and on the 24th once more arrived in Georgetown.

Mr. Sheriff Daly sent a lengthy report to the Governor, enclosing a bitter letter from Mr. Hollingsworth, both of which were handed to me for perusal. I immediately sent a rejoinder, couched in such terms as a true-born Englishman would be likely to use in dealing with such narrow-minded zealots. The Governor, I am sure, was satisfied with my defence, for I heard nothing more of the matter. Thus ended the miserable opposition to our cause in Berbice; and the shot that secured its death was fired by my own hand.

The resources of our West India Missions were crippled by Imperial Legislation in 1846. Eight years previously the House of Commons paid twenty millions sterling to the so-called owners of slaves; and now, in 1846, in a frenzy of folly, it passed an Act for admitting the sugar of slave-producing countries into competition with our own free sugar, in the markets of England. The craze to bring this about was irresistible, and this staple of our own colonies was sacrificed. It cannot be pled that the mechanical and peasant classes of Great Britain clamoured for cheap sugar at the price of Christian consistency and political justice; but, on the contrary, tens of thousands of them would have preferred to forego this small delicacy than to have encouraged Cuba and other slave-producing countries in any shape whatsoever. Like many other questions of Imperial policy, this vital question to the comfort and loyalty of all classes of our West India fellow-subjects could not be considered upon its own intrinsic merits. Too many interested and unprincipled men were behind the scenes, and were stealthily working their own nefarious ends through the House of Commons. 'The weakest,' of course, 'went to the wall;' and, as the immediate result, there followed, throughout the whole of our West India possessions, an insolvent proprietary, bankrupt firms, increased taxation, and a dearth of employment for the emancipated classes. And nowhere were these sad reverses more generally witnessed than in the hitherto prosperous British Guiana. Several plantations were thrown out of cultivation, and the streams of commercial intercourse were dried up.

Is it any wonder, then, that the Parliamentary 'break' being suddenly applied, we came to grief? It was cruel to the planting interest; but it was diabolical to the peasant classes, whose 'life' depended upon the prosecution of their great industry of sugar-growing. Not a tear that I ever heard of was shed in England over the wrecked condition of our West Indian colonies, occasioned solely by the legislation of 1846; but denunciations of the severest kind, as might be expected, were poured forth by the ruined classes upon the heads of those in England who brought such mischiefs upon them.

The Wesleyan Mission in British Guiana for many years had been self-supporting. And it was our justifiable boast that in this grand province we could do without 'grants' from the London Committee. But now my journal records the existence of financial difficulties, which had been brought upon us by our imperious masters at St. Stephen's.

July 25th.—Held our Quarterly Meeting to-day, and found the circuit still in debt. These are hard times for conducting the West India Mission, thanks to the famous legislation of the mother (?) country. 1846. This year, surely never will be forgotten in the annals of West India history. I could write many pages on the evils of the legislation referred to; but I forbear. The penalty will be paid some day in full tale. . . . I trust, however, that the Lord will again smile upon our people, and overrule and overturn the fiscal legislation of the Imperial Parliament for these colonies. Their encouragement of slavery (as before noted) hath beggared thousands upon thousands, and caused many to withdraw their loyalty from the parent state. This is Lord Harris's opinion, the popular Governor of Trinidad. Very many also of our once respectable females have been so bereft of employment, that they have been obliged to earn a living by means from which their very souls revolt. It is dreadful to think of the untold miseries the infamous Act of 1846 hath occasioned to these once valuable appendages of the British Crown.'

But underlying this question is an important principle of Imperial legislation. What right, we may ask, has the English House of Commons to pass certain fiscal laws so disastrous to the best interests of the colonists, without their consent or even privity? As British subjects, living abroad, we have no right of representa-tion, personally or by proxy, in the Commons of England, and yet that House, by its legislative action, may inflict untold evils upon us before we can become aware of its bad intentions. What can we do in the presence of so mighty a factor—a self-imposed master—as is the Imperial Parliament? 'Grin and bear it,' said a Dutch gentleman to me, on one occasion, in Demerara; but that is no remedy for political injustice. One thing is certain, that under the conditions we have noted, the affection of the colonists, and the loyalty of the emancipated classes themselves, have been so strained, as to render the tie that holds the West Indies to the Crown very weak indeed. But there should be no necessity for such an ordeal! Let the English Parliament 'do justly,' which is a high command; unjustly—and the colonies will rebel. The bargain, as between the Imperial Parliament and the colonies, has two sides to it. And the stronger should always act in justice to the weaker. This is the old and tried way for securing mutual confidence, trustiness, and satisfaction.

Aug. 19th.—The yellow fever epidemic visited Demerara this year. The first person I was called upon to visit was a Captain S. T. Gibbons, from Baltimore. I was taken to him in the forenoon by a Mr. Hicks, a Christian merchant, to whose firm the ship's cargo was consigned. I found the captain very ill. He had to me a strange appearance. I learnt that he had the black-vomit, which accounted for the change in the expression of his countenance. I conversed with him, in as tender a manner as possible, on his dangerous condition, and knelt down for prayer with him. I had not offered more than a few sentences when he raised himself up in his bed, and exclaimed, 'Oh, my God! This man is a Roman Catholic priest.' I came, of course, to a halt, and, rising from my knees, I addressed him in suitable terms, assuring him that I was a veritable Wesleyan missionary, connected with the English Conference. He was satisfied, and desired me then to pray for him. At 3 p.m. I visited him again, and found that during the interval he had received an answer to his prayers. He testified, in the presence of Mr. Hicks and me, that the Lord in His mercy had forgiven him all his sins. He asked to have the Holy Sacrament before he died. 'I do not expect the ordinance,' he said, 'to save me; but I want to show my love to my Saviour Jesus Christ. I have been to sea all my life, and I have neglected it.' It was a solemn and gracious time. All in the room communicated, and 'the Lord was made known to us in the breaking of bread.' Before I left the room his poor mind was unhinged, and he became so violent that two strong men were necessary to keep him in bed. This dreadful fever makes awful havoc when it seizes the brain, and the strongest man soon succumbs. He died at twenty minutes to 11 the same night, leaving in Baltimore an affectionate wife and one child to mourn their loss.

'*Aug. 20th.*—To-day I buried the remains of poor Captain Gibbons; a great many gentlemen attended the funeral. Dr. Blair informed me that, from the *post-mortem* examination, they had come to the conclusion that Captain Gibbons had left Baltimore with typhus fever in his system, and that his illness at sea and in the colony resulted from this cause. There were not all the outward manifestations of typhus fever; but this peculiarity may be attributed to the influence of the tropics on his physical system.'

A few particulars of the history of Captain Gibbons may be inserted here. I learnt from him that he was the son of Methodist parents, and that he had been nursed in Methodism; that he had not served his father's God, but had cast off His fear. The Lord, however, had laid His hand upon him, and that he hoped in His mercy alone. Two or three advantages I observed to result from the training Captain Gibbons had received in the doctrines and duties of Christianity: his clear views of the plan of salvation he possessed; 'Christ crucified' was his sheet anchor.

The Foreign Missionary Meetings were duly attended to. In the month of October they were held in the city, T. A. Spooner, Esq., and the High Sheriff, George Bagot, Esq., brother of the late Captain Bagot, of North Adelaide, presiding. The weather was hot, being 95 degrees in the shade, and 124 degrees in the sun, which necessarily affected the attendance. And then the lassitude induced seemed to be a burden of life hard to bear. In November I went to Abram Tuil, Essequibo, accompanied by Mrs. Bickford, in the interests of the foreign missions. I preached three times on the Sabbath, and spoke at three meetings during the week. At the Abram Tuil meeting our day-school teacher, Mr. Thomas Trotman, informed us of the introduction of the 'swinging-pole' by the coolies. The resident missionary, the Rev. Joseph Biggs, told us that 'he had gone to see it.' Mr. Trotman spoke also of other idolatrous practices the coolies were introducing, and exhibited one of their 'gods.' A case of African cruelty was also reported. A black man, a negress, and three boys were working together in the cane-field. The man inveigled one of the boys into the canes, and commenced with a piece of notched iron hoop to cut the boy's throat. The cries of the poor boy brought the necessary help, and he was saved before it was too late from the would-be murderer's hands.

Our campaign being over, we returned, being accompanied by the Rev. William Heath, in the *Murray* schooner to Georgetown. It was a trying time for us—headwinds all the way and excessive heat. Our faces and hands were literally scorched. In beating up the river *Demerary*, we came under the lee of the ship *Fame*, a fine vessel laden with Coolies. They appeared to be contented with their new condition; they were mostly boys and girls. We are importing into the colony all kinds of grossest superstition, ignorance, and depravity, so that we are on the high road of becoming once more a heathen land. Hence the necessity of an increased missionary staff, with more of the 'power from on high' for counteracting the threatened evils arising in our midst.

For excitement, probably no place under the sun can surpass Demerara. The following jotting from my journal sets forth one of its elements :—

'*Nov. 25th.*—Preached yesterday at Kingston and Trinity. When offering the last prayer I heard the shout of "Fire, fire!" and before the Benediction could be pronounced the congregation crowded to the door. I hastened into the parsonage to get my pilot coat, and then returned to the church to see after Mrs. Bickford's safety. I found her at the vestry door, in company with Mrs. Cameron, Mrs. Van Watt, and Captain MacEachem. Having seen Mrs. Bickford safe, I went forward with the crowd to the 'place of destruction.' It was a fearful sight. It would be in vain for me to attempt a description of its fury and volume. Four houses were consumed, and one life was lost. I returned to Werk-en-Rust Parsonage about 10 p.m., and found Mrs. Bickford sitting with her bonnet on, ready to depart if necessary. I read Psalm xci., and offered prayer at our family altar, and then we retired to rest under the safe protection of Him who "never slumbers nor sleeps."'

'*Dec. 2nd.*—A Coolie young man came this afternoon with a candle, which he had purchased to be burnt in the church to cure his bad leg. I told him that the burning of the candle would not cure his sore, but, if he would come next day, I would examine it and give him some ointment to cure it. He promised to come, and seemed grateful. "Kindness melts the savage breast," it has been said ; but I perceive that it also touches the superstitious mind.'

'*Dec. 12th.*—To-day I posted to the Rev. W. L. Thornton, M.A., London, a manuscript memoir of the late Meinhaard Retemeyer for publication in the *Methodist Magazine.* It has run to the length of twenty-six pages of foolscap, and cost twelve shillings postage. This amount was generously paid by order of the Governor, the subject of it having been for so many years a highly respected servant of the Crown. I have had much chastened pleasure in preparing this memoir, and sensible communion of soul with my departed friend. I often felt that it was a very thin partition that separated him from me. Oh, blessed religion of Christ ! What hopes or joys can equal those Thou inspirest ? '

'*Dec.* 14*th.*—I had a long conversation to-day with Mr. H——, one of our Georgetown merchants, on Surinam slavery. He appeared to maintain that the slaves were happy ; and that it was better for them to be slaves and be provided for than to be let loose upon the country, no one caring for them. A few remarks were sufficient for convincing him that slavery was an evil—a great and monster sin. He then told me of a case of crying cruelty which had come to his knowledge in Surinam. The proprietors of the plantations have what are called 'Bush-days,' once or twice a year, to hunt up and catch runaway slaves. On the occasion he was referring to, they came upon a settlement where were several of these unfortunate creatures. They had located there for some years, and had erected a small sugar mill, and had many comforts about them. On the approach of these white wolves, the more agile of the negroes ran away, but the young and decrepit were unable to escape, and so fell into the clutches of their merciless persecutors. They were at once conveyed to Paramaribo. And as they could not now be identified, they were forfeited to the Dutch Government. These slave-hunters then set fire to the negro establishment, notwithstanding the many years of toil it had cost to bring it to what it was. Poor unhappy slaves of Surinam ! Oh, that the Lord would arise for their deliverance ! '

Mr. H—— bore his testimony to the valuable services of the Moravian missionaries in Surinam. He had attended one of their services, and was much interested in the manner of the worship and in the demeanour of the congregation. I wish from my very heart that we had a mission in Surinam. Two grand objects would be accomplished by it : (1) The extinction of slavery in two or three years ; (2) the ingathering of thousands of coloured persons, for whose souls, at present, no one cares. There are, I am informed, eighteen thousand of these, who are without the Gospel and the blessings of the Christian pastorates. The Moravians attend to the blacks ; the coloured would fall to us.

The Christmas season entails many additional duties upon the ministers of so large a circuit as was that of Georgetown, Demerara. The annual examinations of the day-schools, which came off at Christmas, was a time of great interest. At the Werk-en-Rust examination the Governor, Sir Henry Barkly, the High Sheriff, George Bagot, Esq., and some other gentlemen were present. Nothing could exceed the condescension of Sir Henry to the coloured and black children, as they came up to him with their copy-books and slates for him to see what they were able to do. The ready replies of the pupils in mental arithmetic, English grammar, geography, and spelling, were most satisfactory to our distinguished visitors. The special service on Christmas Day, the ' Watch Night,' New Year's Sabbath, the ' Renewal of Covenant,' followed by the Lord's Supper, constituted the Church's great festival season for the year.

1851.

The Berbice Mission called me away during the month of January. On the 22nd, I sailed in the *Governor Barkly*, which was full of passengers. We had a tedious passage, and I was very sick. On the Sabbath, early in the morning, I preached at Cumberland, on the Canji Creek, and gave the Sacrament. Returned rapidly to New Amsterdam, and held service at 11 a.m., and in the evening I preached again to a large congregation. We had the Sacrament at the close of the service. The next day, I had an interview with Roelof Hart, Esq., the leading official of the Dutch Church. Mr. Hart again informed me of the earnest desire of the Vestry to have an ' ordained ' minister as their pastor. He offered me, in addition to the free occupancy of the manse and the untrammelled use of the church, £100 per annum to secure such an appointment. This is a clear providential call to us; and yet, hitherto, it seems impossible to convince the London Committee that it is so. Hence their stolid refusal to allow us to occupy the place for the benefit of nearly one hundred members, who will have no other ministry but ours; together with many of the Dutch families, and other white persons, who plead and pray for our ministrations. But we shall see, sooner or later, that our persistency will alter the views of the Committee, who will then consent to our and the people's wishes.

In preparing the statistical information for the coming District Meeting my feelings were of a mingled character. Through the generous help of several friends the circuit debt was paid off. But the number of Church members was less than the previous year. Nearly a hundred had been removed from the class books because of their non-attendance at the weekly fellowship; besides which, it had been a year of great mortality among our adherents. Such a result was very discouraging, in remembrance of the toils and troubles we had passed through. But never were my sympathy and indignation more excited than when I heard of the death of the unfortunate C. I——. She had been a girl of beautiful form and many charms, but decoyed from her pure home in Barbadoes by a young white scoundrel—a sprig of the law, I believe. As long as she pleased him there was a cruel kindness in his conduct. But, a few months before I saw her, he had cast her off, in a land of strangers, unpitied and unknown:—

> 'Woman,' cried the seducer, 'hold thy tongue,
> For thou art weak, and I am strong.'

C. I—— was *in extremis* when I was called in to minister to her soul in its agony of distress. I did all that I could—and she died. Her last words were, 'I do hope Christ will wash my guilty soul in His precious blood.' Poor Magdalene! how I pitied thee! and prayed for thee! 'More sinned against,' in the first instance, 'than sinning;' thy guiltiness could not overleap His 'uttermost.' May I so hope and believe!

The annual voyage from Demerara to one of the Windward Islands to hold the usual District Meeting was to us a salutary and beneficial change. Never did I want it more than in the beginning of this year, 1851. Mrs. Bickford and I had passed through several attacks of fever, and we naturally looked forward to two or three weeks at sea, and to the society of friends in the District Island, with pleasurable hopefulness. Accordingly, on the 10th of February, our little company, consisting of the Revs. Limmex and Heath, and our respective wives, went on board the brigantine *Agnes*, for Barbadoes. We made a fair start from the 'lightship,' and nothing special occurred until we were off the east coast of Tobago. Mr. Limmex and I occupied the two 'dog-houses' upon the quarter-deck, so as to be near at hand in case of an emergency. We had a sudden wind upon us of hurricane strength, which would have capsized our struggling vessel but for the wakefulness and nautical experience of Mr. Limmex. The *Agnes* was heeling over dangerously when I looked out for my friend on the lee quarter. I saw him spring forward and 'let go' the main-sheet, when the brig rallied to her rightful position. Captain Stanley, at the time, was 'for-ard' helping the men to shorten sail. The man at the helm was skilfully steering through the terrible seas; and, but for Mr. Limmex's timely interposition, we must have come to grief. He was the only man to see the danger, and by his help we escaped a watery grave.

We reached Carlisle Bay on the 16th. Here, on landing, a new trouble began.   The land-sharks, *alias* 'Barbadoes' porters, were ready to devour us.   But with the help of the Rev. John Corlett, the resident senior missionary, and a few obliging policemen, we succeeded pretty well in escaping their extortionate demands.   In the evening of the same day, the Revs. Messrs. Bannister (Chairman of the District), Hurd, Horsford, D.D., Binks, Butcher, Brown, and Wrench, arrived from the 'leeward' per royal mail steamer.   The next day the sessions of the District Meeting began, and in six days we got to the end of our business.   It was a most harmonious and successful meeting.

On the 27th Mr. and Mrs. Banfield and Mr. and Mrs. Limmex, Mr. Heath, and I left by the *Iris* for Demerara.   Mrs. Bickford, who was much reduced in strength, was left behind for quiet and the advantage of sea-bathing.   Mrs. Cameron, a dear Scotch sister in Christ, remained also as her companion.

March 2nd.—We arrived in Georgetown in time for Divine service in Trinity Church.   Messrs. Heath and Banfield preached morning and evening.   At the close, we took the Lord's Supper once more together.   There was a large number of communicants.   Thus we began a new Methodistic year.

March 28th.—The R.M.S. *Derwent* arrived from Barbadoes, but without our lady friends.   I was informed by one of the gentlemen that two boats with passengers were within the swell of the steamer, but that the captain would not wait.   His act was un-English and cruel.   Great was our disappointment in Demerara.

I now give a few extracts from my journal, indicating some of the larger questions which crowded this ecclesiastical year :—

'*April 28th.*—Since my last entry, I have been incessantly engaged in Church and colonial business.   Mr. Attorney-General Arrindall having originated the idea of an Orphan Asylum for British Guiana, Mr. Sheriff Bagot called a public meeting at the court-house to take the subject into consideration.   His Excellency, Sir Henry Barkly, with his accustomed readiness, took the chair. I attended and spoke on the general question, and I observe that my suggestions have been adopted by the committee appointed to carry out the details of the scheme.   I was thankful to have an opportunity as a Wesleyan minister to express my views on the benevolence of Christianity, and on the duties of all Christian people in relation thereto.   Bishop Austin (Anglican) spoke a few words very gracefully.   On Wednesday evening, a tea meeting was held in Trinity schoolroom to raise funds to aid in paying for the outbuildings.   About three hundred persons were present.   With the exception of the conduct of a few ignorant, ill-trained youths, the meeting was well and happily conducted.   On the Thursday our Ministerial Quarterly Meeting was held. Messrs. Limmex, Heath, Banfield, and I were present. We had to consider several important matters, viz. Friendship Station and Day School, now vacant through the lamented death of Mr. Thomas S. Maddison, a worthy and excellent officer of our Church ; Berbice Mission, and the continuous cry of the Dutch Vestry for the appointment of a resident 'ordained' minister ; the recently promulgated scheme of the Educational Commissioners ; and the application for a missionary to the Coolie immigrants, many thousands of whom were now in British Guiana. Mr. Limmex and I sat up till a late hour in preparing a document for the Governor and Court of Policy on the new scheme of Education. Wrote the London Committee also, beseeching that one or more of the General Secretaries should forthwith interview Lord Grey, Secretary of State for the Colonies, on the Education and Coolie questions. Wrote a few more letters, and then settled with the workpeople for the outbuildings. Mr. James Rogers, of Rome, was my foreman for carrying on the work. He was a very reliable man.'

' " In labours more abundant." I find such questions as the following pressing upon me : (1) What avails all this labour as to myself ? I trust that although I am so constantly going round the circumference of duty, I still feel that my permanent dwelling place is at the centre : " All my springs are in Thee." (2) As to the church. Here, I say, my work is the Lord's, and I leave it with Him to give what prosperity it may please Him to grant. (3) As to the cause generally. An impression in this province in favour of religion under the form of Wesleyan Methodism. Lord, I am Thy unworthy servant : I appeal to Thee ! '

' *May 5th.*—In reviewing the last week, I have much to be thankful for. I visited Golden Grove and Mahaica to consult with Messrs. Limmex and Banfield on the Berbice and Friendship Stations. On returning to the city, I found that I had to leave immediately for the " Supply " Station, fifteen miles up the Demerara river, for important ministerial duties. Whilst there, I heard of a dreadful murder committed by the villagers upon a Kroo man, who had, with several others of his own tribe, been plundering their provision grounds, and keeping them in constant dread of their lives by their prowling about armed with murderous weapons. I gathered up the facts, and wrote his Excellency Governor Barkly upon the whole case. I specially requested that the necessary steps might be taken forthwith for clearing the Bush districts of these bloodthirsty wretches.'

' *May 6th.*—This day I am thirty-five years of age, more than thirteen of which have been spent in the West Indies and British Guiana. The Rev. W. Fidler and Mrs. Fidler, the Rev. W. Cleaver and Mrs. Cleaver, and Mr. J. L. Savory, our teacher at Werk-en-Rust, dined and took tea with us. " Bless the Lord, O my soul."

And now dear friends were leaving us for the old country. On the 13th, George Ross, Esq., and on the 14th, the Rev. William Fidler, Mrs. Fidler, and their two youngest daughters, sailed for England. The latter were passengers in the ship *Laura*, Captain J. Le Messurier, a good Guernsey Methodist. It is impossible to

describe the feeling of melancholy sadness which steals over one's soul
as friends leave for the dear old country, and we are compelled to
remain to contend with the exhausting climate, fever, and death.

May 23rd.—Went on board the *Clyde* for Berbice, and arrived at
the Cauji Creek, in the Berbice river, the 24th.   The next day
had a long conversation with Roelof Hart, Esq., on the sore business
of placing an ordained minister in New Amsterdam.   Rode to
Cumberland, preached at 7 a.m., and gave the Lord's Supper to the
members.   Returned to New Amsterdam, and preached at 11 a.m. and
6.30 p.m.; renewed the tickets of membership of sixty persons, and
finished up by administering the Lord's Supper to the Lutheran and
Methodist adherents.   It was a hard day's work, but a happy
one.   Spent the whole of Monday in pastoral visitation, and saw
Mrs. Obermüller and her four fatherless children.   We lost a true
friend in Mr. Obermüller; he was the Secretary of the Dutch
Vestry, and always sympathized with us in all the discussions on
the subject of appointing an ordained minister in New Amsterdam.

The captain of the *Clyde* told me of a horrible case of cruelty
on the Waterloo estate in Surinam.   A poor slave, he said, was
chained to the 'copper-hole' by the leg, and remained there, with
very little intermission, day and night.   He is compulsorily the
fireman of the sugar-works.   Previous to this punishment, he ran
away several times, seeking to achieve his freedom.   But he was
always captured, and this was his punishment.   The owners on the
plantation, or their representatives, had erected a shed over him
to shelter him from the sun, and this is the only consideration
shown to this courageous man.   Oh, Slavery, thou monster of
cruelty; surely, if there be a God who heareth the cry of the
captive, thy days are numbered !

'*June* 11th.—Mrs. Bickford and I sailed for the Arabian Coast, and arrived
off Lorg, and stuck on a sandbank until 11 p.m.   We landed, and walked to
the church at 12.30 p.m.   I then walked to Abram Tuil, a distance of three
miles, and knocked up the Rev. W. Heath, who instantly harnessed his horse
and fetched Mrs. Bickford from Lorg at half-past two in the morning.   Returned
to Georgetown on the 21st, just in time for the Sabbath services at Kingston
and Werk-en-Rust.'

The term of service for European missionaries in the West Indies
was ten years.   But I had been able, 'by reason of strength,' to add
a few years to that number.   Still I now began to feel that the

time was come when I should make known to the London Committee my earnest desire to return as soon as convenient. Accordingly, under date 'July 11th, 1851,' I wrote to the Committee asking permission so to do after the next District Meeting, which would be held in February 1852. Supposing my request were granted, I would then have laboured fourteen years in a tropical climate. But I was not tired of the work, for I loved it. My whole energies, and brain, and prayers, had been given to the mission all this time ; but I was now painfully conscious of the existence of mental and physical enervation, which rendered the financial and spiritual care of the Georgetown Circuit a burden I could no longer sustain. Mrs. Bickford, also, from many attacks of fever, and the trying character of the climate, had become the subject of a weak and nerveless state most distressing to witness. I sent no medical certificates, or recommendations from my dear missionary brethren, but simply told my own tale, and left the final decision with the Committee. The result will appear farther on.

In the month of July also an important public question engaged the attention of Governor Barkly, the Court of Policy, and the pronounced educationists of British Guiana. It had been felt for some time that the then arrangement was insufficient ; and, yet, during the first years of the *régime* of freedom, it seemed to be the only practicable one. The Mission Churches had done the bulk of the work, which was in part supported by an annual *per caput* payment of two dollars for each pupil under tuition. Of course this small sum did not meet the cost of salary, books, and buildings, necessary for carrying on the work.

It was now proposed, as the consequence of Mr. Commissioner Dennis's investigations in Europe and America, to set aside the existing denominational schools, and to institute in lieu thereof a national system, providing secular education only. So serious and unexpected a departure from the arrangments which had obtained ever since freedom had been established was at once opposed by the Anglican, Presbyterian, and Wesleyan bodies. The discussion came on on the 12th, when three petitions were presented against the Bill, which was down for a second reading. The first speech was from Sir Henry Barkly, who generally explained the principles of the proposed measure in a fairly reasoned manner. But the second speech did the business of the day. The High Sheriff, George

Bagot, Esq., smote it 'hip and thigh.' It was then held in abeyance, and the protesting documents were referred to the Commissioners for report. Believing that Mr. Attorney-General Arrindall would be glad of as much information as he could get upon the question now in such sharp dispute, I called upon him and begged him to read Watson's great sermon, entitled 'Religion, a part of Education,' which he politely promised to do. Mr. Arrindall was the Chairman of the Commission, and a man of impulsive and forceful character. It was, therefore, very desirable, if possible, to get him on our side.

Our action was severely commented upon by the Editor of the *Colonist.* I accordingly addressed a letter to him, demanding that our 'memorial' should appear in its columns, that the thinking public might be able to judge between us. This was done, but the Editor—editor-like—would have the last word, in which he poured a heap of abuse upon me.

The position of the Wesleyan missionaries in their relation to the Education question, then so fiercely contested in British Guiana, must be briefly stated. It was not with us, at that time, a question as to the comparative merits of the two systems of public education—the denominational and the national. Indeed, our personal predilections, if we had any, scarcely entered into the matter at all. We—each one of us—were 'under law' to the British Conference, whose representatives and servants, in a filial and Christian sense, we were. The Conference of 1840 laid down certain principles, which, as far as practicable, were as binding upon us in British Guiana as they were upon our ministers and day school committees in England. Such as—

'The Bible, in the Authorized Version only, shall be the basis of all the religious instruction ; and a certain portion of every day, at least, half an hour each morning and afternoon, shall be set apart for the devotional reading of the Holy Scriptures, with explanations by the teacher or visitor.'

'The Conference records its deep and solemn conviction of the duty and necessity of providing the means of obtaining, in week-day schools, an efficient education in scriptural and other useful knowledge ; and would regard, with much satisfaction, any public measure which would secure this desirable object, on just, tolerant, and liberal principles.'

'The school duties shall uniformly begin and end with prayer.'

And much more to the same effect.

We might have gained, in some quarters, a temporary popularity

FALLS OF DEMERARA.

by adopting a contrary course to that we felt bound to follow; but that would have been no compensation for disloyalty to the English Conference and the traditions of English Methodism. We took, 1 am sure, under the conditions of the whole question, the right course; but we had not yet reached the end. The feeling that binds the British Empire together, is the outgrowth of a common interest in the unity and prosperity of the whole. So it is with large Christian bodies. The Wesleyan Methodist Connexion is no exception to this remark. The reception, at the Georgetown Mission House, on July 11th, of the intelligence that through the reform agitation 55,000 members had been lost to our Church, caused much distress, followed by tearful prayers, that the 'God of our fathers' would, in His great mercy, interpose and cause that good might come out of this great trouble.

How chequered was my Demerara life! It was panoramic in a wonderful degree. 'Fightings without,' if not 'fears within,' mostly filled up the 'cup' of my every day's experience. I had been preaching on the evening of July 24th, at Trinity Church, on the 'Life and death of Dorcas,' and had returned to the parsonage, when I was hastily called to go to Kingston, in the eastern part of the city, to see Mrs. Thomas Spooner, who, whilst spending the evening with our friends, the Rev. William Cleaver and Mrs. Cleaver, was taken alarmingly ill. On reaching the place, about a mile distant from Trinity, I found her dying. We united in prayer and commended her soul to God. The next day she 'passed away,' in the fortieth year of her age. The day following, we followed her dear remains to the grave; which had been prepared in the officers' burial ground. Mrs. Spooner was a Christian woman, and was brought to God under the ministry of the Rev. W. L. Binks, a few years previously to her last sickness. She was a true missionaries' friend, as was also her devoted husband, Mr. Thomas Spooner. She was one of the white 'stars,' gathered into brightness and beauty by the untiring labours of our missionaries.

'*Aug. 2nd.*—This has been a busy week. On Monday attended to Society business, met my large class, and from 10 a.m. to 9 p.m. was incessantly employed. On Tuesday attended to the brethren's wants in the country circuit; and purchased the lumber wanted for the new school-house at Kingston. On Wednesday, Mrs. Bickford and I left for Mahaica, that I might be present at the Quarterly Ministerial Meeting, when I addressed the congregation in the evening. Thursday: we spent the day with our dear friends,

G

the Rev. W. Limmex and Mrs. Limmex. Mr. James McSwiney, a stipendiary magistrate—"a just man "—was one of our party. Friday : we left Mahaica for Golden Grove, the residence of the Rev. James Banfield and Mrs. Banfield. I preached a commemorative sermon on August 1st to our people in the Victoria Church. In the evening we went to the tea-meeting at Friendship, and returned to Golden Grove at 1.30 a.m., wearied and spent. On Saturday we returned by train to the city well in health but greatly fatigued.'

The Rev. William Moister was my first Superintendent in the West Indies, and to him I still have, notwithstanding the lapse of fifty years, grateful remembrance of his interest in me. I was as a 'pupil' under him ; and, in various ways, he helped me very much. Mr. Moister after his return to England was sent by the Missionary Committee to the Cape of Good Hope, as Chairman and General Superintendent of Missions in that district. But he did not forget me, as the following quotation from my journal will show :—

'*Aug. 8th.*—Received to-day a budget of papers, pamphlets, and letters from the Rev. W. Moister, now stationed at Cape Town, in South Africa. His correspondence was truly acceptable and welcome. He is a valuable missionary of the " Cross of Christ ;" and I have no doubt that in the day of the Lord very many will be the seals of his ministry. He invites me to join him at the Cape, and suggests that I might take the English congregation as my charge. But my inclinations are towards Australia, in the event of my returning to England after the holding of our District Meeting.'

The subject of Coolie immigration had become in 1850-2 a very serious business in British Guiana. The Governor and Court of Policy were at their wits' end to know what to do with the several thousands of Coolies who had been imported into the colony under agreements with the East Indian Governments. To utilise this new increment of labour on the sugar plantations, and to secure for the immigrants 'a fair day's wage for a fair day's work ; ' to see that such accommodation was provided as would be preservative of health ; to defend them in courts of justice ; and to keep in the immigrants' view their right of return to India after five years of indentured work, were problems in Coolie social life not easy of interpretation and practice. There was not an Englishman in the colony of such repute for character, linguistic ability, and of Christian sympathy with the Coolie people, as could help the Government in its praise-worthy efforts to do justly by these thousands of immigrants, who were spread over the province, and occasionally swarmed into the city.

How to Christianize these heathen strangers, and to bring them into working harmony with their new conditions, was the problem which awaited solution. I am sure that none of the good men now living, who were in Demerara in 1850-1-2, will accuse me of assuming an unwarrantable position when I affirm that, besides the Wesleyan Methodist, no other Protestant section of the Church showed either adaptability, or desire, to contribute towards the smoothing away of the Coolie difficulty. And I do no injustice to my own brethren when I say that the whole burden of negotiating with the London Committee, and, subsequently, with the Court of Policy, fell upon me rather than upon any of them. But I think, however, that I was providentially led into it through the conversion and 'baptism' of a Hindu gentleman, in whose case God made me the honoured instrument. He took the name of Samuel Johnston, in the presence of a large and sympathizing congregation in Trinity Church. Mr. Johnston prepared an interesting letter, signed by himself and many of his countrymen, to the London Committee, earnestly praying that a missionary might be appointed for their special benefit. The Rev. J. E. S. Williams, who had been a missionary in Ceylon, prepared a reply in Tamil. On the 11th of August the English mail arrived bringing this very letter to my address, which I delivered to Mr. Johnston and his co-signatories. Such correspondence was bound to bear fruit. Hence, on the 28th August, I received a beautiful letter from the Rev. Dr. Hoole on the spiritual condition of these Coolie immigrants, and encouraging me to hope that a missionary would be sent as soon as possible for their evangelization.

Sept. 26th.—The English mail came in. I say in my journal, under that date,—

'Received my mail letters, and was glad of affectionate renewals of regard and love from Revs. John Corlett, Joseph Biggs, and W. L. Binks. The English Conference had closed, and I had not heard one syllable from the Committee in reply to my application to return to England. A press of business, no doubt, and other causes, have prevented the usual courtesy of a reply. But I am much disappointed. I must wait a little longer, and all will be explained. The Committee's reply to our District Minutes will have a reference to it, I am certain, and, till then, *orare et laborare.*'

One of the oldest and ablest ministers in Demerara was the Rev. Joseph Ketley, a Congregational 'standard-bearer.' By invitation, I went to the Old Agricultural Rooms to hear from him a lecture

addressed to the Athenæum Society. There were three divisions:
(1) Science, in its general principles; (2) Literature, in its outlines
and advantages; and (3) Arts, which he described as the application
of science to the purposes of life. The subject was most skilfully
handled, and I was thankful that the young men present had such
an opportunity of being instructed by such a master.

Oct. 7th.—The true idea of a missionary's relation to his flock is
that of a father, and to any afflicted or troubled family, therewith
connected, that of a sympathizing friend. In both these aspects I
had to appear under the above date. Amongst our respectable
coloured families in Georgetown were a Mr. E. N. Pieters and
Mrs. Pieters, with whom Mrs. Bickford and I had been guests at
one of our District Meetings. Their kindness was so simple and
abundant that I became quite attached to the whole family.

At this time we were much engaged in providing buildings and
apparatus for the education of the children of our people. On
October 8th we opened the new schoolroom at Kingston, when
two hundred and fifty persons took tea together. The addresses at
the after meeting dealt with the all-engrossing subject of *Combined
Education*, a principle to which we felt ourselves committed in the
best interests of the emancipated classes, and as missionaries under
the direction of the English Conference. On the 13th the Rev.
W. Heath and I preached, at Kingston and Trinity, the annual
sermons in aid of our Foreign Missions. In the afternoon of the
same day we held a special service at Trinity, when two hundred
and fifty children and young people were present. Mr. Heath,
Mr. E. N. Pieters, the superintendent of the school, and I gave
addresses. Edward Pieters, junr., the secretary, read the rules of
the school. It was a time of much interest and good feeling.

Hitherto I had had pretty plain sailing in Demerara. I had
made and had retained hosts of friends. How much, therefore, was
I surprised when, on October 13th, I received a confidential note
from the Hon. Richard Haynes, a coloured gentleman of high
character and mercantile standing, informing me that a letter had
been addressed to him, as the intended Chairman of the Trinity
Church Missionary Meeting, to the effect that I was 'prejudiced
against the coloured people,' and requesting him (Mr. Haynes) to
demand from me, at the public meeting, a distinct disclaimer of any
such feeling. I was at a loss for the clue to this foul accusation,

until I remembered that I had, a few days previously, a somewhat spirited conversation in my study with a young coloured man on the subject of the utility, or otherwise, of debating societies—my contention being that such as he, and those he represented, did not need to be taught how to argue upon difficult questions; but rather to commence at the foundation of real mental work, by threading their way through the elementary lessons of English literature, and acquire thereby a confidence in root-truths, and an aptitude in using correctly English forms of speech. I had no intention either of discouraging or offending the young man in question, and this Mr. Haynes most thoroughly believed.

But I was grievously pained, and could not but ask whether so cruel an assumption held good with the character I had borne during thirteen years of voluntary residence in a tropical climate, and with the sacrifice of health and many comforts I had made to serve the people, one of whom had so cruelly maligned me!

The missionary meeting was held under the presidency of the Hon. Richard Haynes. His was a Christian and comprehensive speech. The congregation was large, and the feeling deep. But there were no clapping, no noises: the utmost decorum obtained, just as if it were a Sabbath service. This was an improvement on the missionary meetings in England and in the islands.

As an inevitable outgrowth of freedom, money became somewhat plentiful in the hands of the wages-receiving labourers on the plantations. This improvement in their social position enabled them to form large associated bodies for purchasing abandoned estates from the English proprietors on the east coast, on the southern side of the river Demerary, and in other parts of the colony. Several such properties were purchased, calling into existence a new form of political and social life, which was designated 'The Village System,' whose slow but sure growth occasioned much concern to the Government. A form of queries was drawn up, and copies were sent with the *imprimatur* of the Governor to all the clergy, the missionaries, and the stipendiary magistrates for information, showing to what extent this system had reached, the acreage purchased, the kind of cultivation carried on, and the number of the population who had come under this novel form of co-operativism. Suggestions also were invited for the governmental control and development of such associations.

The question, it was admitted, was extremely difficult, because of the self-created and self-controlling functions these new proprietary bodies assumed and exercised. In the islands the case was different. Take, for example, St. Vincent's, where a new proprietaryship came into existence; but there it was the purchase by an individual free labourer from an individual proprietor. Whereas, in British Guiana, there were in these transactions combinations of men and consequent community of interests, which gave formidableness to these bodies, and required attention from the Government. It must be confessed that the Governor and Court of Policy had not, *pari passu*, launched any system of municipal or police control to meet this novel state of things; and yet it should have been anticipated, because when the free labourers became possessed of money, they would no longer be content to remain in great numbers upon the estates where they had once been slaves.

To illustrate, *ab inconvenienti*, the nature of the conditions upon which 'The Village System' was sought to be built, we may take as a typical case the plantation 'Friendship,' on the east coast of Demerara, which was purchased for seventy-five thousand dollars by one hundred and forty (black) proprietors. One of the conditions of sale and purchase was, that no white man should ever legally become joint proprietor with the original purchasers. The idea of a number of head men to be over the remainder could not work; therefore, one was chosen to be manager, or 'Boss,' to conduct the general business of the plantation. But up to this point there need not have been any practical difficulty, provided that the whole number of the proprietors agreed. But a new and unexpected *crux* arose, and in this way. One of the original owners became insolvent, and in due process of law his interest in the proprietary was sold at public auction by the Provost Marshal at the court-house steps in the city of Georgetown. The purchaser happened to be one of the prohibited class. It need hardly be observed that the 'Act of Insolvency' was stronger than was the private compact of the one hundred and forty proprietors. The compact was overridden, and justice was done.

A second embarrassment arose in which the Wesleyan missionaries were involved. A large Logié, originally used for drying coffee, had been fitted up for Sabbath worship and Sunday and day school objects at considerable expense. When the plantation passed from the original owners to the new proprietary body, it was felt that our tenancy was insecure. Hence, after some negotiations, the Rev. James Banfield, the Superintendent Minister, purchased the building, not the land, with the free consent of the proprietors at one of their business meetings. About three months afterwards, at another of their meetings, when the proceeds had to be divided, there came to the surface the bitterest opposition of eighteen of the proprietors. The dissentients took legal proceedings for setting aside the action of the head man as their representative and executive officer, and gave us considerable trouble.

We had 'fallen among thieves,' but the end was not yet. I find in my journal the following entry :—

'Mr. Banfield, Mr. Cleaver, and I have been engaged in getting up a " report," in obedience to the judge's " order," on a petition presented to the " Court of Justice " by eighteen of the proprietors of *Friendship*, praying that the sale of the *Logie* may be prohibited. Mr. Banfield had bought this building three months previously, when these very men were apparently satisfied with the transaction, until the appropriation of the money took place. What the result will be it is impossible to divine.'

Numerous other cases of difficulty, provocative of expensive litigation, were constantly arising in different parts of the colony. Legislation, therefore, ensued and solved many a perplexity. The Court of Policy at that time, with Governor Barkly as president, had some very able men in it. The Bill that was passed arrested needless litigation, and provided against future vexatious proceedings. The colony generally, but especially the emancipated classes, were laid under great obligations for the intervention of the law members of the Court of Policy, and to Governor Barkly, who gave much earnest attention to this perplexing subject.

Nov. 2nd.—My journal entries are now showing that the elasticity of my spirits, as well as my bodily health, were seriously giving way. To get out of the city, and have only one day free from worry, was a perfect Eden to me. We had a sweet retreat about a mile up the river in the Ruimveld sugar plantation. Our dear friends, Mr. and Mrs. George Ross, at their beautiful home, afforded the relief Mrs. Bickford and I so much needed. We would drive out in the morning and enjoy the cool river air, and in the evening we would return to Werk-en-Rust quite refreshed.

Nov. 8th.—Mr. Robert G. Ross and I sailed for Abram Tuil to attend to the interests of our Foreign Missions. Our congregations were good. We were some twenty-four hours on our return voyage, and I suffered terribly from the sun. Mr. Ross was a native of Tobago, an excellent man, lay-preacher, and had been a day school teacher. I had engaged him for Berbice when the London Committee did not choose to send an ordained minister.

As an interim supply, Mr. Ross did us good service. On the death of Mr. Maddison, the Rev. J. Banfield engaged him for the Friendship Station.

'*Nov. 9th.*—Preached twice yesterday from Acts ii. 38, 39. A good day, but much wearied from the exposure and fatigue of the previous week. Heard this morning of some, from whom I had expected better things, who had gone to the races. May the good Lord take not His Holy Spirit from them.'

'*Nov. 24th.*—Last week was one of extreme agony of mind occasioned by home correspondence. What can be the design of Providence in thus afflicting my relatives in their circumstances, and opening sources of discomfort to us all such as we have never been accustomed to? " Lord, Thou knowest." '

'*Nov. 27th.*—Returned this morning from Supply village in torrents of rain, and wearied almost to death.' "

'*Nov. 30th.*—Went to Nismes and preached. I baptized twenty-two adult Africans, and three infants. I renewed the membership tickets of sixty persons, and administered the Lord's Supper. Arrived at home at half-past 4 wearied and hungry. Preached in the evening at Kingston, to a large congregation. Two months more and then I shall go (D.V.) to another sphere of labour in the Lord's vineyard.

The ' rise and progress ' of the cause at Nismes are worthy of a passing notice, as illustrative of what one really good man may do in the cause of Jesus. This out-station was situate about five miles up on the north side of the Demerary river, and about half a mile from the Herstelling plantation on the opposite side. The congregation was composed wholly of free (black) labourers. The head man in our society was known by the title of Father Liberty; he had a family of grown-up children, and he was anxious that each of them should follow in his footsteps. Said he one day to my predecessor, the Rev. William Hudson, ' Massa Hudson, before you do leave the colony, me want you to build one new church at Nismes.' 'That I fear,' replied the minister, ' is impossible. Where is the money to come from?' 'Oh, if dat be all, then me go and see.' The very next day, to Mr. Hudson's grateful surprise, who should be at his office door but Liberty, with a Bristol tripe jar on his head. ' What have you got there?' said Mr. Hudson.

'Massy going to see!' And he turned the contents of the jar out upon the table, amounting to $750, equal to £156 3s. 4d. The old man explained: 'Dat money be saved for me children, but they no love de religion. So me say, "Me build for them one house of God, and they will be no able to spent Him."' And the church was built.

But Father Liberty's good work did not end with the princely gift just noted. On our Sabbath and weekday visitations to Nismes, the old man would come with his *batteaux* across the river to the Herstelling jetty to take us over and back. He never failed when we wanted him. He felt that he was doing service for his Master Christ, and this conviction strengthened his arm and will, in spite of wind, rushing tides, or a scorching sun. 'Me cannot preach de Word of God,' said Liberty to me one Sabbath morning, as we were gently proceeding out of the creek towards the rushing river, 'but me can take preachers to do it.' 'Oh, yes, Father Liberty,' I replied, 'and you are doing God's will in what you do as much as we, in what we do, in coming to Nismes.' These words cheered the old negro's heart.

The Rev. George Osborn (now Dr. Osborn) had been appointed to the London *secrétariat* of our Foreign Missions, and on December 18th, I had the pleasure of receiving my first letter from him. It was not a business, but a friendly, brotherly communication, which was a great comfort to me. By the same mail I received a letter from Peter J. Bolton, Esq., one of the Secretaries of the 'British and Foreign Anti-Slavery Society,' on the subject of the further equalization of the sugar duties. The House of Commons was about to inflict a further injury upon the West Indies, and this just and humane society was awake to the importance of helping us to prevent any further wreckage being done. There were two aspects in which the matter had to be viewed: (1) In the interests of the defrauded and oppressed slaves themselves, who were still held in bondage in Cuba and other countries; and (2) in the interests of the West Indian proprietors, and of the emancipated classes. The Home cry, it was affirmed, was that of the British people, who wanted still cheaper sugar, no matter that it would be at the cost of prolonged suffering and of political righteousness. But what could we do? We could only cry to heaven in our weakness; for to memorialise the Imperial Parliament, under the circumstances, would be of no use whatsoever. We had thus to wait in indignant silence for the paralysing blow.

Dec. 19*th.*—The annual examination of the Werk-en-Rust Day School came off. Sir Henry Barkly, as was his custom, presided, and did us good service. The Hon. William Walker, colonial secretary, John Lucie Smith, barrister, and W. B. Pollard, Esq., members of the Board of Education, and George Ross, Esq., were present. The pupils were in fine form and did well. In mental arithmetic their skill in calculating surprised us all. The writing of two black children—a brother and a sister—were specially good, and specimens of their penmanship were requested by the Governor. Mr. John J. Savory, the master, and Miss Blair, the first assistant, won great praise to-day.

We had visitors during this month with whom we were much pleased. Mr. and Mrs. Thomas Carter, from Luton, England, and Captain Furze, from Mevagissey, Cornwall, were among the number. Away, from year to year, from the dear old Mother Country, and residing in the tropics, it was quite a Godsend to have now and then intelligent persons in one's domicile. Mr. Carter was an able local preacher, and Captain Furze was a Methodist of the true Cornish type.

Dec. 25*th.*—Christmas Day has always had a red letter in the calendar of West Indian Christians, by whom it is gratefully and religiously observed. My Journal jottings say :—

' Preached at 5 a.m. in Trinity Church to a large congregation. Mr. T. Carter preached at 11 a.m., and kindly took the service in consequence of the pain in my chest.'

' *Dec.* 28*th.*—The last Sabbath in the year. Preached at Trinity and Kingston. Was very poorly in the morning, and had hard work to get through the services of the day. A year of toil and mercy.'

1852.

Jan. 1*st.*—Praise the Lord for crowning another year with His goodness. The ' Watch Night Service ' was a solemn season. The church was filled to overflowing. Mr. John J. Savory assisted me. This year may I live to God alone. Lord, help me ! On the 5th the usual ' Renewal of Covenant Service,' and the Lord's Supper were duly observed. It was a good beginning of the year's services.

The feelings of my heart are correctly expressed in our beautiful hymn,—

' Oh, happy day, that fixed my choice,' etc., etc.

Jan. 10*th.*—' And in the garden there was a sepulchre.' This singular association of a ' garden ' with a ' sepulchre ' represented the beautiful but suddenly changed home-life of the Rev. W. Cleaver and Mrs. Cleaver, at Kingston, in this city. During the year just closed, no member of the mission family had died of yellow fever; but, in the first month of this year, one death from that fearful scourge took place. It was little Charles Carlton Cleaver, only son of my colleague, Mr. Cleaver, who had passed away. He died in the morning, and in the evening we buried him under the branches of the lovely tamarind-tree in the Lodge burial-ground. Precious dust! In sure keeping until the resurrection morn.

Jan. 26*th.*—In the absence of further information from the London Committee, we concluded that our application for permission to return to England after the District Meeting could not at present be granted; and that my prospective appointment to Barbadoes would take effect. We accordingly commenced packing and otherwise to ' set our house ' (circuit) ' in order,' so as to be ready for our removal. If our health could have permitted it, there were some very good reasons why, at that time, we should have remained two or three years longer in Demerara. But that seemed impracticable, and hence our preparation for a removal to the salubrious climate of Barbadoes, which had become, in our estimation, a providential sanatorium for the worn-down and fever-stricken missionaries from the southern stations of British Guiana.

This was, of necessity, a time of much anxiety to us. I had, because of the non-arrival of the royal mail steamer from England, to arrange to go to the District Meeting, to be holden in St. Vincent's, without Mrs. Bickford, although she had been again so dangerously ill from the terrible Demerara fever. We were much ' perplexed.' At length the steamer arrived, about midnight, and we were informed that she would leave again at 4 in the morning. So that my colleagues and I were greatly hurried to get away by her. We had a fine run across to Carlisle Bay, Barbadoes, arriving there at 1 p.m., on February 5th. I was most kindly welcomed by the Rev. John and Mrs. Corlett, at

Bethel Parsonage, and I was their grateful guest as long as I remained on the island.

I spent two Sabbaths in Barbadoes, and preached at James Street and Bethel. On the 9th, Mr. Corlett and I called at Government House to pay our respects to His Excellency Ker Baillie Hamilton, whom I had so intimately known in Grenada. We also called on Mrs. Doctor King. I was much affected at seeing her, now bereft of her affectionate husband, but full of Christian resignation and good works.

Feb. 13*th.*—Left per steamer *Derwent* for St. Vincent's. On stepping on to the deck, great was my joy at meeting my old friends, the Rev. Henry and Mrs. Hurd and their children, the Rev. Mr. Silifant and Mrs. Silifant, and the Rev. J. E. S. Williams and Mrs. Williams. Mr. Williams was sent on a special mission of evangelisation to the Hindus in British Guiana. Mr. Silifant was a Baptist clergyman, on his way to labour in Jamaica, and was a brother to Mrs. Hurd.

From my reverend brother, Mr. Hurd, I learnt that he had been charged by the General Secretaries to assure me of the affectionate sympathy of the Committee, and that it was with the greatest regret they saw that the way for my immediate return was not quite open; that it was mainly at my earnest request the Rev. Mr. Williams had been sent as their missionary to the Coolies in Demerara, and that the Committee feared that my removal at this juncture from the colony might seriously imperil the success of the enterprise. Besides which, the Education question was far from being settled; and it was believed that my absence, when the matter came again before the Court of Policy for discussion and settlement, might result in damage to thriving and numerous mission schools; that I was requested to return to Demerara for a fourth year to guide in the arrangement of these important questions; and, generally, still to help in prosecuting the glorious work of our missions in British Guiana; and, further, if Mrs. Bickford's health, as well as mine own, were insufficient to bear the strain of a full year's residence in Georgetown, then I was at liberty to use my own discretion and return to England, when it might become absolutely necessary. All of which suggestions seemed so reasonable and just that I could not but say, 'The will of the Lord be done.' 'God helping me,' I said, 'I will remain at my post and do my best to justify the confidence the venerated fathers in England repose in me.'

Feb. 18*th*.—The Rev. William Bannister, Chairman, commenced the business of the District Meeting. We had a blessed prayer meeting, and the business went on comfortably all day. The Rev. Mr. Williams was introduced to the brethren by the Chairman, and he was conducted to a seat according to his seniority. The Rev. Mr. Silifant was welcomed as a visitor, and requested to be present at the sessions when it suited his convenience.

The official reply of the General Secretaries to the Minutes of the previous District Meeting is always received with becoming respect and gratitude. I have sometimes thought, when listening to those famous manifestoes from our head-quarters, that there is more of the minute in them than there need to be. Every report of the state of religion and education in the several circuits, and the expenditure of the grants from the Committee and of locally raised moneys for carrying on the work, evidently had been subjected to a watchful criticism, the result of which appeared in the yearly official communication. Sometimes there is such an appearance of severity in the comments, that a nervous, thin-skinned brother would feel it to be a trying ordeal. But no 'bones' are 'broken;' and, upon the whole, it must be admitted that such a review of the internal life and working of a foreign district is healthful to the brethren's own tone of spiritual life, and sustaining to the administration of our *Episcopus*, as the executive officer of the Committee, in the faithful discharge of his onerous, and sometimes very unpleasant, duties.

From the official letter, dated January 2nd, 1852, we copy so much as refers to the appointment of the Rev. J. E. S. Williams as missionary to the Coolie immigrants in British Guiana. It has never been printed, although worthy of a place in the missionary literature of this remarkable century. It marks also the beginning of one of the most merciful missions the great men at the head of our affairs at that time in London ever had the honour of undertaking :—

' The state of the Coolies in Demerara has occupied the serious attention of the Committee, and encouraged by the experience of Mr. Bickford that the Colonial Government were disposed to make provision for the support of a missionary among them, they have decided upon sending Mr. Williams, a returned Indian missionary, and his wife, in company with Mr. Hurd, by the packet of the 17th inst., who shall devote his time to the work of preaching the Gospel to them in their own language. Mr. Hurd and Mr. Williams, in repeated conversations which we have had with them, are made fully acquainted with the Committee's views upon the subject, and the strictest adherence to those views will be expected. Mr. Williams is sent in his proper character as a missionary of the Society, not as a Government agent ; and will receive his allowances, and fall under the general district regulations, the same as all the other missionaries. The mission among the Coolies must be undertaken and conducted as a Wesleyan mission, in which the character of the Society is involved ; and the Government is not to be applied to, to provide for it as a State institution, but to make annual grants to enable the Society to support its own mission. The Committee are encouraged to commence this mission to the Coolies, because they regard it as an especial act of Christian charity to send the Gospel to these poor outcasts of society, and under the persuasion that a well-conducted mission will strengthen the credit and influence of the Society among the friends of religion and humanity in general ; it being an undoubted fact that the wretched state of the Coolies has taken a strong hold upon the Christian philanthropy of this country. Still, however, the undertaking must be with the strictest regard to 'economy, and the utmost exertions must be made to supplement the annual grant of the Government by local subscriptions, which we are led to expect may be obtained from parties in the colony, who feel deeply interested in the welfare of the Coolies, some of whom have even hesitated to continue their subscriptions to our general mission fund, because we have hitherto neglected to provide for those degraded and destitute strangers.'

There was no mistaking the meaning of this document. The District Meeting accepted the responsibility of the appointment of the Rev. J. E. S. Williams as the missionary to the Coolies in British Guiana ; and, in a few days, he and Mrs. Williams embarked with the Demerara brethren, for this new field of labour.

March 1st.—Sailed from Kingstown Harbour, St. Vincent's, at 4 p.m., in the sloop *Nautilus,* thirty tons burthen. We were a large party, and had to arrange as best we could. We had an opening made through the partition which separated the 'hull' from the cabin, and in the 'hull' we laid mattresses and hung up sails for the ladies' night-quarters. The brethren looked out for themselves—lying on the cabin floor, or stretching themselves on the softest planks on deck. It is really wonderful how English people can accommodate themselves to strange and trying conditions. We were as jolly and content as if we were in nice quarters on board one of the princely royal mail steamers.

The party consisted of the Revs. J. Banfield, W. L. Binks, John Wood, B.A., and J. E. S. Williams, with Mrs. Banfield, Mrs. Binks, and Mrs. Williams. I was a kind of supercargo, and catered for the whole party. We were in for a dead beat for the night, and tried to adjust ourselves to our 'environments.'

March 2nd.—All the party are very ill from the tossings of the sea.

March 3rd, 10 p.m.—We arrived off Barbadoes, and agreed to go on in the *Nautilus* to Demerara. Captain Stanley laid down his course, which was S.S.W. Carlisle Bay then bore east.

March 4th.—We had a beautiful day and fair wind.

March 5th.—We are still going on delightfully towards our ' desired haven.' We caught a fine barracuda to-day, which our good captain had cooked for the use of the passengers and crew.

March 6th, 12 a.m.—The captain has just taken the latitude, and we find ourselves sixty miles from the lightship. 6 p.m. : We are full of anxiety about making the land. It is so low that it is dangerous on account of sandbanks and strong currents to approach too near until the lightship has been seen.

March 7th.—Praise the Lord. We saw the ship *Hirunda* bound for London and spoke her. The captain informed us that the mouth of the river Demerary bore south. He also told us of the lightship. We then made direct for the river, took a pilot from the lightship, and sailed straight into port. We anchored at ten in the forenoon, just in time for the service at Trinity Church. The Rev. W. Heath was preaching a sermon full of sweetness and beauty from St. John xx. 20. It was so good after our voyage, which that morning had so happily terminated.

An interesting incident occurred as we were threading our way among the anchored shipping in the port of Georgetown. The ship *Lucknow* was right in our way in the stream. It was suggested to our pilot to pass close under her lee, as there appeared to be a great number of Coolies on board. ' Brother Williams,' said I, ' here are some of your sheep just about returning to Madras after the expiration of their five years of apprenticeship. Give them a right hearty salaam. It will cheer and please them.' Instanter Mr. Williams sprang on to the near bulwarks of our little craft, and shouted to them in their own tongue, much to their surprise. The emigrants rushed to the ship's side, wildly vociferating, and expressing their delight. The passing conversation closed with an understanding that Mr. Williams would go on board the next day before their departure for Madras.

March. 9th.—' Promptitude being ' the soul of success,' I lost no time on the morning of the day in taking the necessary steps for bringing the fact of the Rev. Mr. Williams's arrival before the Government and the community. Accordingly at 11 we started off for the public buildings to interview Sir Henry Barkly. The Rev. John Wood, M.A., accompanied us that he might be introduced also to the Governor. Mr. Williams carried over his head in true Eastern fashion his Indian umbrella, made of the bamboo, and which was artistically and beautifully ornamented. As we approached the court-house, he, with his vegetable parachute, became the object of staring surprise to the spectators. A few of the more respectable of the Hindus were standing about, so I said unto him, 'Give them a salutation ;' which he immediately did in their own Tamil, with such a full yet sweetly modulated tone, that it echoed along the corridors with magical effect. The delight of the missionary was ecstatic ; and from that hour he became the accepted friend and religious teacher of the Coolie immigrants.

Our interview with the Governor was all that could be desired. Sir Henry was very kind, and spoke freely to Mr. Williams on the subject of his mission to the Hindu population, and promised his support in every practicable manner. The Hon. W. Walker, Government Secretary, was also pleased to see Mr. Williams, and spake words of encouragement to him. In the evening Mr. Williams, accompanied by Mr. Wood, went on board the *Lucknow* to see the Coolie passengers. He went round amongst them, speaking in familiar terms to each, giving them tracts in Tamil and Hindustanee, and commending them to the care of their common Father in heaven. The joy of these wandering Shemites was unbounded in finding, after five years' residence on the sugar plantations, a white Englishman, who could and would speak to them words of wise counsel and kindly feeling.

All classes of the community seemed gratified that, by the arrival of the Rev. Mr. Williams, the sin and shame of neglecting the spiritual condition of the Coolies were to be removed. It was, therefore, hardly a surprise that our memorial to the Combined Court for a grant of salary to Mr. Williams was so successful. Our expectations were not large, because at that time the mission was simply an experiment. But we were careful to set forth the whole case, and leave the Court to deal with it on its merits. It was on the 11th, two days after the advent of the missionary, the memorial was considered. My jotting under that date is very jubilant :—

'*March* 11*th.*—The Hon. Richard Haynes moved, to-day in the Combined Court, and the Hon. George Booker seconded, that £200 sterling be put on the estimates in aid of salary to Rev. Mr. Williams. and £100 to defray travelling expenses ; which was unanimously agreed to.   Ebenezer ! Ebenezer ! '

Mr. Williams now entered upon his work ' with a will.'   He was plainly a man who could do nothing by halves, and seemed possessed of all those qualities for the mission upon which his whole heart was set.   A missionary to a weak and despised race, yet a man of ripe intellect, great conversational powers, ready resources, and of a quick, fine temper.   I was pleased to see how he made the question of the fair treatment of the Coolies by their employers one of essential importance to the success of his work.   The first plantation I visited with him was Nismes, where there was a large batch of the immigrants employed under a contract of five years.   The evident sympathy he manifested in the best interests of these poor strangers and the adroitness of his remarks greatly pleased me.   At the close of his address, one of the head men entered into a discussion with Mr. Williams.   The main point of his argument was that there were no two things in nature exactly alike—then why should there be a forced similarity in religious beliefs?   Holding out his right hand, he said, ' See these fingers, how they differ both in lengths and uses ! Yet each is equally needful to the construction of the hand, and each has its own functions.   So with religion.   The English have their own, and so have we.   They have their long finger, and we have the shorter one.   But because the two fingers differ in length, shall I cut off the shorter one and cast it away?   No : both are necessary—both useful—both good.   So with religion.   Why throw ours aside for yours, when it has been good for our people, the same as your religion has been good for your people ? '   The discussion, of course, was in Tamil, so that it was not till afterwards that I knew the exact character of the contention.

The effect of the objections of the head man upon the whole personality of Mr. Williams was most striking.   In reply, he treated the symbol of the ' two fingers ' somewhat playfully, and then proceeded to deal with the ' thing signified ' with due seriousness. He had, he said, something better for them than they had ever previously had ; and he was come all the way from England to make it known to them.   Then, by a process of incontrovertible facts, he proved to them that the religion of ' the white man of the

7

West ' was a more powerful factor for removing all the ' evils that
are in the world ' than was any system of religion that India had
ever produced.   He would tell them of that better thing if they
would listen to him ; besides which, he would help them in any
other way that lay within his power.   We were standing all the
time on the edge of the verandah in front of the ' big ' house, and
the Coolies crowded on the steps leading up to it.   At the close
Mr. Williams was thanked for his visit, and the immigrants returned
to their work.

As we walked together from the plantation to our Nismes Church,
about a mile away, for an evening service, Mr. Williams manifested
much anxious concern for the salvation of these poor strangers.
However, he had begun an attack upon the citadel of an ancient
superstition, and had secured the respectful attention of his auditors.
Even the short dialectical battle was to him an omen for good.

Mr. Williams's next visit was to the Industry sugar estate, about
three miles from Georgetown.   The manager, Malcolm McNabb, Esq.,
was a hospitable Highlander, and a regular worshipper at our Trinity
Church.   We were quite a party on the occasion, consisting of Mr.
and Mrs. George Ross, Mr. and Mrs. Allan Cameron, Mrs. Williams,
Mrs. Bickford, the Revs. John Wood, J. E. S. Williams, and myself.
The Coolies were collected in front, and Mr. Williams spoke to them
for half-an-hour or so.   It was a beautiful spectacle : the visitors in
the background, Mr. Williams and Mr. McNabb a little in advance
of us, and in the verandah and on the steps were the immigrant
hearers.   A few of the free labourers, black and coloured, were on
the margin.   It was a grouping which, if it could have been photo-
graphed as we were all under the spell of the missionary's impassioned
speech, would have possessed an historic interest of no mean value.
The Coolies thanked Mr. Williams, and said it was very kind of him
to come and speak to them.

I will here express, a second time, my conscientious belief that the
labours of our missionaries have been a known blessing to the white
colonists as well as to those of the sable race.   This remark specially
applies to the two classes as they existed in my time.   It may be that
there was a degree of repugnance of feeling among the more respectable of the whites to mingle with the so-called inferior race in our
large city congregations in Demerara and Barbadoes ; but then there
was always a sprinkling of such through whom our names became

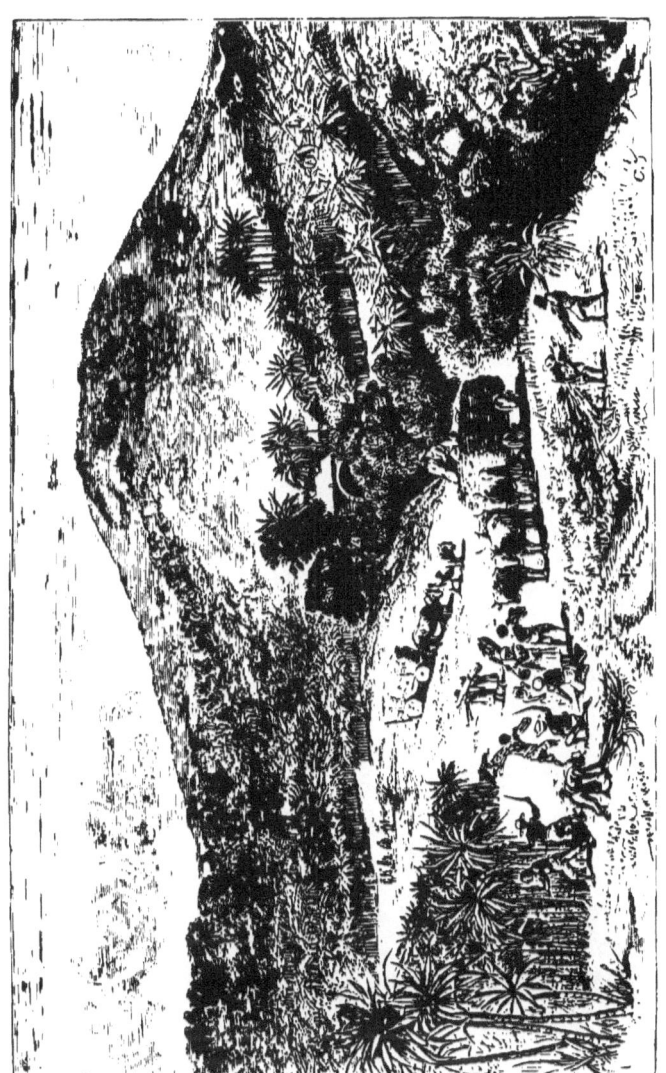

SUGAR PLANTATION.

familiar, and the influence of our characters were felt in the best circles of white society. And this influence begot a confidence in our piety and far-reaching knowledge of spiritual experiences, which were availed for times of affliction and seasons of bereavement. This was very much the case in the city of Georgetown, during the period of my incumbency as pastor of Trinity Church. As a sample only I quote the following from my Journal :—

'*March 23rd.*—The Hon. George Booker called this morning to ask me to visit the Hon. John Croal, who was very ill. He is an old and respectable colonist, and if he be taken off he will be greatly missed from the colony. I called back again at 5 o'clock, and found Mr. Croal a little better.'

'*March 24th.*—Called again on Mr. Croal. He was considerably improved, and hopes to leave for Barbadoes by the steamer now expected. May a gracious Providence interpose in his behalf !'

The case of the Hon. John Croal and my visits to him in his dangerous illness should have some explanation. There were two gentlemen in Demerara, John Croal and Peter Rose, who had been, as members of the Court of Policy, a difficulty, if not a terror, to many an English Governor sent to the colony. Acting together, they could so control the votes of the Court as to create at will a ' deadlock ' in all legislative action. They were men of stalwart size, strong in purpose, and powerful in debate. When they would have their own way they always had it. The Governor, although backed by the Colonial Office, and supported by numerous officials, was powerless to resist them. The deadlock in 1849, from which the colony suffered so much, was their united creation. The points in dispute were the reduction of the enormous Civil List, and the making a legislative provision for the introduction of thousands of Hindu Coolies to assist in keeping the sugar plantations in a state of efficient cultivation. There was, however, reason in what some people called Rose's madness, as the events clearly proved.

The strain upon Mr. Croal was such that ultimately his health gave way, and he was laid aside by a terrible illness. When his friend, the Hon. George Booker, called upon me to visit him, I was taken by surprise. I asked to know how it was that I had been selected for this painful duty, when Mr. Booker informed me that on that very morning the doctor had advised the calling in of a Christian minister to give spiritual counsel to the sick man. Further, that the names of several clergymen had been mentioned, and that

Mr. Croal had selected me. Thus armed, I went in the name of the Lord, to minister to this ardent politician in his distress. I found him lying in a hammock in the centre of a beautifully furnished room, surrounded by a number of sympathising friends. 'Mr. Croal,' said I, 'I have come at your request to see you. Would you like me to explain to you in a few sentences what the Heavenly Father is willing to do to help persons situated as you are?' 'That is what I want,' he replied; 'I am very ill, and I may die and I am not prepared.' 'Oh, my God,' I inwardly said, 'this is the crisis of his soul; help me to lead him to Thee.' I then explained to him the plan of salvation; assuring him that if he would accept a free and full pardon for all his sins, he would have that blessing even now. 'Will you accept?' I said; 'there is nothing else.' You become a child of God by being forgiven, but all for Christ's sake.' I then knelt down and commended him in prayer to God.

I was deeply penetrated with the belief that the Almighty Father would hear prayer for the removal of the fever which had so mercilessly prostrated this hitherto very strong man. I expressed this belief when I returned to the Werk-en-Rust Parsonage. During the next five or six days I was constant in my visitations to Mr. Croal, when, to our great relief, the R.M. steamer arrived, and our friend was carried on board and left for England, *via* Barbadoes, if so advised on his arrival in that island. But Mr. Croal had so much rallied during this short voyage, that his physician recommended he should stay in the mild climate of Barbadoes, in the belief that that would be sufficient. I received during his stay a grateful letter from him, in which he mentioned the rapid progress he was making towards the full restoration of his health. In due course, Mr. Croal returned to Demerara, and, on the very next day after his arrival, he was driven up to our house, that he might personally thank me for my sympathy and prayers 'in the hour of his distress.' He also stated to me his earnest desire to do something for the permanent support of our mission, by providing in a 'Clergy Bill,' which he intended to lay before the Court of Policy, an annual endowment, in recognition of the invaluable services the Wesleyan missionaries had rendered to the Government and the general community by their unostentatious and disinterested labours. As such provision would be exclusively for the educational and spiritual good of the emancipated classes, I accepted, in behalf of my brethren and the London Committee, the aid so generously proffered. But Mr. Croal had been for many years an annual subscriber to the funds of the Wesleyan Missionary Society, and in many other ways had showed his friendly feeling towards the honoured men who had superintended the work in British Guiana.

I now insert a few jottings from my Journal :—

'*March 27th.*—I attended by invitation a meeting of the subscribers to the New Orphan Asylum, held in the court-house, when eight directors were chosen from the contributors. But such had been the indifference of the Nonconformists to this humane institution, that we could not even elect one director. This is too bad ; and I felt thoroughly ashamed.'

'*April 4th.*—Preached this morning at Trinity, and in the evening at Kingston. A splendid prayer meeting at the close of the service was held at Trinity. This is the day appointed by the District Meeting to pray for the outpouring of the Holy Spirit upon our congregations and churches in the district.'

'*April 5th.*—This morning I felt very happy, and I could say : " Now, Lord, I feel that I have only one desire to live, and that is to do good." I was much blessed yesterday. My prayer has been answered and now I am wholly Thine. Oh keep me, gracious Lord, in this state all the days of my earthly pilgrimage ! Henceforth this shall be my motto : "This one thing I do, forgetting those things which are behind, and reaching forth unto those things which are before, I press toward the mark for the prize of the high calling of God in Christ Jesus." '

I am not sure that I had received the grace of a ' perfect ' consecration to God, in the same measure, before the period just noted. It was a baptism of 'holy fire' from Christ's mediatorial altar. And what was its merciful purpose? But to prepare me for the terrible ordeal of suffering which was shortly to come upon me. I was to be suddenly arrested in the midst of a series of labours and responsibilities which were being borne, but only for Christ's sake. As long as I had full strength it was a pleasurable toil ; but the 'last feather' was laid on, and the 'back' broke.

I was sitting at my desk in the upper or third storey of the house, writing an important official document on the subject of the Coolie Mission for the Governor and Court of Policy, when, suddenly, the *cerebrum* came within the grasp of power which paralyzed all further effort. I could only compare it to what would probably be the effect of a strong man standing before me with a pair of extended pincers, with one claw gripping one side of the forehead, and with the other claw gripping the other side. My power of further mental action collapsed, and my pen dropped from my hand. I crawled to my room and was laid on the bed. The doctor came in a few minutes, and recognised the case at a glance. 'Twenty grains of calomel and twenty-four of quinine,' said he; 'and in three hours two-thirds of a tumbler of castor oil.' For a desperate attack a desperate remedy was needed. The sufferings I endured for the next three days no tongue can tell. The news that I had been seized with the yellow fever spread like wildfire through the city. During the forenoon of the third day it was reported that I had passed away. But it was not so, God having more work for me yet to do in His vineyard.

'*May 1st.*—Since my last entry, I have been on the east coast for a fortnight for the benefit of my health, but, at Mahaica, I had a relapse and was obliged to call in Doctor Miller. I was again much prostrated. On the evening of the 26th, Mrs. Bickford and I returned to the city, as weak as when I left a fortnight previously. The whole of this week I have been improving, and I have now the prospect of being able to engage in the blessed work to-morrow.'

'*May 3rd.*—Yesterday I preached at Kingston from the words, "It is good for me that I have been afflicted;" after which I gave the Lord's Supper. Returning to Werk-en-Rust, I learned with much pleasure that Mrs. Cameron, our dear friend, had taken the Sacrament with us.'

'"In the midst of life we are in death." Henry J. Sawyer, a young gentleman recently from England, and who had been Sheriff of Essequibo, died on Saturday and was buried yesterday morning. He died at Government House, having been stopping with his cousin the Governor. He died of the yellow fever : hundreds of others also have been cut off by the same dreadful scourge. I trust the merciful God has pitied them and saved them.'

'*May 6th.*—This day I am thirty-six years of age. Another year of mercy and goodness. This will be a year of change if my life is spared. Whether the time is come for us to return to England, or to take the prospective appointment in St. Vincent's, I can hardly say.'

'*May 13th.*—The full effects of the Demerara fever do not altogether cease with the apparent removal of the cause. Frequently a strange affection of the brain remains, which is most painful to bear. I had to call in again Doctor Blair to help me, if possible. He prescribed sixteen grains of calomel and sixteen grains of compound extract of colocynth. I was very ill, and Mrs. Bickford and I spent the remainder of the week with our kind friends, Mr. and Mrs. Ross, at Ruimveld plantation. Mr. and Mrs. Cameron were there also, and ministered to our comfort.'

'*June 1st.*—Death, fire, and fever ! Such is the record. My dear and venerated father, John Bickford, yeoman, and formerly of Modbury, Devon, died at North Rhine, South Australia, on the 25th of November, last year, and his precious remains were interred in the little cemetery at Angaston, there to await the resurrection of the just.

'The new Orphan Asylum has been destroyed by fire. It was a mournful spectacle. Mr. Attorney-General Arrindall was the benevolent projector of this humane institution. I called, as in duty bound, on him to tender my condolence, which he received for himself and Mrs. Arrindall with much feeling. The destruction of the asylum was a great calamity to our orphan poor.

' The Rev. John Wood, my colleague and inmate at Trinity Parsonage, was taken ill with fever. On the 25th Dr. Blair said it was decidedly a case of yellow fever, and that next day would be a critical time for him. In the night he was apparently approaching death. Mrs. Bickford and I rushed to his help, I holding him up in an erect position, and she bathing his poor forehead with eau-de-Cologne to prevent his fainting away. It was a crucial moment, and we feared the worst. But, in God's mercy, a copious flow of perspiration broke out, and immediate danger was over.

' The Rev. James Banfield, at Golden Grove on the east coast, has been ill from the same scourge twelve days. We had given up all hope in his case, as the black vomit had set in. But what in so many instances had been the precursor of death was in Mr. Banfield's case the turning point of his recovery. I went up to see him, and soon detected symptoms of coming restoration to health. But, it seemed to me, judging from the details Mrs. Banfield gave me of those twelve days of prostration and suffering her husband had passed through, that the sparing of his life at that time was a physical miracle wrought by God, in mercy to the tried Mission families, " lest we should have sorrow upon sorrow."

' Mr. Wood is pronounced to be nicely convalescing. Thank God for prompt medical skill and the Divine blessing upon the means employed.'

July 5th.—My Journal records—

' Preached to-day at Trinity Church on the conversion of the Philippian gaoler, and gave the Lord's Supper. In the afternoon I visited a Scottish Presbyterian lady, a Mrs. MacIntosh, who was very ill. In the evening at Kingston, just after the commencement of the sermon, the cry of " *Fire* ! FIRE ! FIRE !" was raised, and the congregation had to be dismissed. A fortnight ago, a similar cry was raised just as the evening service closed, and a rush to the doors took place. Last evening, the house of a Mrs. Thomas was burnt down : her daughter was very ill at the time, but she escaped unhurt. She is a member of my class. Mr. Wood was able to preach yesterday, and seems no worse for it this morning.'

' *July 15th.*—To-day, Sarah Jane, daughter of the Rev. W. L. Binks, died at Mahaica, on the east coast, of yellow fever. I hastened up by an early train to comfort and to assist our dear friends in this hour of their great trouble. On arriving at the mission house I was much distressed at the appearance of Mr. and Mrs. Binks themselves. They had both " been down " with fever, and were prostrated with weakness. An immediate change from the fever-hole, which Mahaica, at certain seasons of the year was known to be, was a dire necessity. But the first thing to be done was the interment of the remains of the dear child, whose pure spirit had fled to the " arms of Jesus." After consultation with the sorrow-stricken parents, I got the sexton to dig a grave under the floor of the school-house, and therein we deposited all that was mortal of that once beautiful child. This solemnity being over, I secured the loan of a carriage, and we drove off for Golden Grove and rested there. By the evening train we proceeded to the city, and arrived at our humble home in due course. The afflicting scenes of that day are so impressed upon my memory that they can never be forgotten. It was, indeed, a day of sadness : our sun appeared to be covered with a cloud.'

'*July 30th.*—Mr. Williams, our Coolie missionary, returned from Berbice this morning very ill. Dr. Blair was called in and prescribed twenty-four grains of quinine and twenty of calomel, to be followed in two hours by the usual quantity of castor oil. A malignant fever is still raging, and the "faculty" prescribe these large doses in the beginning to save time.'

'*Aug. 1st.*—Mr. Williams is convalescing very assuredly to-day. Praise God.'

'*Aug. 3rd.*—My last visit to the Arabian coast. Mrs. Bickford and I went on board the *dredging* schooner, the *Pheasant* : but, leaving the river somewhat late for the falling tide, we were not clear before it began again to wash. We had therefore to come to anchor on the Zeelandia bank for the night. With the rolling of the vessel and the effluvium from the bilge-water, I suffered much pain in my head, and was very sick. Mrs. Bickford bore the strain much better than I. Reached Lorg the next day. On the 4th, 5th, and 6th, I attended three tea and public meetings, and spoke at each. On the 9th, I preached at Lorg, Queenstown, and Abram Tuil. It was a good day in every respect, and I trust the congregations were comforted and edified.'

On the occasion of my visits to the country parts of this wide and laborious circuit, I always pressed into them as much work as I could. I did not omit either to call upon the local gentry, who were friendly to our missionaries. Such visits were much valued; and, oftentimes, left a blessing behind. Therefore, 'on the day after the Sabbath,' I waited upon the Rev. William Austin, an Anglican clergyman, and brother to Dr. Austin, Bishop of Guiana, Mr. Bagot and family, and other gentlemen, both coloured and white. At the close of the day's exercises I was much fatigued, but I was comforted in the belief that the time was not by any means lost. We returned by sea to Georgetown, reaching our home at midnight on the 13th, and found all well.

The arrival of the fortnightly mail steamer is an event of commanding interest in Demerara to all the Europeans. For days together sometimes, our eyes would be strained by using our telescopes for reading the semaphore at the east end of the city. When, at length, the north arm would fall, that was to say that a steamer was in sight; when the south arm, that was to the effect that it was the royal mail steamer from England. On the 24th, the assuring T appeared, and the whole city was on the *qui vive*. No letter from the Missionary Committee came to hand; but my old friend the *Watchman* did, and was full of Conference news. Mrs. Bickford and I eagerly inspected the official 'Stations Sheet,' and therein we saw the welcome words—

'JAMES BICKFORD IS RETURNING HOME.'

The answer to my prayers and requests, which these five words brought me, seemed to re-nerve my hand for answering letters, as well as to inspirit my heart for attention to other duties. Under date *August 25th*, my Journal says :—

'Wrote by this mail to the following friends :—Mrs. Furze, Mevagissey, Cornwall ; Captain James le Messurier, Guernsey ; the Rev. W. L. Thornton, 14, City Road, London ; and my niece, Miss Boon, Modbury, Devon. And in the islands to Rev. John Corlett, Barbadoes ; the Rev. Henry Hurd. St. Vincent's ; the Rev. W. Limmex, Trinidad ; Sidney Stead, Esq., Buxton Grove, Antigua ; Mr. Edward Drew, a student in the Mico Institution, Antigua. So much correspondence is a heavy matter, but it must be attended to. I have been much impressed with this view of correspondence since reading the " Life of William Wilberforce," one of England's greatest philanthropists and Christian statesmen, who, when embarrassed with " an immense accumulation of letters," remarked, " How can I clear away the arrear ? It will cost me a month to do it. Yet courtesy is a Christian duty, and I must write to those who may fairly claim answers." So will I—" giving no offence in anything, that the ministry be not blamed." '

During my absence in the West Indies my parents had emigrated to South Australia. My father had died there, and my widowed mother was still living in the colony. I was sorely distressed on her account, and on August 31st I wrote the London Committee offering, on our return to England, to go out as one of their Australian ministers. The rush to the goldfields had set in, and the English Conference was anxious to strengthen its staff of preachers, especially in New South Wales and Victoria. I quote from my Journal :—

'Wrote a letter to-day (the 31st) to the Committee, offering to go out to Australia for these reasons: (1) I have from the time of my conversion in 1832, felt my sympathies to be in that direction, and these have been strongest when my soul has been most alive to God and to the welfare of my fellow-men ; (2) I prefer colonial to the English work, and I could not but with extreme pain consent to settle down at home and thereby sink, or set aside, the experience and information I have obtained from fourteen years of residence in the colonies ; (3) I strongly desire that my next field of ministerial labour should supply a home for myself and dear wife for our lifetime ; (4) The climate of Australia is of a medium character, and therefore better adapted to us after so long a sojourn in the tropics ; (5) I would add that the remains of my late venerable father are interred in a cemetery at Angaston, South Australia ; that my yet widowed mother is still resident in the colony. . . . I crave your forgiveness for adding that it would be a mournful satisfaction to see my father's grave, and "o'er it drop a tear ; " to be with and aid by my sympathy and prayers my mother in her declining years ; and to use my best endeavours, morally and spiritually, to benefit my brothers and sisters and their families, now in Australia, by my presence and ministrations.'

'*Sept. 4th.*—This day Mr. Wood is again ill. He is very unwell of the fever.'

'*Sept. 5th.*—"Deep calleth unto deep." Mrs. Bickford, Mr. Williams, and Mr. Wood are prostrate with fever. In the afternoon I buried our dear friend, Miss Fisher, late sister of Mrs. John Evans. She died of yellow fever.'

'*Sept. 14th.*—Mrs. Brown, the overseer's wife at Thomas estate, died yesterday, and this evening her remains were interred. She has been called to seek the Lord about eighteen months, and she walked obediently in God's statutes. Her affliction was a deeply painful one, but her soul was happy. She has gone to heaven to be with Jesus.'

'*Sept. 17th.*—Returned yesterday from the Supply village (up the river), to which place I had gone for services the day before. I was overpowered with heat. and was compelled to lie down in the *batteaux*. I was very ill as the consequence of this exposure, and had to take strong remedies.'

' *Oct. 10th.*—Received a kind letter to-day from the Rev. George Osborn, Junior Missionary Secretary, on the subject of our return to England, but not one word about the appointment of an ordained minister for Berbice, nor concerning the circuit whose superintendency I am so soon to vacate. This is very perplexing.'

'*Oct. 25th.*—The Annual Missionary Meeting was held at Kingston : Thomas A. Spooner, Esq., in the chair. It was a deeply interesting time.'

' *Oct. 26th.*—The meeting at Trinity Church came off ; Sir Henry Barkly presided with great ability. The Hon. W. Walker and the Hon. W. Bruce Ferguson spoke for our Foreign Missions. The Revs. J. Banfield and J. E. S. Williams assisted. The Governor told me at the close how much he had been pleased. He said "that such sustained eloquence as he had heard that night he had never known surpassed ; not even in the English House of Commons. That evening would always be a pleasant memory to him." '

'*Oct. 27th.*—After nearly four years of pleading with the London Committee for the appointment of an ordained minister for Berbice, we succeeded in our request. Another illustration of the famous maxim : " All good things come to those who wait." Dr. Hoole communicated this pleasing news to me. He said in his welcome letter : " The Committee has concluded to send a missionary to Berbice." That was all, but it was enough.'

'*Nov. 3rd.*—And now it became necessary for me once more to visit Berbice, for I had good news to tell our Dutch friends and our own people. I therefore left in the steamer *Tyne*, and made a quick passage from port to port. We took only seven hours and twenty minutes. Surely there is nothing like steam for speed and comfort in traversing the sea ! Mrs. Dalgliesh, wife of the Rev. John Dalgliesh, London missionary in New Amsterdam, had just returned from Scotland, and was one of our passengers. She lent me her copy of Mrs. Stowe's world-renowned book, entitled " Uncle Tom's Cabin," which I read all the way up. By turns I laughed and I cried ; yea, I almost cursed as I learnt of the senseless and brutal conduct of the Legrees, on the southern plantations, towards the black and coloured people. In my soul, I hope, I did not sin, but I was on the very edge of doing it. I was enraged at the tale unfolded by Mrs. Stowe. "Is the story true," said I. Well, upon this point I will get corroborative or condemnatory evidence from the lips of the old planters still living in these once accursed slave-holding lands, and the world shall know the result. Alas! alas! I found that there was hardly an incident of wickedness told in 'Uncle Tom' that could not be paralleled in the earlier history of British Guiana. *Mutatis mutandis.* And Mrs. Stowe's story would be true of the slave *régime* in these once unhappy lands!

'On this occasion of my visit, I spent nearly a week in preaching and visiting. On the evening of the 3rd, the day of my arrival, I preached in Mr. Dalgliesh's church to 130 persons. On the 4th, I visited our members and Scotch and Dutch friends, and preached in the Lutheran church in the evening. On the 5th, I did more visiting, and in the afternoon I went out to Cumberland and held a religious service. On the 6th, I passed over the river to the west coast, and spent the day very profitably with the Rev. Mr. and Mrs. Roome, at the London Missionary Station. I returned to New Amsterdam by the evening boat, and went directly to the house of Mrs. Hancock's son, to christen it, as it was called. This is a good custom, and I tried to encourage it. On the 7th, I preached in New Amsterdam twice, and once at Cumberland. Besides, I renewed the tickets of ninety-five members, and gave the Lord's Supper at both places. It was a busy, but a happy day. On the 8th, I returned overland in the mail waggon for Georgetown, a distance of seventy-five miles. Our good people at Berbice are blessing God that at length a minister is to be appointed for them. I praise God also with all my heart.'

A gap of twelve days occurs in my Journal. On the 20th, I say—

'Since my last entry I have been laid aside with fever, superinduced, no doubt, by the heavy labours in Berbice, and the fatigue of the overland journey. Last Sunday I was unable to preach, and Mr. J. J. Savory and the Rev. J. E. S. Williams took my appointments. On Tuesday Mrs. Bickford and I went up to the "Industry" plantation, at the invitation of Malcolm McNabb, Esq., the hospitable manager. I improved very much by the change, and came home last evening pretty well. Oh, that the Lord in mercy may "prop the house of clay" a few weeks longer, when I hope to leave the tropics for a more salubrious clime!'

'*Dec. 4th.*—A busy week; employed in collecting the annual subscriptions for our Foreign Missions, and in superintending a lot of mechanics about the premises. Mr. James Rogers, one of our best men, employs and directs these workers, and I pay them every week. Preaching and visiting the sick have also been attended to. The temporal and spiritual prosperity of the mission lies near my heart.'

'*Dec. 5th.*—A very wet day, and congregations small. We have had great sorrow to-day from the following circumstance: Captain John Smith, of the barque *Gratitude*, belonging to Messrs. J. Lidgett & Son, London, shipowners, a good man, who had rendered himself very dear to us, was to be buried to-day. He was taken ill on Friday on board the vessel, came on shore on Saturday, and died on Sunday. He sent for me, but it was too late. As I was leaving our house, a second messenger (one of our members) came with the melancholy news of his death. His last Sabbath was spent with us, and the last sermon he heard was from my lips. The text was: " The Master is come and calleth for thee." He died of the prevailing fever, which has taken off many of the sailors, especially the captains of vessels lying in the river.'

' *Dec.* 10*th.*—This morning the "mate " of the *Gratitude* died after two days' illness ; also the " mate " of the *Phœnix*—both of the yellow fever. Mr. Murray, one of our respectable merchants, called on me to perform the funeral service over them, which I did, but it was a mournful sight.

'News came to hand that the Revs. Chatterton and Rotherham have succumbed to the relentless foe—both young men and full of promise for usefulness, but they are gone. When will the Heavenly Father stay His hand in mercy to the white life in Demerara and Barbadoes? When ?' . . .

' *Dec.* 16*th.*—To-day in the Court of Policy the battle was again fought over the " Secular Education " project, which, if carried as provided in the Bill, would have crippled and ultimately destroyed our mission day-schools. We could not stand quietly by and allow such a *finale* to come about without a strong protest. The clerical educationists mustered in great strength in the Court whilst the discussion was going forth. We heard the " memorials " read ; and, from where we sat, we could watch the effect upon the countenances of the members. The three best speeches were those of the President of the Court, Sir Henry Barkly, Mr. Secretary Walker, and the Hon. Thomas Porter. The feeling of the Court evidently was that the religious bodies, which had for so many years expended money, and time, and ability, in aid of the educational work of the colony, were entitled to be heard, and to have justice done to them ; and that no case had been made out by opposing parties for ruthlessly arresting the good work they were doing. Besides which, it was felt by several of the members that such a system as that proposed would cost more than the colony at that time could bear. Beyond, therefore, the providing for a more careful and vigorous inspection of existing schools, and the gradual introduction of such improvements as Mr. Commissioner Dennis might suggest, nothing more of a practical or destructive kind was done. But a principle was affirmed, which should apply to any prospective legislation upon the subject, as follows : " That in all schools deriving any portion of their support under the provision of such Bill, religious instruction founded upon the precepts of Holy Scripture be imparted to the pupils." By this resolution of the Court of Policy the position of the Wesleyan missionaries in their relation to this question was upheld, for, in the absence of specific instructions from the London Committee, we were not at liberty to diverge from those principles the English Conference had adopted.'

' *Dec.* 17*th.*—By the mail I had the satisfaction of hearing from the General Secretaries on the subject of the Coolie mission ; also a kind letter from the Rev. Dr. Hoole on matters of a personal and circuit character. I received another letter from the Rev. John Corlett detailing the particulars anent the affliction and death of Brother Rotherham.

'The Rev. J. E. S. Williams and I called upon Governor Barkly to lay before him certain particulars relating to the Coolie mission. We had to tell him that the London Committee threw the entire support of the mission upon the

Government and Christian friends and well-wishers in the colony. We required to rent and furnish a house, as the parsonage at Kingston was no longer available. He was very kind, and promised us £50 in aid of the expenses of the mission.'

'*Dec.* 24*th.*—The annual examination of the Werk-en-Rust School came off to-day. There was a large attendance of pupils, nicely clad, and looking healthful and happy. His Excellency Sir H. Barkly, Chief Justice Arrindall, and several other gentlemen were present. The result of the examination was most satisfactory to our distinguished visitors.'

As this was the fourth and last time I expected to be at this annual demonstration, I was anxious that the Governor and the Chief Justice should know what we were really doing for the mental and moral improvement of the pupils of this large and influential city school. And they were greatly pleased. Nothing could exceed the beautiful simplicity and practical value of His Excellency's address to the scholars and teachers at the close of the exercises. The pupils cheered him heartily as he left. It was a proud day for Mr. Savory, Miss Blair, and the assistant teachers.

1853.

Jan. 1*st*, 1853.—I quote from my Journal :—

' " Praise the Lord, O my soul, and forget not all His benefits." The last two hours of the last year were spent at the 'Watch Night Service,' at Trinity Church. The Rev. J. E. S. Williams preached an eloquent discourse from Dan. v. 25. His studies when a missionary in the East greatly helped him in his exposition. I followed with an exhortation, urging an immediate abandonment of all sin, and a renewed consecration to God. It was a solemn time for both ministers and people. I do not remember ever to have had such a delightful sense of God's goodness as when I rose from my knees, and congratulated the congregation by offering to them in the Name of the Lord "A Happy New Year."'

'*Jan.* 2*nd.*—Preached at Trinity Church to a large congregation. We then renewed our covenant to be the Lord's, and sealed it at the Lord's Table. It was a solemn and blessed time.'

'*Jan.* 12*th.*—I had now to pay my final visit to Berbice : Mrs. Bickford accompanying me. We had a nice passage up, and were received with much affection by Mr. Thomas Fraser, Miss Dow, and other Wesleyan members. When not holding public services, I visited the Society and our Scotch and Dutch friends. I preached as usual three times on the Sabbath ; twice in New Amsterdam, and once at Cumberland. I renewed the tickets of membership of nearly one hundred members, and gave the Lord's Supper twice.

' I cannot refrain from mentioning the names of those dear friends who were most hospitable and kind to us on this occasion of our last visit : Mr. and Mrs.

Roelof Hart, Mrs. Dr. Koch, Mrs. Obermüller, Mr. Thomas and Mrs. Fraser, and the Rev. John and Mrs. Dalgliesh. I preached my last sermon in the Dutch Church. on the evening of the 17th, to an immense congregation. *Vale!*'

We returned by sea to Georgetown on the 20th, and found that during our absence Mrs. Williams had been very ill. The Rev. W. L. Binks, who, after ten years of incessant and useful labour and many personal and family afflictions, has obtained permission to ' return home,' came from Mahaica that we might consult over the affairs of his circuit. We had no practical difficulty in making arrangements for the caring of the work until a successor arrived. We also agreed that we would go by the same ship from Demerara direct to London.

The Annual District Meeting was this year to be held in St. Vincent's; but, in consequence of the prevalence of that dreadful scourge, the yellow fever, it had to be postponed. The Rev. R. Ridyard, a promising young missionary, had died at Calder, and a Miss Handley, a Christian young lady employed as governess in one of the mission homes, had died at Calliaqua; whilst Mrs. Bannister, the wife of the Chairman, was hopelessly ill. The Rev. Mr. Pritchard was laid aside also. The early months of 1853 set in with a heavy cloud over the whole of the white people, and we seemed as walking upon the very edge of eternity.

We in Demerara were under very great pressure, and every day of delay in our departure for England, appeared to imperil our very lives. Therefore, on February 23rd, Mr. Binks and I went on board the barque *Cleopatra*, Captain McEachem, and took our passages for London. We wrote a joint letter to the Rev. W. Bannister, Chairman of the District, informing him of our inability to be present at its sessions this year.

March 5th.—I copy from my Journal as follows :—

'Visited my much-respected and venerated friend, the Hon. George Bagot. Old age and ailments have come upon him, and his time cannot be long. His mind appears to be in a tranquil state. He rests alone for salvation upon the atonement of our Lord Jesus Christ. I also called upon my friend, the Hon. W. B. Ferguson, who, with his family, expects shortly to leave for London. The friendship of Messrs. Bagot and Ferguson were to me, under some trying responsibilities, a source of strength and of much comfort. I cannot but believe that God " raised them up " for my aid in conducting the important mission entrusted to me in British Guiana. Mr. Sheriff Bagot was an Irish Episcopalian, and Mr. Ferguson was a Scotch Presbyterian—both representative and Christian men, whose friendship I both needed and valued.'

In order that the work of the mission might be sustained and even prosecuted with greater vigour than ever, we brought all the influence we reasonably could to bear upon the Combined Court, whose annual session was to be held this month. To our former clients, the emancipated classes, we had now to add the Coolie immigrants, whose civil and spiritual condition lay heavily upon our hearts. With no grants from the London Committee for any branch of the English or other work in the Province, we were again compelled to look to the Colonial Treasury for the pecuniary help required. Memorials to the Court were accordingly prepared, and confided to the financial representatives for presentation at the proper time. The result is noted in my Journal :—

'The Combined Court has sat, and much business has been got through. The Court has been very liberal to us. It has granted $1,840 to the Coolie mission ; $250 to aid in building a "Chapel-schoolhouse" in Stanley village, near Mahaica ; $250 to aid in establishing a Wesleyan day-school in New Amsterdam; and $500 in "aid of children of indigent parents" in Georgetown.'

The Coolie mission met with great favour from the Government. And no wonder ! For the presence of the Rev. Mr. Williams was a great relief to the authorities in dealing with this imported increment of our mixed population. Soon after Mr. Williams's 'arrival,' there was a murder case to be tried, in which one or more of the Coolies were concerned ; when the services he alone could render were availed of as sworn interpreter. It was a long and painful trial ; and, for the first time, the judge expressed his satisfaction that they now had a gentleman of high character and linguistic ability to help the Court in the administration of justice. In the preparation of official documents relating to the social conduct of the immigrants ; their obligations as indentured labourers on the sugar plantations to the managers and the free blacks ; together with a number of other questions arising out of their location amongst us, and their amenability to our laws, Mr. Williams was a willing and invaluable assistant. Indeed, he was soon known and recognized as the Coolies' friend as well as spiritual guide.

Every day now spent in Demerara brought the time of our expected departure so much the nearer. It was, therefore, because trending in this direction, that I felt considerable relief when, on March 11th, our brethren, the Revs. W. Heath and J. Banfield, sailed in the R.M.S. *Derwent, via* Barbadoes for St. Vincent's, to attend the session of the

Annual District Meeting, thereby relieving me from all further official connexion with it.   All the necessary documents I had prepared, and I committed them to the custody of Mr. Heath for presentation to the Chairman of the District.   I had also arranged for paying to the Treasurer of the District all Connexional moneys which, once in every year in our West India districts, are required to be settled.   'John Mason's' book account, and the annual subscription for the London *Watchman,* had to be included, or the Missionary Committee would know 'the reason why'!   I purchased a bill, at par, on the Colonial Bank, in London, for £308 15s. 4d., and committed it to the custody of Mr. Heath to pay over at the District Meeting. This transaction settled all my monetary relations to the St. Vincent and Demerara district, of which I had been a member fifteen years. The sense of conscious relief I experienced seemed as if Godsent.

My interest in Demerara had not yet completely gone.   For instance, at the ordination of the Rev. Mr. Murray in the Scotch Church, 'by the laying on of the hands of the Presbytery,' I could not but feel a deep concern.   This church had suffered much for many years, and now it was hoped that a 'time of reviving ' and re-establishment of the good cause would be witnessed.   On the 15th I attended, by special invitation, the official opening of the 'Orphan Asylum and School of Industry,' when, at least, 400 persons were present. I was much delighted with all that I saw and heard.   On the 25th, we heard of the death of the Rev. Mr. Pritchard, at Calder, St. Vincent's, of yellow fever.   When will this 'Reaper' cease his desolating visitations of our much weakened missionary staff? Lord, when?

'*March 28th.*—This is my last officiating Sabbath in the city of Georgetown. I preached at Kingston and Trinity on Acts xxvi. 22, 23.   At the latter service we had an overflowing congregation, and I was much affected.   My physical strength was unequal to the effort, and my soul was "cast down and disquieted within me."   The thought that this is the last time for me to preach to this dear, loving people quite overwhelmed me.   Four years of preaching, making in all over seven hundred times, and with what result?   I will not afflict my already burdened heart with unprofitable regrets ; but hope for the best.   I have gone "forth weeping bearing precious seed ;" shall I not, when the harvest time comes, appear "rejoicing," with "sheaves" of success?'

The remainder of my tale is soon told.   The missionaries, Messrs. Banfield, Heath, Biggs, and Wrench arrived in Georgetown on the 29th March.   They brought to us comforting news respecting the new appointments for British Guiana. The Rev. John Corlett, a man of impulsive nature and fine disposition, well-cultured and eloquent in the pulpit, was by the District Meeting sent to succeed me in the Georgetown Circuit. His colleagues were Messrs. Biggs and Heath. The Rev. John Wood was appointed to the Berbice Mission, and Rev. R. Wrench to the Mahaica Circuit. The Rev. J. Banfield was continued in the Golden Grove Circuit, and the Rev. W. Heath in the Abram Tuil Circuit. All the circuits were provided for in this manner. On April 1st I prepared a Circuit Balance Sheet, and committed it to the custody of Mr. Biggs for presentation to my successor on his arrival. On this being done, I gratefully say in my Journal :—

'My mind is greatly relieved, and I am now looking forward to next Monday, when we expect to embark for our native land. It was the casting off a heavy burden, which I was unable any longer to carry.'

My reverend brethren assembled at the District Meeting were so good as to place upon their Minutes an expression of their respect and love for me, and of the work in the several circuits in which I had laboured for the term of nearly fifteen years, being five years over the usual term of service for English missionaries. The resolution is as follows :—

'The brethren acknowledge with thankfulness the kind permission of the Committee for the return home of Brother Bickford. He has laboured in this District upwards of fourteen years with great acceptance and usefulness, and his removal will be long and deeply felt by us, and also by our people in the different circuits where he has been stationed. They affectionately commend him and Mrs. Bickford to the kind attention of the Committee, and to the ever-watchful providence of our covenant God.'

'*A Roland for an Oliver.*'—The historian, J. A. Froude, recently took a hasty run through the West Indies, since when he has written a book, in which he says : 'You must not trust the negro with political power ; remember Hayti. . . . A religion, at any rate, which will keep the West Indian blacks from falling back into devil worship is still to seek.' Mr. Froude ought to have known better than thus to have written. He little thought, as he was preparing his scandalous libel on the character of the Queen's coloured subjects in the West Indies, that, at the very time, there was living in Trinidad, an educated black gentleman, a Mr. Thomas, who, like a modern Nemesis, would scourge him for his audacity 'with many stripes.' A book, having the appropriate title of 'Froudacity,' was published, in which the insulted author stingingly says : 'Away with your criminal suggestion of the hideous orgies of heathenism in Hayti, for the benefit of our future morals in the West Indies, when the political supremacy which you predict shall have been an accomplished fact.' But let us see how this question really stands? Why, such has been the steady progress of our West Indian Missions, that in 1884 the English Conference gave them a constitution for managing their own affairs by a general triennial conference, and two colonial annual conferences, subject only to an affiliation with the parent body in England. There are, at least, one hundred and seventy-five thousand persons in our schools and congregations ; and, inclusive of the Moravians and other Christian denominations, there will probably be a million of the black and coloured races under the preaching of the Gospel, and guided by the faithful pastors in all matters of faith and morals. Instead, therefore, of retrogression—'a falling away'—as Mr. Froude basely insinuates, there has been marked advance all along the lines.

THE VOYAGE HOME.

'They that go down to the sea in ships . . . see His wonders in the deep.' The prevailing reason why Mr. Binks and I chose to go home by a sailing ship and not by the royal mail steamer was that it would cost less money ; besides, it would be more direct than by making the islands' route as far west as St. Thomas's, before finally leaving for London. But if we could have foreseen what would be the disagreement on board the *Cleopatra*, we should have gone by steam. Still, we got over the voyage safely ; but roughly, as must be admitted by all the passengers.

The Journal jottings possess even now a freshness of interest for the writer ; and, possibly, as showing what a sea voyage was like thirty-six years ago in one of our West India sugar-carrying vessels, they may have some interest for modern sea-travelling missionaries, in the magnificent steamships of the present time. We can only give briefest extracts :—

'*Cleopatra, April 4th.*—We went on board, and the anchor was raised at 2 p.m. The Revs. Biggs, Williams,* Banfield, and Wood accompanied us.

---

* In the month of August 1853, this devoted missionary, in the fulfilment of his duties to the Coolie immigrants, again visited Berbice. Whilst there he was attacked a second time with the yellow fever. On the news reaching Demerara, Mrs. Williams, accompanied by the Rev. John Corlett, hastened by the overland route to Berbice, just in time to see this eminent man pass away. He died on the 27th. A chastened grief pervaded the whole colony, and all classes of persons bewailed the public loss in his early removal from his beloved work. Governor Barkly, in a touching communication to the Colonial Minister, Earl Grey, bore testimony to the high character and great usefulness of the labours of the deceased missionary.

Mr. J. N. Pieters came alongside in the Customs' boat, once more to thank me for some little kindnesses to himself and family. Our old friends, Mr. George Ross, Mr. Allan Cameron, and Captain Millard remained until we were some six miles beyond the lighthouse. The pilot is a Mr. Adams, a short, black man, well up in his calling, but it is easy to see that his "word of command" is not liked by the white sailors. It is too authoritative and vehement, they say ; and is like nigger driving. We got on a bank and anchored for the night. We got again "under weigh" the next day and reached the lightship at 10 p.m., when the pilot left us, on the 8th ; we made Barbadoes, covering the distance from Demerara in sixty-eight hours. Captain McEachem, fearing that he could not weather the island, bore away N.N.W., and passed between St. Vincent's and Barbadoes to the north. We are now away from the sight of land. The certainty of our severance from our West India friends we now realized with much acuteness and affectionate regrets. Mrs. Bickford and I sat down in mute wonderment at the mercifulness of God's providence in permitting both of us to have lived through our West India term, and to be now on our way back to the fatherland, from which we had gone out so many years before.'

' *April* 10*th*.—This is the first Sabbath on board, but so different from those spent in Trinity Church, Georgetown. Everything is quiet, and the captain, officers, and crew are showing their respect for the Sabbath by putting on their black coats, and otherwise presenting a cleanly appearance. We had Divine service on deck, and in the evening family worship.'

' *April* 13*th*.—By a sudden squall our ship was thrown aback ! By the captain's prompt action we were soon out of danger "of going down by the stern." We made a complete circle in getting right again.'

' *April* 17*th*.—Holy Sabbath. Mr. Binks preached on the "Parable of the wise and foolish virgins." It was a faithful and excellent discourse.'

' *April* 24*th*.—The Holy Sabbath. There had been so much unpleasantness on board, that I preached on the subject of God's love to a lost world, in the hope that the hearts of all present might be softened toward each other. Mr. Binks at the close offered up an affecting and solemn prayer.'

' *May* 2*nd*.—Last night, at eleven o'clock, we had a heavy squall. All hands were called on deck, and the studding sails were got off. Some injury was done to the sails, and one of the bumpkins was wrenched from its place. 4 p.m. : We are carrying only one double-reefed topsail and a foresail. Wind furious, and sea tremendous. Nevertheless, we are making seven and a half knots on the right course.'

' *May* 3*rd*.—12 a.m. : The wind came suddenly from the north-west, and had hurricane force. In the midst of this awful storm we narrowly escaped a dreadful collision. We showed our light at least ten minutes before it was apparently recognised by the passing ship. At the last moment our captain "kept away," and the threatening intruder passed close under our stern. The captains exchanged some words not of the most complimentary kind.'

' *May* 4*th*.—The *Cleopatra* is a spectacle of distress, with nothing hardly but bare poles. We had only one able seaman capable of steering over these tremendous seas, and he kept to the helm until the danger was over. Such an instance of physical endurance I never saw at sea before. I thanked him for his devotion to duty. Our captain, too, behaved admirably all through this trying time. His skill and steady courage were beyond all praise. I should think that for forty-eight hours he was not ten minutes together absent from the deck.'

'*May 6th.*—To-day I am thirty-seven years of age. I seem to have lived long : although I am some years from the period accepted as the meridian of English life, say from forty to fifty. "God be merciful to me," and direct my future steps aright.'

During the remainder of the voyage nothing of special notice occurred. We had, as is usual, fair, foul, strong winds and calms in irregular succession. The distances, kindly furnished to us by the captain, marked the gradual but sure approach of the *Cleopatra* to the end of her voyage :—

'*May 16th.*—We are four hundred and eighty miles from the Lizard.'
'*May 20th.*—We are one hundred and twenty-five miles from the Start.'

My last jotting is—

'"Praise the Lord." We at last see the Eddystone, thirteen miles distant. At 3 p.m. we left the ship, and went on board a Cowes cutter, and in four hours we landed at Plymouth. Once more we were in our beloved native land. "So He bringeth them unto the haven where they would be."'

THE RETROSPECT.

Mr. Wesley, after having been two years and eight months in Georgia, returned to England in 1738. Reviewing his mission, he says, 'I went to America to teach the Georgian Indians the nature of Christianity, and what have I learnt myself?' Mr. Wesley found Georgia to be a severe disciplinary school, but his experiences were turned to good account. 'God showed him,' in that unfriendly land, 'what was in his heart.' In like manner, many of Wesley's sons have learnt in the discipline of the foreign field many lessons tending to develop a fitness for the onerous duties of a mission station, which could never have been gained in the stereotyped routine of English Methodist circuits. Personal observation, extending over many years, suggests the desirability of a certain class of our young men beginning their ministerial life by a 'breaking-in,' in such countries as may climatically and intellectually suit them. Some very sage and earnest men have even suggested, not ill-naturedly, but in view of the greater influence of young ministers, that a 'breaking-down' also could not fail of being of the greatest use. Many of our ablest, noblest and sense-endowed men, now in English Methodism, had their earliest training in India, Africa, the South Seas, the

West Indies, and British Guiana, who, on returning to England at the close of their terms of honourable service, have taken influential circuits and the highest official positions ' the British Conference' can confer upon its most trusty members.

What have I learnt myself ? My answer is :—

(1) I have learnt from incontestable evidence that God, in His providence, gave to English Methodism a vocation to carry the Gospel of the 'common salvation' to the black and coloured populations of the British West Indies ;—the conversion of the Hon. Nathaniel Gilbert, Speaker of the House of Assembly in Antigua, in 1760, under Mr. Wesley's preaching in London ; the advent of Mr. Baxter, a local preacher, into Antigua, in a responsible position in His Majesty's dockyard ; the emigration of an Irish Methodist family for Georgia, but driven by stress of weather to Antigua ; and, at last, on Christmas Day, 1786, Dr. Coke himself, with three missionaries, originally designed for North America, were compelled by wind and storm to make for this elect island. These incidents, in our judgment, are links in a Divine chain of causes and effects, for giving force to the purpose of a merciful God in making known in this part of His vineyard the glorious Gospel of Christ. The further proof is found in the generous willingness of the English Methodists to subscribe the funds for fostering and extending the good works ; also, in the chivalrous spirit shown by a succession of missionaries, of eminent piety and ability, whom God has raised up for carrying on this loving enterprise. ' It is the Lord's doing.'

(2) I learnt to respect and love the black and coloured people in the West Indies. Amongst them I had generous and loving friends. I never had any sympathy with the cruelly absurd and depreciating remarks made by cynical and ungenerous white people, in regard to their mental powers and capacity for appreciating and practising the doctrines and precepts of Christ, as recorded in the New Testament. And the names of very many are still present to my mind as synonyms of all 'that is lovely and of good report.' As leaders of classes, male and female, in my belief, they have never been surpassed for faithfulness and loyalty by any of their co-officials in England or elsewhere. Many of the young men, mostly of the coloured class, have given themselves to the Ministry, and are effectually helping the English missionaries in carrying out the work of the Lord with credit and success.

(3) When the social evolution wrought by the Emancipation Act in 1838 was fully realized, complexional distinctions died out ; and as years succeeded to that blessed event, a clear and broad road was created for all classes to respectable professions, intermarriages, and the acquirement of material comforts, without prejudice or distinction. Absolutely there was no bar to the improvement and happiness of the West Indians, but such as those they might unwittingly throw across their own path.

(4) I learnt that my mission had not been ' a fool's errand.' Every truth of Divine revelation I accepted during my student days, and which I firmly held at the time of my ordination in 1838, I tested in the presence of numerous congregations to whom I sustained the responsible relation of ' pastor and teacher' for about fifteen years. I found that human nature was the same, and that the needs of the human soul were the same, in the sable and white races, without exception or qualification. I proved to a demonstration their equal eligibility to experience a sure process of personal reconciliation with God, and heirship to eternal life. ' There was no difference : ' ' Christ was all and in all.'

(5) I have no regrets at having given the best years of my earlier manhood to this portion of our great mission-field. True, the West Indies had ' the beginning of my strength.' My residence there, as English life goes in the tropics, seems to have been a protracted period ; but I do not begrudge it. The gratitude and the love of our people are an abundant reward.

(6) In the civil elevation and spiritual improvement of what was once the slave population, we have both the pattern and the pledge of what may yet be done for Afric's sons and daughters on their own great continent, as well as for other sable races in different parts of the world. The experiment of a hundred years of evangelising and civilising appliances, in these once benighted islands, for the salvation and elevation of all classes of the people, has been a gratifying success. The slave has sprung up into a freeman of Jesus Christ; the Creole has shown the possession of an innate force of character for which he had gained no credit ; and ' the white man ' has put away his mean and foolish prejudices, and now lives in peace and harmony with those he once oppressed. There has not been witnessed, as yet, the welding together of these varied races into one solid, social mass, as may be hoped and prayed for ; still, all things considered, the conspicuous

advancement of Negroes and Creoles alike to the position of a law-abiding, contented, and religious people is such as should gladden the hearts of all philanthropists and Christian workers in every part of the civilised world. ' He hath visited and redeemed His people : ' ' Blessed be God ! '

ENGLAND, *May* 1853 *to January* 1854.—My health was too feeble for me to do much work during the above period. However, I managed to preach over sixty times in the South of Devon, Cornwall, and in London. I spoke, as I had opportunity, at missionary meetings; but I was unable to place myself at the disposal of the London Committee for deputation work. I was frequently the subject of distressing fever pains, consequent on biliary derangements, which laid me low during their continuance. Mrs. Bickford also was very unwell, and we needed each other's help a good deal. The good Methodist people in Devonshire had to take the ' will for the deed ; ' for active, effective service was for me impossible at that convalescing, transition period.

AUSTRALIA.

1853—1888.

THIRD PART.

BY the English Conference, August 1853, I was appointed as one of the ministers of the Melbourne Circuit, Victoria. It was expected that I should be in my new circuit in the early part of 1854, so that Mrs. Bickford and I would have only about eight months for ' pulling up' our health and for visiting our kindred and friends. We took in regular order Kingsbridge, Salcombe, Modbury, Ivybridge, Ashburton, Plymouth, and Camelford, where we had brothers and sisters or acquaintances. At each of these places, I either preached on the Sabbath, or church anniversaries, or missionary meetings. I attended the Annual Conference at Bradford, and had the great pleasure of being the welcome guest of the Misses Pickles and Townend at Great Horton. I and three other West Indian missionaries, Messrs. Bannister, Hudson, and Binks, spent many a happy hour at the Marsdens, in their beautiful home. The Rev. John Lomas was elected President, and the Rev. William Barton, Secretary. The platform was filled with venerable men, whom for many years I had longed to see. I may mention Doctors Bunting, Newton, Beecham, Dixon, the brothers Thomas and Samuel Jackson, the Revs. George Marsden, George Osborn, and William Arthur. Dr. Beaumont was on the floor of the ' house,' and so was Joseph Fowler, a keen and fearless debater. Everything I saw and heard greatly interested me. The preaching at the Conference was of a high order. The first sermon was from Dr. Hannah, on " Jesus Christ, the true Foundation ; " the second was from Dr. Jobson, on " Sowing and Reaping ;" and the third was Thomas McCullagh, then a young preacher, on the " Power of the Holy Ghost." Dr. Jobson's sermon was the most telling attack upon the conscience of the sinner I ever listened to. Such specimens of earnest and soul-saving preaching made me feel very small; nevertheless, I glorified God in them.

1854.

The months passed rapidly away.

Jan. 12*th.*—Mrs. Bickford and I left Kingsbridge for London. We joined the train at the 'Kingsbridge Road Station,' and sped our way to England's metropolis. A little after the start, I said to Mrs. Bickford, 'Give me the Bible from your bag, and I will read the chapters for the day. Perhaps some words of comfort may come to us.' The first of the three chapters to read, according to our custom, was Genesis xii., in which these words occur: 'Get thee out of thy country, and from thy kindred, and from thy father's house, unto a land that I will show thee; . . . and thou shalt be a blessing.' Our hearts were very soft, and no wonder; for the second farewell to our kindred was worse than the first. But the comfort came!

Jan. 17*th.*—The valedictory service for our party was held in City Road Chapel. The Rev. Dr. Hoole conducted the devotional part, and the Rev. Charles Prest gave the address. I remember how he strove to impress upon us the necessity of close application to our great work, and to keep clear of the political questions which would agitate, more or less, the Australian communities. Good advice, no doubt, I thought, but not always to be followed. The great matter in settling new countries is for wise and good men to prevent the transmission to them of the abominable feeling of *caste*, class legislation, unjust laws, and other meaningless disabilities; to say nothing of the poverty, intemperance, and impurity, which for so many centuries have cursed England and embittered the lives and homes of tens of thousands of her sons and daughters. I inwardly felt sure that, if God permitted me to land in Australia, it would be with me 'an obligation of Providence' to do whatever in me lay, to secure for the Antipodean communities full religious liberty and equality, just laws, fair taxation, and the unchallenged right of every family-man to a reasonable share in the public estate. Justice, freedom, progress, and everything else that is true, were bound to have my uncompromising advocacy and support. This might be done quite consistently with the conscientious discharge of the higher obligations which my 'ordination' devolved upon me.

I append a few jottings from my Journal :—

'*Jan.* 22*nd.*—I heard Bishop Blomfield preach this morning, and Dr. Cumming in the evening—both great men on their own lines ; but I liked the Bishop better than the Doctor. The first sermon had the great merit of scholarly plainness, was orthodox, and practical ; the second was pedantic, very theoretical and unspiritual.'

'*Jan.* 29*th.*—This morning I heard the Rev. H. L. Church, at St. George's-in-the-East, preach an excellent sermon from the story of Caleb. Mr. James Nibbs Brown, from Grenada, was present also. After the service we walked in company, and conversed mostly on West Indian affairs. It was a very great pleasure for me once more to see my friend and co-worker in our Lord's vineyard after so many years of separation. In the evening, I heard the Rev. John Farrar, in Jewin Street, with much satisfaction. Clear in intellect, and full of spiritual power, he could not fail to hold his audience as if under a bewitching spell.'

As showing the reckless manner in which large ships, *quasi-*'emigrant,' were despatched from England to Australia, say, thirty-five years ago, I record the following facts :—

Jan. 30*th.*—This morning Mrs. Bickford and I journeyed to Gravesend, to join the *American Lass*, commanded by Captain James McKellar, of Glasgow. As soon as our friends had left us, the chief steward called me aside and informed me that the ship was not properly provisioned for the number of passengers who were on board. Our party alone was eight first-class ; and there were many other passengers, both first and second. The steward further stated that he had made known to me how things were so as to avoid trouble during the voyage. I was much perplexed, and laid the whole matter before the captain. In the evening I sent Mr. Vanderkiste, one of the young ministers, to London in charge of a letter to Dr. Hoole, setting forth the predicament we were in, and that we were resolved not to go to sea until we were satisfied that the stores were sufficient for all the passengers for so long a voyage.

Jan. 31*st.*—This morning Mr. Vanderkiste returned from London with a letter from Dr. Hoole, authorizing me to purchase such supplementary stores as might be necessary, and to charge the cost to the mission house. I went on shore accordingly, with the captain, and bought 4 cwt. of fresh beef, 10 cwt. of potatoes, 2 barrels of flour, 1 cwt. of ling fish, 500 eggs, and some other articles of food. The captain made some purchases also. In the meantime the Emigration Agent had gone on board, and found fault as follows :—

(1) The ship had been cleared as carrying one class of passengers

only, whilst there were two classes; (2) the provision was for sixteen weeks, whereas the law was that it should be for twenty weeks; (3) the number of passengers had been reported less than they actually were, and the stores were laid in for the lesser number; (4) the agent complained that the London agent had deceived the second-class passengers, by telling them that there was to be no difference between them and the other (first) passengers; (5) he took exception also to the dietary scale, and finally refused to allow the ship to proceed to sea.

The captain had to proceed to London to see the agent, and to procure additional supplies for the second-class passengers. A clerk was sent from the office to further look into the matter. He took the names of the second-class passengers, and paid each one shilling per day for the time they had been detained in London. The ship had to be re-cleared. The Emigration Agent informed the clerk that his principals had laid themselves open to heavy penalties for making false entries, and for obtaining a clearance under false pretences. It seemed an unaccountable thing to me that a respectable London firm could have been guilty of such conduct as this narrative of facts discloses.

Feb. 3rd.—We were taken in charge by a tug, and on the 5th we reached the Downs. We were now away from any further disputings between the charterer of the ship and the Emigration and Custom-house officers. We were thankful for this deliverance. We were detained by foul winds until the 9th, when, at 3 p.m., we finally got away with a fair wind.

The incidents of this our first voyage to Australia will best be learnt from my Journal :—

' *Feb.* 10*th.*—At 5 p.m., we were off the Start, and at 9 p.m. we were abreast of the ' Eddystone.' In passing, we saw Bolt Head and Salcombe Harbour. Mrs. Bickford and I thought much of our ' kith and kin ' as we ran rapidly through these waters. It was but nine months ago, on our return from Demerara, we first saw the Bolt Head, and now, in obedience to a Providential call, we are passing away from it to unknown scenes in far distant Australia.'

Selfishness and cowardice are closely allied in some men. A striking proof is found in our ship-life this evening. We were informed that the London broker (*alias* agent) had confided to the captain secret instructions to be observed in dieting our party. The nature of these will appear from the terms of the letter we immediately addressed to the captain :—

' SHIP, " AMERICAN LASS,"
' *February 10th*, 1854.

' CAPTAIN JAMES MCKELLAR,—

' SIR,—We the undersigned first-class passengers bound for Sydney, having learnt that Mr. Alexander Milne, the broker in London, has sent for your observance a dietary scale for us, do hereby respectfully protest very strongly against our food being supplied to us by weight and measurement. We are compelled to add that, should you determine, notwithstanding our protest, to subject us to such an indignity, we shall, on our arrival in port, hold you responsible for any ill consequences which may thereby have resulted to our health during the voyage.

' (*Signed*) JAMES BICKFORD, R. W. VANDERKISTE,
LONSDALE ABELL, HANS MACK,
JOHN GALE, THOMAS ANGWIN,
WILLIAM KELYNACK, WILLIAM
CURNOW, FANNY BICKFORD.'

The cowardliness of the intended action is seen at once. For if we had been made acquainted with the existence of a sealed instruction, to be acted upon when we were out at sea, before we left Gravesend we could have left the ship or have insisted upon its cancellation ; but when it was sprung upon us we were in a sense helpless ; still, knowing what was right and honourable, we addressed the captain as above, and threw all responsibility upon him. The captain felt his position, and we heard nothing more about the matter.

We had now before us a long voyage through, to us, untravelled oceans. All our surroundings had become dire realities. We committed our 'way in the sea' to the care of God. We did not forget the earnest prayers which had been offered up for us by our reverend fathers at the London mission house. These prayers ever accompanied us as an inspiration against the fear of destruction and death. My Journal up to this time tells of fair winds, freedom from gales, undisturbed worship, and good health.

' *Feb. 16th*.—The captain remarked at the table to-day that he had crossed the Atlantic (west or south) forty-seven times, and he had never had so fine a run as at this time. From the time of our rounding the South Foreland, we had not had to 'bout ship, or reef a sail. He even said he believed the God of missions was with us and giving us His favour.'

' *Feb. 18th*.—We have run 208 miles since yesterday. The supply of potatoes was finished seven days ago ; and the vegetables the captain put on board at his own expense were finished to-day. As far as the charterer of the ship was concerned, his provisioning was shamefully cruel, and yet we are informed that his profit from the voyage will be over one thousand pounds.'

'*March 8th.*—South latitude 0° 44', west longitude 28° 17'. This is the holy Sabbath. I preached on the main deck, and afterwards in the saloon I baptized Mr. and Mrs. Pass's two infant children. Several of the sailors came to witness the administration of the ordinance. I also gave the Lord's Supper to the mission party and to some of the passengers.'

'*March 10th.*—The thermometer to-day was 87° in the shade. The awning was not spread for us, although we asked that it might be. We went from one part of the ship to another seeking shelter from the sun's rays. On the 11th we secured this favour, and the relief afforded was very great, but especially to the sailors who worked under its shade. Still, the condition of the exposed men was the cause for the spreading of the awning, and not the inconveniences of the passengers in the least degree.'

'*March 13th.*—Several of our party are ill, and it is no wonder. Our potted meats and fruits are unfit for use. Yesterday, when a pot of the former was opened, the stench was so dreadful that the passengers ran for shelter to their cabins or to the main deck. Several bottles of fruit had to be thrown overboard. Not a third of our voyage is yet done, and this is the state of our stores.'

'*March 15th.*—The thermometer in the saloon to-day stood at 102°. We could hardly breathe.'

'*March 16th.*—The atmosphere has undergone a complete change. The rain has fallen heavily ; the wind has come from every point of the compass, and the sea is as if it had been boiling in a caldron. These phenomena indicate the failure of the south-east trade-winds, and suggest that the 'variables' are solely caused by atmospheric influences. Every appearance above, around, and below is confused and wild. 5 p.m.: For the first time since we left the Downs, on the 9th February, we have tacked ship and reefed topsails. It is blowing very hard and foul, compelling a south-south-east course.'

'*March 19th.*—The stormy weather continues. We had a gale of wind this morning, and the fore-topsail was split from top to bottom. We are now running under double-reefed topsails, forecourse, jib and spanker. Nearly all the passengers are ill.'

'*March 20th.*—Close-hauled and a gale of wind.'

'*March 23rd.*—(Dead reckoning) South latitude, 32° 18', west longitude 23° 50'. Wind changed in the forenoon from east-south-east to south-west. This is a dangerous part of the ocean from "wind-checks," and our captain is anxiously watching so as to be prepared for them should they come. The sea has an imposing appearance this morning, reminding us of certain passages in Job: "He maketh the deep to boil like a pot ; He maketh the sea like a pot of ointment. He maketh a path to shine after Him : one would think the deep to be hoary." A stream of fire seemed to follow the wake of the ship whilst tearing through these terrible seas.'

'*March 28th.*—Saw the Magellan clouds and the Southern cross. Both brilliant and beautiful. Who could look for the first time upon these and remain an infidel or atheist ? Dark indeed must be the mind, and corrupt must be the heart, of the man that failed to recognise in such magnificent constellations the wisdom and the goodness of the great Creator of "all things."'

'*March 31st.*—Obscured sun. Wind again foul. We are off our course, and are compelled to run at the rate of seven or eight knots an hour. This is now the fiftieth day from the Downs, and we want nearly two thousand miles of being half over the voyage. "O Thou, who art Lord of the winds and seas, mercifully interpose for us."'

'*April 1st.*—The wind still foul. This is now the sixty-fourth day since most of the passengers joined the ship in St. Catherine's Dock, and, naturally enough, fears are being awakened in some minds that both provisions and water cannot last to the end of the voyage. The second-class passengers are to-day put on short allowance. Mr. Vanderkiste is very poorly.'

'*April 2nd.*—Tristan d'Acunha is in sight this morning, bearing west by south. It is 8,000 feet high, and is pyramidal in form. It is cheering to see even a solitary rock amidst these trackless deeps. But how came it there? and wherefore? Is it a primitive creation? or is it the work of ages upon ages? evolution, or something of that kind?'

'*April 3rd.*—Still foul wind. We divided into two companies, and "gave ourselves to prayer."'

'*April 7th.*—The captain intimated this evening that, as the voyage would be unusually long, we having been out seventy-five days already, it would be necessary to reduce the water for each to half-a-gallon *per diem.* so as to provide in time for any emergency which might arise. I at once intimated our willingness to leave the matter implicitly in the captain's hands.'

'*April 8th.*—A day of thanksgiving and joy. We have now a fair and strong wind. Speed nine knots.'

'*April 9th.*—"Rejoice with trembling." A small bolt having worked out of its place, the foretop-gallant mast and yard broke, and left the fore-rigging a perfect wreck. What a change in a few hours! Most of the sails had to be taken off with a view to repairing damages. This has been the Sabbath Day. Messrs. Angwin and Gale preached, but it has been almost a lost Sabbath to me. Oh, for the Sabbaths on shore! I hope I shall love and prize them more if permitted again to have their hallowed hours and hallowing worship.'

'*April 10th.*—Sun obscured, consequently no sights could be taken. The captain and carpenter are engaged in making a new mast, and the "watch" in making preparations for rigging it. What a change in twenty-four hours!'

'*April 11th.*—The new foretop-gallant mast was put up this afternoon, and the yard is being spliced. The wind is from the north-west, and is tolerably fresh.'

'*April 13th.*—The Albatrosses have been flying about our ship to-day, with much apparent confidence in our kindly feeling towards them. Two or three were unusually large, and, under their wings and over and around their bodies, as white as alabaster. The upper parts of their wings were of a dark grey colour, and from "tip to tip" were from ten to twelve feet. The sea has been rolling heavily. We have had scarcely twelve hours of carrying wind since we passed the equator.'

'*April 14th.*—The ship is under double reefed topsails, and close hauled to the wind. The gale has been furious; but as we are passed the meridian of the Cape we may expect to have steadier winds. In the night, the passengers, who were about, cheerfully assisted in taking off the canvas so as to ease the ship. The ladies were much alarmed, and not without reason. In the afternoon we saw, "sporting in the deep," five whales, taking their pleasure as if they were the monarchs of the sea. How strange it is that these ocean monsters should so often fall a prey to other sea-animals inferior to them in strength and size. One of their enemies is a small shell-fish, which insinuates itself beneath their fins, where, in security, it feeds on the thick layers of fat. But the most terrible foe of the whale is the sword-fish, at whose approach, in dread of the battle that must ensue, it exhibits an extraordinary degree of agitation, and seeks to retreat in the opposite direction. Having no instrument of defence but the tail, this inoffensive monster is ill-adapted for conflict with the sharp tooth-edged beak of the rapacious sword-fish, which, darting first on one side and then on the other, lacerates and mangles its huge frame with impunity. These whales were from ninety to one hundred and twenty feet in length. We also saw to-day an enormous shark, whose fearful equipment of teeth renders its possessor an enemy to be much dreaded. These teeth are arranged in six rows, in a wedge-like figure, and are one hundred and forty-four in number. Sailors have a mortal dread of the shark.'

'*April 14th.*—South latitude, 41° 55', west longitude, 21° 43'. 8 p.m.: This is Easter Sunday, the comforting memento of our Lord's resurrection from the dead. Messrs. Abell and Angwin conducted the services. 11 p.m. :· Before I had any personal experience of sea-voyaging, I thought the life of a sailor was one of comparative ease, but I have since observed it to be a life of laborious toil and of undefinable hardships. The people who live in comfort on shore little think of the risk to life and health undergone by mariners, to procure for them the productions of foreign countries. With too many *upstarts* of men, the sailor is little better than a "dog;" but I have found him to be brave, kind, and generous.'

'*April 18th.*—Wind strong, cold and fair. We are now running up our "Easting" with some rapidity. Our longitudinal degrees are now about forty-three or forty-four, so that we have a prospect of doing from five to six daily. A few years ago the mariner, who would go so far south, as we now are, and expect yet to be, would be regarded as mad, but scientific knowledge of the most satisfactory kind, has constrained the adoption of this track as not only the easiest but the shortest by several hundreds of miles. The principle is that known as the "Great Circle;" and to those who have studied the rotundity of our globe it will be easily understood. In fact, it is simply "going round the hill instead of going over it." The *Marco Polo* ran the distance, on the Great Circle course, from the Cape of Good Hope to Melbourne in twenty-seven days.'

'*April 19th.*—The captain is now getting good observations. The last of our sheep was killed to-day : she would eat no food ; suitable fodder having been all used some time ago. The fowls, pigs, and sheep have had to be fed upon soaked biscuits. So much for the generosity of the London broker. His covetousness has even afflicted the poor brutes we had on board. To be starved or eaten was the alternative. The sugar, too, for more than a fortnight we have had for our tea was the commonest, undrained muscovado, which shows how grievously our Missionary Committee have been taken in. I begged of the steward for Mrs. Bickford a little of the sugar sent to the forecastle, and now she is able again to take her tea. The captain told us this evening that he would not send to his men the sugar put upon our table for £50. If he were to do so, he said, in the first place they would throw it overboard ;

and in the second, on arrival in Sydney, they would every one desert the ship.

'Mr. Curnow preached this evening an able sermon from Psalm cxix. 160. I am struck with the apparent inability of the young brethren to adopt a ready, simple, and elementary style of preaching, as that which is only appropriate on board ship.'

'*April* 20*th.*—South latitude 45° 12', east longitude 38° 40'. Wind fair and cold. An immense quantity of birds have followed the vessel to-day. This may be proof that we are not far from "Cavern" and "Prince Edward's Islands." A sight of them would gladden our eyes and hearts.'

'*April* 22*nd.*—Wind strong and cold. Run 244 miles since yesterday. We have been much perplexed that *Noray* and the Admiralty chart differ in more than three degrees, *re* the longitude of Crozer's or Desert Island. It would be well for the English Government to send out a surveying party to ascertain the exact position of this island, that mariners might know where danger is and how to avoid it.'

'*April* 23*rd.*—To-day for the first time we have seen the Cape pigeons. They are about the size of the English pigeon, have webbed feet, and have four large spots of white on their wings. They appear to have no fear of us; but fly all around the ship, and even over the quarter-deck, doubtless in search of food. Here, far away from the haunts of civilised men, the very birds seem to live in primeval harmony; but, would it be not so with them if perchance they lived in those portions of the globe "where men each other tear!"'

'*April* 25*th.*—We have escaped a frightful accident to-day. Through the rolling of the ship a large jar of vitriol broke away from its lashing, and a portion of the main deck was covered with a wave of liquid fire. The two remaining pigs were severely burnt, and one of them, maddened with pain, whilst we were at dinner, rushed into the saloon and from thence into our state-room. It was at first intended to kill the animal right away, but by throwing a quantity of salt water over it, the pain decreased. How dangerous it is to carry large jars of this fiery liquid on board a ship which, at the same time, was carrying such a quantity of gunpowder in her hold! Mr. Allardice, the chief mate, got his hands and boots burnt in trying to arrest the surging vitriol on the ship's deck. There seems to be no end to our troubles. For example, the water we have for drinking to-day is very bad. It has the smell of rotten turnips; but we have no alternative, for it is that or none. There is a large supply of excellent water in the tank, but the captain has forbidden any more of it to be used for the present. His idea is to reserve it as a supply in stormy weather, when access to the puncheons could not be had. The precaution seems to be reasonable, but the privation is hard.'

'*April* 26*th.*—To-day, at the dinner table, Captain McKellar remarked on the water as being much affected by the climate, to which Mrs. Bickford replied "that it was very bad, and that it was impossible to drink it." Dr. James then suggested that a small quantity might be taken from the tank for our use at dinner, which called forth a rejoinder from the captain to the effect "that he would not receive any suggestion on the matter." Messrs. Angwin and Mack reiterated the request for a small portion daily, solely for drinking purposes. But the captain firmly refused, saying, that if a gale should overtake us, and carry our casks away, we should have the cistern to fall back upon. In this style the conversation proceeded, and when I was afraid of high words ensuing, I suddenly rose and returned thanks. Catching the captain's eye, I retired from the table. I heard, but somewhat indistinctly, sharp words between the captain and the doctor, but what they were I only know by report. In the evening of the same day, Mrs. Bickford came to me with the information that the water had become quite good. Whereupon I went to the steward for an explanation. He told me that another cask had been opened. It was now as good as could be desired ; and had it therefore been given to us all the unpleasantnesses of to-day would have been prevented. However, we need to exercise the utmost precaution in the article of water, because of the great distance we have yet to go. Possibly some circumstances may yet arise which may show us after all that the captain was prudently right.'

' *April* 28*th.*—Dead calm at 3 a.m. The sails were in danger of being injured by flapping heavily against the masts and yards. At 8 a.m., the wind sprang up, but was dead ahead. 10 p.m. : Our ship is now going her course, and the rain is falling in torrents. We have a dreary night before us.'

' *April* 29*th.*—This evening heavy rain. Ship under double reefed topsails, and two points off our course. At 12 a.m. to-day we were about a degree east of St. Paul's.'

' *April* 30*th.*—Terrible gale all last night, and portion of the bulwarks were carried away. We lost also a pipe of water. No service this morning beyond singing a hymn, reading Psalm cvii., and prayer. It has been a day of anxiety and alarm. The fore and main topsails are double reefed, and the forecourse is held down with chains. This is all the sail we can get at present. The cross-seas come tumbling in upon us, and threaten to break our ship in pieces. Several big jars of oil of vitriol had to be thrown overboard ; the captain most wisely removing the danger by casting the whole lot into the sea. The ladies and other passengers were much alarmed at seeing the liquid fire, for a second time, running from side to side of the ship's deck, and no one daring to go near it.'

' *May* 1*st.*—Blowing almost a hurricane. The same canvas on as yesterday. At 10 p.m. it was almost a calm, when the ship rolled heavily in the troughs of the sea. South latitude 46° 33'.'

' *May* 2*nd.*—In the middle watch there was a terrific squall. This morning we shipped a sea over the stern, and through one of the stern windows. All the cabins as well as the saloon were deluged. The " dead-lights " were put in for the first time.'

' *May* 3*rd.*—This afternoon we had a heavy gale and showers of hail. The ship has been under the canvas called ' long-reaching,' *i.e.* close-reefed maintop-sail and forecourse. The ladies are much dejected, and wearied out with anxieties and the ship's motion.'

'*May* 5*th.*—The gale came on again this morning from the north-west, and the sea has been very high. The captain told me to-day that during the forty-five years he has been to sea he had not had such bad weather as during the past week. The question is as to whether we should have come so far south as we have done. Probably 43° or 44° south latitude would have been better for us than 46°.'

' *May* 6*th.*—My natal day. I am now thirty-eight years of age. The past year has been crowned with lovingkindness and mercy. We have visited our native land ; have seen those of our kindred yet living ; and now we are braving tempestuous seas for another sphere of Christian enterprise. May the merciful God be with us in Australia, even as He was with us in the West Indies ! We shall require much grace ; but it will be given "in the time of need." '

' *May 8th.*—We have had a gale all the'day, and heavy rain. 10 p.m. : This evening we had the most terrific gale I ever saw. Nothing could be done during its fury but to commit the safety of the ship to the care of the Most High. The Ice point of the foreyard dipped three times in the sea, so fearfully did the vessel careen over. The " whisker " on the lee-bow was carried away. We are now sailing under close-reefed fore maintopsails and the foresail. Not a rope has given way or sail split, notwithstanding the tremendous gale we have encountered. If the *American Lass* had not been of immense strength, she never could have weathered the storms she has encountered in the Southern Ocean. I deeply sympathise with Captain McKellar in the harassing cares and exposures he has to wade through.'

' *May 10th.*—Very fine day, with the wind from the north-west, which s too "sharp up " for us for making much progress. 10 p.m. : The wind now threatens to increase to a heavy gale : the topsails are again double reefed, and other sails have been taken off. How strange it is that, in the *Australian Directory*, it is said, that in these latitudes the gales are from the south-west to the south-east, whereas ever since we left the meridian of the Cape of Good Hope, all the gales we have had came from the north to north-west. There appears to be no uniform law for the winds and the waves ; concussion disturbs the atmospheric phenomena above us, and these terrific outbursts occur to restore the equilibrium which has been disturbed. I would have expected here, in the Australian Bight, that the land to the north of us, being two thousand miles in breadth, would so rarify and moderate the wind as to make it of less density than the ocean wind, and as a consequence retire from the latter ; but it is not so. Instead of prevailing south-westerly winds, we have had them from the north.

' Mr. Kelynack preached this evening on the words, " Not by might, nor by power, but by My Spirit, saith the Lord." An eloquent and highly-pitched discourse ; but totally inappropriate to our little congregation.'

' *May 13th.*—South latitude 40° 00', east longitude 132° 01'. Last night the top-gallant sails had to be taken in, and the topsails single reefed. The rain fell heavily. But this morning, as the weather cleared, the long-expected south-west wind came ; since when we have been making good progress. Another week is gone, but how little I have done for the improvement of my mind, or for the growth of holiness in my soul. Many Christians, who have never been to sea, think that seclusion from the world for so long a time would be followed by much mental and spiritual advancement; but it is not so with me. We are nearly sixty souls on board, and we are in such close contiguity to each other, that the usual privacy and application enjoyed on shore are unattainable here. Hence, retrogression, rather than advancement, is more generally the consequence of a long sea voyage than the contrary.'

' *May 14th.*—We are now about two hundred and forty miles from Cape Otway. Messrs. Mack and Gale preached to-day. We then had the Lord's Supper together, which would be the last time on board the *American Lass*.'

' *May 15th.*—We had a delightful time at our weekly class to-day. The brethren appeared to be in a good state of mind.'

' *May 16th.*—South latitude, 39° 20', east longitude 144° 00'. A day of great mercy and goodness. At 2 p.m. we saw Cape Otway bearing north of us. The captain altered the ship's course to east, direct for Curtis' Island. "Bless the Lord, O my soul, and all that is within me, bless His holy Name."'

'*May* 17*th.*—This day at 9 a.m. we sighted Curtis' Island. At 2 p.m. we passed Kent Group. These islands are of peculiar appearance, and look as if destitute of all verdure.'

'*May* 18*th.*—This morning we made the land on the Australian coast. The wind became very light, and we remained in sight of Cape Howe all the day. As night came on, the wind became northerly, and drove us out to sea.'

'*May* 19*th.*—At 10 a.m. we tacked ship, and made the land a little to the south of Cape Dromedary. The wind is dead ahead. We saw a colonial steamer running for Cape Howe. We are about one hundred and sixty-five miles from Sydney.'

'*May* 20*th.*—We are now one hundred and forty-six miles from Port Jackson Heads. Wind still from the north.

'Twelve months to-day we landed in Plymouth from Demerara. I view the country to which we are going with deep emotion. There is no romance in this undertaking. It will be hard and stubborn fact, and will impose upon me duties of a serious and affecting nature.'

'*May* 23*rd*, SYDNEY.—By the good providence of God, we came into this harbour to-day. We had a trying time of it up from Cape Howe, except for the last ninety miles, which we ran with a leading wind. We were one hundred and three days from the Downs to Port Jackson.

'It was some time after we passed through the Heads before the pilot came on board and took charge. We had to beat up to the anchorage, and for six hours each man of our party, except poor Mr. Vanderkiste, who was still ill, nobly helped the captain to work the after-sails of the ship, and it was the hardest work I ever did. I almost feared my arms would be pulled away from their sockets. At last, the welcome words were shouted out by the pilot, " Let go the anchor ! " and out ran the chain with a rush and rapidity that made the old *Lass* shake from stem to stern. But the voyage was over, and we were anchored in the waters of one of the most beautiful harbours in the world.

'In the afternoon, I went on shore to report our arrival. I soon found my way to the Prince's Street Parsonage, and called upon the Rev. Stephen Rabone, the second minister of the York Street Circuit. He courteously received me, and promised to see the Rev. W. B. Boyce, the General Superintendent of our Missions in Australasia, and inform him that Mrs. Bickford and I, with seven young ministers, had just come from London. I then returned to our ship.'

'*May* 24*th.*—The Rev. S. Rabone and other brethren came on board to take us to friends' houses on shore. Mrs. Bickford and I were kindly welcomed by Mr. and Mrs. John Caldwell, in Pitt Street, with whom we remained until we sailed for Melbourne, Victoria.'

Mr. Boyce came in due course to Mr. Rabone's, where we assembled to meet him. The Rev. T. N. Hull was also there. At the request of Mr. Boyce, he addressed us in terms of encouragement and thankfulness. Mr. Boyce followed in one of his characteristic addresses. It was full of practical wisdom, and delivered in a brusque, conventional style. To me he was pleased to say, 'that he did not expect to see me in such good health. He had supposed that I was a fever-stricken, worn-out West Indian missionary, whom the Committee had sent to Australia to save their funds.' If he had known, he said, that I was so physically capable for the Australian Circuits, he certainly would have kept me in New South Wales. He had thought that, possibly, I might have been a confirmed invalid, and would be wanting to be carried about in a sedan chair, and much more of the same kind. I heard it all, and, without moving an expression of my face, simply told him that the English Conference had appointed me to the Melbourne Circuit, in Victoria, and that I intended going thither by the first opportunity. And so the conversation ended.

But there was nothing unkind in all this. It was his manner, and Messrs. Chapman, Hull, and Rabone enjoyed it vastly. But I think, nevertheless, that there is 'a more excellent way,' in certain conditions, which might be followed. One of our party, I know, was much surprised at the character of the interview. It was so evidently different from what he had expected. He had likely imagined the General Superintendent, who was a veritable and venerable *episcopus*, at least, among his own people, to be the symbol of a dignified ecclesiasticism, with garb and speech in full keeping with it; but, herein, he was much mistaken. Mr. Boyce was too erudite in scholarship; too greatly endowed with good common sense; too sure of his scriptural position as a leader and teacher in his own Church; and too much in sympathy with the free, democratic kind of all society in New South Wales, to put on any foolish airs, or to assume any superiority even over the weakest of his brethren. He was a great man in his very humbleness, and a wise man in his condescending affability towards all classes of religionists among whom he moved. At the bottom, he was one of the truest, best men I have ever known.

The Australian Connexion had to purchase its independence, by becoming responsible to the English Conference for the support and extension of its prosperous missions in the South Seas. This was a somewhat perilous compact on our part, and involved generous giving, if not sacrifices, from our people. The arrival in Sydney of so large a number of ministers as our party represented had therefore to be turned to some account. The Rev. Thomas Adams, a brother of the famous astronomer of that name, and both hailing from Cornwall, had just come up from the Friendly Islands, full of information, love, and zeal. Mr. Adams and I were despatched to the Hunter River District, to preach sermons and hold meetings in aid of the good cause. During this visit Mrs. Bickford and I were the welcome guests of Mr. and Mrs. Little of Maitland, whose hospitality was in keeping with that for which Austral-Irish Methodist families have been always distinguished.

We traversed the whole of the Hunter River District, and did our utmost to strike such a keynote as should vibrate in every Circuit in the colony. The result was £400, or a few pounds more. The people gave with a princely munificence, especially at a small place 'Bulwarra.' The Rev. F. Tuckfield, the resident minister at Maitland, helped us with a true heroic courage, and chaperoned us throughout his extensive circuit.

On our return to Sydney, for a few weeks before leaving for Melbourne, I preached at York Street, Prince's Street, Surrey Hills, Chippendale, and Wooloomooloo, and was much cheered by the evident appreciation of the intelligent congregations to whom I ministered. A second and last Sabbath was given to York Street, when sermons were preached by the Rev. T. N. Hull and myself in aid of our South Sea Missions. The annual meeting of the York Street branch was held on the Monday evening, when the Hon. G. Allen, M.L.C., an old and true friend of Methodist missions, and lay-treasurer of the society, occupied the chair. The Rev. W. B. Boyce read the report. Mr. Hull and I were the only speakers. The interest was kept up to the end, and the financial response was very good. With this meeting ended, at that time, my public appearances in our churches in the Mother City of Australia. I was anxious to be in my Circuit in Victoria; for, although my time had been well occupied in New South Wales, I felt I was a minister without a charge—a shepherd without a flock. With me the pastoral office was in abeyance! I availed myself, therefore, of the first steamer for Melbourne, and had not long to wait. Although thirty years have elapsed since these occurrences took place, yet I cannot forget the great kindness of the Rev. S. Rabone and Mrs. Rabone, Mr. and Mrs. Caldwell, to us during this our first sojourn upon Australian soil.

MELBOURNE, VICTORIA.

It was on *July 8th* that we, early in the morning, passed through Port Philip Heads, and made our way up the Bay for Cole's Wharf. We overhauled an emigrant ship, and took from her as many passengers as crowded our deck in every part. This was far from being agreeable, but we had to submit. On reaching the world-wide reputed Cole's Wharf, how was I disappointed to find that it was only a bank of hardened mud, shaped by the ebb and flow of the Yarra Yarra, and flattened on its surface by the tread of many thousands of immigrants.

We had all our material belongings with us, and all in a heap, with that of scores of others, in the fore part of the steamer's deck. The stern order was soon given: 'All passengers on shore and their luggage.' And then the helter-skelter began. I never before saw such a confusion; and I certainly feared, not without very good reason, that some few of my twenty-eight packages would get into wrong hands. So I requested Mrs. Bickford to stand by, and see that our luggage was handed on to the wharf, and I would keep watch over it when once there. Luckily the largest and heaviest of my boxes came first on shore, on which I had had my name painted by a coloured youth before I left Demerara. This name I saw was immediately recognised. A young farmer-looking man was not only interested, but seemed made fast to the spot. Here is a chance of some help, thought I. So looking straight into his fine, open face, I said, 'Is there anything in that name that possesses any interest for you?' 'Oh, yes,' he replied, 'I know it well, and yesterday I saw your brother Nicholas, who is expecting you.' 'Where did you come from?' I enquired. His reply astonished me: 'From Wakeham, about four miles from Modbury.' 'Then your father and mine rented under the same landlord, Archdeacon Froude; is it not so?' An affirmative reply made us friends at once. 'Take care of these packages for me, will you? whilst I go on board to look after Mrs. Bickford (who was standing amid a Babel of talk), and bring her ashore.' This was quite a providential help for us, for without it we may have fared badly.

My young Devonian friend, at my request, called a 'trolly' (Eng., wain) to take us and our belongings to the Wesleyan Parsonage in Collins Street, where resided the Rev. John Egglestone. The trolly

BOTANY BAY.

being loaded, the next thing to do was for Mrs. Bickford and I to mount to the top of the luggage, and hold on for very life, lest we should topple over into the 'slush,' some twelve inches thick at the very least, which then covered Flinders Street.

I told the driver where we had to go; but, instead of going up Elizabeth Street, he chose to go up Flinders Street, then up Russell Street, and then turned down Great Collins Street. Just opposite to what has been for a number of years the *Melbourne Thunderer*, *i.e.* the *Argus* office, we were bogged, and came to a stand. We had to dismount and make enquiry, so unfortunate had we been. Messrs. Allison & Carter, drapers, whom we had intimately known in Barbadoes and Demerara, had their shop close by. I went into the shop, and my appearance was a great surprise to them. They gave the driver the necessary directions, and once more we made a start for the Collins Street Parsonage. Arriving here, I met for the first time the Rev. William Butters, the Chairman of the Victorian District. At first sight I was drawn to him, and I placed myself at once under his fatherly and official guidance. The next thing to do was to get Mrs. Bickford down from the trolly, in which Mr. Butters assisted. Of course we were introduced to the Egglestones, who gave us a truly Christian welcome. Mr. Butters informed me that the Melbourne District Meeting had made certain alterations in the boundary of the City Circuit, and that I was appointed to the superintendency of the new Circuit of Brighton. It was a salubrious marine township, about six miles to the south of the city, lying within 'Dendy's Survey.' Mr. Butters thought that it would save both expense and time, if the man in charge of the trolly were sent at once along to Brighton with our luggage, to which I agreed. I thought, 'This looks like business, and provided it be one of the conditions of service in Victoria, under Mr. Butters' administration of our Church affairs, I shall like it all the better.'

On the evening of the same day, July 8th, we found ourselves quietly ensconced in the hospitable home of my former Kingsbridge friends, Mr. and Mrs. John Wills, Moore Street, Collingwood. Here also I had the unspeakable pleasure of again meeting my dear, aged, widowed mother, and my brother Nicholas, whom I had not seen for about sixteen years. My parents, after I left for the West Indies in 1838, emigrated to South Australia, and my father died at the age of seventy-five at North Rhine. To see my mother, and, with my brother and sister, assist her in her widowed life, was the strongest motive I had for coming to Australia.

BRIGHTON CIRCUIT, 1854.

We went to our Circuit on *July 13th*, and on the 17th I opened my commission by preaching at East, Little, and Great Brighton. In the evening, at the latter place, I administered the Lord's Supper. 'It was a good day, rather cold in travelling, and fatiguing to the body' (Journal). I was now entered upon the full work of an Australian Circuit, and I resolved to spare no pains to preserve the good work as I found it; and also to extend it to localities outside the Circuit proper, where as yet there was no preaching nor churches, nor day nor Sabbath schools. My time and strength I consecrated anew to God and to the salvation of all the people in the district.

A few jottings from my Journal will show how I attempted to do this work, as well as to indicate some incidents of a family kind :—

'*July 22nd.*—We have heard of the death of my sister Rebecca (Mrs. Treby). She died in hopeful trust of God's mercy through the merits of our Lord Jesus Christ. The first of the band of nine brothers and sisters is removed : the chain is broken, the links are separating. May we not hope for a re-uniting by-and-by!

'I have been across the country to see my brother Nicholas, at Gardiner's Creek. He has made a nice selection as to locality, but the soil is poor. All the industry he could put forth in a lifetime in England would have been insufficient to procure the necessary means for purchasing so much land, and to have become so nicely settled.'

'*July 26th.*—At Little Brighton to-day I saw two brothers of the Rev. Joshua Jordan, a West Indian missionary. They are small farmers, and well-to-do. I visited in the afternoon our day school at Little Brighton—Mr. John Webb, master. I did not think the children were so sharp and intelligent as they ought to be. Mr. Charles Stone, the senior Circuit Steward, kindly accompanied me.

'To-day the Revs. Isaac Harding and John Egglestone came out to see me. Mr. Harding, who is an ardent educationist and great worker, has a wish to establish a Wesleyan Grammar School in Geelong, and believes it would be a great success. Both appeared to be excellent and affectionate brethren. I much enjoyed their visit.'

'*July 28th.*—This morning I went to the house of a Mr. Campbell, beyond Little Brighton, to see a Mrs. Carvill, whose husband was killed yesterday by blasting the underpart of a big gum-tree. I tried to comfort her with the promises of the Heavenly Father.'

'*July 30th.*—This has been a trying day. I again visited Mrs. Carvill, and performed a short funeral service on the remains of her late husband. All the friends present appeared deeply to feel the painfully mournful event which had occurred. I preached at the three Brightons as usual, to attentive congregations, and was much blessed.'

'*Aug. 3rd.*—This has been a very solemn day. In accordance with the proclamation of the Governor, Sir Charles Hotham, we have devoted its hours to fasting, prayers, and charity. I preached from Isa. xxvi. 9. A collection was made on behalf of the widows and orphans of the brave men who have fallen in this cruel and unjustifiable Crimean war.'

'*Aug. 7th.*—Pastoral visitation at East Brighton, and spent several hours in walking from house to house. Twelve souls had been recently converted, and joined the church.'

'*Aug. 17th.*—Pastoral visitation at Moorabbin. I called upon every member, and prayed in every house. I also visited non-members, *i.e.* hearers and worshippers with us. Several incidents of an interesting kind came up, and suitable conversations took place. Will not God bless the sowing of this seed? So I believe.'

'*Aug. 18th.*—Went to Collingwood to-day amidst clouds of dust. We had the pleasure of seeing the young T. T. Wills, who had just arrived from England with his wife. They had stood the voyage pretty well.'

'*Aug. 19th.*—Mr. Butters preached twice to-day with great acceptance. He told me of the resignation of the Rev. W. Byrnes. He is going over to the Anglican Ministry, which will be a great grief to his old Methodist father at Paramatta. But if he be discontented in our Ministry, he had better go.'

'*Aug. 22nd.*—Mr. Hawkins and I went to Melbourne to solicit subscriptions for our new church. Messrs. Pascoe and Cocker advised us to defer our appeals until a later period.'

'*Aug. 24th.*—Went to Beaumaris to see Mr. Charland, who is anxious to have religious service established in his neighbourhood. He offers a piece of land upon which to build a church-schoolhouse, which I accepted. I arranged for Mr. Charles Stone to open preaching services on the coming Sunday evening.'

'*Sept. 6th.*—I went to Melbourne to-day to solicit subscriptions for our new church at Brighton, and succeeded pretty well. In the evening I attended a church meeting at Prahran, at which were the Revs. W. Butters, J. Egglestone, and J. S. Waugh. It was a very fine meeting, and the whole debt on the building was subscribed.'

'*Sept. 8th.*—An awful storm of hail to-day. I measured one of the stones, which was one inch and a quarter in diameter. The lightning was very vivid, and the thunder rolled heavily over our heads. I was reminded of some of those terrific thunder-storms peculiar to the islands lying near the Spanish main. I am convinced that the winds and clouds were from opposite directions, and that the sultry atmosphere of the morning caused the wind to come from the north and north-west, whilst the cold above brought the wind from the south and south-west. These phenomena appeared to be over our house, and greatly alarmed us. Blessed be God, we were preserved from all harm.'

'*Sept. 13th.*—To-day, Mr. William Head and I rode over to Oakleigh, a small township about seven miles from Brighton, to see if there were any religious services held. We found that up to this time there were none. But there were three public-houses, and that the desecration of the Sabbath was dreadful. We called upon several of the families, all of whom were anxious for us to provide for their spiritual wants. There is an "open door" here, but as soon as we shall enter it we shall have many adversaries.'

'*Sept. 21st.*—Opened tenders this evening for roofing the new church at Brighton. A large undertaking for our few people, but the work has to be done.'

' *Oct. 8th.*—I preached at Beaumaris, and took Mr. Butters to see my cousins, Mr. James Bickford Moysey and Mrs. Moysey, and dined with them.'

' *Oct. 10th.*—A great tea meeting at Brighton on behalf of the new church. The Rev. Mr. Butters greatly helped us. Some four hundred persons were present, and the financial result amounted to £120.'

' *Oct. 19th.*—I went to Oakleigh to meet the people about building a church-schoolhouse, who subscribed then and there £30.'

' *Oct. 22nd.*—This Circuit is full of backsliders, who are hard to be affected for good. To-day in one of my congregations I had one of this class, who for sixteen years had been a leader in England. Drink has been his bane. Alas ! for his poor wife and children.'

' *Oct. 24th.*—The *Marco Polo* has arrived from London, bringing six hundred souls. A three months' voyage and full of discomfort. My dear friends, Mr. and Mrs. Allan Cameron, of Demerara, were passengers, whom I shall bring to Brighton for a few weeks.'

' *Oct. 28th.*—Heard to-day of the death by cholera of the Rev. W. Bannister and two of his children in Barbadoes. This dreadful plague has killed some fifteen thousand of the island population.'

' *Oct. 30th.*—The Annual Missionary Meeting at Collins Street. Collection £40 1s. I met Mr. Ramsay from St. Vincent, who, with his family, has come to Victoria to settle.'

' *Nov. 6th.*—The first Melbourne Exhibition was held. Mr. and Mrs. Isaac Groves. Mrs. Bickford, and I went. We were much pleased at seeing what the country could produce under the industrious operations of the colonists.'

' *Dec. 1st.*—I went for the first time to Keys Station, Mordialloc. about twelve miles from Brighton, to establish religious services. Mr. Battrick drove me thither. Here I found a thriving Irish Methodist family ready to welcome me as Christ's messenger. There were Mr. and Mrs. George Keys, the aged parents ; Mr. and Mrs. William Keys, Mr. and Mrs. Isaac Keys, Thomas Keys, and several neighbours. After dinner, the preaching service was commenced, and at the close the class-meeting was held. It was a unique spectacle in the midst of the Australian forest,—a nucleus of light and moral force for the whole neighbourhood.'

' *Dec. 3rd.*—Preached missionary sermons at St. Kilda, and gave the Lord's Supper. The Hon. A. Fraser and Mrs. Fraser were my hosts.'

' *Dec. 6th.*—A dreadful conflict, which had been long foreseen by thoughtful men, has taken place between the military and miners on the Ballarat Gold-fields. The harrowing and insulting behaviour of certain officials, in searching for mining licences from the men whilst engaged in working their claims, was at the bottom of the disturbance. The soldiers and the " diggers " joined issue at Eureka Hill, when some fifty of the miners were shot down at once. Mr. Peter Lalor, one of the leaders of the resisting force, was shot through the arm, which had to be amputated. There were serious casualties among the military also. Martial law was proclaimed in the *Government Gazette*, and copies were posted all over the district. But the excitement was fearful all over the colony, and great indignation was felt at the administration of the Chief Secretary, Mr. Foster, and the troubles he had brought upon the country. He was super-seded, and he returned to Ireland.

' The *Argo* arrived in sixty-two days " from land to land," and brought the news of the taking of Sebastopol by the allied armies. It may be hoped that this is the beginning of the end of this useless, cruel, and wicked war. With John Bright's sentiments in reference to this war every Christian statesman must agree. It is a great national sin.'

'*Dec. 24th.*—A fine day for Brighton. The Revs. W. Butters, J. Egglestone, and J. S. Waugh dedicated by prayers and worship our new church to God. In erecting this sanctuary, we have been generously helped by Methodist gentlemen in Melbourne, St. Kilda, and Brighton ; also by the gratuitous labours of Messrs. Hawkins, Baker, Gifford, German, and other brethren. Without their personal services, the building could not have been ready so soon after our arrival in the Circuit.'

'*Dec. 26th.*—The tea and public meetings were a great success. Every table, most abundantly supplied, was given, and about three hundred persons sat down to tea. In the evening the church was crowded. The senior Circuit Steward, Mr. Charles Stone, presided with much kindness and ability. Messrs. Butters and Waugh helped us with excellent addresses. We had a good collection and subscription list, which seemed to put heart into our dear people for the work so auspiciously begun.

'We had nearly reached the end of the year. All the customary services of Christmas, " Watch Night " and " Renewal of Covenant," were held as in England. In the observance of these, we got a gracious help from " on high " for the arduous enterprises of the New Year.'

1855.

The Annual District Meeting, for the whole colony, was commenced on *January 3rd*, the Rev. William Butters presiding ; the Rev. John Egglestone was elected as Secretary. Besides the brethren mentioned, there were, as members of the meeting, Messrs. Harding, Symons, Lightbody, Curry, Raston, and Hart, with Messrs. Waugh, Hill, Wells, Taylor, and Bickford, who had come from England during the year. Under the genial guidance of Mr. Butters the ordinary business was soon despatched. This District Meeting has an important historical bearing on the future constitution, permanence, and extension of our Church in Australia. A jotting from my Journal will explain this :—

'The various subjects placed before the meeting were of an interesting nature, and supplied strong inducements for yet more abundant effort in the Lord's work. A very spirited discussion took place in the financial District Meeting, on a proposal made by Mr. J. R. Pascoe, and seconded by Mr. H. Cook, that lay-representation should be an element in the constitution of the Australian Conference. The ministers allowed them full scope for the discussion of the principle ; and, on the motion of Mr. Walter Powell, it was referred to a Committee, to be empowered to sit during the year and to report to the next District Meeting.

We give the Statistical Returns from the District Meeting Minutes, as they may serve a purpose of comparison with those of subsequent years. But, it must be observed, that at that time we had a responsible charge in respect to public education, and these ' returns ' will be useful as showing how we utilised our own buildings for day school purposes, and thereby correspondingly relieved the Government from a large expenditure of money in erecting school buildings, especially on the Goldfields. We also heartily assisted the Board of Education in the administration of the system then in vogue.

The ' Returns ' I have summarised as follow :—

' Churches, 30 ; other preaching places, 40 ; ordained ministers, 13 ; assistant missionaries, 2 ; catechist, 1 ; church members, 1,055 ; on trial, 85 ; Sabbath school teachers, 401 ; Sabbath school scholars, 3,527 ; local preachers, 151 ; day schools, 37 ; day school teachers, 59 ; day school scholars, 3,007 ; buildings used for day school purposes and Divine worship, 15 ; total adherents, 18,897.

These glorious results had been the work of less than twenty years of prayerful and generous toil : ' So mightily grew the Word of God and prevailed.'

1856.

Jan. 12*th.*—One of the most painful yet necessary duties of the pioneer ministers at this date, was to find and shepherd lone women and their families in the bush. The men for the most part would be away for weeks together, engaged in carting goods from Melbourne to the Goldfields, that they might get a little ready money for the support of their families, and paying for the small allotments of land they had purchased. To the loneliness of the situation, must be added the fear of bushrangers, whose very presence was a terror to unprotected settlers. A sample of the effect of such circumstances I discovered, as I was riding through the forest to fulfil my monthly engagement at Keys Station.

' *Jan.* 13*th.*—Our house accommodation has been very poor since we came here in July last. One-half of the building has been used as a church, literally, " a church in the house," as in earlier times. But now, the whole space being available as a domicile, we have had several tradesmen employed making the necessary alterations. For six months my usual studies have been interrupted. New stations always impose inconveniences upon the ministers and their families, especially when it is attempted to make the homes what they ought to be. The respectability of the Ministry is often gauged from the character of the establishments over which they are placed. A good appearance has a great deal to do with the success of the cause '

'*Jan.* 25*th.*—We are making history. Our beautiful new church was honoured to-day with its first marriage. J. C. and A. D. were joined together by me in holy matrimony. A marriage in the Lord, on both sides, according to the Apostolic injunction. Here is the guarantee of a happy union and blessings from God.'

'*Jan.* 28*th.*—Hot winds at last. Thermometer in the shade 110°. The air was heated as if it had come from a "fiery" furnace. To the south and east of Beaumaris there was a raging fire devastating the whole district. Had not the wind suddenly changed the whole township would have been consumed. I was in the neighbourhood on ministerial duty, and saw a poor settler, his wife, and one child, who had been burnt out. Their little all was gone. The poor woman had not time even to get her bonnet ; she could only snatch up her child and fly for her life. The clouds of smoke could be seen for miles stretching away towards Mordialloc and Dandenong.'

The old settlers take but little notice of these hot winds. But to those English persons, who are doing the novitiate of a first or second year's residence, they are almost unbearable. And were it not for the heavier south-west winds, rushing in to fill the vacuum created by the heat and storm of the north wind, they would be hardly able to retain either elasticity or power of motion. But when the change comes, so great is the relief, that the dreadful ordeal is soon forgotten, and the pleasure of existence is again enjoyed.

'*Feb.* 5*th.*—The great gathering place of new arrivals of Methodists from the old country was our church in Collins Street, Melbourne. I preached there this day, morning and evening, to good congregations. After the morning service, I saw Mr. Richard Major, whom I formerly knew in the Kingsbridge Circuit. He and his family have come to settle in Victoria. I met Mr. Ick also, a long standing Methodist from Antigua. He has arrived with a family of twelve to share in the fortunes of Australia-Felix. I visited Mr. and Mrs. Henly, formerly of Torquay, and other Devonians, at his house. These new arrivals little know of the difficulties they will have to contend with in this, as yet, unsettled country. The colony, from a number of causes, is in a fearfully abnormal condition: an unwelcome contrast to the quiet, prosaic sort of life, these friends had been accustomed to in their English and West Indian homes.'

'*Feb.* 18*th.*—At the invitation of the Rev. Isaac Harding, I preached to-day in the Yarra Street Church, Geelong, the annual sermons in aid of the Trust Funds.'

This being my first visit, Mr. Harding took me to see a few of the principal friends—Mr. and Mrs. John Lowe, Mr. and Mrs. Thomas Forster, Mr. and Mrs. Rix, and some others. Of this visit, my Journal says :—

'There were good congregations, and a fruitful effort in finance. Mr. Harding entertained Mrs. Bickford and myself with much Christian kindness. Geelong and the surroundings are very picturesque and beautiful. It well deserves to rank as the second place in the colony. I like our Wesleyan friends in Geelong very much. They are a hearty and sensible people. I should think they are a happy flock to shepherd, with truth and grace.'

'*Feb.* 28*th*.—Special efforts at Little Brighton this evening for meeting the expense of stuccoing the church. Mr. T. Vasey, from Collingwood, presided. The debt altogether was £85, which we raised. Mr. Hurlstone, senr., gave £20.'

1857.

At the Sydney Conference, held in January last, under the New Constitution, great changes were made in the appointments of several of the senior ministers. Those which most affected Victoria and South Australia, were changes in the positions of the Rev. William Butters and the Rev. D. J. Draper. These zealous and able men had been for some years respectively in Melbourne and Adelaide, and it was felt by the Conference that a change was desirable. On *February* 14*th*, a breakfast-meeting was held at the 'Home' as a farewell recognition of Mr. Butters' mportant services in Victoria. We presented to our ex-Chairman a valuable gold watch and a massive chain, with an appropriate address. The Rev. Mr. Chase (Anglican) and the Rev. Dr. McKay (Scotch Free Church) were present with us. Mr. Butters' reply was manly, affectionate and broad, but evidencing deep emotional feeling at his leaving us for another field of labour.

Church Extension had been our keynote since our advent to this Circuit. But now the time was come for church solidification, by erecting inexpensive buildings for 'church and school' purposes in the localities we had taken up. On *March* 20*th*, therefore, I rode up to Beaumaris, and laid the first block on which the sill of the new building would rest. We came into this neighbourhood before any other religious body showed any interest in the spiritual welfare of the people or of their children. By precedence of action, therefore, this place belongs to us.

'The same process has begun at Oakleigh. I have been over, and accepted a tender for erecting a "church-schoolhouse." There is a Building Committee, who will see the work faithfully carried out. Our heads and hands are getting quite full of enterprises connected with the Church in this Circuit. And God will bless the work.'

'*March* 3*rd*.—Educational progress is the order of the day. This morning I went to Melbourne to see Mr. Colin Campbell, the Secretary of the Board of Denominational Education, that I might apply (1) for a master's and sewing-mistress' salary for East Brighton; (2) for a sewing-mistress' salary for

Moorabbin ; (3) for a master's and sewing-mistress' salary for Brighton. There is nothing like having "plenty of irons in the fire." I find it alike good for body and soul to be always pushing, always employed. I have just concluded my quarterly visit to the day schools, and find them in a satisfactory condition.'

'*April 1st.*—God's own day, and preached three times as usual. After the service at Moorabbin, a fine young man came to me for an interview. He told me that he had been five years in the colony, and had been only once in a place of worship before that very day. But the Lord had brought him there, he said, and he was determined to serve Him. He is a native of Hampshire, and I judge he had known of the grace of God before at the parental home. The sermon was founded on Titus iii. 4-7, and powerfully touched the young man's conscience.'

'*April 6th.*—The Rev. D. J. Draper opened our little church at Beaumaris to-day. The place was packed ; I could not even get a seat inside myself. Our friend, Dr. MacNicol, from St. Kilda, presided at the after meeting.'

'*April 16th.*—How the work grows ! "More preachers !" is the cry from every part of the colony. Mr. Draper has a wonderful faculty for detecting moral and mental worth in young men, when they come in his way. Joseph Dare (afterwards Dr. Dare) was one of his captures in Adelaide, and now his keen scent for labourers has brought him into contact with a young man of the name of Dyson, whom Mr. Draper thinks God has called for the work. We had a special meeting of ministers, and examined the young man, and approved of his being employed in the Castlemaine Circuit.

' I afterwards attended a meeting in the Mechanics' Institute, called by some influential citizens, for protesting against the influx of Chinese into the colony. It was a noisy and disgraceful meeting, and could have no effect in the direction sought. It was so one-sided, and so narrow, that I do not see how any just and cosmopolitan Englishmen could side with the speakers.

' The inevitable tea and public meeting were held. Charles Stone, Esq., took the chair, and Messrs. Reynolds, Barker, and Sykes addressed the after meeting. The people expressed their gratitude to us for our attention to themselves and their children. Mr. Reynolds has been appointed as master of the school.'

' *May 28th.*—Our financial economy for carrying on and extending the work is being rapidly developed. The present move is for establishing a " Church Extension Fund," so that we may be able to overtake certain Connexional and Circuit funds. I think this effort first took form in the Brighton Circuit, when the Revs. D. J. Draper and J. S. Waugh preached the sermons. At the public meeting subsequently held, the Rev. J. Egglestone was the chief speaker, and eloquently pleaded for the people's practical sympathy. We collected in all £21 10s. for the fund.'

' *June 5th.*—I rode over to Oakleigh on business connected with the new church and school. On my way back my good horse " Rusty " fell, and caught my right leg under him. I extricated myself, but not until I had felt the heavy pressure of the sprawling beast in a most painful manner. I feared at first that I had sustained serious injury ; but, after a while, I was able to remount and pursue my way. I turned aside to visit a " backslider," upon whom the hand of God was laid. He was penitent, and before I left him he promised to retrace his steps to the good old way, *i.e.* his church.'

'*June 7th.*—A bit of bush mission work again to day. I rode to Kingstown, and preached to fourteen adults and seven children. This is charity and mercy too. Leave bush settlers to themselves, and they rapidly degenerate, and in the end become dangerous elements to the peace of the social body. It is in such accidental groupings of men, far away from the influences of civilisation and religion, where the class known as " bushrangers " are manufactured. Are they not, under such conditions, more to be pitied than shunned ? '

'*June 8th.*—This day I buried the mortal remains of the late James Hurlstone. He died in the Lord.'

'*July 8th.*—I have now completed twelve months' work in this Circuit. We have had both enlargement and prosperity. I have preached two hundred and thirty-two times ; pastorised the Circuit with regularity and fidelity ; looked after every matter, great and small, with assiduity and carefulness ; have made many friends, and, thank God, not one single enemy.'

The record of the remainder of my work in the Brighton Circuit was but matter of routine ; and only such incidents as are of an important or public nature will now be noticed.

'*August 6th.*—I preached at Williamstown yesterday in aid of the Church Extension Fund ; and this morning the resident minister and I called upon Mr. and Mrs. Mason and other friends. We afterwards went to see the unfortunate convicts, as they were working in " chain-gangs." I felt a deep, deep sorrow for them. It seemed to me that this so-called "Prison Discipline," instead of being corrective and reformatory, must have the contrary effect. And the " life-long " sentenced men, in particular, must become yet more hardened, because for them there is no hope in this life. Good for such men if they had not been born.

'At the public meeting held in the evening a Captain McKay presided. The Rev. D. J. Draper made an excellent speech. The collection was £15.'

Sept. 4th.—The Rev. J. S. Waugh, the Superintendent of St. Kilda Circuit, became much interested in a young local preacher, who was resident therein, of the name of Samuel Knight. Mr. Waugh was impressed that he had both the piety and the gifts for becoming a minister of our body. He accordingly sent him up to Brighton, that I might hear him, and advise upon the case. Mr. Knight came and preached. My Journal note is the following :—

'Mr. Knight, from St. Kilda, preached here this evening on the " new birth." He is a promising young man ; and, judging from appearances, as a whole, I think we should encourage him to prepare for the full work of the Ministry.'

'*Sept. 14th.*—I buried at Beaumaris the remains of my second cousin, Sarah Jane Moysey, who was just eight years of age. Her knowledge of Christ's history was wonderful, and she loved Him as only a regenerated heart could. The most constant couplet upon her lips was : " I the chief of sinners am ;—but Jesus died for me." She was the first ripe fruit gathered from the children's " flock " at Beaumaris.'

NATIONAL GALLERY

MELBOURNE PUBLIC LIBRARY

AND SCIENCE MUSEUM

THE PUBLIC MUSEUM AND LIBRARY.

'*Oct.* 21*st.*—The Rev. J. W. Crisp preached here this evening, and at the after prayer meeting five dear young sisters came up to the communion rails, and found peace with God. Miss Elizabeth Baker led the way.'

'*Oct.* 26*th.*—Church Extension towards Western Port. Preached at Mr. Patterson's station, to settlers who came from miles round to hear the Gospel. I was much impressed that it was our duty to establish religious worship at Dandenong and Western Port. Mr. Sykes accompanied me.'

'*Nov.* 23*rd.*—To-day the New Constitution was proclaimed, and we have now "Responsible Government." Thanks to Providence, we shall be out of the "leading strings" of the Colonial Office, and be directly responsible to the Crown.' *

'*Nov.* 28*th.*—The Annual District Meeting was commenced this day in Geelong, under the presidency of the Rev. D. J. Draper. I was elected Secretary of the District, and the Rev. William Hill, Assistant Secretary. On this day, too, the Rev. W. L. Binks, Mrs. Binks and child, and the Rev. George B. Richards and Mrs. Richards arrived from England. The reception of these honoured brethren by the District Meeting was most hearty. Thomas James, originally from near Lelant, Cornwall, was received as a candidate for our Ministry. He approved he said, of the Constitution of the old Body, and desired to exercise his ministry under the direction of the Australasian Conference. The increase in all departments of the work was most encouraging. We were in session until December 4th, when the Minutes were read and signed. The Binkses came to Brighton to remain with us until they were appointed to a Circuit.'

1856.

'*Jan.* 3*rd.*—Church Extension is still our "Watchword." This day, Rev. Binks, Mr. T. Reynolds, Mr. W. Head, and I visited Wellington, Mordiallock, and Damper Springs, with the view of providing the inhabitants with religious ordinances. We met with much encouragement, and resolved that services should be commenced the very next Sabbath.'

'*Jan.* 4*th.*—The funeral of the late Governor, Sir Charles Hotham, took place. There were many thousands of persons watching with mournful looks the procession, as it passed from Toorak to the Melbourne Cemetery. The administration of His Excellency had not been a success, through a want of adaptedness for ruling over the democratic population of the colony. In the department of public service, which he had chosen, and for which he had been trained, doubtless he did as well as any of his compeers; but the qualities for governing a free

---

* The New Constitution had been prepared by the old Legislative Council for endorsement by the Crown. It provided for two elective chambers. Thus nomineeism was for ever dismissed. We had some very able colonial statesmen at that time, among whom may be mentioned Sir William Stawell, Mr. Fellows, Sir Charles Sladen, Mr. W. C. Haines, Mr. Ireland, and Sir John O'Shanassy. Mr. R. Heales, Sir Graham Berry, Sir James MacCulloch, Mr. Higinbotham, and Mr. James Service had not then come to the front. Mr. Haines was the first Premier under the New Constitution.

and independent province he did not possess. He did his best, but it was a poor best. He was too "high-metalled" to be an acceptable Colonial Governor. Civilians are better adapted for the position than military men can ever be : especially if they have had some years of experience in the English House of Commons.'

'*Jan. 9th.*—Held the Quarterly Meeting, and we decided that the junior minister, the Rev. John Catterall, should reside at Moorabbin, and be charged with the pastoral care of that part of the Circuit.'

'*Jan. 24th.*—The Second Australasian Conference was commenced in Melbourne to-day. The Rev. W. B. Boyce, who had been appointed by the English Conference, presided. The Rev. W. Butters was elected Secretary. There were about thirty brethren present.'

'*Feb. 9th.*—The Conference was closed. The formality of reading and signing the Minutes was observed as in the English Conference, all the brethren standing when the President and Secretary affixed signatures. Upon the whole it was a fairly successful Conference.'

'*Feb. 18th.*—We are making a beginning at Dandenong. Mr. Binks and I this day have been over and laid the first of the corner blocks for the new building. We knelt down upon the grass, and Mr. Binks fervently prayed to the Heavenly Father for His favour upon the undertaking.'

'*March 18th.*—The Rev. J. S. Waugh opened the church-schoolhouse at Dandenong to-day. Mr. and Mrs. James Webb, James Webb, junr., Mrs. Bickford, and I made up the party from Brighton. We had an excellent sermon from Mr. Waugh, and a large congregation. Mr. Webb presided at the after meeting, and Mr. Waugh and I addressed the audience. It being St. Patrick's Day, Mr. Waugh took for his subject the Irish saint and the evangelist of Ireland. The people were greatly interested.'

May 6th.—I quote in full from my Journal under this date :—

'I am this day forty years of age. I have therefore reached the meridian of life. I now feel that, with my constitution, it behoves me steadfastly to look at this fact, and prepare for those yet undeveloped events which may occur in the course of God's providence. "If I live, I live unto the Lord; if I die, I die unto the Lord: living or dying, I am the Lord's."

'" O may life show forth His praise,
   Who died a shameful death, to raise
      A rebel to His throne :
   May every act, and thought, and word
   Be to the glory of my Lord ;
      I'd live to God alone."

This day I have given myself anew to God and His Church. The Lord help me !'

'*May 14th.*—Old Mrs. Wellard died to-day. She had been a member for over sixty years, and received her first ticket from Wesley himself. Her sheet anchor in her dying hour was Rom. iv. 5: "But to him that worketh not, but believeth on Him that justifieth the ungodly, his faith is counted for righteousness." Her views of personal acceptance through the great atonement were as clear as sunlight. I never saw a happier death.'

'*June 8th.*—Is not this a brand plucked out of the fire? The aged Mrs. Sykes is gone. She lived without God for more than eighty-four years, and then she was awakened to a deep sense of her danger, and she sought salvation and died in peace. An answer to her son's prayers, I have no doubt.'

'*June 11th.*—This night that dear young Christian, Elizabeth Baker, departed this life in the faith and hope of Christ. She had been laid aside ten whole months, during which period I saw her once or twice a week. Only on one occasion did she manifest a want of resignation to the will of the Heavenly Father ;—when, seeing her younger sister and a number of young ladies going out for the Sunday school picnic, she exclaimed: "Oh, that I could go ! Is it not hard that I should be denied this pleasure ? " But it was only for a moment. The feeling of impatience passed off, and never again did she show anything but the completest resignation. Her early happy death created a salutary impression amongst the young people of the Brighton Church.'

'*June 25th.*—Thank God for good news. We have just heard that on March 30th, at Paris, the plenipotentiaries of England, France, Austria, Prussia, Russia, Sardinia, and Turkey have signed the "Treaty of Peace." But why could not these Powers have agreed to keep the peace, and thus escaped the great wickedness of going to war at all ? '

'*July 5th.*—To-day the mortal remains of the Rev. Walter Tregelles were buried in the Melbourne Cemetery. All the ministers in and about Melbourne were present. Mr. Draper conducted the service at the grave.'

'*Aug 15th.*—This morning at 4 o'clock, Mr. Edwin A. Bignell, formerly of Kingsbridge, Devon, died of chronic imflammation of the kidneys. His sufferings were intense. I was with him all through his last illness, and I believe his end was peace. Mrs. Bignell and her large family had arrived only fourteen days before this bereavement came upon them. But they will have many sympathising and helping friends.'

'*Aug 19th.*—We are now electing members for the Southern Province under the New Constitution. There were eleven candidates, for five of whom I voted. May God be gracious to this land ! '

Nov. 1st.—Not having yet seen Ballarat, I accepted an invitation to the circuit in the interests of our Foreign Missions. I left Melbourne by Cobb & Co.'s coach. We started from Bourke Street with splendid horses, and turning by the Post Office we went up Elizabeth Street at great speed. We went through Bacchus Marsh, where I saw the finest field of English clover my eyes had ever beheld. Somewhere about the Black Hill we had the trouble of being bogged, in an attempt to rush through a water-soaked gully. The two leaders turned quick round, broke the pole, and became so entangled with the wheel horses, so that we were in danger of making no further progress for the day—' Every one off the coach,' cried the driver, 'and help to get the horses free.' We all helped as desired, repaired the damages as far as possible, and, after perhaps an hour's detention, we made another start. We at last reached the 'Spread Eagle,' where man and beast were alike refreshed. I now commenced a conversation with the driver on the profanity of the language he had been using all the way from Melbourne. I reminded him that he ought to have some regard to the feelings of his passengers. Instead of turning upon me with abuse, he frankly acknowledged the badness of the habit, and apologised for his ill manners. I engaged to nudge him each time during the rest of the journey if he broke out, and, by the time we had got to Ballarat, I had almost cured him of his profanity. He was a Canadian by birth, and, I think, from certain admissions he made, he had been religiously brought up.

The journey from Melbourne to Ballarat was about one hundred miles; and I must say that it was the roughest I ever undertook. That we reached, late at night, the great Goldfield at all, with sound limbs and decent apparel, is to me a wonder.

I was the welcomed guest of the Rev. Theophilus and Mrs. Taylor —the one, a man of fine intellectual powers and a great pioneer worker; the other, a beautiful specimen of the real English lady in manners and hospitality. They were well-yoked; drawing together with loving unity in carrying on the Lord's work.

Nov. 3rd.—I preached at the Township to about five hundred persons. There was no choir, but a Mr. John Davy, one of the miners, led the singing—and it was singing, such as those Cornish men and women could render with unrivalled power. After the sermon, I baptized several infant children, among whom were ' Cissy,' the firstborn of Mr. and Mrs. Taylor; and a child of Mr. and Mrs. William Couch, formerly of Aventongifford, Devon.

I attended missionary meetings at Creswick, Mount Pleasant, Magpie, and Ballarat. On my return journey, I spent a Sabbath at Geelong, and held religious services.

Nov. 19th.—To-day we finished the sessions of the District Meeting, which had been held under the judicious guidance of Mr. Draper. The routine business was soon disposed of, and in a highly satisfactory manner.

The question of public education had already become crucial, and it was therefore necessary that we, as a recognised ecclesiastical educating ' body,' should put forth our views as to the general principles and guards we were prepared to adopt. We agreed to the following :—

1. All schools supported in whole or in part by the State to be called ' Public Schools.'

2. Not less than four hours consecutively in each day shall be devoted to secular instruction.

3. A portion of the Bible to be read at the commencement or close of the school, or both, and the school to be opened and closed with the Lord's Prayer, or some form of prayer approved by the Local Board.

4. No child required to be present during these religious exercises if the parents (in writing) object to it.

5. No attempt whatever to be made to disturb the particular religious tenets of any sect, and no catechism peculiar to any Church to be used by the teacher.

6. That no person appointed as teacher in any school, without a certificate of moral and religious character shall have been laid before the Local Board from the minister of whose Church such teacher is a member.

7. That one minister of religion from each denomination to be, *ex officio*, members of the Local Board, and permitted to give religious instruction on any school day, according to previous arrangement during the period allotted to religious instruction.

8. After a period to be named, no teacher shall be appointed to. or retained in, any ' Public School ' who shall not have submitted to an examination, and received a certificate of qualification from the Central Board of Education.

9. A Central Board of Education, consisting of five members representing the different Churches, to have the direction of the education of the colony.

10. Public Schools to be open to the inspection of the Central Board. but only in reference to secular teaching.

11. No school to be entirely built or supported by the State, except it be a Normal Training School or Schools.

12. Provision to be made by the State for the gratuitous education of orphans, and the children of destitute parents.

The debate which took place in the preparation of these resolutions was earnest and able ; and I well remember Mr. Draper expressing his regret that a shorthand writer was not present to take down the speeches. Of course, it was assumed all through that the Denominational system was the only practicable one; and, further, that it was only in connection with those Churches which were willing to expend both time and money in the work, that public education could be carried on at all. This was certainly the prevailing conviction, and all the conditions of the question justified it. Such a resolution as the ninth of the series could never have been passed in the absence of such a belief.

' *Dec.* 23*rd.*—Our new Governor, Sir Henry Barkly, arrived in Melbourne to-day, accompanied by Lady Barkly and children. We are fortunate in having

Sir Henry appointed in succession to the late Sir Charles Hotham. Our New Constitution requires further adaptation to the unique circumstances of the colony. We want vote by ballot, manhood suffrage, the abolition of the property qualification for the House of Assembly, the throwing open of large areas of land for selection and settlement, before or after survey, as the Parliament may decide, and the passing of a bill for legalising mining on private property. Sir Henry Barkly is just the man to see what are the real exigencies of our social and political environments, and he will be ever ready to assist the Council and Assembly in making legislative provision for meeting them. I am sure of this, that he will act judiciously, justly, and with due consideration in upholding alike the prerogatives of the Crown and the rights of the people. To have had, in our present circumstances, so wise, and strong, and good a man to rule over us, is evidence to my mind of the continuous care and love of God over us in this new and difficult country.'

1857.

'*Jan. 1st.*—This day begins a new epoch in my laborious and anxious life. The Christmas and New Year's festivals have been of deep interest to me. As it respects my future, I use Wesley's own words, "Lord, I appeal to Thee." I had the great pleasure of seeing Governor Barkly to-day. I found him as affable and courteous as he used to be in Demerara several years ago. He answers exactly my ideal of what the finest type of an English gentleman is and should always be.'

'*Jan. 20th.*—We have a large addition to our ministerial staff by the arrival from England of Messrs. King, Lough, Lane, Mayne, Fidler, Beasley, Dubourg, Lloyd, and Dawson. Also Mr. and Mrs. Ingram and Mr. and Mrs. Hessell. Misses King and Boundy were likewise of the party. They came by the *Walmer Castle*, and are all in good health.'

'*Jan. 26th.*—I preached at Dandenong and Western Port. We have gathered in some precious souls already in this extensive district, over whom I have appointed as leader Mr. William Sykes, a man admirably adapted to the office.'

I carefully watched over the interests of the Brighton Circuit until March 3rd, when my connection with it ceased. On the 6th, a tea and public meeting were held to say farewell to Mrs. Bickford and myself. Mr. Charles Stone presided, and Messrs. T. Wellard, John Webb, James Barker, Edward Barker, W. Sykes, and T. Reynolds addressed the meeting. A purse of fifty sovereigns was presented to me in acknowledgment of the earnest service I had rendered in the Circuit, and all felt deeply the sorrow of parting.

BALLARAT.

I was appointed to the charge of this metropolitan Goldfields Circuit by the Adelaide Conference. My colleagues were the Rev. James W. Crisp, who was to reside at Creswick, and the Rev. Charles

Lane, who was to be my assistant in Ballarat. We arrived on the evening of the 6th of March, free from accident in travelling from Melbourne, *via* Geelong, to the place of our destination. At the parsonage several friends had gathered to give us a hearty welcome. Our cottage was of weatherboard, having six very small rooms; and most of the cooking, washing, etc., had to be done outside. But it was as good as most people had, and better than many could get. In the cold winters, we were almost blown away by the strong, gushing winds which came up from the flats in the south; and in the summer, especially when we had hot winds from the north, it was hard indeed to endure the strain.

The 'Church Reserve' had been turned into a 'paddock,' and was well taken up by miners' tents; whilst on the north side, about halfway down the hill, was the Waterloo claim, sunk to between two and three hundred feet deep, and was worked night and day by the Company. Anything more unlike a decent Church establishment could hardly be found under the sun. Our 'church' was a schoolhouse, into which were crowded from Sabbath to Sabbath some five hundred people. In this building also were conducted a Sabbath and day school. Behind the building stood a cottage occupied by Mr. and Mrs. George Knox, the master and mistress of the school. Below the slope of the hill stood the tent of Mr. Dimsey, who was our sexton, groom, and gardener. Right in the centre of the 'paddock' was the large tent once occupied by Mr. John Hoiles and family, but now used as a classroom on Sunday afternoons; Mr. Hoiles himself being the leader. There was also a garden plot, worked by Mr. Dimsey, whose privilege it was to grow vegetables for the minister's family and for his own. There was also a rough stable on the south of the parsonage, on the same level as itself, for the two horses which had to be kept for working this part of the Circuit.

The 'Waterloo Company' had entered into a contract with the trustees for sinking a shaft inside the north fence, and to pay a royalty of $2\frac{1}{2}$ per cent. on the net proceeds of the mine. But in an evil hour another company started sinking a shaft on the outside of the south fence, intending, when they had bottomed, to work towards the centre of our 'paddock,' where the 'gutter' lay, and the gold was to be found. But this was strongly objected to by the Waterloo Company, as it meant, according to the understood rules of mining, intrusion and robbery. There was no law to regulate such operations, consequently the Waterloo Company, the *quasi*-legal occupiers of the ground, determined to take the matter into their own hands.   During the dinner hour on a certain day, they went across the ' paddock ' in a body, and took forcible possession of the new shaft.   They then broke down all the machinery and other appliances, and threw the whole into the shaft, and then returned to their own company's ground.   The vigilant eyes of the police watched the whole transaction, and, the next day or so, summonses were issued against the leaders of the adventure.   The presiding magistrate, Mr. Clissold, gave it against them, and they were bound over to take their trial in the Supreme Court.   There was great excitement throughout the Goldfields; and it was clearly seen that the Parliament would have to pass some bill for regulating ' mining on private property.'

The second day after my arrival, a public meeting, attended by three thousand miners, was held in an open space outside Her Majesty's gaol.   The leading politicians of the district took the question up, and spoke with great cogency and power.   Resolutions were passed condemnatory of the non-action of the Government, in not having provided by Parliamentary intervention for the serious difficulty which had arisen.   Expressions of sympathy with the men of the Waterloo Company, who had defended their just rights, although in an improper manner, from invasion, were also heard. Each miner in voting held up both hands, the effect of which was very imposing.   Mr. James Oddie, J.P., an influential citizen, and I stood in the midst of this vast assemblage, and watched the proceedings with intense interest.

The more I pondered over the case, the deeper was my conviction that the prosecution of the men ought to be abandoned.   I therefore wrote the Governor, Sir Henry Barkly, a long, confidential letter, in which I pointed out the unchallenged fact that the ' Waterloo ' men had no other course open to them than that they had taken for protecting their rights.   And I asked for three concessions : ' (1) That the Crown Prosecutor should be instructed by the Cabinet to enter a *nolle prosequi,* and so let the matter drop ; (2) That the Government should immediately introduce a measure into Parliament for validating agreements entered into between owners of private property and mining companies ; (3) That the Crown should demand a small royalty on the net proceeds, so as to be a party to all such contracts.' The prosecution never came off; but nothing was done to prevent breaches of the peace in the future under like conditions.

Ballarat itself was an abnormal Goldfields town. The old land and population marks have not been altogether obliterated by the 'civilization' which has set in in these later years. There are still old Golden Point, Gravel Pits, Specimen Hill, Black Hill, Bakery Hill, Brown Hill, Soldiers' Hill, Mount Pleasant, and Canadian Gully; places and localities where much of the yellow dust used to be gathered, and which has made Ballarat the wonder of the world. Here also have been seen some of the grandest triumphs of the grace of God ever witnessed. To be made the Superintendent, *i.e.* 'Bishop,' of this great circuit, was at that time the heaviest responsibility the Conference could have put upon me.

I soon found that I and my colleagues had much work cut out for us. We were three men in full physical vigour, and were much in earnest to 'spread scriptural holiness' throughout the whole district. The area was extensive, and may be thus described: from Mount Bolton to Mount Egerton, and from Spring Hill to Scarsdale. Any English county, with the exception of Yorkshire and Devonshire, might be put within these outposts, leaving a pretty large margin for unimportant excursions.

A few details from my Journal may be given :—

' *March 8th.*—I opened my commission by preaching at Magpie and Ballarat. In the afternoon I visited the school, and found only a few children in attendance.'

' *March 15th.*—I rode out to the Warrenheip 'Sawmills,' some fourteen miles from Ballarat. After much difficulty I found Mr. and Mrs. Biddle at this place. I did not think at first I should be a welcome visitor, for Mr. and Mrs. Biddle, before leaving England, had been strong partisans of the Everett "reform" movement. On my way back to Ballarat, I fell in with a prize-fight. It was a brutal sight. It was said that there were a thousand persons present. I duly reported this breach of the law to the authorities.'

' *April 17th.*—This morning I heard of the melancholy death of Lady Barkly. I wrote immediately a letter of condolence to Sir Henry. His reply was very touching, and worthy of his fine character.'

' *June 1st.*—Preached twice at Creswick, and addressed the Sunday school in the afternoon. Monday : Mr. Crisp and I walked out to Mangilla, the residence of Mr. and Mrs. Whitfield Raw. Mr. Raw is our senior Circuit Steward. In the afternoon we went to the top of "Cattle Station" hill, from which we saw the historic "Seven Hills," innumerable dales, and extensive grassy plains. It was a beautiful panorama. In the evening I rode to Ballarat, and was much bewildered in my progress by the new fences which are springing up in every direction, so rapid is the settlement of farms as the result of success in mining in this matchless auriferous district.'

'*June 24th.*—To-day I have ridden to Mount Mercer, Messrs. Crombie and Davies' station. I preached to a small company in the hall, and formed a class of six members. We agreed to build a church-schoolhouse at Hardie's Hill, on a site generously presented to the Conference by Mr. Thomas Dunstan. In going and returning I visited a number of families, who received me with thankfulness.'

'*Sept. 6th.*—This day we consecrated to the worship of God the new church at Lake Learmouth. May this the first sanctuary erected in the whole of this extensive district, be filled as time rolls on with grateful and holy worshippers ! In the after part of the Sabbath I rode to Spring Vale, and held Divine service in Mr. Maiden's barn. This neighbourhood is the most lovely I have seen in England or Australia. It is perfectly "Edenic" in charm ; and the soil is rich indeed.'

'*Sept. 13th.*—This morning I preached at Mount Pleasant to a fine congregation. After which I rode to Durham Lead, and opened the new building for the worship of God.'

'*Nov. 9th.*—The holding of the Annual District Meeting was a welcome relief to me from the toil and anxieties of the Ballarat Circuit. My travelling companions to the meeting were Messrs. Crisp and Lane. The coach was driven over to the Parsonage that we might be sure of seats. Our final start was from the "Charlie Napier," in the main road or street, then up Specimen Hill, and away to Melbourne, *via* Warrenheip. We were sixteen passengers in all. Everything, except the severe "bumping," went on well until we were some ten miles on our journey. Our driver was one of those venturous Americans, who, in those days, were the "whips" between the Goldfields and the city. I fear the optic nerve of our "Jehu" had been disturbed, so that its measuring faculty was at fault, for, unexpectedly to us, at least, we had an unpleasant capsize through his driving against a "stump." An immediate spring by the inside passengers, though the uppermost window-door, was an amusing sight. There was but one slight injury, the remainder escaped with a fright and shaking. All helped to right the coach, when the horses were re-harnessed, and we made another start. We had other casualties, such as the breaking of the linchpin ; and the aft wheels were on fire through the want of grease for several miles, as we neared the end of our journey. However, we got into Melbourne at last, and thankful we were that nothing more serious had happened than the breakage and fire before noticed.'

From the 10th to the 18th of November we were engaged in the District Meeting ; the Rev. D. J. Draper, Chairman, and the Rev. W. L. Binks, Secretary. No business of special importance came up, and the sessions were pleasantly passed. Messrs. Draper, Binks, and I were elected as representatives to the ensuing Conference. Mr. Lane and I returned to Ballarat on the 20th, safe and well.

'*Dec. 20th.*—To-day we have at Miners' Rest and Wendouree consecrated to the Lord two additional places of worship. I preached again in the evening at Ballarat. It was a hard day's work. The cause is prospering in our hands, which sweetens the toil.'

1858.

The Ballarat Goldfields were discovered in 1851, from which period the population steadily increased. The time, therefore, appeared to have come for erecting a building in the township for accommodating from twelve to fifteen hundred persons. We supposed the cost would be some £4,000. The necessary steps were accordingly taken for inaugurating a financial scheme for accomplishing our object. A tea and public meeting were held, presided over by the Rev. Theophilus Taylor, at which over seven hundred pounds were subscribed.

Jan. 19th.—The foundation-stone was laid by Sir Henry Barkly, when from fifteen to twenty thousand persons assembled from all parts of the district to welcome the Governor, who that day was to make his first entry into the metropolitan Goldfield. It was a day of great rejoicing for his suave bearing and his able speeches. The trustees of the new church, Messrs. Oddie, Doane, Creber, Francis, and Couch, to mark their appreciation of the kind services of Sir Henry, presented him with a suitably inscribed trowel, made of Ballarat gold, whose handle of native wood was ornamented with small quartz nuggets, most artistically arranged. The Building Committee, consisting of fifteen gentlemen, acted with commendable generosity in the presentation of this valuable memento to His Excellency, in association with the trustees.

The 'stone,' having been 'well and truly laid,' by Sir Henry, he gave to the surrounding crowd an excellent address, in which he complimented the Ballarat Methodist Church for its zeal in undertaking, in the general interests of that large district, the erection of so costly a building. He also spoke of the sincere pleasure he felt in meeting again his former friend, the Rev. James Bickford, whom he had known and esteemed as a Christian minister in the colony of British Guiana, when he was Governor there some few years before. Other speeches followed, and the ceremony of stone-laying was over.

At 5 p.m. on the same day, I left by coach for Melbourne, and took the steamer the day following for Hobart, Tasmania, to fulfil my duty as one of the representatives of the Victoria District to the Australasian Conference. I arrived on the 22nd, and entered the Conference at 2.30 p.m., and was heartily welcomed by the Reverend President Butters and the assembled brethren. I preached at O'Brien's Bridge, at Melville Street, and, on my way home, at Launceston. The President's official sermon was delivered before the Conference and a large audience on the evening of the 27th, for which he received the hearty thanks of the Conference. I left Launceston by steamer on February 9th. Mr. and Mrs. Allan Cameron, formerly of Demerara, Mr. Norman, and Mr. John Munroe, came on board to wish me *bon voyage.* On the 12th, I reached Ballarat, and found all well at home.

March 25th.—The new church at Black Lead was opened. Mr. Roberts, a Welsh lay-preacher, and I officiated. I baptized eleven children in connection with the service. On the 29th, we held a tea and public meeting at Spring Hill, and paid off the church debt. On the 30th, a similar effort was made at Belfast in aid of the new church-schoolhouse erected there.

May 15th.—At the request of the Building Committee, I have been to Melbourne financially to arrange for carrying out our great enterprise at the Township. Mr. Draper accompanied me to see Mr. Henry Miller, the responsible manager of the Bank of Victoria, in the colony. Mr. Miller, when he found it was a Church transaction we were seeking accommodation for, unhesitatingly granted our request. I returned to Ballarat with 'a light heart,' in possession of a letter to Mr. Robertson, the local manager, to honour our cheques for the new building.

July 18th.—A memorable day for Ballarat. The Rev. Mr. Draper came up from Melbourne, and dedicated our beautiful church to the worship of God. At the public meeting on the 19th, we raised £341 9s. 7d. On the 25th, the Rev. Joseph Dare, from Sandhurst, preached twice. At the prayer meeting, at the close of the evening service, several penitents came forward to seek salvation. Every one of us present felt that the 'Ark of the Covenant' was 'in the house of the Lord.' Mr. Dare also gave us, on the 26th, an able lecture on the adaptability of the Methodist Church to the condition and spiritual needs of our Australian population. In writing to Mr. Draper, *re* Mr. Dare's visit and service, I gave as my opinion, that the reverend preacher, at whose feet I had been sitting, would be the future 'Robert Newton' of the Australasian Methodist Church.

'*Sept.* 19*th.*—I improved this evening the melancholy death of Hugh Anderson, who was killed behind the "Charlie Napier." There were about one thousand persons crowded into the church. A black man, from Jamaica, is accused of the murder of Anderson, but he accused two others, whose names he has given.'

'*Oct.* 3*rd.*—A hard day's work. I preached twice at the Township ; baptized seven children, and married a couple. There were one hundred and fifty communicants at the Lord's Supper at the close of the public service.'

'*Oct.* 21*st.*—This evening I gave a lecture at Durham Lead on Total Abstinence. Seventeen took the pledge.'

I much regret that I did not, when I was a missionary, give some portion of my time to this branch of Christian work, as well as to preaching the Gospel.

Nov. 1*st.*—I attended in Melbourne Gaol the execution of Thompson and Gibbs. Both died protesting their innocence. If really so, would not the pitying Christ, who saved the malefactor on the Cross, show mercy to them also? I had previously visited both in gaol, and tried to prepare them for the dreadful death the law had condemned them to.

Nov. 2*nd.*—The District Meeting commenced in Melbourne. Mr. Draper presided, and the Rev. T. Williams was elected Secretary. The business was soon despatched in a satisfactory manner.

Nov. 27*th.*—At Mr. Draper's request I went to Ararat to assist the Rev. W. Woodall to establish this new circuit. At Fiery Creek I found that there had been no religious service for over two years. I visited, in order, Pleasant Creek, and held service in a calico building; Great Western, Cathcart, and Ararat. I preached six times, met five Societies, and pastorised several families. I decided that Mr. Woodall should, for the present, reside at Great Western Diggings, it being central to his work. He has a fine, unchallenged field for his ministrations, and 'no adversaries.' The people throughout this scattered district seemed to 'esteem him highly for his work's sake.'

Dec. 10*th.*—This evening a public reception meeting was given to the Rev. Thomas Binney, from London. Mr. Oddie presided. The resolution of welcome was moved by me, and seconded by the Rev. Cooper Searle (Anglican). Mr. Binney's reply was grand and good. We were all vastly interested. On the evening of the 12th he preached in our new church, it being the largest in Ballarat. My Journal jotting of this service says :—

' The building was thronged, and hundreds had to go away, being unable to get within hearing distance of the great preacher. His text was: "And every man stood in his place." Mr. Binney exhibited a profound acquaintance with human nature, and gave us wise lessons on our duty in this new country. "I never preached," said he, "to such a congregation before. There is not an old man amongst them. The best sinew and brains from the Mother-land are gathered together here. Their intelligence and force of character beam in their very countenances."

It was a grand service. At its close, the Lord's Supper was administered.

1859.

'*Jan. 4th.*—A great shadow has fallen upon us. Mr. Taylor's health had failed under the heavy labours of establishing the Ballarat Circuit. He died this morning in the presence of Mrs. Taylor, Rev. C. Lane, and myself, without a struggle. His end was peace.

'About ten days before this melancholy incident occurred, he opened his mind to me as follows: Now that death was rapidly approaching him, he felt, he said, no fear. His soul was full of gratitude, and thankfulness, and peace. If the Lord were to put it to him whether he would prefer to die or live, his preference would be the former. The glory at God's right hand he longed to enjoy. He had been, he said, reserved in his communications to others of his experience of religion. He had considered it too sacred a thing to be talked about. He had had, nevertheless, a "spring under a spring;" the upper had been his official life and through that he had gone without fear or timidity. No hesitation or hanging back had ever marked that department of his life; whilst underneath it had lain "a spring" of sweet enjoyment and strength. This was unseen, and often it had been thought that his was an official piety, but it was not so. "I could never be converted in those meetings yonder; 'it pleased God to reveal the Son in me' was the manner of my conversion, and in secret. I shouted for hours, 'Glory! Glory!' My soul was full to overflowing. I feel it now, although my disease considerably affects my mind and gives it a false colouring, and makes me irritable. But I am on the Rock—I give up all to Him—I am safe." We knelt down and prayed. It was a deeply solemn time. Mr. Taylor's responses were clear, hearty, and appropriate.'

'*Jan. 6th.*—The funeral of our late brother, Mr. Taylor, took place to-day. After an affecting service in the church, we proceeded to the New Cemetery, Creswick Road, and laid all that was mortal of this pioneer preacher on the Goldfields in their last earthly resting-place. There was a great assemblage of mourners of all denominations, who were anxious to show their love and respect for this faithful servant of God. On the 9th, I improved the death of our dear departed brother. My text was Isaiah xl. 6, 7, 8. Mrs. Taylor was graciously sustained throughout all the distressing incidents, thus briefly stated, by the presence and love of Him who is the widow's Husband and the Father of the orphaned.'

'*Feb. 16th.*—To-day I opened the new church at Clunes for Divine worship. We raised at the public meeting on the Monday £120 towards the expense of the building.'

' *March 6th.*—The Rev. William Hill, from Geelong, visited us for our Township Sunday School Anniversary. He preached two eloquent and suitable sermons to large congregations. The collections on the Sunday and on the Monday evening showed the great interest the people took in Sunday School work. The Conference of this year appointed the Rev. J. G. Millard, of Sydney, as my colleague. He comes to us with the reputation of being an able preacher, and a successful soul-winner.'

In the settlement of some of our agricultural districts, serious misunderstandings frequently arose among the purchasers, or lessees, in relation to the boundaries of each other's holdings of fee-simples. I felt that it was quite within the scope of my duties, as a minister of peace and righteousness, to assist in preventing as much as possible expensive litigation amongst such parties. Besides these, misunderstandings often arose among members of our own church, who, with their families, had settled on small farms bounded by each other's farms; having only logs of wood, 'dog-leg' fences, or post and rail, for dividing between them. Such a condition of things only made mischief in the midst of the families in their relation to each other.

Notwithstanding the enormous calls upon our people on the Gold-fields for local contributions, they could not ignore the obligation we owed as a prosperous branch of the Australasian Church to our Foreign Missions. In recently making up the returns for the Ballarat Circuit, I was thankful to find that the noble sum of £301 4s. 5d. had been raised. I had been, during the quarter, as a deputation in the interests of the missions to the Carisbrook and Castlemaine Circuits, where I found amongst the ministers and congregations a fine missionary spirit.

The wear and tear of mining life, especially in the deep sinkings of Ballarat, soon brought to the painful notice of the leading men of the city, the necessity there was for some generous provision of a benevolent kind being made for an increasingly large increment of prematurely old, unfortunate, and indigent persons within the district. Private funds under the direction of a large committee, had been distributed for a few years as occasion required; but this, as a means of out-of-door relief, was found to be altogether unsatisfactory. It may appear somewhat invidious to mention anyone's name in particular when so many nobly helped; still the name of 'James Oddie' cannot be overlooked. To him, more than to any other

gentleman of that time are we indebted for the capacious and handsome building, known as the Ballarat Benevolent Asylum, in the
western part of the city.   On the occasion of the laying the foundation stone, on March 17th, by Mr. Oddie, there were about five
thousand persons present.   The Revs. Messrs. Potter (Anglican),
Henderson (Presbyterian), and I, gave addresses on the duties and
privileges of Christian benevolence.   The cosmopolitan objects of the
institution commended it to the paternal assistance of the Government, whose aid was generously rendered.

'*March* 18*th* (8 a.m.)—I was at Mount Mercer Station. and after family
worship with Mr. and Mrs. Cromby, I came over to Hardie's Hill, and marked
off the land given by Mr. King for the new school-house.   Messrs. Wilson,
Dunstan, Thomas, and Roach were with me.   We all knelt down on the
ground, and prayed that God would bless the project.   It being the end of
the quarter. I visited the Durham Lead, Magpie, and Mount Pleasant Day
Schools on my way back to Ballarat.

Our greatest ecclesiastical event of this year was the division of
the circuit, by forming into a new charge Creswick, Spring Hill,
Clunes, Mount Bolton, and Lake Learmouth.   The Rev. George
Daniel was appointed superintendent, with the Rev. Charles Lane
as his colleague.   The Conference had been generous in its gifts,
for both ministers ranked among our best men.   The Quarterly Meeting for carrying this division into effect was held at Creswick on
April 4th.   There was a large attendance, and forty-two brethren
sat down to a real English dinner of roast beef and plum pudding.
The arrangement of the finances took up a great deal of time, and
we found that we had a deficiency of £51 10*s.* 8*d.*   This amount the
Ballarat Circuit agreed to take over.   We appointed stewards for
both circuits, and broke up in harmony.   It was not a case of the
stronger throwing off the weaker, but of mutual adjustment in
the common interest of the cause.   Six day schools went off with the
division.   We agreed that the Rev. J. G. Millard should reside at
Ballarat East, and that his salary should be £300 per annum.

'*April* 13*th.*—Mr. and Mrs. Millard, four children, and servant arrived in
Ballarat.   The Stewards not having as yet provided a house, we took them in,
and did our best to make them feel at home with us.'

'*April* 20*th.*—We had a reception meeting for Mr. Millard.   About four
hundred persons sat down to tea.   It was a capital meeting, and realised
£20 16*s.* towards Mr. Millard's removal expenses from Sydney to Ballarat.
During the evening Mr. Daniel arrived from Geelong on his way to Creswick.

He was lamed through the upsetting of the coach. It was well that he escaped with so little hurt.'

' *May* 24*th.*—A busy day as usual. I went to the hospital and admitted ten applicants, and dismissed five or six. I called on Widows Barker and Evans. In the afternoon I rode out to the Warrenheip railway works to the church opening services. We had a fine meeting, and paid off the whole cost of the building. Messrs. Guthridge and Little have liberally helped us in making a home for a Methodist Church at this station.'

' *June* 2*nd.*—The Rev. Mr. Buzacott, a London missionary, from the South Seas, preached this evening and interested us greatly. We made a collection of £5 10*s.*, which was handed to him for his glorious mission. Mr. George Howe, of the George Hotel, whom I have been visiting for some weeks in his great illness, took the Sacrament from me to-day. God is showing him His salvation.'

On the 4th Mr. Howe died. I was much distressed at not seeing him again. 'Saved by mercy' I humbly believe. Mrs. Bickford and I went to the 'house of mourning' to condole with Mrs. Howe. Her dear Lucy came home too late to see her father alive. It was a crushing sorrow for the child. On the 7th the mortal remains of my late friend were interred. The Rev. C. Searle (Anglican) read at the grave the usual service, and I addressed the sympathising audience, and offered extempore prayer. I was very unwell afterwards, and had to call in Dr. Nicholson. My pulse was 106 degrees. On the 8th I was too ill to leave my room.

' *July* 25*th.*—I have had severe headache all day, occasioned by the cold of yesterday and heavy labours. In the evening I met my Bible class. I am worried almost out of my life with our day schools. Under this Denominational System we have to find all the buildings and appurtenances, appoint and superintend the teachers, examine and report on the condition of the schools, and preside at all meetings of the Local Boards. In this district I am myself the Corresponding Secretary with the Central Board in Melbourne of some fifteen or twenty schools; have to examine and sign all returns, receive the grants, and pay the teachers their salaries. Large packages of books and *plant* come to me, for which I have to account from quarter to quarter to the Central Board. Indeed, it is a heavy burden—*a troublesome* " department "—requiring much time and method of action to keep matters straight.

' My pastoral and preaching duties are almost as nothing compared with the constant attention and care these schools impose on me. I wish that I could be rid of this burden by some *new* legislation, through which the churches would be freed from all further connection with so responsible and thankless a work. My friend, Mr. James Bonwick, is the District Inspector, but his duties are quite distinct from mine. And were it not for his judicious suggestions and countenance, I certainly would be compelled to retire from all further connection with the administration of the Denominational System of education in this extensive district.'

' *July* 28*th.*—A singular example of the effect of *deep conviction* of sin upon

11

the physical man occurred to a Mr. Langley at the Wendouree Swamp, who had become both blind and speechless for some thirty or forty hours. I was sent for, and promptly rode up to see him in his now quiet cottage home. Messrs. Hoiler and Morgan had spent much time in prayer for him. When I came into his presence, I found that he could see and speak, and was saved. The first words he uttered were in testimony of that great spiritual change ; God had forgiven him, he said, and he was now happy. In sad contrast to this "incident of grace" was the case of a man—a complete stranger—who called on me in Lydiard Street, and disclosed a melancholy tale of wretched conjugal and colonial life. A sadder case I never heard of. Poor fellow ! He is to be pitied ! But on whose side is the fault ?

'I went to the hospital and admitted ten patients, and spent the rest of the day in pastoral visitation. At the meeting of the Benevolent Association I was elected a member of the Committee of Management.'

'*August 5th.*—We had been contending with the Eastern Council for many months about our site at the Gravel Pits, which we had occupied in the usual manner for several years. But now the Council sought to dispossess us of our land, and use it for the purpose of a town hall, institute, and library. Mr. Belford, the mayor, had no sympathy with our church, so he determined to seize our chosen ground. Finding that the longer we corresponded the more entangled the matter became, I prepared and despatched a letter to Sir Henry Barkly, our Governor, upon the whole case. It was our only hope for a just settlement.'

'*August 23rd.*—My first visit to Smythesdale and Brown's Diggings. At 7.30 I preached in the Primitive Methodist Church to about one hundred persons. I supped at Mr. John Davey's tent, and slept at Mr. Mitchell's. The next morning, after breakfasting with Mr. and Mrs. Harris, and family worship I sallied forth on pastoral work until 1 p.m. I dined at Mr. Frost's and baptized his youngest child. I then started for Ballarat, and got lost in the ranges for nearly two hours. At last I fell in with a couple of wood-splitters, who informed me that I was going in the opposite direction from Ballarat, and kindly put me on the track for Cherry Tree Hut. I got home at 7 p.m., and went into the church and preached. I was much tired, and my whole nervous system was upset.'

'*Sept. 16th.*—This day Mr. Belford, on behalf of the Eastern Council, and I, in behalf of the Wesleyan Church, met at my house, and we settled the dispute about the Gravel Pits site, after two years of smart and obstinate contention from both sides. We erect entirely new premises on the other side of Barkly Street, upon a new site to be granted by the Government, and the Council would erect their buildings upon our old site. We were to receive a monetary payment from the Council as compensation.'

On the 19th I went to the Gravel Pits to see the miners, and arranged with them for clearing away from our new site. I had not much trouble with them about compensation.

'*Sept. 28th.*—I learnt to day that there are 17,050 persons on the Smythesdale and Brown's diggings without a resident minister of any kind.'

Oct. 4th.—Went to Mount Mercer, and attended a *post-mortem* examination of the late Mr. Crombie. He was shot by a Prussian labourer, over a disputed five pounds which he claimed for sinking a dam for Mr. Crombie. It was beyond doubt an unjust debt, but better it had been paid. Mrs. Crombie is left with one son and two daughters. Deeply did I sorrow for them, but that brings not back the dead to life.

We lost another excellent Christian man in the death of Mr. Thomas Guthridge. He died at the Warrenheip railway works after a painful, lingering illness, and entered into rest.

Oct. 5th.—We held our Quarterly Meeting. The deficiency on the quarter was £54 12s. 6d., which, with the balance of £139 for furnishing Mr. Millard's house, made a total deficit of £193 12s. 10d. I had to leave the meeting to inter the remains of the late Mr. John Crombie. The funeral procession was large, and the crowd most sympathetic. Mr. Draper, in a letter to me, under date Oct. 21st, only expressed the general sentiment when he said, ' Poor Crombie! I mourned over the sad tidings of his barbarous murder for days. I never heard of anything more truly appalling. Surely the wretched murderer must be an incarnate fiend.' The murderer was subsequently adjudged to be of unsound mind, and did not therefore forfeit his own life for that he had so cruelly taken.

Nov. 1st.—' The Bonwick Testimonial.' As an inevitable result of the harassing labours of our ' District Inspector of Schools,' the health of Mr. James Bonwick completely broke down, and a special fund was forthwith started, to enable this most valuable public officer to take the needed rest and chance of being again set up for his beloved work. Mr. Bonwick was an educationist by inspiration and special endowment. To permanently lose him from the district was regarded as a great public loss. In mentioning this painful case to the Rev. Mr. Draper, who had known Mr. Bonwick for many years, he replied as follows :—

' Mr. Bonwick's case is very distressing. I hope he will get something substantial from the public, and from such private friends as have it in their power. I wrote to him yesterday, and shall see him before he leaves for England. He is a genial soul. You will scarcely meet with a more cheerful and intelligent man ; one in whom the greatest confidence may be placed. I never had reason to doubt his genuine sincerity as a Christian man, and as a friend.'

In a few weeks we raised over one hundred guineas to enable our friend to visit England, which, as treasurer of the fund, I had the pleasure of handing to him.

The Annual District Meeting this year was held in Geelong. There were six of us attending from Ballarat and adjoining Circuits. We commenced on *November 8th*, under the presidency of Mr. Draper, and concluded on the 15th. By appointment, I preached the official sermon in Yarra Street Church, choosing as my text 1 Cor. xv. 58. I received the next day the warm thanks of the ministers for the service. We had had a prosperous year in every department of the work. On the 15th I had the pleasure of again seeing my aged widowed mother, at my brother's, at his house in the Crown Lands Office, and returned in time to Geelong to address a large crowd at the Institute, on the Christian duty of abstinence from the use of intoxicants. At 10.30 p.m. the Rev. W. Woodall and I left by coach for Ballarat. The night was cold, dark, and fatiguing.

Dec. 3rd.—I went to Sandhurst in the interests of the Foreign Missions. I preached twice on the Sabbath, and attended four meetings in the week. I reached home on the 11th, and heard of the particulars of two desolating fires which had occurred in the Main Road during my absence. The Rev. T. Williams had come up from the city as a deputation in aid of our South Sea Missions. He preached on the Sabbath, and spoke with much effect at the public meetings. Messrs. Daniel and Millard also assisted.

1860.

The time had now come for the erection of a hospital at Ballarat. A number of influential gentlemen met for initiating the movement, and it was agreed to send a memorial to Sir Henry Barkly, asking for a grant for the object. At the request of Mr. Lynn, solicitor, I agreed to take charge of the document, and hand it to the Governor on my arrival in Melbourne. On *January 14th* I left Melbourne for the Clyde, beyond Dandenong, to open the new church. I was the guest as usual of Mr. and Mrs. Alexander Patterson, who received me with much courteous attention. I preached on the Sabbath, and spoke at the public meeting on the 16th, Mr. Patterson presiding. We had a large attendance of kind friends from many miles round. It was the first meeting of the kind ever held in the Western Port District. Mrs. Dunbar, of the Dandenong Hotel, entertained me, free of charge, on my way back to the city.

Jan. 17*th.*—The Stationing Committee, consisting of Revs. Messrs. Manton, Butters, Buddle, Draper, Harris, Cope, and myself, met at Wesley Church. On the 18th the Connexional Committees met and got through much business. The Conference was opened on the 19th ; the Rev. John Egglestone, President, and the Rev. D. J. Draper, Secretary. On the 21st and 22nd we had scorching hot winds, much to the discomfort of all the brethren. The Conference closed on *February* 3*rd*, and I left for Ballarat. Reached home at 6.30, a.m., the next day, and found heaps of arrears awaiting my attention. The Rev. John Egglestone, the President, and the Rev. John Thomas, from the Friendly Islands, came in the evening for missionary purposes. Mr. Thomas was our guest, and his whole demeanour convinced me of the thoroughness of his character as an honoured missionary of the society.

Feb. 10*th.*—The 'foundation-stone' of the new church at Creswick was laid to-day by the Hon. A. Fraser, M.L.C., from St. Kilda. We had a fine after-meeting, and the people nobly responded to the call for contributions.

Feb. 18*th.*—At last we are able to accept a tender for the new church, Barkly Street. It may be hoped that our troubles, *re Gravel Pits*, are nearly at an end. On the 20th I arranged with Alexander Morrison, Esq., manager of the National Bank, for such advances as we should need for carrying out the work.

Feb. 25*th.*—Preached at Smythesdale to open the new church, and to inaugurate the new circuit. The Rev. Ebenezer Taylor had been appointed by the Conference to the charge of this extensive district. On our way up to the new church, on the Sabbath morning, Mr. Taylor and I came up to a tent, in front of which a miner was lustily engaged in splitting small logs of wood. Said I to Mr. Taylor, 'If you want to do any good at Smythesdale you will have to get into the way of reproving men who may be engaged on the Lord's Day morning, as is this man. Now let me see how you would deal with such a case.' 'Very well, I will try,' he replied. So, making up to the man's tent, he said, 'We have kindly called to enquire if you have any children you and your wife' (she was peeping out of the tent door) 'would like to send to the Sunday School, to be established next Sunday at the top of the hill there?' The man was taken 'all aback,' and his axe fell behind his back. Then, turning to his wife, he said, 'These men are going to start a Sunday School

up in that new church ; I think we may send our children after a
week or two.' ' It is very good of them,' she rejoined, ' and we sha'll
be glad to send some.'   So much gained, Mr. Taylor proceeded, ' I
have been appointed the minister of that church, and to-day this
gentleman ' (pointing to me) ' has come all the way from Ballarat to
open it for Divine worship.   Will you come to the service this
evening ? '   The man made a kind of half-promise that he would try
to do so.   We then proceeded on our way.   ' Brother Taylor,' said I,
' you have managed that man admirably well.   I looked on all the
time, watching you in your attack upon him.'   ' Well,' said he, ' I
have learnt this, that if you want to get at the hearts of parents you
must do it through their children.   If I had reproved him at the first,
it is likely he might have resented it, and insulted me; but now I
think that have made him my friend.'   Happy man, I thought,
to be able thus to combine ' the wisdom of the serpent with the
harmlessness of the dove '!   The services passed off well, and the next
day I held a local preachers' and quarterly meeting.   The evening
meeting was well attended, the subscription list came up better than
expected, and the Scarsdale Circuit was started on old Methodist
lines.   It was midnight before I could retire to rest.

March 30th.—Met my class for the last time.   The members
presented me with a beautifully bound Bible in token of their love.
The next day I was very ill, being completely run down with the
burden of toil and anxieties I was carrying.   My good and skilful
doctor, George Nicholson, had to be called in.   He prescribed for
me, and gave me excellent counsel in regard to my future health.

April 2nd.—Held the last Quarterly Meeting in Lydiard Street.
It was largely attended, and the finances came up well.   The brethren
said many kind things of Mrs. Bickford and myself.   Messrs. Bell,
Biddle, and Gillingham—formerly connected with the, so called,
English Reformers—bore grateful testimony to my conciliatory,
administrative conduct, whereby they had been restored to the
Church, and many blessings had come to their families.   What
they thus volunteered touched me deeply.   Mr. Millard, my
colleague (*sotto voce*) said to me, ' I wish such acknowledgments
could be circulated throughout our whole Connexion.'   The membership was 738.   The superintendency of the Ballarat Circuit now
devolved upon Mr. Millard, and the Rev. Thomas Roston was
appointed as second preacher.

The usual 'farewell meeting' was held on *April 4th*, and was attended by official representatives from every part of the Circuit. Mr. James Oddie, the senior Steward, presided, and was supported by Mr. Joseph A. Doane, the junior Steward. The Rev. J. C. Symons, who was on his way to the Amherst Circuit, took his seat on the platform. Ministers of other Churches were also present, and took part in the meeting. A beautifully embossed address, with several valuable presents, were handed to me. An unexpected surprise came upon the meeting, in the appearance upon the plat- of a coloured brother, a Mr. Edmondson, from Jamaica, who, for himself and some ten or twelve other coloured persons, presented me with an address, and Mrs. Bickford with a handsome silver cake-basket. As an old West Indian missionary, I had done my best to make them feel at home with us in Ballarat, where the cursed colour prejudice was happily unknown.

Thus ended my official connection with the Ballarat Circuit. The three years of my incumbency had been marked by much blessing from God and much extension of the work. We had built our churches and school-houses in every part of the district; our ecclesiastical organisation was complete, and our local preachers and leaders were devoted and excellent men. My journal shows that I had preached five hundred and eighty-two times, besides lectures and other ministerial work. *Laus Deo!*

SANDHURST.

April 5th.—We left Ballarat this morning for Sandhurst, *viâ* Creswick and Castlemaine. It rained heavily when we started; still we had to go, for such are the exigencies of the Methodist itinerancy. Our kind friends, Mr. J. A. Doane and Mrs. Edmondson, went with us as far as Creswick. The journey from this township to Castle- maine was rough and trying, from the unmade condition of the roads, and the swollen creeks through which we had to pass. At Yandoit the passengers had to leave the coach, whilst the driver, at full tilt, dashed into a creek, and swam the horses over. The coach itself was partially submerged, and had become quite unfit for our further occupancy. We, the passengers, had to ford the creek with the aid of fallen trees, and otherwise do the best we could for our- selves. We ultimately got round to where the coachman pulled up, rejoined the coach, and proceeded on our wretched journey. We reached Castlemaine at 5 p.m., cold, weary, and dispirited. The next day we left for Sandhurst, and reached the parsonage at 6.30 p.m. Mr. Allingham, the senior Circuit Steward, was there to receive us. I opened my commission on the 8th, by preaching at Eagle Hawk and White Hills, and had good congregations. On the 21st, Mr. Allingham and I accepted a tender of £102 for improvements to the parsonage, being indispensable to our health.

I certainly had hoped that, in coming to Sandhurst, I should have escaped many of the difficulties I had had in Ballarat in connection with the day schools. Our chief trouble, however, arose from the action of the ' Central School Board," in their appropriation of the Annual Grant. The full sum for the year 1860 was £125,000, ' with power reserved to the Board to re-distribute equitably, after October 1st, with the sanction of the Governor in Council, any sums for the expenditure of which provision may not have been made.' After deducting from the gross amount of grant £32,500 for the ' National Board,' the remainder was thus apportioned :—Denominational Board: Salaries, Normal Inspector and Secretary, £1,000 each ; six inspectors—four at £600 each, and two, at £300 each ; Church of England, £35,461 9s ; Roman Catholic, £16,258 13s. 1d. ; Presbyterian Church, £14,622 14s. 6d. ; Wesleyan Methodist, £11,068 ; other Protestants, £6,831 18s. 2d. ; Jewish, £464 1s. 1d.

The fundamental error of this scale of appropriation was that it was made not on the basis of the number of children each of the educating denominations actually provided for and instructed ; but, on the ' General Census ' of the entire population, which was taken for another purpose entirely, and upon which the ' State Aid to Religion ' Grant of £50,000 was made to those of the denominations who chose to accept it.

The ' General Census ' gave the Wesleyan body, as one of the accepting denominations, one-fifteenth part of the State Grant as its share in aid of the support of the Ministry, and other Church objects ; whereas, by adopting as the basis of distribution of the Grant for Public Education, the Official Returns of attendants at our schools, we should be entitled to one-fifth of the amount set apart for Denominational Schools. And whilst we were thus cramped in our educational work by this unjust appropriation the other bodies had a larger amount to their credit, than they had schools to take up.

WESLEY CHURCH, MELBOURNE.

In common fairness to the Roman Catholics, Presbyterians, and 'other Protestants,' it should be stated that they were no parties to the pressure the Anglican bishop, Dr. Perry, brought upon the Central Board to withdraw all support from Wesleyan Schools requiring assistance outside what the 'General Census' gave to the denomination. Hence several of our schools were in danger of immediate disendowment, to the disadvantage of the teachers, and to our discredit as an educating body. We fought the battle of right and justice with the Central Board, and, in the end, its Secretary, with the consent of the Government, informed the Rev. Mr. Draper, the 'Head' of our Denomination, that if the other 'Heads of Denominations' would consent thereto, a part of the unused portion of the vote might be applied to what was offensively called the 'Surplus' Wesleyan Schools. The only opponent to this righteous solution of the question was Dr. Perry himself. We, in Bendigo, then took the matter into our hands, by placing three of our schools under the wing of the Rev. Dr. Nish, the Presbyterian clergyman, and two under the Rev. W. R. Fletcher, M.A., the Congregational minister. Thus we saved five schools to the district.

The annoyance and vexation caused to us by the Anglican bishop, naturally produced in our minds a set determination to upset, at the earliest possible moment, the then Dual system of public education. And I distinctly remember Mr. Draper remarking, with considerable emphasis, that the only effectual remedy for removing the unfairness of the present administration of the parliamentary grant, was the abolition of the two Boards of Management, by the substitution of a thoroughly National System, free from all ecclesiastical interference, and to be under the sole direction of a Minister of Education directly responsible to Parliament.

The River Murray District, lying to the north of Bendigo, was as yet untouched by effective evangelistic labours. Accordingly, on the morning of *May 25th*, I left by coach for Echuca, and arrived at my destination at 5.30 p.m. Messrs. Watson and Powell kindly welcomed me, and arranged for my stay at Mrs. Redmond's hotel. The next day we secured the Court House for the Sabbath services. The first Methodist sermon preached at Echuca was from 1 Tim. i. 15, and the second was from Rev. vii. 14. I made the acquaintance of Mr. and Mrs. Hopwood, Mr. and Mrs. Sabine, Mr. Veale, Mr. Tomline, and some others. On the 28th, I returned to Sandhurst and had the honour of finding Mr. and Mrs. Draper as guests at our house. The Sandhurst Church Anniversary was held at this time, and Mr. Draper greatly helped us.

June 9th.—Received this morning a letter from the Chief Secretary. ' No more schools for us this year.' Surely ' the triumphing of the wicked shall be short.'

June 23rd.—Mr. Dowling drove me to Tarnagulla. On the 24th I preached twice, and on the 25th I held the Quarterly Meeting at Inglewood. There are in the Circuit 117 members. At the public meeting in the evening we raised £48. On the 26th we held the Church Anniversary at Tarnagulla, when 350 persons sat down to tea. The Revs. Beer, Adams, Bunn, and I, spoke. Mr. Pybus also helped us with a fine speech. On the 27th I returned to Sandhurst.

An important meeting was held at Sandhurst by the local clergy, to consider the advisability of commencing a series of religious services in the ' Lyceum,' for the special benefit of the non-churchgoing portion of the people. We also agreed to call upon the merchants and shopkeepers to come into an arrangement for shortening the hours of business. Messrs. Hart, Fletcher, and I, made the appeal. On the 23rd, I preached in the ' Lyceum ' to a crowded audience, on Ezek. xxxiii. 11.

Sept. 15th.—I again left for Echuca, and reached Runnymede at 11.30 a.m. Here I was disappointed in not finding a coach to take me on. I therefore arranged with Mrs. Stephenson for holding a religious service in the hotel parlour in the evening. I spent the afternoon in visiting all the families in the neighbourhood, and invited them to the service. I preached to twenty-five adults. On the 16th I preached twice at Echuca and once at Moama, on the N. S. W. side of the Murray. On the 22nd, I was again at Sandhurst.

Sept. 23rd.—I had again to leave for Inglewood. Preached twice on the Sabbath, and addressed the Sunday School at 3 p.m. On Monday I held the Quarterly Meeting, and found the Circuit free of debt. We passed, after the usual examinations, the brethren Collins, Davies, Jenkins, and Tucker as full local preachers. Messrs. Jenkins and Davies will likely enter the Ministry after a while. Mr. Bunn was the young minister in charge.

October 1st.—We held the Sandhurst Quarterly Meeting, and Mr. Hart and I were unanimously invited to remain a second year.

Nov. 13*th.*—The District Meeting was commenced in Melbourne. We were in session eight days, and I returned to Sandhurst on the 24th.

The time had now come for us to give an ecclesiastical form to our work at Echuca. I accordingly went up again on *December 8th.* I preached and gave the Sacrament and married two couples. I selected as our first trustees, Messrs. Henry Hopwood, Oliver Veale, George James Walker, and George Charles Watson. These with myself made the number the Government required before granting sites for churches.

Dec. 15*th.*—I once more visited the Tarnagulla and Inglewood Circuit. I preached on the Sabbath, held the Quarterly Meeting next day, and lectured on the West Indies in the evening in aid of the Circuit funds. The business was interrupted in the afternoon by two miners finding a corpse in an abandoned shaft between the church and the Main Street. It was so decomposed that identification was impossible. The case was duly reported to the police.

1861.

The usual solemn service was held last night. My first Journal entry is:—

'Praise God for the commencement of a new year. May it be a renewal of mercy to my spirit, and may I be more useful than hitherto in saving souls and in promoting the glory of God!'

The Conference of this year, beginning on *January 17th*, was held in Sydney; the Rev. S. Rabone, President, and the Rev. T. Buddle, Secretary. We had the pleasure and advantage of the Rev. Frederick Jobson, D.D., who had come to us on matters relating to the Foreign Missions, and the claims of those of the Australian ministers who are still members of the English Annuitant Society. Dr. Jobson proved himself to be an apt *diplomat* in the management of these questions; they were soon satisfactorily arranged. Dr. Jobson's official sermon before the Conference was a masterly exposition of the doctrine of our Lord's Priesthood, and was delivered with much effect. It was a beautiful specimen of Methodist preaching in her Augustan age in the Mother Country. The York Street congregation hung upon the preacher's lips for the full hour, during the delivery of this never-to-be forgotten sermon.

By this Conference, on the motion of the Rev. W. L. Binks, I was appointed as Superintendent of the Melbourne Fourth Circuit, of which St. Kilda was the head. My former colleague, the Rev. C. Lane, was appointed as second preacher. I had not the least idea of so early a removal from Bendigo; but when the change was proposed, I accepted it, on account of the heavy financial cares and harassing journeys I had had throughout the year. I could not have borne the strain much longer without permanent injury to my health.

Feb. 12th.—I sent the first of a series of papers to the Rev. J. S. Waugh, Editor of the *Wesleyan Chronicle*, entitled 'Missionary Recollections,' in the hope such reminiscences might be useful to the young men of Methodism, in fanning in their souls a holy flame of love to our own South Sea Missions.

March 9th.—I went by coach to Castlemaine, to help the Rev. John Harcourt in holding his Foreign Missionary anniversary meetings. We had a vile set of drunkards as fellow-passengers, one of whom shall be nameless because of her sex. Reached Mrs. Harcourt's at a late hour. Preached on the Sabbath; attended two public meetings, and returned to Sandhurst on the evening of the 13th, quite well though much fatigued.

April 1st.—I held the last Quarterly Meeting for this Circuit. The Rev. R. Hart, my good and faithful colleague, and twenty-four brethren were present. The income paid all demands for the quarter, but there was still the standing deficiency of £160. Important resolutions were passed for clearing off the debt occasioned by the additions and repairs to the parsonage, and for preventing future circuit debts. The Rev. George Daniel had been appointed as my successor, and Mr. Hart as second minister. On the 9th, we left for our new Circuit.*

After visiting Ballarat, Geelong, and Melbourne, we reached

---

* The departure of the Rev. J. Bickford, from Sandhurst, is thus referred to in the *Bendigo Advertiser* :—" The crowd that gathered at the evening Sabbath service was attracted by the farewell sermon of the reverend gentleman, who is leaving Sandhurst for St. Kilda. At the public meeting held next day, a resolution, expressive of the deepest regret at the removal of the Rev. J. Bickford from Sandhurst, and breathing earnest wishes for the future welfare of himself and his lady, was unanimously carried. The Revs. Butler, Smith, Nish, Fletcher, and Messrs. Fizelle, Hooper, Coombs, and Marrarck, addressed the meeting. A few parting words from the Rev. J. Bickford, full of deep emotion, followed, when the meeting was closed with singing and prayer."

St. Kilda on the 13th, and received a warm welcome from the Hon. A. Fraser, M.L.C., Mr. John Whitney, Mr. T. J. Crouch, and other officials and friends. In the evening, my mind was much exercised about this new sphere of work, and my feelings were much excited as to the success or otherwise of this appointment, I now found that the time had come for me to give effect to the Rev. Thomas Binney's famous maxim, which he gave us in his great sermon in Ballarat some few years ago, viz. : 'To do anything worth while in religious and philanthropic works, a man must first believe in his God, and then in himself.'

St. Kilda.

I did not retire to rest until 11 p.m., by which time my mind was made up as to three courses of action : (1) I resolved to be a pastor in a more persistent manner than I yet had been ; but, especially, in relation to the artisan classes and poor families ; (2) that I would regard as sacred to God a sufficient proportion of my time for preparing for the pulpit, so as to have new and stimulating truths ; thereby keeping in the congregations an expectation of instruction and interest ; and (3) that I would devote as much time as possible to the Sabbath schools, and to such other means of improvement for the young men and women, as might help them in the acquirement of studious habits and intellectual strength. I felt convinced that each of these might be secured by a rigid economy of my time, and with the blessing of God. I was aware that, being now in close proximity to Melbourne, I would likely have to take my share of committee work for the general benefit of the Connexion ; nevertheless, I resolved thoroughly to work the Circuit, and not to permit such a diversion for any other purpose as would interfere with my success in winning souls.

April 14th.—I began my ministry by preaching at St. Kilda and Prahran, on 1 Thess. iii. 1. It was an appeal to the congregations for their sympathy and help. The routine work of this compact Circuit came upon me as an every-day duty. I commenced on the 15th, and preserved the even round until the 22nd, when Mrs. Bickford and I went to Richmond to see our afflicted friend, Mr. Samuel Merrick, who was dying. Mrs. Merrick was heart-broken. One short year of beautiful conjugal life was to be suddenly closed. We sorrowed deeply for her.

April 28th.—I opened our new church at Keysborough, and next day I assisted at the public meeting. It was largely attended. We raised, in all, £130. I simply went to fulfil an old promise.

The question of the Day Schools seemed to baffle all settlement. I accordingly wrote an article, headed ' Public Education,' for the *Wesleyan Chronicle* on the subject. I quote one portion of it :—

' The present time is opportune for the extinction of the two rival systems of education, and for the introduction of a general system in their stead. We have no hesitation in saying, that it is our solemn conviction—in view of the jealousies which have existed now for several years between the two Boards : the envious and checkmating spirit which has, in numberless instances, marked the conduct of one denomination towards another ; the use which has been made of school-grants to build churches, and work out thereby ecclesiastical objects : and the needless expenditure of public money in supporting two executives, and two (sometimes even more than two) schools in localities where one would be sufficient—that the present rival systems should close with the present year.'

God has put it into the heart of a young Methodist Christian, Mr. John Watson, to do something for the soldiers at our Barracks, near Prince's Bridge. He enlisted me in the work, and on the evening of *May 4th,* he and I walked over to see those of the men who were ill. We read and prayed with them, and arranged for holding a Bible class there on Fridays at 8 p.m. Serjeant-Major Hurworth would be our mainstay in these services.

May 10th.—At the request of the Rev. D. J. Draper, I accepted the office of Missionary Secretary for the Victoria District.

June 19th.—I forwarded to the editor of the *Wesleyan Chronicle,* an article on the dispute which had arisen at Castlemaine and Sandhurst, in connection with the interment of the dead by their own ministers in the public cemeteries. The contention had thriven so much in intensity, and to such an extent, that Bishop Perry had appealed even to Sir H. Barkly for legislative interference. He informed the Governor that ' several of the clergy,' including the ' Archdeacon of Castlemaine ' had complained of ' persons ' violating the ' law of the Church of England, not belonging to her communion. And what was all this stir about ? That certain mourning relatives had seen fit to choose certain unoccupied portions in the public cemeteries in which to inter their dead, and to call in any minister they chose to officiate at such interments. In this free country, in which there was not, and would never be, a State Church, it was a great oversight for Dr. Perry to ask that the Attorney General should get the Act so amended, as to make it a 'penal offence, punishable in a summary manner by the Magistrates,' in the event of such interments being made. The foolish stir, as might be expected, ended in smoke.

June 26th.—I visited the Female Refuge, at Prahran, and conducted a service with the inmates. Mrs. Perry (the bishop's wife) was present.

July 1st.—I attended the annual meeting of the Victoria Anti-Liquor League. The Hon. R. Heales, Premier, presided; Dean Macartney, the two Fletchers (father and son), Dubourg Kean, and Ramsay spoke. It was a glorious meeting. My first Quarterly Meeting was held to-day; the Circuit is out of debt.

July 8th.—A drunken mother, in St. Kilda, this day cut her child's throat. Is not drink a devil?

Aug. 3rd.—Mr. Draper to-day, at my request, made an application to the Government for a grant of land at Elsternwick for church purposes.

Aug. 25th.—I preached twice at Ballarat, and next day attended a public meeting in aid of the new church at Soldiers' Hill. We raised £147.

Nov. 12th.—The District Meeting was begun to-day at Brunswick Street, Fitzroy. The Rev. D. J. Draper in the chair. We had a long discussion on the marriage question, and we agreed to be uniform in the administration of the ceremony. We spent much time in preparing a station sheet for the forthcoming Conference. The official sermon was preached by the Rev. Thomas Williams. It was an admirable discourse. The meeting thanked me for my services as Missionary Secretary and re-appointed me to the office. We closed on the 22nd.

Nov. 24th.—John King, the only survivor of the Burke and Wills party, came to St. Kilda to-night. He was a mere shadow, and his whole nervous system was unhinged. On *December 5th*, I accompanied Mr. King to Melbourne, and introduced him to Sir William Stawell, the Chief Justice, who received from him Mr. Burke's note book. His last record was, 'King has acted nobly.' Sir William appeared to be deeply affected. He made many enquiries of King, to whose replies he paid the closest attention. I then went with King to the Parliament House, and left him there for examination before the Committee of Enquiry. On the 6th I went to the house of Henry Jennings Esq., to meet several ladies and gentlemen who were favourable to the establishment of a Moravian Mission at Gipps Land.

Dec. 18*th.*—I attended the funeral of the late Rev. William Fletcher. The Rev. R. Connebee gave the address in the church. ' A good man and a just ' has gone to his reward, and the church-life of St. Kilda is all the poorer for his removal. On the 19th, Mr. Draper and I waited upon Sir H. Barkly, to ask him to pre-side at our Missionary Anniversary. He readily agreed to comply with our request. On the 21st, I finished the series of ' Missionary Recollections,' nine in number, and sent it for publication in the *Wesleyan Chronicle.*

Dec. 31*st.*—I copy now a Journal jotting :—

' This year has been full of mercy and goodness from the Lord. The future I leave with Thee ! May the Lord undertake for me ; guide and protect me and mine. Also, may the Holy Ghost rest upon the ordinances of His house, making them wells of salvation to the souls of the people ! '

1862.

Jan. 6*th.*—The first of the United Prayer Meetings was held in our church this evening. The Rev. Mr. Seddon (Anglican) gave the address, the Revs. Moir, Poore, and I, offered prayer. These services are bound to be a blessing.

Feb. 10*th.*—I wrote another article on ' Public Education ' for the *Chronicle.* The object was, in part, to keep this still unsettled question before the friends of education and the Victorian Parliament. In the second paragraph of the article I say :—

' The present Systems stand condemned for their extravagance, sectarianism, and rivalry. Not only have we two Boards, officered at great expense, but, in almost every part of the country, schools under both are set up in opposition to each other, and, in some instances, schools under the same Board are established in the same locality, sometimes even on opposite sides of the same street ; as, in the Bendigo District, greatly to the surprise of Her Majesty's liege subjects, to the deep injury of the teachers, who are thereby reduced to a mere pittance for support, and to the creation of hatred and jealousy in the children's minds of the one as against the other school. "See how these children hate one another," is the remark of the passer-by. "Beautiful training this," they say, "of the rising generation of the Colony." Alas ! Alas ! '

Feb. 21*st.*—John King asked me to go with him to Castlemaine, where he was to be entertained at a public banquet. It was largely attended. I spoke of Burke's last experiences as told me by King, which touched the guests deeply. In reply to the address which was presented to King, he modestly said 'he had nothing to boast of, for he had simply done his duty.' Noble fellow! A true man was he!

The Conference this year was held in Adelaide. It was begun on January 26th; Rev. James Watkin, President, and the Rev. J. B. Waterhouse, Secretary. It seems to have been a happy and successful Conference. There are two paragraphs in the Address which are worth transcribing, as follows:—

' We think no body of men more happy than ourselves. Our work is honourable; we regard our position, as Wesleyan ministers, as being the most honourable in which God could place us. We are happy in that success with which, year to year, He has crowned our labours, and in beholding the many evidences we have of your piety, your zeal, your liberality, your affectionate esteem of us, your order and stability, and your growing intelligence.' . . . 'On the subject of dress we exhort you to be plain. Let not the poor dress themselves in costly apparel, and let not the rich adorn themselves in such a manner as to excite the envy of poorer members. Let your dress be such as shall not attract attention. Do not strive to be first in following the changing and often foolish fashions of the day. Be yourselves patterns to others, and let the world imitate the church rather than the church the world. How can you indulge in costly apparel, while so many about you are destitute and afflicted? Let your dress be such as shall not unfit you for visiting the homes of the poor and the bedside of the dying.'

This is very apostolic and seasonable advice.

March 14th.—Amongst all the other duties I have managed, by changing the weekly Bible class service to a Tuesday evening, to get the Friday evening for a theological class. I began in my study with nine young men, all members of the church. I hope this weekly exercise will be good for the students, and be of use to me also. I much need a systematic acquaintance with our standard theology, so as to be upsides with the scepticism of the age.

March 15th—Mr. John Whitney informed me that Mr. Walter Powell, now in London, has engaged to give £500 towards the reduction of the debt on the St. Kilda Church, on condition that we raise £500 ourselves. We gratefully accept the condition.

May 9th.—I finished the first of a series of papers on the ' Wesley Family' for the *Chronicle.* The subject was,—the Rev. Bartholomew Wesley, the great-grandfather of John Wesley. He was a very fine man; full of wit and wisdom.

12

May 20th.—I called on Sir Henry Barkly, and informed him that John King, the explorer, wished to have granted to him six hundred and forty acres of land on the Flinders River.

I then went to see the Hon. John O'Shanassy, Premier, on the Education question. He was very courteous and fair with me on this and two or three matters on which I consulted him. On the 22nd I wrote another article on 'Public Education' for the *Chronicle*. The question had now become crucial, and must be settled. Two Bills were brought before the House of Assembly, one by Mr. O'Shanassy, whose principle was payment by results; the other by Mr. Heales, which was based on payment upon numbers. The former was rejected, and the latter, entitled 'The Common Schools' Bill,' received the Royal Assent in due course. So that from the date of the new law one general system of education will be established throughout the colony. We had further gratification by the publication of the 'Census Returns' of 1861, which gave us 46 per cent. increase on the previous census, and we are now one-ninth of the entire population.

There was not much room for church extension in the St. Kilda Circuit. Still, we had one promising outlet in the direction of Glen Iris, lying between Gardiner's Creek and Oakleigh. By previous arrangement I went over on *September 9th*, and held a religious service. I visited, previous to the service, Mrs. Kent, Mr. and Mrs. Bainbrige, Mr. and Mrs. Robinson, Mr. and Mrs. Glanshot, Mr. and Mrs. Mann, and thereby secured a nice congregation. I conversed with the friends upon the subject of having forthwith Sabbath services, and the erection of a church for the neighbourhood. This was the beginning of the work at Glen Iris.

The fruits of our efforts for the young men were now beginning to be shown. At the local preachers' meeting, held at Prahran, on the 24th November, young Thomas Grove, who, having preached an excellent trial sermon, was examined in the usual manner and passed. Other young brethren were also taken by the hand, viz., Brothers R. M. Hunter, John Moorhead, J. Cooper, and Andrew, who were received as exhorters on trial. We were having prosperity on every hand. The membership had risen to 227, with 12 on trial. Balance in hands of stewards, £42. By an unanimous vote, I was invited to remain a third year as Superintendent of the Circuit.

The District Meeting of this year was marked by important

discussions. It commenced on the 11th of September, and ended its sessions on the 22nd. The subject of our financial arrangements occupied much time, and several resolutions were adopted. As Secretary of the Educational Committee, I had to present a full report of the new legislation which had become law, the number of schools, and their general condition. The report was adopted. On the motion of the Rev. W. L. Binks, we agreed to a scheme of the division of the district, which had become so unwieldy, and the interests of the country circuits so many and diversified, that nothing less than the creation of three districts would meet the requirements of our so rapidly extending work.

1863.

The usual 'Watch Night' and 'Renewal of Covenant' services were held in St. Kilda Church, and I think we had a good beginning of the year. On New Year's Day, Mr. Smith called and presented to me an alphabet which he had constructed of the ancient Assyrian (the Cuneiform), and their equivalents in the Greek, English, etc. This self-taught man seems a linguistic marvel. If he were in England instead of Australia, he would have a chance of turning his talents to good account.

Jan. 9th.—'I attended a meeting of Superintendents in Melbourne for the examination of Brother Martyn Dyson, who offers for the missions. We agreed to recommend him to the Conference as a suitable candidate for our itinerant work.

The Conference of this year was held in Hobart Town, Tasmania. It began on January 20th and closed on February 2nd; the Rev. T. Buddle, President, and the Rev. J. Bickford, Secretary. The official representatives from Victoria were Messrs. Draper, Butters, Bickford, and Daniel. In consequence of severe indisposition, the Rev. Mr. Butters asked for permission to return to England, which was granted. It marked the high estimation in which this honoured servant was held by his brethren, that he was cordially appointed as the Representative of the Australasian Church in the British Conference. The 'Address' was prepared by the Rev. Father Watkin, from which I copy a paragraph of much practical value :—

'The Class Meeting is one of the greatest helps and incentives to personal religion. We have scriptural authority for the practice. It is one of the bulwarks of Methodism. It has been an unspeakable blessing to multitudes.

All who have reaped benefit there cannot discontinue the practice without loss . . . You perhaps think it a privilege to be accounted a Wesleyan Methodist. Bear in mind that none are members with us who do not meet in Class. It is not likely that so prudential, so salutary, a regulation will ever be altered.'

During our stay in Hobart Town, Mrs. Bickford and I were the guests of Mr. and Mrs. Dickenson, at Sandy Point. They were to us a generous host and hostess. We arrived again at Melbourne on *February* 6th. The Rev. C. Lane, Messrs. Whitney, H. C. Fraser, T. J. Crouch, J. Oldham, and J. Watson, were at the Wharf to receive us. In the evening the young men, W. Jennings, R. M. Hunter, Read, and Thomas, called to welcome us. Mr. President Buddle came with us to be our guest until he should leave for New Zealand. On the 12th, Mr. Butters and his family sailed in the ship *Essex* for London. All our ministers in and about the city went down to Sandridge Pier to see them off. We had worship in the saloon, and commended our dear friends to the loving care of the Heavenly Father. It is not likely that we shall see Mr. Butters again in the work in Victoria : but he has rendered to the Church much valuable and effective service in the past. His record and reward are on all.

The easy transit of Anglo-East Indians to Australia, by means of the royal mail steamships, for recreation, sightseeing, or improvement of health, is quite a temptation to many a would-be traveller. Our missionary brethren in India take advantage of the mail arrangements, for visiting us even when on their way to England. One more of these honoured men, the Rev. E. Jenkyns, M.A., favoured us in this manner. On the 20th I called upon him at Windsor, and spent an agreeable hour with him. I was impressed with his intellectuality and profound acquaintance with the ancient superstitions of India. The East Indian mission-field is no doubt a favourable sphere for men of genius. Mr. Jenkyns, during his stay with us, may be of great benefit to the ministers and congregations as *quasi*-missionary in their training and sympathies.

April 25th.—I travelled in company with five members of parliament to Ballarat. There was discussion, easy chat, and repartee, beyond the ordinary range of railway travellers. My good friend, Mr. Oddie, was at the station to receive me. Preached at Ballarat East (Barkly Street) to good congregations. At the public meeting on Monday we raised £100.

May 19*th.*—A grand commemoration day on the marriage of the
Prince of Wales with the Princess Alexandra. There were about
a thousand children of St. Kilda assembled at noon to partake of a
sumptuous treat. In the evening we went into Melbourne to see
the illuminations. The whole city was etherealised : gas, candles,
and designs, everywhere to be seen, which must have cost thousands
of pounds. Such a display of enthusiastic loyalty, outside England,
I believe was never before seen. It is highly creditable to our
democratic community. But, then, we have no political grievances !
How, then, could we be disloyal?

June 23*rd.*—As I was the secretary of the Wesley Grammar
School Committee, I had, with other secretaryships, much clerical
work to do. On the occasion of my going into Melbourne, to
attend an important meeting of the committee for the first time, I
heard the Rev. William Taylor, from California, preach in Wesley
Church. I was much interested in the service, and felt a strong
hope that his visit to Australia would be a means of reviving and
extending the kingdom of Christ. His style of preaching, and
methods of working, are in forceful contrast to our prosaic and quieter
style of working. But there is much attraction in his personality
and singing, and the crowds are bound to hear him. I shall watch
with intense solicitude the effects of the labours of this honoured
evangelist's ministry.

July 13*th.*—Mr. Taylor opened fire at St. Kilda. There was
much enthusiasm connected with his mission to our Circuit. On the
Sabbath, and during the week, the congregations were large. There
were several, who for years had been regular hearers, and to all
appearance had got little if any good, who rose, in response to his
appeals, and declared themselves to be on the Lord's side. Many
persons, day after day, called at the parsonage to speak of their
spiritual troubles. There was truly a great awakening amongst the
people.

The time had now come for the colony to lose the invaluable
services of Sir. H. Barkly as our Governor. When laying the
foundation stone of the new church at Emerald Hill, a few weeks
ago, I asked His Excellency if I might have the honour of presenting
to Lady Barkly a Conference picture of ministers belonging to the
Australian Church, which Mrs. Bickford had set up in an elegant
leather-work frame. He was pleased to signify that her ladyship

would much value such a *souvenir* of our esteem. Accordingly, on *September 9th*, I drove up to Toorak, and presented the picture to Lady Barkly. She received it most courteously, and expressed her admiration of the handsome frame and its Gothic style of ornament. The next day, the Rev. D. J. Draper and the city and suburban ministers waited upon Sir Henry, with an address on the subject of his departure from the colony. He seemed much to feel the attitude of esteem and affection which our presence and address evinced for himself and Lady Barkly. He shook hands with us all. He had been a good Governor for Victoria.

'The King never dies!' Sir Charles Darling, formerly Governor in the West Indies, was appointed by the Crown as successor to Sir Henry Barkly. On September 16th, I went to Melbourne to attend the *levée*. There were, it is said, nine hundred gentlemen present. Such a demonstration of loyalty must have been very gratifying to the new Governor.

Oct. 2nd.—Attendance at class is the sure unerring test of the success, or otherwise, of such a series of revival services, especially such as those of the Rev. William (now Bishop) Taylor at St. Kilda. At the Quarterly Meeting we found that our membership had increased to 273, with 112 on trial. The next day, at the ministers' monthly meeting, it was reported that in the circuits in which Mr. Taylor had been preaching there were 797 meeting on trial. We all felt that the Great Head of the Church had wonderfully blessed the special services which had been held.

We had not yet come into touch with Gipps Land, an extensive country lying to the east of the Western Port District, and stretching far away even to Cape Howe. We had many Methodist families at Port Albert, Tarraville, Sale, and Stratford, but somehow we had not gone as yet to look after these 'sheep in the wilderness.' At length, at Mr. Draper's earnest request, I undertook this mission of inspection.

Oct. 21st.—I left Melbourne for Port Albert by the steamer *Keera*, and arrived next day at noon; Messrs. Parr and Wood were at the wharf to welcome me. I became the guest of Mrs. Parr, who showed me much kindness. The next day Mr. Parr drove me to Tarraville, that I might call upon the people, explain to them the object of my visit, and inform them of my intention of preaching in the township on the Sabbath. I began at the first house on the right of the roadside. A knock at the door soon brought the mistress to me. Said I: 'I am a Wesleyan minister, just come from Melbourne to have a look at the people settled here, with the view of ascertaining if the Methodist Church has anything to do in the way of providing religious ordinances for the people of this district.' She was a plain country-woman, brusque and self-possessed in manner, with a somewhat inviting facial expression. 'Are you really a Methodist preacher?' she enquired. 'Yes,' I replied, 'there can be no doubt about that,' at the same time I handed to her my card. 'Well, I never,' she ejaculated, 'it was only this morning that I was saying to my man' [husband], 'I wish we had such a parson as Mr. Butters to preach to us here.' 'Why,' said I, 'do you know Mr. Butters?—he is one of my brother ministers, and we are very great friends.' 'To be sure I do,' she rejoined; 'didn't he use to preach to us at Campbell Town, on the other side? [Van Diemen's Land.] Bless the dear gentleman, I wish we had him.' 'Where is your husband? can't you call him? I want to speak to him also.' Off she went to the vineyard at the back of the house, and I heard her lustily shouting for her 'man.' We had an interesting conversation and prayer. 'Will you have a drink of wine?' enquired the gladdened matron. 'No, thank you,' I replied, 'I never drink wine.' She and her husband looked surprised, but I think that in their heart of hearts they were pleased.

I then called at the next house—the next—and the next, and so on, until I had seen the whole of the people. I remember the following names: Mr. and Mrs. Disher, Mr. and Mrs. T. Frost, Mr. Wood and Mrs. Howden, senior. I found, much to my surprise, at Tarraville, a small colony of Tasmanians, who had worshipped with us at Campbell Town and Ross in that colony. On the next day (Saturday) I called on Mrs. Black and several other families, and informed them of the arrangements for the Sabbath services. I accidentally met the Rev. Mr. Stretch (Anglican), who was coldly polite in his manner and remarks. I could not think he was pleased at my advent into the district.

As this was purely an official visit, I reported, in substance, to the Rev. D. J. Draper, after my return to St. Kilda, as follows:—

'On Sabbath, *October 25th*, I preached at Tarraville, at 11 a.m., in the large room at the Manse, to a most attentive audience; in the afternoon I addressed the Sunday School, and in the evening I preached at Port Albert, in the Presbyterian Church, to a large congregation.

'On *October 26th*, Mr. Hobbs kindly drove me to Tarraville, when Mr. Disher, a generous Presbyterian friend, rode with me some distance to see me on my way to Sale, distant fifty miles from the port. Two young men, bullock drivers, soon overtook me, and finding that they were on their way home several miles onward, I got into conversation with them, with a view to their directing me towards Sale. The road, if such it may be called, was the most lonely, uninteresting, and wretched I ever saw. I reached Hill-top—a place separated from Sale by a frightful morass—about 5 p.m. I abandoned all hope of getting to the end of my journey that evening, and turned aside to a squattage about two miles distant from Hill-top. I was most warmly received by Mrs. Campbell, and soon found myself quite at home. Mr. John Campbell soon came and expressed himself pleased at seeing me. There was a young (Hobart) lady, the governess of the children, from whom I had learnt that she had been connected with Melville Street Sunday School, and was still retaining the fear and love of God. I spent with this hospitable, godly family, a quiet and profitable evening. Some of the men came in for family worship, when I read one of the Psalms, gave a short exposition, and offered prayer.

'The next morning I left Glencoe Station, when Mr. Campbell kindly piloted me across the inland sea of water-mud and morass, and never left me until he saw me safely in Sale. The first gentleman I saw was the Venerable Archdeacon Stretch, who spoke to me words of kindness and respect. He is a man of a different spirit from his brother at Port Albert; so I would judge. I soon found the house of Mr. and Mrs. Nehemiah Guthridge, from whom I received a truly Hibernian welcome. In the afternoon Mr. Guthridge and I called upon a Mr. George Ross, an Inverness Methodist, and a Mr. Stead, the son of the Rev. Thomas Stead, then stationed in Liverpool. We visited some other friends as well. In the evening I preached in the Mechanics' Hall to about one hundred people. The singing was led by Mr. William Little, who had come in from Stratford, a distance of twelve miles, to see me and to attend the service. The Guthridge and Little families were for many years connected with Wesley Church, and were amongst our most generous friends and sincere supporters. After the public service, I desired all who felt an interest in my errand to stay and hear what I had to say in explanation of it. About thirty stayed, who, after hearing my statements, expressed an earnest wish to have a Wesleyan minister forthwith appointed to reside amongst them.

'Having collected all the information I needed relative to the population in and about Sale, I left on the morning of the 28th, and proceeded on horseback in company with a young Irishman, of the name of Michael Dillon, and reached Mr. Parr's in the evening. I had been in the saddle some twelve hours, and was much fatigued with the journey.

'On the 29th, I rode out to Yarram Yarram, an agricultural district, about nine miles from Port Albert, and spent several hours in visiting. I called upon the Devonshires, Mr. and Mrs. Gray, Rendall, Huntingdon, Collis, Fisher, Carpenter, Barlow, Ostler, and spoke to the children in the day school. Five of these families were Wesleyans; the others were Independents or Baptists. Mrs. Devonshire pressed me to go across the paddocks to see a young married woman, who the day before had been confined of twins. The hut, in which she and her husband lived, was perhaps ten feet by six, and was destitute of every comfort. A portion of the hut was portioned off as her room. I found her with her infants clinging to her breasts, as if they were sucking her life away to save their own. The husband was outside trying to split up a tree for sale as firewood. He had been unfortunate up the country, and had taken refuge in this bit of forest land. His wife had come from a comfortable home; having been born on a farm a few miles outside St. Austell, in Cornwall, I prayed with this poor creature, gave her my card at her request, with the date of my visit written thereon, and a few shillings to help her in her present distress. The sorrowfulness of that scene haunted me for many weeks; nay, for some months.

· In the evening of this to-be-remembered day I preached in the Presbyterian Church at Port Albert, to a large and highly respectable congregation. I met the leading Wesleyan friends after the service : fully explained the object of my visit, after which they signified with one consent their strong desire for the ordinances of their own church, and pressed upon me to use every possible exertion to secure for them and the neighbourhood the services of a Wesleyan minister.'

After all the fatigue and exposure in my journeyings in Gipps Land, the most trying and dangerous part was the return voyage to Melbourne. I had written to Mrs. Bickford that I expected to be at St. Kilda about 4 p.m., on the 31st, in time for the Sabbath services the next day. I went on board the *Keera* at 10 p.m., on the 30th, and we steamed away from Port Albert, with calm weather, and full of hope for a speedy voyage. But during the night we were met with a strong head-wind, which soon increased to a gale. To save our little struggling steamer, ourselves, and a valuable cargo, from destruction, Captain Lapthorne put in at Western Port Bay, and took shelter under the lee of Rabbit Island. We were detained by the heavy weather in that position until the following Tuesday morning. During all this time we could have no communication with Melbourne, and the worst fears were felt for our safety. In our humble home at St. Kilda there were much distress and many tears ; and when at length I turned up on Tuesday evening, I met Mrs. Bickford so overcome as to be scarcely able to speak. At last she said, 'I had given up all hope of ever seeing you again.' I could see at a glance, by the disturbance of her usual placid countenance, how much agony of suspense she had suffered.

Nov. 10*th.*—The District Meeting was commenced to-day: the Rev. D. J. Draper, Chairman; Rev. John Harcourt, Secretary. I reported my visit to Gipps Land, and obtained a grant of £150 to assist in establishing one minister at Port Albert, and another at Sale. Mr. Thomas Grove was unanimously recommended by the District Meeting as a candidate for our ministry. Rev. E Jenkins, M.A., preached an able sermon in Wesley Church on the words, ' A servant of God.' The District Meeting accepted a series of resolutions which I submitted, on the appointment of a Committee of Privileges and the establishment of a Theological Institution. My official report on the day schools was well received. On the 17th, the sessions closed in the usual manner. In the afternoon of the same day, Sir Charles and Lady Darling opened the Bazaar for the new church at Prahran. They were both complacent and liberal. Sir Charles had intimately known the Rev. Jonathan Edmondson in Jamaica, and took much pleasure in speaking of him as ' My friend Edmondson.' On the 19th, Sir Charles took the chair at Wesley Church, when Dr. Jenkins gave his noble lecture on India.

Nov. 30th.—Yesterday I preached in Ballarat in aid of our foreign missions. This evening, in the Lydiard Street Church, the Rev. Samuel Waterhouse gave a most effective speech on Fiji. I never heard a better address on that interesting mission. The Rev. J. S. Waugh the Superintendent of the Circuit, called an aggregate meeting of the local committees and day school teachers, that we might consult together on the still perplexing subject of Public Education. As the secretary of the general committee, I had much information to give the assembled brethren. On the motion of Mr. (now Dr.) Waugh, I was heartily thanked for my address. In the evening we had a fine missionary meeting at Barkly street, when Mr. Waterhouse and I were again the speakers.

Dec. 24th.—One of the dearest old men I have met with was Mr. Parr, of South Yarra. He was formerly a leading Methodist in Manchester. Mr. Parr was a great help to the Prahran Church, and he was much loved both by ministers and people. His latest affliction was one of great acuteness. I went this day to administer the Lord's Supper to my dear friend. He was much blessed in his soul. He said that he felt the presence of Christ to be with him; but that his distressing bodily weakness was as much as he could bear. He had no fear of death, and was assured that all would be well. On the 28th, we concluded the St. Kilda Church Anniversary. The result, in cash and promises, was £379 1s. 2d.

At the Watch Night Service the Rev. C. Moir, M.A. (Presbyterian), gave us a good and faithful exposition of God's Word. I concluded the service with an address and the accustomed solemnities. It was a profitable time. Praised be God for the mercies of another year !

1864.

As a sample of nearly every day's engagements at St. Kilda, I copy from my Diary for that day, *January 1st*, the exact record :—

'Read Genesis i.; 2 Chronicles i.; and St. Matthew i. Received letters from Revs. J. B. Waterhouse and J. Watsford, S.A. The latter paid me £7 16s. for "Minutes of Conference." Mr. Matthew Burnett called and conversed with me for two hours. Wrote upon Joshua xxiv. 15. Two ladies and seven children called, and threw us into all sorts of confusion before they left. Mr. John D—, from Scarsdale, called and sat more than an hour and a half in my study. Went to Mr. Burnett's, and baptized his child. Attended the Sunday School treat at Mount Erica, and distributed the prizes. Came home at 10.30 p.m.'

Where, it may be well asked, is the leisure to be got, in the face of such ever-recurrent engagements for pulpit preparation, pastoral visitation, and general reading, as the record of this day presents? 'Echo answers, Where?' The Methodist Superintendent, in some positions, has to swim against wind and tide! If he happen to be a prominent public man he is to be pitied.

Jan. 12th.—The Rev. T. Buddle came from Auckland. He is to be our guest during the holding of the Conference. I was occupied most of the day in preparing the forms for the Stationing Committee. I held the Quarterly Meeting in the evening. We had £40 in hand after paying all demands upon the Board. The membership had increased to 536, with 21 on trial. The Hon. A. Fraser and Mr. T. Nicol were appointed Circuit Stewards, and Mr. John Whitney as Secretary to the Quarterly Meeting.

On the 13th, I went to Prahran to hold the local preachers' meeting. Our young brother, R. M. Hunter, preached on 'Justification by Faith' (Rom. v. 1) much to the satisfaction of the brethren. The sermon was well thought out, exactly Wesleyan in its theology, and delivered with sober and convincing effect. The examination at the close was equally satisfactory, and Mr. Hunter was received by an unanimous vote as a fully accredited local preacher.

Jan. 20th.—The Conference commenced to-day; Rev. J. Buller, President, and the Rev. J. S. Waugh, Secretary. An alteration was made in my appointment, as recommended by the District Meeting and Stationing Committee, so that instead of going to the Melbourne First Circuit (Wesley Church), I was appointed to the Sydney Second Circuit (Chippendale); and the Rev. J. Egglestone, who was anxious to leave the Foreign Missionary Secretaryship, in Sydney, was appointed in my stead to Wesley Church, the First Melbourne Circuit. Three important resolutions were passed at this Conference relative to the Jubilee of the Foreign Missionary Society in London.   The first related to the establishment of a Central Theological Institution ; the second, to the commencement of a mission in New Guinea ; and the third, for the relief of burdened trusts and for the erection of new churches.   A carefully worded resolution was made of the invaluable services rendered to the Methodist Church by the Rev. William Taylor ; and also of the able services of the Rev. E. E. Jenkins.

In the Conference Address we have a strong recommendation upon a much neglected duty amongst our congregations :—

'Let Infant Baptism be much more with you than a form or a domestic festival.   Let your efforts and prayers for the early conversion of your children be unceasing.   Let there be a church in every house, and let a priestly sacredness elevate and guide parental relationship.'

Mr. Taylor preached before the Conference on the subject of 'Perfect Love.'   The platform was full of senior ministers and Conference officials, and Wesley Church was crowded.   When the hymn,

'Ye who know your sins forgiven,
And are happy in the Lord,'

was sung, high notes of 'true believers' rose higher still in pæans of praise to God.

'On the soul of each believer,
Let the Holy Ghost descend :
He is coming : He is coming !
Glory—glory—to the Lamb !'

was the beautiful climax to this Pentecostal service.   On *February 4th* this glorious Conference closed.

Feb. 11th.—A day of mournfulness caused by the early death of Master George Watson, through accident.   I buried his dear remains in the St. Kilda Cemetery.   It was a largely attended funeral.   In the evening, I wrote a letter of condolence to my afflicted friend, Mrs. Watson, to comfort her concerning the loss of her son.   This day I handed to Mr. Draper bank deposit receipts for £624 17*s.* 9*d.* for the new church at Prahran.   The Rev. Francis Neale, my colleague, should have the credit of getting most of this handsome amount.

March 1st.—I went once more to Sandhurst, at the invitation of the Rev. George Daniel. After calling upon several of my former friends at California Hill and Eagle Hawk, Mr. Daniel and I went to the White Hills to attend a meeting for raising funds for building a new church : £100 and gratuitous labour, with some materials, were promised. It was a capital meeting, and the friends were glad to see me again.

The next day Mr. Daniel and I drove out to Myrtle Creek, to see my brother George and his family. I baptized three of my brother's children, and spent a comfortable time with them. We went to Golden Square in the evening, and spoke at the missionary meeting. Messrs. Richards, Allingham, Lyle, and other brethren were glad to see me again.

April 6th.—The time had now come for us to say 'good-bye' to St. Kilda. This evening the usual valedictory meeting was held; and my old and faithful friend, the Hon. A. Fraser, presided. The speaking was confined to our own Circuit officials, whose words were kind and generous. My reply was short, but quite enough under the sorrowings of a 'farewell' to so affectionate a people. I was presented with a massive inkstand of silver, and Mrs. Bickford with an elegant desk. The theological class presented me with a beautiful address, and a valuable book, with the names of the members inscribed.

With this meeting was closed my official connection with this comfortable Circuit, and its many, many dear friends.

New South Wales.

We rose early and got ready for our voyage to Sydney. Arriving in Melbourne, we found Revs. Draper, Millard, Harcourt, Dare, Neale, and several other Methodist friends waiting to see us. We sailed at 1 p.m., in the *City of Adelaide*, in charge of Captain Walker, an experienced commander in the company's service. We had many passengers. I had been so many years in Victoria, that it was no wonder that I felt such a sense of oppressive solitude as we steamed down Hobson's Bay. An itinerant ministry is scriptural; but the wrench which it inflicts is hard to bear. It was particularly so in this case.

We did not reach Sydney till the morning of the 10th, when we were met at the wharf by Mr. Charles Caldwell, who took us to his parents' home in Pitt Street. Mr. and Mrs. Caldwell gave us a genuine Irish welcome, and we had to remain with them until late in the week, when we took possession of our house in Cleveland Street. The day after our arrival I got all our luggage from the steamer, and had it conveyed to our new home. I preached my first sermon at Chippendale on the Tuesday evening, and held a leaders' meeting to nominate officers for the Sunday School Committee. It was a novel business to me. I found in existence a code of local rules for managing the schools of the circuit.

The Circuit of which I was now put in charge was small in extent. It had only five preaching places :—Chippendale, Hay Street, Bishopsgate Street, Toxteth, and Mt. Lachlan. But the population was large. Sydney (proper) had 59,719, and the suburbs 40,543. The births, for the first three months of the year, had been 1,864 ; and the deaths 681. My colleague, the Rev. Richard Sellors, had had his training in Richmond College, London, and was a young man of considerable promise.

Being new to the Colony, I saw that my time and services would not be required for much Connexional work. I therefore determined to be diligent in preaching and pastoral work, in helping the Sunday schools, forming a theological class for young men, and Bible classes for the elder pupils of day and Sunday schools, Bands of Hope and other Temperance work. By proceeding upon a given plan, as to every day's work, I saw that I would be able to resume a class of studies which for many years had been impossible in my busy Victorian life. I cast myself upon the Lord for His grace and help in respect to each and all these several departments of ministerial duty.

I was comforted in the belief that the day school question would not be a trouble to me as it had been for many years in Victoria ; but the Sunday school institution I saw was bound to be, because of the constitution under which they were worked. The first of a series of disputes came up on the 15th, being only five days after my arrival in the Circuit. I had to meet the General Committee for the election and appointment of the Sunday school officials in the Circuit. It was a spirited affair. But the trouble specially arose from the fact that this committee was a ' Court of Appeal ' and a case of long standing from Bishopsgate Street had to be heard. We sat until a late hour, when it was agreed that I should hear the parties

SYDNEY, FROM PYRMONT.

implicated at Bishopsgate Street itself on the following Monday evening. By changing the venue, and limiting the court to the smallest number, I hoped to curtail any spread of bad feeling throughout the Circuit. This object was happily secured; for at the adjourned meeting the whole matter was satisfactorily arranged.

The Allens, at Toxteth, were very influential in religious circles in Sydney. The Hon. G. Allen, M.L.C., and Mrs. Allen, were specially the friends of Wesleyan ministers; Mrs. Allen was, as a child, a member of the first Methodist class, formed in 1815, in Sydney. From that period, during all the intervening years, she had been a true Methodist and a devout follower of Christ. Mrs. George W. Allen and Miss Allen were also members. On Saturday evenings there were select gatherings of clergymen of all denominations, and godly ladies and gentlemen, who met there for religious intercourse. I attended one of these 'socials' on the evening of the 24th, and spent a few hours very agreeably. The whole Allen family laid themselves out for promoting the ease, comfort, and profit of the visitors.

On the 25th, I attended the Financial District Meeting, the Rev. S. Rabone presiding. On the 26th, I went to the City Cemetery to see the grave of the missionary Spinney. I knew him as a young man, resident in the parish of Loddiswell, Devon, before he entered the ministry. At that time he was a stalwart man capable of much physical exertion. But he died in Sydney of consumption after all. His career in Fiji was short, but it was eminently useful. I also went to Darlinghurst Gaol to have an interview with Frank Gardiner, the notorious 'bushman' and highway robber. The jury had acquitted him of the capital charge. I saw John Vane privately, and talked and prayed with him. Misguided young man! His sentence was fifteen years with hard labour. I promised him a Bible.

May 27th.—I went over to Toxteth to meet the class. We met always in the 'chapel of ease' the Hon. G. Allen had built, and in which he officiated on Sunday mornings; ordained ministers (Wesleyan and others) officiated on Sunday evenings. Mrs. Allen took me to see two afflicted sisters, tenants on the property. I called afterwards upon Mrs. Boxell and Mrs. Sprod. I gave the Lord's Supper to old Mrs. Gillard. I began the theological class this evening : three came. Mr. and Mrs. Springthorpe, formerly of St. Kilda, and Mrs. Flashman, formerly of Modbury, Devon, came and spent a couple of hours with us this evening. We had a profitable conversation.

June 5th.—We held a Circuit tea meeting to raise money for putting the parsonage in order, and for furniture: £95 was the result.

June 10th.—Five came to the theological class this evening. I expect much pleasure and profit from this weekly exercise. My papers are based on Richard Watson's 'Institutes,' because there are none better. I read to-day the Rev. Thomas Smith's Life by himself. I do not wonder, but am grateful, that the Bishop of Sydney suppressed this publication. Smith was a 'brand plucked from the burning.'

June 17th.—I met the Bible class for the first time; thirty were present.

June 25th.—This morning I went to Toxteth (Hon. G. Allen's) to join several friends in meeting the Rev. William Taylor (*alias* 'Californian Taylor'), with whom I was greatly pleased. He seems full of the Spirit of God.

June 28th.—Mr. Taylor came as our guest during the time he will be working at Chippendale. The leaders met him in my study, for counsel and prayer relative to the revivalistic services to be held in our Circuit. Mr. Taylor appeared to great advantage as he unfolded his plan of working, and sought the co-operation of the brethren. He speaks as a 'master in Israel' only could speak on the winning of souls for Christ.

July 4th.—Mr. Taylor preached from the words : 'Do ye now believe?' The church was crowded, and thirty penitents found peace with God.

July 5th.—Mr. Taylor preached famously this evening, and the names of twenty-eight seekers were taken down. Mr. White and Mr. McCoy, senior, were brought to God at this service.

July 7th.—Mr. Taylor gave us a forceful and impressive sermon on 'Christian Perfection.' We made this evening a collection of £18 17s. for the 'Church Extension Society,' whose object is to spread the blessings of the Gospel throughout the colony.

July 8th.—Mr. Taylor and I went to Darlinghurst Gaol to hear the trial of Frank Gardiner. The court was crowded in every part.

THE BOTANICAL GARDENS, SYDNEY.

We were accommodated with chairs by the side of the Chief Justice, and could watch the proceedings with effect. In addition to the apparent indifference of the prisoner, there was a levity of manner in the court, which, if not expressive of actual sympathy with Gardiner, was highly unbecoming. It looked much like an endorsement of crime. We did not stay to the end of the trial. In the evening Mr. Taylor preached again, and with 'great power.' We have good reason to believe that, at least, one hundred and eighty souls have been savingly benefited by Mr. Taylor's labours in this Circuit.

July 19*th.*—I held my first Quarterly Meeting. There were twenty-one brethren present. The finances had greatly sprung. The meeting, by unanimous votes, fixed the Superintendent's salary at £275, and the second minister's at £160 per annum. All things considered, these allowances were equal to those paid in Victoria.

July 20*th.*—I went to the recognition services of the Rev. John Graham, Pitt Street Congregational Church. There were twenty-five ministers present, and a 'full house.' It was a very fine time.

The Rev. Samuel Leigh landed in Sydney on August 10th, 1815. Hence this is the jubilee year of the mission of our church in Australia. Mr. Leigh landed from the ship with a heart full of peace and hope and gratitude. He said, in his first l 'ter to the London Committee:—

'The signal is up for our arrival in sight, and the wind is more favourable for us. It is 12 o'clock, and we are now in sight of the cove and town. Sydney has a good appearance from our situation. Its first view exceeds my expectation. At 3 o'clock I landed at the King's Wharf, from which place I was conducted to Mr. Bowden's, in good health, and in the enjoyment of peace with God through our Lord Jesus Christ. Surely goodness and mercy have followed me all the voyage, and it is of the Lord that I am brought unto my desired haven. What shall I render unto Thee, the King of Saints? May all the days of my life be devoted to Thee!'

Such was the spirit of full consecration to God, and dependence upon the care and love of His providence, in which this pioneer missionary of the Cross entered upon his great work in this Australian continent.

July 26*th.*—My daily routine work is now fully within my grasp. As a specimen, I give the Diary's record for this day:—

'Did a good Hebrew and Latin exercise. Visited Mrs. Clissold (a confirmed invalid), Mrs. Wright, Mrs. Gray, Mrs. Hayden, Mrs. Oliver, Mrs. Swinball,

13

and Mrs. Wearne. Went to Bishopsgate Street and preached ; returning, 1 heard more than half of the Rev. Thomas Smith's lecture on "Ups and Downs." Mr. Buckland and I sat together, and heard the reverend lecturer with great pain. It was a performance worthy of an ecclesiastical buffoon rather than of an Anglican clergyman. Read Stevens's " History of Methodism " until 11 o'clock. I wrote notes of invitation to several persons to become members of the "Young Men's Mutual Improvement Association " which we had established at Chippendale.'

The Rev. William Taylor began a series of services at Hyde Park on the evening of the 28th, for the spiritual benefit of the unsaved multitudes. We had a platform erected, and gas laid on, and other conveniences. We adjourned to York Street Church, for gathering up the results.

July 31st.—This morning the Revs. W. Taylor, S. Rabone, W. Moore, and J. Dunn, who had just come up from Fiji, and myself, also Messrs. Wearne and Ducker, went to see the Mint. We saw the whole process of coining from the beginning, and handled sovereigns then and there minted. I then went to see the *John Wesley*, and was pleased to find the good ship which had done such valuable service in the South Seas. In the evening I went with Mr. Taylor to the Hyde Park and York Street services.

Sept. 5th.—Following up Mr. Taylor's convincing lecture upon ' Total Abstinence' last week, at St. Barnabas's (Anglican), we formed at Chippendale this evening a society, when twenty-eight gave in their names to be members. We appointed Mr. Richard McCoy secretary, and Mr. Dorsett treasurer.

Sept. 8th.—Mrs. Bickford and I went to Newington College to see the Rev. Mr. Manton, the Principal. We found him very ill. He was trusting in the blood of Christ for final salvation. He quoted with a full confidence the words : ' Yea, though I walk through the valley of the shadow of death, I will fear no evil : for Thou art with me ; Thy rod and Thy staff they comfort me.' I prayed with him, and commended him to the faithful and merciful God. In the evening I heard young Robert Johnston preach, who did well. This is the first-fruits of our Theological Class.

Sept. 10th.—We buried the remains of dear Mr. Manton to-day in the Paramatta Cemetery. His last words were—' Saved at last !' He was the founder of the College, and in his removal we have suffered a great loss.

Sept. 12th.—I wrote this day to the Hon. Dr. Wilson, Commissioner of Lands, setting forth the great need there was at Chippendale of a larger church site for our congregations and schools; and requesting that the Government would make us the necessary grant of an unoccupied piece near our property.

Nov. 3rd.—The District Meeting was begun to-day; the Rev. S. Rabone, Chairman; the Rev. C. W. Rigg, Secretary. At this meeting we carefully considered the plan for creating Colonial Annual Conferences. We also inaugurated the Jubilee movement by a largely attended breakfast meeting, a love-feast, and a glorious assemblage in the evening. The Hon. G. Allen, M. L. C., presided. Most interesting reminiscences of the early ministers and the work were given by the Rev. Ralph Mansfield, who, himself, was the fourth Wesleyan minister the British Conference sent to New South Wales, and arrived in Sydney in 1820. Mr. Robert Iredale and I were appointed treasurers, and Mr. C. W. Rigg, secretary. The giving was most liberal. It was a glorious day for New South Wales Methodism.

Dec. 11th.—Our new church at the Glebe was opened for Divine worship to day. The next day at the tea 500 persons were present, and at the after meeting the building was crowded. We raised by these services £171 4s. 10d. On the 14th I breakfasted at the Rev. Dr. Steele's. The Revs. J. Graham, Adam Thompson, and J. Voller were there also. We agreed upon a plan for united religious services during the first week in January. On the 17th I buried the remains of our late afflicted brother, David Moon, in the same grave as had been laid those of his good father, Jesse Moon, some years ago. On my pronouncing the Benediction, an old friend of the family, looking into the grave where father and son were now sleeping in death, said, audibly, and with much emotion: 'The prayers of David, the son of Jesse, are ended.' It was a unique expression, and touched many hearts.

Dec. 29th.—Mrs. Bickford read the usual Lessons, and Sutcliffe's Commentary, in consequence of my being very poorly. Indeed, I am quite run down with labours of Circuit and Connexional cares. My good friend, Dr. O'Reilly, came and prescribed for me.

1865.

New year's Sabbath I preached twice on the subject of 'The Barren Fig Tree.' I hope it was a good beginning of the year.

The next day the Young Ladies' Bible Class held a 'Social,' at which sixty members were present. I was presented with a beautiful inkstand and address in token of their gratitude.

Jan. 16th.—The Conference was opened to-day; the Rev. J. S. Waugh, President, and the Rev. H. H. Gaud, Secretary. I was requested to report the business of the Conference for the *Daily Press.* Our old friend, Mr. Binks, was our guest. On the 27th I went to the Land Office, and saw the word 'Approved' written on the margin of the official record of the grant of the new site at Chippendale. We had now full scope for a complete church establishment.

The Rev. D. J. Draper obtained from this Conference a year's leave of absence for visiting England. He had rendered good service to our Church for more than thirty years in New South Wales, South Australia, and Victoria, and deserved his holiday. His fine character and devoted labours well merited the complimentary notice in reference to him. On the 11th Mr. Draper called to bid us good-bye. My prayer is that he and Mrs. Draper may have a pleasant voyage to the dear old country, and a safe return, at the time appointed, to Australia.

There is a way for making up to our invalid members the loss they suffer from deprivation of the means of grace. I found that on entering upon the duties of this Circuit, my predecessor, the Rev. S. Rabone, had paid almost a daily visit to one of God's dearest children, Mrs. Clissold. This obligation I inherited and fulfilled. But our sister wanted something more than the simple pastoral visit; she wanted the fellowship and worship combined, with the Lord's Supper also. The first of the kind I arranged for. There was a gathering of 'elect sisters' in her room. The service was a miniature one of those held in the church hard by. At the close, Mrs. Clissold said 'the service had been precious to her soul.'

March 2nd.—The Crown Surveyor laid out our grant of land at Chippendale this morning; so that we are now in legal possession, and the way is cleared for commencing the erection of our new church. It is to cost about £4,500.

March 31st.—We held our Quarterly Fast by a prayer meeting at 7 a.m., and another at noon. The latter was a season of deep and earnest supplication; especially for the prosperity of the Circuit.

April 5th.—I examined the Chippendale Day School to-day. Messrs. Joseph Wearne and T. Reeve were present, members of the Local Board. There were 145 pupils in the classes. Mr. and Mrs Burrows are doing well in this school.

On the 8th, I prepared five sheets of catechetical lessons for the public examination at Easter. On the 18th, I attended a valedictory meeting for the Revs. W. Moore, J. E. Moulton, and J. Rooney. On the 20th the *John Wesley* sailed for the South Seas with these valued brethren and their wives. There were many friends to see them off. We wished them 'good-bye' near the 'Heads.' On the 27th I was present at a committee meeting of Newington College. There was a large attendance of gentlemen, and, amongst other important matters of business, it was agreed that my nephew, Edmund Sorrel Bickford, who was daily expected from the Westminster Training College, should be employed as Fourth Master if deemed eligible by Mr. President Fletcher.

I heard this afternoon that the notorious Ben Hall, burglar and murderer, had been killed. 'Whoso sheddeth man's blood, by man shall his blood be shed.'

May 6th.—This is my forty-ninth birthday. The Lord has been forbearing and gracious during the past year to me.

May 8th.—Being in the city I learnt that the *Dora* was inside the 'Heads.' I hired a boat, and went down our beautiful harbour to meet the good ship with my nephew on board. I saw him on the quarter deck, and instinctively recognised him. 'Surely blood is thicker than water.' He had grown during the eleven years which had elapsed since we parted at Kingsbridge in 1854, to be a full man. We hastened to the parsonage in Cleveland Street, where his aunt was impatiently awaiting his arrival.

This is my Diary jotting for May 11th :—

'Went to Newington with my nephew, E. S. Bickford, to introduce him to the Rev. J. H. Fletcher, the President, and Mr. Thomas Johnston, the Head Master. They conversed with him on various subjects embraced in college work, and were pleased with him. He is to enter upon his new duties on May 15th.'

On the 26th I went by steamer to the Hunter River. I left the wharf at 11 p.m., and reached Newcastle the next morning. I spent the day with Mrs. Creed, visited several families, and in the evening spoke at the missionary meeting ; Mr. Daniel, brother of Rev. George

Daniel, presided. On the 27th I went on to Maitland, and was the guest of Mr. and Mrs. Owen. I found that the visit of the Rev. William Taylor had been a great blessing in the town and district. After preaching on the Sabbath, and attending three meetings, I returned to Sydney.

June 17th.—Mr. James Hooke, formerly a schoolmate of mine at Ivybridge, Devon, called to see me. We much loved each other as youths. How strange that we should meet again after more than thirty years of non-intercourse or knowledge of each other's whereabouts! It is very surprising that we could so easily bridge over the incidents which had filled those thirty years.

June 24th.—Sad news from America! President Lincoln has been assassinated. A great man has fallen, and the whole world mourns the loss.

On the 29th I prepared a statement of the Rev. W. Taylor's Sydney financial affairs; after which I attended a committee of ministers and laymen, for considering how we should fittingly recognise the soul-saving labours which he had rendered to the congregations and people of Sydney and neighbourhood. We agreed to hold a public meeting, and present an address and a purse. We cannot do too much for this great and much honoured servant of God.

July 3rd.—My nephew, E. S. B., is beginning to evidence a preference for preaching to teaching at the College. I therefore requested him to prepare a manuscript sermon, and read it to me. The first of the kind he read this evening. It was in the rough, but I liked both its theology and diction.

On the 4th we held our Quarterly Meeting. We had a good increase of membership, and a balance in hand of £42.

July 11th.—The Rev. W. Taylor sailed to-day. He has done a good work for his Master in New South Wales. May God be with him!

Sept. 13th.—After many delays and annoyances in arranging for the erection of our Chippendale Church, the Building Committee this evening resolved to return to its original intention of spending about £5,000 for the building. To accomplish this object we had to get an entirely new set of plans and specifications. What a plague architects sometimes are to trustees and committees! In this particular case we were much tried. The lowest tender for the first plans was £6,700, whereas our instructions were for a building to cost £5,000 at the farthest. At length we accepted a tender at our own figure, and the work proceeded.

July 18*th.*—English telegram : 'Old Pam is still in the ascendent.' In the evening I attended an ' Ordination Service,' when the Rev. J. S. Austin was solemnly set apart as a missionary to the Navigator Islands. The veteran Rev. James Calvert gave the charge. It was a season of blessing.

Oct. 5*th.*—Held the Quarterly Meeting. The increase of members was 106, and the credit balance was £45. Mr. Robert Johnston was recommended for the Ministry.

Oct. 22*nd.*—I preached at Wollongong in aid of the ' Church Sustentation Society.' The next morning the Rev. George Hurst and I went to the American Creek to inspect the Kerosene Works. We went into the mine, conducted by Mr. John Graham, one of the proprietors. It was a wonderful deposit. The works, now in course of erection, will cost £2,500. On the 25th Mr. Hurst and I went up to Mount Keira to see the coalmine. We literally ' went into the mountain,' guarded from danger by the standing walls of coal which sustain the superincumbent weight. Layers of purest coal, six or eight feet in depth, stood across our track, in the front of which were men with their picks and shovels working at the lowest part, when all that had been affected by the strokes came tumbling down. Tramways were laid all along the mine for conveying the coal to the mouth, where it was shot into a connecting shoot, and whisked along to the vessel lying more than a mile off at the Wollongong Wharf. The New South Wales coal-beds are the marvel of scientific men, and are rather different in their form from those found in the North of England. I attended meetings at Wollongong, Bulli, and Mount Keira. On the 26th I left by the steamer *Hunter*, and reached Sydney on the evening of the same day.

Nov. 7*th.*—The District Meeting was begun to-day. On the evening of the 8th I preached the official sermon in York Street Church. We took the Lord's Supper at the close of the service. We had an increase of 480 members, with 299 on trial. We had four candidates, two of whom passed. Messrs. Manning, Sellars, Wiles, and Gillmore were examined by Mr. Fletcher, and were ultimately recommended to be taken into full connexion at the ensuing Conference. The Rev. William Curnow was elected

Representative. The sittings were closed on the 16th. On the 18th Mrs. Taylor and her three sons arrived from San Francisco; I went to Dr. Moffatt's to see them, and sent a telegram to Mr. Taylor, then at Willunga, South Australia, to come to Sydney forthwith.

Dec. 4th.—Went to Parramatta to attend the Missionary Meeting. This place is full of old Methodist families. I visited the Oakeses, Watkinses, Byrneses, Martins, and Bowdens.

Dec. 16th.—English telegram: 'Lord Palmerston is dead.' Irish by birth, and English by sympathy, he served his country well, and upheld the honour of England in every Cabinet and Court in Europe. Finished another article for the *Advocate*. Subject, 'Public Morals.'

Dec. 30th.—This year has been one of mercy and blessing.

1866.

Jan. 1st.—We had an auspicious beginning of the new year. Mrs. George Wigram Allen laid the memorial stone of the new church at Chippendale. We called it 'Wesley Church,' in honour of our founder, and to indicate to the public its character and claims. The ceremony passed off with much *éclat*. About £370 was then subscribed for the new building. The next day I called on Sir John Young, the Governor, and asked him for a subscription for our new church. It was amusing to hear him say that it was a principle with him to give to nothing that was local; and that, if he were to give anything to me, he would violate his principle and be besieged for every enterprise in the city. I could not but contrast Sir John's conduct, in this case, with that of Sir Henry Barkly in Victoria. On my way back from the 'domain' I called on Mr. George Wigram Allen, and told him of my disappointment. He spoke encouragingly to me to persevere in my efforts, and promised me £50 as a subscription.

Jan. 7th.—Rev. Jabez Bunting Waterhouse preached an admirable sermon at Chippendale. The Covenant Service was especially good. 'My God, I am thine! O save and and keep me!'

Jan. 8th.—I attended an executive committee meeting for missions. Captain Walsh explained to us the circumstances of the wreck of the *John Wesley*. He stood by the wheel to the last minute, and

when she began to break up, he sorrowfully exclaimed ' Poor Johnny ! ' We pitied the Captain very much.

Jan. 9th.—I held the Quarterly Meeting, which was well attended. We had in hand £56, after paying all demands. The appointments for the year were : Superintendent, Rev. James Bickford ; second preacher, Rev. Henry Gaud. This arrangement was to be forwarded to Conference by Mr. Joseph Wearne, senior Steward.

Jan. 28th.—I received a letter from the Hon. Alexander Macarthur, London, promising me £50 towards Wesley Church, Chippendale.

Feb. 5th.—The Station Sheet came to hand. We are to go to Geelong in Victoria. If this be the will of God, then it will be all well. There is strong feeling in the Circuit about this change.

Feb. 14th.—I had a long conversation with the Rev. Stephen Rabone on the subject of my removal from the Circuit. He told me that Mr. Gaud moved in the Stationing Committee that my name should stand for the Goulburn Circuit. My appointment to Geelong was an after consideration, and arose out of the pressure of Sydney First for Mr. Draper.

Feb. 22nd.—To day I received a kind letter from Messrs. James Wood and T. B. Hunt, Circuit Stewards of the Geelong Circuit, and enquiring as to the time of our probable arrival.

March 5th.—Sydney is full of the wildest excitement to-day. Mr. and Mrs. Draper, Dr. Woolley, and between two and three hundred persons had been drowned in the Bay of Biscay, through the foundering of the steamship *London*, on Friday, January 5th. We were struck dumb at the crushing forcefulness of the blow. All Sydney clothed itself in mourning.

March 19th.—I attended a meeting of Sydney ministers, to provide a Superintendent of the York Street Circuit in the place of the lamented Mr. Draper. We agreed that the Rev. William Kelynack, the second preacher, should take charge.

March 21st.—I paid Mr. Rabone £251 8s. 6d., being the contributions of the Sydney Second Circuit to the Foreign Missions for 1865. It was a noble contribution from a generous-hearted people.

March 24th.—At the earnest request of Messrs. Rabone and Chapman, I preached in York Street Church a funeral sermon for the late Mr. Draper. There was a large and sympathetic congregation.

I took as my text, Acts xx. 24, thinking St. Paul's great courage as an Apostle of Christ was typical, in many respects, of Mr. Draper's loving sacrifices and blessed toil for more than thirty years in Australia. And his conduct at the last momentous hour of his life, in that ill-fated ship, was worthy of Paul himself in the presence of his cruel martyrdom. Mr. Draper forgot himself in his last efforts to save the souls of his fellow-passengers. So died Daniel James Draper.

March 26th.—A valedictory service was held at Chippendale for Mrs. Bickford and myself, this evening. A dear friend, Mr. Alderman Murphy, who was brought in under Mr. Taylor's preaching at York Street, presided. Mr. Richard McCoy, another dear friend, presented me with a beautiful timepiece, suitably inscribed, as a memento of the true esteem and affection of our people. My heart was indeed sad at parting from my many loving and attached friends.

March 27th.—I held my last Quarterly Meeting. The membership had risen to 428. Balance in hands of stewards £81. A resolution, in which grateful mention was made of my two years' labour, and wishing Mrs. Bickford and myself every blessing from the Heavenly Father in our future Circuits, was unanimously passed, and duly signed by Joseph Wearne and Thomas P. Reeve, Circuit Stewards.

On the 28th we set apart another missionary for the South Seas. The service was held in York Street Church. At the request of the Chairman of the District, I delivered the charge, based upon the words of St. Paul: 'I speak concerning Christ and the Church.'

April 2nd.—I attended the Sunday School Anniversary at the Glebe. There was a good attendance, and an excellent meeting. At its close, Mrs. Bickford and I went on to Toxteth Park, and spent the night in the Christian home of the Hon. G. and Mrs. Allen. The next morning we called upon Mrs. G. W. Allen, Mrs. McAfee, Mrs. Lewis Moore, and other friends.

The Diary jotting for *April 4th* is as follows:—

'Left Sydney to-day for Geelong, Victoria. Mr. Murphy most kindly drove us to the wharf. Many dear friends were there to see us off and to say good-bye. We passed through the "Heads," and proceeded at a moderate rate towards Hobson's Bay, Victoria.'

More than twenty-three years have elapsed since the recurrence of the events just recorded. My forcible removal from Sydney, at the end of a two years' term of service, has in it an element of mystery I have never been able to grasp. It had been our intention, after spending a few more years in the Ministry, quietly to have settled down in a supernumerary position in one of the city suburbs, and there have ended our days. But, without our concurrence, or knowledge, until the Station Sheet came to hand, we were sent back to Victoria, there to begin a second term of itinerancy amongst old and new friends. Did God so appoint? The experiences of the next seven years must answer this question!

Arriving at Sandridge Pier, about noon on *April 7th*, we had the pleasure of meeting our brother, Mr. Nicholas Moysey Bickford, James Arscot Bickford, and Annie Bickford, and Mr. Thomas Wills, who were there to receive us. We went straight to the Crown Lands Office, and found my dear aged mother, Mrs. Bickford, and a group of children, all in good health.

GEELONG.

We spent three days in Melbourne in visiting our former friends. How we seemed to bridge easily over the chasm of a two years' absence from them! On the 11th, we started for Geelong, and arrived in due course at the station. The Rev. J. W. Simpson and the Circuit officials were awaiting our arrival. We quickly proceeded to the parsonage in Yarra Street, where Mesdames Crombie, Brown, Hunt, and Messrs. Wood, Hunt, Balding, and Hitchcock were to present us to our new home. Messrs. Crisp and Simpson conversed with me on several Circuit matters which required immediate attention. In the evening I preached at Newtown, and had a nice company to join with me in a *quasi*-recognition service.

It is a singular coincidence, that the very Circuit, of which I often thought before leaving England as that *one* I would like some day to be in charge, was this very Geelong Circuit. I seemed to have been drawn to it; and now that I was really there, I resolved, by the help of God, to do my 'level best' for its prosperity. There were several families at that time in Geelong for whom I had for long felt affection and respect, and I was naturally desirous for closer acquaintance with them than was possible during the time I was itinerating on the Victorian Goldfields. I will name only a few of those whom I found in Geelong, but who have since gone to their rest in heaven! The Hon. John and Mrs. Lowe, Mr. and Mrs. Thomas Forster, Mr. and Mrs. Rix, Mr. and Mrs. George Wright, Mr. W. Thacker, Miss Quinan, Mrs. Silas Harding, Mrs. Mowbray, Mr. Burrows, Mr. and Mrs. Dennis, Mr. Gaylard, and Mr. Wyatt. To be associated with such a company of good and holy men and women as I found in this Circuit was to me a great privilege. Indeed, the Geelong Circuit as it was twenty-five years ago was one of the most coveted prizes in the gift of the Conference any minister could receive at its hands.

In geographical extent the Geelong Circuit came next to the Ballarat Circuit. It extended from Murgheboluc to Kensington, and from the Duck Ponds to Jan Juc. The town of Geelong was the base of operations for overtaking the work in this large area. There was a settledness and strength in the Circuit which made me feel that, if we were not prosperous, the fault would certainly be our own. The routine work would not be troublesome if dealt with in a systematic and vigorous manner. A judicious administration, with the Divine blessing, would, I felt assured, be crowned with success.

April 15th.—This was my first Sabbath. I preached at Chilwell and Yarra Street. God gave me this very day the ear and heart of the people.

On the 23rd it was notified to me, by the Secretary of the Board of Education, that I had been appointed 'Corresponding Secretary' for the Yarra Street and other schools in connection with the Board. I was called late this evening to see a very old minister, a Mr. Higgins, at Newtown. He died while I was commending him to God in prayer. Lectures, Bible classes, preaching and pastoral work occupied the remainder of this month.

May 6th.—This day I am fifty years old. God be praised for all His mercies to me and mine!

May 16th.—I accompanied Messrs. James Oddie and Joseph A. Doane to Melbourne, to interview the Commissioner of Lands, Mr. Grant, about the Lydiard Church Reserve in Ballarat. In his absence we saw Mr. Ligar, the official head of the Department, and Mr. Brough Smyth, the head of the Mining Department. We laid the whole matter before these gentlemen, and then went to the Book Depot in Lonsdale Street, to prepare the required document to be laid before the Government. This being done, we all three signed it on behalf of the trustees and congregation concerned.

June 2nd.—I accepted the position of President of the Geelong Temperance Society, in the hope of acquiring increased influence in dealing with questions affecting the sobriety of the people. Mr. Benjamin Short, from Sydney, called on me. He is an interesting, well-informed, and godly man. Matthew Maddern, a young man who seeks to enter our Ministry, preached a *quasi*-trial sermon to-night, and did very well.

June 18th.—I read John Bright's famous speech on the 'Extension of the Franchise in England.' I read other great speeches also. England's future strength, as time must show, lies in that direction.

June 23rd.—I went to Ballarat to the Lydiard Street Church Anniversary. We had a successful time. In connection with the Monday evening meeting was inaugurated a fund for the erection of a new church.

I returned to Geelong on the 26th, and went straightway to the anniversary at Newtown. The Revs. D. Annear and S. Knight gave excellent addresses. We raised about £60.

June 28th.—I went to Drysdale, to hold the Quarterly Meeting. We had a good attendance, and a fine spirit was manifested. I returned to Geelong in time to hear young Henry Moore preach; his text was: 'Beloved, now are we the sons of God.' It was a creditable effort.

June 29th.—I examined the Yarra Street Day School, and was pleased with the result.

July 3rd.—The Newtown School I examined to-day. In the evening Mr. Simpson and I went to Chilwell, to the Annual Meeting of the Young Men's Mutual Improvement Society. It was a grand affair and a great success.

July 5th.—I held my first Quarterly Meeting. Messrs. Crisp and Simpson were present. The brethren were in excellent spirits and the business was soon disposed of. In the evening I preached from Rom. i. 16, when there was a gracious influence of the Divine Spirit resting upon the people for their good. The brethren from the country would return to their respective societies all the better for their duties by this baptism of grace and love.

July 9th.—Special services at Yarra Street all this week. I preached every evening except Saturday, when we had a 'testimony' meeting. The apparent results were small, but much good was done in the quickening of the Church, and in enlisting the sympathies of our people with their ministers in carrying on the Lord's work.

July 21st.—I went to Portarlington to open the new Church. Mr. and Mrs. Widdicombe gave me a hearty Christian welcome We raised £87 at the services.

July 24th.—I went to the Hospital to make Brother Scholes's will, who is dangerously ill. We prayed earnestly to God for the prolongation of his life.

July 27th.—This evening I met in a theological class the young brethren, Moore, Maddern, Legge, and Bonner. Our subject was the 'Trinity of Persons in One Godhead.'

July 28th.—I have been quite poorly to-day from too much work and worry. Thank God for the success which has attended the special services at Newtown. Several seekers have found salvation.

July 30th.—I attended a meeting of gentlemen at the Hospital, to arrange for collecting subscriptions for erecting the new building, as the accommodation was inadequate for the needs of the district.

July 31st.—I read to-day Disraeli's speech on the new Reform Bill. England has still her great men : Gladstone, Bright, Derby, Disraeli, etc. The Constitution is so safe in the hands of such men, that the electoral franchise may be extended to millions of men who are at present disfranchised. And what for? This is the question that stares the English nation in the face and demands a reply.

Aug. 1st.—I went to Kensington and visited ten families. Preached in the evening to a full congregation as the result of pastoral attention. Baptized a child and gave the Lord's Supper.

Aug. 2nd.—Mr. Scholes died to-day. I am sorely afflicted at this loss. May the Lord comfort the widow and her five orphaned children.

Aug. 6th.—Mr. Currie (squatter) and I, to-day, finished our collecting for the Hospital new building. We got, in small sums, £20, chiefly from the mechanic classes. I read Taylor's book, 'How to be saved,' this evening That is the great problem we are now trying in connection with our special religious services.

Aug. 14*th*.—We have collected in all £560 towards the Hospital. We did not meet with one refusal.

Aug. 17*th*.—This afternoon, at the request of the Rev. J. S. Waugh, I prepared a document, for the Board of Education, for the continuance of Mixed Schools as an essential part of our system of public education. We seem never to have done with contentions over our educational policy in Victoria.

Sept. 20*th*.—I attended a meeting of ministers at St. George's Church, to arrange for the 'Ragged Schools' and 'Biblewomen's' Annual Meeting. These are necessary institutions and a high charity. We must help those who cannot help themselves. At our preachers' weekly meeting to-day we agreed to nominate to the Quarterly Meeting, as candidates for our Ministry, Henry Moore, Matthew Maddern, and George Minns.

Sept. 25*th*.—Hearing that Thomas Learmouth, Esq., was at the National Bank as a guest of Mr. R. Gillespie, I called upon him. After a pretty full conversation upon the most prominent political topics of the day, I wished him success in his praiseworthy efforts to gain a seat in our Legislative Council. Mr. Learmouth is not only a pious, but a strong man ; and his presence in the Council would be a steadying power for good.

Sept. 27*th*.—I held the Quarterly Meeting to-day. I nominated Messrs. Moore, Maddern, and Minns as candidates for our Ministry. They were cordially recommended. Mr. Crisp and I were invited to remain another year in the Circuit. Mr. Simpson was asked if he wished a second year's appointment ; if so, the meeting would be glad to invite him. He, in reply, said that as he was a young beginner he would prefer a change. Whereupon, Mr. R. M. Hunter was appointed as third preacher for the ensuing year.

Oct. 22*nd*.—I attended a Conference of Ministers on Public Education. It was unanimously agreed to recommend to the Government the retention of Local Committees and Religious Instruction in all Denominational Schools.

Nov. 6*th*.—I attended the District Meeting in Ballarat; the Rev. W. L. Binks, Chairman ; Rev. J. Bickford, Secretary. We had a good beginning. Mr. Binks affectionately addressed the brethren, and several prayed. The Sessions closed on the 14th.

Dec. 3*rd*.—The Rev. S. W. Baker called, and he gave much information about the mission work in Tonga. He is to preach and speak in the interests of the Tongan Churches.   He seems to be full of the spirit of his work, and much good must result from his visit.

Dec. 5th.—I received a letter from Mr. Butler, inviting me to Jan Juc for Christmas Day.   As this was another opening for extending the ordinances of the Church, I engaged to go.   Only ten called this forenoon.   In the evening I heard the Rev. Oswald Dykes speak to ' Young Men.'   It was in many respects a famous lecture, but I thought it wanting in outspokenness of belief in the Divinity of Jesus Christ.

Dec. 17th.—I went to Melbourne to attend the Stationing Committee.   In the evening I wrote to twelve brethren, informing them of the Circuits for which they were recommended for appointment by the Conference.

Dec. 18th.—I went to Ballarat, on my way to the Scarsdale Circuit, to attend missionary services.   The Rev. Henry Baker drove me from Ballarat to Linton's, where I was the guest of Mr. and Mrs. Matthews, who showed me great kindness.   Here I met, for the first time, the published account of the 'Irish State Trials,' with which I was deeply interested.   The mixture of Irish wit and legal lore which characterised this trial, followed by the acquittal of Daniel O'Connell and his co-patriots, must render it memorable in significance in British jurisprudence for years to come.   I returned to Geelong on the 21st, and in the evening I presided at the Speech Meeting of the Central School.

Dec. 25th.—At 11 a.m. I preached in Yarra Street Church, when 150 persons assembled to join with me in commemorating the ' Incarnation.'   At midday Mrs. Bickford returned from Melbourne, bringing my nephew, Edmund Sorrell Bickford, who had just arrived from Sydney, with her.   My nephew had passed the District Meeting as a candidate for our Ministry, and had consequently resigned his connection with Newington College.   He seemed unwell, but the salubrious air of Geelong, with home comforts, will soon restore him to former strength.

Dec 27th.—I held the Quarterly Meeting.   We had £19 to the good.   Membership had risen to 875, with 33 on trial.   The next day the Rev. J. S. Waugh, President of Wesley College, came to Geelong to canvass for subscriptions towards Wesley College Building Fund.   As he knew none of the leading friends, I had to accompany him.   We soon got £25 promised.

Dec. 31*st.*—Watch Night Service. Messrs. Hunt, Balding, and Barker (N.S.W.) assisted in the service. It was a solemn and heart-searching time. I hope good was done.

1867.

Jan. 8*th.*—This morning Mr. Hunt and I drove to Barwon Park, and breakfasted with the hospitable Mr. and Mrs. Austin. We then went over to the Winchelsea Township to meet the gentlemen of the Shire Council about our Church Reserve. We agreed to yield sixty-six feet of the north-west corner, so as to render the approach to the bridge safe and convenient. The difficulty between the Shire and the Church is now overcome.

Jan. 15*th.*—I arrived in Launceston, Tasmania, this night at 11 o'clock, when the Rev. J. Egglestone and I went to Mr. Gleadow's as guests during the Conference. I was very ill during the voyage over, with sea-sickness. Indeed, I lost my voice for two or three hours. The steamer was more like a hospital than a pleasant sea-boat for passengers.

Jan. 16*th.*—The Conference was opened to-day. The Rev. Henry Honey Gand was President, and the Rev. Benjamin, Secretary. At this Conference our four young brethren in Geelong were accepted as candidates,—viz., Messrs. Brown, Maddern, Minns, and E. S. Bickford. Mr. Egglestone asked permission to visit England for one year. A touching 'In Memoriam' of the late Daniel James Draper was inserted in the Minutes, concerning his heroic death. At this Conference was nominated for the Presidency in 1868.

Feb. 1*st.*—I reached Geelong at 10.30 p.m. with a heart full of thankfulness to God for His mercies to me by land and sea. During my absence at Conference, the Hon. John Lowe, M. L. C., of Hampstead, died. He was a man who 'feared God above many,' and he was a true friend to Wesleyan ministers and to Methodism. His removal is a great loss to the Circuit. The day after my arrival home, I rode out to see Mrs. Lowe, now a widow, and her only daughter at home, Emma Lowe. It was an affecting interview, and my soul felt something of 'the sorrows of death' for my bereaved friends.

Feb. 14*th.*—The Rev. Benjamin Field—a choice man, a Methodist theologian, and an excellent preacher, but an invalid—is coming to

14

Geelong to-morrow for change of air.   I called on my friends, Mr. and Mrs. Silas Harding, to ask them to entertain him during his visit.   Both seemed glad to have such an opportunity for showing kindness to so eminent a servant of God.

Feb. 17*th.*—I attended the Church Anniversary at Great Brighton. We raised £59 in aid of the Trust.

Feb. 23*rd.*—I went to St. Albans to select a site for a new church. Mr. Maley directed me to a most convenient allotment, which Mr. J. G. Carr, the proprietor, would give to the Conference for such an object.

Feb. 25*th.*—Messrs. Balding, Hunt, Moore, and I went to the Duck Ponds, to a Church Anniversary.   We had a fine meeting. We were in great danger in returning to Geelong, because of the dense darkness of the night.   I reached home at midnight.

March 11*th.*—Having accepted the invitation of the Trustees to take part in the opening services of Wesley Church, Sydney, I left by steamer to-day.

At 11.30 a.m., on the 13th, we made fast to the company's wharf, and found Messrs. Murphy, McCoy, Curtis, and Loudin, awaiting my arrival.   I went on to the Murphys', and had a warm welcome. I spent the next three days in visiting old friends.   On the evening of the 16th I was waited on by the Circuit Steward of the —— Circuit, who asked me if I had said 'I would not take another Circuit in New South Wales?'   To which I replied 'No.'   'Whether I would accept a Circuit in New South Wales, if I were invited?'   To this I gave no pledge.

March 17*th.*—Wesley Church was opened to-day.   I took the evening services only.   There were fine congregations.   The tea and public meeting the next day was a great affair.   We raised £227.

Before leaving for Melbourne, my successor, the Rev. H. H. Gaud, called my attention to two or three subscriptions to the new church, which were marked 'paid,' but which, he said, were not accounted for !   I quietly asked him if he had enquired at the bank in Parramatta Street, if the amount in question were there?'   He said, 'No.' On the way to the steamer I called myself, and found that the exact amount had been lying there for twelve months to the credit of the Church.   Mr. Murphy promised me to tell the troubled treasurer, Mr. Gaud, of this 'nest egg.'   On board the steamer I had an interesting conversation with Mr. George Coppin, of theatrical notoriety. I found him to be a man of fluent speech and great information. His account of social life in San Francisco was very distressing. The Rev. W. Taylor's description of the 'gambling hells' of that newest of American cities, had not been at all over-drawn. I reached Geelong on the 22nd, and found all well.

March 25th.—We lost by death a truly 'elect sister,' Mrs. Sargeant of Ashby. Her last words were, 'I am going to the land of the pure and the holy.'

March 28th.—I held the Quarterly Meeting to-day. The income was £83 above the expenditure. Membership, 792; on trial, 62. The brethren were in fine spirit.

March 31st.—I preached the Church Anniversary Sermons at St. Kilda. The next day I dined at Wesley College. Dr. Waugh, Dr. Corrigan, and I went to Brunswick to see Mr. Overend. Poor man! he is suddenly arrested in his career of honour and usefulness. Afterwards I attended a meeting in St. George's Hall, on behalf of the 'Early Closing' movement. It was a grand meeting. On my way back to Geelong on *April 3rd*, I had a long conversation with my old neighbour, the Rev. John Potter, M.A. (Anglican), of Ballarat, on social and ecclesiastical questions. I think Mr. Potter is not so narrow as he was formerly, when we were together in Lydiard Street.

May 14th.—J. G. Carr, Esq., presented me with a 'Bill of Sale' of three allotments of land at St. Albans, as a site for a Wesleyan Church. Mr. Solicitor Maley had been instructed to prepare the usual conveyance without any cost to the trustees to be appointed.

May 19th.—Mr. Thomas Pybus preached the sermons in aid of the Trust of the Newtown Church. At the public meeting the next day, he gave us an eloquent speech on the 'Non-failure of Christianity.' We raised £100 7s. 7d. On the 22nd, I wrote a letter to the *Argus*, on the 'Public Instruction Bill' now before the House of Assembly.

May 25th.—We held the Highton Church Anniversary this evening. There were about 200 persons at the tea and public meeting. We inaugurated the movement for a new church, and £102 were promised.

June 1st.—At the request of the Rev. A. Mackenzie Fraser, M.A., I preached in the High Church (Presbyterian) this afternoon. The service had reference to the six-monthly celebration of the Lord's

Supper, which was to come off the next day. This is what our Scotch friends call 'fencing the tables;' a necessary precaution, no doubt, for preventing improper persons for coming to the Lord's Table.

June 7th.—My nephew, the Rev. E. S. Bickford, gave a lecture this evening to the 'Young Men's Literary Society,' Yarra Street, on 'Egypt in the Time of the Pharaohs.' It was well received, and the lecturer was thanked.

June 24th.—I went to Inverleigh to select a site for a church. Messrs. Bickham and Due accompanied me from Murgheboluc. We called upon several families who were formerly in connexion with us. The next day I wrote Mr. Waugh, to make the usual application to the Government for a grant of the land.

June 27th.—We held the Quarterly Meeting to-day. The Circuit is still prospering in every respect. In the evening I preached to a full congregation, and held a building committee and leaders' meeting. I returned to Yarra Street at 11 p.m. A hard day's work.

July 8th.—I drove Mrs. J. B. Smith, who had been visiting us for six weeks for the benefit of her health, and my niece, Alice Bickford, to the station. In the evening, I began reading 'Stanhope's Life of Pitt,' with the view of understanding the reasons for the provoking continuance of the war with the First Napoleon, after he was willing to come to terms, and for depriving the Irish nation of its Parliament.

July 23rd.—I buried the remains of the late Mr. Southey to-day. I humbly trust he found mercy from the Lord before he passed away.

July 29th.—Mr. Hunt and I went this afternoon to Wellington to select a site for a church. Mr. Hopkins met several of the resident settlers in the evening, and promised us the land we wanted if we would erect thereupon a stone or brick building. We accepted his generous offer. The sum of £40 was immediately subscribed.

Aug. 8th.—Mrs. Daniel died to-day. The last words she said to me were: 'The next time I shall meet you will be in heaven.' This is another sanctified soul gathered from the Yarra Street Church to the home of the blessed.

Aug. 14th.—Finished reading Pitt's life to-day. The battle of Austerlitz killed England's great minister.

Aug. 15*th.*—I went to Ashby to see Mrs. Dennis, who was ill, but on finding that she belonged to the Primitive Methodists, I called on her minister and informed him of the case.

Aug. 21*st.*—N. McC—— was sentenced for forgery to-day to seven years in Melbourne Gaol. It may be questioned, I venture to think, whether so severe a measure would have been taken against him by the bank, but for the strong political feeling existing between certain parties at the time. In the interests of abstract justice I am obliged to say thus much.

Aug. 27*th.*—I finished reading the memoir of Archbishop Whately. I was much interested in the character and work of this logic-headed ruler of the Irish Church.

Aug. 29*th.*—I paid my accustomed visit to the Hospital. Mr. George Brown was with me. Each ward was visited, and all the suffering patients were spoken to. I thus spent profitably a couple of hours in merciful work.

Sept. 3*rd.*—We accepted tenders to-day for erecting a new church at Highton. On the 9th we began a special effort at Ashby for a new church, and raised £100. Messrs. Crisp and Greenwood spoke well. I paid to the local treasurer of the Bible Society, as our contribution for Geelong Wesleyans, £22 13*s.* On the 10th we held the Annual Meeting of the 'Biblewomen's Mission.' Six hundred persons partook of the tea. It was a great success.

Sept. 12*th.*—I finished reading my 'Dixon's New America' to-day. It is a marvellous disclosure of the social condition of the people, and should be creative of great effort by the American Churches to remedy it.

Oct. 3*rd.*—I held the Quarterly Meeting. There was a large attendance of brethren. Members 800; on trial 7. We had a credit balance of £16. The invitations for the next year were Revs. J. Bickford, F. E. Stephenson, and E. S. Bickford. A fourth minister was asked for the Barwon. Church Extension is to the 'fore;' this is right.

Oct. 7*th.*—The Rev. W. D. Lalean came to preach at our Chilwell Church Anniversary, and did us excellent service. We raised £108 towards the extinction of the Trust debt.

Oct. 11*th.*—I wrote Mr. Matthew Burnett, the Yorkshire Evangelist, and pressed him to come to Geelong, and commence his mission on the 21st November. His reply was, 'Can't come until next year.'

Oct. 13th.—I buried poor Mrs. Wilson. Another holy woman has ' swept through the gates ' into the presence of her Saviour.

Oct. 19th.—The three-masted schooner, *John Wesley*, made fast to the wharf in Corio Bay to-day. We had an enormous gathering of children to see this beautiful craft. The visit happened to be whilst the District Meeting was being held, which gave additional interest to the incident. I took from the missionary-box on board the sum of £9, and made advance payments to some of the men.

Oct. 23rd.—Mr. Binks and I heard W. H. Fitchett preach this evening. The sermon was clever—founded on the words of our Lord : ' Beware of the leaven of the Pharisees, which is hypocrisy.' Mr. Fitchett is only in his second year, and promises to be one of our ablest men. The next evening, my nephew, Edmund S. Bickford preached at South Geelong. Messrs. Binks, Williams, Daniel, and Blamires were present. A formidable bar of triers for a young man in his first year. The sermon was well thought out; but the voice was not well managed. A few lessons in elocution will correct that defect. On the 31st the Sessions closed.

Nov. 1st.—Busy with foreign missionary matters. I finished reading to-day the second volume of Charles James Fox's Memorials and Correspondence. Pitt and Fox ; a strange juxtaposition of men, providentially raised up to help the nation in her troubles.

Nov. 4th.—I met the Committee of the Ladies' Benevolent Society, who guaranteed £135 worth of goods for the forthcoming bazaar.

Nov. 11th.—I laid the foundation-stone of the new church at Highton. Mr. Robert Gillespie ably presided at the public meeting. We raised £50.

Nov. 13th.—English telegram : There is imminent danger of conflict between Italy and France on the Romish question. I requested the Rev. Mr. Waugh to make application to the Government for an allotment of land at Jan Juc for Wesleyan Church purposes. The missionary meetings are being got over. The Rev. Henry Greenwood has rendered us good service.

Nov. 18th.—I went to Stieglitz to attend a missionary meeting. Messrs. Greenwood, Edwards, and I were the speakers.

Nov. 19th.—Mr. Waugh informed me of the grant of two roods of land at Moranghurk for our church.

Nov. 20th.—Dr. Jakins, a Wesleyan M.D., from London, called to consult me about his settlement in this colony. I advised him to try

Ballarat, as presenting him a wider field and less competition than Geelong could be. I gave him letters of introduction to Mr. Oddie and other old friends.

Nov. 21st.—I presided this evening at the Mechanics' Institute meeting to receive Mr. M. Burnett. There were from 350 to 400 present. Mr. Burnett spoke. It was an enthusiastic time, and augurs well for the success of his visit to the Circuit.

Nov. 23rd.—The Duke of Edinburgh is at the 'Heads.' My heart welcomes the Queen's son to Australian soil. The *Galatea* is gone up the Bay.

Nov. 26th.—I went to Melbourne to attend Prince Alfred's *levée.* It was largely attended ; a gratifying evidence of the genuine loyalty of the democratic Victorian people to the Queen.

Dec. 2nd.—The Prince came to Geelong to-day. As a member of the reception committee, I had to be close to him as he stepped on the wharf. He was sweetly affable, as a son of Queen Victoria ought to be. The procession through the town was witnessed by a great multitude of people, with respectful demonstrations of affectionate loyalty. In the evening, Mrs. Bickford, Miss Amelia Parker (our West Indian friend) and I went to see the beautiful fireworks and the illuminations. There never had been such a sight, nor such rejoicing, in Geelong before. Viscount Canterbury, our Governor, accompanied the Prince.

Dec. 3rd.—English telegram : Italy in a state of insurrection ; the days of the Pope's temporal power are numbered.

Dec. 7th.—I went to Drysdale, taking Mrs. Bickford with me. The next day I preached missionary sermons, and on Monday, I spoke at the Missionary Meeting. In the forenoon, the Rev. T. Kane drove me to Queenscliffe to make proper arrangements for the new church. We dined with Mr. and Mrs. Hawse, who were very hospitable to us.

Dec. 10th.—We went to Port Arlington, and spent the day at Mr. and Mrs. Widdicombe's. I attended the Missionary Meeting, and spoke for seventy-five minutes. ' Too long by half : ' but then I was the only speaker. Hastened back to Geelong on the 11th, to see the local Commissioner of Lands, Mr. Belcher, about the Queenscliffe Church Reserve, which, by some mischance, had been gazetted for sale. He immediately withdrew it from sale.

Dec. 31st.—I attended a meeting at St. George's Church, to arrange for holding the United Religious Services in the first week in the New

Year. Thus I finished the work of 1867 in the spirit of love and unity with all who love our Lord Jesus Christ, who is both theirs and ours.

1868.

Jan. 1st.—My Diary jotting is as follows :—

' I have entered upon the new year in Yarra Street Church. It was a solemn time. I endeavoured to consecrate myself anew to God. I have heavy responsibilities in prospect of the Presidency, but I will cast myself upon the wisdom and aid of the Holy Spirit, and I shall be helped.'

In the afternoon Mrs. Bickford and I went to Fyan's Ford, and spent a nice time with Mr. and Mrs. Wyatt. Returned home at 9.40 p.m.

Jan. 2nd.—We opended tenders for the enlargement of Ashby Church. We conditionally accepted one for £703. I buried the drowned boatman—poor Robinson—to-day. The ' Sons of Temperance ' attended to show their respect for the deceased. I received a kind letter from my friend, the Hon. A. Fraser, M.L.C., relating to our Conference arrangements. I am thankful for his sympathy and good wishes.

Jan. 9th.—We held our Quarterly Meeting to-day. The membership was 873, with 32 on trial. Credit balance, £85. The appointments, in part, as recommended by the Stationing Committee, were rejected by the Quarterly Meetings, and the invitations, as agreed to by the September Meeting, were reaffirmed.

Jan. 13th.—Yesterday I preached at Clunes and Creswick, and attended their missionary meetings. On reaching Geelong, on Wednesday, I found letters awaiting attention from the Rev. Dr Hoole, the Rev. W. Butters, and Rev. J. Eggleston.

Jan. 20th.—I went to Sandridge to receive my niece, Christina Flora Pascoe, who had come from Kingsbridge, Devon, to live with us.

Jan. 22nd.—I went to St. Kilda to be the guest of Mr. and Mrs. Fraser during the Conference. The Revs. H. H. Gaud, J. S. Waugh, and W. Hill called in the evening. The next day, in Wesley Church, Melbourne, the Conference was opened at 10.30 a.m. This was the largest Australasian Conference that had yet assembled. From 125 to 130 ministers were present. The brethren received me as their

President very kindly, and I was thankful for their sympathy and good wishes. The usual prayer meeting was a good time, and great grace rested upon the people. After dinner the business was commenced in real earnest; we broke up at 5 p.m. Conference Sabbath, the 26th, I preached in Wesley Church, the Rev. John Cope, the Superintendent Minister, read prayers. I took as my text the words of Joshua : 'As for me and my house we will serve the Lord.' On the evening of the 29th I preached the official sermon from the words : 'These things saith He that hath the seven spirits of God, and the seven stars; I know thy works' (Rev. iii. 1). It was followed by the Lord's Supper, both ministers and people communicating.

We had no heroic legislation at this Conference. But we reported progress. An increase of 12,000 members greatly rejoiced our hearts ; they were 'the seals of our apostleship.' There were fifty thousand children in our Sunday schools, which the 'Address' designates 'an imposing fact.' Seventeen probationers were received into 'full connexion' with the Conference, and ten were on trial.

There is a passage in the 'Address,' on the subject of our Missions in the South Seas, of much value to us even now :—

'We again solicit from the members of our colonial churches a deeper and more constant interest in our Polynesian missions. Foreign missions we can scarcely call them. It is certain that at present they cannot dispense with our aid. In proportion to their resources they have contributed towards the support of the work among themselves : and God has raised up amongst them a native ministry which, for soundness in the faith, for deep devotedness and piety, and for success in winning souls, will bear favourable comparison with any body of Christian ministers in the world.'

Feb. 8th.—I returned to Geelong much fatigued in body and mind. My prayer was : 'May the Lord help me in the discharge of the high and responsible duties connected with the Presidency of the Australasian Wesleyan Methodist Connexion this year.'

Feb. 10th.—The Rev. H. P. Burgess, from South Australia, came this morning. My nephew, the Rev. E. S. Bickford, readily drove him about 'to see whatever could be seen.' We were much pleased with our guest. Mr. Dennis died to-day. Mrs. Dennis died some months ago. At my suggestion, Mr. Dennis had appointed Messrs. F. B. Hunt and N. H. Brown guardians of the now orphaned family, and executors of the estate.

March 2nd.—Yesterday I opened the Queenscliffe Church, and to-day I assisted the local treasurer in making up the balance sheet. We had a soirée, which was a great success. Mr. Hugh Pattison, of Melbourne, generously gave us £50 towards the undertaking.

March 25th.—David O'Donnell, a young local preacher from Ballarat, called and presented his credentials. He wishes to offer for our ministry.

March 26th.—I held the Quarterly Meeting to-day. Credit balance over £100. Members 897, with 24 on trial.

April 3rd.—I laid the 'Foundation Stone' of the new church at Wellington. We had a largely attended tea and public meeting in the evening. I reached home at 11 p. m., wearied and poorly.

April 20th.—I preached at Chilwell, and held the leaders' meeting. As far as we can estimate, 173 persons have joined the classes as the result of Mr. Burnett's mission.

April 29th.—I went to Highton and preached. At the after meeting we had twenty penitents; fifteen of whom found peace.

May 4th.—We held the South Geelong Church Anniversary, and raised £107.

May 5th.—I went to Jan Juc and preached to eighty persons. Twelve gave in their names for membership. I appointed Brother Bland, Leader; Brother Musgrove, Society Steward; and Brother Gundry, Poor Steward. This forest church has now a complete organisation.

May 6th.—This day I am fifty-two years of age. In the quietude of a chamber in Mr. Grundy's house, I once more consecrated my whole 'body, spirit, and soul to God.' Lord, 'I am Thine,' now more than ever. I spent most of the day in pastoral visitation, which was a new, but grateful, experience to those Bush families, and pleased them very much. On my way back, I turned off the direct road to lecture at Mount Duneed, in behalf of the Sunday School Library. Dr. Heath took the chair. We raised £5 15s. 6d.

May 18th.—A great work is being done at Ceres. Mr. Burnett, assisted by my nephew, E. S. Bickford, is carrying on special services there. It is reported that 135 persons have received spiritual good.

May 25th.—I went to Melbourne to attend the *levée* in honour of our good Queen. Afterwards I called at the Crown Lands Office, to see about church sites.

May 27th.—I went to Chilwell to hear David O'Donnell preach.

I was favourably impressed, and shall probably recommend him to the next Quarterly Meeting as a candidate for the itinerant work.

June 1st.—Mr. Burnett and I drove to Murgheboluc. We had a glorious time. There were several penitents seeking salvation. We came home at 11.30 p.m. News arrived by telegram that Gladstone had defeated Disraeli on the Irish Church question by sixty votes. There is now some hope that the anomaly of a State Church Establishment, kept at the national expense for a minority of the people, will be removed. This should be one more step towards welding the several races on Irish soil into one strong nationality.

June 4th.—I went to Melbourne to see the Commissioner of Lands about the affiliated college land, being a part of the section set apart by the Government as a University Reserve.

June 8th.—English telegram : Glorious Budget as a whole : ' The right man in the right place ' once more. This is England's will.

June 11th.—I went to Ceres, preached and held a leaders' meeting. I appointed additional leaders, and the stewards were re-elected. The precious souls gathered in by Mr. Burnett's labours must be shepherded in classes, or they will fall back again into the world.

June 25th.—I went to Melbourne to meet the committee on the ·' Old Preacher's Fund ' business. We had several suggestions before us, claiming our closest thought. We sat all day.

June 27th.—I finished reading Taylor's ' South Africa.' What a wonderful work of God was wrought in that country through the labours of this modern Apostle to the Gentiles !

July 1st.—I went to Jan Juc, and preached to a ' full house.' I met the new converts, when twenty more joined the classes. Reached home at 11.40 p.m. A more lonely sixteen miles' journey at night than this I do not know.

July 7th.—This evening Messrs. M. Burnett, E. S. Bickford, S. Ham, and I were received as honorary members of the ' Sons of Temperance.' I hope this step will be a means of additional usefulness to each of us.

July 8th.—I went to Melbourne to preside at the Loan Fund Committee. It took us all the day to get through the business. In the evening, I went up to the House of Assembly, and found the MacCullock party refusing supplies. So that the dead-lock is not over yet.

July 9th.—I held the Quarterly Meeting. Cash in hands of steward, £98. In the evening young Macmichae preached. He did very well. He shapes for the Ministry as well as most, and deserves a trial.

July 11th.—A new Ministry is formed. The 'Macs' are triumphant once more. The 'dead-lock' is over for the present. In the evening we held a society tea-meeting at Chilwell, when we inaugurated a movement for the enlargement of the church. The friends promised £112.

July 14th.—I wrote a long and pressing letter to the Missionary Committee in London, on the claims of Queensland for monetary and ministerial help.

July 15th.—I was after church sites to-day : one in the Warrnambool Circuit, and one at the Leigh Road Station.

July 17th.—I left by the midday train for Ballarat, and preached in Lydiard Street to a large congregation. We held a prayer meeting, which continued up to ten o'clock. I sat up until nearly twelve o'clock conversing with Mr. Oddie and the Rev. George Daniel, upon church and political questions. I left early on the 18th for Pleasant Creek. The morning was cold, and the journey was wearying. The Rev. John and Mrs. Catterall received me most kindly. I talked with Mr. Catterall for a couple of hours, and retired at 11 p.m. I preached three times on the 20th. We had a large gathering the next evening, when we raised £130 towards the new parsonage. I returned to Ballarat on the 22nd. My good friend, Mr. Oddie, was at the coach office to receive me.

July 24th.—The Rev. John Watsford lectured at Chilwell this evening. It was an admirable lecture, and was most useful in its aims.

July 27th.—A deputation of gentlemen and day school teachers, with the local committees, came for consultation about the new rules of the Central Board of Education. We sat until 11 p.m.

August 1st.—I accompanied this morning a deputation of Wesleyan day school teachers to Melbourne, to interview Dr. Corrigan, our representative at the Board, on the new rules of the 'Common Schools.' He was most complaisant, and promised to do all he could for insuring justice to the teachers. I then went to the Cremorne Private Lunatic Asylum, when the obliging proprietor, James T. Harcourt, Esq., M.P., showed me over the buildings and grounds.

I returned to Geelong in time to attend a special meeting at Ashby for raising money for building a transept to the Church and for other improvements. We raised £200.

On the 24th I went again to Melbourne to preside at a meeting of the Educational Committee. There was great diversity of opinions. We passed four resolutions; but I was not satisfied with the result. We afterwards held a meeting of the Book Committee. We agreed to purchase the first issue of the Rev. Benjamin Field's 'Handbook of Christian Theology.' This very able compendium of our standard doctrines will be of great use to the local preachers, Sunday school teachers, and candidates for our Ministry. It ought to have a large circulation in these Colonies, for it is the best thing of the kind we have yet had.

August 25th.—I went to the Barwon Heads, and preached in Mr. Johnston's farmyard. It was the first religious service ever held there, and it was unique and romantic. I stood in a waggon as my platform, and the people, composed of several denominations, utilizing the dinner-hour for the purpose, gathered around it. We had hearty singing, and every appearance of a sincere desire on the part of the audience 'to worship God in spirit and in truth.' The farmyard that day was 'holy ground.'

August 30th.—I preached in Forest Street Church, Sandhurst. After the public service, nearly to a full congregation, I gave an account of the glorious work of God in the Geelong Circuit, mainly through the labours of Mr. Burnett. I encouraged the people to expect similar blessings during the Mission he was about to conduct in the Bendigo District. At the public meeting held the next evening we raised £102. On this occasion I visited my former friends at Long Gully, California Hill, Eagle Hawk, Golden Square, and in Sandhurst itself.

Sept. 1st.—Returned to Geelong, and in the evening I went out to German Town to a special meeting in aid of a new church. We raised £104.

Sept. 12th.—I went to Melbourne to consult Messrs. Egglestone and Waugh on the Bright Church Property case. We agreed to a course of action, which I consented to carry out. I ran out to Malvern to see Mesdames Ross and Cameron. Mrs. Ross and her fatherless children have come from Demerara to settle in Victoria. These dear ladies were special friends of Mrs. Bickford's when I was labouring in British Guiana. Messrs. Ross and Cameron were amongst my most true and generous acquaintances in that magnificent colony. They were also regular communicants at Trinity Church, and supporters of the Wesleyan Mission.

Sept. 15th.—I went to Wabdallah, and appointed a building committee to raise money for erecting a church. I was much pleased with the spirit of these Christian gentlemen.

Sept. 16th.—I baptized Mrs. Ash *with* water, i.e. by affusion after the New Testament precedents. I believed in her sincerity, and thus admitted her into the ' body ' of Christ's Church.

Sept. 17th.—A young man, Benjamin Gilbart Edwards, from Stieglitz, preached in Yarra Street Church this evening. He gave promise, I thought, of usefulness. I conversed with him at large the next day, and encouraged him to persevere in his studies with the view of his coming into our Ministry.

Sept. 21st.—I went up to Stieglitz and held the Quarterly Meeting. B. G. Edwards was nominated as candidate, and was recommended for the Ministry. During my stay I was the welcome guest of Mr. and Mrs. Osborn at Emily Park.

Sept. 23rd.—I buried the remains of Mrs. Auld in the West Cemetery. Another redeemed spirit gone to the Golden City—' from sufferings and from woes released.' The Revs. Shirley W. Baker and E. J. Watkin were our missionary deputation this year ; both able speakers on the glorious theme.

Sept. 29th.—I prepared the examination papers for the fourth-year men to be taken into full connexion at the ensuing Conference. I went to the church opening service at Wellington. We raised £80.

Sept. 30th.—I went to Cowie's Creek, held a service, and baptized eleven children and one woman. To-day I received a letter from Mr. Bee, senior Steward of Wesley Church Circuit, asking me if I were prepared to accept an invitation to the Superintendency for next year. Should I be so appointed by the Conference, it will be the most responsible position I have yet had as a Circuit minister.

Oct. 1st.—I went to see poor Moore, who has been shot in the back of his head. Unfortunate man ! May God have mercy upon his soul ! I buried to-day the remains of the late Mr. Bowman— a man of little faith ; still he died safely trusting in Christ. By the English mail to-day I received from the Rev. Dr. Jobson, a copy of his beautiful memoir of the late Dr. Hannah, Theological Tutor at Didsbury College. It is a well merited testimony to the ability, learning, and apostolic character of this great Methodist preacher.

Oct. 2nd.—The Rev. S. W. Baker was present at our ministers' weekly meeting. We were much delighted with his manly bearing, his shrewdness, and his zeal for the Tongan Mission. He is a very fine man, and an able preacher in English as well as in Tonguese. If superior qualifications and great success in the work go for anything, then, beyond all doubt, we have in Mr. Baker a true successor of St. Paul.

Oct. 5th—The Rev. John Watsford preached yesterday in behalf of the Yarra Street Trust. We raised £137 14s. Mr. Watsford's sermons and speech at the public meeting were much appreciated.

Oct. 8th.—I held the Quarterly Meeting. Every interest in the Circuit is healthy and prosperous. I nominated David O'Donnell for our Ministry, which was sustained by the vote of the meeting. We held a great meeting in honour of Mr. Burnett in the evening. Thank God for the blessings of this day.

Oct. 12th.—The Rev. Joseph Dare gave us a lecture on 'True Manhood,' which was fruitful in pecuniary results.

Oct. 16th.—This evening I lectured at Newtown on 'The Bible : a Revelation from God.' We had a good and sympathetic audience. Retired to Yarra Street, and commenced reading Liddon's Bampton Lectures. It is a mighty work, and ought to be studied by all ministers of religion.

Oct. 21st.—I went to Ballarat to preside at the District Meeting. The Rev. G. Daniel was elected secretary. At this meeting Messrs. Edwards and O'Donnell, after the usual examinations, were recommended to the Conference as suitable candidates for our work. Robert Walter Campbell and Abel Marsland were also received for theological training at Wesley College. It was, from beginning to end, an excellent meeting. On arriving at home on the 30th, I found two copies of the English Minutes awaiting me. I read with pleasure that my old West India friend and fellow-worker, the Rev. W. L. Binks was appointed President of our Conference for 1869. In the evening the Rev. T. F. Bird lectured on 'Mahomet.' It was an able deliverance in every respect.

Nov. 13th.—I received a letter from the private secretary to the Governor, in answer to my appeal in behalf of the unfortunate

W. N. McC. The case is referred to the Minister of Justice for reconsideration. I now have some hope.

Nov. 16*th.*—I wrote to Mr. Burnett to see if he can give a fortnight's services to Yarra Street when he has finished at Sandhurst. His reply, received next day, was in the negative. He wants rest, and will not disappoint the Superintendents of the Western Circuits.

Nov. 20*th.*—I left for the presidential annual tour to the Western District, which occupied me until December 5th. I preached and spoke in aid of the Foreign Missions in each Circuit in the District The utmost kindness was shown me by friends and ministers all along the line. I much enjoyed the trip, and having completed my visitation, returned home at the appointed time, none the worse for the fatigue I had undergone.

Dec. 8*th.*—I went to Melbourne to attend the meeting of the Stationing Committee. We sat two days, and closed the business.

Dec. 10*th.*—Busy all day preparing the accounts of the Children and Education Funds. The next day I closed up the accounts of the Church Building and Loan Fund, and the Jubilee Fund. I sent cheques for balances to the respective treasurers, so as to have the funds off my mind. In the evening I wrote to Mr. Commissioner Grant about the threatened sale of our Church Reserve at East Melbourne. I was much tried with the mental toil of the day, and at midnight I retired to rest.

Dec. 12*th.*—I left for Sebastopol, and was received by Mr. and Mrs. Robinson with much Christian urbanity. I preached in aid of the Trust at 11 and 6.30, and the Rev. R. M. Hunter at 3. The next day the public meetings were held, and the attendance was good.

Dec. 15*th.*—I read Baxter's 'Reformed Pastor,' and began writing the 'Ordination Charge' for the Conference in Sydney. There are several probationers to be received into full connexion, and, as ex-President, the preparation and the delivery of the Charge falls upon me. I wrote the Government about our Church Reserve at Newton Hill. The Hon. C. J. J. had been moving the Commissioners to sell it, on the ground that we had made no use of it. I asked Mr. J. G. Carr and Mr. Quinan to help me in resisting this robbery of 'God's acre.'

Dec. 19*th.*—I completed the Annual Statement of the 'Old Preachers' Fund' for the treasurers, and sent a cheque to Rev. J. S. Waugh for £361 12*s.*

SYDNEY UNIVERSITY.

Dec. 31*st.*—I held the Watch Night Service at Yarra Street, and thus closed the busiest and most responsible year of my Australian Ministry.

1869.

Jan. 1*st.*—I entered upon this year in the Yarra Street Church. It was solemn: a time of self-examination, confession, prayer, and consecration. Surely our vows will be noted in the ' Book of His remembrance.' By the first train I hastened to Melbourne to attend the funeral of the late Mrs. Hill, for many years the devoted companion and fellow-helper of her husband, the Rev. William Hill. It is a terrible blow to him, and an irreparable loss for the now motherless children. The whole ministerial circle is deeply touched with the suddenness and sadness of this bereavement.

Jan. 7*th.*—I held the Quarterly Meeting to-day. We still report numerical and financial progress. The membership has risen to 1,477, and the stewards have a credit balance of over £200. In the evening the Union Prayer Meeting was held. The Rev. G. Goodman (Anglican) gave the address. The church was full, but the singing was very poor.

Jan. 13*th.*—I left for the Conference to be held in Sydney, which was opened on the 21st: the Rev. W. L. Binks, President; and the Rev. B. Chapman, Secretary. Messrs. R. M. Hunter and C. T. Newman were received into ' full connexion,' and Messrs. B. G. Edwards, James Read, D. O'Donnell, and P. C. Thomas were received as ' preachers on trial.' We had to mournfully record the martyred death of the Rev. Thomas Baker, in Fiji, on July 21st, 1868, by the cannibal heathen. He was a holy man, and zealous in his Master's work. His companions, native Christians, fell also under the clubs of the savages. The net increase of membership for the year was 1,517, with 8,953 on trial.

The Ordination Service was held in Wesley Church, Chippendale, when the charge, founded on 1 Cor. ix. 27, was given by me as ex-President. It was a time of acute distress to me, for I feared it had fallen much below what was expected. After the service, however, the Rev. Father Watkin spoke words of comfort, and thanked me for the discourse. No ex-President ever received greater relief than that which came to me the next day, when the Secretary, Mr. Chapman, moved: ' That the thanks of the Conference be presented to the

15

ex-President for the very valuable charge addressed by him to the newly-ordained ministers, and that he be earnestly requested to furnish it for publication.'

On *February 5th* the Sessions closed, much to the relief of us all, for the heat had been very trying, even to the strongest man amongst us. By this Conference, I was appointed to the Superintendency of the Wesley Church Circuit, Melbourne, having as my colleagues the Revs. W. D. Lalean, Martin Dyson, and E. J. Watkin. On the 8th, I was once more at home in Geelong and found all well. Our passage from Sydney to Sandridge Pier was made in fifty hours, and was quite a pleasure trip all through.

March 2nd.—I left by first train for Newlyn, *via* Ballarat, to lay the 'foundation-stone' of our new church. The building committee presented me with a handsome silver trowel, commemorative of the event. The Rev. Edward B. Burns, Mrs. Burns, and Mrs. Sadgrove accompanied me from Creswick to Newlyn. We had a large attendance at the tea and public meeting, and a generous response in aid of the building. We got back to Creswick at midnight.

March 25th.—We laid the 'foundation stone' of a new church at German Town. The usual after meetings were held.

March 27th.—I left for the Mortlake Circuit, and reached Pyneyup in the evening. Mrs. and the Misses Shaw, whom I had known in Geelong, received me most heartily. I preached twice the next day, in aid of the Circuit funds.

On the 29th the Rev. T. F. Bird, the Shaws, and I went to the stone-laying ceremony of the new Mechanics' Institute. In the evening we held a meeting in our church, when we raised £25 for the Circuit. On the 31st, Mr. Thomas Shaw drove me to Camperdown, where we joined the coach and reached Geelong in the evening. The Shaws showed me great kindness.

April 1st.—I held the Quarterly Meeting. We were from 11 a.m. to 6.30 p.m. It was a capital meeting. Members 1,489; and on trial 30; removals 47. We have still a large credit balance to the good of the Circuit. The next day I went to Ballarat to an 'Ordination Service.' Messrs. T. F. Bird, R. M. Hunter, Edward A. Davies, and James J. Watsford were to be ordained to the full Ministry by the 'laying on of the hands of the Presbytery' as in apostolic times. The Rev. George Daniel gave an excellent charge.

April 6th.—A valedictory meeting was held this evening in Yarra

Street for myself and nephew, the Rev. E. S. Bickford, whose terms of service had expired. Substantial tokens of love and esteem were made to both of us. Thus closed my official relation to this loving people, and to their extensive and prosperous Circuit.

April 8th.—We left at 1 p.m., by train for Melbourne. The Hunts, Browns, Hitchcocks, Lowes, and some other friends saw us off. Mr. Edward Whitehead, Circuit Steward, and brother of my former fellow-worker in the West Indies, the Rev. Francis Whitehead, was at the Spencer Street Station to receive us. At Wesley Church Parsonage, Mesdames Whitehead and Burrows were awaiting our arrival. I met the Minister's Class in the evening, and presided at a meeting of the Sunday School Committee. We retired to rest at 11 p.m.

April 9th. [Diary Jotting]—' We are all very much tired. Oh, this itinerancy! The longer I live the more I object to it. Our removals are oftentimes not only very expensive, but inconvenient and unfortunate. I hope the principle will yet be considerably modified.'

April 12th.—I preached at Wesley Church in aid of the Sunday School, and next day I presided at the public meeting.

April 13th.—I attended the Church Anniversary at Sandridge and presided at the evening meeting. I find that Mr. and Mrs. Roalman have much helped our Church in this seaport.

April 16th.—I entered upon my beloved pastoral work and visited twelve families.

April 19th.—The Rev. John Egglestone, having resigned the position of ' Acting Clerical Treasurer ' of the ' Old Preachers' Fund,' and I, having been requested by the other treasurers to assume that position, and accepted it, to-day the large 'iron safe' with all books and papers were handed over to me. This will be an additional responsibility; but with the available counsel of my co-acting treasurer the Hon. A. Fraser, M.L.C., in all matters of loans, and the assistance of Mr. Hewitt as accountant, occasionally, as his services may be required, I hope to be able to do the work.

April 26th.—Mr. E. Taylor and I went to the Education Office, to secure a day school connected with our church at Carlton, as well as to speak to Mr. Kane, the secretary, about the Central School in Geelong.

May 3rd.—I received a letter from the Rev. B. Chapman,

Secretary of the Conference, covering resolutions of Conference, anent the relation of two of our brethren, members of the Irish Annuitant Society, and of one brother n South Australia, who had joined our Ministry at the age of forty years about, as to terms upon which they may be received as members of our Annuitant Society. The resolutions embody a principle which shall apply to these and to similar cases as they may hereafter occur.

May 6th. [Diary Jotting]—'My birthday to-day. I am now fifty-three years of age. My heart is the Lord's, and so is my life His. May the coming year be one of much happiness!

May 13th.—The Rev. J. S. Waugh called to tell me of the dreadful murder of our dear brother minister, the Rev. W. Hill, at Pentridge Stockade, by a life-long prisoner, Ritson, when Mr. Hill was in his cell praying for him. We then went to Victoria Parade to break the sad news to Mrs. Holmes, the mother-in-law of Mr. Hill. We called also on Mrs. Gallagher, a good, kind sister in Christ, who had seen much trouble, to go at once to the house of mourning, and comfort and help the distressed family. Messrs. Egglestone, Dare and others called at the house in the evening. We are all overwhelmed at the terrible calamity which has come upon us : 'We are troubled " deeply," but not in despair.'

May 15th.—The mortal remains of our late Brother Hill were to-day interred in the Melbourne Cemetery: 'Devout men carried him to his burial and made great lamentation over him.' Mr. Waugh, at Brunswick Street Church, preached a solemn and instructive discourse on the death of Mr. Hill. The church was densely packed.

We met the Circuit officials after the service, to make arrangements for carrying on the work of the Circuit until the next Conference. The Rev. Mr. Waugh engaged to do his best, and other ministers proffered help. The next day I was asked by the Book Committee to take Mr. Hill's place as Book Steward, and the Rev. George Daniel to act as co-editor with the Rev. B. Field of the *Wesleyan Chronicle.* I moved that a memorial volume of sermons, as preached by Mr. Hill, be published, which was agreed to. At the instigation of the Premier, Sir James MacCulloch, a handsome provision for the education and support of the Hill orphans was made, and to continue until the youngest of them reached the age of twenty-one.

The Christian people showed their sympathy in a very substantial manner. All was done that could under such circumstances be desired.

May 24th.—I attended the *levée* in honour of our beloved Queen. In the evening I read with intense interest in the London *Watchman* a report on the ' Irish Church ' question, which had come off in the House of Commons. The result upon my own mind is that Mr. Gladstone is undoubtedly an ' elect servant ' of God for working out great social, political, and ecclesiastical reforms in Great Britain.

June 7th.—We accepted a tender for the erection of a new church at Carlton, and the next day we accepted a tender for erecting a new parsonage at Sandridge. We can't stand still, even if we were to try. Besides which, not to advance in Church Work is to recede ; and that we must not do.

June 21st.—Mr. Lalean and I went to Sunbury to visit the Government Industrial School. Altogether it is an enormous establishment, and appears to be well conducted. We held a religious service. In the evening a tea and public meeting were held in the interests of the new church. The debt on the building will be only £17.

June 23rd.—This forenoon I entered upon a new sphere of duty. It was at the Melbourne Gaol, where I first preached to about two hundred male prisoners. I saw in the audience a convicted Catholic Priest, an ex-Baptist Minister, a son of a Wesleyan Minister, an ex-editor of a newspaper, and I hardly know whom besides. An intelligent, fine young man, but one of the unfortunates, presided at the harmonium, and joined in singing right heartily. It was a sad spectacle. After this service, in another part of the gaol, I met some eighty to a hundred women, who were in durance vile for bad conduct of many kinds. I waited in one of the cells, set apart for the purpose, to converse with any of these women who might choose to do so. Several came, and I gave the pledge to three of them. The effect of the services upon me I cannot describe. I was distressed and prostrate in body and soul.

June 26th. [Diary Jotting]—' This has been one of the most trying weeks I have ever experienced. "When my heart is overwhelmed within me ; lead me to the Rock that is higher than I." '

June 30th.—I held my first Quarterly Meeting in this Circuit—

income £439 19s. 4d., being a small increase upon the previous quarter. But we have a big debt caused by refurnishing parsonages. The brethren were full of hopefulness.

July 3rd.—Is it possible to have 'too many irons in the fire?' Well, it has to be done sometimes. To-day I had to conduct the second 'Female Prayer Meeting' in Wesley Church, when 250 ladies were present. I gave the address, on 'Woman's Work in the Church.' It was well received. In the evening I went to Sandridge to raise funds for the new parsonage. We got over £100. Mr. and Mrs. Poolman are a great help to us here.

July 12th.—Mr. Burnett called. I was really glad to see him, and took him to see Mrs. Holmes, the foster-mother of the orphaned Hills. The conversation was highly spiritual, and we had a sweet time in prayer. I preached in the evening at North Melbourne. The after meeting was full of Divine power.

July 20th.—I lectured this evening in the Temperance Hall, Russell Street, on 'Total Abstinence.' The place was full of people.

July 21st.—I went to Maidstone and Albion. I preached in the evening at Albion to thirty-eight persons, and baptized two infants. Previous to the service I called upon many families and invited them to church.

July 24th.—I wrote Revs. Dare, Egglestone, Catterall, King, Cope, Bird, Daniel, and Neale requesting their kind supervision of 'Industrial School' children located in their respective districts. Mr. Duncan, the head of the Department, and I are acting together in the children's welfare.

July 28th.—This day I made up the subscription list for the Hill orphans. Mr. and Mrs. William Horder kindly contributed £50 towards this fund.

July 29th.—Mr. S. G. King, J.P., laid the foundation-stone of the new church at Carlton. The meeting at 7 p.m. was largely attended, and the response was most generous. For safe custody, I sent to day to Mr. Waugh, our custodian of Church Deeds, all documents, papers, and letters, which had come to me from the Crown Lands Office during my Presidential year.

Aug. 2nd.—I prepared and sent to supernumerary ministers' widows and ministers' widows their quarterly annuities direct. There were 150 present at the prayer meeting this afternoon. In the evening the Rev. Dr. Tucker (Anglican) gave us in Wesley

Church a learned lecture on the Abyssinian captives. Dr. Corrigan presided with suavity and ability.

Aug. 3rd.—Ritson, the murderer of the late Rev. W. Hill, will be executed this time. From the hour of his conviction he has been attended to by the Revs. W. D. Lalean, Watkin, and Neale ; may we hope with good effect ? So Mr. Lalean believes.

Aug. 8th.—' Honour thy father and thy mother.' My father died some years ago in South Australia, but my mother is still living and in her eighty-seventh year. This morning Mrs. Bickford, my niece Christina Pascoe, and I went to Whittlesea, to see her. She was as well as could be expected at her great age. In the afternoon Mr. Wyett drove us to see the Yan Yean, which is an immense reservoir, from which is drawn the water that supplies the city of Melbourne and suburbs. It was a grand sight, and a wise provision for the health and comforts of the ' city-ful.'

Aug. 19th.—Mr. Taylor and I went to Footscray and Stony Creek to visit among the people. We were kindly received, and we promised them that on the next Sabbath afternoon a religious service should be held.

Aug. 20th.—At our Preachers' Weekly Meeting to-day, James Ah Ling, the Chinese catechist, was present. Mr. S. G. King finds his salary, and I supervise his work. May we not believe that amongst these so-called Heathen Chinee, our Divine Lord shall ' see of the travail of His soul ' ?

Sept. 1st.—Our dear brother, the Rev. B. Field, departed this life in peace and hope to-day at 10.45 p.m. He had been writing for the *Wesleyan Chronicle,* of which he was senior editor, up to 9.30, when he laid aside his pen, and went to his bed and died. How sudden, ' yet how safe.' On the 4th, we interred the remains of our dear brother, B. Field, ' in sure and certain hope.'

Sept. 8th.—In the afternoon I attended the funeral of the late Hon. John Fawkner, M.L.C. the founder, it is claimed, of the city of Melbourne. He was an eccentric, adventurous man, and an ardent Colonial and politician. He was much venerated as 'Johnny Fawkner,' and he went down to his grave full of honours and blessings.

Sept. 17th.—We held a meeting of Wesley Church Trustees to consider the financial condition of the Trust. We raised £120 towards the £500 required.

Sept. 18th.—Young Thomas Adamson preached this evening, with a view to his nomination for the Ministry. It was a creditable discourse.

Sept. 19*th.*—The Rev. William Taylor preached in Wesley Church to a densely crowded congregation. The next day (Monday) a tea and public meeting were held. We raised £353 12s. 10d. Mr. Taylor greatly helped us.

Sept. 25*th.*—I heard David S. Lindsay preach an acceptable discourse. He will be a candidate for the Ministry. We met the new converts after the service, and put them in classes for fellowship and counsel.

Sept. 27*th.*—I went at 5 p.m. to see Mr. Glass, and remained with him until he died. This is a sad bereavement for our sister, Mrs. Glass, and her sisters.

Sept. 29*th.*—I held the Quarterly Meeting this evening. Income £470 16s. 8d. being £42 3s. 7d. over expenditure. This reduces the debt to about £100. The invitations for next year were myself as Superintendent, M. Dyson, E. J. Watkin, and R. C. Flockart.

Oct. 1st.—I copied from the *Argus* this statement :—

'Messrs. McCulloch and Sellers have in stations 375,540 acres, for which they pay £1,800 per annum, seven-eighths of a penny per acre. Besides which, they have a reservation of 9,000 acres.'

Here would be something for Mr. George, of ' Land Nationalization ' notoriety, to do. This is only one among many cases of a similar kind.

Oct. 21st.—I went to the House of Assembly, and heard an acrimonious debate led on by Mr. George Higinbotham. I greatly admired the bearing of the Chief Secretary, Mr. John Macpherson, who is very able in reply and courteous in speech. I wish in this respect there were more like him in the House.

Oct. 28th.—I attended a meeting of clergymen of different denominations, called by Bishop Perry, for forming a ' Society for the Promotion of Morality.' Such a society should be a factor for good.

Nov. 3rd.—The District Meeting was begun to-day; the Rev. J. S. Waugh, Chairman, and the Rev. George Daniel, Secretary. The Rev. William Taylor preached in the evening in Wesley Church to a full congregation. My nephew, the Rev. E. S. Bickford, came to-day, and we sat up until 12 o'clock, conversing mainly on the spiritual condition of the Circuits, and the prospects of the Methodist

Church in these Colonies. I am delighted that he is taking such an interest in the general affairs of our great Connexion. On the 6th, the three young men from the Wesley Church Circuit, Messrs. Adamson, Brown, and Lindsay, were passed as suitable candidates for our work. On the 10th, the regular order of business of the meeting was suspended at 12 o'clock, when we had a gracious sacramental ordinance. In the evening, the brethren from the country gave an account of the work of God in their several Circuits. It was a fine meeting and full of blessed influence.

Nov. 11th.—The sessions of the District Meeting were closed to-day, when we went to Cremorne at the invitation of James Harcourt, Esq. M.P., and Mrs. Harcourt, to spend the afternoon. We were treated with much genuine hospitality. Rev. T. F. Bird lectured on 'Past and Present,' in Wesley Church in the evening. It was a noble and grand effort, and took the people by surprise. He is a brilliant fellow.

Nov. 12th.—I had to break a lance with the Rev. J. W. Inglis (Presbyterian), who had stated in the Assembly that the Wesleyans were decoying Presbyterian parents and their children from their own Church, by means of our Sunday Schools, and I took my letter to the *Argus* for publication. On the 13th, there appeared a reply from the pen of the Rev. George Mackie, explanatory of the accusations of Mr. Inglis. I accepted the rejoinder, and so ended the matter.

Nov. 16th.—The Rev. W. H. Fitchett and I travelled to Geelong together, and we had much profitable conversation. He will be some day one of our ablest men. Mrs. Hitchcock received me with much Christian cordiality. In the afternoon I went to pay my respects to my kind friends, Mr. and Mrs. Silas Harding. In the evening, I accompanied Mrs. Harding and Miss McLellan, to the special religious service at Chilwell. I commenced the meeting with prayer and reading the Scriptures, and the Rev. W. Taylor preached with wonderful power. I remained in Geelong until the 20th, visiting old friends, and helping Brother Taylor in his great work. I returned to Melbourne by steamer, and was all the better in health for my Geelong visit.

Dec. 13th.—I went to the Land Office to see about the Footscray Church site, and the Carlton Parsonage site. I also attended the Bazaar in the interests of the Benevolent Asylum, when I handed to the Treasurer a cheque for £129 odd, as our contribution to the Fund. The Treasurer was not a little surprised. The next day I attended a meeting of the Stationing Committee.

Dec. 16th.—I went to Footscray with Mr. Harding from the Land Office, and Mr. Adamson the architect, to mark out the Church Reserve, and to take the levels of the ground. I also attended the Wesley College Speech Day, and was much pleased with the performances and artistic works of the young gentlemen.

Dec. 21st.—We laid the foundation-stone of the new church at Footscray. Mr. Gresham, the Mayor, did us the kindness of laying the stone. We had a tea and public meeting in the evening, when good financial help was promised.

Dec. 25th.—I preached at 7 a.m., and the Rev. Dr. Tucker at 11 a.m. His text was taken from Isaiah ix. 6, 7. The sermon was a very able exposition of the great Gospel text, and was listened to by a large audience with deep and delighted interest. I need not add, that to me, who have no chance of often hearing brother ministers, it was 'a feast of fat things, a feast of wines on the lees, of fat things full of marrow, of wines on the lees well refined.'

Dec. 27th.—I went to Gardiner's Creek, and preached a funeral sermon for my late friend and county man, James Woodmason. He was the embodiment of an honest Devonshire yeoman, and a generous supporter of the Church.

Dec. 29th.—We held the Quarterly Meeting, and found ourselves in debt to the tune of £220, occasioned mostly by an additional outlay on the Sandridge Parsonage. We shall clear this debt also before my term of service closes, if the recurrence of such extras can only be prevented.

Dec. 31st.—We held the Watch Night Service in Wesley Church. I was assisted by Messrs. Wilton and Hodgson, two of our excellent local preachers. It was a profitable service.

1870.

Jan. 1st. [Diary Jotting]—'I commenced this year in Wesley Church. The concluding part of the Watch Night Service was very solemn. May the Divine Spirit confirm the resolutions into which I, with the congregation, entered. Many letters and papers this morning, an earnest of what I may expect this year. But I look to Heaven for help, and shall not be disappointed.'

The case of T. W. D. has caused me an agony of distress all this day. He is in gaol, awaiting his trial for embezzlement of moneys at the Bank. I saw him in the gaol yesterday, pitied him, and prayed with him.

Jan. 3rd.—We held the Union Prayer Meeting in Wesley Church this evening. The venerable Dean Macartney gave the address. It was full of wise counsels, such as might be expected from a man of his spirituality, deep experience, and ability. The Spirit of God seemed to rest upon the other ministers who led in prayer. It was a good time to us all.

Jan. 5th.—We were plagued with beggars all the forenoon. We need one domestic to answer to the door. Such a thing as ministerial privacy cannot be had in this house.

Jan. 7th.—To-day Ebenezer Taylor was examined in Committee by the Chairman, the Rev. J. S. Waugh, who was well satisfied. Mr. Taylor was unanimously recommended to be taken into the itinerant work.

Jan. 8th.—I buried the remains of dear Mrs. Stanford this afternoon. It was a melancholy scene! Poor Stanford is heart-broken. Short wedded life of only eight months. How mysterious are thy ways, O God!

Jan. 11th.—Busy indeed, and plagued with persons calling to stay, when one has no time to attend to them.

As showing the strength of the Connexional principle in the Wesley Church Circuit, I may here give the gross totals, for 1869, of the several funds, as follow : Church Building Fund, £47 16s. 9d. ; Education Fund, £37 13s. 4d. ; Church Extension Fund, £74 4s. 1d. ; Foreign Missions, £281 15s. 9d. ; Chinese Mission (fifteen months), £187 10s. 0d. ; City Mission and Bible Woman Agency, £18 6s. 9d. ; total, £647 6s. 8d.

Jan. 12th.—I left per steamer for the Adelaide Conference. Judging by the number of ministers on board, we appeared to be taking the Conference to the sister colony to sit. I was the guest of Mr. and Mrs. J. H. Kaines, at Halton Brook, during my stay. Mrs. Kaines is the daughter of the Rev. T. W. Smith, a Wesleyan Minister in England, who, when travelling in the Kingsbridge Circuit, Devon, conducted my theological studies, and recommended me to the Conference for the foreign work. No wonder that I was much at home with my Halton Brook friends! The Conference was opened in Pirie Street Church, January 20th; the Rev. George

Hurst, President, and the Rev. B. Chapman, Secretary.   The Rev.
W. H. Fitchett, of Victoria, and the Rev. J. T. Simpson, of
South Australia, with fifteen other probationers, who had honourably
completed their four years' ministry, were received into full connexion.   Sixteen young men were accepted as candidates for the
ministry.   The net increase of members for the year was 3,384,
with 10,091 on trial.

Feb. 1st. [Diary Jotting]—'Closed the Conference this evening at 9.45.
Upon the whole it has been a happy Conference, although we had some
difficult work. The President, the Rev. George Hurst, did well, and the
Secretary, the Rev. B. Chapman, was ready with the minutes as soon as
required.'

Feb. 2nd.—I left Halton Brook for Adelaide this morning to see
my kinsfolk, the Bickfords, and some other friends.   Mr. Kaines,
my generous host, with his daughters, Bessy and Laura Kaines, saw
me into the train at the North Terrace for Port Adelaide, where our
steamer lay.   The Kaines' were most kind to me, and I parted from
them with much gratefulness of feeling.

Feb. 4th.—I arrived at home after a somewhat rough passage.
Indeed, I was ill from sea-sickness all the way over.   The Rev. B.
Chapman came with me to be our guest *en route* for Sydney.   The
Chairmen of the New South Wales Districts settled with me their
accounts for the Old Preachers' Fund before sailing on the 9th.   On
the evening of this day our dear Father Watkin preached in Wesley
Church.   It was quite a treat to hear so original, quaint, and telling
a sermon from the dear old man.

Feb. 18th.—Mr. and Mrs. Kaines came from Adelaide to be our
guests for a while.

March 3rd.—I spent an agreeable time with Dr. Pinnell, the
American Consul, and Mrs. Pinnell, taking tea with them.   They
are members of the Methodist Episcopal Church in the United
States, and Mr. Pinnell is a lay preacher ; I am sorry that they
cannot 'fall in love' with the colony to which they have come in a
representative capacity.

April 1st.—The 'children of Shem' are coming to Christ.   The
first-fruits we had in Wesley Church to-night, when I baptized two
converted Chinamen in the name of the Holy Trinity.   James Ah
Ling, our catechist, translated their own accounts of their respective
experiences, when, after answering certain questions put to them

through James, we received them into the Christian Church. There was deep feeling in the congregation. I gave each a copy of the New Testament in Chinese, with a little charge as to their future conduct.

April 3rd.—I preached at Ashby, and examined the Sunday School in the afternoon. On the Monday I visited my old friends, and in the evening I spoke at the public meeting. I returned to Melbourne by the last train, and reached home at 11.30 p.m.

April 6th.—We held the Quarterly Meeting to-day. We had a fine attendance. The finances were well up, so that we reduced the Circuit debt to £153 15s.

April 7th.—We have been in this Circuit twelve months to-day. It has been a year of incessant engagements of a Circuit, Connexional, and public kind ; but my health, through God's great mercy, has been good and pretty well equal to the strain. But it is a painful draw-back to the pleasure one might otherwise have felt on reviewing the year, that the Superintendent of this Circuit cannot command the time necessary for making such preparations for the pulpit as the intelligence of a city congregation demands. This remark does not apply to the Superintendent's colleagues, whose principal time should be occupied in pastoral visitation and in pulpit preparation.

April 11th.—Our first anniversary for the new ecclesiastical year was held at Wesley Church. The services on the Sabbath were well attended, and on the Monday evening we had quite a demonstration in favour of Sunday Schools. Our friend, Dr. Cutts, presided with much ability, and the Revs. Flockart, Symons, Watkins, and Hayward spoke with fine effect. It was a good beginning.

April 15th.—For some years I have availed myself of the aid of the Presbyterian Clergy for my Christmas and Good Friday services. In this way I have had the opportunity twice a year, at least, to hear doctrinally stated their views of the Incarnation and Atonement of Christ. From the time of his arrival in Melbourne, Dr. Adam Cairns had always shown the most friendly feeling towards the Wesleyan ministers, and I accordingly invited him to take the pulpit at Wesley Church on this day. The Doctor took as his text : ' It is Christ that died.' About three hundred were present. We had an able exposition of the death of Christ for ' the sins of the whole world.' It was the ' strong meat ' by which mature Christians are fed, and do grow.

May 5th.—It is a source of much comfort to me that my Society class keeps up so well. There were twenty-eight present this evening. The quickening grace received under the Rev. William Taylor's special services has continued with these precious souls. It is a great honour to be the means of leading men into the Church; but it is the greatest of all good work afterwards to keep them within the Church's fold.

I am reading with keenest interest the Memoir of Madame Guyon. 'She was,' says Wesley, 'undoubtedly a woman of a very uncommon understanding, and of excellent piety. Nor was she more a lunatic than she was an heretic.' With such a recommendation, it is no wonder that I read the book with much attention. I was much struck with the controversy between Bossieu and Fénélon. My sympathies are with the latter, who, no doubt, was a truly good and great man. The former was able, but he was a despot; he seems to have been anything but what a bishop should be. My mind was greatly excited over this controversy.

May 6th. [Diary Jotting]—' I was unwell, and could not therefore rise at my usual hour. I am this day fifty-four years of age. This morning, in my chamber, I solemnly gave myself, just as I am, to my God in Christ for service —for life, for death. Oh, that the Holy Spirit may perfect what is lacking in me, so that I may "stand perfect and complete in all the will of God"!'

In the evening I presided, as usual, at the Young Men's Association Meeting, when Mr. R. Hodgson, the vice-president, gave a clever essay upon ' Death : Before and After the Fall.' My friend is fond of the abstruse and the difficult, but it is his way. The after discussion was spirited and able.

May 9th.—I went to Albion, and lectured at a Temperance Meeting: forty took the pledge.

May 19th.—The social condition of Melbourne was one of the subjects for the consideration of the ' Society for the Promotion of Morality,' of which Bishop Perry is president. This morning I was one of a deputation who went to the Chief Secretary about the deplorable state of the city. He received us courteously, and promised his help.

May 24th.—Attended, as I was in duty bound, the Governor's *levée* in honour of Her Most Gracious Majesty. I think it is most important in this democratic country that all respectable English people should pay this mark of respect to the representative of our good Queen.

June 10th.—In our Young Men's Meeting this evening the subject of discussion was: 'Are Forms of Worship desirable in Public Worship?' We had a stirring time of it. The negative was carried by sixteen to eight. This is quite in sympathy with the feeling in great part of the Wesley Church congregation, where Mr. Wesley's Abridgment is used. It will have to be discontinued, I expect; but not during my superintendency.

June 13th.—I attended the Church Anniversary Meeting at North Melbourne. We raised £343 odd. It was a noble contribution to the Trust.

June 16th.—On a Thursday afternoon, when I could afford the time, I used to run up to the Parliament House to hear the debates. To-day four of the ablest men in the House spoke: Messrs. Fellows, Francis, Langton, and MacCulloch. It was time well spent. The Rev. W. Taylor returned from Adelaide this evening, looking well after his campaign in soul-saving in South Australia.

June 17th.—The Rev. Joseph Dare lectured at Carlton on 'Wesley. The Hon. J. A. MacPherson, M.P., in the chair. It was an eloquent dissertation on the character of the great and good man. About three hundred were present.

June 22nd.—Preached again at the gaol, and spent two hours and a quarter among the prisoners. This is a terrible ordeal for me. I felt nerveless and ill when I returned to the Parsonage.

June 27th.—I went to the Land Office to see about Keilor and Essenden Church Reserves.

June 30th.—I wrote again to the Land Office for a grant of land at Northcote as a Parsonage Reserve.

July 1st.—We had a fine discussion at the Young Men's Meeting this evening on the question, 'Should the Parliament pass a Permissive Bill?' I examined to-day 'Replies to Essays and Reviews.' They are keen, and much to the point. I hope the poison in the 'Essays' will be neutralised by these 'Replies.'

July 6th.—We held the Quarterly Meeting to-day. Income £483 5s. 11d. Debt remaining, £142 11s. 5d. Members 1,011; on trial, 45. The next evening the Rev. W. R. Fletcher gave a lecture to the Young Men's Association. About two hundred persons were present. The lecture was much appreciated.

July 14th.—I was engaged all the forenoon in preparing a set of resolutions for the Consultative Committee, upon the new state of things sprung upon us by a new measure, entitled, 'Repeal of State Aid to Religion Bill,' now before the Parliament. My proposition of vesting a portion of our Grant was rejected, and Mr. Daniel's, for spending all during the next five years, was accepted.*

Afterwards the Rev. John Cope and I conversed at large on the 'Old Preachers' Fund' business, and, at his request, I engaged to prepare certain data to aid him in his calculations.

July 15th.—The Rev. William Taylor returned from Beechworth, and lectured in the evening to eight hundred and fifty persons. The next day, the Rev. Father Watkin, his son, E. J. Watkin, Mrs. Watkin, and a dozen at least besides, called to see Mr. Taylor. He is much and deservedly beloved.

July 19th.—I received a letter from Lady MacCulloch, acknowledging, for Sir James, the Rev. W. Taylor's present of his book on South Africa. It is a beautifully written and well-expressed note.

July 20th.—I went with Mr. Egglestone to see Mr. and Mrs. James Harcourt, who have just heard of the death of their son Charles, in Fiji. It was a mournful scene. The Rev. J. S. Waugh joined us in condoling with our friends and praying with them. In the evening I worked upon the statistics of Methodist itinerant life

---

* The Cessation of 'State Aid,' under the McCulloch Government, imposed a heavy responsibility upon the Wesleyan Connexion, to raise by collections and subscriptions such a sum as would carry on the work which had come into existence by the aid of Government grants. The amount of £50,000 was provided under the 53rd clause of the Constitution Act, and was to be distributed under certain conditions. (1) That in supplementing stipends, it had to be shown by the applicant that the amount he claimed had been duplicated by his congregation. (2) That the amount claimed for churches and parsonages had been duplicated in the same manner. But a large proportion of really ' godly ' persons objected to its continuance : 1, Because truth and error were equally subsidised ; 2, That in the appropriation, great injustice was done to the Presbyterians and Wesleyans, whose Census ' Returns ' were *bonâ fide*, whereas one of the denominations could not so aver ; 3, Then there were the Congregational, Baptist, and Minor Methodist bodies, who, from conscientious motives, would not take any money from the public exchequer. As might be expected, the continuance or the non-continuance of the ' Grant in Aid ' became a burning question. The contention was brought to an end by the Government, subject to a diminishing scale spreading over five years, when it ceased altogether. Since that notable period, 'a fair field and no favour' has been the unchallenged right of every religious denomination in the colony.

for Mr. Cope's guidance, in his attempt to fix the principles of our Annuitant Society upon sound and safe principles. It is a great and difficult work he has undertaken.

July 30*th.*—To-day James Ah Ling and Leong on Tong called about a matrimonial errand to China. I gave Leong on Tong a letter to the Rev. George Piercy, our missionary at Canton, including three bills for £20, £10, £10, to be used in the interests of James Ah Ling, in the event of Leong succeeding in his mission for him.

Aug. 9*th.*—I went to hear Dr. Bromby (Anglican) lecture on 'Pre-historic Man.' Of course, it was clever in its way, but unsound in its theology; and, in a metaphysical aspect, most erroneous. I returned home distressed in mind for the sad effects such statements are sure to bring about amongst a certain increment of our city population. As an example, two mechanics, who were working in Russell Street, on the next morning were heard thus to converse: 'I say, Jack, did you hear what Dr. Bromby said last night in his lecture?' 'No,' said Tom, 'what was it?' 'Why, man,' rejoined the other, 'that if we die without being converted there will be an end of us. So we have nothing to fear.' And much more was said on the same line. The learned and eccentric doctor cannot ever know in this world how much mischief his lectures have done.

I went to Brighton, and baptized three children of the Rev. J. B. and Mrs. Smith. The parents are attached and true friends. But my pleasure was rudely disturbed, later on in the day, by the sad intelligence of the sudden death in Melbourne of Mr. James Webb, who for many years had been a strong supporter of our Church in Tasmania and Victoria. Worry was the cause of his death. I am sorry—deeply sorry. What will the family do? May the Heavenly Father undertake for them.

Aug. 16*th.*—I was engaged with Wesley Church business all the morning, when I prepared a plan for the distribution of the £513 11*s.* received from the estate of N. & R. Guthridge & Co., and enclosed it to the Treasurers of the Trust. This is the last payment, I suppose, from the Old Collins Street property.

Aug. 24*th.*—I took my letter on Dr. Bromby's mischievous lecture to the *Argus* for publication. I had waited to see if Bishop Perry, or Dr. Cairns, or the Rev. J. S. Waugh, would call the doctor to account, and finding that they had not done so, I was constrained to do my little best. With what effect, I cannot divine.

Aug. 25th.—I again attended the sick at the Hospital, and afterwards visited Mr. Miscamble. Poor man ! He is much afflicted, but he is very happy. I saw the venerable Dean Macartney, at the ' Promotion of Morality ' meeting, who thanked me for my letter on Dr Bromby's lecture. ' How is it,' said I, ' that you have no dogmas in the Thirty-nine Articles upon " Future Punishment" ?' He replied, ' If there is nothing in the Articles, there is in the prayers.' ' Yes,' I rejoined, ' we do pray in the Litany to be saved from that " wrath and everlasting damnation." But there should have something in the Articles themselves, as expressive of the Church's belief.' I think he ully acquiesced in my remark.

I began reading again Hamilton's ' Rewards and Punishments,' with the view of obtaining more information on this awful doctrine of the Scriptures. I do not think anything better can be had at the present time.

Aug. 27th.—In the *Argus* of to-day Dr. Bromby's answer to my letter appeared ; if it can be called an answer, which is doubtful. However, I now drop the matter, and leave the controversy to those of ' The Brethren,' who have more time and more polemic ability than I have for further discussion. This has been an anxious and oppressive week, and I am feeling quite ill. Mrs. Bickford and I, therefore, are going out to St. Kilda to see what its salubrious air and quiet will do for me.

Aug. 29th.—Telegram from England—' War has broken out between France and Prussia.' As far as I can judge the Emperor is entirely wrong ; and if he be he should suffer severely.

Aug. 30th.—This evening I presided at a meeting for forming a Temperance Society in connection with Wesley Church. Messrs. Callaghan, Hodgson, Marshall, and Platt spoke effectively. Between twenty and thirty signed.

Sept. 15th.—To-day I finished my lecture on ' Wilberforce,' which will be given, in the first instance, to the Wesley Church ' Young Men's Society.' I consider my subject under three aspects : (1) As a Christian ; (2) as a Statesman ; (3) as a Philanthropist. I hope it will do some good. 1 have now in course of reading ' Power on Universalism,' as I find I must get the grip of this question in all its varying aspects. Melbourne, at the present time, is afflicted with a polemic spirit.

Sept. 19th.—We held the opening services of the North Sandridge Church. We raised £50 10s.

Sept. 20th.—I went to Geelong to attend the ' Sons of Temperance ' Meeting. I travelled with Messrs. Longmore, Burtt, and Cope, M.P.'s, and Mr. D. Matthews from Echuca, the friend of the Aborigines, together with Mr. Poole, ex-editor of the *Herald.* We had a lively time of it all the way. In the afternoon I visited several of my old friends, and took tea with Dr. and Mrs. Machin, and had a baptismal ceremony. I afterwards spoke at the Mechanics' Institute Meeting, where we had a large audience. From thence I went to the *Advertiser* office to know of the latest telegrams, when I learnt that so far the Prussians had completely beaten the French. I returned to Melbourne on the evening of the 21st in time to hold the Local Preachers' Meeting. James Ah Ling and Mr. Restorck were received as full local preachers.

Sept. 24th.—I received a letter from Mr. George Smith, Circuit Steward, Ballarat, and one from Mr. James Oddie, my old and true friend, asking me if I will accept an invitation to that Circuit as Superintendent for the coming year ? I replied by telegram, ' I am not expecting to leave this Circuit; but if I were I would accept with pleasure.' Startling news to-day. The Napoleonic dynasty is at an end.

The Rev. T. McKensie Fraser, M.A., from Geelong, lectured this evening in Wesley Church on Dr. Bromby's ' Theory of Annihilation ' to some four hundred persons. It was a very able lecture, in which the author, as I think, refuted point by point the doctor's unscriptural and unphilosophical theories. Mr. Fraser was listened to throughout with closest attention.

Sept. 30th.—I gave ' Wilberforce ' this evening to the ' Young Men's Association,' and was well received.

Oct. 3rd.—A kind of red-letter day. I started in the morning for Sunbury by an early train, and officially visited the Government ' Industrial School and Reformatory.' I was much pleased with Mr. Scott, the superintendent. I conducted a pretty full religious service, and then returned to Mr. Smith's at Sunbury. In the evening I preached to a nice week-night congregation, and returned to Melbourne, reaching home at 11.30 p.m. A hard and happy day's work.

Oct. 5th.—We held the Quarterly Meeting. The motion for a division of the Circuit was negatived by forty-four against forty votes. The four ministers were re-invited with a young preacher for Carlton.

Oct. 12th.—I attended the Loan Fund Committee, when £150 was voted to the Carlton Church. In the evening we met again for forming a Sustentation Society. We sat until 10 p.m. I was very cold, and wearied with the labours of the day.

Oct. 13th.—I prepared a fair copy of the 'Rules and Regulations' for a 'Home Mission and Contingent Fund Society,' for submission to the District Meeting and Conference. I attended in the evening a Temperance Meeting at Coburg, and spoke for half an hour. There are now forty-five adult members.

Oct. 14th.—The proposed 'Rules and Regulations' for Sunday Schools were agreed to by a Committee this evening. I read Lothair until 12 o'clock, and again on the 15th, when I finished it. It is a surprising book. The characters are well drawn, and the Satanic depth of Jesuitism is scathingly exposed. Disraeli is a bold man to publish such a book at such a political crisis as is this. But good and not evil the book must do, especially in Great Britain and Ireland.

Oct. 18th.—I read a second time the Rev. J. C. Symon's tractate on Christian Baptism. It is well reasoned, and there is no waste of words. It seems to me to be most conclusive on the side of the pedo-baptist usage.

Aug. 22nd.—I wrote Mr. Duncan, the head of the Industrial Schools, informing him that we had arranged for holding religious services at the Prince's Bridge establishment. This means more work, but it must be done. It is the only chance these unfortunate 'waifs' and 'strays' have.

In the afternoon I went to Cremorne private Lunatic Asylum; particularly to see Mr. E. and J. T. Poor wrecks! My soul was sore for them. What is diabolical possession? Mr. Harcourt told me of a young lady in England, and of another at Cremorne, born in godly homes, and reared in association with religious culture of a somewhat high order, who, when the fits of madness came upon them, would give utterance to such profane and obscene language as would make even wicked men to blush. How is this to be accounted for? But in this way most likely;—with reason dethroned, the ' evil one' enters and takes possession ; and hence the insanity and blasphemous outcome we have noticed. Does this theory throw any light upon demoniacal possessions we read of in the Gospels?

Aug. 25*th.*—Under the auspices of the ' Society for the Promotion of Morality ' a congress was held to-day ; Bishop Perry presided, and excellent papers were read and impromptu speeches were given. It was a grand day for sobriety and righteousness.

Nov. 2*nd.*—The District Meeting was begun to-day. We continued in session until the 10th. It is a great comfort to me to see how smoothly we get through the business of this large district.

Nov. 15*th.*—I heard Dr. Bromby lecture this evening in answer to his critics. Probably 2,500 persons were present. As a reply to his critics it was unsatisfactory and weak. It is hard to say what he really believes.

Nov. 24*th.*—I went in the afternoon to the Land Office to see about a church site at Lauriston. I also spoke to the Hon. J. A. MacPherson about the three-cornered allotment at Emerald Hill. He told me that we could proceed with the buildings if we liked at once, for the site would be gazetted as a Wesleyan Church Reserve in two or three weeks. This evening I had twenty-nine members present at my class. It is quite a task to meet them as one would like.

Nov. 28*th.*—I baptized, in Wesley Church, two Chinese converts, Thomas Ah Foo and Simon Tuck Sat. There was a large attendance of sympathizers with this Christian mission.

Dec. 2*nd.*—I spent the whole of this evening in seeing some of the members of Wesley Church Choir, who are grievously offended at an article which appeared in our *Chronicle* last week. The occasional admission of irritating articles into our official organ is a great mistake and offence. At all events, I cannot afford to spend my time in attempts to smooth away vexatious feelings, as in this instance ; and I hope I may not have to do it again. John Colton, Esq., M.P., from Adelaide, called and spent half-an-hour with us. I know more of South Australian Methodism now than I did before he called.

Dec. 8*th.*—Mr Taylor and I went to Maidstone to inspect the ' Meat Preserving Company's Works.' We were politely shown over the whole establishment. Strong, fat cattle would, in the morning, be driven into the slaughter-house, and in the evening of the same day the meat is tinned and packed ready for shipment to China, India, England, anywhere. This should be a renumerative industry. We visited several families, and had a preaching service at night. The next day I lectured on ' Wilberforce ' at Footscray in behalf of the new church. My zealous colleague, the Rev. R. C. Flockart, has charge of the finances of this undertaking, and is succeeding admirably.

Dec. 15*th.*—I went to the Legislative Council to see the Hon. T. T. A. Beckett, about the ' Wines, Beer, Spirits, Statute Amendment Bill.' I saw also the Hon. John O'Shanassy about the same thing. We are anxious for the passing of this Bill. There is a provision in it in favour of ' Local Option,' for preventing the multiplication of hotels and public-houses where not necessary.

Dec. 21*st.*—The Bill for the Payment of Members was passed after a pretty stiff debate. The ' Rupert ' of the Chamber was Mr. O'Shanassy. His best speeches reminded me much of those of Sir Robert Peel in their nice and comprehensive arrangement of facts, which he marshals with an easy fluency and persuasiveness of appeal. Sometimes, however, he can storm, and then his opponents have to look out. I have seen him rise in the Assembly, when he was our Premier, at the end of a debate, which may have lasted for hours, and reply, without a single note taken down, to each opponent in turn, and make a clean sweep of the whole lot. About this payment of members policy, I may say, that when it was first mooted I was greatly opposed to it. But the more I weighed the arguments, *pro e con,* the more was I convi...ced that, in a new country like Victoria, it was desirable. It is an experiment truly ; but the principal being right, we can have nothing to fear.

Dec. 31*st.*—I spent most of this day in pastoral visitation—Mrs. Pascoe, Mrs. Russell, the Misses Palmer, Mr. Fenton, and Mr. Hackett. Mrs. Hackett, after much suffering, which she bore with true Christian resignation, escaped to her heavenly rest. This closed my pastoral work for the year.

A BATTLE OF GIANTS.

1871.

The years 1869 and 1870 will be remembered as those in which a battle was fought in Melbourne between certain metaphysicians, theologians, and scientists. It was under the auspices of the ' Early

Closing Association ' that this contest began, and by whose patronage it was continued. The Rev. J. E. Bromby, D.D., Principal of the ' Church of England Grammar School,' gave three lectures, entitled : ' Creation *versus* Development,' ' Pre-historic Man,' and ' Beyond the Grave.' Of these lectures every minister of Christ had reason to complain. It was not an unfriendly, but a brotherly hand which wrote of the doctor and his lecture as follows :—

' He has launched a theory which carries the gravest moral consequences with too evident haste ; he has put to sea without carefully examining into the sea-worthiness of his vessel, without any definite idea of the course ; and I fear that he, and those who have embarked with him, will make shipwreck of their faith.'

The Bishop of Melbourne (Dr. Perry) came out with a very able lecture, entitled, ' Science and the Bible,' in which, ' by a few gentlemanly, polished sentences, he swept each hypothesis out of scientific existence, and courteously consigned it to the limbo of all error.'

Much service was done on the same side by the Editor of *The Wesleyan Chronicle* (Rev. John Christian Symons), who, in a series of articles, by closest reasoning and clear statement, showed the unsoundness and danger of Dr. Bromby's theories. Three anonymous publications also issued from the press, entitled, ' No Annihilation ; or, Scripture Evidence of Eternal Punishment ;' ' The Theory of Annihilation,' and ' A Modern Moloch ; or the Painless Non-existence of Materialists,' which did good service on the Scripture side of the controversy. But the conflict was not confined to Melbourne. The Rev. James Nish, D.D., Sandhurst, gave three interesting lectures on ' Universalism, Examined and Refuted ;' and the Rev. T. McKenzie Fraser, M.A., in Geelong, also gave a lecture on ' Dr. Bromby's Theory of Annihilation,' which he afterwards delivered in Wesley Church, Melbourne. Every city pulpit, for months together, became a vehicle for dogmatic pronouncement on the questions which Dr. Bromby had so thoughtlessly made an arena of strife. Possibly we should never have known what an amount of learned, critical ability lay hidden in the cultured minds of our more prominent ministers, and educated laymen, but for this battle for the truth.

Jan. 1st.—I began my ministry by preaching at North Melbourne and Wesley Church. In the afternoon we had the ' Renewal of

Covenant Service' and the Lord's Supper. It was a blessed time : 'My God I am Thine.'

Jan. 2*nd.*—I sent the quarterly annuities to all the claimants on the 'Old Preachers' Fund' outside the colony. Sending these allowances early in the quarter is like giving : 'he gives twice who gives quickly.' In the afternoon I buried the remains of our dear Sister Hackett : 'happy soul thy days are ended.'

Jan. 7*th.*—Mr. Courtney, from the College, came at 8 a.m. to tell me of the death of our dear Dr. Corrigan. An able and useful man is gone from us in the midst of his days. Our loss is very great. On the 9th we buried the mortal remains of the late Dr. Corrigan in the Melbourne Cemetery. The Rev. Joseph Dare was the officiating minister, assisted by Messrs. Waugh, Mackey, and myself. It was a largely attended funeral, and every countenance we saw in travelling from St. Kilda to the city cemetery appeared stricken with sorrow.

Jan. 11*th.*—We held a meeting of the Treasurers of the 'Old Preachers' Fund,' when I submitted the balance sheet for the year, which was at once passed. It was an agreeable and satisfactory meeting. The next day I left for Launceston to attend the Conference. We were fourteen ministers in all. Arriving on the 13th, I was glad to find that during my stay I was to be the guest of the Rev. John and Mrs. Harcourt. The next day I visited the Gleadows, Harts, Norwoods, and Grubbs. We made a small party in the afternoon for some outing. Mr. Robe drove Mrs. Robe, Messrs. Williams, Harcourt, Cope, and me, to the Cora Linn Water Falls, which were fine and imposing. We took tea at Mrs. Robe's, and spent the evening with Mr. and Mrs. Grubb. It was a most enjoyable time.

Jan. 19*th.*—The Conference was opened in Hobart Town to-day, under the presidency of the Rev. John Watsford. At this Conference my nephew, the Rev. E. S. Bickford, with fifteen others, was received into full connexion, and twenty-one were received on trial. We continued in session until the 31st, when the Journal was read and signed. It was a successful Conference, and the hospitality of the friends was beyond all praise. During the Conference I visited Bushey Park, *viâ* New Norfolk, and preached on the Sabbath. Mr. and Mrs. Shoobridge showed true Kentish hospitality. What a lovely spot it is ! A perfect hive of industry, and a home of the highest type of family godliness. Mr. Shoobridge, on our way back, took me to see the 'Salmon Fish Ponds.' Who will not hope that this Governmental enterprise may be a success, and that some day the cool and picturesque rivers of fair Tasmania may be as much alive with this 'king of fishes' as are the romantic rivers of grand old Scotland?

Feb. 1st.—This morning I left Hobart Town, in a hired steamer, with 320 friends for New Norfolk for a day's recreation and enjoyment. Miss Smith and I went to Valley Field to see Mr. and Mrs. William Shoobridge. We went all through the beautiful gardens, and admired the cultivation. I saw many other things calculated to please the eye and to excite gratitude in our hearts. I reached Hobart Town in the evening, and spent a profitable time with my kind host and hostess, Mr. and Mrs. James Smith. Miss Smith took me to Kangaroo Point to see the Browns, who are particular friends of the Frasers of St. Kilda. Mrs. Brown was feeble, but was in a happy state of mind.

I settled up affairs with the Commercial Bank, and took a draft for £1,304 4s. 5d., to be paid to the credit of the Old Preachers' Fund in Melbourne. After visiting Mr. and Mrs. Vanstone, Mr. and Mrs. Heyward, Mrs. Crouch and Miss Crouch, I left by a night journey for Launceston, and arrived at 8.30 the next morning. At 10.30 a.m. the Conference party went on board the *Derwent*, when I at once turned in so as to avoid sea-sickness. We had a pleasant trip down the river, and fine weather out at sea. The next day I reached Melbourne, and found all well at home.

Feb. 7th.—I made large deposits to the credit of the Old Preachers' Fund; the next day I met the treasurers, and reported the state of affairs. In the evening the Rev. George Woolnough, M.A., preached in Wesley Church on 'Jacob's Vision.' It was a clearly conceived and well-delivered sermon.

Feb. 15th.—After preaching at North Melbourne, I gave the congregation a short address on the business of the late Conference. I think to do this is good policy as a ministerial duty.

The ex-American Consul, Dr. Pinnell, and Mrs. Pinnell left by the steamship *Macedon* to-day. I do not think they felt much at home in Melbourne, and that they will be glad to get back to America. I parted from them with regret.

March 2nd.—I left for Marathon Station, Sutherland's Creek, to

see Mrs. Dow, who is very ill. In the evening Mr. Dow and I went
to the Anakies, to hear the Rev. Henry E. Merriman lecture on
' Representative Women.' It was a thoughtful and instructive
lecture, and was well received. Poor Mrs. Dow was about able to
recognise me, and that was all. We knelt by her bed and commended
her to God in prayer and faith.

March 5th.—I preached at Yarra Street, Geelong, in aid of the
Sunday School. At the public meeting I spoke on (1) Public
Education, (2) Publicans' Bill, (3) The Permissive Bill. I think I
had a pretty good grip, and succeeded in interesting the audience,
which was large. My object was, in most part, to influence public
opinion in the expectation of a general election.

March 8th.—The Loan Fund Committee met. We voted to
churches and parsonages over £3,000. This amount was fairly
distributed as between ' Town and Country.'

March 14th.—The news of ' peace ' between Prussia and France
reached us this morning ; but dearly bought on both sides. I began
reading Tyerman's ' Life of Wesley ' to-day. It would be curious to
know how many biographies of this great man have been written.
I understand that Tyerman's is the best amongst the whole lot ; but
of this I shall be able to judge after perusal. One thing is certain,
that the reverend author makes his subject a little more human
than do some of the writers ; which, I think, is wise, and a strong
recommendation of the work.

Feb. 20th.—Messrs. Ebenezer Taylor and Henry Moore were
ordained to the full work of the Ministry in Wesley Church this
evening. It was a good service, and the Great Head of the Church
sanctioned the ceremony with His own blessed Presence.

Feb. 21st.—We held the Church Anniversary Meeting this
evening at Emerald Hill, when Mr. Thomas Pybus gave us his great
speech on ' Is Christianity a Failure ? ' Here is a case of a man, of
singular endowments, missing his way into the highest service of the
Church, through the pernicious influence of ministerial agitators
some years ago in the North of England. Methodism, in the past, has
had her troubles, but they always begun amongst a few able but
unreasonable men amongst the ministers themselves. This ought
not to be. We raised at this Anniversary £150 for the Trust.

Feb. 24th.—I was again in Geelong to attend an Ordination Service,
when my nephew, the Revs. E. S. Bickford, H. Catford, T. E. Ick,

M.A., and W. Weston, were thus set apart for the Ministry. The Church was well filled, and it was a very fine service.

Feb. 26th.—I preached twice at St. Alban's Church to-day. On Monday I was at Mr. Lowe's, enjoying a quiet day and rest.

March 28th. [Diary Jotting]—" This morning I went to St. Alban's Church, and, assisted by the Rev. F. E. Stephenson, I married my nephew, Edmund Sorrell Bickford, to Emma Lowe. The church was full of friends. The Rev. John Cope, on behalf of the Sunday School, presented to the bride an address and an elegantly bound Bible and Hymn Book. We spent a pleasant afternoon, and I, with my niece, Christina Pascoe, returned to Melbourne by the evening train."

The Rev. D. Annear called. He feels deeply and justly his non-appointment to a Circuit this year.

March 31st.—I held the Local Preachers' Meeting; Messrs. Willis, T. Leslie, Kirk, Johnstone, and Cowperthwaite were examined, and received as full local preachers.

April 5th.—We held the Quarterly Meeting to-day. The income was £471 13s. 6d. Debt reduced to £37 1s. 9d. We had an encouraging and happy meeting.

April 7th (Good Friday). — I heard the Rev. Mr. Edwards preach to a very good congregation. Mrs. Bickford and I went out to Heidelberg and spent a quiet evening. I was unwell from hard work and worry, and needed rest and change.

April 10th (Easter Monday).—A delightfully quiet day. Melbourne is ' out of town.' I wrote two articles for the *Recorder*, and in the evening I read Tyerman's ' Life of Wesley.'

April 16th.—The Rev. J. F. Horsley preached a good sermon in Wesley Church, which I much enjoyed. It was a famous specimen of the logical style which well becomes our principal pulpits.

April 21st.—A busy day. I wrote five letters to England, and attended the Female Refuge, Protestant Orphan Asylum, Wesley Church Sunday School, and Sunday School Union Committees.

April 24th.—Through the Christian generosity of Mr. S. E. King, the Rev. D. Annear, who was left without a Circuit at the last Conference, has come to Wesley Church as a Home Missionary for one year. I went with him, therefore, in search of a house in which he should begin his work.

May 9th.—The Chinese Mission is prospering. This evening in Wesley Church I baptized three converts from the teachings of

Confucius to the faith of Christ.   There was a fine congregation.
We had all the Chinese members on the platform, when, led by
James Ah Ling, they sang 'Rock of Ages' in their own tongue.
There was deep feeling.   We collected £6 8s. 6d for the Mission.

May 12th.—I went into Collins Street on Old Preachers' Fund
business.   I tried to arrange for a loan of £5,000 on a first mortgage,
but did not succeed.   I also attended a great meeting in the Town
Hall in aid of the Saturday Half Holiday Movement, when I conversed with Sir James MacCulloch and the Mayor on the fearful
prevalence of the larrikin element in the City.   They entered very
fully into my views, and were willing to co-operate in any well-
directed efforts for removing this social plague from our midst.

May 16th.—I went up to the House of Assembly to hear the
Treasurer, Mr. Francis, give his Budget speech.   He spoke for two
hours and twenty minutes with much clearness and grasp of his
subject.   There was a good deal of pleasurable excitement in the
House.   Are politics an easy game to play?   If not, on what
principle can we explain how it is that a gentleman, who has spent
his whole life in commercial transactions, can stand up with so much
self-possessedness before his compeers, and deliver himself as Mr.
Francis did to-day?   I suppose this is the solution: the Treasurer
knew beforehand what he had to talk about, and he stood up and
said it.

On the 17th the Rev. Mr. Beecher (Anglican) and I tramped
the streets of Melbourne, soliciting subscriptions for furnishing a
temporary home for fallen women.   We met with some success, and
the Heavenly Father will reward those who so generously helped
our object.

May 22nd.—I was busy to-day in pastoral visitation, which was
very pleasant to me.   In the evening I attended a great meeting
for forming a 'Young Men's Christian Association.'   The speaking
was very fine.

May 24th.—I went as usual to the Governor's *levée* in honour of
the birthday of our dear Queen.   May God bless her!

June 3rd.—I left by train for Scarsdale, *vià* Ballarat, to help at
several religious services.   The next day (the Sabbath) I preached at
Linton's, and was the guest of my kind friends, Mr. and Mrs.
Matthews.   We held the tea and public meeting the next evening,
and raised £35.   Here I met with the published account of the

'Irish State Trials.' Daniel O'Connell and his patriotic friends were acquitted. How much better for the English Government to have listened to the complaints of the Irish nation, and devised remedies for their removal, than to have run the risk of a 'State Trial' of the men who were seeking to save the nation !

June 6th.—My nephew, the Rev. E. S. Bickford, and I went to Rokewood, and found Mr. and Mrs. (Ashby) Hill and Mr. and Mrs. Musgrove all well. The Revs. I. Steele and Iddeson assisted at our public meeting. On our way back to Scarsdale, we passed the solitary place where Burke killed an unfortunate wayfarer for his money. I shuddered as I passed the blood-stained spot. I returned to Melbourne on the 8th, arriving at home at 11.30 p.m.

June 24th.—I left at 1 p.m. for Keysborough, and arrived at 4.50 p.m. Mr. and Mrs Keys, Senr., received me as usual with full-hearted Irish hospitality. I spent a pleasant evening with Mr. and Thomas Keys and other members of this family. The next day I preached at Keysborough, Dandenong, and Berwick. During this visit I attended 'Church Extension Meetings' at Mornington, Clyde, and Keysborough. I had the pleasure to once more visit my friends, Mr. and Mrs. Sykes, Mr. and Mrs. Patterson, Mr. and Mrs. North, and Rev. Thomas and Mrs. Kane. I returned to Melbourne on the 30th, and found a heap of important business letters awaiting attention. The business that has to be attended to by the Wesley Church minister baffles all description.

July 8th.—The *Weekly Times* came out to-day with my portrait, and a sketch of my personalty and style of preaching. This is the penalty I am paying in being mixed up in the wretched controversy with Dr. Bromby. The 'sketcher' points out many defects in my discourses, but he gives me great credit for my pastoral habits, and attention to the sick, the poor, and the aged. Well, this is something to the good. If I am not too old to change in the style or substance of my pulpit performances I would try to improve. We shall see.

July 17th.—I renewed my conversation with James Mathieson on the subject of his going into our mission work. I think, physically, he would do well for the Tropics; and I have also a strong belief in his natural ability and piety.

July 19th.—I began reading Dr. Pusey's lectures on 'Daniel the Prophet.' From what I can see it is a learned and able work. In the evening I read in Wesley Church Bishop Simpson's great sermon on Isaiah xlii. 4. Mr. Duncan and I had to-day an interesting conversation on gaol discipline, including regular religious services for the spiritual benefit of the prisoners. It is quite comforting to find an 'Inspector of Gaols,' as is Mr. Duncan, enthusiastically holding to the belief that Her Majesty's 'imprisoned' subjects are capable of reformation, yea, even of salvation.

July 21st.—I read in the London *Watchman* the account of the Exeter Hall Meeting. It was a great refreshing of soul to me. I wonder if I shall ever have the privilege of attending one such meeting 'before I go hence.'

July 22nd.—I began again reading Bishop Butler's 'Analogy of Religion,' feeling that it is of much importance that I should keep in touch with this masterly exposition of the *credo* he has accepted, and was bound to defend.

July 25th.—I attended a meeting of Christian gentlemen for selling good literature throughout the Colony. Surely, next to pulpit and Sunday School work, this comes of great importance. We shall prevent the reading of bad books by settlers, miners, and others, by supplying to them, at reasonable prices, readable, pure literature.

Aug. 14th.—I read the *London Quarterly* for two or three hours. I like our periodical better than I do any of the others that come to us from London. But I am much grieved that so few of our leading men, and ministers even, ever see it. It must be a great loss to them.

Aug. 18th.—At our Preachers' Weekly Meeting to-day we had two Chinese catechists present. Their report of their work was encouraging, and there appears to be a wide field before them in these Colonies. It was good to have these men with us.

Aug. 31st.—Messrs. James and Garrett, M.P.'s, called about our petition to Parliament on the 'Prohibition' question. In the afternoon Mr. President Watsford and I went up to the House, and handed our petition to Mr. James for presentation in favour of the Bill. In the evening I presided at the 'Daughters of Temperance' Meeting. About four hundred were present on the joyous occasion. Upon the whole it was a gratifying success.

Sept. 5th.—There is no end of trouble over our Day School matters. To-day I had to go up to the Board of Education to see the Secretary

(Mr. B. F. Kane) about the Carlton, Coghill's Creek, and Wesley Church Schools. The next day I finished my second copy of the 'Wilberforce Lecture.' It has been quite a means of instruction and good to me to prepare this lecture. May the Lord bless it to others! (D. J.)

Sept. 11*th.*—I accompanied a deputation to the Chief Secretary about closing the ship *Cerberus* to the public on the Lord's day. The right is on our side, but the might (the 'world-power') is against us. But we shall see.

Sept. 23*rd.*—I left for Sebastopol, and arrived in the evening. I was the guest of Mr. and Mrs. Robinson, who made me most welcome. The next day I preached at 11 a.m. and 6.30 p.m. to good congregations. The usual public meetings came off the next evening. I spoke for three-quarters of an hour on the proper work of the Church in two branches, viz., the preaching of the Gospel, and the religious training of the young. The brethren were more than kind in their references to my former labours in the Ballarat District. On Tuesday evening I lectured for an hour and a half on 'Wilberforce' with much freedom. Not only from natural instinct, but also from a long residence in the West Indies, I seem always to feel an unexplainable sympathy with the humane efforts for the African race which this great Christian philanthropist put forth. I went into Ballarat, and slept at Mr. Oddie's, so that I might be ready to leave for Melbourne by the first train next day.

Sept. 27*th.*—This evening Orlando Knee and James Matthieson preached in Wesley Church with a view to their nomination at the ensuing Quarterly Meeting for the work of the Ministry. They did very well.

Sept. 30*th.*—This afternoon the foundation-stone of the new Temperance Hall was laid by his worship the Mayor in Russell Street. At the evening, meeting, the Revs. Dare, Mackie, and I, with Messrs. Munro, Callaghan, and Beauchamp spoke. It was a very good meeting, and augurs success.

Oct. 3*rd.*—A notable day in the interests of the Christian Sabbath. A great meeting was held at St. Enoch's of a stormy kind. But that was to be expected. We carried the whole of our resolutions, and appointed a Sabbath Defence Association.

Oct. 4*th.*—We held our Quarterly Meeting. There were sixty-five brethren present. I nominated Brothers Knee and Matthieson.

They were passed with the condition of both having a year's training at Wesley College. We concluded our meeting after midnight.

Oct. 6th.—I left for Echuca by the 11.40 train, and arrived in the evening. I spent an agreeable hour with the Rev. J. F. and Mrs. Horsley, and I slept at Mr. Brown's. The next day I visited Mr. and Mrs. Heyward, Mr. and Mrs. Stephenson, Mr. Payne, Mr. Forbes, Mr. and Mrs. Redman, and Mr. Matthews. At 3 p.m. I left for Deniliquin, and reached this 'City of the Plains' at 9 p.m. Mr. Hunter, formerly of St. Kilda, was there to receive me. I was to be the guest of Dr. Jones, who, with Miss Jones, gave me a gracious welcome. I was much tired; the bush road was simply execrable. I opened the new Church the next day. I saw in the congregations several of my former friends in other Circuits. The usual meetings were held on the Monday, when the Mayor, Mr. Robertson, occupied the chair. We raised about £40. On the 10th I rode with the Rev. Charles Jones to Landall's Station to see the sheep-shearers. There were eighty men at work. It was to me a novel and exciting sight. I was told that some of the men will shear as many as a hundred sheep *per diem;* but such shearing I never saw before. It seemed to me to be wasteful and cruel. In the evening I gave 'Wilberforce' at Deniliquin; Mr. Gordon, the police magistrate, in the chair.

It is not often that a minister in the full work of a Circuit can have such a treat as I had in a quiet two hours' talk with my generous host—Dr. Jones. Here in this out-of-the-way place I found one of the best read, the best informed, of men, on all matters affecting the future of the Australian Colonies, and the trend of social and political thought in Europe, it had ever been my privilege to fall in with. Besides which he was a Christian gentleman, and Editor of the *Pastoral Times.* No wonder, therefore, that although I had had a day which sorely taxed my physical and mental strength, I sat up with him until midnight before I could retire to rest. On the 11th Mr. Horsley and I left in a buggy for Echuca, and reached his home at 4.30 p.m. I called on Dr. and Mrs. Allen, who are Church members. Dr. Allen is the son of the Rev. John Allen, a minister of the English Conference. In the evening I lectured to a fair audience, but I was too much tired to do justice to my theme. On the 12th I left for Melbourne. At Sandhurst the Rev. W. P. Wells, an old and dear friend, met me at the station, and drove me to the parsonage for lunch. I spent a nice time with him. I left by train in the afternoon for Melbourne, and reached Wesley Church all well. I found waiting my arrival Mr. S. G. King and the Rev. Josiah and Mrs. Cox, from China. Mr. Cox will be in the Colony for some time, looking into our Chinese work, meeting the catechists and the converts in Christian fellowship, and holding services in the City and in those parts of the country where the Chinese are located.

Oct. 17th.—I went to the Assembly, and heard Messrs. Duffy, Langton, McGregor, Vale, and O'Grady speak. There was much feeling in the House. But the Government in the end beat their opponents by two votes to one. After this trial of strength, perhaps the Government of the country may be carried on without further obstruction.

Oct. 23rd.—The Rev. E. Taylor and I left for Sunbury. At Flemington we conversed with Mr. James Robertson about the land he has for sale adjoining our Church site. At Bullar we called on Mr. and Mrs. Saunders, who were kind to both 'man and beast.' We reached Sunbury at 6 p.m., and went at once to the Public Meeting, which was well attended. We returned to Melbourne *via* Keilor. In the evening I went to Footscray, to the new church tea and public meeting. I returned at 11.30.

Oct. 25th.—I met the Flemington Trustees, who agreed to purchase fifty feet to Mount Alexander Road at £1 per foot and one hundred feet at the back for 10*s.* per foot. This will give us an excellent church and school site.

Nov. 1st.—The Annual District Meeting was commenced to-day; the Rev. John Watsford in the chair. During the sessions we held a special public tea and public meeting in the interests of the Chinese Mission. The object was to raise funds for purchasing a site, and for erecting a mission church, in Little Bourke Street. Mr. Cox was the principal speaker, and the response to his appeal was immediate and generous. We raised £266. The Financial Meeting was held the next day, when the Circuit Stewards came prepared with a number of resolutions affecting the finances of the Connexion. It was quite a field day. The freest scope was allowed in the discussions, and eventuated in the withdrawal of the resolutions *in globo.* We sat until 10 p.m., when we parted on good terms with each other. We spent a whole day in considerations, recommendations to Conference, and in examining Messrs. Nicholson, Robin, B.A.,

17

and Schofield for full connexion. On the evening of the 6th the Rev. J. C. Symons preached the annual sermon to the young. It was a highly practical sermon, and was well received.

At the District Meeting much prominence was given to the claims of the ' Home Mission and Sustentation Society.' The public meeting was held at Brunswick Street, and the young brethren did capital service. We closed our sittings on the 8th. Under the guidance of Mr. Watsford we had a successful and profitable District Meeting.

Nov. 29th.—Still involved in the Church Sites question. We have formed a new trust for Sandridge property, and now the trouble is about the Crown Grant. I went again to-day to the Crown Solicitor's office about it. The ' red tape ' observed in Government offices is a terrible trial to men of practical minds. I wanted to get Mr. Sutherland to insert in the ' Certificate of Title ' two or three lines for recognising the principle of trusteeship in the Title, so as to do away with the necessity of a supplementary document of ' Declaration of Trust.' I did not get this concession, but Mr. Sutherland promised me the usual Title this week. At the same time I called upon the Treasurer, Mr. Graham Berry, to express my sympathy with him in the death of his daughter. I had a nice interview with him. I also attended a meeting of friends, called by the Rev. Adam Cairns, D.D., to consider the question of starting a religious newspaper as an organ of the Evangelical Churches, of which there is great need.

Dec. 12th.—We met to-day to make the Conference Plan. This is a difficult business, because of the uncertainty of brethren being with us from the distant colonies. This may be remedied some day, it may be hoped. I heard this morning of the death of the Rev. George Mackie, of South Yarra. It is a great loss to us. Mr. Mackie was a good minister of Jesus Christ, an ardent worker in the Temperance cause, and a genuine philanthropist. He and I had been close friends since our first acquaintance in Ballarat some years ago, and we had often stood side by side in defending religion and sobriety.

Dec. 14th.—I went to the funeral of the late George Mackie. It was largely attended; a public testimony to the moral worth and great usefulness of our departed friend. The Rev. Alexander Cameron's address was full of deep Christian feeling, and touched many hearts.

Dec. 25th.—By invitation, the Rev. D. Nimmo preached this morning in Wesley Church, and gave us a sermon full of rich thought, and delivered with calmness and judgment. I much enjoyed it. For a Christmas Day the congregation was very good.

On the 26th I went to Carlton to see John King, the explorer. Poor, dear fellow, he is done for this world. He is going to heaven. Since his return from Cooper's Creek and settlement in St. Kilda I have had much opportunity of knowing him. A man of stricter probity, I believe, never lived.

Dec. 31st.—I closed the hard work of this year by holding the usual Watchnight service in Wesley Church.

1872.

Jan. 1st.—Through God's mercy I have entered upon another year. I look to heaven for assistance and grace. May our way be directed from on high !

Jan. 2nd.—Held the Quarterly Meeting. We had a breezy time, but no bad blood.

Jan. 6th.—I looked through Dr. Gregory's 'Life of the late Walter Powell,' and found it to be a highly suggestive work. It should be read by all young merchants who wish to succeed in life.

Jan. 10th.—I went again to the United Mid-day Prayer Meeting. Bishop Perry presided, and gave an excellent address. The prayers were hearty, and the feeling was very good. I also, at the request of the Bishop, addressed a few words of counsel and encouragement to the congregation.

Jan. 15th.—We heard to-day of the dangerous illness of the Prince of Wales. We are waiting with trembling anxiety for the incoming Suez mail. I wrote to-day to the Hon. Graham Berry, informing him of John King's death ; pointing out that the Government should undertake the entire expense of the funeral, and send one or more of the officials to follow the corpse to the place of interment. Mr. Berry's reply was to the effect that the Government would allow the sum of £40, and leave the entire matter in my hands. We buried the mortal remains of this intrepid man in the Melbourne Cemetery, when many friends gathered around his grave and wept over his death. The Government all along has shown the utmost generosity to this only survivor of the unfortunate Burke and Wills exploring party, the leaders of which perished at Cooper's Creek in 1861.

The Conference of this year was an important one, as marking a new era of ecclesiastical development. It was opened at 10 a.m.

on January 18th by the retiring President, the Rev. John Watsford. After his address, the Rev. Benjamin Chapman took the chair, and the Rev. John Cope was chosen as Secretary. The Conference Sunday was a high day for Wesley Church. The President, according to custom, occupied the pulpit in the morning, and gave us a richly evangelical and earnest discourse. The Rev. James Buller, from New Zealand, preached a good sermon in the evening. It was stately and scholarly, as are all his public utterances. On the 22nd the Annual Missionary Meeting was held. The brethren spoke with much power and beautiful eloquence. The collection amounted to £31 8s. 3d. On the 24th we had a great breakfast meeting in the interests of the Chinese Mission, and raised £355. In the afternoon the Rev. Josiah Cox addressed the Conference in an admirable speech, on the duty of the Australasian Methodists assisting the British Churches in their efforts to evangelise China. The Ordination Service was held in the evening, when Messrs. Fitcher, Jones, Robin, Schofield and Nicholson were fully 'set apart' to the work of the Ministry. Mr. ex-President Watsford gave the 'Charge,' which was excellent and impressive. On the 29th the first Methodist Conference Temperance Demonstration came off in the Town Hall. It was a great affair. Much good must result to all Australia from this committal of the Conference to the Temperance cause. On the 31st the Rev. William Kelynack lectured in Wesley Church, Sir James MacCulloch, M.P., in the chair. The Cathedral Church of Australian Methodism looked well with its crowded audience. The collection was £50.

The plan for holding, in 1873, instead of one Australasian Conference as at present for the whole Connexion, four Colonial Annual Conferences was earnestly debated, and ultimately passed. This plan provided also for the holding of a Triennial General Conference, as the Supreme Court of Legislation of the Australasian Wesleyan Methodist Church. Although good reasons were shown why this change in our form of government and administration should be made, yet there was a powerful minority, not in numbers certainly, but in ability beyond all doubt. The names of the dissentients are as follow: Messrs. Gaud, Hurst, Quick, J. G. Turner, Piddington, N. Bennett, Ironside, S. Williams, J. B. Waterhouse, Sellors, Nolan, Wilson, F. E. Stephenson, J. B. Stephenson, and Woolnough. Seventy-four voted for the Plan, and so it was carried.

We had a great discussion on the case of the Rev. Thomas Guard, then a missionary in South Africa. His name had been brought before us by the Rev. William Taylor, who had seen him in that country, and knew his worth. The Conference finally adopted a resolution, which I give *verbatim*, that the Methodist people may know the terms on which similar cases may be dealt with :—

" Resolved :—That the Chairman of the Melbourne District be permitted to negotiate with the Rev. Thomas Guard, in reference to his joining the Australasian Conference on the following conditions, which the depressed state of the Connexional funds, and the finding of stations for married ministers, render necessary, viz :—(1) That such financial arrangements be made by Mr. Guard's friends in Victoria without prejudice to those funds ; (2) That the Circuit seeking Mr. Guard's services shall take him as an additional married minister, without having the previous four years' service of single men, in addition to defraying the expense that may be incurred in bringing Mr. Guard and his family to Melbourne."

These terms were accepted, and £500 were raised to secure Mr. Guard's advent amongst us.

The news of the murder of Bishop Patteson and the Rev. J. B. Atkin, in Polynesia, called forth the deep sympathy of the Conference, and a resolution of condolence with the Church Missionary Society was passed relating thereto. It was as follows :—

" Resolved :—That this Conference record its deepest sympathy with the Directors of the Melanesian Mission in the great loss they have sustained by the deaths of Bishop Patteson and his fellow-labourer, the Rev. J. B. Atkin, who fell by the hand of violence while prosecuting their self-denying labours among the islands of the South Pacific ; and also expresses its strongest condemnation of the traffic in human beings which is now being carried on among the islands, and which there is reason to believe has been the main cause of the murder of these devoted missionaries, is likely to lead to many similar acts of violence, and to interfere most prejudicially with missionary labour."

It is not to be wondered at that such an expression of sympathy came welling up from many a soul, as this painful disaster was under consideration, when we call to mind that in the Conference there were so many veterans who themselves had often been 'in perils among the heathen.' For, if it be true, as was remarked by the lamented Dean Stanley, that ' the vast literature of the nineteenth century had become the real bond and school of the nation, beyond the power of educational and ecclesiastical agitation to exclude or prevent; ' then how much more true has the association of God-honoured men of different Churches, in the outlying portions of the world, tended to cement them as 'one' in Christ's love and pity for the lost. I am sure that if Bishop Patteson and Mr. Atkin had been our own missionaries, the great sorrow which moved the Conference could not have been stronger or more sincere.

Feb. 7th.—The Conference broke up, and the next day I accompanied the Rev. Stephen Rabone, the General Secretary of our Mission, and Mr. President Chapman, to the steamer, in which they soon left for Sydney.

March 4th.—I went to Hotham Hill to select a site for church, and school purposes. The population is rapidly gathering here, and no time must be lost in choosing a God's Acre for the people's benefit. On the 7th we accepted for the new church in Little Bourke Street, for the Chinese immigrants. We shall build forthwith. Financial success is secured. In the afternoon I visited eight families, which was a real pleasure to me.

March 16th.—The news of the death of the Venerable Dr. Dixon reached us. I went at once to condole with Mr. James Dixon and Mrs. Dixon. A great preacher, 'old and full of days,' has gone from us.

March 19th.—I held an important meeting at Carlton. We had associated with the 'Five' trustees, gazetted by the Government, several influential seat-holders as a Building Committee. I conceived that their duties were fulfilled in the completion of the church. I called this committee together to hear the balance sheet, which was accepted and signed, when I informed them that the affairs of the church would have to be managed in future by the legal trustees. On the 25th I met the trustees of the Footscray Church, and presented the account for the erection of the building. We had spent £686 3s. The Rev. R. C. Flockart, my excellent colleague, had raised, by a series of lectures, £55 of this amount.

March 29th (Good Friday).—The Rev. Andrew Robertson preached in Wesley Church this morning, taking as his text the words, "And now, O Father, glorify Thou me with Thine own self with the glory which I had with Thee before the world was.' He was grand in dwelling upon the glory of the eternal Divinity surrounding and penetrating the humanity of Christ. In the evening I went to St. Francis' Cathedral, and heard the Rev. MacGullicardy pronounce an oration on the sufferings of Christ. His text was, 'Is it nothing to you, all ye that pass by? behold, and see if there be any sorrow like unto My sorrow, which is done unto Me?' In the recess behind the daïs there was suspended from the wall a large and beautiful painting of 'Christ Crucified,' and, as he proceeded in developing his great theme, he would frequently turn round and point to the crown of thorns, the pierced 'hands and feet,' and the streaming 'blood.' It was, but not in an offensive sense, powerfully histrionic; and the feeling throughout that vast assemblage reminded me of a West Indian sea, heaving and swelling preliminarily to an earthquake or a hurricane breaking forth. We had a full hour's impassioned, emotional declamation, and I was held as under a spell. The choir, I understood, was composed of 'professionals,' and its rendering of the pieces was wonderful. To my heart, yea, to my very soul, it was in pathos, in depth, in fulness, in harmony, and majestic volume, inconceivably superior to anything of the kind I had ever heard in churches or cathedrals in the old country. I would like to have seen Mr. MacGullicardy at the close to have thanked him for his great service.

April 13th.—Another of itinerary farewells I have just passed through. The last Conference appointed me to the Ballarat East Circuit, and to the Chairmanship of the Geelong and Ballarat District; but the closing of various accounts of which I had held the treasurership, and the resigning of positions in the philanthropic, Temperance, Young Men's Societies, and Connexional offices, seemed to me to be a work for days instead of hours. The Valedictory Meeting at Wesley Church was very gratifying. The Venerable Dean Macartney, the Rev. J. S. Waugh, Dr. Cutts, Mr. Callaghan, and Mr. Hodgson, and some others, spoke with much affection of my labours in the City. The Circuit was, in due course, handed over to the Rev. W. A. Quick, my successor, and the Acting Clerical Treasurership of the 'Old Preachers' Fund' I placed in the hands of my co-treasurers, when the Rev. J. C. Symons was chosen in my stead. I was now free from further responsibilities, and I hastened to the hospitable home of the Harcourts at Cremorne for a few days' rest and recreation. Mrs. Bickford went to Carlton on a visit to Mrs. Pascoe, who had been for years a great sufferer from chronic rheumatism. I got to Ballarat in time for the religious services of April 14th, when I entered upon my new sphere of labours.

BALLARAT EAST.

I commenced my labours in this Circuit by preaching at Brown Hill and Niel Street, when 1 found my old friends glad once more to sit under my ministry. I do pray the Heavenly Father to bless me and my young colleague, the Rev. David Perry, in our ministrations to this people. The next day I arranged my study, and made everything straight. I paid in advance my subscription to the 'Reading-room,' and spent the afternoon in pastoral visitation. On the 18th Mr. Walsh, formerly of Barbadoes, W. I., died. He was present at my marriage in James Street Church, Bridgetown, on May 6th, 1841, and now, after all these years, we meet in Ballarat, and I attend him in his dying hour. The next day died Mr. Bennett, one of our good Cornishmen. Two good members in our first week are taken home.

April 25th.—The Venerable Dr. Lang was visiting Ballarat, and Mr. Oddie kindly asked me to meet him at tea, which I did. I anticipated much pleasure from this historic man; but I was disappointed. He would not talk; so, after tea, I left him to his thoughts.

May 1st.—I preached at Little Bendigo to forty persons. I had a wet, dark ride back after service. To-day I wrote a long letter to the *Star* on Public Education. The drift of it was to prevent, if possible, any further meddling with the present Act.

May 8th.—I went to Melbourne, to the business of the Loan Fund and Sustentation Society. We sat for ten hours, and finished our work.

May 11th.—I prepared the statement of the Home Mission and Contingent Fund Society for the Annual Report.

May 15th.—I went to Bungaree for the first time, and preached to thirty-eight persons. I visited several families before the service. The road was awful. I came home at 11 p.m. cold and wet.

June 7th.—I have often felt that the magistracy of the Colony had not in its ranks as many intelligent, godly men as it ought. I, therefore, wrote the Premier, asking that, when any new appointments were being made, my friends, F. Poolman, Esq., Sandridge, and S. G. King, Esq., of North Melbourne, might be included. To-day I received a letter from the Hon. Howard Spensley, Solicitor General, informing me that my request had been granted.

June 14th.—I commenced reading the 'Life of Lord Brougham,' because I find political biography extremely instructive. I should think that the noble lord was too erratic and impulsive to 'work in a team,' and too communicative to be associated in Cabinet.

July 5th.—I rode out to Mount Egerton to attend the Quarterly Meeting. It was poorly attended, and every interest seemed much depressed. In the evening I preached to an attentive congregation, and made an effort of finance for the Circuit. The Rev. W. M. Bennett is our minister in charge.

July 18th.—His worship, the Mayor of Geelong, wrote me that the gentleman I had recommended as superintendent of their Botanical Gardens had been appointed. I am happy that I was able, with some others, to do a good turn for my friend, Mr. John Raddenburg.

Aug. 2nd.—I had an interesting interview with Dr. Jakins, originally from London, who acted upon my advice given him in Geelong to seek a practice in Ballarat. He is succeeding well, and is much respected. In the evening I read a report, published in pamphlet form, of a famous discussion : ' Was St. Peter ever at Rome ?' The combatants were a converted Italian priest, who had become a Wesleyan clergyman, and of an Ecclesiastic from the Vatican. The Methodist, I think, had the best of the argument. But such a discussion in Rome, under the very eyes of the Pope, is one of the wonders of this wonderful century.

Aug. 12th.—I wrote the Hon. A. Fraser, the Commissioner of Works, a long and as pungent a letter as I could write upon the subject of the Government undertaking forthwith a series of public works, so as to give employment to the working-classes who had nothing to do. In this matter I was only following the example of Wilberforce, who wrote Mr. Pitt to do the same thing for the starving poor in London.

Aug. 22nd.—I again visited Mr. Woolcock at Mount Pleasant. As he is not long for this world, I made his will. Referring to the state of his soul, he said, 'Religion is a glorious fact. It is solid rock. I am safe. With great humility, but with confidence, I can say,—

> ' " O Love, thou bottomless abyss,
>   My sins are swallowed up in thee !
> Covered is my unrighteousness,
>   Nor spot of guilt remains on me,
> While Jesu's blood, through earth and skies,
> Mercy, free boundless mercy, cries."

' Covered : yes—covered ! I do not see the full glory yet right through, but I shall ! Yes : I shall ! Hallelujah ! Abundant entrance into the everlasting Kingdom.' It was a glorious testimony ; I never heard a clearer or more triumphant confession of ' victory through the blood of the Lamb.' Old Samuel Wesley, Rector of Epworth, as he lay upon the bed of death, addressing his poet son Charles, said, ' Be steady. The Christian faith will surely revive in this kingdom. You shall see it, though I shall not.' And what the grand old Rector meant by the ' Christian faith' is explained in the few words he had strength enough to speak to his son John Wesley, ' The inward witness, son, the inward witness, that is the proof, the strongest proof of Christianity.' This same lesson of ' steadiness' I again learnt from the lips of Brother Woolcock on the subject of my pastoral ministry ; whilst the cogent demonstration of its living power over the acutest sufferings—the very ' swellings of Jordan,'—and of his consciousness of peace and safety in Christ, was simply glorious. That is the ' Faith' to be revived in all Australasia.

On the 24th I went out to Clunes in the interests of the Home Missions. I preached on the Sabbath, visited old friends, and took tea at my nephew's, James Bickford Boon's ; after tea I baptized seven children. I spoke in the evening for nearly an hour. We raised £18 5s.

Sept. 12th.—I read an article in *Harper's Magazine* entitled, ' Republicanism in Europe !' This is a stirring discovery. ' It is a dream,' say some ; others, ' It will surely come '! But God reigns.

Sept. 29th.—I went again to Stieglitz for the Sabbath, and to hold the Quarterly Meeting next day. I gave a lecture in the evening, Mr. John Osborne in the chair. We raised £15.

Oct. 4th.—The Barkly Street Church sustained a great loss to-day in the sudden death of our senior leader, our dear brother, Peter Johns. He was going his rounds with vegetables, and when near the hospital he was seen to fall forward, and died immediately. I went straight to Mrs. Johns to condole with her in her sorrowful bereavement.

Oct. 5th.—I held the Quarterly Meeting, which occupied all the day. In the evening we held a fine Meeting in aid of the new school-rooms ; at night I was much tired with the worry of the day.

Oct. 9*th.*—How rapidly the months fly! Here I am again in Melbourne attending the Connexional Committees. After which I went to the House of Assembly, and heard part of the debate on 'Public Education.' What an interminable question this is; but it should be settled this time. The Bill now under discussion contemplated a system of 'National Education,' on the basis of a free, compulsory, and secular foundation. The father of the Bill was the Hon. Wilberforce Stephen, Attorney General of the MacCulloch Government. It ignored Bible or Religious Instruction in all State-paid schools, and thus removed the 'religious difficulty' to the direction and care of Christian Churches, and to the action of parents as the natural guardians of the children. This accomplished by direct legislation, the way was cleared for an effective administration of the Act. It was a great charge the Parliament assumed, for there were of children, at that time, 281,876 of school age, and 205,502 were in attendance at public schools. About 10,000 had night schools established for their special benefit. Two objects by this Act were sought to be secured. (1) To place compulsorily within the reach of every boy and girl in Victoria, free of expense to parents and guardians, instruction in the elements of a good English education; and (2) to bring about, as soon as practicable, the abolition of every vestige of the 'Denominational System,' by establishing a complete network of efficient Secular Schools under the supervision of a Minister of Education solely responsible to Parliament.*

Oct. 16*th*—To-day I buried the mortal remains of the dear good man, Brother Woolcock. His end was simply blessed.

The next day I visited the Chinese Camp at Golden Point. I saw in one of the rooms the *fan-tan* game of chance in full swing. These rooms are visited for gambling purposes by young white men, who

---

* Mr. Attorney General Stephen took great satisfaction from the passing of this Act. He was a staunch Episcopalian ; still, his belief was that such a measure was absolutely necessary for securing to the rising generation of Victoria a good elementary training at the national expense. It must have been to him a sore remembrance of the conflicts he had passed through that led him on February 24th, 1874, thus to refer to the part he had taken in the preparation of this measure :—'Sectarianism would never again, he believed, endanger the success of the System, for the antidote for the poison had been found in the principle of free education. Without the strong motive power of free education, he did not think that the hydra-headed monster of denominationalism could have been got rid of.'—*Speech at Maryborough, Victoria.*

are being ruined by, and are enchanted with, this vice. They are very dens for debauchery, cheating, and every other abomination. A plague-spot in the midst of our Colonial life, which should be mercilessly swept away.

Oct. 19*th.*—English news. We are mulcted in £3,100,000 damages for the *Alabama's* exploits in cruelly robbing and destroying American merchant vessels. But, if Lord Russell had prevented the escape of this pirate ship from Liverpool, which he might have done, we should have been saved from much trouble, indelible disgrace, and this enormous fine.

Oct. 30*th.*—We began the Annual District Meeting, and all the brethren were present. We reached the sixteenth question before we adjourned. In the evening I preached the official sermon, after which we partook of the Lord's Supper together.

Nov. 5*th.*—We had a stiff discussion over the protest of the Neil Street Trustees, against the occupancy by the Lydiard Street Quarterly Meeting of the 'Free Methodist Church,' Macarthur Street, for religious worship, seeing that it was only three hundred to four hundred yards from the Neil Street establishment. Mr. J. T. Phillips, Circuit Steward, Barkly Street, spoke in favour of the protest, and Mr. Henry Bell, M.P., against it. Both speeches were able, and were well received. It was finally decided, on the motion of the Rev. E. J. Watkin, 'that as there had been no violation of boundaries this meeting cannot interfere.' An impotent conclusion, and very risky as to consequences.

In connection with the reading of the 'Liverpool Minutes,' a spirited conversation ensued on the subject of an endowment of power, as a specific condition to success in the Ministry. Our reverend brother, Mr. Ussher, struck out some original thoughts on the subject. Referring to the passage, Acts i. 8, he maintained that the last great promise of the ascending Lord assured that essential gift to us as God's servants. That 'gift' was not the ordinary grace of the Holy Ghost which all penitent believers receive in their adoption and sanctification; but, over and beyond that grace, it was a special endowment for persuading men to consent to be saved. He thought the grace of holiness was the only basis upon which the gift of power could rest. The Rev. Joseph Dare contributed wise and fervent counsels in the discussion, and insisted upon the possibility of every one of us receiving this blessed 'Baptism of power' then and there.

THE FEDERAL COFFEE PALACE, COLLINS STREET WEST, MELBOURNE.

I think that every brother present was impressed with the season-ableness and importance of this 'conversation,' and was encouraged to expect greater things than those previously received from the risen Saviour. Taken altogether, I think it was the best conclusion to that particular part of our sessional business I ever attended.

Dec. 12th.—I went to Melbourne to attend the Stationing Committee. We worked all day, and finished our duty.

Dec. 27th.—The new Education Act having come into force, and finding that there was much diversity of opinion abroad as to some of its provisions, I thought it advisable for me to prepare a syllabus of the Act, and publish it for general information. This I did, and published the document in the *Star* and *Courier*, Ballarat papers, and thereby secured a very general circulation. I think the syllabus was copied into the columns of the *Age* also.

The Watch Night Service was duly held, the local preachers taking part with me.

1873.

Jan. 2nd.—We held the Quarterly Meeting. Income £148 3s. 3d. Expenditure £195 3s. 5d. Total Circuit debt, including previous deficiencies, £79 7s. The Barkly Street Society did well; still, it was impossible to meet our expenses. The Circuit was due for a second married minister at the ensuing Conference, but the brethren, by a unanimous vote, declined to take up the obligation. I could not blame them. On the 16th I was in Sydney attending the Conference; the Rev. Thomas Williams, President, and Rev. John Cope, Secretary. Important action affecting some ministers took place at this Conference. The Rev. Joseph Nettleton, who, having been in Fiji for nearly thirteen years, had permission to return to England, and the Rev. J. Hutcheon, M.A., a minister of the British Conference, would reside in Melbourne. We had great difficulty with some of the Stations, and it was hard work to get the great wheel of our Itinerancy to revolve at all. The Rev. Thomas James was appointed to Port Adelaide, which created great dissatisfaction among his friends in Adelaide and Ballarat, and I was removed from Ballarat East to Pirie Street, Adelaide. But these are only a sample of the changes which had to be made. One would almost suppose that Bishop Short had written with the Methodist Conference in view as an extenuation of the supposed hardships of the

Itinerancy, as follows, 'Much good incidently arises from such changes, which tend to modify the torpor sometimes resulting from a lengthened incumbency, or other grounds of discontent.' The itinerant principle, in its operation, is sometimes exceedingly inconvenient for ministers and ministers' families, disappointing and trying to Circuits; nevertheless, it was one of Wesley's wise arrangements for perpetuating Methodism 'so long as the sun and moon endure.'

This was the last of the Australasian Conferences to be held. The new plan for holding Colonial Annual Conferences would come into operation in January, 1874, as agreed to by the British Conference. On February 3rd the sessions closed, and all were glad when our President pronounced the Benediction. We left per steamer for Melbourne the next day, leaving our Sydney friends with much regret. We had two excellent services on board. The Rev. K. Johnstone, Sailors' Chaplain at Sandridge, preached once on 'The Banner of Truth,' and the Rev. J. C. Symons also once on 'Heaven.' We reached Sandridge on the morning of the 7th, and after breakfasting with the Poolmans I left for Ballarat, and reached home at 4.30 p.m. Mrs. Bickford had remained behind in Sydney for a few weeks with our dear Christy, previous to our removal to South Australia.

March 10*th*.—The Board of Education informed me, through Mr. Venables, 'that the Local Committees of Non-Vested Schools, carried on under Clause 10 of the new Act, are still recognised as Committees of Management; but Trustees of School Properties can supersede them, if so disposed, as they have the control of the buildings.' Exactly so, Mr. Venables; but the suggested supersession is more easily made than done!

March 17*th*.—I went to Creswick, and lectured on 'Wilberforce.' We had a good attendance. Afterwards I had an interesting conversation with Messrs. Cooper and Gardner on public questions of a national and an ecclesiastical kind. It is not often that one can meet with gentlemen in a country township possessed of so much general knowledge.

March 25*th*.—I packed my books in five large cases. Alas! too many by one-third for our wandering life.

April 7*th*.—I sent off my luggage, and settled up all accounts. I left by the evening train for Melbourne, and spent the night in the hospitable home of my friends, Mr. and Mrs. Thomas Osborne.

The following Comparative Statistics have been courteously procured for me by the Hon. J. L. Dow, M.P., Commissioner of Lands, from the Government Statist, W. H. Hayter, Esq., showing the progress of the Colony ecclesiastically and materially for the period named :—

1. Population (mean) 1854—267, 371 ; 1873—765, 511. Increase, 498, 140.
2. Churches 1854—187 ; 1873—2.284. Increase. 2,097.
3. Registered Clergy 1854 (no return) ; 1874—654.
4. Day Schools 1854—391 ; 1873—1.731. Increase. 1,340.
5. Day Scholars 1872—160, 743 ; 1873—226, 255 ; 1874—238, 592. Increase in attendance, through abolishing school fees, first year, 65,512 ; second year, 77,849.
6. Sabbath Schools 1854 (no returns) ; 1873—111,973 children.
7. Crown Lands sold, or selected, to end of. 1854—1,369.382 acres ; 1873—13,263.600 acres.
8. Acres under Cultivation 1854—54,905 ; 1873—964, 996.
9. Squatting Runs 1854 (no returns) ; 1873—894 runs = 25,830,641 acres.
10. Imports 1854—£17,659.051 ; 1873—£16,533,856. (Imports reduced under a Protective Policy.)
11. Exports, 1854—£11.775,204 ; 1873—£15,302,454. (Exports increased under a Protective Policy.)
12. Gold produced 1854 —2,392,065 oz., value £9,568.260 ; 1873—1,241,205 oz., value £4,964.820.

---

13. Churches 1887—4.223. Schools, 2,660. Scholars, 268,705.
14. Population 1887, males. 550.044 : females, 486,075 = 1,036,119.
15. Primary Education 1888. Schools, 2,077. Scholars, 197,115. Cost, £641,993. Per child, £4 6s. 6$\frac{1}{4}$d ; including buildings, rent, scholarships, etc. Total is £787,860.

The Gold has done it all. This gift of Providence has attracted population, and set in motion such vital forces as have created the richest gem in the British Crown. And 'Victoria' is only on the fringe of her destined greatness. 'Hail Victoria !' the golden land ; the happy home of free, self-sustaining churches : of free education ; and of 'Home Rule,' as the conceded boon of England's 'Reformed' Parliament to a loyal, contented, and grateful people.

GOD SAVE THE QUEEN.

SOUTH AUSTRALIA.

April 8th.—At 1 p.m. Mrs. Bickford and I went on board the steamer *Aldinga* at the Queen's Wharf, and soon started for Adelaide. The Revs. J. Watsford, J. C. Symons, J. Harcourt, and a few other friends were there to say 'Good-bye.' We got through the 'Heads' before dark; and being now once more on the high seas I contentedly 'turned in.' The next day the weather was charming, the wind fresh and fair, and the passengers agreeable. What more could be desired? Well, nothing except that,—although I had been an 'itinerant preacher' for about thirty-five years, yet, I could not get so used to it as to like it. It was to me, with my friendly instincts so strongly embedded in my very being, a crucible not always in its operation of a very satisfactory kind. The question put by the President of the Conference at our 'Ordination,' 'Will you reverently obey your chief ministers, unto whom is committed the charge and government over you?' oftentimes becomes difficult, if not galling, as a first duty to Conference authority. Still, obedience is an essential part of our compact; therefore, in now journeying to a neighbouring Colony in the exercise of my ministry, I was fulfilling it. Duty was mine; consequences belonged to the Conference and to God.

We reached Port Adelaide on Thursday the 10th, when we were greeted by the Rev. W. L. Binks, James Scott, Esq., and Mr. Martin, Circuit Steward. These ministerial changes are designedly made at fixed times, so that the out-going minister, having vacated the parsonage premises, the in-coming one may on arrival enter without delay his new habitation. But not so in our case. We went, therefore, to the hospitable home of Mr. and Mrs. James Scott, to await the departure of my predecessor, the Rev. Thomas James, and the preparing the house itself for our reception.

April 11th. (Good Friday)—I greatly prize a religious service in commemoration of our Lord's Crucifixion, and not being quite in charge of my new Circuit, I asked Mr. Scott to take me to hear Dean Russell at St. Paul's. I liked the discourse, and I was glad to have had the opportunity of once more worshipping in an Anglican Church —the Church of my ancestors in the old country. In the evening I went by invitation to Norwood, and gave a short address at the Sunday School Anniversary. The Circuit ministers and the friends gave me a hearty reception.

April 13th. (Easter Sunday)—There is a great deal of agreeable curiosity arising out of the first appearance of a new minister in his Circuit. Possibly this feeling is mutual; as I think it ought to be. I certainly was anxious to see what the congregations at ' Draper Memorial ' and Pirie Street were like, and I was not disappointed. There was a ' savour ' of Christian ' goodness ' in the people perceptible to me, of a most encouraging kind. I felt I had come amongst a people who would ' receive with meekness the engrafted word.' I essayed to begin my work as I knew I could continue it. I was fortunate in my co-pastor, the Rev. G. W. Patchell, M.A., who would share with me the obligation of ministering the word of life to the congregations, and in the Rev. W. P. Wells, the President of Prince Alfred College, whose Sabbath services were to be given exclusively to the Pirie Street Circuit. And I had a very fine staff of local preachers as helpers in the work. But, the Circuit being large, it would require a nice adjustment of appliances and of ' times ' to overtake all its requirements. The pastoral work, I saw, would need to be systematically done, and Mr. Patchell and I were resolved upon doing it.

I cannot account for the circumstance; but it, nevertheless, was true, that I felt more oppressed with my new environments than I had ever been previously in taking charge of my circuits. The Pirie Street congregation was large, and had had some of our ablest men as Superintendents. But I resolved to assume this ' burden of the Lord,' and do my very best for preserving our hold upon so large a constituency, and to maintain the reputation my predecessors had won among their clerical compeers in the city. I had no new character in which to appear; I could not be in the pulpit either a philosopher, scientist, politician, or Biblical critic, so much as to be a ' Methodist Preacher ' of an earlier date and style—plain, expository,

18

evangelical, earnest, and soul-saving. This was my ideal of what Christ expected me to be; besides which, it was what I believed would accord with the aspirations of my congregations, and the genius of South Australian Methodism. In these respects I have not miscalculated 'the fitness of things.'

The first attempt I made at preaching was in 1834, at East Allington, near Kingsbridge, Devon, from the words, ' And that He died for all, that they which live should not henceforth live unto themselves, but unto Him which died for them, and rose again.' The ' Fall,' the ' Atonement,' the ' Resurrection,' and the ' New Life,' were the main points of my juvenile speech on that occasion. I have tried their strength many times since; and to use Bishop William Taylor's apt simile, I may say, ' I know how far they will carry.' I began in that very manner at the 'Draper Memorial Church,' on April 13th, 1873, but taking as my text, ' And I, if I be lifted up from the earth, will draw all men unto Me.' In the evening of the same day, at Pirie Street, I took the words, ' Have ye received the Holy Ghost since ye believed?' My subjects, and the manner of their treatment, gave our city congregations a pretty good idea of the ' manner of speech ' they would be likely to hear from me during the period of my incumbency.

Within the first fortnight I attended several Anniversaries, and thus had an early introduction to the greater part of the leading workers of our City and Suburban Circuits. The balance sheets of the Trusts and Sunday Schools gave me a good idea of our financial position, and of the monetary ability of our numerous adherents to sustain the work.

On the 26th—that is, sixteen days after our arrival—we took possession of our new home in Pirie Street. The Scotts had shown us much kindness during the time the Parsonage was being cleansed and renovated. I much enjoyed the society of this nice, genteel, Christian family.

For the first time in my long career, I had the full gratification of labouring where perfect ' religious equality' obtained. It was provided in the accepted Constitution of the Colony: (1) 'That it was never to be a charge to the Mother Country;' (2) ' That there was never to be a State Church recognised;' and (3) 'That the transported prisoners from Great Britain were never to be admitted to its shores.' So that, in the absence of a Presbyterian or Anglican

'State Church,' the various sections of the one South Australian Church have equal rights, privileges, and powers. 'A fair field,' therefore, 'and no favour,' is the legal, national, and ecclesiastical birthright of all religionists throughout the length and breadth of the land. And there is a true unity amongst all these religionists; but it is the unity of the beautiful rainbow, whose distinctions of colour so sweetly blend as to make a perfect whole. Our unity is real because it is spiritual; 'One is our Master, even Christ, and all we are brethren.'

It will be known to the careful readers of early Methodistic history, that Mr. Wesley had always before him the purpose of supplying to the families of his Societies a high class of education. This praiseworthy object of our founder has never been lost sight of in England (since his death in 1791), or in America, or Australasia. In South Australia, as early as 1854, at the Adelaide Annual District Meeting, presided over by the lamented Rev. Daniel James Draper, it was resolved that efforts should be made to establish such an institution as Prince Alfred College now is. But it was not till 1865 that really definite steps were taken, by the purchase of a block of land of fifteen acres, which was then being offered for sale at Kent Town for £2,750. His Royal Highness the Duke of Edinburgh laid the foundation stone of the new College on November 7th, 1867, in the presence of a large assemblage of the *élite* of the Colony. The main building was occupied for educational work a few months later, when an Inaugural Meeting was held in connection therewith, under the auspices of Sir James Fergusson, then Governor of the Colony.

When I arrived in Adelaide, in 1873, I found that Prince Alfred College had gained a firm footing as one of the higher class of educational institutions. The South Australians had given to it their confidence, and the general public its warm support. The first Head Master was Samuel Fiddian, Esq., B.A., who, having honourably fulfilled his engagement with the Committee, was succeeded by J. A. Hartley, Esq., B.A., B.Sc. Mr. Hartley served two terms, greatly to the advantage of the College, when he accepted from the Government the position of Inspector General of the State Schools. This College met a great want, and has secured the good opinion and generous support of all classes of the community. The subsequent additions to the main building of the 'Waterhouse' and 'Colton' wings, for providing larger accommodation for boarders and day, pupils, is proof of the high estimation in which the College is held. The present master is Frederick Chappel, Esq., B.A., B.Sc., whose conduct of the institution has been one of unbroken success.

May.—One month in Adelaide has shown me, that in our Australian cities it is simply impossible for ministers in prominent positions to settle down, as they can in English and Scotch large towns, to the ordinary routine work of a Circuit. In a new country, as is South Australia, this is very much the case. The Chairman of the district, the Rev. W. L. Binks, was in receipt of letters from the Northern Areas, in which was pointed out the difficulty of obtaining sites for church and school purposes. At Mr. Binks's request, the Rev. W. P. Wells, Mr. Colton and I accompanied him to the Chief Secretary, Sir Henry Ayres, to lay their case before him. Sir Henry, who is the politest and most liberal Premier I know, received us with courteous consideration, and listened to the statements of Messrs. Binks and Colton. When I thought that we were not making much progress with our case, I presumed to lay before Sir Henry the *modus* by which similar difficulties were got over on the Victorian Goldfields, by our 'squatting' on suitable sites, erecting our buildings, and then applying to the Hon. Commissioner of Lands to offer such sites at public auction, with full valuation for the improvements. This form of settlement, I contended, was gradual, easy, inexpensive, sufficient, and inflicted no loss on the Government or local communities. To my surprise, Sir Henry asked whether such a course of action would not be interpreted as ' State Aid.' ' And you know,' he said, 'that we are prohibited from doing that in any form whatsoever.' The utmost that could be done, he thought, would be for the ministers and their friends to make selections in the meantime of such sites as were suitable for their objects, and the Government would not allow of any interference with their action. We gained all we wanted, and thanked the Chief Secretary for his readiness to help us.

In the evening I preached in Pirie Street Church to 100 persons, which was a large attendance for an ordinary week-night congregation.

May 9th.—My first patient was a Mr. Morecombe in Waymouth Street ; I attended him all through his illness. He ' received the Spirit of Adoption,' and was made happy. The last words he spake were, ' Glory be to God.'

May 26th.—The Queen's *levée* was held to-day. I attended with Mr. Binks, and thus showed my loyalty to the best of Sovereigns.

June 9th.—Our new Governor, Sir Anthony Musgrave, was sworn in to-day in the Town Hall. I went of course to witness the ceremony, which was imposing. He is a fine, benevolent-looking man, and made a good impression upon the large audience which had assembled to welcome him. On the 25th I held the Quarterly Meeting. There was a large attendance of brethren. We reported a decrease of membership; but the income met all expenses of an ordinary kind.

July 3rd.—We held a meeting for establishing a mission in the Northern Territory. We raised £88. Mr. James Scott and I were appointed Secretaries to this Mission.

July 8th.—Mr. Colton and I went to Glenelg to seek for a convenient Church site. We pitched upon a central spot, and Mr. Colton agreed to make enquiries about the price.

July 10th.—Mr. Angas, senior, sent us a cheque for £50 in aid of our Northern Territory Mission. I prepared the circulars, and sent thirty-seven to New South Wales and Victoria inviting aid. Mr. Scott and I prepared a memorial to the Rev. W. B. Boyce, Mission House, London, asking for a grant of £300 towards this Mission. As the expense of establishing this Mission would be considerable, and too much for South Australia to bear alone, we were obliged to look where we could for help.

July. 23rd.—This afternoon we held a private Ordination Service in Pirie Street Church, and ' set apart ' for this important Mission the Rev. R. T. Boyle, in whose piety, prudence, and ability we had the utmost confidence. In the evening, at a public meeting, we commended Mr. and Mrs. Boyle to ' the grace of God.' On the 26th they sailed in the steamer *Tararua* for Palmerston, Port Darwin. May God preserve and bless them !

July 24th.—The circular is bearing fruit. James Campbell, of Ballarat, sent £5 5s., S. G. King, at Melbourne, £2 2s., James Robin £5 5s., J. H. Angas £10 10s., Thomas Moyses £1 1s., Hon. G. Bagot £5 5s. Money came in from many quarters, and we felt justified in incurring such expense as was necessary for efficiently working this distant mission.

Oct. 6th.—We held the Pirie Street Church Anniversary, and raised £250.

Oct. 16th.—Some official men are too broad, and others are too narrow. Of the latter class is Mr. B. To-day he came to me, and said that he had been nursing his grievance for some days. That grievance was that at our Young Men's Society's entertainment, 'Dickens,' as an author, had been praised. He had read the report of the Meeting in the paper, and he objected to the name of 'Dickens' being mentioned in such a connection. I talked with him at large, but it was of no use. I expect he will resign his connection with our Church. The next day he sent me his letter of resignation. I hope, on reflection, he will regret the hasty step he has taken. Unfortunate Superintendents! They have to do with all 'sorts and sizes' of God's creatures, and are expected to preserve their equanimity, preach like apostles, and suffer as martyrs. But are they not 'flesh and blood' like other men? Have they no feelings to be considered? Eh?

Oct. 21*st.*—The Annual District Meeting was begun to-day. The Rev. W. L. Binks presided. We went rapidly through the ordinary business, and concluded on the 24th. It was a happy and successful meeting.

Nov. 14*th.*—Mr. G. W. Cotton called to tell me that Mr. Colton, Mr. J. D. Hill, and himself had purchased a new site at Glenelg for £320. 'It is well.'

Nov. 19*th.*—Finished my review of Thomas Cooper's Bridge of Nineteen Arches;' being an 'Historical Argument' in defence of the Christian religion. It has run out to fifty pages; too long by half. I was taken with terrible vertigo just as I finished this heavy work. I rallied sufficiently to give the paper in the evening to the 'Young Men's Society;' it was a great effort. At the close I was nervously prostrate. Too much pressure on.

Dec. 9*th.*—This is the ninth day of hot winds. We are simply enduring life. In the evening we had a thunder-storm and heavy rain. The change generally comes when our feeling is that we are near the last gasp.

Dec. 10*th.*—I went again to Her Majesty's gaol to see Mrs. W., who is under sentence of death for the alleged crime of having poisoned her husband. She had been earnestly seeking, she said, the Divine mercy in Christ, and that her prayers had been answered. I examined her closely, and felt greatly relieved by her statements.

Dec. 12*th.*—I received a letter from the Governor of the gaol, requesting me to see the young man R., who was yesterday sentenced to death for the murder of his mate B.

Dec. 17*th*.—Mrs. W. handed to me to-day a sealed letter to be opened after her death. Poor unfortunate woman ! She seems to contemplate her sad end with a calm fortitude. Her trust is in God.

Dec. 29*th*.—Again at the goal to give the Holy Sacrament to the penitent Mrs. W. 'If good works,' she said, 'were necessary, my soul would be lost.' What a mercy for her that she learnt the plan of salvation in the Sunday School, and that now, in the time of her great need, she has embraced it. R. was in tears, reading the Bible. He confessed his crime to me this very morning, and there was now hope for him. We both earnestly wrestled with God in prayer for his salvation.

' *Dec.* 30*th*. [Diary Jotting]—I went with Mrs. W. to the scaffold, and saw her executed. It was a sad, sad scene. In the afternoon I buried her mortal remains within the precincts of the gaol ground. The law is satisfied ! What more ? . . . The next day I handed to the Editor of the *Register* the letter which had been confided to me. It was a sorrowful tale ; and thus was ended the romantic story of Mrs. W.'s short life.'

1874.

' *Jan.* 1*st*. [Diary Jotting]—I attended the execution of poor R. He told me that he had made his peace with God. I went with him to the scaffold, and prayed with him and for him there. He affectionately kissed me after prayer ; the bolt was drawn, and he died immediately. I buried the corpse close to that buried a few days ago : and, on returning to Pirie Street, I wrote the Chief Secretary, Hon. Arthur Blyth, M.P., a full statement of the facts of the case. The close of the year and the beginning of the next one were mournful, and intensely painful to me.

The next day, the 2nd, I received an official letter from the Chief Secretary, thanking me for my assiduous attention to W. and R., and expressive of the sympathy of the Government in the anxious solicitudes through which I had passed.

On January 20th, at 10 a.m., the first South Australian Conference was begun ; the Rev. W. L. Binks in the chair, and the Rev. W. P. Wells, Secretary. We started with 39 ministers, 285 local preachers, 370 leaders, 1,843 Sunday School teachers, and 4,865 Church members. We had 170 churches, 168 Sunday schools, 12,381 Sabbath scholars, and 33,626 attendants on public worship. The educative effect of our attending the Australasian Conferences, for about twenty years, was seen in the ready and effective manner in which the business of this, our first Colonial Conference, was taken up and carried through.

We were comparatively small, but we were not faint-hearted. Our trust was in the 'God of our Fathers,' and in His Name we 'set up our banners.' In our 'Annual Address' we say :—

'The recent legislation of our Church has placed us in new and endearing relations to you . . . We have committed to us unitedly the administration of our ecclesiastical polity in this land ; and our review of the past gives encouragement and hope of prosperity in the future.'

In this, our first Conference, a difficulty arose in the interchange of ministers ; but it was finally arranged that the Rev. Thomas James, of South Australia, should be transferred to Victoria, and that the Rev. R. W. Campbell should come from Victoria to us.

On February 4th a public 'Ordination' Service was held, when Brothers William Henry Rofe and John Hosking Trevorveen were fully set apart to the ministry. The giving of the 'Charge' devolved upon me, as an ex-President of the Australasian Conference, after which the ministers and members partook of the Lord's Supper. A good and wise discussion ensued upon the subject of 'Lay Representation' to Conference, and it resolved :—

'That we, as a Conference, agree to deal with the recommendations of the Melbourne Committee on the subject in our sessions of next year, in order that our views may be laid before the General Conference in May 1875.'

The conversation upon the work of God was searching and salutary. We say, 'It is a source of deep regret to us to learn that many of those whose names are on the class-books so frequently absent themselves from that mode of Christian fellowship which, under God, has been one of the principal means of the spiritual life and power of the Methodist Church from the commencement ;' and the leaders were urged 'to visit absentees,' and seek ' to restore such as have backslidden from God.' The dangers of the times respecting spiritual beliefs, and the necessity of fidelity in our profession, as Christians, are well set forth in the following words, ' We feel compelled to guard you against the unsettling theories which go under the name of "Modern Thought"—theories which are subversive of the authority of Scripture, and derogatory to the God of Revelation.' Followed to their legitimate conclusions, they all terminate in a common darkness and uncertainty, while the Gospel system raises up in every believing heart an assurance indisputable as the testimony of God on which it is based, 'He that believeth on the Son hath the witness in himself.' The name of the Rev. A. J. Boyle appears on the Minutes as our minister and representative in the Northern Territory.

Fifteen years have elapsed since the holding of this Conference. It was the 'beginning of our strength' as an independent Colonial Conference; although, of course, affiliated to the General Conference, and dependent upon it for legislative action. Our faith in the loyalty of our leading officials was strong, and not misplaced, as events have fully shown. The Conference was closed on February 11th. On the 15th I was at Goolwa, preaching Church Anniversary sermons. The next day Captain Johnson and I went over to Port Elliott. I was surprised to find it so boisterous and exposed. As a watering-place for invalids, and for families during the summer heat, the want of a land-locked harbour is a serious drawback. In the evening I gave my lecture on 'Wilberforce,' and we raised £25 for the Trust. I much enjoyed this visit; and much of that pleasure arose from the great kindness of the Rev. James and Mrs. Allen, with whom I was a guest.

March 2nd.—I was under the disagreeable necessity of writing an article in our Magazine—of which I was the senior Editor—on the Rev. Silas Mead's attack on Mr. President Binks, for some remarks in his recent address to the Conference, on the subject of the relation of the children we baptize to our Church. He also attacked me for what I said in my 'Charge,' on the custom of 'child-communion' in the early Church. Mr. Mead poses as the apostle of immersion, as the only form in which that sacrament is to be administered, and, of course, only to such as personally profess faith in Christ. I 'rebuked him sharply,' because he was to be blamed for his unprovoked interference with us. It is difficult to live in peace with some sections of the Church, even in this land of religious freedom and of equal denominational rights.

On the 12th I went out to Mitcham to select a church site. Messrs. Viney and Mouldon assisted me. I visited Mrs. Barron and some other families.

March 13th.—Several lay and ministerial brethren met to consider the advisability of our starting a weekly religious paper, in the interests of morality and general church work. We agreed as to the advisability, and adjourned the meeting for a few weeks.

March 18th. [Diary Jotting]—' This is mother's birthday. She is ninety-three years old to-day. May the good Lord be gracious unto her during her remaining days, and prepare her for all His will ! '

March 19th.—A busy day. I examined Mr. George Crase's journal of City Mission work, and conversed with him for an hour on several phases of his honoured calling. I received Mr. Boyle's journal of his work in the Northern Territory, and revised it for the press. Mr. Nicholson's sermon on ' Joining the Church ' I examined with a view to its publication, believing that it would be useful to our young people. The next day I wrote a review of the Rev. W. A. Quick's sermon entitled, ' Baptism Viewed in its Relation to Infants,' and sent it on for the Magazine. At the Local Preachers' Meeting this evening I examined Walter H. Hanton and George Crase, both of whom were received as full local preachers.

March 25th.—I held the Quarterly Meeting, and thirty brethren were present. The income was £287 6s. 11d., and expenditure £241 8s. 5d.

March 26th.—I received to-day from —— £8, ' conscience money,' to be paid to ——, which will be done.

March 27th.—I wrote to-day my friends, Messrs. John Colton and James Scott, who are in England. I feel it to be my duty, arising out of my ministerial relation, to keep in touch with these honoured brethren by means of an occasional letter to them. I commenced reading to-day ' Personal Life of George Grote.' It is a fine book, and full of deepest interest to politico-historic readers. The lamented Charles Sumner, one of America's best statesmen, on the receipt of the news of Mr. Grote's death, telegraphed to Mrs. Grote, as follows, ' When the electric cable flashed across the Atlantic the news of this great loss, the whole of this vast continent vibrated with sympathy for you.'

March 29th.—I preached the Church Anniversary Sermons at Gawler. The next day the Rev. R. S. Casely took me to see several of our friends. At the public meeting we raised, with the Sunday Collections, £140. I was the guest during this visit of Mr. and Mrs. Wincey, whose children much pleased me.

April 1st.—We accepted Mr. Carey's proposals for the publishing of *The Methodist Journal.* In the evening I attended the ' Draper Memorial Church Anniversary,' and spoke for half an hour. We raised £80. I got the ' Deed of Declaration of Trust ' for the

Glenelg Parsonage site signed to-day, and handed it to Mr. Opie for registration.

April 2nd (Good Friday).—I preached at 7 a.m. in Pirie Street Church from the words, 'Who is he that condemneth? It is Christ that died.' At 11 a.m. I went to St. Paul's to hear Dean Russell on 'The Lamb of God.' The sermon was atrociously read. The want of naturalness, distinctiveness, and the 'eye' always on the manuscript, spoilt it all. And yet the 'enthusiastic' Dean is a man of great ability, and could wield much power if he would only leave his manuscript in his study.

April 15th.—Mr. Patchell and I were appointed 'Editorial Council' of the new paper to-day. How to squeeze out sufficient time for doing this additional work as it ought to be done it is impossible to divine.

April 16th.—I wrote an inaugural address for the new 'Sunday School Union;' subject, 'The Sunday School and its True Work.'

April 29th.—Mrs. Bickford and I went to Clarendon for a few days.

In the evening I began again to read Daniel Isaac on 'Infant Baptism.' This is a fine old work, and is thoroughly exhaustive in its treatment of its subject. I have heard an account of the cause of this sledge-hammer publication, as follows: 'When, many years ago, the Rev. Daniel Isaac was stationed in Bristol, a Baptist minister, of a disputative turn of mind, happened to be stationed there also. This man, unfortunately for himself, commenced an onslaught on the 'Pedo-Baptist' ministers, in which he ridiculed the usages of their Churches in relation to infants and very young children, and predicted, as the consequence of his greater knowledge and influence, their speedy overthrow. Mr. Isaac, believing that much could be said, and conclusively said too, on the other side, set himself to this task. The work was published in due course, and fell like a thunderbolt upon his Baptist assailant; who, in his alarm, called together a number of his ministerial brethren for counsel and defence. Of this number was the celebrated Robert Hall, of Leicester. The frighted men, in order, gave their views, which were of course strongly condemnatory of Mr. Isaac's book; but the great preacher maintained an ominous silence. He was challenged for his opinion, and, it is said, that he rose to his feet, and looking round, eyeing particularly the head-centre of the conclave, he gravely said, 'Brethren, if you value having sound skins, I advise you to leave Mr. Isaac alone, for if he take any of you in hand he will flay you alive.' It was enough; from henceforth the stalwart polemic went on his way in peace, whilst the disturber of the concord, which had previously prevailed in Bristol, had ' to hide his diminished head.'

May 6th. [Diary Jotting]—' This has been my fifty-eighth birthday. The last one was one of comfort to me in my ministry. My health has stood it pretty well. May the merciful God be with me during the ensuing year.'

May 12th.—Mr. Patchell and I re-examined my manuscript sermon entitled, 'The Double Baptism,' and passed it on to the printers. This is the last blow I administered to my neighbour and brother minister, Silas Mead, who will, I think, in the future, leave his Wesleyan brethren alone.

May 27th.—The Methodist Journal is now *fait accompli.* To-day I wrote the first review for its columns, on Mr. Tapling's new work on the Narringeri tribe of Australian blacks. It is an interesting book, and could only have been written by a man who was in strong sympathy with these original owners of this island continent. We have taken their country from them, and it is a small matter to give in exchange a few blankets, rations, protection, education, and religion.

June 1st.—The Rev. Thomas White Smith, my ecclesiastical father, and dearest ministerial friend in England, does not forget us. To-day I received from him a long and beautiful letter, and full of affectionate kindness.

June 15th.—Yesterday I preached at Coromandel Valley at 11 a.m., and at 3 and 6.30 p.m. at Upper Sturt. To-day the 'foundation-stone' was laid by the Hon. John Carr, M.P.; the Revs. Joseph Nicholson, Mr. President Binks, and I took part in the proceedings. We raised £39.

June 17th.—A great blow has fallen upon the Rev. Silas Mead in the death of Mrs. Mead. Mr. Binks and I attended the funeral. I never saw more feeling than on this occasion. Mr. Mead was prostrate, and every one sincerely pitied him. The dear man, the next day, sent us a letter expressive of his sense of our sympathy and brotherly love in being present on so mournful an occasion.

June 19th.—I am confined to the house through a violent attack of lumbago. I sent for Dr. Whittle to see if he could give me anything to help me for the Sabbath duties. Instead of helping me in that direction he ordered me not to leave my room.

June 23rd.—Being still confined in the house, I held the Local Preachers' Meeting in our dining-room. There was a good attendance. I retired at 11 o'clock, but not to sleep through sheer excitement and prostration.

June 24th.—After a week of sickness I am again in my study. In the afternoon I held the Quarterly Meeting. Income £272 0s. 4d. ; expenditure £251. We rapidly did the business, and closed at 5 p.m.

July 3rd.—Mr. T. S. Carey issued the first number of *The Methodist Journal* to-day. It is indeed a venture, but with our large constituency it ought not to be a failure. May God bless its circulation throughout these Colonies !

July 6th.—No increase of work could lead me to neglect the visitation of my people. The Pastor's office comes first with me. My Diary for this day says :—

'Busy all the forenoon. Went in the afternoon to see Miss Lawrence, Mrs. Marshall, Mr. Good, Miss Marsh, Miss Franklin, Misses Ingram, etc. I attended the Building (Connexional) Committee at 4 p.m., the Unley Trustee Meeting at 5.30 p.m., the Pirie Street Trustee Meeting at 6.30 p.m., the Leaders' Meeting at 8.30 p.m., and the Good Templars' Demonstration at 9.30 p.m. Tired at last ! '

July 25th.—I wrote a review of a lecture on ' Secularism and Atheism ' for our *Journal.* This follows two papers on ' Public Education ' and ' Our Day School Teachers.' If we do not succeed with our paper it will not be because we have not tried for it.

Aug. 8th.—This evening I went to the ' Come and Welcome ' Good Templars' Lodge, and was installed as ' Worthy Chaplain.' I must endeavour to do some good here.

Aug. 10th.—Mr. John Rounsevell called for me to go to Glenelg to see his sick father. I spent more than an hour with him in conversation and prayer.

Aug. 17th.—I wrote an article for the *Journal* on Gritton's ' Christianity is not the Invention of Impostors or Credulous Enthusiasts.' Many of our constituents maybe will read a short article on a tough subject, when perhaps the book itself would be thrown aside as cumbersome and ' dry.'

Sept. 2nd.—I received to-day from Rev. S. Knight a cheque for £200, being a donation from that good man, Mr. T. G. Waterhouse, now in England, for the 'Strangers' Friend Society.' The 'blessing of those who are ready to perish' will come upon this benevolent remembrancer of our poor.

Sept. 22nd.—I attended the funeral of the late Mr. Theophilus Robin, and offered prayer at the grave. It was a mournful sight. The next day I held the Quarterly Meeting. We have now a credit balance of about £90. Thank God for freedom from Circuit debt.

Oct. 7th.—I attended the funeral of the late Mr. Rounsevell. I read and prayed in the house, and the Rev. C. Manthrope officiated at the grave. It was a solemn and somewhat imposing funeral. I returned to Pirie Street, suffering from a severe attack of lumbago. We resolved to-day to proceed forthwith with the erection of a parsonage at Glenelg.

Oct. 10th.—I was at Moonta, at the Rev. R. S. Casely's. In the evening he conducted me to Captain Hancock's, where I enjoyed the evening very much. I preached the next day at the Mines, and addressed the Sunday School in the afternoon.

Oct. 12th.—Captain Hancock took me to see the works, which are elaborate and expensive. The Public Meeting came off in the evening. We raised £85.

Oct. 15th.—I went to the House of Assembly to hear the discussion on the 'River Murray Railway Bill.' During the discussion, the Chief Secretary, the Hon. A. Blyth, came to me in the Speaker's Gallery, and told me that the Fiji Islands were ceded to the British Crown. This news set me a-thinking pretty much in this strain : Is it true, I asked, that Christian influences were brought to bear for the first time on Cannibal Fiji not quite forty years ago ? Is it really true that the Revs. Cross and Cargill, M.A., landed in Lakembor so late as October 12th, 1835, and that a sapping of the basis of the cruellest forms of Heathenism the world has ever seen was successfully prosecuted by these intrepid men ? Is it true that in one short year Mr. Cargill could write the London Committee as follows :—

'Preaching is established in many places, and classes are formed of persons who are enquiring "what they must do to be saved." Day and Sunday Schools were instituted, and the sacred rites of marriage were being observed ?'

'Sappers and Miners,' in an Apostolic sense! No marvel, therefore, that in so short a period as forty years the whole system of Cannibalism was destroyed, and the Christian religion, as formulated by the Wesleys, became the accepted belief and practice of the whole Archipelago . . . . And who prepared these outlying portions of the world to become integral parts of the great British Empire, but these very Wesleyan Missionaries and their noble successors in the Christ-like enterprise?' 'Founders of Empires' and 'Ambassadors of God' at one and the same time. In Africa, India, New Zealand, and Fiji, they have hoisted the grand old flag of England, and Aboriginal races have learnt to 'fear God and to honour the Queen.'

Oct. 17th.—I read one hundred and fifty pages of the 'Life of the Rev. James Dixon, D.D.' How 'great this man was in his day and generation,' none can tell but those who have sat under his wonderful ministry, and drank in a knowledge of 'the deep things of God,' as they listened to the 'wisdom' with which he clothed his mighty thoughts.

Oct. 19th.—The Annual District Meeting was begun to-day; Mr. President Binks, Chairman, the Rev. H. T. Burgess, Secretary. All the ordinary questions were disposed of on the first day. At this Meeting Mr. Binks applied to become a Supernumerary at the Conference of 1875. Seven years of active work in South Australia had told upon his health, and he needed a spell of rest. The Methodist Church, under his direction, had taken possession of the Northern Areas, and had extended her ordinances even to the western portion of the Northern Territory. He had proved himself to be a worthy successor of Daniel James Draper, William Butters, and John Watsford. A veritable *Episkopos*, whose burden was that 'which came upon him daily—the care of all the churches.' I moved two resolutions, which, being accepted by the Meeting, our recommen-dation was duly recorded for presentation to the Conference.

Mr. William Rhodes and I were the Conference Treasurers for the 'Old Preachers' Fund.' Our Church Loan Fund had already a capital of £780·7s. 2d., and the Church Extension and Home Mission Fund of £334 4s. 11d. This was the 'day of small things;' but, as our people had accepted these as essential parts of our Connexional Finance, we could have no doubt as to their growth and permanence. On the 23rd our sessions closed.

We went on 'the even tenor of our way' until November 3rd, when all Adelaide was astir through the arrival overland of the Forrest Exploring Party from Western Australia. I went to the

Town Hall balcony with a number of other gentlemen to be close to the elder Forrest, and to hear his address. The party in their terrible journey had suffered nearly 'the loss of all things;' but, under Divine Providence, sustained by the love of life, and the force of the heroic sentiment within them, these intrepid men 'fought their way through,' and were rewarded in Adelaide 'with an abundant entrance,' and acclamations of welcome. The Brothers Forrest had done a splendid service for Western and Southern Australia, and should be handsomely paid.

Dean Russell and I were great friends. This was evidenced in his readiness to write articles on social and ecclesiastical subjects for *The Methodist Journal*, but also in active co-operation 'in good works.' We mutually watched the arrival from England of shipments of female immigrants; and on the 6th we met at the Servants' Home in Adelaide, and held a religious service for their benefit. I thought the good Dean shone more as a Christian teacher in his familiar remarks to these anxious 'strangers,' than he did in his scholarly, laboured expositions in St. Paul's pulpit. Speaking of valuable help we had in preparing the weekly matter for the *Journal*, not only the Dean, but other ministerial friends contributed also. The Revs. A. Rigg, S. T. Wittrington, H. Mack, H. T. Burgess, L. B. Stephenson, and Joseph Nicholson wrote articles for us. My co-editor, the Rev. G. W. Patchell, M.A., and I both felt that the literary value of our *Journal* was much increased thereby.

A striking episode occurred at this time. I received two letters from England, anent two young men who were coming to the Colony without their fathers' consent. When, on the 17th, the young man, L., called, I handed to him his father's affecting letter to read. It was a touching appeal to his son, and made him weep. C. also came a day or two after with his friend L. I conversed with them at length, and offered to be at their service should they require my assistance. Mrs. Bickford and I, finding that they knew neither where to go nor what to do, invited them to our house. We conceived a great affection for these fine, adventurous young men; and we deeply sympathised with their parents, who had suffered much on their account. L.'s father had entrusted to me a bill for £40, for sending his son to a coffee plantation in Ceylon, which I accordingly did. C. had no such luck; but, through the kind assistance of the Hon. G. W. Cotton, Land Agent, etc., C. got employment on a squatting station in the Port Lincoln District. It was a strange freak of the young men, and they paid dearly for their violation of the Fifth Commandment.

The claims of the Pirie Street Trust now pressed heavily upon us, and the trustees resolved upon a great effort. I called upon the Hon. John Colton, M.P., to head the subscription list. Sitting opposite to each other at his office table, he enquired of me what I thought would be a proper amount for him to give. I replied that so uniform and generous had been his contributions to the Trust that I could not presume to make even a suggestion. 'Well, then,' said he, 'I will give you £125 for myself, £25 for the firm, and £25 for my partner, Mr. Longbottom.' £175 in all. This was a noble helping. We went together on a begging excursion among the Pirie Street pew-holders and other friends. We finished up with a grand Anniversary Meeting, and we had the pleasure to report the raising of £480.

Dec. 21st.—The Quarterly Meeting was held to-day. Income £269 5s. 3d.; expenditure £253 14s. 6d.; entire credit balance £109 1s. 7d. Mr. James S. Green went out of office as Steward after two years' term of generous service. The Stewards for the ensuing year were Mr. Henry Codd and Mr. A. A. Scott; two worthy men who had the confidence of the Circuit.

As we were now rapidly nearing the end of the year, I wrote an article entitled, 'The Retrospect,' and a second on the Chief Secretary's speech at Gummeracha, for the *Journal.* The next day, the 23rd, I visited fourteen families at Unley, and prayed in each house. At 6.30 I met the Bible Instruction Class, and at 7.30 I preached on Isaiah xl. 11, to a fair congregation. The determination I came to, when I accepted the position as responsible Editor of the *Journal,* that its claims should never interfere with my Circuit relations, I religiously carried out.

Dec. 25th (Christmas Day).—A happy day. At 7. a.m we had a good service in Pirie Street. At 9.30 I attended the great gathering of the Sunday School children at the Town Hall; and at 11 I heard Dean Russell on the words, 'When the fulness of the time was come, God sent forth His Son.' I spent the afternoon and evening in reading and quiet thought.

Dec. 26th.—I wrote a review of 'Orthodox London,' which occupied me until 4 p.m. I was much wearied and beaten with the heat.

19

The next day, in the hope of having a good paper for the first issue in the New Year, I wrote two articles, entitled, 'The Prospect, 1875,' and 'On Identity.' My last engagement for the year was the Watch Night Service, Pirie Street Church. I preached as usual, and Messrs. Burton and Berry offered prayer. Thus was closed one of my busiest years.

1875.

Jan. 1*st.*—The New Year was ushered in under the auspices of great Sol's fiercest rays. At the observatory, on the 5th, the thermometer stood at 156° in the sun and at 115° in the shade. A trying time for the strongest, but much more so for the ailing and the ill. I was called to see Mrs. G. W. Coombs, who was dying, and at a quarter to 10 a.m. she passed away. On the next day we buried her mortal remains, and on our return to Mr. Coomb's house I baptized the now motherless babe by the name of George Uriah. It was a mournful ordeal, and deep was the sympathy felt for the bereaved father and his family.

The news of the effect produced in England by Mr. Gladstone's pamphlet on the impossibility of English Catholics, under the new dogma of the 'Infallibility of the Pope,' being loyal to the Crown, as it was their duty to be in every part of the Empire, reached us on the 9th. All honour to this great Christian statesman for this thunderbolt cast into the Vatican. After this daring feat, it may be hoped that his political opponents will be slow to renew their vile insinuation that 'W. E. G.' is a 'Jesuit in disguise.' But politics in Great Britain are a lying and cruel game, and the marvel is that men of high and generous feelings consent to be mixed up with them.

Jan. 14*th.*—I wrote for the *Journal* an article entitled, 'Mr. Gladstone's Expostulation.' My object was to justify his interference, and to uphold the grounds he had taken. Besides which, I wanted South Australian readers to understand something of the fierce ecclesiastical conflicts in which British statesmen and the leaders of religious thought are occasionally involved. As ecclesiastics we do not seek quarrels; but when assailed we have only one course to follow.

Jan. 26*th.*—The South Australian Conference was opened to-day I was chosen as President, and the Rev. S. Knight as Secretary.

The chief difficulty we had to contend with was the stationing of the ministers. But it is no wonder, because we have no fixed principle on which to proceed. The Circuits in Australia have the same right of inviting ministers as in England; but our number is so small that we cannot dispose of our staff upon the invitation system. In some cases the preferences of our Quarterly Meetings were suitable enough, and the Conference would save itself much harassment by adhering to them. But then election of some carries with it as its counterpart reprobation, as Calvin would say, of the other. It was not until the fourth day of the Sessions that we could get a second reading, and not even then without a great deal of cross-firing and unpleasantness.

Feb. 1st.—I returned from Gawler this morning, and presided over the Conference. One item of business was at least satisfactory. By a unanimous vote Messrs. Patchell and I were thanked for the manner in which we had conducted the *Journal.* This was our only pay, but it was enough. On the 8th we read the stations for the third time, and the next day the Minutes were signed.

At this Conference we sanctioned the formation of a Home Mission and Contingent Fund Society; we also adopted a set of revised rules for the Church Loan Fund. The Connexional Committee submitted a plan for 'Lay Representation to Conference,' which was accepted by our Conference, and ordered to be sent on to the General Conference. The Rev. W. L. Binks was made Supernumerary, and a suitable record of his high character and work was entered upon the Minutes.

Feb. 15th.—I paid an official visit to the Gunneracha Circuit to arrange the terms upon which the services of the Rev. Matthew Wilson, a venerable Supernumerary minister, might be secured for one year. After considerable discussion it was agreed that the Circuit should pay Mr. Wilson £150 per annum, to include salary, rent, and house expenses. The Connexional claims were to be met and the travelling expenses of the local preachers paid by the Circuit.

Feb. 2nd.—I came to the conclusion that in South Australia we ought to have an Act passed for the payment of Members in Parliment as in Victoria. The experiment has been a success ' over the Border,' and I therefore strove to get our Legislature to follow in the same steps. Hence, an article in the *Journal,* which I had carefully prepared, entitled, ' Payment of Members of Parliament,' was inserted. I can claim, I think, the credit of being the first public advocate of that just and righteous principle in this Colony.

Feb. 24th.—'The New House of Assembly' was my next leader for the *Journal*. Mrs. Bickford and I went in the afternoon to Glenelg to call upon Miss Poolman, from Sandridge, after which we drove round to Dunrobin to take tea with our kind friends, Mr. and Mrs. Keyner.

March 3rd.—Great excitement in the city at the news of the loss of the steamer *Gothenburgh* on the Barrier Reef off Queensland. Much valuable life is doubtless lost.

March 10th.—I attended a meeting in the Town Hall in aid of the families deprived of their husbands and fathers by the loss of the *Gothenburgh*. I gave two guineas; but I would that I could have given twenty.

March 22nd.—I attended a meeting of ministers, when we agreed to invite Moody and Sankey to come to South Australia. In the afternoon I went to the 'Stone-laying' ceremony of the new church at Brompton.

March 24th.—I held the Quarterly Meeting. Income £287 8s. 7d.; expenditure £239 16s. 1d. Credit Balance in all £155 15s. 8d. We agreed to expend this accumulated balance in furnishing the new parsonage at Glenelg. We certainly had a fine meeting. With such a condition of finance every official brother was pleased, and not a word of grumbling was heard.

March 26th (Good Friday).—I heard the Rev. Mr. Symes preach a beautiful sermon in Stow Church, when I hastened off to hear Bishop Short in St. Paul's. A sermon in the old orthodox style—'good roast beef and plum pudding' at one and the same time. In the afternoon I went to Sir John Morphett's grounds to join in the picnic of the Pirie Street Sunday School. About five hundred children and young people were present, and a large number of teachers and friends besides. I came home desperately tired, and lay down in my study, sleeping right away for two whole hours. Sleep is my remedy for excessive fatigue and nervous prostration. It never fails me.

March 31st.—I drove Mrs. Bickford to Port Adelaide to embark for Melbourne. The heat of Adelaide had for some time been most oppressive, and she needed change of air and scene.

April 21st.—We have been in the itinerant 'swim.' The Rev. G.

W. Patchell is gone to the Burra, and the Rev. W. P. Wells to Kent Town. Mr. Burgess and Mr. Nicholson have come to the Pirie Street Circuit, and this evening we had the usual welcome meeting; Mr. James Greer, the senior Steward, presided. There were, at least, two hundred persons present. A hearty reception was accorded to the 'new' men. Under the inspiration of this joyous meeting I wrote an article for the *Journal* entitled, ' The Wesleyan Itinerancy.' The principle of the Itinerancy may be thus stated : ' When He ascended up on high He received gifts for men.' One of the most precious of these ' gifts ' is that of ' pastors and teachers ; ' and the aim of the Itinerancy is to distribute this agency over our whole Connexion, as occasion may require. The well-balanced mind of Wesley caught hold of this idea, and he ordained its observation by the Conferences he created. We, of the Australasian Church, have taken no such power from the original ' Poll Deed,' as would permit of such changes as would ' do away with the Iterancy of our ministry.'

May 12th.—I am once more in Melbourne ; this time to attend the First General Conference, held under our amended constitution. My co-representatives are the Revs. S. Knight, W. P. Wells, W. L. Binks, T. Lloyd, J. B. Stephenson, and R. S. Casely. The proceedings were opened by the Rev. S. Wilkinson, the President of the New South Wales Conference. In the ' Address ' to the British Conference, we say :—

' By an interesting coincidence, the Senior President of the Conference, whose duty it was to open the first session, was able to tell us that though not the first Wesleyan minister who preached in Victoria, yet he was one of the first, having been appointed as a Wesleyan Missionary here thirty-five years ago. Thus, within the few years of one ministerial history, are gathered the planting, the robust outgrowth. and the almost completed self-regulation, of the Methodism which assembles now at its first legislative Conference in this city ; itself the product of social forces, acting with great energy, and within a very brief period.'

The Presidents of the Colonial Annual Conferences presided in rotation, and conducted the routine business from day to day. Several important principles inherent in our ecclesiastical polity were re-affirmed, or formulated for the first time, as follows :—

1. For guarding the pastoral office from invasion or injury by the proposed introduction of laymen into our Colonial Annual Conferences. The Rev. James Swanton Waugh (now Doctor Waugh) prepared the following declaration :—

' That this Conference distinctly asserts its maintenance of the New Testament doctrine. that the ministry derives its existence from Christ, and that upon Christian ministers, to whom is entrusted the duty of taking "heed to all the flock. over which the Holy Ghost hath made them overseers, to feed the Church of God," devolves the solemn responsibility of enforcing godly discipline, and administering the pastoral government of the Church.' . . . 'That in the admission of laymen as members of the Conferences, this principle must be held to be sacred and inviolable.'

2. For insisting upon the maintenance of the historic condition of members, as set forth in the ' General Rules of the Society.' There are three distinct provisions :—

(1) We take no power to ' revoke ' (*i.e.*, to recall ; to repeal ; to reverse) the ' General Rules of our Societies.'

(2) We agree in the conviction, that no mode of facilitating and promoting fellowship among Christians approaches so nearly to the requirements of the New Testament as the Class Meeting, which, under God, has so greatly contributed to our spiritual vitality and success ; and we resolve to adhere to it as a test of membership in our Church.

(3) To secure correct returns of the number of members in the several Circuits, it was agreed to call the attention of Superintendents to the law of 1837, as follows: ' The Superintendents are directed to return, in their Quarterly Schedule, the precise number, without any abridgment or deduction, of those to whom, after due and sufficient probation, they or their colleagues have actually given tickets in their respective Circuits.'

3. On Direct Representation to Conference, it enacted that ' the Quarterly Meeting of each Circuit shall be entitled to elect one lay representative, who shall be elected by ballot at the Quarterly Meeting next preceding the session of the Conference to which such Circuit pertains.'

4. The condition of ' baptized children ' is thus stated : ' By baptism you place your children within the pale of the visible Church, and give them a right to all its privileges, the pastoral care of its ministers, and, as far as their age and capacity will allow, the enjoyment of its ordinances and means of grace.'

5. The Inter-Colonial changes of ministers was provided for, by empowering the General Conference ' to make. or direct the Annual Conference to make, all necessary changes and interchanges of ministers between the several Annual Conferences.'

6. The pastoral authority of each Annual Conference was recognised in the direction given to them to issue a ' Pastoral Address ' to the Societies under their care.

The Minutes of the First General Conference, as published under the able guidance of the Rev. J. B. Waterhouse, its Secretary, do not show that much work of a legislative kind was done. Still, being *ab initio*, I think we did enough. The plan for popularising our highest Church courts, by the introduction thereto of representative laymen, under safe and wise conditions, was no ordinary task. That the British Conference accepted our plan without amendment, and, in Colonial Office phrase, left it to its operation, is surely evidence of the carefulness with which it had been prepared. It is now the recognised Magna Charta of the Australasian Wesleyan Methodist Church, securing alike to ministers and laymen New Testament rights, and free action in the prosecution throughout the Southern World of a peaceful and soul-saving mission.

The Minutes were signed as under:—

SAMUEL WILKINSON,
President of New South Wales and Queensland Conference.

JAMES BULLER,
President of New Zealand Conference.

JAMES BICKFORD,
President of South Australia Conference.

JOHN HARCOURT,
President of Victoria and Tasmania Conference.

JABEZ B. WATERHOUSE,
Secretary of General Conference.

June 1st.—I went on board the steamer *Aldinga* at the Queen's Wharf at 1 p.m., and sailed for Port Adelaide. After a delightful run of forty-eight hours I landed, and at once hasted to Pirie Street, and found all well.

I held the Quarterly Meeting on the 23rd, when for the first time this year we were in the midst of some 'troubled waters.' And wherefore? Alas for the 'Plan'! Was it an uprising of old conservative ideas against the action of the General Conference? Or what? Well, let the truth come out—we had not gone far enough. Resolutions were passed condemnatory of our action, and some hard things were said. But it is not at all unlikely that three-fourths of the meeting had not even read the 'Plan,' or knew anything about it.

June 23rd.—I wrote a strong article on the Northern Territory, in which I insisted, among other matters deserving the immediate attention of the Government, that it should be constituted an electoral district, and have the constitutional right to send one or more representatives to both chambers of the Legislature in Adelaide.

July 6th.—To reform the Church, even in the direction of liberalism seems to be more difficult than to reform a Parliament. Our recent proposed legislation is still 'a bone of contention' in some quarters. I therefore wrote a long article for the *Journal* on 'Wesleyan Polity,' and justified the action of the General Conference. On the 12th I wrote a second article, and still more strongly defended my brethren. And there the matter must rest.

July 15th.—The Education question is again to the front. I gave, therefore, much of my time to its consideration. This afternoon I went to the House of Assembly to hear the debate. Mr. Rowland Rees spoke with great ability. I prepared besides an article on the subject for the *Journal*. In the evening I went to Edwardstown, and met as usual the Bible Class at 6.30, preached at 7.30, and then met the Church Committee.

July 16th.—The three students came from Prince Alfred College for their weekly lecture. At 8 p.m. I presided at the Young Men's Literary Society. Busy day—all the day—until 11.30 p.m.

July 19th.—I attended the funeral of the late Mrs. Ingram, relict of the Rev. W. Ingram. Another holy woman, and one much tried, has gone to God.

July 22nd.—We held a meeting of the Education Committee, to consider the Bill now before the Parliament. We passed three resolutions generally approving of the Bill.

July 26th.—At the Draper Memorial Church Anniversary this evening we raised £175 17s.

July 31st.—All sorts of letters come to me. A troubled husband has just sent me an anonymous letter, in which he complains of his wife's neglect of reading the Bible, and requests me to preach a sermon for her admonition. Poor man !

Aug. 3rd —I went to the House to hear the Treasurer's Budget Speech, and the next day I spent three whole hours in writing an article upon it. The difficulty was mostly in 'trotting' out the figures, calculations, etc., and making them agree with each other.

Aug. 9th.—I went to the Servants' Home to see the new immigrants. I found amongst them a Mary Michelmore from Totness. I took her case in hand, and got her into a good home. I wrote to the Chief Secretary about the male immigrants having nowhere to go on their arrival in the Colony. He politely replied, and asked me to see the Premier, Mr. Boucaut, and lay the case before him.

Sept. 13th.—The ' Singing Pilgrim ' (Mr. Philip Phillips) sang in

Pirie Street Church this evening. About eight hundred present. On the 14th he sang in the Town Hall. The audience was grand, and the 'Pilgrim' acquitted himself in style.

Sept. 16*th.*—Mr. T. S. Carey and I went to the Church Opening Services at Clarendon. We raised £100 10*s.* I supped and slept at Mr. Fox's, who 'is worthy.'

Sept. 17*th.*—Mr. A. A. Scott called with Messrs. S. F. Prior and H. H. Teague, who have just arrived from England to join our ministry in South Australia. On the 20th I got them enrolled as ministers authorized to celebrate marriage in this Colony.

Sept. 21*st.*—I went to the Church Anniversary at the Wallaroo-Mines, Kadina. The Rev. A. Rigg met me at the coach-office, and I spent a delightful evening with him and Mrs. Rigg at the Parsonage. I preached the next day at the Mines' Church to two large congregations. On the Monday morning Captain Anthony drove Mr. Rigg and me to the smelting works at Wallaroo. They are extensive, and give employment probably to two hundred men. We had a successfully conducted Anniversary, and raised £85.

Sept. 23*rd.*—The Quarterly Meeting was held to-day. Income £333 7*s.* 6*d.*; expenditure £280 0*s.* 5*d.* We returned 550 members, with 71 on trial.

Oct. 11*th.*—Angaston Church Anniversary to-day. I preached twice to interesting, but not large congregations. The next day I called upon Mr. and Mrs. Pepperell, who are distantly related to our family. I visited the Keyne and the Angas families. The Angases (father and son) sent unsolicited two five-guinea cheques for our evening meeting. Mr. Keally took me to the old cemetery to see my dear father's grave. It was on September 28th, 1851, at the age of seventy-five, that my father died. On returning next day to Adelaide, I ordered from Mr. Thomas Martin a small marble headstone to mark the spot where my venerable and kind father sleeps in peace. Mr. Prior, who was with us, whilst I was away at Glenelg in the evening, heard from Mrs. Bickford several particulars of my father's life and character, and penned the following epitaph for the stone :—

> 'An honest and brave old English yeoman,
> Ready of hand, and true of heart and kind,
> Mild and affectionate, belov'd by all,
> Lieth below. The day of life is o'er,
> And God hath given to His beloved sleep.'

The Denomination System of Education, established in 1852, thoroughly collapsed in 1875. It broke under the pressure of its own weight. Not a tear, of which I ever heard, was shed over the demise of this expensive, irritating, and effete system. On October 15th, this very year, ' An Act to Amend the Law relating to Public Education ' was assented to by ' A. Musgrove, Governor.' There are only twenty-five clauses, so that much of detail would have to be dealt with by ' Regulations.' Three of the clauses of the Act merit special notice :—

' 8. A public school may be established in any locality where the Council shall be satisfied that there are at least twenty children who will attend such school.'

' 9. In every public school, four and a half hours at least shall be set apart during each school-day for secular instruction only ; and such schools may open in the morning a quarter of an hour at least before the time fixed for such secular instruction to commence, for the purpose of reading portions of the Holy Scriptures in the Authorised or Douay Version. The attendance of children at such reading shall not be compulsory, and no sectarian or denominational religious teaching shall be allowed in any school.'

' 14. Notwithstanding any regulation for the payment of school fees, any child whose parent shall be unable to pay such fees shall not on that account be refused admission into a public school, but shall, on the inability being shown in the prescribed manner, be received and instructed in the same manner as the other pupils attending such schools.'

The Government was fortunate in securing the efficient services of the Head Master of Prince Alfred College, for piloting through the ' sea of difficulty ' which awaited the introduction of the New Act. But the feat has been accomplished ; and to-day there is not in all Australia a better system of Public Education than that in this Colony.

Nov. 19*th.*—The Rev. Samuel Antcliffe, D.D., a Primitive Methodist Minister from England, called. We were quite a clerical party for the occasion. The Rev. J. Goodwin, P.M., introduced the Doctor, and Rev. Messrs. Stephenson and Nicholson were also present. We were much pleased with our titled visitor from the dear old land. The next day I prepared the address of welcome we had agreed, as a body of ministers, to present to the reverend Doctor.

Dec. 1*st.*—I wrote an article for the *Journal*, subject : ' The Parliamentary Collapse.' To say the least, the Ministry had deserved a better fate.

The Rev. Henry Greenwood, formerly one of our missionaries in the Friendly Islands, did us good service in deputation work this year. His sermons were finely evangelical, his speeches were racy and full of anecdote, and his intercourse with our friends was modest and spiritual.

Dec. 5th.—The expenses of our late General Conference amounted to £523 10s. 11d. We thought to have saved expense in working the 'Connexion' on the new plan; but we shall find, I fear, as we go on, that we have greatly increased it. But 'the die is cast.'

Dec. 24th.—The Quarterly Meeting was held to-day. The income was £355, and the expenditure £301 11s. 11d. As my three years' incumbency would terminate at the next Conference, the Rev. S. Knight was invited to succeed me in the superintendency of the Circuit.

Dec. 25th.—The Rev. James Lyall (Presbyterian) preached an admirable Christmas sermon at seven o'clock this morning.

Dec. 27th.—I went to the 'Servants' Home,' and held a religious service with the female immigrants. Poor creatures! I wonder what will become of them?

Dec. 29th.—I wrote for the *Journal* the last leader for this year. Subject, ' 1875.'

1876.

Jan. 2nd.—I copy from my Diary :—

'This is the first of another year. Twenty-two years ago Mrs. Bickford and I spent the corresponding Sabbath in London, awaiting the sailing of the *American Lass*, for Port Jackson, New South Wales. We landed in Sydney on the following May 24th. During all the years I have been in Australia my health has been equal to the strain of the work. But I have now reached a point in my itinerant life which compels an examination of the situation, so that I may provide against a "break-down" in my work. To rest for a year or two seems the dictate of common sense, of religion, and of Connexional relations. But whether that course be practicable remains to be seen. I love my work as much as ever; although the Itinerancy has become inksome and trying to me. To-day I have done my work much as usual. The "Renewal of Covenant" Service and the Lord's Supper were specially helpful, and I hope much good will follow from these godly exercises.'

Jan. 25th.—The Conference was opened to-day; the Rev. N. P. Wells, President, and Rev. C. H. Goldsmith, Secretary. In the afternoon a strong discussion ensued upon the standing of two of the ministers who had been transferred to the Victorian Conference. At length the President ruled that the brethren, in question, were members of the South Australian Conference until the time came for their removal as fixed by the General Conference. On the same day I formally applied to be made a Supernumerary minister, that I might visit England this year. The next day my request was granted, and the following record was ordered to be inserted in the Minutes :—

'REV. J. BICKFORD.

' The Conference takes the occasion of the Rev. J. Bickford's visit to Europe, to express to him the most sincere sentiments of Christian esteem and confidence. In view of thirty-eight years of faithful labour in the Christian Ministry, and twenty-two years of devoted work for God in Australia, this Conference rejoices that Mr. Bickford has sought needed rest and recreation while in the possession of sufficient health and energy to bear the fatigues of foreign travel. Mr. Bickford has earned his merited relief by a singularly laborious life. His three years of labour in this Colony have been successful in the highest degree. At Pirie Street there has been the feature of increased congregations, uninterrupted peace, and financial prosperity, resulting in large reduction of the long-standing debt on that property. The denominational organ has found in his indefatigable editorship the largest contributor. Mr. Bickford's occupancy of the Presidential chair, for the second time, has justified the trust of the Conference in his administrative abilities. We hope that Mr. ex-President will be able to render us invaluable aid during his visit to England. We wish Mr. and Mrs. Bickford a pleasant voyage, and a speedy return to this land.'

The heat at this Conference was intolerably oppressive, and to it the Rev. Matthew Wilson, on the 29th, succumbed. He died alone, in his son's house, at East Adelaide. But to him ' sudden death was sudden glory.'

Feb. 4th.—The Sessions of the Conference closed to-day. I was completely wearied out with the heat and the excitement occasioned by matters of difficulty the Conference had had to deal with. Mr. Wells made an admirable President; he ruled justly, without fear or favour.

Feb. 9th.—I was busy all the day in making inquiries for a ship for England. I finally engaged the cabin, No. 13, in the *Lady Jocelyn,* bound for London.

Feb. 14th.—To-day I settled all Connexional and District business with Mr. President Wells, and gave him a cheque for all balances then in my hands. I am therefore loosing my hold upon South Australian Methodism ! Be it so ; if it must be so.

Feb. 15th.—My dear niece, Mrs. J. G. Pascoe, child and servant, left us to-day for Sydney. I felt more than sad at parting with her.

Feb. 16th.—I joined the Bible Christian Conference in their official service. The Rev. James Way, a venerable and faithful minister, preached an excellent sermon on the 'Atonement.' I joined with the brethren at the close in partaking of the Lord's Supper.

A valedictory tea and public meeting were held this week, at which an address was presented to me, and a purse containing eighty-five sovereigns,—an expression of sympathy, confidence, and generous recognition of service, very gratifying to my feelings.

March 8th.—Our last day in Adelaide. At 1.30 p.m., I handed the key of the parsonage to the senior Circuit Steward, Mr. A. A. Scott, and we then proceeded to the North Terrace Station. I have found this departure from Adelaide a cruel ordeal. It has almost broken my heart. About two hundred persons accompanied us and the other passengers to the ship lying off the Semaphore. The parting scene was more than we could bear. The affectionate kindness of the South Australian friends to me and Mrs. Bickford can never be forgotten by us.

As I did not consent, although requested by the General Conference, to be associated with the Rev. J. Buller, as a joint representative to the British Conference, I had to obtain from the President and Secretary of my own Conference a 'letter of commendation' to the English Conference. The following is a copy of the document given me by these honoured brethren :—

'ADELAIDE, *February 9th*, 1876.

'To THE REVEREND GERVASE SMITH, M.A.,
  " President of the British Conference.

' REVEREND AND DEAR SIR,—

'We have great pleasure in commending to you the Rev. J. Bickford, ex-President of our Conference, who is about visiting England. Mr. Bickford was President of the Australian Conference in 1868 ; of the South Australian Conference in 1875 ; and one of the Presidents of the First General Conference held in May last. He has for upwards of twenty years occupied our foremost positions, and is one of the representative men of Australian Methodism. We have reason to believe that, had it been known that Mr. Bickford would have been visiting England, he would have been associated with the Rev. J. Buller as a representative from the General Conference to the English Conference. Mr. Bickford will be able to furnish, if desired, reliable information to the Committee on Australian affairs, in regard to the constitution of our Church. Whatever attention you may be able to show Mr. Bickford, and whatever position you may be able to accord him in your Conference, or elsewhere, will be a gratification to the ministers and churches in these Colonies.

'We are, reverend and dear Sir,

'Your obedient servants,

'WILLIAM P. WELLS, *President,*

'CHARLES H. GOLDSMITH, *Secretary.*'

As I had been in correspondence with the Premier, the Hon. J. P. Boucant, M.P., on the subject of my giving a series of lectures, during my intended visit to England, on South Australia as a promising field for British emigrants, I received from the Treasurer, the Hon. J. Colton, M.P., an official document on the subject, to be presented by me to Mr. Dutton, the Agent General, resident in London. It was as follows:—

'THE TREASURY, ADELAIDE, SOUTH AUSTRALIA,

'*March 1st*, 1876.

'SIR,—

'This will serve to introduce to you the Rev. James Bickford, who is a much respected minister of the Wesleyan Church, and a personal friend. My principal object in asking your kind offices is that he takes great interest in public affairs in general, and our Colony in particular. During his temporary stay in the old country, he will use his best endeavours, in various ways, to make the Colony known as much as possible, with a view to getting suitable persons to emigrate: and, especially so, in his native county, Devonshire. Anything you can do to facilitate his movements, I shall regard as a personal favour. I may add, that this Government have given him every information which will be of value in his contemplated project.

'I am, Sir,

'Your obedient servant,

'JOHN COLTON, *Treasurer.*'

March 10th.—I was on deck at 2.30 a.m. to see the *Lady Jocelyn* make a start. Of course, the songs and trampling of the men prevented sleep.

On the 13th we lost sight of Cape Borda, and entered the Australian Bight. I had been asked by the captain, Mr. George Jenkins, to act as semi-chaplain during the voyage, consequently I preached on the first Sabbath, and instituted morning family worship. To the latter, as a daily religious observance, the gentlemen passengers, Messrs. Gurner and Gall, for themselves and their families, promised their attendance. We ran rapidly through the 'Bight' (the Australian 'Bay of Biscay'). On the morning of the 16th, whilst at breakfast, the conversation turned upon the extraordinary fact that as yet no lighthouse had been erected at Cape Leeuwin. Whose fault can it be? All the shipping coming down the Indian Ocean for the eastern colonies pass here, and yet there is no lighthouse. Surely the Lords of the Admiralty should see to this.

March 31st.—We weighed anchor three weeks ago to-day, since when we have come 3,080 miles. Sometimes it has been very hot, and our strength has been unequal to the fierceness of the climatic ordeal.

April 6th.—The weather is now beautifully fine, and we are running at ten and half knots, without almost any perceptible motion of the ship. The second-class female passengers are still dissatisfied with their food. What a pity it is that there should be on board the same ship, on a long voyage, two, or more, grades of passengers!

April 9th.—I took the cool air on the deck before breakfast for an hour and a half, and I find this habit beneficial every way to my health. We have now come 4,634 miles.

April 12th.—I had an interesting conversation with Captain Jenkins on the atmospheric disturbances, occasioned by the conjunction of the moon and the planets. To-day there is such a conjunction with the planet Jupiter. A great deal might be learnt from such an intelligent man as Captain Jenkins on the beautiful science of navigation, and cognate subjects.

April 19th (latitude 32° 57′, longitude 31° 6′).—This evening, at seven o'clock, in the south-east, an appalling electric cloud was visible from the ship's deck. The base lay along the horizon about a third of the quarter circle, and reached more than halfway up to the sky's meridian. So near was it that it did not interfere with our six-knot breeze. With every new flash the dense cloud was revealed, and showed out in mountains piled upon mountains, from the base to the topmost line. Layers of clouds, resembling primeval forests, were occasionally seen; and, whilst the eye admiringly rested upon the new phases of phenomena, the fiery fluid issued forth in all kinds of forms—curved, serpentine, forked, and straight, some of the lines dipping into the sea. Our gallant ship, all the time, majestically sailed along, apparently on the outer fringe of the terrible cloud. Every countenance, together with masts, sails, and rigging, were lit up with a blaze of light. The passengers and crew ranged along on the port side, the subjects of wonder, admiration, and awe. As the phenomenon passed away, the religious service, as appointed, was held in the second cabin, when we sang, with becoming solemnity, Paul Gerhardt's hymn :—

> ' Give to the winds thy fears,
> Hope, and be undismayed ;
> God hears thy sighs, and counts thy tears ;
> He shall lift up thy head.
>
> Through waves, and clouds, and storms,
> He gently clears thy way ;
> Wait thou His time—thy darkest night
> Shall end in joyous day.'

Such a phenomenon, for grandeur, sublimity, and wonderfulness, I cannot expect again to see. It was, indeed, an awful display of the power of creation's God. But, whether upon the sea or the land,—

> ' This awful God is ours ;
> Our Father and our love.'

On *April 25th* we saw 'Table Mountain' rising in majestic height from behind Cape Town. We soon rounded the 'Cape of Storms,' and with a fair wind headed up for the South Atlantic Ocean. 'Captain,' said I, 'what about running into Cape Town harbour for a change ?' ' Well,' good-naturedly replied the captain, ' if I had any business there I would do so; but as I have none, I am not going in. Besides, if I were to do that, "Jack" would want to go on shore too ; and who can tell what trouble I might have again to get him on board. But I will stand in a bit, and you can use your " glasses," and see all that is worth seeing.' There was no use in arguing with Captain George Jenkins in such a case; so we were content to strain our eyes for a while, and then, as if by general consent, we stood away for St. Helena.

May 8th.—We saw this historic island. From the Cape our voyage had been most trying, from prevailing calms, light winds, and heavy seas which came rolling up from the Southern Ocean. I now copy from my Diary :—

' Sighted St. Helena at 6 a.m. So called by the famous navigator, Ivao da Nova, Galego, who discovered it on August 15th, 1502, being the anniversary festival of St. Helena. It has been uninterruptedly in the hands of the English since 1674. It is about nine miles in width, and twenty-seven in circumference ; and it is situate about 1,200 miles west of Benguela in South Africa ; and 1,800 miles east of Brazil, in South America.

' The passengers were soon on deck, and a grand object presented itself to our wondering gaze. Our gallant ship in fine trim and sail came boldly up to the east side, making Saddle Point. We " hauled to." and rounded Barn and Sugar Loaf Points, when Jamestown with its batteries, signal station, its road of steps, and spiral church, came in view. There were lying close in shore, under the protection of precipitous cliffs, a " man-o'-war," several foreign barques, and a few smaller craft. The captain sent up the British ensign, followed by a set of flags, giving our name, number of days from Port Adelaide (fifty-seven), where bound, with the assuring words, " All well." Our communication was promptly recognised from Flagstaff Hill, and a promise to report us in London was given. We then bore away on a north-north-west course, with a fine breeze, and full of hope for the rest of the voyage.

' It is impossible for a reflective Englishman thus suddenly for the first time to drop upon this singularly formed island in mid-Atlantic, without deep emotion. It is to my mind another remarkable proof of the mercifulness of the great Creator, for His sea-going creatures, that this island should be placed exactly in the highway of the ocean for ships in their homeward route from India, China, Australia, and South Africa. For repairs to ships, for obtaining water and provisions, and for postal and telegraphic purposes, it is the most convenient provision the great Father could have made. But with the historic association, as the island-prison of the First Napoleon, it must ever hold a place in the grateful memories of the brave-hearted British people in all parts of the world.'

May 11th.—Our captain is a great favourite. He embodies in his own personality the manners of a gentleman, the grace of a Christian, the intelligence of a traveller, and the skill and courage of the English sailor. We could not therefore allow this day to pass without some expression of our respect. It was in fact his fifty-first birthday, and he was still strong and hale. I presented to him early in the morning an excellent work entitled ' God's Word Written,' as a memento of my affectionate esteem. Mrs. Jenkins invited the ladies to tea in the ' stern-villa,' and Messrs. Gurner and Gall invited Captain and Mrs. Jenkins, and the lady and gentlemen passengers, to an evening banquet. Such amenities on ship-board have the effect of softening asperities of feeling, and of bridging over the inevitable estrangements common to a long sea-voyage.

May 12th.—To-day, for a couple of hours, I read the ' New Zealand Handbook.' The writer evidently has a bitter animus against all missionaries, forgetting that he and other British immigrants are mainly indebted to this class of pioneer workers, who made New Zealand a desirable and prosperous field for the settlement of white people. Samuel Marsden, Samuel Leigh, Archdeacon Williams, Nathaniel Turner, John Hobbs, Bishop Selwyn, James

Buller, Thomas Buddle, may be taken as representatives of the army of early missionaries who subdued New Zealand, and prepared the way for its becoming the fairest gem of England's crown, and the chosen home of over half a million of British people. The man, therefore, who can ignore such facts, is entitled to no hearing, or credence, as a chronicler of the progress of this 'Southern Britain.'

The Great Bear rose high to-night. Venus, too, was gloriously bright—a little moon in fact; Jupiter came out in majestic splendour; whilst Sirius seemed to look down upon us with a kindly recognition as we wander over this trackless ocean.

After enduring much inconvenience for several days from heavy rains, and the necessary closing of the portholes making our fine saloon an enormous vapour bath, on the 21st, in latitude 6° 59′ N., and longitude 20° 18′ W., we caught the north-east trade winds, and were able to steer a north-west course. On the 22nd I saw for the first time this voyage the North Star. It is now about twenty-three years since I last saw this useful constellation. The Great Bear revolves around this powerful polar centre.

May 24th.—Queen's birthday. Although we were so far both from England and Australia, our loyalty sprang to the surface and received appropriate recognition. At the family altar we devoutly prayed for her gracious Majesty. The captain invited the saloon passengers to a supper-entertainment in honour of the day. Long life and happiness were lovingly desired for the Queen, and grace and goodness for the Prince and Princess of Wales and the Royal Family. We toasted the owners of the *Lady Jocelyn*, also, to which our worthy captain replied. From principle, I drank water, and not wine; still my goodwill was the same.

I examined to-day an invaluable work, entitled 'The Stars: how to know them, and how to use them.' It was kindly lent to me by the captain, and I much valued his courtesy. On the 26th our good friend, Mr. Gurner, gave us 'An Hour with Neptune:' a piece written by himself for our amusement. It was cleverly done, and evidenced considerable ability.*

---

* The following characteristic notice Mr. Gurner prepared for circulation among the passengers:—

'LADY JOCELYN SALOON.

'On Thursday evening, May 18th, at 8 o'clock, will be produced for the first

May 29*th.*—We have now run, I find, since we left the Semaphore on March 10th last, 11,903 nautical miles.

The 30th May has a special notice in my Diary :—

‘ Rose at 4 a.m., and went on deck to see the “ Great Bear ” (*Ursa major*). It had well-nigh completed its circle around the Polar, or North Star. It consists of seven stars, two of which are called “ Pointers,” which always point the voyager where to find the Pole Star. The “ Southern Cross ” (*Crux*) was not to be seen. It had “dipped” some nights before below the horizon. Thus are we reminded of our advance northwards to the higher latitudes, and of our complete severance from the sunny lands of the southern hemisphere. I could not but remark on noticing these transitions above us, What a wonderful economy is this which these starry heavens exhibit ! I am filled with admiration and praise ! “ HE made the stars also.” ’

June 3*rd.*—Rose at 5 a.m., and went on deck. The air was healthful and bracing. Read and wrote a couple of hours before breakfast. We are now a little over 1,200 miles from Flores, and 2,148 from the Lizard.

June 6*th.*—Much signalling and speaking to other ships to-day. This is a pleasant break of the monotony of our sea life. At 8 p.m. the surroundings of the moon were unspeakably gorgeous. The setting of the sun and the rising of the moon were truly wonderful. The clouds were ‘ full of glory.’

June 7*th.*—At 8 p.m. I gave my new lecture on ‘ South Australia, in relation to Emigration from the Mother Country.’

June 12*th.*—There are two sea routes for sailing ships from Australia to England. One is by the ‘ Horn,’ the other by the

---

time, and written expressly for the occasion, a nautico-musical extravaganza, entitled :

‘“ AN HOUR WITH NEPTUNE.”

‘ Neptune, god of the sea, but a somewhat amphibious monarch, to whom a certain latitude must be allowed ; who from longitude has taken his degree, and is second to none in his attachment to the briny.

‘ *Lady Jocelyn*, registered AA1 at Lloyd’s, a fast sailing clipper, with a grievance, and determined to ventilate it. Zephyrus, the west wind, sometimes called, the “ Gentle Zephyr ”—an airy nothing, and never about when it is wanted.

‘ *Scene*—“ ON THE BOTTOM OF THE SEA.” ’

It need hardly be added that the evening was enjoyably spent. Indeed, all seemed to value the efforts made for contributing to the pleasure of the whole company. This was the order of things : Literary and Scientific Subjects, Mr. Robert Gurner ; Singing and Music, Miss Clara Brown ; Lectures, Preaching and Worship, Rev. J. Bickford.

'Hope.' Anchored in the river at Port Adelaide was the iron ship, *Old Kensington*, which was to leave for London about a week after us. On the morning of the 12th of June this vessel was near us on our lee. We were pleased to see that our Port neighbour, who had come by a contrary route from us, was as far on the voyage as ourselves. But now the light winds and calms prevented progress; indeed, for eight days we had only made eighty miles. But a change took place on the 14th, when, with a strong, fair wind, we bounded through the 'Roaring Forties' at ten knots. And yesterday we were in company with twenty-four ships, but to-day only one of them is visible.

The 21st of June will always be a 'red-letter day.' We had come 14,766 miles, and were now in the 'chops of the Channel.' At 4 p.m. we saw the Start, then Berry Head, and a long line of hazy English coast. We had a fair wind up Channel, and at 10 p.m. we saw the Portland lights. A small cutter came alongside, and the master with the help of a rope, climbed on board. He handed to the captain a late newspaper, which we were all glad to see. Oh, how friendly our visitor was ! 'Will you take our letters and post them for us ? ' we inquired. 'Most gladly, gentlemen, I will oblige you.' 'What will you charge ? ' 'Well, ten shillings a letter.' 'Come now,' said I, 'that's too much ; we won't give you that price.' He finally agreed for two shillings a letter. As soon as he got his budget, he got over the ship's side, and we saw him no more.

On the 22nd, at 2 p.m., when off the Isle of Wight, our captain reported the arrival of the *Lady Jocelyn*, one hundred days out, to the signal master, so that in the papers of to-morrow morning the news will be telegraphed all over the kingdom.

June 23rd.—We came to anchor off the Margate Sands at 1.30 a.m., which was a great relief to us. I turned in and slept until 7 a.m.

June 24th.—We got 'under weigh' at 8 a.m. We were being towed by a struggling little steamer, when our un-'giving' steel hawser tore away her gear. We then gave a hempen hawser, in place of the other, and everything went on well. We reached the London Dock in due course, and at 8.30 p.m., Mrs. Bickford and I were with our friends, the Rev. William Butters and Miss Butters, at Brixton Hill. *Consummatum est.*

I should here remark that, strange as it may appear, I was not the subject of the strong emotional feeling I expected should God permit me again to see Old England. But I had been too long away : indeed, it may be said, my heart was still in Australia; and I had more friends, and even more kindred there, than I now had in my native country. Still I was deeply grateful that our long voyage had ended so propitiously, and that my earliest Australian ministerial friend was still alive and well. On that evening, as we gathered around the family altar at Upper Tulse Hill, I praised my Heavenly Father, that I and my dear companion, in many lands and for many years, were again at Home.

ENGLAND.

LONDON, 1876.

June 25th.—A 'day of days' this has been to me. Surely some-thing of the inspiration of David, the King of Israel, possessed my soul this morning as we wended our way from Upper Tulse Hill to the Brixton Hill Church. The Rev. William Gibson, M.A., was the preacher. The attractiveness of Christ was the theme. There was a fine congregation to hear a very beautiful sermon. In the evening, Mr. Butters and I went to 'Newington Butts' to hear England's Spurgeon, and we were not disappointed. There were 6,000 people to begin with; congregational singing and great devoutness; and an able sermon founded upon the words: 'And he appointed certain of the Levites to minister before the ark of the Lord, and to record and to thank and praise the Lord God of Israel.' The gist of the discourse was on the subject of defective memories in relation to matters of religion, and the cure of that mental disability. I confess I never heard so much hard hitting and so much shrewd common sense squeezed into one sermon before. At the close, Mr. Butters inquired, 'Do you wonder now that Mr. Spurgeon is so great a power in England?' 'No,' I replied; 'the greatest wonder in my judgment would be if that were not so.' It was a most profitable Sabbath.

The Centenary Hall and Mission House was my first place of call on Monday morning. Mr. Butters chaperoned me to the old loved spot. I saw the senior Secretary, the Rev. W. B. Boyce, and entered into conversation with him. Acting as Deputy Treasurer, he was very busy; which, at first sight, he did not fail to inform me. Then he proceeded to a little good-natured banter, quite *à la* Australian. 'Well,' said he, 'you are a great fool to come home, Brother Bickford!' 'How so,' I inquired, 'when I am only follow-ing your example!' 'Exactly, but then I am going back again in

September.' 'I intend also to go back, but not so soon as that. So that we are in the same boat so far.' 'Can I do anything for you?' he good-naturedly inquired. 'Not to-day, thank you,' I replied. Mr. Butters and I then ascended the great staircase to see for the Rev. G. T. Perks, M.A., who was at his desk apparently in deep study over something. How nice he was in his inquiries for Mrs. Bickford and myself, after our long voyage! The interview was short, but I think I succeeded in securing Mr. Perks as our friend in dealing with our Australian affairs. After we left, I said to Mr. Butters, 'I shall stick to Mr. Perks as long as I am in England. He has, I am sure, the grip of our difficulties, and will help us in their settlement.' 'You can't do better,' said my sage friend.

June 28th.—Mr. Butters accompanied me to Westminster, to see the South Australian Agent General (Mr. Dutton), and present to him the official letter I received from our Government. Also I left with him a copy of my proposed Emigration lecture. About ten days afterwards, Mr. Dutton returned me the manuscript of my lecture, enclosing a cheque for its publication and postage, with an offer of the most obliging kind to help me in any practicable way in my 'praiseworthy' efforts to send suitable emigrants to South Australia. From that time, to the day of his lamented death, only a few months afterwards, Mr. Dutton was to me a sincere and generous friend.

This was a busy day. Mr. Butters and I called upon Dean Stanley, at the Abbey, to whom Dean Russell, of Adelaide, had given me a letter of introduction. Dean Stanley was still mourning over his loss of the beautiful Lady Stanley. He appeared to be in feeble health, and was much 'cast down' in soul; but, said he, in the language of Charles Wesley's grandest hymn, 'I see the morning breaks.' He added, 'If I am spared for a little longer, I intend to say something more than I was able when the ceremony of unveiling the statue of the "Brothers Wesley" took place in the Abbey.' It was a precious interview from beginning to end. We called in at the three Courts of Justice, and saw no less than seven venerable and learned men meting out justice to foolish litigants, who cannot agree among themselves to settle their own misunderstandings, without recourse to expensive courts of law. We also went to the House of Commons, and heard a debate on the 'Entail of Property' in England. Much was said on the importance of upholding the ancient families and their great estates from spoliation by a division of them amongst the junior members of families. It was the ' grip of the dead hand ' which the Liberals assailed, but which the Tories upheld. The latter, being on the right of the Speaker, had the vote. Mr. Disraeli, Mr. Gladstone, Sir Stafford Northcote, and John Bright did not speak.

July 2nd.—I preached at Thurlow Park and Penge. At the Park, I was brought into contact with a custom unknown to us in Australia. In the vestry, after the service, said the Church Steward, ' Will you take a glass of wine, sir ? ' ' Excuse me,' I said, ' but I never take wine, nor anything that is intoxicating. But, on such a hot day as this, if you have any cold water near, I shall be glad of a drink.' I drank, and was refreshed. After the service at Penge, in the evening, we made our way to Upper Tulse Hill. Alas for me ! I had walked six miles, was dripping with perspiration, and was completely ' run down.'

In the afternoon, as Mr. Butters and I were walking up the hill near the Crystal Palace, we saw about a dozen youths out on a Sabbath spree. ' We must speak to these youths,' I said. ' Yes,' said my friend ; ' round them up, and I will tell them a story.' They were caught with the idea, and gathered around the fine old man. ' About forty years ago,' said he, ' I was stationed at Hobart Town, Van Diemen's Land, when a dreadful incident occurred to a youth about the age of one of yourselves. He had been a good Sunday School scholar, and promised to be a fine and useful man. But a band of burglars persuaded him to join them, under a promise of secrecy and a share in the spoil. He was to be used as a spy to find out when families were absent from their homes, and then, when the way was clear, to be hoisted to the windows so as to open the doors from the inside to the robbers. But, after a while, the boy was caught in the very act ; was tried, convicted, and sentenced to be hung. He would not disclose the names of the vile band ; no matter what persuasives were used. I visited him several times in the felon's cell, and deeply did I pity him. He confessed to me that the first step to his ruin was when he forsook the Sunday School, and, with other boys, went bird-nesting and stealing fruit from the people's gardens. ' Ah, my lads,' said Mr. Butters, ' beware of first beginnings of evil. Keep the Lord's Day, attend the Sunday School, and revere and love your parents.' Several of the youths were much affected, and promised to attend the school the very next Lord's Day.

July 4th.—' Westward Ho ! ' A friendly cab-owner lived near. I therefore engaged him to take us for an early train at the Waterloo Station. I cannot describe the variety of landscape we saw, as we rushed along through the intervening counties until we reached the grand old cathedral city of Exeter. ' Living-green,' hill and dale, with pretty peeps at the blue waters of the Channel, as we threaded our way through Devonshire, met my delighted gaze, and filled my grateful heart. This is England at its very best, I thought; it was, indeed, a beautiful best for my Australian eyes.

' Kingsbridge Road Station ! ' shouted the guard, and the train pulled up. Yes; so it was; for there in the crowd stood my eldest brother, John Bickford, whom I had not seen for nearly twenty-three years. In a trice Mrs. Bickford was in the coach, and my brother and I were in a gig, starting for ' Kingsbridge town.' We talked so much by the way that we reached Coombe Royal and capped Knowle much before I had expected. At 6.30 p.m. we reached my brother's house, and now I felt that I was indeed at home. At 9 p.m. my brother, Mr. and Mrs. Jarvis, and I surrounded the family altar, where we united in thanking God for the Fatherly care He had shown to us. But one was not; my sister-in-law, Mrs. John Bickford, died in 1864, and entered into rest. She was a woman ' who feared God above many.'

July 6th.—I had a pleasant run, with Mr. W. Quarm, down the Kingsbridge River to Salcombe. What a sweet, pretty place this has become ! All the old scenery, reaching from Halwood Point right away to the Bolt Head, retained its former charms and interest, and I was much delighted. I visited a few of the Methodist members I left here in 1838, and was greatly disappointed in not seeing Mr. and Mrs. James Vivian, who had ' joined the great majority.' My nephew and niece, Mr. and Mrs. Baker, at Snape's Farm, were very glad to see me again. I returned by the little steamer *Reindeer* in the evening to Kingsbridge. On the 8th, I visited the new cemetery at Highhouse Point. This very eligible freehold had been purchased by the inhabitants of Kingsbridge and Dodbrook, so I understood, as a general burial-ground for their dead. Mr. Quarm, who accompanied me, and I made straight for the ' mortuary chapel,' where the first oddity that challenged notice was a partition wall erected right across inside the building. 'Halloa,' exclaimed I, 'what's that for? This looks like "a middle-wall of partition." I suppose there is some reason for its erection: pray, what is it?' 'Yes, of course there is,' he replied; 'it was put up at the bidding of the Bishop of Exeter, to shut off the Dissenters from Churchpeople; and he would not consecrate the ground until it was done, as you see it.' 'What,' said I, 'you people bought and paid for the land, and submitted afterwards to this bigoted and cruel prejudice! You must be idiots.'

On the 9th I delivered my lecture in the Town Hall; Mr. Solicitor Hurrell, senior, in the chair. At its close, I was subjected to a number of questions relating to the summer heat of South Australia, and the want of rain at certain seasons of the year. One of the inquirers actually asked, with all seriousness, if we had any water in Adelaide? Another, What could an emigrant do for his family when he arrived at Port Adelaide? My answer was, 'Let him leave his family on board, and go on shore, and seek for work and a couple of rooms as a temporary home, and then take them on shore.' I think my answers, and they were many, satisfied the audience. The next day, Mr. C. Tope, my nephew, displayed some hundred splendidly executed photographs of South Australia on the walls of the building, for illustrating the condition, resources, and progress of the Colony. These works of a beautiful art were kindly sent to me from Adelaide, by Sir Henry Ayres, Chief Secretary, to aid me in my lecturing tours up and down the country. My lecture brought forth good results.

On the 15th I went over to Modbury (my native parish), and saw the Flashmans, the Gills, the Luscombes, the Matthews, the Lethbridges, and my kindred. I preached the next day three times, and on Monday evening I again lectured on South Australia; Mr. Stidstone of Kingston, a gentleman farmer and a staunch Wesleyan, took the chair. By public resolution, I was thanked for my lecture.

On the 18th my brother, Edmund Whiteway Bickford, and I went to Plymouth, when I made arrangements with Mr. John Smith, Old Town Street, to print a thousand copies of my lecture for free distribution in England and elsewhere.

July 21*st.*—Mrs. Bickford and I left for Ilminster, on a visit to the venerable and Reverend Thomas White Smith, my ministerial father and friend. It was thirty-eight years since I saw him before, when he was in the zenith of his power. Now I found him feeble, and very aged in appearance. Oh! it was good to see him again.

Mrs. Smith had died some years before this visit, and the dear old man had only an unmarried daughter, Miss Smith, and the faithful Lizzy for companions.

On the 24th I left for the Conference at Nottingham. I was to be guest of Mr. and Mrs. Curtiss, a choice family with whom I was much at home. The next day I attended the Connexional Committees of Review; the Rev. Gervase Smith, M.A., in the chair. The place was crowded, and there appeared to be no ventilation, so that I was much inconvenienced. Mr. Curtiss and I soon left, and in the evening we went to hear the Rev. Doctor Williams' Fernley lecture on the Priesthood of Christ. It was able, and well read. In the pew before me was seated my old West India colleague, the Rev. David Barley, and by his side sat his son, the Rev. A. L. Barley. Mr. Barley and I had not seen each other since we parted in Demerara twenty-five years ago.

On the 26th the Conference was opened, and the Rev. Alexander McAulay was elected President, and Dr. Williams, Secretary. The building was so crowded that I hied my way to the gallery, and took a seat where I could be seen right in front to the platform. The Rev. ex-President Perks, M.A., saw me, and sent one of the Brothers Hartley to request me to take a seat on the platform. This honour I accepted, and was only too thankful to Mr. Perks for his kind consideration. This was just before the election of the President; and, being a member of the Conference, I exercised my right to vote.

July 29th.—This was a day of fat things for me. I had the great privilege of hearing the Rev. Benjamin Gregory, M.A., and the Rev. Dr. Punshon preach. It was no small treat.

Aug. 4th.—The great debate on Lay Representation began to-day. As I intended going to the West in the morning, I asked the President's permission to say a few words. I had an influenza cold upon me, so that I could scarcely speak to be heard ten yards from the platform. But as the official reporter was sitting below, I persevered in the hope that what I said would appear in the *Watchman.* Of course I spoke on the question then before the chair, informing the Conference that we in Australia had, after about three years of earnest and prayerful thought, adopted the principle then under discussion. I stated that the presence of the lay brethren in our Conference would steady our action and give weight to our decisions. I expressed the hope that the English brethren would speedily find their way to the same desirable issue; which, in Australia, I felt sure, would give us both consolidation and enlargement as the years rolled by. As I retired to my seat at the rear of the platform, one of the Irish representatives said in an undertone to me, 'Some will not be obliged to you for your speech.' 'I cannot help that,' I meekly replied; 'it is the simple truth.'

The Ordination of forty young men to the full work of the Christian Ministry, according to the usages of our Church, was an imposing ceremonial. Of course, there were many of the 'fathers' of the Connexion present, whose earnest countenances indicated how much they valued this service as the perfecting circumstance of the young men's probationary course. The Rev. Gervase Smith, M.A., as ex-President, gave the 'charge,' which was on 'Preaching,' *i.e.* 'Who should preach?' 'What to preach?' and 'The end of preaching.' In his great discourse, Mr. Smith evidenced a thorough acquaintance with the Roman and Anglican theories of 'Apostolical Succession;' he unsparingly exposed the gaps and breaks of the lineal chain, together with the corrupt character of many of the so-called Successors of the Apostles. He brought out the true character of the 'eldership' as recognised in the New Testament; Mr. Wesley's right to transmit to his 'assistants' the power of Ordination in his Societies, and the unbroken line of ministerial 'orders,' generally, through the 'laying on of hands,' from the death of Wesley to that very year. The 'charge,' clothed in 'words of fire,' went home to the young ministers' hearts, and produced, it may be believed, in them a fuller consecration to their holy work. The 'charge,' in fact, may be characterised as a defiant and trenchant setting forth of the basal principles of the historic English Reformation, and of the great Evangelical Revival of the eighteenth century, in the face of the nation and of the world. It was, in short, the outcome of a sanctified heroism in the interests of truth and righteousness; the old Spartan spirit baptized and softened by the love of Jesus Christ. But the subject and its environments both created and called it forth.

Aug. 5*th.*—I soon tired of Nottingham, through being unable to bear the fatigue of sitting in the Conference from day to day. A few men did all the speaking, which made the business very monotonous and tedious. It seemed to me that far more of detail should be done in the District Committees, and that the main attention of Conference might be given to what is purely legislative business. 'Great bodies move slowly,' and here was proof of the truth of the maxim. I left early in the morning for Ilminster, and was twelve hours on the journey. The next day (Sunday) I heard the venerable **T. W.** Smith preach from the words: 'I have no greater joy than to hear that my children walk in truth.' It was a sweet and beautiful discourse. I preached in the evening, from the 'choice of Moses,' to a good congregation. It was by previous arrangement, and at my dear old friend's request, that we thus took the services.

Aug. 8th.—Mr. Smith, Miss Smith, Mrs. Bickford, and I went over to South Petherton to see Mrs. Smith's grave. It was a mournful visit for us. We took tea at Mr. Benjamin Hebditch's, a nephew of Mr. Smith's; after which we returned to Ilminster.

On the 9th we left for Plymouth, and domiciled at my nephew's, Mr. Joseph Grainger, Exeter Street. The next day my nieces, Mrs. Evans, Miss Bickford, and Mrs. Grainger, accompanied me in a trip around the Eddystone. I was struck with the appearance of the lighthouse, its scientific character and stupendous strength. But the heat was great, and I felt unequal to stand against its exhaustive pressure. 'How is it,' I asked myself, 'that I, who have "pulled through" so many Australian summers, am so "run down" here?' And I concluded that it was not intensity, but humidity, of the atmosphere that robbed me so easily of my usual strength.

On the 11th, after calling upon the Revs. Messrs. Jones and Jenkins, and my cousins, Mr. and Mrs. Nicholas Moysey, we left by the steamer, and reached Kingsbridge at 10 p.m. The 'Bolt Head' and 'Tail' came out in fine view as our little craft rounded the grand promontory, preparatory to our entering Salcombe harbour. I much enjoyed the trip across, as the air was cool and refreshing.

Aug. 19th.—I went by appointment to Stonehouse, and was the guest of Mr. and Mrs. Luxor at Emma Place. The Rev. Mr. Twells came over to see me. I preached at Stonehouse the next day. After the evening service, as there appeared to be a gracious feeling in the congregation, I called for a Prayer Meeting, and about three hundred persons remained.

On the 21st I called on Mr. Weeks at the Emigration Office, and left with him one hundred copies of my lecture on South Australia for free distribution. I was much disappointed in not meeting at the office the Rev. John Thorne, who had been appointed by the South Australian Government as emigration agent in England. I returned to Stonehouse, and prepared for the meeting in St. George's Hall, at which I had been announced to lecture on Australasian Methodism. I spoke for an hour and a half with much freedom, and I hope I interested the large audience who had come to hear what I had to say.

The next day I returned to Mr. Grainger's much exhausted, and I had to sleep for several hours before I could do anything at all. My brother-in-law, Mr. William Tapp, was very ill, but so happy that his desire was to be with Christ.

The 23rd was an interesting day. I dined at Mr. Barker's, who heard me preach at Ugborough in 1838, just as I was leaving for the West Indies. The Rev. Hugh Jones, the Chairman of the District, and Mrs. Bickford were there also. In the afternoon we drove to the Hoe to see the swimming matches. There were at least four thousand people present, and in the steamers, which were constantly flitting to and fro, there was quite 'a cloud of witnesses.' In the evening Miss Barker and I attended the episcopal service at St. Andrew's, and heard the Rev. Mr. Guinness preach an evangelical sermon.

Aug. 27th.—I preached again at Salcombe, and the next evening (Monday) I spoke at a Bible Society's Meeting, at which the Rev. Mr. Fieldwick attended as a deputation. Mr. Benjamin Balkwill, of Kingsbridge, took the chair. In my short speech I justified the claims of the Bible Society for support from the Christian public, because of its practical sympathy with our missions in the West Indies, Africa, India, and Australasia. It was a very good meeting. I took a terrible cold in returning to my niece's (Mrs. Baker's), at Snape's, from the rain which had been falling all the evening.

Sept. 2nd.—I was again at Modbury. In the afternoon I visited the churchyard to see the graves of some of my kindred. The epitaphs, in several instances, were quaint and touching. I climbed the ancient ladder up into the belfry, that I might see Mr. Joseph Flashman wind up the great clock. I spent some time in the church, where my parents and nine of us, brothers and sisters, used to worship 'the God of our fathers.' A funeral occurred during my visit, and I joined in the procession and solemnities at the grave. As I had been desirous of obtaining a certificate of my baptism, I thought this would be a good time for getting it. So I followed the Vicar into the vestry, presented my card, and asked him to furnish me, from the register, with a copy of my baptism. He courteously inquired for the year and month, which I gave him. He opened his eyes when I told him ' 1816,' and that very likely the month of May would give it. It was immediately found, and a form was duly filled in. ' What is the charge, Mr. Green ? ' said I. His answer surprised and pleased me. ' You are a minister, are you not ? ' he inquired. I said, ' Yes.' ' Well, then,' he rejoined, ' I make no charge. But the certificate requires a penny stamp,' said he. I confess that I was a little nonplussed, not having to pay for stamps in such matters in Australia ; and never carrying anything less than a threepenny silver-piece in my purse, I, of course, was unprepared to pay. ' But I have no penny,' said I ; ' what's to be done ? ' ' Oh,' said he, ' I have a stamp here,' which he at once fixed on the document. I thanked him for his kindness, and as I walked over the flags, which my boyish feet once trod when attending Mr. Wreford's school, I could not think but that in the Modbury Vicar there was a beautiful blandness, notwithstanding his High Churchism and ritualistic antics.

Sept. 3rd.—I preached at Kingston, and was the guest of Mr. Stidston, a gentleman farmer, and a good Wesleyan. Mr. Stidston was converted under the preaching of the Rev. P. C. Turner many years ago, during his visit to this rural locality for a church anniversary. My brother, Edmund Whiteway Bickford, and my nephew, James Bickford (his son), were with me all the day.

Sept. 5th.—I filled up a second batch of applications for free passages to South Australia. Mr. and Mrs. Samuel Shepheard had already gone, and now I was making applications for eleven more.

Sept. 9th.—I left for Ivybridge this morning, where I am to preach on Sunday. As we drove through Edmeston Farm, where I was born and lived until I was fourteen years old, I thought much of my dear parents and kindred. We have been scattered the ' wide world o'er.' I was the guest of Mrs. Badham, at the parsonage, who treated me with much Christian hospitality. I called on a few early friends, whom I knew in my schooldays. I preached the next day in the beautiful church built at Mr. Allen's expense, and given by him to the Connexion. I dined at Mr. Allen's, and met Mrs. Dingley there. It was a pleasant and profitable Sabbath.

After spending all the time we could spare at present in Devonshire, and wishing to be near the Agent General for South Australia, we went up to London on the 15th, and took furnished lodgings at 36, Maitland Park, Haverstock Hill, occupied by Mrs. Sillifant, whom I had formerly known in the West Indies. It proved, in every respect, an economical and a comfortable arrangement for us.

Sept. 16*th.*—The Coolie Mission in Demerara was still dear to me. So that on learning that the Rev. H. V. P. Bronckhurst and Mrs. Bronckhurst were at Dalston 'on account of health,' I went this evening, piloted by Mrs. Hurd, to see them, and to inquire about the progress of the Mission. I was much pleased with the information I received from Mr. Bronckhurst, who had been employed in the Mission since 1865. It was interesting to me to learn that Mrs. Bronckhurst was a Miss Patterson, formerly connected with Trinity Church, and who was appointed to take charge of Mrs. Bickford's class when we left Demerara, for England, twenty-three years ago. She had been a worthy helpmeet to her husband in the Coolie work.

Sept. 19*th.*—I attended the Financial District Meeting, Dr. Osborne in the chair. I thus had an early opportunity of becoming acquainted with the London Ministers. I could not but observe that the subject of lay-representation to Conference was the *bête noire* of the meeting. Mr. President McAulay presented me, on the second day, with a beautiful copy of our recently issued Hymn Book. It bore the following inscription :—

'Presented to the Rev. James Bickford, President of the South Australian Conference. 1875, from the British Conference assembled in Nottingham, in 1876.—A. McAULAY, President.'

Sept. 24*th.*—I preached at Toddington in aid of the church funds. On Monday evening I lectured on Australia to a good audience. The Rev. John Rodwell was the Circuit Superintendent; his wife, 'Fanny Bickford Hurd,' was baptized by me in St. Vincent's, and was my god-daughter. 'I baptized their infant child, and thus identified myself still further with this delightful family by giving him my name as godson to me. We visited about, took tea at Mr. Gadston's, and drove through the grounds at Woburn Abbey.

Sept. 27*th.*—I went over to the Westminster Training College, and was courteously received by Dr. James H. Rigg. He took me over the extensive and well-arranged buildings, and showed me the College

Church also. The apparent haughtiness of the Doctor to strangers entirely disappears in close contact with him. To me, he became so bland and so interesting, that I would have liked half-a-day with him instead of a couple of hours.

Sept. 29th.—Mrs. Bickford, Mrs. Sillifant, and I went to see the Prince of Wales' jewels at the Kensington Museum. It was a great display of the finest art and of untold wealth.

Oct. 1st.—I preached missionary sermons to-day at Colchester, and addressed the Sunday School in the afternoon. The public meeting came off in the evening of the next day. Mr. Coleman from Chelmsford presided with effect. The Revs. G. Terry, B.A., T. Thompson, T. Llewellyn, and I were the speakers,—too many by two for a good meeting. Of course I visited the ruins of the old historic castle. I was the guest of Mr. and Mrs. Sargisson, who showed me much kind attention.

Oct. 4th.—I ran down to Plymouth to say ' good-bye ' to my kins-folk, Mr. and Mrs. John Jarvis and family, who were about to sail in the *Robert Lees* for Port Adelaide, South Australia. I also attended the funeral of my brother-in-law, Mr. William Tapp, who had, after much suffering, died, even as he had lived for more than forty years, ' in the full assurance of faith.' The next evening I went to the depot, and held a semi-religious service for the South Australian emigrants. There were about three hundred present, to whom I spoke on the conduct proper to ship life, and on their duties when they landed in Adelaide. They appeared very grateful for the counsels I gave them, as well as for the ' notes of introduction ' to be used by them in the colony. On the 6th, Mr. Smith, the despatching agent from the London office, and I went through the ship, and saw the arrangments for the emigrants. In the evening, my brother, E. W. Bickford, from Modbury, and I went to St. Andrew's, to hear Bishop Perry, formerly of Melbourne, preach. His text was 1 Cor. x. 1-5. The venerable man struck hard at the theory of ' Baptismal Regeneration,' drawing his arguments from the sad case of the ancient Israelites as mentioned in the text, and earnestly exhorted his congregation to trust alone for conversion to the baptism of the Holy Ghost. It was a telling and seasonable discourse ; being delivered during the holding of the Anglican Congress, there were several of the ministers and representatives of that Church present in the town.

21

Oct. 8th.—I preached at 'Ebenezer' this evening, at the earnest request of the Rev. Hugh Jones, the Superintendent; and the next evening I spoke at the Missionary Meeting, held at Wesley. On the 10th, I returned to London, none the worse for my journeyings and labours in the west.

Oct. 14th.—My next visit to Baddow Park, near Chelmsford, for services on the Sabbath. Mr. Coleman met me at the station, and drove me to the Joneses, whose guest I was to be. The old Mr. and Mrs. Bradshaw, formerly of Geelong and Ballarat, were staying with their son-in-law, Mr. Jones, and Mrs. Jones, their daughter. On Monday morning, Mr. Jones kindly drove me some twenty miles, to see the surrounding country, which was very fine. In the afternoon we walked to Great Mascal Farm, to see Mr. James Duffield, brother to the Hon. T. Duffield, near Gawler. We had a most agreeable interview with this gentleman farmer and his family. The next day, Mr. Jones and I went to Chelmsford, it being market day. I was introduced by my friend to Mr. Solicitor Duffield, whom I found as well versed in Australian affairs as if he had been a resident. 'Then you have no State Church,' said he, 'in South Australia?' 'No,' I replied, 'and the right thing too in a new country. We are doing very well without.' 'Well; yes,' he rejoined, 'in a new country certainly. And it will be the same thing in this country too when you have a majority in the House of Commons.' He was not at all afraid of the voluntary principle in religion; they were now acting upon it in the parish church : the public collections were most generous, and they had plenty of money for all their claims. They had no Church rates, and were better without them.' Mr. Duffield was certainly the most liberal Churchman I had met with in England; but it was no wonder, for his intelligence seemed to be the measure of his good-sensed broad-heartedness.

It was a treat to meet with such a man. We dined at Mr. Coleman's; the Rev. John Jones (D) and Mrs. Jones joined us. I found Mrs. Coleman a very choice Christian lady. We went through the works, which were very extensive.

Oct. 18th.—I dined by invitation at the Rev. Richard Roberts's, and met Dr. Egerton Ryerson from Canada there. In the evening we went to Harrow-on-the-Hill to hold a Missionary Meeting; General Crawford in the chair. The Rev. H. G. Hellier, Dr. Ryerson, and I did the speaking. Messrs. R. Roberts and Ishmael

Jones were also present. I suppose it was a pretty good meeting.

Oct. 20th.—I attended a School Board Committee Meeting at Regent's Park, to select candidates for the ensuing election. We agreed to nominate the Hon. Lyulph Stanley, Dr. Angus, and Mr. Watson, a former member of the Board. It was believed that the election would cost at least £600, and liberal offers of contributions were made. We held an after-meeting of the ' Preparation Class ' in the vestry of Dr. Angus's church; Colonel Griffin presided. I spoke for twenty minutes on the compulsory, free, and unsectarian nature of public education in Victoria. The meeting was evidently taken by surprise at the account I gave. It seemed ' to be too good to be true,' even in an Australian Colony.

Oct. 21st.—I wrote an indignant letter to the London *Echo* on Churchyard grievances, as detailed from time to time in the daily press. I could not believe that the exclusive claims some of the incumbents set up, in regard to these ancient national cemeteries, could be sustained in law. If so, the question arises, Would there not be more honour in breaking it than in obeying it ? In Australia it would be swept out of existence in twenty-four hours.

It is our happiness in Australia not to be weighted with a State Church ; there is, therefore, a complete freedom from all those petty annoyances and cruel disabilities experienced even in English-speaking countries where State Churches are known. The absence in Australia of all Parliamentary recognition of ecclesiastical establishments, has been creative of a very full sympathy of the various religious bodies towards each other. The Episcopal clergy, with a few unimportant exceptions, are included in this remark. And I do not believe that there is any serious desire on the part of the dignitaries of that body ever again to have recourse to State aid for upholding and extending the Episcopal form of worship in any part of Australasia. All the religious denominations have accepted the principle of voluntary support as right ; whilst the principle of a complete religious equality has been so firmly established, that the general public would never tolerate the slightest practicable departure from it.

Oct. 22nd.—Great Queen Street Church anniversary. I heard the Rev. Theophilus Woolmer preach the morning sermon, which was one of great excellence. Its pure diction, earnest thought, and dignified utterance, suited me exactly. In the evening I preached at King's Cross; Mr. Gall, a young gentleman of colour from Barbadoes, walked with me, for I cannot travel by rail, or tram, on the Lord's Day.

Oct. 23rd.—At the Exeter Hall Juvenile Missionary Meeting to-day, Mr. H. H. Fowler, the Revs. Dr. Punshon, G. T. Perks, and W. O. Simpson were the speakers. Exeter Hall looked well, and the meeting was a grand success.

Oct. 24th.—I went to Westminster to see Mr. Dutton, the Agent General, on several South Australian matters. He was very accessible, and presented me with a cheque to recoup me for my expenses in the service of the Colony. I could not take a shilling as 'emigration agent' for South Australia; but I did expect to be indemnified for personal expenses in travelling, lecturing, and seeing the ships off at Plymouth.

Oct. 29th.—I went to Keyworth near Derby, to preach anniversary sermons. Mr. T. E. Cawdell and I went to the parish church in the morning. The service was simple and evangelical, as became an establishment connected with the Protestant Reformed Church of England. My services were in the afternoon and evening. Here I met with a respectable but very poor widow and her daughter, who had not tasted a bit of animal food but once or twice for two years. But they were 'content,' although so poor. They were of that class of Christians of whom St. Paul speaks, as 'having nothing, and yet possessing all things.'

On my return to London, I found an affectionate and beautiful letter from the venerable minister, the Rev. John Corlett, who succeeded me in Demerara. Mr. Corlett was a native of the Isle of Man, and entered our Ministry in 1824. Somehow he was not known in our Connexion as his abilities deserved; but he was, nevertheless, a great Methodist preacher, a famous theologian, powerful in prayer, an earnest missionary, and a genuine philanthropist. We have but few such men as was Mr. Corlett in our West India Missions.

Oct. 30th.—I went this evening to Hampstead Church anniversary; the Rev. John McKenny in the chair. My reference in my speech to the Total Abstinence question, pleased the congregation very much. I was glad to tell them that the young ministers in the Australian Conference were, for the most part, total abstainers and anti-smokers.

They were careful to contract no bad habits, and they generally gave promise of great usefulness. It was a great comfort to me, as a somewhat old minister, to bear this testimony.

Nov. 1st.—I took tea at Mr. A. Russel Johnstone's, 101, Long Acre, and from thence went to the Missionary Meeting at Great Queen Street. The Revs. M. C. Osborn, G. Adcock, and I, were the speakers. I got on but poorly somehow; the fact was, that the two preceding speakers occupied all the time before I had my chance to speak on our Polynesian Missions. I was much dissatisfied, and annoyed with myself for having attempted to speak at all.

A ministerial convention at Jewin Street was a hallowed season. Dr. Osborn presided with much tenderness and ability. The subjects were ' Ministerial Privileges,' by Rev. Samuel Walker; ' Ministerial Dangers,' by Dr. Osborn; ' Ministerial Difficulties,' by Rev. E. E. Jenkins, M.A.; ' Ministerial Duties,' by Rev. F. W. Macdonald; and ' Ministerial Responsibilities,' by Rev. M. C. Osborn. Each paper was followed by judicious remarks from the brethren. We concluded by taking the Lord's Supper, at which I and Rev. James Buller assisted.

Nov. 3rd.—Captain Bagot, of North Adelaide, gave me a letter of introduction to his son, Mr. Solicitor Bagot, 40, Chancery Lane, and I went with him this evening to his beautiful home at Mortlake to dine and spend the night. Mr. and Mrs. Maturin and Miss Maturin were there to meet me. We were a nice little party of South Australians. I spent a delightful evening with this select and genteel company.

Nov. 4th.—Mrs. Bickford and I left for the Rev. W. G. Pascoe's, Belvidere Road, Liverpool. The next day I preached at St. John's and Garstang; and I attended Missionary Meetings at both places. Of course we visited Prince's and Sefton Parks, the miles of docks, the forest of shipping, the landing jetty opposite Birkenhead, and scores of other places and objects of great interest. On the 8th we took tea, with a large party of friends, at Mr. and Mrs. Johnstone's, true friends of our Missions. At the meeting, in the evening, Mr. Samuel R. Healey presided. Mr. Healey was a strong Conservative, and I am afraid that some of my statements, political and ecclesiastical, were not welcome to him. I spoke an hour, after which I went with Mr. McQuie to his country house, and spent two lively hours with Mrs. McQuie, Mrs. Malcolm, Mr. McQuie, and family. The next morning I saw the dear old Mrs. Posnett and her widowed daughter, and had a nice season of prayer with them.

Nov. 12*th.*—I was at Horsham on Mission business. At the public meeting the Rev. Mr. Hugill presided. As I was the only speaker, I had to make two speeches. On my way back to the parsonage I was accosted by a Mr. Sergeant Witham, who inquired if I knew his brother-in-law, Mr. Baseby, at North Adelaide. We had a long chat about his friends in South Australia.

Nov. 18*th.*—I left for the Isle of Wight. The Rev. William Moister met me at Cowes, and I accompanied him to Newport. It was thirty years ago since we last met. As we looked upon each other, we were much excited, and the feeling in both was gratitude to God. Reaching Mr. Moister's sweet little cottage, Mrs. Moister repeated the kindness of thirty-eight years ago, in Port of Spain, Trinidad, by giving me a hearty, Christian welcome. We spent a delightful evening in conversing upon a multitude of topics of a personal, ecclesiastical, and national character. On the 19th I preached twice at Newport to capital congregations. My old and first Superintendent, Mr. Moister, was one of my hearers in the evening. The next morning I went to Shide Mill to see my niece, Mrs. Alice Treby. We took tea at Mrs. Dore's, the Methodist home for ministers and Wesleyan visitors from time to time. In the evening I gave a lecture on ' Total Abstinence, the only Cure for Intemperance,' when my venerable friend, Mr. Moister, presided, and made touching references to our former association in the mission-field. The Rev. Mr. Connor, Vicar of Newport, and one of the Queen's teetotal chaplains, made a good speech. When replying to the vote of thanks, I took occasion to refer to South Australia as an encouraging field for English emigrants.

After our return to Mr. Moister's, the subject again came up. I was strongly advised, by my generous host, to employ any leisure time I might have, whilst in England, in extending, in the form of a portable volume, the substance of my lecture at the Institute. He thought, he said, it would serve the object I had in view, in the matter of inducing a stream of eligible persons in Great Britain to seek their fortunes in the Southern World. It would, he also observed, be a permanent memento of my visit, which my many friends in England and elsewhere would much value. I promised to think about it on my return to London.

Nov. 22nd.—The Rev. James Gillman, a venerable Irish supernumerary minister, called. I had often heard of his eloquent
discourses and great ability, and it was a great treat to me to listen
to the conversation between my friend and him. The next day
Mr. Moister accompanied me to Woolston, *via* Southampton, that we
might together see our West India friends, the Rev. George Ranyell
and his estimable wife. We had a very profitable interview. In
the afternoon Mr. Moister returned to Newport, and I went up by
train to London.

Nov. 25th.—I left for Ilminster to do deputation work, and reached
the Rev. T. W. Smith's in the afternoon. The next day I preached
twice, and specially addressed the 'Society' and young people at
the close of the evening service.

On Monday, Mr. Smith and I went to Dillington Farm to spend a
little time with Mr. Obed Hosegood and his estimable family. In
the evening we held the first of the series of Missionary Meetings;
Mr. Smith presiding. The next day we went to Martock, when a
choice party met us at Mr. Bradford's to tea. We had a fine
meeting in the evening. Our next meeting was at South Petherton,
Mr. S. Hebditch in the chair. In my speech I referred to the
Swantons, Bakers, and Giffords, who were formerly resident in the
neighbourhood, as friends of mine in Victoria. Such allusions are
pleasing to our people in England. An interesting incident was
named to me here. It seems that it was a little more than one hundred years ago that the Rev. Dr. Thomas Coke, then curate of South
Petherton, rode over to Kingston to see Mr. Wesley. He, in a few
weeks, cast in his lot with the great evangelist, and placed his
fortune and his life at the disposal of Christ. Eternity alone will
show the results of that interview upon the best interests of the
Church and the world. The next meeting was held at Crewkerne.
I spoke on the Australian and Polynesian Missions; giving, at the
same time, some valuable information upon the advantages of
emigration of certain classes of the people to South Australia.
I was asked by a gentleman in the audience if I were 'a paid
agent of the Government.' My prompt reply of 'No' satisfied my
interlocutor.

Dec. 1st.—I went to Milbourne Port to see old Mrs. Coombs,
mother of Mr. W. G. Coombs, of Rundle Street, Adelaide. I saw
also Mrs. Fudge, Miss Fudge, Mr. E. Coombs, Mr. Enson (known to

me in Melbourne), and the Rev. Mr. Holland.   In the afternoon I left for Plymouth to fulfil engagements at Stonehouse on the 3rd. I preached twice to capital congregations, among whom were a good sprinkling of the military profession.   On the occasion of this visit, I spoke at Missionary Meetings in Stonehouse and Morrice Town, Devonport.

Dec. 6th.—I went to the Emigration Depot, and spoke to about three hundred people.   The Rev. John Thorne, from South Australia ; Colonel Hickman, from Kentucky ; Dr. Sherfy, from New York ; and the Rev. W. Holderness (Anglican) took part in the service. In the evening my nephew, Mr. Grainger, and I went out to Stonehouse to a Good Templars' meeting.   The question of Coloured People's Lodges in America was agitating Good Templarism throughout Great Britain and the United States, and strong, angry feeling was shown.   I must say that I thought the Colonel's vindication of the side his party had taken was complete.   I need not say that, from the associations of my West Indian life, my sympathies were with those whose complexions are regarded as a social disability.

On the 7th I travelled in company with Colonel Hickman and Dr. Sherfy to London.   We had exciting and beneficial conversations all the way up.   It was not often that I had in my journeys such companions as they were on this occasion.

Dec. 8th.—A day of considerable excitement in London.   The great meeting in St. James' Hall on the Eastern Question came off. Of course I went, and for six hours I listened to some of the ablest leaders of socio-political thought in Great Britain.   There was an amazing earnestness displayed throughout the day.   Mr. Gladstone spoke in the evening, and it was a grand spectacle from the gallery to look down upon some five thousand intelligent people as they hung upon the lips of this great English statesman.   When he rose to speak, the audience became the subject of a hurricane of excitement.   The whole multitude rose *en masse* to testify its faith in him, as the trusted exponent of the feeling of England towards the oppressed nationalities of South-eastern Europe.   He contended that England should not spend one shilling, nor sacrifice one life, for upholding the territorial integrity of the Porte ; further, that Turkey should never again have the power to oppress, rob, or murder the Christian populations of European Turkey.   'I am far,' said Mr.

Gladstone, 'from saying that we have taken out a commission of universal "knight-errantry;" but this is not a case where we act on the principle of benevolence. This is a case in which we have given a conditional support to the Turkish power, in which the conditions have been forgotten and betrayed. It is a case, therefore, of positive obligation; and when, under the stringent pressure of that obligation, the long-suffering and long-oppressed humanity in those provinces has at length lifted itself from the ground, and is beginning again to contemplate the heavens, it is our business to assist in the work; it is our business to acknowledge our obligations, to take our part in the burden; it is our business to claim for our country a share in the honour and in the fame. The acknowledgment of duty, this attempt to realise honour, is at least what we are attempting to obtain from our Government. And with nothing less than this, I believe, we, who are here assembled, will not under any circumstances be persuaded to be content.' It was some considerable time before the rustling flood-tide of excitement subsided.

Dec. 10th.—This Sabbath morning Mrs. Bickford and I went to Prince of Wales Road Church to hear the Rev. R. Roberts, Superintendent Minister, preach. Text: 'Praise is comely for the upright.'

In the evening of the same day I went to Dr. Landels' Church, Regent's Park, in the hope that I might hear him. In this I was disappointed, but I heard instead an extraordinary sermon from the Rev. Frederick Tucker, of Camden Town. There was, I thought, a singularity about him, which rather discouraged in me the expectation of anything superior to the general run of the London ministers. But I was mistaken, for here was a man of no ordinary talent: a great preacher was indeed in the pulpit.

Dec. 18th.—I heard the Rev. Doctor Donald Fraser, of London, lecture on 'John Knox and his Times," which was full of interest— historical and ecclesiastical.

Dec. 24th.—I again heard the Rev. Richard Roberts. Text: Isaiah xliv. 22. Thus within one week I was privileged to hear two sermons from this eloquent preacher. But I confess that his week-night discourses, which had no aroma of midnight oil about them, were much fresher, pointed, and feeding to one's soul than were his Sabbath discourses, which were oftentimes very long, and unnecessarily discursive. I often told my friend that in preaching so long he talked away his great power, and to that extent defeated his otherwise very able ministry.

We spent the Christmas Day of this year with the Butterses at Upper Tulse Hill, Brixton Rise. Our Methodist 'Gaius' (the Rev. Mr. Butters) had invited also the Rev. J., and Mrs. and Miss Buller to be there also. So that with the family we made rather a large party. We had a most agreeable time. On the 29th we were invited to dine and spend the evening at the Rev. Dr. Jobson's, Highbury Park. The Revs. J. A. Armstrong, T. Allen, their wives, and a Mr. and Mrs. Parry, from Cornwall, were there also. The good Doctor presided with all the urbanity and heartiness of an old English rector or country squire; whilst Mrs. Jobson did her part with a pleasant affability. It was a very choice gathering of really godly, intelligent persons. It seemed to me that the Rev. W. Butters and Dr. Jobson were the generous hosts of official ministers, and Sir W. McArthur, M.P., of influential gentlemen, visiting London from the outskirts of the empire. No doubt they had their reward.

I finished up the year by preaching at Prince of Wales Road Church at 6.30 p.m., and we did our Watching at Maitland Park, by prayer and reading of the Scriptures at the midnight hour. Thus ended this year of 1876.

The correspondence since our arrival in England on the emigration business, the monthly letter to *The Methodist Journal*, Adelaide, and the travelling up and down the country in the service of Methodism and of South Australia, had been one unbroken burden of work. But, God be praised, it seemed to be helpful to my health, and gave me an elasticity of spirits, which, had I remained in London most of the time, I could not have had. The only drawback was that Mrs. Bickford could not travel very much with me, through the lack of physical enduring power; but she never once complained, feeling that I was doing my duty to my Church, the Foreign Missions, and to the colonies of Australasia.

1877.

Jan. 1st.—At 1 a.m., on my knees, and with all my heart, I gave myself again to my Lord and Master for active service or for suffering, for honour or dishonour, for England or for Australia. This year will probably be more eventful to me than 1876 has been. But 'my times are in Thy hands.'

Jan. 2nd.—The stupid Turks have rejected the proposals of the Combined Powers. What next? The 'sword' in deadly duel between Turks and Russians. May the God of justice defend the right!

Jan. 4th.—I heard the Rev. Joseph Parker, D.D., preach at his midday service to a large congregation. His text was Gen. xx. 9. His first sentence, 'This is the second lie Abraham told Abimelech,' put me against him, and I heard the sermon in a spirit of antagonism. It was clever, of course; but its ethics, I venture to think, were somewhat dangerous. It seemed to me that the discourse was a kind of apology for the *laches* of good men. There were of course some very fine passages in it. The Rev. Edward White, in an after meeting, read an able paper 'On the loss the Church has sustained through the absence of a continuous exposition of the Scriptures in the pulpit.' The essay I thought looked rather in the direction of an abrogation of all theological standards and creeds. Its refrain was, 'More sea-room, if you please!'

Jan. 7th.—I preached at Great Queen Street on 2 Kings v. 25, which I thought suitable for the first Sabbath morning of the New Year. I was at the Covenant Service at King's Cross in the afternoon; and in the evening I heard the Rev. Charles Kelly preach an excellent sermon. It was to me a thoroughly good day.

Jan. 10th.—I could not complain of being overlooked—'left out in the cold'—by the London official ministers when any matter of public interest was on the *tapis*. Hence, in the forenoon of this day, I went by invitation to the Centenary Hall, to attend the monthly meeting of the Executive Committee of our Foreign Missions. On my way to the Chalk Farm Station, I fell in with my old friend, Mr. James Bonwick, from Melbourne. I was both surprised and pleased. The Rev. G. T. Perks, M.A., the senior Secretary, conducted the business with much suavity and prudence. The Rev. President McAulay presided, and the room was well filled. There was an air of earnestness pervading this influential Committee which impressed and delighted me. When gentlemen meet to transact the important business of our Foreign Missions, I like to be able to recognise grip, seriousness, and generousness in their spirit and action. I attended a second meeting in the afternoon, which had been called by the President to consider the question of raising funds for establishing and strengthening Methodism in the smaller towns and villages in the kingdom. Sir William McArthur, M.P., generously gave £2,000 ; and the sum of £37,500 in all was promised. The lay gentlemen gave like princes, which they are in our Methodist Israel.

I preached at Prince of Wales Road in the evening, and continued the service until 9.30. Thank God, in the inquiry room, we had four penitents seeking the forgiveness of their sins.

Jan. 11*th.*—I found the Rev. William R. Williams, D.D., a gentlemanly and affectionate brother. As Secretary of the English Conference I had often seen him, and I always found him so kind and so considerate of my wishes. I was not therefore surprised this morning to receive through the post a copy of his critical and comprehensive Fernley Lecture on the Priesthood of Christ. In the evening I heard the Rev. John Bond preach an earnest sermon at Prince of Wales Road in connection with the special services. We had a fine prayer meeting at the close. Good is doubtless being done.

Jan. 20*th.*—At the earnest request of Dr. Jobson, who was ill, I consented to go to Louth for the Sabbath services. Mr. Bennett, of the Cedars, was waiting for me at the station, and I accompanied him to his beautiful home. Besides the Bennett family, there were, Mrs. Sharpley, and Mr. Sharpley, her son, and the Rev. B. B. Waddy, the Circuit Superintendent. We spent together a delightful evening. The next day I preached twice to excellent congregations. In the vestry, previous to the service, one of the Church Stewards said to me : ' We don't like long services here ; our time for closing in the morning is 12 o'clock.' ' Agreed,' said I, ' you shall be out at that time.' As I was ascending to the pulpit, I looked round the capacious building to see how my presence was relished, seeing that, at that time, Dr. Jobson was the most popular minister in that county, when I thought I saw expressions of disappointment traced on the countenances of the people ; so before I gave out the first hymn I said : ' I wish to tell the congregation why I am here in the place of your friend, Dr. Jobson. I am sorry to say that the Doctor is so ill as to be unable to leave his bed, and so, to prevent collapse, I have come in his stead. Now I have hope that we shall have a good time together.' I felt instanter that the congregation was within my hold, and I proceeded with the service. At about seven minutes to twelve, I suddenly stopped and remarked that I had been informed that the congregation did not like long services, and, that I would, with much regret, 'break off'' at once; but that as I hoped to preach again in the evening, we would have more time, and we could remain as long as we liked. In the vestry I was asked, in a rather abrupt manner, why I had concluded so soon? I then stretched out my hand to the brother who had spoken to me before the service, and referred to him for the reason. I simply added that 'when I am from home, I always make it a point to obey orders.' In the evening we had a fine congregation, and at the close I invited the people to remain to hear a short address on Australia. I should think that eight hundred at least remained behind. The collections for the day amounted to £20 for the Circuit Funds.

The next morning, the Rev. Thomas Champness breakfasted with us. He spoke to me about casting in his lot with us in Australia. I gave him no encouragement, as far as the South Australian Conference was concerned, because of the great difficulty we had in providing for married ministers, but that New South Wales Conference laboured under no such difficulty. I remember one expression of his which amused me very much. Speaking of preaching under powerful impulse, he said, 'that he never saw the land again after he had once started, until he had got to the end.' As a description of the *abandon*, the rush, and tear, of his sermonic performances, I suppose the figure was most appropriate. He appeared to be a racy, good-natured, well-informed, and zealous man.

Jan. 29th.—I preached at Stow-on-the-Wold yesterday, in aid of the Church Trust; and this evening I lectured on South Australia. The friendly Rector, Rev. Mr. Hodgers, presided. The Rev. Joseph Payne, our minister, took me to see the Rev. Henry Badger, a former West Africa Missionary, who is very ill. He made 'a good confession,' and his hope was sure and steadfast. He inquired most affectionately for the Revs. B. Chapman, T. Roston, W. A. Quick, and R. Hart, his former colleagues, or fellow-workers 'in the Dark Continent.' The grace of an enduring friendship is largely bestowed on missionaries; it generally ends only with life.

Feb. 6th.—I attended the Mixed Committee on Lay Representation to Conference. It was a large gathering of the best men in English Methodism. The Rev. James Buller and I were permitted to be present by an unanimous vote of the Committee. I cannot speak too much in praise of the thorough impartiality of

Mr. President McAulay, and of the adroit manner in which he put the main points of numerous amendments, and disposed of them by a 'yea' or 'nay' vote. There was the finest spirit throughout, and it was specially gratifying to see how resolved the Committee were to do the very best thing that could be done to popularise the entire movement, and thereby secure the warm and sincere suffrages of the entire Connexion.

It is impossible to over-estimate the historic value of this great discussion. The crucial points were :—(1) The provision for securing a continuity of the lay element in the Conference, answering to the Legal Hundred, as provided in the Deed Poll. The Rev. W. B. Pope spoke on this point in a clear and impressive manner. The provision was accordingly made, on the motion of Dr. Punshon, 'That one-eighth of the lay representatives shall from time to time be elected by the Conference, when composed of ministers and laymen.' (2) The Quarterly Meetings remained untouched, although Dr. Rigg and Mr. H. H. Fowler spoke at great length for a representative to the District Meetings, in addition to the two Circuit Stewards. (3) A long debate ensued upon the point whether membership in one district, and trusteeship in another, would qualify for a seat in Conference, provided the District Meeting, composed of ministers and laymen, elected such to the Conference. This was carried by a large majority. (4) It was provided that the business to be transacted by the Conference, when consisting of ministers only, shall be completed before that which is to be transacted by the ministers and laymen be entered upon. Mr. Buller and I much enjoyed these discussions.

It was pretty well at the close of the business that the Rev. John Rattenbury came to where Mr. Buller and I were sitting, behind the President's chair, and accosted us as follows : 'Why can't you men out there' (Australia) 'leave well alone? We are indebted to you for all this trouble about lay representation !' I suppose there must be something in my Devonian blood that is easily roused, for I answered him too sharply, I fear : 'We have studied this very thing for three full years, and have got to the end without any serious friction, and for the best, as succeeding years will show, I have no doubt.' This was enough for our friend. Good and earnest man, and a great preacher, too, when he was in his prime; still, somehow I could not take to him as I could have wished.

In the evening Mr. Buller and I went to the Memorial Hall, Farringdon Street, to hear the Rev. J. Guinness Rogers lecture on 'The Rev. A. Tooth and the Church.' The hall was packed with men who were intensely interested in the proceedings. There were certainly many clerical representatives present of the two great parties now disturbing and dividing the Anglican Church. The behaviour of the respective parties, under Mr. Guinness's heavy fire, showed on which side they ranged. The lecture was worth travelling a thousand miles to hear.

Feb. 8th.—Mr. Hays, senior clerk at the Mission House, sent me a memorandum to-day, showing the entire cost of establishing and working the Australian and Polynesian Missions, from 1815 to 1875 inclusive, as £720,281 12s. 1d.; less, by local contributions, £269,365 13s. 4d., leaving as the cost to British Methodism £450,915 16s. 10d. A noble contribution surely to the Southern World!

On the 10th Mrs. Bickford and I visited Westminster Abbey. As we stepped inside the wicket-door, Mrs. Bickford seemed overcome with the gorgeousness of everything she saw. 'What a wonderful place is this!' she exclaimed. 'Yes,' I replied, 'you will indeed say so when we have seen all that is to be seen.' We were taken by a guide through the private chapels, and for a full hour we were on our feet following in the track of our loquacious guide. What a marvellous monument is the Abbey to the memories of the mighty dead! Also to the genius and mechanical skill of the great intellects of the past and present centuries. Of course there is but one Westminster Abbey in the world,—even as there is but one London. The most affecting of the sights, however, was the chaste enclosure in which are those touching memorials of the death of the Dean's late wife, Lady Stanley. We saw the beautiful statue, erected by the Dean's kind permission, within the precincts of the Abbey, for John and Charles Wesley. It gratified us very much to see this imperishable memento of two of England's greatest sons in this grand old Abbey.

I only attended one high ritualistic service whilst I was in England. This was on the evening of the 11th, at St. Mary the Virgin's, Primrose Hill. There were eight candles burning upon the altar-table, a crucifix in the centre, and other insignia of the most expressed forms of Roman worship. The parade of incensing the Rev. Newton Smith, the curate, was curious, and even disgusting. The vessel was held up to his nose, to his ears, waved across his forehead, and around his head, until he was scented all over. His calm dignity as he sat in his chair, and his gesticulations as sacrificing priest, were amusing. The sermon lasted for fifteen minutes, but it was long enough. It consisted of a rehash of elemental science as affecting certain material changes in the natural world; and closed up by exhortations to the people to prepare by penitence and prayer to meet death. The name of Christ was not once mentioned, from the beginning to the end of this miserably weak discourse. I must pass over a number of small ceremonials, and only add that the sisterhood were apparently more devout than were the brotherhood. Both gazed at a large crucifix suspended in a conspicuous place, and, in the processions up and down the church, the priests and others always nodded as they passed a little image of Christ suspended from a wall. To me, who in my youth was accustomed to worship with my parents in the parish church in Modbury, and who, even now, can well remember the dignity and beauty of the services as conducted by the Rev. Mr. Stackhouse, the saintly vicar, the performance at St. Mary the Virgin's pained me greatly, and will remain with me to the end of my life as an awful travesty of what should be the most scriptural and effective of all the forms of public worship known and celebrated in any part of the civilised world.

Feb. 17*th.*—I read this morning the report of the great debate last evening in the House of Commons. The Rupert of the discussion was Mr. Gladstone, whose reply to Mr. Chaplin was not more crushing and complete than he deserved. Party buffers have some use, I suppose, even in the House of Commons, and sooner or later, they will be rewarded with office, if possible. In the afternoon Mrs. Bickford and I went to the British Museum, and were well repaid for our trouble. A palace of wonders is the Museum. The exhumations of the ancient world are God's own revelation cut in stone, and shaped in statuary. What did Chaldæa think of God? The winged-headed ' Bull ' is the reply! Intelligence, strength, and ubiquity here embodied exhibit the old nation's idea.

The Ministers' Monthly Meeting in London is among the greatest treats an Australasian can desire. About eighty to a hundred are generally present, with the President, or an ex-President, in the chair.

The conversations on the condition of the Circuits are free and out-spoken. At the last of these meetings I attended there were collateral subjects, which engaged much of the time of the brethren. (1) The forthcoming City Road Church Anniversary, when an effort was to be made to pay off £2,000 of debt. What an ever-absorbing subject of interest and affection is this 'mother church' of Methodism to all Wesley's true sons in the Gospel! (2) The Rev. J. Smith Spencer's Circular, *re* the forming of a 'Young Men's Improvement Associa-tion,' of an aggregate character for the whole of Methodist London. It was a noble idea, and received much sympathy. (3) On the practical difficulties of class-meeting membership. The question was delicately touched, but the meeting itself was very fine; and I could not but think how great were the privileges and ad-vantages of the younger ministers, thus to be associated with the Methodist fathers in these monthly gatherings for conference and prayer.

Feb. 26th.—I received a polite note from Mr. J. R. Langley, of the Westminster Training College, inviting me that evening to a meeting of the Royal Geographical Society to be holden in the London University. Mr. Langley was on the look-out for the Rev. James Buller and myself. He got for us seats directly in front of the *dais.*

Sir Rutherford Alcock presided. The first paper was by B. D. Young, Esq., R.N., on the Lake Nyassa, which he found to be an inland sea four hundred miles long, and having close in shore, on the eastern side, a depth of water beyond soundings. The details were of the most exciting character. The second paper was by the Rev. Mr. Price, of the London Missionary Society, who had traced a new route from the coast right across two hundred miles to Ujiji, on a high plateau, free from all malaria. Sir Bartle Frere, Dr. Cotterill, Bishop of Edinburgh, Sir Samuel Baker, and other distinguished men, took part in the discussion. And the venerable Dr. Moffat was there also; whose tall, fine form, long, flowing white hair, and striking features, were a beautiful picture. The evening was well spent.

As I was now fairly launched in an attempt to prepare an account of 'Christian Work in Australia,' I wrote a short note to the Right Reverend Charles Perry, D.D., late Bishop of Melbourne, soliciting the favour of any information he had relating to the rise and present

22

condition of the Anglican Church in Victoria. I transcribe his reply :—

'38, AVENUE ROAD, REGENT'S PARK, N.W.,
' *February 28th*, 1877.

' MY DEAR MR. BICKFORD,—

' I am just now so much engaged, that I have not time to put on paper the particulars you ask for, and I fear that I shall find it difficult to search them all out; but I will, please God, endeavour to do so in a few days.

' If you should be coming this way, I should be most glad to see you.

' Your brother in Christ,

' CHARLES PERRY, *Bishop.*

' The Rev. James Bickford,
' Haverstock Hill, N.W.'

In about a week after the receipt of this courteous and dignified note, I called upon the venerable Bishop, who, with Mrs. Perry, did their utmost to supply me with the information I was wanting.

March 18*th*.—For the first time since my arrival in England, I mustered sufficient courage to read the Liturgy used in our beautiful church at Highbury. I got through without difficulty; prayed *extempore*, and preached with much liberty. Speaking of the liturgy, as used in many of our London churches, reminds me of an amusing colloquy which took place about twenty years ago at City Road, during an ordinary morning service. A Mr. and Mrs. W. and family, from the Brighton Circuit, Victoria, were visiting England; and, as in duty bound, they made their first appearance in Methodism's mother church. Sitting close to the side of the matronly mother was her firstborn son, J., who soon became much disconcerted by the kind of service which was going on. The fact is, that a lay functionary was ' reading prayers,' and J. could not understand how that was. Said he, in a quiet undertone, ' Mother, is this church or chapel ? ' ' Hush, my boy, be quiet ; we shall have chapel presently, I suppose.' J. submitted, but not with a good grace. Appealing to his mother a second time, he blubbered out, ' Mother, it is neither church nor chapel ; let us go.' Poor disconcerted youth, he had never before had his prayers done for him, and he would not have it then ! But, it may be believed, that hundreds of good people from our churches in Australia, since then, have had similar experiences through the compulsory endurance of a long, dreary, liturgical service in our London churches. Australian Methodists like short, sharp, decisive services ; and ' do prayers' for themselves.

I took advantage of a leisure evening to attend the Rev. Edward White's service at Kentish Town. The Rev. F. W. Cox, of Adelaide, Mr. White's brother-in-law, had given me a letter of introduction to him. The service was to me one of great·interest. Notwithstanding its length and mental strain, Mr. White himself sang most heartily. 'Let us sing,' said he, 'as if we meant it. Don't let us be sleeping over it.' And they did sing. The congregation was large, and attended earnestly to the preacher's argumentative and telling sermon. I do not suppose there was present one of the so-called ' upper ten thousand ' in the congregation ; but there was something better in the marked facial form, the intellectual expression, and the subdued earnestness of the people. They were, I understood, mostly Scotch mechanics, which accounted for the intellectuality and judicial pose of the audience. To keep such a cause together requires an able minister ; and, in my judgment, Mr. White is the very man.

March 21st.—I left London this morning, *en route* for deputation work in Cornwall. The next day I went to see the *Airlie,* an emigrant ship, lying inside the Breakwater, Plymouth. I was pleased to be associated with Mr. S. Deering, the acting Agent General since the lamented death of Mr. Dutton, in examining the arrangements for the comfort of the emigrants. I cannot speak too much in praise of Mr. Deering's carefulness in regard to this matter. He assured me that the ship should not go to sea until he was satisfied that everything possible was done for the safety and well-being of the 463 souls on board. I held two religious services, of a somewhat informal kind, because of the confusion arising from getting the ship ready for sea.

I tarried by the way for services at Aveton-Gifford and Modbury. It greatly gratified me to be holding services in both places, among my own kin and the few surviving friends of my young manhood. On the 30th I reached St. Ives, and preached the next day (Good Friday) to a true Cornish congregation. My co-delegates were the Rev. William Hirst, London, and the Rev. James Hartwell, formerly a West Indian Missionary. We took the usual round of Circuits, viz., St. Ives, Marazion, Penzance, St. Just, Camborne, St. Keverne, Helstone, Hayle, and Redruth. At each place we were received with genuine hospitality, had large sympathetic congregations, and princely contributions. The spirit of Wesley still lives in Cornwall.*

April 25th.—I was in the cathedral city of Exeter preaching Missionary sermons. The Rev. James H. Cummings was my colleague in the North Devon campaign. We held meetings, in succession, at Torquay; Exeter, Bridport, Taunton, Bridgewater, Barnstaple, and Bideford.

At Torquay a pleasant surprise came upon the meeting in a spontaneous gift of £25 from a gentleman who was present. Mr. Cummings and I had spoken, when, on resuming my seat, an open letter was handed to me.

'TORQUAY, *April 16th*, 1877.

'SIR,—

'The enclosed five £5 notes (£25) are intended for the benefit of the Wesleyan Missionary Society. To ensure their coming safe to hand, will you kindly acknowledge the receipt of them at the meeting to-night.

'Yours, etc.,

'ANONYMOUS.

'To the Chairman of the Meeting.'

No one knew, as far as I could learn, who this generous donor was.

We were received everywhere with much affection. I got back to London on the 26th of the month, having been absent thirty-six days. I was much fatigued, and wanted rest.

April 28th.—Mrs. Bickford, Messrs. Butters and Buller, and I, went to the Missionary Breakfast Meeting. Good speaking enough, but utterly void of such Missionary facts as an English Wesleyan audience desires to hear. And it seemed to me a strange oversight

---

* The thrift and love of the Cornish Methodists for the Mission cause were shown at one of the meetings by the following list of contributions, which was read out by the local secretary : 'Butter box, £1 10s. 9d.; sale of flowers, £1 5s.; a happy working man, £1 5s. 11d.; a young man who believes in Providence, £1 10s.; the Master's money, £1; for prosperity in business, £1 5s.: two tiresome boys, £1 1s.; three old-fashioned Methodists, £4 10s.; smoke money, £2 17s.; lady's dress-ring, £1 5s.; fruits of temperance, £1 10s. 6d.; a clergyman of the Church of England, £5; the gleaners, £3 10s.; conscience money, £2 8s. 9d.: in memory of our precious boys, George and Freddy in Heaven. £1 1s.; the offering of an artizan, £1; lambs' wool, £3 11s.; pig, bee-hive, and chickens, £2; fragments, £2 1s. 7d.; hair-cutting, £1 12s. 6d.; produce of peach-tree, £1.' Now these are examples which might be imitated with advantage by those friends whose pecuniary means are somewhat limited.

that Mr. Buller, who had spent forty years in the Maori and English work in New Zealand, was not included in the list of speakers. He could have told that audience, as I am sure no other man in England could, of the subjugation and uplifting of the Maori race, through the preaching of the Gospel by the Wesleyan Missionaries, into the light and peace of Jesus Christ. But the opportunity was unfortunately missed; and, in that respect, the meeting was a decided failure.

Tarrying in Plymouth a few days, I had the rare pleasure of hearing the renowned Peter McKenzie in King Street Church. It was in the afternoon, and the sermon was based upon Isaiah's 'feast of fat things.' I must say that in my judgment he did singular, characteristic, and ample justice to his subject. In the evening, in the same place, he lectured on 'Queen Esther,' and the lessons her history teaches. No one who has seen the Rev. Peter on the platform will ever forget either his physique or his antics; but, as to his mental portrait, who can successfully sketch it? Well, he is a natural mimic, full of enthusiasm, impulsive, eloquent. He wants the culture a great platform speaker should possess; still he has his *forte*, overflowing with pointed wit and sarcasm, with unmatched originality and dash. In bearing and style, he is, I suppose, one of the most popular lecturers in England. There is not his like in the English Conference; perhaps, one only of his kind is enough. Shaking hands with me in the vestry, he exclaimed, 'I consider this the greatest honour. I now see a real live ex-President of the Australasian Conference.' In making his salaam, he bowed nearly to the floor, and then he stood erect and spake like a man. 'Could I get to Australia for a hundred pounds?' he inquired. 'Yes,' I replied, 'and for less than that. We could frank you through from colony to colony, and put you in the way to get all that it would cost you for the whole round. The Australian Methodist people would like to see you, Mr. McKenzie, out there.' 'Oh, would they? then we will see!' Mr. McKenzie is one of the Lord's 'chosen vessels to bear His Name before the people,' and one of nature's noblest sons.

April 28th.—This is emphatically the Missionary season. The Rev. William Butters and I were on the 29th at Barnet preaching on behalf of our Foreign Missions. We were the guests of Mr. and Mrs. T. G. Waterhouse. What a beautiful place this good man has secured, to say nothing of his great wealth, as the result of his commercial industry in the city of Adelaide! Nothing like the Colonies for honest and persevering men 'climbing up the hill.'

April 30th.—The dream of my life—the May Missionary Meeting. Mrs. Bickford, Mrs. Sillifant, and I went. S. D. Waddy, Q.C., presided with ability. It was a grand meeting, and was not over until 4 p.m. Income £146,231 2s. 1d. A princely contribution for the conversion of the heathen!

May 1st.—Mrs. Bickford and I went this morning to pay our respects to the Hon. A. Blyth, the newly appointed Agent General for South Australia. He was very polite, and promised to help me in my efforts to send out suitable emigrants to the Colony.

May 5th.—Once more on the wing. This time Portsmouth for Sabbath services, and an address on Australian Methodism. My kind friends, Mr. and Mrs. Watkins, took me on Monday morning to see the dockyard. The *Minotaur* and the *Inflexible* are marvels of mechanical skill and strength. The war-spirit seemed to dominate this great establishment. The town itself was full of rollicking sailors and soldiers. I would be very sorry to be compelled to reside at Portsmouth.

' *May 6th.* [Diary Jotting]—This day I am sixty-one years of age. What a wonderful year this has been to me and my wife! Here we are in England once more. This morning (at Portsmouth), I re-consecrated myself—' body, soul, and spirit '—to the service of my God and Saviour. May the Lord help me to be diligent and useful to my country-people this year!'

May 9th.—Emigration business this morning. In the afternoon, I went to the London University, and saw the most knightly man in England, Lord Granville, hand the prizes to the successful graduates. 'Robert Lowe,' and Mr. Childers, were also present. It was a beautiful sight.

May 11th.—I went to Slough, and was met at the station by my old West India friend, the Rev. William Limmex, after a separation of some twenty-five years. We soon felt as if we had not been away from each other at all. How wonderful is this bridging over great distances, by the two-fold action of the mind—obliviousness of long absences, and a consciousness of renewed unity! Who can fathom the depth of this mental philosophic action! In the evening we took a walk to Turner's gardens, where I saw some of the finest groupings of floral beauty my eyes had ever beheld.

May 12th.—Mr. Limmex and I went to see Windsor Castle. The gratification I felt no tongue can tell. From the 'Round Tower' we saw the Queen, the Marchioness of Lorne, and Princess Beatrice. At the station, in the evening, we saw the Duchess of Edinburgh— a very fine woman. I returned to London, and found a cheque awaiting me, 'as a gratuity for services rendered in lecturing, distributing "Forms of Application," travelling to and from Plymouth, etc.,' which I was well entitled to, as the slenderest acknowledgment for services I had rendered to South Australia since my arrival in England.

May 15th.—I went to the 'Second London District Meeting,' and remained all day with Messrs. Butters and Buller. In the Financial District Meeting, the question of lay representation was again discussed. Dr. Rigg presided, as if 'to the manner born.' On the 22nd, at the request of the Rev. John Kilner, I went into Yorkshire in the interests of the Foreign Missions. The Rev. R. N. Young was my colleague in this work; we visited in turn Driffield, Bridlington, Howden, and Hornsea. At the Hull Meeting we had eleven ministers on the platform, and as many laymen. On the 29th, the Rev. David Barley accompanied me to the Pier Head, when I took the steamer for crossing the Humber. I went by train to Great Coates, and proceeded from thence to Mr. Sowerby's, where I was kindly received. I preached in the afternoon, and addressed an enthusiastic meeting in the evening. We raised £30 by the services. At Grimsby, I learnt of the lamented death of the Rev. G. T. Perks, M.A., which took place at Rotherham very unexpectedly. My soul is sore distressed for the loss of my true friend.

June 3rd.—I preached at Bromley and Widmore. I was the guest of Mr. Radman, whose intelligent intercourse I much enjoyed. At Widmore, inside and above the front door upon the wall, are printed in red letters, the words : ' Onward '—' Upward '—' Heavenward'—' Homeward.' Yes, quite true—' The holy to the holiest leads.' What a curious pedigree this little sanctuary has ! It was erected in 1776, in a garden abutting on a narrow private lane, and here Mr. Wesley often preached. When 'Adam Clarke ' was stationed in the City Road Circuit, in 1813, he used to walk from thence to Widmore, a distance of twelve miles, to his appointments on week evenings. His afternoons he spent among the Methodist families, would preach to his rustic congregation in the evening, refresh himself at a friend's house with a cup of milk, and then, staff in hand, trudge back to London. Thus this learned itinerant did his country work; and by such men, and by such means, was village Methodism established throughout England.

The 'Order of St. Michael and St. George.' Under date, May 31st, 1877, Her Majesty was pleased to honour with distinguished notice several of her faithful servants 'at home and abroad;' and among the number was included the Hon. Arthur Blyth. The list appeared in a 'Supplement to the *London Gazette,*' and reached me in due course. Alas, for my inconsiderateness! I had occasion to write our worthy Agent General about a Mrs. Scotcher, a kind, Christian woman, of South Australia, for her to have a confidential position in the next emigrant ship for Adelaide, when I omitted to recognise the new address of my friend. This 'fault' brought me, by next post, the following letter :—

> '8, VICTORIA CHAMBERS, WESTMINSTER,
> 'LONDON, S.W., *June 5th*, 1877.

'REVEREND AND DEAR SIR,—

'I have handed a copy of Mr. Harcus' book for transmission to you, and have scolded the clerk for not replying to your letter, which came when I was down at Plymouth. I am sure you will not think that I am unduly "puffed up" when I say that you appear not to have noticed the compliment paid to the colony in my person, as the Queen has made me a K.C.M.G. Hoping soon to see you,

> 'I am, yours very truly,
> 'ARTHUR BLYTH.

'P.S.—Mrs. Scotcher goes as matron of the *Forfarshire.*'

I liked this note. I was justly blamable on the oversight pointed out by Sir Arthur. I apologised; and there, of course, the matter ended.

One source of pleasure I had, whilst in London, was to see Missionary brethren from the West Indies. Amongst this number was the Rev. John A. Campbell, from Demerara, the son of a Mr. and Mrs. John Campbell, respected Creoles, who formerly were the head master and mistress of our day school in St. George's, Grenada. When I had charge of the Grenada Mission in 1846-7-8, young Campbell was one of his father's pupils; but, on receiving the 'grace of conversion' during his early manhood, he gave himself to self-culture, and ultimately entered our Ministry. Being a native of the West Indies, he naturally wished to see the Mother Country, and to become acquainted with the General Secretaries in London and with English Methodism. He came frequently to Maitland Park to see us. At the Bristol Conference, at the request of the Rev. John Kilner, he attended the ' Recognition of Missionaries' Meeting ' at Bath, and spoke with effect. On the 11th I went to the ' Wickliffe Commemoration ' Meeting at Exeter Hall ; the Bishop of Meath presiding. The three principal speakers were Canon Farrar, Joseph Angus, D.D., and Mr. Mursell, from Birmingham. It was a very fine meeting.

June 19th.—Good news this morning. In the House of Lords last night, the Earl of Harrowby's amendment,—*re* ' The Burials Bill '—giving the right to Nonconformists to bury their dead in the parish cemeteries, was carried by a majority of sixteen. One more of the laws of barbarous exclusiveness enacted by Tory Churchmen is swept by that vote from our Statute Book ; and there are more to follow.

One of the most pleasant visits of this month was to Shooter's Hill, Kent, for a Sabbath's services. I was the guest of the Whelmptons. Here I met Miss Corduroy and sisters, whose parents I well knew at Williamstown, Victoria, many years ago. At Plumstead Common, I met with Sergeant Hurforth and his wife, whom I had known in Melbourne. There were some others who used to worship with us in Wesley Church in that city. I went with Mrs. Whelmpton to her class, and met it for her. Master George Whelmpton, now the Rev. George Whelmpton, M.A., our minister-in-charge at Hâvre, France, took me round to see Mrs. G. P. Harris, relict of Mr. Harris, an Adelaide merchant, and member of our Kent Town Church. The interview was very pleasant.

June 21st.—Mrs. Bickford and I went by invitation to the Haverstock' Hill Orphan Institute. Samuel Morley, M.P., presided. There were 400 fine, healthy boys in the gallery. The drill and bathing were splendidly done. The anniversary was a success.

July 17th.—The Rev. H. H. Teague called with a certificate from his doctor, to the effect that he was fit to return to his Circuit work in South Australia. The same day, I received a letter from John Watts, of , Outwell, near Manchester, expressive of his readiness to go to South Australia. I had not seen this young man, but as his testimonials were satisfactory, I requested him to be ready by the 28th current.

July 24th.—I left London for the Bristol Conference. Mr. G. B.

Dare, formerly of Kingsbridge, was at the station to receive me as his guest.

In the evening we went to hear the Fernley Lecture on ' Atheism : its Promises and Prospects,' by the Rev. E. E. Jenkins, M.A., which he handled with great skill.   As I listened to his glowing words, I felt more than thankful that we had in our ranks a man who could deal with the materialistic philosophy of the age in so acute, masterly, and comprehensive a manner as he did.   Of course, his experience gained in India, where we have the oldest recorded thought in the world, outside the Scriptures, was a great help to him in the preparation of his great essay.   The next day, the 25th, Mr. Buller and I, as Australian ex-Presidents, took our seats on the platform.   The Rev. William Burt Pope, D.D., was elected President, and the Rev. Dr. Williams, Secretary.   After some preliminaries, the business was entered on with much spirit and dispatch.

This Conference was remarkable for its having to deal with some new-fangled notions which had got into the heads of certain young brethren.   Strange to say, these notions struck at, (1) The Divine Inspiration of the Scriptures ; (2) The Atonement of Christ in the sense of satisfaction to Divine justice ; and (3) Torture and Eternal Punishment.   Dr. Osborn, as might be expected, came out in his strength.   He spoke twice, pretty much as follows: holding up in his right hand a copy of our new Hymn Book, he maintained that the man who could not, *ex animo*, say

> ' I must be born again.
> Or die to all eternity,'

could not occupy a Methodist pulpit.   The time had come for the Conference to put down its foot, and be as firm as eternal rock to the truths of which they had been the inheritors.'   The great Doctor is the veriest champion of orthodoxy.   He spoke with wonderful force and solemnity.   'I shall not be much longer among you,' he impassionably exclaimed, ' but my protest shall be among you ; we must have no " open " questions as touching the testimony we have received.'   The President (Dr. Pope) followed.   The brethren, by scores, rose to their feet and bent forward, so as not to lose a word. He maintained ' that, upon the disputed points, the Methodist theology was in agreement with the Word of God.   He asserted his belief that when the nebulous clouds, which had gathered around the faith of some divines of other denominations, had cleared away, the full orb of truth would be seen shining out with peculiar clearness and beauty more than ever.' Dr. Punshon said, 'that they wanted a good book upon the subject,' strangely forgetting that the Rev. Marshall Randels had prepared such a work, entitled, 'For Ever.' Dr. Osborn then recommended to the young ministers a work by the Rev. Matthew Horbery, B.D., written and published in 1744, in which, said he, 'the whole question was dealt with.' Two ministers were lost in this theological fog, and thus the Methodist Brotherhood was, to that extent, purged.

The open Conference was largely attended. The Rev. William Tobias spoke for Ireland; the Rev. William Cornforth for France; Dr. Lowry for America; and the Rev. William Kelynack for Australia. Racy, sedate, earnest, and beautiful were the speeches. The Ordination Service was conducted by Dr. Pope with matchless dignity; the ex-President's (Rev. A. McAulay) charge was extemporaneous, and full of earnest evangelism. The number of probationers who were ordained was seventy-one. Dr. Jobson offered the concluding prayer. It was fervent, pleading, and comprehensive, and the whole congregation seemed bowed down by the power of God. If the young men did not get a baptism of the Holy Ghost to qualify and commission them for their work of saving souls, then it would be difficult to say how it was to be obtained.

Aug. 10*th.*—The Conference closed to-day; and I had to leave my kind friends, Mr. and Mrs. Dare, for Malvern, where I was to preach on the Sabbath. Mrs. J. B. Goulding, a former Ballarat friend, was to be my hostess. What a romantic spot is this!

I have fallen in with an eccentric epitaph, first written in Tobago, in 1820, by the missionary Smedley, on the death of his wife :—

> 'Where all I once lov'd, or dreamed of worth.
> Now charmless lies, a mould'ring heap of earth.'

Does relentless death do all that to those we have loved as our own soul? Echo asks, Is it so?

Aug. 18*th.*—At last I am able to fulfil my promise to Mr. Alderman Rees, J.P., of Dover, to spend a Sabbath with him. The Alderman met me at the station, and conducted me to his home. Mrs. Rees had died a few months before in the true faith of Christ. We spent an interesting evening together.

On the Sunday I preached twice, and was pleased with the congregations. On the Monday we visited the Pier Head and about the town. I wrote Mr. Rowland Rees, M.P., and Chief Justice Way, from this charming home.

Sept. 8th.—Important routine work has employed the whole of my time for the last three weeks. But at this date I went a second time to Newport (I.W.), to preach Sunday School sermons. I was the welcome guest of Mr. and Mrs. Dore, whose establishment is regulated by high Christian principle. The assistants, male and female, are treated as if belonging to the family.

Sept. 15th.—I was at Redhill, and was the guest of Mr. Ives, senior, and Miss Ives, one of my most respected friends in St. Kilda and Geelong, some years ago. I preached twice on the Sabbath, and, at the earnest request of Mr. James Duncan, addressed the Sunday School in the afternoon.

On my return to London on the 17th, I attended a meeting of ex-Presidents on Australian affairs.

Sept. 18th.—I attended the Financial District Meeting; Dr. Rigg in the chair. The whole of the business was done in four and a half hours.

Sept. 19th.—I ran out to Redhill, to lecture in aid of the Poor Coals Club; Mr. Hadley in the chair. We had a sympathising audience, and raised £4 15s.

Sept. 22nd.—I left for Cross Hills, near Leeds, to help the Rev. J. S. Fordham in his Foreign Missionary Meetings. I was the guest of Mr. George Parkinson, Rycroft House, who, with Miss Parkinson, showed me no little kindness. We held meetings at Cross Hills, Silsden, Icomschock, and Conalty. I went into Bradford with Mr. Parkinson, to see the Misses Pickles and Townend, kind friends with whom I stayed at the Conference of 1853. I called on the Rev. John and Mrs. Hartley, whose acquaintance I had made at the Nottingham Conference the previous year. Mr. Hartley after we had dined, took me to see the town. The improvement in the last twenty-two years was truly surprising. I called also upon Mrs. (widow) Marsden and Miss Marsden, known to me through the Rev. John and Mrs. Wood, formerly in the West Indies. I had a great treat also in going over a large manufactory, accompanied by my friend, Mr. Fordham. The whole process of wool-combing, spinning, and weaving was explained to us. Several bales of wool were labelled ' Botany Bay.' I asked an explanation, when I was informed that the label simply meant Australian wool. I protested against the false custom, and informed my guide that Botany Bay was simply an inlet of the sea on the east of Australia, into which Captain Cook ran, and anchored his fleet, in 1770 ; but that the whole district was so barren that it would hardly feed rabbits, much less flocks of sheep. I asked that the misleading label should be discontinued.

Oct. 2nd.—I make grateful mention of Lord Carnarvon, whose ready kindness was extended to me in the matter of my having free access at Downing Street to official documents, for obtaining information anent Australasian affairs. I was ushered into a big room, in which were piles of ' blue-books ' and ' despatches ' of various kinds. A gentleman was in attendance to help me in securing the information I required. This is the courtesy that Austral-Englishmen like when visiting great London officials. And it pays ! I called also on Sir Arthur Blyth, on emigration business. The open-minded Agent General and I soon got into an earnest conversation, *re* the ecclesiasticism and religious opinions so rife in certain quarters, and which had occasioned much anxious thought to even Lord Penzance, in the Court of Arches. Arthur Tooth's eccentric tactics were then to the front. To me his whole behaviour, as a minister of the Protestant Reformed Church of England, was so recreant to the principles upon which the Reformation was based, as to merit the highest censure and condemnation. He posed as a martyr ; but the ' stuff ' of which martyrs were made was not in the Rev. Arthur Tooth. Besides, his prison door had its bolt on the inside.

Oct. 14th.—I preached at Romford twice, and addressed the Sunday School. My good host and hostess were Mr. and Mrs. Davey, Market Square. I hastened to London on the Monday morning, that I might be present at the Ministers' Monthly Meeting. Dr. Jobson presided. After the meeting Mr. Butters spent three hours with me in examining my account of Victoria and South Australia. His suggestions were invaluable to me.

Oct. 21st.—I preached at Chelmsford in aid of our Foreign Missions, and attended meetings at Chelmsford, Braintree, and Maldon. My associates were the Revs. Thomas Chope, R. Winterly Crouch, and John Jones (D). I much enjoyed the visit.

On the 31st I was at Alton for the Foreign Missions. We held

the public meeting in the Town Hall. The Rev. H. H. Teague
spoke admirably, and the Rev. Joseph Payne also addressed the
friends. I supped and slept at Mr. Dyte's. At supper there were
from fifteen to twenty young persons, who were assistants in the
establishment. We all united in prayer at the family altar. I saw
on the wall a picture which attracted my attention. It had six
portraits of eminent men: Mr. Gladstone, Lord Granville, Marquis
of Hartington, Robert Lowe, Mr. Forster, and John Bright. Said
I, to my generous host, 'May I be pardoned if I ask for that picture
to take with me to Australia? I would value it very much; and
the place of honour it shall have in my Australian home, if you will
entrust it to me.' 'Yes,' he replied, 'you are quite welcome to it.'
I did thank him with the warmest expressions I could command.
But there was one drawback to my pleasure in my visit to Alton.
I copy from my Diary:—

'I had a nice walk with the Rev. Joseph Payne. He told me of two
oppressive cases. The first from a lord landowner; the second from the
parish minister. The former refused a bit of land as a site for a Wesleyan
place of worship; and the latter had threatened the withdrawal of pay from
the poor rate, because the recipient was a "Dissenter." I often heard of similar
cases in the agricultural districts.'

Nov. 7th.—Dr. Punshon informed me that the Missionary Committee would send three young ministers to South Australia, on the
condition that I guaranteed repayment of the expense in three
instalments. In behalf of my Conference, I accepted the offer with
thanks.

Nov. 8th.—I read three great political speeches:—Mr. Gladstone's
at Dublin; Lord Hartington's at Glasgow; and Mr. Bright's at
Rochdale;—the English triumvirate; each a trusted tribune of the
people.

Nov. 12th.—I preached at Tunbridge Wells for the Missions. The
rain spoiled our congregations. The next day, the Rev. Joseph
Hargreaves dined with us at the Learoyd's, with whom and Mrs.
Learoyd we were much pleased. There were four teetotal ministers
present at the Missionary Meeting—Messrs. Hargreaves, Smith,
B. Brown, and myself. I was much delighted with my visit to this
beautiful spot.

Nov. 17th.—I left for Woolwich. The Rev. Richard Hardy
accompanied me to Mrs. Harris's, Shooter's Hill. I preached twice

the next day, and left for London on the Monday. Mrs. and Miss Harris went with me in their carriage to Blackheath Station. We had a nice conversation by the way.

Nov. 20th.—I preached at City Road, and held the Leaders' Meeting. The Rev. John Baker, M.A., the Superintendent, has not allowed this important institution to become obsolete in this the mother establishment of English Methodism.

Nov. 26th.—I went to Horncastle to advocate our Missions. The Rev. Thomas Baine and young Mr. Roberts were at the station awaiting my arrival. I had to preach in the afternoon, and address the public meeting in the evening. There were also the Revs. Jabez Marrott, William Henderson, R. W. Little, and Samuel Joll. Mr. Marrott gave an excellent speech on our West India Missions, and I kept to Australia and the South Seas. I was the guest of Mr. R. Roberts, whose family pleased me very much. I called to see Mrs. Watson,—'a widow indeed'—the sister of the Rev. Thomas Williams, of Ballarat, Victoria.

Dec. 23rd.—In the early part of this month I was under the medical treatment of Dr. Smith, and was confined to the house. My last preaching services for the year were at Greenwich, where I was the guest of Mrs. Archer, formerly of Adelaide. I held two services and a lovefeast. It was a profitable day. This was my last public work for 1877.

1878.

Jan. 1st.—I copy from my Diary :—

'Through the mercy of God I enter upon the duties and responsibilities of another year. Here, in the quietude of our own home, my dear wife and I kept our "Watch Night," and together implored the descending blessings of God upon us and our kindred. Oh, that the new year may be a time of visitation to them as well as to us!'

My literary exercises began with a careful reading of the *London Quarterly* on this very day. The first article is very able, but I was more than interested with the review of the Rev. W. Arthur's book, 'The Pope, the King, and the People.' The author has a marvellous grip of the subject in all its phases. It is a work over which high ecclesiastics and leading European statesmen would do well to ponder. On the 2nd I read in Earl Russell's 'Recollections,' with much avidity and satisfaction. Eminent statesmen, like eminent poets, are not made, but born.

Jan. 21st.—The Rev. Thomas Bird, a probationer in one of our Scottish Circuits, having replied to my advertisement for a young minister of two or three years' standing for Western Australia, expressive of his willingness to go, I informed Dr. Punshon, who, in reply, was pleased to say that Mr. Bird was the sort of man for the place! But the transfer was not to be obtained as easily as might have been expected.

Jan. 31st.—The war spirit is in the ascendant. Disraeli seems determined to plunge the country into a murderous conflict with Russia over the Turkish embroilment. But many Christian Englishmen are resolved that this shall not be. Circulars were therefore sent to certain influential men 'in Church and State' to attend a meeting at the Memorial Hall, Farringdon Street, to oppose the war vote of £6,000,000, proposed by the Government. The Rev. James Buller and I attended. We both felt that, although we were very Australian in our sympathies, we had not lost our early love and jealousy for the honour of the country of our birth. Hence our earnest opposition to the vote. The Rev. Guinness Rogers struck the key-note in earnest and burning terms; the Rev. Newman Hall followed in a calm, strong speech. With bated breath and solemn pause at the close, he said: 'If England goes into this war, then I for one will not be able on my knees to ask my Father, God, to give success to the British arms.' It was a ponderous utterance, and fell like a thunderclap on the audience. We afterwards went to the Cannon Street Hotel to attend a similar meeting. But the 'Jingoes' came full-primed for a row, and in the end prevented the meeting being held. The scent in their nostrils for blood and plunder was very dreadful.

Feb. 7th.—I went to hear Dr. Parker preach, and to attend an after-meeting on Mission work in London. His text was: 'He shall go free for his tooth's sake.' There were three leading thoughts: (1) God cares for everything He has made; (2) The Old Testament treats mostly of Divine providence in its care for the body; (3) The New Testament shows God's great love for the soul. Injury to others, sooner or later, brings the penalty of Divine chastisement. At one point in the discourse I certainly expected the preacher to put in a plea for the Christian Principalities of Turkey, but he lost the opportunity. At the after-meeting the Earl of Shaftesbury presided. The best speakers, I thought, were 'Edward White' and 'Joseph Parker.'

Feb. 15th.—In the House of Commons this evening Mr. Morgan's resolution for throwing open the National Cemeteries (*alias* 'Church-yards') to the people for the interment of their dead, without interference from rectors, vicars, *et hoc genus omne*, was lost by a majority—For, 227; against, 240. I wrote a strong letter to the *Daily News* on the 'Burial Question,' in the interests of religious equality and the rights of British citizenship.

Feb. 19th.—I heard Dr. Punshon lecture at Hampstead on 'Daniel in Babylon.' For fervid eloquence, solidity of thought, and aptness of illustration—grand principles upon which to build the character and virtue of statesmen, of social reformers, and Christian men generally—I never heard its like before. Its elocution was faultless, the language simply beautiful, the humour natural and smart, and the occasional hits equal, if not superior, to any I have heard from Dr. Parker, or Mr. Spurgeon. I returned to Haverstock Hill well pleased.

Feb. 20th.—I ran over to-day to the Great Northern Hotel to inquire for Mr. T. G. Waterhouse, and found him rapidly improving. The doctors were right, when they remarked upon his bruised and battered appearance after the terrible accident: 'There is some chance for him because he is a teetotaler; we may be able to pull him through.'

Feb. 23rd.—I went to the Centenary Hall to see the young ministers, Messrs. Teague, Bird, Moreland, and Ince, who are about to sail for Australia. Mr. Samuel Adams and I went to the ship to see that everything was comfortably arranged for them. I afterwards left for Woolston to preach in behalf of the Church Trusts the following day. I was the guest of Mr. and Mrs. Louney, at the Laurels, whose kindness it will be impossible for me to forget.

On the 25th I lectured on 'Christian Work in Australasia,' the Rev. Mr. Poultier presided. The Rev. George and Mrs. Ranyell were much gratified to see me again at Woolston.

The 'Colonial Marriages Bill' was read a second time last night in the House of Commons. There were for the Bill, 182; against, 161. It was of course opposed by the Tory Government, as is every other measure proposed by the Liberals in favour of the non-franchised and nonconforming portion of the British people.*

March 19th.—I went to the ' Royal Colonial Institute,' and heard an able paper read by Sir Julius Vogel, an ex-Premier of New Zealand, on the present condition and resources of that wonderful Colony.   The Duke of Manchester presided.   The Hon. Mr. Casey, from Melbourne, spoke sharply in defence of Victoria, which had been unfavourably alluded to by Sir Julius.   How is it that public men are unable to learn that ' comparisons are odious '?

March 20th.—I had the great gratification once more to see the Rev. Henry Hurd, who after forty years of good work in the West Indies, had ' returned home.'   It was about twenty-six years ago since we last saw each other at the St. Vincent's District Meeting.   The Rev. William Dawson, whose health had been seriously impaired by the malaria fever of Trinidad, came with him to see me.

March 25th.—The Melbourne *Spectator* and *Argus* came to hand to-day.   The Conference had been successfully held, and Dr Gervase Smith was continuing to win golden opinions.   He will render great service to our Australasian Church.

April 3rd.—I went to Exeter Hall to attend the Wesleyan Education Meeting ; William E. Forster, who spoke with great ability, in the chair.   Dr. Rigg, F. W. Macdonald, and W. O. Simpson followed.   It was a splendid demonstration in favour of Wesleyan Day Schools.

April 5th.—This evening I heard the Rev. Dr. Dykes preach the opening sermon of the new Oxenden Presbyterian Church, Haverstock Hill.   He took his text from Hebrews xiii. 7.   He had two heads: (1) The advantages of piously remembering the pious dead ; (2) The dangers connected therewith.   He insisted that our only safeguard was the presence in the Church of the ever-living Christ, and a strong spiritual life in each follower of Christ from day to day.   It was a

---

* We take another example.   Last month in the House of Commons, Mr. Meldon called attention to the restricted nature of the Borough Franchise in Ireland, as compared with that existing in England and Scotland, as a subject deserving the immediate attention of Parliament, with a view of establishing a fair and just equality of the franchise of the three kingdoms.   The case is as follows : Borough Franchise in England, £4 ; Ireland, £6 : County Franchise, English and Scottish, £12 ; Ireland, £16.   Mr. Meldon's motion was rejected by 8 votes—For, 126 ; against, 134.   What shameful injustice is this !

beautiful exposition of a subject not often heard in our pulpits. I had a nice interview with him at the close of the service.

April 10*th.*—I attended the meeting of the Missionary Committee. We had before us important documents from South Africa upon the Scriptural right of the Colonial Churches to govern themselves. After a long and earnest discussion a committee was appointed to prepare a reply.

April 13*th.*—I left for Ripon for missionary services. Attended meetings at Galphay, Ripon, Rainton, and Markington. The Snows, Aslin, and other friends, showed me much kindness.

On the 17th I went over to Harrogate to see Mrs. Vasey, relict of the late Rev. Thomas Vasey. Miss Vasey took me to the springs ; I drank, and was refreshed. Mrs. Vasey was bed-ridden, but patient and happy.

April 25*th.*—The Missionary season has come. I attended at the great room, Centenary Hall, to hear the Reverend President, W. B. Pope, D.D., preach the first of the sermons on behalf of the Society. Text : Rev. i. 9 ; of course, the sermon was read. (But why of course ?) It was a great service taken altogether ; but its effectiveness was marred by the too close use of the paper.

April 26*th.*—I heard the Rev. Dr. Thompson, of Edinburgh, preach the official sermon at Great Queen Street. Dr. Punshon read prayers, and this eminent preacher followed with an able discourse. This also was read. I wonder how it is that when so many ministers of the Gospel become ' D.D.'s,' they appear to lose the gift of *extempore* speech. Better do without the ' D.D.' than sink to the level of mere ' readers,' instead of being preachers of sermons ' with the Holy Ghost sent down from heaven.'

April 27*th.*—China Breakfast Meeting. Said I to the Rev. J. K., ' Why don't you go on to the platform, and take your rightful place among the great officials and " M.P's " up there ?' He replied, ' I don't belong to the Brahmins ; I am of a lower caste, and am content with my position.' ' Indeed !' I rejoined. Perhaps this interjection would be more forcible, as showing the absurdity of the situation, than any words I could employ.

April 29*th.*—Off to Exeter Hall, Mesdames Hurd, Rodwell, Sillifant, and Bickford accompanying me. ' It has been a capital meeting,' said Mr. S. D. Waddy, Q.C., the popular chairman. But a greater treat was in reserve for the evening at City Road, when

the annual missionary lovefeast was to be held.   The grand old
sanctuary was full of godly Methodists, and the influence was sanc-
tifying.   I had the high honour of conducting this blessed service.
The Revs. Buller (New Zealand), Greenwood (Victoria), Hartwell
(West Indies), and Dr. Lowry (America), took part, and testified to
the triumphs of the Gospel in their respective fields of labour.   On
the 30th, I attended the annual meeting of the ' Church Missionary
Society' at Exeter Hall.   We had a nobleman in the chair, and
several bishops on the platform.   But the cynosure of all eyes was
the black Bishop Crowther, from Western Africa.   His was a fine
story, and he told it well.   The evangelical element was strong and
outspoken.

May 6th. [Diary Jotting]—'I am this day sixty-two years of age.   This
morning I renewed my consecration to God.   May the good Lord this year
direct and bless me and mine.'

May 8th.—This forenoon I attended the monthly meeting of the
Missionary Committee.   The Revs. T. Hodgson, E. Rigg, H. Hurd,
and J. Richardson were presented to the Committee.   The insurance
of the Mission vessel, the *John Wesley,* was earnestly discussed, in
which, because of my local knowledge, I took part.   We decided to
continue the payment of the English premium.   In the evening, I
went to the annual meeting of the Liberation Society ; Mr. H.
Richard, M.P., in the chair.   Mr. C. Williams, the Secretary, and
Mr. S. D. Waddy spoke very effectively.   An Anglican clergyman
also spoke, and particularly dwelt upon the desirability of the State
Church being entirely separated from the control of the Crown and
the Parliament.   ' Exactly,' said I.   But will the ' Church ' be prepared to pay the penalty of surrendering ' the loaves and fishes' to
secure this freedom ?

May 23rd.—At the request of Mr. Secretary Kilner, I went to
Rotherham to speak at the Missionary Meeting.   Mr. Wigfield
received me at the station, and drove me to his beautiful home.   The
Mayor of Rotherham (a Congregationalist) took the chair at the
the public meeting.   The Rev. Joseph Nettleton and I were the only
speakers.   In this old Yorkshire town there is a generous Missionary
feeling.   It is the custom of the ' elect' sisters to hold a yearly
bazaar at the anniversary meeting.   This year was raised £140.   We
had a spirited conversation at the tea-table.   The Mayor and I

happened not to be in accord upon certain politico-social queries. But as he had sprung from the people, and had gained his present position by his skill and perseverance, I own that I was sorely disappointed with some of the views he expressed. It was soon evident that he and I were not of the same guild.

How inexcusable are the remarks that some otherwise very kind friends sometimes make to strangers, when about to retire for the night! 'It was in this room, and in this very bed,' said my *femme de chambre*, 'that the Rev. Mr. Perks died twelve months ago, when he was here as a Missionary deputation.' ' Really!' I quietly said. It reminded me of a cautionary warning I received some years ago in the island of Tobago, at the house of the hospitable squatter, Mr. Goldsborough, on my way to the Windward for a Sabbath Day's services. Quasheba, with candle in hand, proceeded to conduct me to my room for the night. As she was leaving, she said, ' Don't be afraid, sir, if you hear noises in the night, for this room is full of rats.' Bless me, I thought, I needed not to be told of such nocturnal companions ; I had rather the room were full of spirits than of rats. But what could I do but contrive to fall asleep, and wait for the disclosures the daylight might make? But it so happened that neither my proboscis nor digits had been nibbled off during the night ; so that, after partaking of a delicious cup of coffee, with the usual breakfast of salt fish and yam, I was able to pursue my long and fatiguing journey to the Windward.

May 24th.—To-day Mr. Edward Young met me at the Newark Station, and drove me to his brother's farm at Collingham. The brothers, Edward and John, were formerly on the Ballarat gold-fields, and 'pitched their tent' in the Lydiard Street Church Reserve. They made their pile, returned home, and re-entered upon farming pursuits. At Newark, the next day, I sought out for Mr. and Mrs. Egglestone's kindred. I saw Mr. and Mrs. Harmston, the Oldhams, and the Knights. I dined at Mr. Edward Oldham's, the brother of Messrs. George and John Oldham, in Victoria. I then proceeded to Loughborough, and was kindly received by the Rev. John and Mrs. Thomas. The next day I opened the new Church at Sheepshed, and was the guest of the Robertses, at Hurst's farm. I was very comfortable with my new friends.

June 4th.—A man not much known in Methodist circles is the Rev. Francis J. Sharr, but who will be as the years of his itinerancy roll on. I heard him lecture at King's Cross this evening to a delighted audience. His subject was 'Man.' It was able, finely original, and well delivered.

June 27th.—I was asked this day at the Mission House, by one of the General Secretaries, if I would go out to the West Indies, and take charge of the St. Vincent's District. I felt pleased for such an expression of confidence; but, because of my connection with the Australasian Connexion, I had to decline the great honour proffered to me.

In the evening the Rev. J. C. Richardson and I went to a 'Prohibitory Permissive Bill' Meeting at Exeter Hall; Sir Wilfrid Lawson, M.P., in the chair. Canon Farrar, Cardinal Manning, and Dr. Richardson, were the principal speakers. The large audience was enthusiastic in their condemnation of the Government in smothering the Bill. But the will of the nation will at length prevail.

June 28th.—I was informed by the Rev. John Hartley, of Bradford, that I was to be billeted, during the Conference, at Miss Townend's, Laurel Bank, Manningham Lane. 'The lines have again fallen unto me in pleasant places.' Fortunate me! In 1853 I was the welcomed guest of the same lady, and of her aunt, Miss Pickles, during the Conference of that year. In the afternoon I prepared, by request, a tabular statement of Australasian and Polynesian statistics for the Missionary Report of 1878, and forwarded the same to Samuel Alder Adams for the use of the General Secretaries.

July 6th.—I preached at Loughborough to-day. The next evening I gave two speeches at the meeting: one, on the Home Missions; the other, on our Foreign Missions. On my way to London the next day, I turned aside for a few hours to call in at Bedford to see Mr. Prior, senr., the father of the Rev. S. F. Prior, of the South Australian Conference. In the afternoon the Misses Prior chaperoned me over the town to see all the historic sights. Of course, everything connected with the heroic life, ministry, and sufferings of John Bunyan, were full of interest to me, who owe so much to the 'Pilgrim's Progress' for light and help when I first began to seek the Lord.

July 11th.—Mrs. Bickford and I went to the Crystal Palace to see the fireworks, which were wonderful for variety and splendour.

July 22nd.—The Rev. T. M'Cullagh was my chum (Australian) at

Miss Townend's happy home. I am much favoured in having the companionship of so enjoyable a man.

In the evening I went with my lady host to hear the Rev. G. W. Olver's 'Fernley Lecture.' The church was crowded. Mr. Olver has his own theory of the future state of the wicked. It is, I believe, that the soul only is punishable in eternity, and that it will be retained in a state of eternal solitude, without hope of redemption ; whilst, as to the body, it will be destroyed 'in the lake of fire!' 'I don't know,' said I to him, 'where you get your theory from ; I do not so read the Scriptures.' The plain fact is, that our learned lecturer, on this question (probably, on this question only), is *in nubibus.* But he is not the first, nor will he be the last. Examples : Edward White, Archdeacon Farrar, etc.

The next morning I went to Conference, and took my seat as heretofore on the platform ; Mr Buller came afterwards, and took his seat at my side. It was a largely attended Conference, and was a grand sight from the platform. We voted for Dr. Rigg, as we both believed that under the new *régime* (the mixed Conference) a man of strength and grip was wanted. The Rev. Marmaduke Osborn was elected Secretary. At the open Conference the Rev. Pasteur Lelièvre and Bishop Bowman spoke with great effect. On the 28th I went, by request, to Morecambe, to conduct the Sabbath services, and to give an address on Australasian matters. Mr. and Mrs. Crabtree were my kind host and hostess. At the close of the evening exercises I held quite a *levée.* One gentleman inquired, 'Do you know the Rev. Matthew Wilson?' Another: 'The Rev. E. S. Bickford was a college chum of mine. Do you know him, sir?' And so they continued until I was tired 'with hearing and answering questions.' I took advantage of this 'outing' to visit the Chamberses at Lytham and the Laceys at Todmorden. I returned to the Conference on the 31st, and remained to the end to see the Minutes signed. The 'John Wesley Conference' was now a thing of the past.

In connection with this Conference, which, as years roll on, will be regarded as one of the most important ever held, a few jottings made at the time may not be without some interest to the future generations of the Methodist people :—

DOCTOR POPE'S CHARGE.

'We receive you into our fellowship with perfect confidence. We send you forth, as we have ourselves been sent forth, in trust that you will surpass us who sent you in everything good. We pray for you that you may prosper in your work, and that it may appear to all, not only in your sound and deep theology, in your faithful and successful administration of our economy, in your earnest and zealous preaching, and in all the gifts and grace that adorn the Christian Ministry. but in, what is above, and beneath, and around all these—your exercise unto godliness.'

The Pastoral Oversight of the Young.

'There shall be established in connection with our Society classes for the religious instruction and training of young people. The names of all such young persons shall be enrolled as recognised members. Each member of such a class shall receive some token or ticket, signed by a minister, to be renewable every quarter. Membership in these classes should be accepted, instead of the ordinary probation of Church membership.'

The Reception of New Members.

' The Conference agreed to adopt some formal method of admitting new members, because such a practice was in accordance with early Methodist usage, and for the purpose of giving all due impressiveness to a member's entrance into the Church of Christ. The Conference, however, did not say when this special service should be held, but it did recommend that it should be public.'

The Laymen in Conference.

' The President avowed himself in entire sympathy with that great development which had gathered them together, and he had been in sympathy with it for many years upon the basis of the charter of rights; there had been a gradual extension, and they now met as pastors and brethren, with no distinction whatever, and only with the assignment of subjects by mutual agreement with the pastoral Conference.'

A Revision of the Liturgy.

' The report of the Committee was presented. Everything went on smoothly until it came to the Prayer of Absolution. It was so amended, as to meet the most fastidious non-sacerdotalist that ever came into the ministerial office. But it would not go.'

Doctor Gervase Smith.

' The returned delegate to the Australasian Churches met with an enthusiastic reception. For an hour and a quarter, with much fluency and connectedness, he detailed the principal events connected with his late Southern mission. He had a good word to say for all the Colonies, and for the Methodist Churches in particular.'

Aug. 3rd.—I left for Ripon, and found my dear friends, Mr. and Mrs. Snow, and family all well.

[Diary Jotting]—' We had a delightful evening. What a lovely family this is ! Miss Keeling and other friends joined us.'

Aug. 10*th.*—I left for Edinburgh, and was received by Mrs. Donald, one of our leaders, with Christian heartiness. I preached on the 11th, and after the evening service I addressed from three to four hundred persons on the work of God in Australia. We had quite a *levée* at the close. The people came round me in shoals, inquiring for their friends in Australia. One of the last to come was a little demure Scotch sister, who said, ' And do you know John Egglestone ? ' ' Yes ; well,' I replied. ' I was converted under his ministry forty years ago in this very Circuit, and I am holding on to this very day.' 'Thank God,' I responded; ' should I see Mr. Egglestone again, I will tell him of you.' Two of my hearers at the Sabbath services were the Hon. John Dunn, M.L.C., and Miss Dunn, of Adelaide. I was much pleased with the grand old northern city.

On the 13th I took train for Montrose, and was kindly welcomed by Mr. Sorrell, the uncle of my nephew, the Rev. E. S. Bickford, of Victoria. The Misses Sorrell soon pressed me into a service of love for the ' waifs ' and ' strays '—the outcast and the fallen—in a *pro tempore* mission-room, which a few young ladies and gentlemen had fitted up for evangelistic work. I went as desired, and spoke to about eighty persons. When I returned to the Sorrells, I found that the young minister (the Rev. Alexander Borrowman) had learnt of my being in Montrose. ' Will you give us a service in our little church to-morrow evening ? ' he inquired. ' Yes,' said I, ' if you can get a congregation.' The next day the town was placarded with bills setting forth the intended service. We had a capital congregation. At the close of the service, I invited all who could stay for a short time to do so, when I would tell them a few things about Australia. Nearly the whole audience stayed.

Aug. 15*th.*—I left for Sedbergh, in Yorkshire, to see my old friends, the Rev. William and Mrs. Moister. On my way, I spent a night at Dumfries, with Mr. and Mrs. Robb, friends of the Leasons in South Australia. At the Sedbergh Station I met Mr. Moister, and accompanied him to his nice, quiet home. My friend is an eminent conversationalist. It was a great treat to me to listen to him, as he drew from his mental storehouse reminiscences of his long, laborious, and eventful missionary life. I left for London the next day.

Aug. 19*th.*—My book at last is published, and I am busy in sending copies all over the kingdom. I shall act under the suggestion of my friend, Mr Moister, viz., 'If you want your book to go, you must look after it yourself.' Exactly : and so I will.

Oct. 4th.—After wading through incessant engagements for the last two months, I was glad to again have a run into Yorkshire. I visited Ripon, and was the guest of my old friends, Mr. and Mrs. Snow. In the evening I lectured on Australia, and had a good attendance.

Oct. 5th.—I left for East Keswick.   Mr. Joseph Lawrence and Miss Lawrence met me at the station.   I preached twice on behalf of our Foreign Missions, and attended meetings at Keswick, Ulleskelf, Blanham, and Aberford.   A good interest was shown in each of these places for the Missions.   Mr. Lawrence's academy is doing a great work in training young men for the Christian ministry.   I was much pleased with the young men I saw at their studies in this preparatory institution.

Oct. 13th.—I was at Cross Hills for Foreign Missions.   The Revs. John S. Fordham and Henry Bunting were with me.

Oct. 17th.—I lectured at Rothwell on South Australia.   The next day I went to Collingham, and was again the welcome guest of Mr. and Mrs. John Young.   I had taken a violent cold, and had to consult a Dr. Broadbent for relief.   He examined me thoroughly, and told me I required complete rest from travelling and preaching. I did the best I could on the Sabbath and on the Monday and Tuesday evenings, and on the 23rd I returned to London.

Nov. 2nd.—I left for Coalville to preach on behalf of the Sunday Schools.   My cough was very trying.

On the Monday evening I lectured on Australasia to a large audience for an hour and a half.   We raised in all £36.   On the 11th, at the request of the Missionary Secretaries, I went to Sheerness to speak at the public meeting ; Sir William King Hall in the chair. Mr. and Mrs. Bobby gave me a true Christian welcome.

Nov. 13th.—I attended an important Committee Meeting at Centenary Hall.   In connection with its business, the Rev. M. C. Osborn received his instructions, *re* his visit of inspection of our West Indian Missions.   The specific object is to prepare the way for constituting those Missions an affiliated Connexion with the Mother Conference in England.   I did not approve of the proposed change, believing that the West Indian Churches could be more cheaply managed from London than among themselves.   We shall see whether I am right.

Dec. 1st.—I preached twice at Romford, and on Monday evening I lectured to about one hundred persons on Australia. The audience was quite demonstrative in their thanks. I was again the guest of Mr. and Mrs. Abraham Davey, who, with their interesting family, treated me with much kindness.

On the 3rd was held the inaugural meeting of 'The Thanksgiving Fund,' at Wesley's own church, City Road. Of all the historic Methodist sanctuaries in England it was the most appropriate of them all for such an object. The Australian representation consisted of Mrs. G. F. Wilkinson, of Lower Mitcham, Mrs. Bickford and myself from South Australia; the Rev. James Buller from New Zealand, and the Rev. William Butters from Victoria. The Rev. James H. Rigg, D.D., presided with great ability, and the Rev. T. B. Stephenson was the honoured Secretary. The devotional services were of the highest order. The hymns were well chosen, and 'sung as in ancient days.' The Revs. A. McAulay, T. Nightingale, T. Champness, G. W. Olver, B.A., John Hartley, and Messrs. J. B. Ingle and W. T. Pocock led the great audience in prayer. The amount contributed during the day, as an expression of the people's gratitude to God for the peaceful and prosperous condition of British Methodism, was £34,680. It was a noble offering by a noble-hearted people.

Dec. 14th. [Diary Jotting]—'Princess Alice died to-day, the seventeenth anniversary of her father's death. The good Queen is in great sorrow. May God comfort her, and touch her heart in mercy for the poor Afghans, whom we are brutally murdering !'

Dec. 15th.—I heard two of the ablest London preachers, the Rev. Edward White and Canon Liddon. For pure intellect, give me the Congregationalist; but for oratory of the loftiest character, give me the Canon. These were the last of England's great preachers I heard before leaving on my return voyage to South Australia.

1879.

Jan. 1st.—Being with Mrs. Bickford at Upper Norwood, as the guests of Mrs. Edmondson, we spent the last moments of the old year in holding a semi-watchnight service. Mrs. Scott and Miss Scott, formerly of Demerara, our kind hostess, Mrs. Edmondson, and the servant, formed the devout party.

On the 2nd I sent to the Mission House, Bishopsgate Street

Within, several valuable packages, to be forwarded to Southampton, and put on board the P. and O. steamer for Glenelg. It was bitterly cold. Whilst standing at the door superintending the delivery of the luggage, I was struck through and through with the biting east wind, and during the evening I became alarmingly ill. The form which my illness took was that known as erythema, and was the accumulation of the colds I had taken in travelling up and down the kingdom in the interests of English Methodism, our Foreign Missions, and the Australian colonies. We called in Dr. F. T. Smith to see what could be done towards getting me ready for the intended voyage on the 9th. The Rev. W. Butters came and offered prayer for my recovery. At my request, he went to see Dr. Punshon, to report my illness, and suggest that the directors of the P. and O. Company should be seen, about our voyage being postponed for a month. This was readily conceded. I do not believe that I was ever so near death as at this time. On the sixth night I said to Mrs. Bickford, 'Matters are becoming very serious with us now. I wish to say that, unless God has more work for me to do in Australia, this illness will see the last of me. But if it be His will that I should return to my beloved people, and work out there, then it can have no power to do that.' To this my dear wife assented, adding, 'Let us do our best. I do hope that you may be spared to me a few years longer.' That night I lay in a helpless condition. The next morning the fever broke, and I felt that a new lease of life was for me.

It was now that I saw how reckless I had been with my health ever since I came home; that I ought to have listened to Dr. Broadbent, who told me that I must have rest from all work, and that my constitution had the appearance of being much older than my years. It did not occur to me until I became convalescent, that, all through the time I was contending with the 'swellings of Jordan,' I did not offer even one prayer to my Heavenly Father for deliverance. The habit of my long life seemed suddenly to have collapsed, and I calmly rested upon God to know His will. But when the pulsation of a new life again penetrated my being, and I felt I was standing on the threshold of a renewed career of life-work, the old habitude asserted its power, and I began again to pray. In my prostration I learnt to be 'still, and to know that He was God;' but in my recovery I heard a 'voice' which bade me ' rise and stand upon thy feet, for I have renewed thee for this purpose.'

The London ministers, through the Secretary of their Monthly Meeting, the Rev. William Hudson, expressed to me in a most affectionate and sympathising letter their regret that at my age, and after so long a term of foreign service, I was again leaving my native land. I was much touched with the recognition it recorded of disinterested and acceptable services rendered to the Methodist Church during the time of my visit to the ' home of my fathers ; ' and it breathed a loving prayer for the preservation of Mrs. Bickford and myself when again on the great deep. It is no wonder that, in the midst of so many tokens of kindness and esteem, I glory in the brotherhood of Methodist preachers as the purest and strongest known in the Christian Church.

Feb. 6th.—We went aboard the *Australian*, 3,663 tons burthen, at 11.30 a.m. The Rev. Joseph Payne, my old and obliging friend ; Mr. Samuel Adams, from the Mission House ; the Rev. George and Mrs. Ranyell, and Mr. Louney, were there to see us off. It was hard to part again from friends so dear.

At 3 p.m. we steamed out of the harbour, and were soon in the Bay of Biscay.

Feb. 7th. [Diary Jotting]--' In the Bay of Biscay. Head winds and heavy seas. Course S.W. The ship rolling a good deal. All the lady passengers are sick. Soundings were taken for fixing our exact position.'

On the 9th, after the Rev. Mr. Lewis (Anglican) had read prayers, which, because of the fierce wind and sea, was all that could be done, as we were sitting at the midday meal, a tremendous wave came on board, pouring itself upon us through the skylight, whilst the second-class passengers in the midships were deluged. Their skylight had been carried away bodily, and they found themselves up to their knees in water. A terrible night followed. We had less sea the next day, but the wind was still a furious gale. It became westerly a point or two, and the mainsail and the jib were set. We were then about midway between Cape Finisterre and Cape St. Vincent. During the night we had a terrible fright. By some mischance the steering gear at the stern unhooked, and the labouring ship ' broached too.' Three awful lurches followed, and I certainly thought the steamer would have gone clean over.` A nautical passenger rushed on deck, saw the danger at a glance, sprang forward and caught the chain with a deadly grip, and made it fast before it was too late. We were ' under the water ' for a while, for the sea was washing from stem to stern, filling the cabins, and causing the hearts of all the passengers to quake with fear.

We reached Gibraltar on the 12th, at 9 a.m. This notable rock is pierced, tunnelled, and planted with guns. The telegram from London was full of bad news : the 24th Regiment, composed partly of native soldiers, had been cut to pieces ; five thousand Zulus were killed in an engagement. What a crime is this restless, bragging, fighting policy of the Foreign Office ! We saw Lord Napier embark in the *Poonang.* The place was all alive with boats and boating, with flags flying, and soldiers playing in red-coats.

Feb. 15th.—We reached Malta. I read the article in the *Quarterly Review* on Cyprus. It is very able, and of course justifies Disraeli in securing it for the Crown. The Rev. Joseph Webster came on board to take us to the parsonage. The last time we saw each other was in Grenada, thirty-two years ago; Mr. and Mrs. Webster were then on their way to the Honduras Mission. The Maltese boatmen were the most exacting of any I have ever met with. They were ready to filch us of every shilling we had. I do think they are quite as bad as the boatmen used to be in Barbadoes.

Feb. 19th.—We reached Port Said, and came to anchor opposite the coalyard. We entered the Canal between two breakwaters, after a detention of three or four hours. This canal is a marvellous proof of what money, skill, and perseverance can do. We are indebted to M. de Lesseps for this ' short cut to India.' The voyage from London to India is by it reduced about six thousand miles. It is 86 miles long, 327 feet wide, and cost over £19,000,000 sterling. It took nine years to do the work. I have been asked, ' Why did you not land at Alexandria, and pay a visit to the Pyramids ? ' The answer is : I have read ever since my youthhood of these huge unsightly, useless erections, and have seen pictures of them, *ad nauseam,* and until some abler engineer than any of the past can give a satisfactory account of the names, and the original intentions of their founders, I am content to remain in blissful ignorance. But a practical work like Lesseps', I could not forego seeing when I had the opportunity. Why, it seems to bring our Eastern Possessions next door to England itself, and revolutionises the commerce of the world.

We reached Suez on the evening of the 20th. A fine-looking Turkish gentleman came on board to sell postage stamps, and to take charge of our letters. The steamer's deck was soon invaded by all kinds of complexioned people for business, hiring donkeys, or to be chaperoned on shore, or to the old city about two miles distant.

Feb. 21st.—Captain Bowers, Mrs. Bickford, and I examined the wharves and docks recently erected by the enterprising Khedive. There were several vessels laid aside through want of trade, or for sale. The next day we made another start, and gallantly steamed down the Gulf of Suez.

Our passengers had increased by the addition of the Right Rev. Bishop Staunton, first Bishop of North Queensland; the Rev. Mr. Flume, and his wife, Mrs. Flume, were also with us. The chaplain, Mr. Flume, introduced the Bishop to me on the saloon deck, in the midst of a number of passengers. I found Dr. Staunton an untravelled but an agreeable man. He pressed me earnestly to take part in the Sabbath services which were to be conducted for all the passengers alike; but I declined the courtesy, and gave as my reason, that the directors of the P. and O. Company had decided that when Anglican clergymen were in their boats, they were to take precedence of all other clergymen in such exercises. But the good Bishop would not be content. He emphatically remarked, 'that it was important, being thrown into the midst of a number of strangers, belonging no doubt to various branches of the Church of Christ, that we show them at the first we were the servants of the one only Master, and that we were united in His great work.' 'Happy bishop!' thought I. 'It will save you from ten thousand annoyances, if you keep to that spirit when you reach the new diocese in North Queensland.'

On the 26th we reached Aden; rugged, sterile Aden! Sublime in her solitariness; another of England's 'strongholds' in the East. The Somali, from the African coast, were all astir, diving for small coins, and otherwise trying to amuse us. Others also, mostly mongrel Jews, came on board to drive a trade in ostrich feathers, bracelets, shells, walking-sticks, and money-changing. The English sovereign had great attraction for them. Poor creatures! As I looked upon them, I could not but feel the force of the question, 'Is life worth living, or having?' At 11.30 a.m. we steamed away for Point de Galle, Ceylon. Running nearly on the equatorial line, we had as much as we could bear, for the next 1,874 miles, in the way of heat.

March 6th.—We made Ceylon at 12 o'clock. Before 1 p.m. we were on board the *Tanjore*, bound for Australia. We went on shore in the afternoon, and soon fell in with the Rev. Mr. Tebb, our missionary, who kindly drove us around this ancient and unique town of Galle. This is the place for professional beggars of all kinds. For peace sake I had to buy off some of them. Several accompanied us to the wharf, annoying us all the way with their cry for 'backsheesh.' I had at last to ask the interference of the water-police, and then we escaped our tormentors.

March 7th.—Again at sea, and bound for King George's Sound. A copy of the *Melbourne Argus* was on board, containing a notice of the death of the Rev. John Egglestone. A good and noble life is closed in peace. Nothing occurred of any importance as we steamed down the Indian Ocean, and on the 20th, in the good providence of God, we made King George's Sound, and passed through the bold Heads into Princess Charlotte Harbour. I went on shore for letters, and met the Rev. John Higgins, our minister in charge of the Albany Station, on his way to meet me. The 23rd was the last Sunday on board the *Tanjore*, when the services were conducted by Bishop Staunton, who preached in the morning, and I preached in the evening. The run through the Australian Bight was pleasant, and we anchored off Glenelg on the 24th, at 1 p.m. 'So He bringeth them unto the haven where they desire to be.'

The distance, as taken by me, day by day, from the ship's log, is as follows:—

Southampton to Gall, 30 days	6,576 miles.
Gall to King George's Sound, 15 days	3,330 ,,
King George's Sound to Glenelg, 4 days	1,007 ,,
	10,913 miles.

The speed, inclusive of stoppages, was at the rate of $237\frac{1}{2}$ miles per diem.

It was a source of much pleasure to me to have fallen in with a very choice company, on board the *Australian* and *Tanjore*, of agreeable co-voyagers. For the first few days, as a matter of course, we are all under a certain degree of restraint, and we do not venture

on anything beyond the veriest 'small talk.' But my supply of that commodity being very soon exhausted, I was glad to make acquaintanceships, which much contributed to temper the tedium of the voyage. Those on board with whom I had most intercourse were Mr. Wilberforce Stephen, Q.C., one of the Victorian judges; Captain Alexander Bowers, of Penang; and Bishop Staunton. My first observation of the judge was when we were in the troublous navigation of the Biscay. He, with Mrs. Stephen, and the Misses Stephen, had been to Europe in the hope of the judge's health being restored. It was cold and damp, and the great lawyer was sitting by a stove in the saloon cabin trying to catch a little warmth. He was so altered that I confess that I did not at first recognise him. But I was struck with his gravity, intellectuality, and calm fortitude.

As we proceeded on the voyage, we became very friendly and communicative, and many an hour we sat side by side on the deck, talking on many subjects. Of course, I can only remember the substance of our conversations. 'Upon reflection, Judge,' said I, 'do you regard with reasonable satisfaction the leading part you took in " drafting " and conducting through the Victorian House of Assembly, in 1872, the Bill for establishing a National System of Education upon free, secular, and compulsory principles ?' 'I do,' he promptly replied, 'it was the crowning act of my political life.' 'How did your Anglican friends look at it? were they pleased ?' said I. 'Certainly not,' he rejoined; 'most of them were opposed to it. But Victoria is essentially democratic, and the people must be educated, cost what it may.' 'What is your opinion,' I inquired, 'on the question of marriage with a deceased wife's sister ? You know that we have had that permission for many years in South Australia !' 'For England,' he said, 'I am opposed to it. Besides, the Church is opposed to it.' 'But what of that, Judge? If you mean that the 'State' or Anglican Church is opposed to it, I have only to say that she has no title to interfere with the wishes of the majority of the English people, and you know that the Nonconformists are now in the majority. The argument from Leviticus (xviii. 18), upon which the opposition of most of the Bishops in the House of Lords is based, goes the other way. Its meaning is as clear as sunlight in our favour. Besides, Judge, look at the question as I will illustrate it.' Holding up my left hand with three of its fingers all in a row, I said, 'I call the *first*, husband, the *second*, wife, and the *third*, sister-in-law. This

24

is their relation to each other in law, and in fact; and as long as the
second stands it must continue so to be.   But, in the providence of
God, this second is removed, carrying with it both the root and link
of the relation as previously existing between the first and the third,
so that now they are as separate and independent of each other as
any other two persons could be.   Where then is the civil or ecclesiastical disability of such persons contracting a marriage if they thus
chose?'   The judge was equal to the position, and good-naturedly
remarked, ' My good friend, you are too subtle.   You ought to have
been a lawyer instead of a parson.'   The conversation then dropped.
Judge Stephen had singular notions as to the relation of laymen to
questions of theology.

   After hearing an earnest sermon, given *extempore*, by Bishop
Staunton, I said to him : 'It struck me as very strange, oftentimes
in England, that sermons to which we had been listening with much
delight, were scarcely ever made the subjects of critical or commenda-
tory remark.   Surely intelligent hearers must have some thoughts of
their own, to which they might give expression on such occasions.'
' Why should they?' he replied ; 'what have laymen to do with
theology?'   ' Well, Judge,' I rejoined, ' there are ladies in London,
and in other parts of England, who are coming to the front as
instructresses of their own sex, in the drawing-rooms and parlours of
the first families.   At such gatherings papers are read on Scriptural
exegesis of great ability and beauty.   Here is a marked change for
the better, and will put many of you gentlemen to shame.'   ' Well,
well,' said my patient hearer, ' all I have to say is this : the Lord
deliver me from theological ladies.'   I could not but inwardly ask
if such were the usual attitude towards Biblical subjects of the
generality of educated laymen to such questions?

   Captain Alexander Bowers was a man of a different stamp.
He was a sturdy, hard-headed, intelligent Scotchman.   He had
been to England on important business connected with steam
vessels employed in the China Seas and the Strait Settlements.
He was thoroughly religious, and had a weakness for theological
discussion.   The Deistical controversy of the early decades of the
last century he had well mastered.   With the theology of Calvin
and Arminius ; Wesley and Fletcher, as leaders on the Arminian
side ; and with the Hills and Toplady, as the defenders of Calvin's
views, he was conversant with on the other.   ' I regard,' said he,

'John Wesley as the greatest theologian of the last century. It was his sermon on "Predestination calmly considered" that killed the Decrees in me.' I lent him Mr. Bonwick's book, entitled, 'Egyptian Belief and Modern Thought,' which he read with the utmost care; making an analysis of its main points and conclusions. He told me that he regarded Mr. Bonwick as a learned Egyptologist.

There was hardly a phase of the religious life of England which Bishop Staunton and I did not converse upon. One day I told him of my occasional visits to the services of the Anglican Church; but that I was becoming quite sick of the shameful way in which the finest liturgy in Christendom was rendered in some of the churches. I noted particularly the wretched reading, or intoning, the liturgy in St. Paul's, which so vexed me that I found it difficult so to regain my equilibrium as to appreciate, as I desired, the learned discourse of Canon Liddon. I told him, that even had I remained in England for a year or two longer, I would have had to give up my occasional attendance at Episcopal Churches, because of the 'sing-song' and unedifying manner of rendering the liturgy. The Bishop coincided with all that I said, which he could consistently do, for his reading of the prayers and lessons was marked with proper emphasis, and free from all foolish affectation.

The Bishop was anxious to gain as much knowledge as possible of the newly-formed diocese to which he was going. I besought him to accept the facts of his new position, reminding him there was no State Church in Queensland, and that the rank and rights of all ordained ministers were equal in the eye of the law; that public education was conducted by the Government upon the secular and compulsory basis, with which the religious bodies, as such, had nothing whatsoever to do; and that the principle of universal suffrage was the law of the land. 'You must "swim with the stream," Bishop, and do not try to breast it,' I impressively said. 'I apprehend,' I added, 'that Queensland is the most democratic of all these Colonies, but you may find it to be a glorious field of usefulness if you happen to get the "right clue."' When we parted at Glenelg, he was pleased to express to me the great pleasure he had had in our free intercourse during the voyage, and of the benefit he had derived from the many practical suggestions I had given him. And I also had received much pleasure and profit from the conversations and discourses of this Anglican clergyman and first Bishop of North Queensland. May God bless him!

Before landing there came on board to welcome us the Revs. T. Lloyd, R. S. Casely, C. Lane, R. M. Hunter, Jos. Nicholson, and A. J. Boyle, Mr. and Mrs. John Jarvis, Mr. and Mrs. G. W. Coombs, Mrs. John Thompson, Mr. Robert Wallace, and some other friends. The Rev. D. O. Donnell was awaiting us on the jetty. As the return mail steamer was anchored in the bay, I hastened to write the Rev. John Kilner, London, informing him of our safe arrival, to be noticed in our papers for the satisfaction of our English friends. We then proceeded to Unley to 'rest awhile' before going to our new Circuit at the Burra.

March 30th.—I preached at Unley and Pirie Street. It was truly a thanksgiving day, and in the evening the sum of £12 was collected for the Circuit Fund. During the next week I visited old friends, among whom I may mention Mr. and Mrs. John Colton, Mr. and Mrs. James Scott, Mr. and Mrs. Kaines, Halton Brook; Mr. and Mrs. Robert Wallace, Mr. and Mrs. William Keynes, Dunrobin; the Padmans, Johnstons, Rastons, Waterhouses, the Hills and Careys, Coombs and Greers, I also called upon.

April 9th.—I attended the funeral of the Rev. George Lee—'a good man and a just'—whom God had taken to Himself. In the evening of the same day, the Rev. Walter H. Hanton was ordained for the Northern Territory Mission. I delivered the charge, founded upon Acts xxvi. 17, 18.

April 12th.—We went by train to the Burra; Mr. F. W. Holder was at the station to receive us. At 3 p.m. we took possession of our humble home for a term of service as the Conference may appoint. The brethren also devolved upon me the Chairmanship of the Middle District, which, with the care of the Circuit, will occupy all my time.

The Burra, from its geographical position, being 101 miles north from Adelaide, would naturally become the base of operations for new townships as the years come on. The Rev. John Harcourt was the first resident minister, as a young man, in 1845. Even at that time there was a noble band of pioneer local preachers, who toiled hard and successfully in the Master's vineyard. Such names as the following are worthy of mention: Messrs. Thomas Thomas, John Boots, John Chapman, Samuel Bray, Joseph Sleep, James D. Bone, and J. R. Stephens. The first leader was good Thomas Moyses; John Dunstone was the first Sunday School Superintendent, and John Roach, one of the first teachers. Thomas Burgess did great service to the young in evening classes; and William Pearce introduced the Temperance cause. A Mr. Thorpe, from Clarendon, used to preach out of doors in his blue serge before the Gospel had a local habitation. He brought potatoes and other vegetables from his farm at Kangarilla for the miners, and preached salvation to them likewise. Mrs. Cotton and Mrs. Sleep (then the Misses Mitchell) and the Misses Mayor, collected the first money for establishing a Sunday School, and afterwards for erecting the first sanctuary in Kooringa (Burra). My circuit I found to be compact and free from heavy debts. Kooringa and Redruth were the dual head; having as outstations, Westbury, two miles; Baldry, fourteen; Baldina eight; and Mongalota, eighteen. I saw plainly that I would have all my afternoons, if I chose, for pastoral visitation, for strengthening and building up the Societies. There was nothing heroic in the administration of the Circuit. It was the quietest routine I had ever had in any of my appointments, and left me all my forenoons undisturbed for study and for Connexional correspondence. My circuit stewards were Messrs. F. W. Holder and John Roach. More agreeable church officers I could not have desired.

May 26th.—We held the Redruth Church anniversary, and raised over £100. Mr. Roach presided, and Captain Paull and I were the speakers.

June 2nd.—I wrote my first letter on South Australia for publication in the *Methodist Recorder*, my object being to supply information to English capitalists, and to those of my countrymen who may desire to better their condition by emigrating to this prosperous colony.

June 20th.—I held my first Local Preachers' Meeting. Messrs. Sleep, Holder, Kitchen, Giles, Crews, and Dr. Brummitt were present. I held the Quarterly Meeting also, when I found that our income exceeded the expenditure by £20. A good beginning!

June 24th.—My official visitation of the Circuits began to-day. I went by train to Freeling, and held the Quarterly Meeting. In the evening I gave my lecture on 'My Trip to England and Back' to about one hundred persons. Mrs. Rankin was my kind hostess.

July 5th.—I went to Crystal Book to preach and lecture on

behalf of the Trust Funds. I was the welcome guest of Mr. and Mrs. Claridge.

July 8th.—I was at Clare for the Home Missions, and on the 9th I was at Mintaro for the same purpose. In this visit I had much pleasure in the society of the Rev. C. T. and Mrs. Newman, and of Mr. and Mrs. Jolly.

July 20th. [Diary Jotting]—'A good day. I had the largest congregation I have yet seen in the Kooringa Church. At the after prayer meeting, Mr. Walker came forward to seek salvation.'

July 24th.—There has been a fall of snow. It was a refreshing sight for my old English eyes.

Aug. 3rd.—I preached at Jamestown on behalf of the Trust Fund of the Church. We raised altogether £112. A Mr. Williams, a well-to-do farmer, promised the proceeds of five acres of wheat. On the 5th, the Rev. P. C. Thomas and I went to Caltowie, where I lectured in aid of the Circuit Funds. We were the guests of Mr. and Mrs. Henry Williams. On my way home the next day, I tarried at Hallett to witness the laying of the 'foundation stone' of the new Institute by Mr. Rowland Rees, M.P., the member for the District. He gave quite a classical speech.

Aug. 10th. [Diary Jotting]—'Laborious and profitable day. Preached three times, gave the Lord's Supper, baptized two children, and held and addressed a prayer meeting at the close. Drove twenty-four miles ; my friend, Mr. Holder, accompanied me.'

Aug. 25th. [Diary Jotting]—'I read over the correspondence anent the young men I sent out from England. The Rev. William Jenkins (P.M.M.) called, and we had a nice conversation about their Connexional matters, their Equalisation Fund, Circuit difficulties, etc., etc. In the evening I attended the " Bible Christian " and " Primitive Methodist meetings," and spoke for an hour and a quarter at both places. I got home at 10 p.m., tired and excited.'

Sept. 5th.—I went to Kapunda, and gave my lecture on 'My Trip to England and Back.' It was the last of a series, and was well received.

Sept. 17th.—I attended the Allocation Committee in Adelaide. We had £1,180 3s. 10d. to distribute for Connexional expenses and for Circuit deficiencies. The Loan Fund income was £1,550. Princely contributions from a grateful and godly people !

Oct. 10th.—The Rev. E. S. Bickford, my nephew, visited us, and preached the Kooringa Church Anniversary Sermons. The next day the Hon. John Colton, M.P., my nephew, and I dined at Dr. Brummitt's. Mr. Colton presided at the meeting in the evening.

Oct. 21st.—We began the Annual District Meeting, when all the ministers were present. The next day the Circuit Stewards joined us. ' We had a short and successful meeting.

Oct. 23rd.—The Rev. R. W. Campbell lectured on ' Burns,' the great Scottish poet. He spoke for an hour and a half without a manuscript or note. It was a very ably composed lecture, and suffered nothing in its delivery. Give me an educated, sympathising Scot to lecture on Scott or Burns, and we may be sure of a treat. My nephew, E. S. Bickford, accompanied Mr. George Sara, a contractor, on his northern fortnightly round, whilst we were at District business. I wanted him to see the Northern Areas, whilst he was over here. He was much pleased with what he saw.

On the 27th, my nephew, E. S. B., my niece, Miss Jarvis, the Rev. R. S. Casely, Mr. and Mrs. Thomas Drew, and I dined at Mrs. John Drew's, when we had a time of most agreeable intercourse. The next day we closed the Bazaar effort for the Kooringa Lecture Hall, and found that we had raised £151 3s. 10d.

Dec. 31st.—The usual ' Watch Night Service' was held at Kooringa. Mr. Holder and I addressed the congregation. It was indeed a season of grace and blessing to us all. And so was closed the year 1879.

1880.

Jan. 1st.—I enter upon the New Year under the influence of a premonition that it will be an eventful one. But I trust in God for both guidance and grace. Père Granion has remarked : ' Sometimes three sacrifices are required by our Heavenly Father, expressed in three Latin words : *tua, tuos, te*—*i.e.* thy goods, thy children, and thyself. In my renewal of consecration this morning, I did give my goods and myself to God; but children to give I have none. I find the clippings I make, in the course of my miscellaneous reading, to be an inspiration of noble and divinest thought in my otherwise lethargic soul. Lord Mansfield's sententious apothegm is suggestive of the spirit in which I should, in the beginning of a new year, enter upon my clerical duties : ' I wish popularity ; but it is that popularity which follows, not that which is run after. It is that popularity which, sooner or later, never fails to do justice to the pursuit of noble ends by noble means.' So may I pursue my holy calling.

It is impossible in these stirring times to sever oneself from the possibilities which await the English race. For example, we, Anglo-Australians, are laying the foundations of a great and prosperous empire in the Southern World. As certainly as the sun rises on the hills and valleys of this Austral land, and the water of the seas lave our shores, so sure will be the increase of the white races from the over-populated countries of northern latitudes, to people and to develop these priceless colonies of the south. Carcour's prediction is receiving rapid fulfilment : ' England's missions have been many, to introduce into the world representative government and free trade, and to keep alive the embers of European liberty. But your great mission is that foretold by Shakespeare, to found empires, to scatter wide the civilised man. Fifty years hence, three or four hundred millions of the most energetic men in the world will speak English. French and German will be dialects, as Dutch and Portuguese are now.'

The Churches of Christ are the heaven-ordained factors for bringing about a world-wide human regeneration. These Churches are the custodians of the ' leaven ' for effecting this glorious trans-formation. And, in all humility, we may venture to say, ' We are able to do it.' What is our numerical strength of English-speaking Christians in this year of grace, 1880? Episcopalians, say, 18,000,000; Methodists, 16,500,000; Roman Catholics, 13,500,000; Presbyterians, 10,250,000; Baptists, 5,000,000; Congregationalists, 6,000,000; and Unitarians, 1,000,000. We confidently ask, Can earth or hell arrest the triumphant progress of Anglo-Saxon civilisa-tion and Anglo-Saxon Christianity?

With such thoughts, I left the Burra on the 19th, for the Annual Conference in Adelaide. I was the guest by invitation of Chief Justice Way, at his beautiful mansion, Montefiore, North Adelaide. At the station, the judge's carriage was in waiting, and I was soon conveyed to my temporary home. The next day, the Conference was opened by the retiring President, the Rev. C. H. Goldsmith; and the Rev. Henry T. Burgess was elected as his successor, with the Rev. J. B. Stephenson as Secretary. The easy despatch of business, and the general order of the Conference, soon showed the wisdom of the choice made of our chief officers. On the 23rd, at the request of the President, I examined, *vivâ voce*, W. A. Langsford, H. H. Teague, and T. E. Thomas, B.A., for ' full connexion.' They were received by an unanimous vote. The thanks of the Conference

were presented to me, 'for my assiduous attention to the best interests of South Australia, during my recent sojourn in England.'

March 1st.—I went to Adelaide to attend a meeting of the Directors of the Wesleyan Newspaper Company. I expressed my dissatisfaction with the old administration, and with the arrangements for the new. The paper before long is bound to come to grief, through lack of support. Our people have taken but little to it; hence our poor subscription list. And yet, as a church, we cannot do without a weekly organ. We want it for giving information of our work, and as a means of defence when we are misrepresented.

March 29th.—I heard to-day of the lamented death of the Rev. Joseph Dare, D.D., in Melbourne. The 'Apollos' of our Australasian Church is gone. A great loss not easily to be repaired.

April 9th.—Great Britain has just passed through the turmoil of a general election. The returns are, Liberals, 343; Conservatives, 177. The latter at present, as a party, is completely broken up.

April 18th.—I preached three times at Port Pirie, in aid of the Trust Funds. I had to return by first train the next morning to inter the remains of the late Mr. Thomas Hosking. There was a large funeral; it was a mournful sight.

April 26th.—English telegram: The Queen has been obliged, after all, to ask Mr. Gladstone to form the new Government. That knightly man, Lord Granville, is Foreign Secretary. Mr. H. H. Fowler, of Wolverhampton, has, I find, been elected to Parliament in the Liberal interest.

June 5th.—The Burials Bill has been read a second time in the House of Lords. The right man is again at the helm.

July 15th.—The Hon. John Colton, M.P., introduced me to our Governor, Sir William Jervois, K.C.M.G., who received us very graciously. I delivered to him a message of respect from Captain Bowers, of Penang. The Governor's references to the old captain were very complimentary.

Sept. 19th.—I went to North Adelaide, to inquire after my old friend Captain Bagot, who was very poorly, but fully prepared for the coming of the Lord.

Sept. 11th. [Diary Jotting]—'Made a copious outline of a sermon for to-morrow. What a comfort it is to be prepared early for the Sabbath services! This discourse on Heb. xi. 1, I began re-writing on Wednesday, and I finished it on Friday evening. This is what I must try to do in future every week. I have read also the *London Quarterly*, and Agnes Strickland's "Lives of the Queens of England," with intense interest. What misery has been inflicted upon Great Britain through the interference of the Parliaments with the people's religion! The Stuarts owe their downfall more to this insane meddling than to any other cause. Why cannot Legislatures, as well as individuals, learn the lesson of our Lord : " My kingdom is not of this world," and practise it also ? '

Sept. 17*th.*—Sitting for many hours at my desk, occasioned a severe pressure of pain in my head. I worked in the garden until it was quite removed. The great Archbishop Whately, of Dublin, used to cleave wood for the same purpose. It is an infallible remedy.

Oct. 9*th.*—I preached at Yarcowie Church anniversary. We raised £55. The Rev. W. A. Langsford and Mrs. Langsford were very kind.

Oct. 19*th.*—I was at Gawler attending the District Meeting. Mr. J. H. Goss successfully passed as a candidate for our Ministry. The business was finished in two days. Mr. and Mrs. Edward Clement were my obliging host and hostess.

Oct. 24*th.*—I was at Kapunda, in behalf of the Sunday School. I gave an address to the teachers, parents, and scholars in the afternoon.

Oct. 25*th.*—At Kooringa Church anniversary, Mr. President Burgess lectured on the nineteenth century discoveries. It was very stimulating, and admirably delivered. We raised £104.

Nov. 14*th.*—The Rev. B. Chapman, General Secretary of our Foreign Missions, preached to-day at Redruth and Kooringa. Mr. Chapman earnestly advocated the Missions in the South Seas. At intervals, some time in each day he was with us, he would refer to the Friendly Islands' District. It was evident to me that the condition of that romantic, and, until recently, glorious Mission was causing him the intensest anxiety.*

Dec. 9*th.*—I held the service at Redruth, and met the classes for tickets. I am greatly distressed at the small attendance of the members at the weekly fellowship. And what to do to cure this

---

* The Rev. Shirley Baker, who for many years had been ' Chairman of the District,' had accepted service under King George as Prime Minister of his kingdom. Such a position, for Mr. Baker, was bound to be a source of entanglement and trouble. And so events have proved.

negligence I cannot tell ! Our membership is loose and inconsistent. But who will take this question in hand ? Who ?

Dec. 31st.—We have got through the heat and ' journeyings often ' of another year. The preaching appointments have been well taken up, and the pastoral work, devolving more particularly upon myself, has been vigorously prosecuted. We held the usual ' Watchnight ' service, which was well attended. Mr. Holder and I gave addresses, and Mr. James Harry acted as precentor. I hope for lasting good as the result of this last service of the year.

1881.

Jan. 1st. [Diary Jotting]—' In the good Providence of God, I enter upon the duties and trials of another year. "Hitherto the Lord hath helped me." This year I intend, morning by morning, devotionally to read the " Portable Commentary " upon the New Testament, two chapters in the Old, and Bates' and Pascoe's Aids and Helps. I must have my mornings at my own command, and undisturbed. I will give heed to the suggestion of the Rev. E. E. Jenkins, M.A., as of great value to me in my Australian ministry : " If you would make sure of the ground upon which your faith rests, cherish the habit of observing a stated time, day by day, for the study of the Holy Scriptures, and for meditation upon God, as well as prayer to God. You have no enemy more dangerous than the temptation that would filch from you the golden minutes consecrated to your private intercourse with God. In everything else judicious solitude is the spring of open services. As a tree attains its strength and loftiness by the unseen and silent ministry of the soil, so great characters are built in secret." To such wise words I am resolved to give heed.

' " My company before is gone." The Rev. Henry Hurd, who knelt with me at our Ordination, and with whom I went to the West Indies in 1838, died at Cardiff, Wales, on the 5th ult. He had served the West India Mission for forty years, and now is reaping his reward.'

Jan. 19th.—The Annual Conference was opened by Mr. ex-President Burgess, and the Rev. J. B. Stephenson was chosen as his successor. The Rev. S. Knight was elected as Secretary. He worked hard, and did a great deal of business. I was requested by the President to examine John Gillingham, Walter H. Hautar, and John Watts, all of whom were cordially received into ' full connexion ' with the Conference. At the Ordination Service on the 26th, the ex-President gave an excellent charge. I returned to Kooringa on the 29th, so as to be ready for the Sabbath services.

Feb. 1st.—In the evening I heard the President of the ' Bible Christian Conference ' preach at the Burra. He reminded me very much of Wesley's famous words, ' I write plain truth for a plain

people ;' but then only an able man can reach that perfection.
Mrs. Bickford and I remained for the after-service, and took the
Lord's Supper. We found it good thus to unite with this dear
people in their sacred services.

Feb. 21st.—No brain work possible to-day, with the thermometer
105° in the shade and 165° in the sun, with a fierce hot wind
blowing as if it came from a red-hot furnace.

Feb. 28th.—I drove out to the Baldina plains to see the aged Mrs.
Pearce. She was very ill, but very happy. 'The love of Christ,'
she said, 'took away her pain.' I called upon the Rogers, the
Bains, and the Tuckfields. In the evening I held the Quarterly
Love Feast, when eighteen believers testified to their conversion.

March 1st.—Mrs. Bickford and I went to Monovea Farm to see
our kind friends Mr. and Mrs. Field and family. We spent an
agreeable time with them. The only drawback was the great
heat.

March 6th.—I preached at Mintaro, and lectured the next evening.
We raised £40 for the Trust Fund. I wrote a letter entitled, 'The
New Theory of Child Salvation,' and sent it to *The Methodist Journal*
for publication.

March 13th.—I preached at Riverton, and lectured on 'My Trip
to England and Back.' Collections for the Trust Funds £66. I
made my home at Mr. and Mrs. Polamountain's.

March 28th.—I held the Quarterly Meeting at Mr. John Dunstan's,
Redruth. We passed several resolutions bearing upon the work
of God in the Circuit. The balance in hand was about ten
guineas.

April 3rd.—After preaching at Kooringa, I drove to Mongalutu,
a distance of eighteen miles, for the afternoon service, and to meet
the class. I spent, as usual, an agreeable evening with Dr. Stephens
and family.

April 16th.—I heard to-day of the death of Dr. William Morley
Punshon. I was struck dumb. The loss to the Methodist Connexion
is great indeed.

April 20th.—Great men are falling fast. By telegram we learn
that Lord Beaconsfield died yesterday morning in the seventy-seventh
year of his age. One of the most trusted servants of the Queen is
gone from her councils, and the Tories have lost the most skilful
leader they have had in this century. His politics were not mine ;

but I throw a wreath upon his grave for his jealous guard over what he thought to be the honour of England.

I exercise my right as a citizen of South Australia in voting for such gentlemen as I please who are candidates for seats in Parliament. My ministerial position, instead of shutting me off from the exercise of my legal vote, in my conviction, seriously increases my obligation to use it. My object is twofold : (1) To keep unsuitable men out of Parliament ; (2) to elect suitable men to that position. Acting upon this principle, I voted to-day for Sir H. Ayres, Sir John Milne ; Messrs. Tartleton, Pickering, Hay, and Buck, for the Legislative Council.

April 23rd.—I finished my reminiscences of the late Dr. Punshon, and sent them to *The Methodist Journal.* I have a feeling of admiration for his superb eloquence, and of veneration for his probity and honour. Like Wesley and Bunting, he has left no successor in our Church.

April 26th.—Mr. John Nairne, a young local preacher from Magpie, Ballarat, called this morning. He is to take charge of the Hanson Home Mission Station until next Conference.

May 2nd. [Diary Jotting]—'Frightful telegraphic news reached us this morning of the loss of the *Waratah,* about twenty-five miles from Bluff Harbour, New Zealand. The Rev. Joseph Waterhouse, Revs. Richardson and Armitage were drowned; also one hundred and four passengers and sailors in all; only about twenty sailors were saved.'

It seemed that the luckless steamer, by an alteration of her course, was steered 'dead on' to the Waipara reef. There were, besides those names above given, Messrs. E. Connell, and E. Mitchell, members of our General Conference. Since the loss of the *Maria,* 'mail boat,' in the West Indies in 1825, no such calamity as this has befallen us.

April 11th.—The General Conference was opened to-day by the Rev. John Watsford, the retiring President, and the Rev. James Swanton Waugh, D.D., was elected as his successor. We met under a great cloud of trouble, and it was difficult so to rise above it as to be able to attend to business. Mr. Watsford's address was impressive and seasonable. We agreed to constitute the Friendly Islands Missions into a separate district of the New South Wales Conference and to be free from the control of the Missionary Committee in Sydney. It was done at the earnest request of King George himself.

Carefully prepared, and affectionately loyal despatches were forwarded to the King upon the subject. The Rev. B. Chapman was appointed for another three years' term as General Secretary of Foreign Missions. The Rev. W. Morley, representative from New Zealand, brought before the Conference propositions for the separation of their Conference from the Australasian Connexion. After a long and earnest debate, they were negatived by a majority of five votes. On the 27th we reached the end of our business. Dr. Waugh requested me to offer the last prayer, and give the Benediction. In parting with the brethren, I was affected to tears, knowing that many of us would see each other no more in this world.

July 2nd.—We agreed to have the Rev. W. A. Bainger as second preacher. A few friends met at Dr. Brummitt's to arrange for meeting this additional expense. £80 were soon subscribed.

July 26th.—I wrote Mr. John Roberts, of Robertstown, about twenty miles from Kooringa, that Mr. Bainger would preach there, on August 14th, if he could secure a congregation. This is our first attempt to enlarge the boundaries of our work. Robertstown is situated in the centre of an agricultural and squatting district, and it will be a great charity to give the people the Gospel of Jesus Christ. Mr. Roberts is, I believe, the founder of the township.

July 30th.—I had an agreeable run to the North; the weather was beautifully fine, and the air was bracing. The Rev. C. H. Goldsmith met me at the Port Pirie Station, and took me to the Parsonage, where I was kindly welcomed by Mrs. Goldsmith. I preached twice the next day to good congregations. On Monday Mr. Goldsmith and I strolled among the wharves, and visited several families. In the afternoon we drove to Lower Broughton, when I was delighted with the wheat-fields, which looked so well. We had a public meeting in the evening. The next day we drove to the Reservoir, and I was much pleased with all that I saw. I lectured in the evening to a small congregation. Admission by one shilling ticket is not popular on the Northern Circuits. I returned home all well, and read sixty-eight pages of McCarthy's 'History of our Own Times,' which I much enjoyed.

Aug. 13th.—I sent off Mr. Bainger to Robertstown with full instructions. I had a severe headache to-day, the result of hard study over my sermon. Read McCarthy on the Kabul massacre, etc. Alas! the whole of this trouble we brought upon ourselves through meddling with the reigning powers of Afghanistan. Surely ours is a 'spirited' foreign policy! But I hope the English Government will be less adventurous under Mr. Gladstone's guidance.

Aug. 21*st.*—I preached a funeral sermon for dear Father Goss, who had grown old and feeble in his Master's service. He was eminently a good man, and departed this life at the age of seventy-five, in blissful hope of heaven.

Sept. 12*th.*—I read in the *South Australian Register* of the death of the Rev. B. Chapman, at Windsor, New South Wales, on the 10th current. No death has occurred for many years in our ranks which has distressed me more than this. Mr. Chapman was away from home in his beloved deputation work, when he became ill, and soon passed away. The greatest sorrow of his official life was the sad condition of the Tongan mission. Indeed, I venture to think, it killed him. A *post-mortem*, if it be reverent so to say, would show deeply cut into his bleeding heart the ominous words, 'Tonga, Tonga.' Nothing could heal the sorrow, or wash away the gore of that heart, but the messenger of Death, whom the Heavenly Father saw fit to send to him. But his record of integrity is on high.

Oct. 2*nd.*—The Rev. F. Langham, our apostolic missionary from Fiji, paid us a visit. He preached and spoke at several places in the interests of the work to which he had given his life. The Rev. A. Rigg also paid us a visit. These 'wise men from the east' contributed much to our enjoyment during the time they spent with us.

Nov. 14*th.*—We inaugurated special services at the Burra, by holding morning and mid-day prayer meetings, and services in the evening. The Revs. Pearce and Burt joined us in these hallowed exercises. Mr. Matthew Burnett came to our assistance, and a great work of God followed. For miles outside the Burra the saving power was felt. With these services on hand, and the care and work of the Circuit to look after, I became prostrate, and had to stand aside.

Dec. 23*rd.*—Mr. and Mrs. Burnett left the Burra for Port Elliot, for rest and rustication. They have left a large blessing behind them.

Dec. 27*th.* [Diary Jotting]—'Dr. Brummitt called to see us. I am better, but Mrs. Bickford had a bad night. She is a great sufferer. I kept out of the sun all the day as I could not endure its intense heat.'

Dec. 28*th.* [Diary Jotting]—'I was poorly all the forenoon through the

fierce, hot wind and heat. We held the Quarterly Meeting in the evening.
The accounts balanced. Mr. Thomas Drew was appointed junior Steward, and
Dr. Stephens as our Representative to Conference.'

Dec. 31st.—The Rev. Charles Lane and Mr. Holder conducted the
' Watch Night Service ' at Kooringa, and Mr. John Lane and I
a similar service in the Primitive Methodist Church at Redruth.
Thank God for all the blessings of the year !

· 1882.

Jan. 1st.—I had a hard day's work in my somewhat enfeebled
condition. I preached at Redruth, Baldina, and in the ' Bible
Christian Church.' The Rev. Charles Lane conducted the services
at Kooringa in behalf of the new classrooms, when £13 2s. 6d.
were collected.

Jan. 17th.—The Annual Conference was opened to-day. The
Rev. R. S. Casely was elected President, and the Rev. R. M.
Hunter, Secretary. John Nairn was received as a probationer in
our Ministry. I took my full share of work in the Conference—
Sunday. At Pirie Street I preached on ' Freedom from Sin ' (Rom.
viii. 22,) and in the evening, at Gilbert Street, on the ' Redemption
of the Soul ' (Psalm xlix. 8), to excellent congregations. It was a
day of special blessing to me.

The Conference incorporated in its ' Annual Address ' a paragraph
as follows, upon the subject of weekly fellowship : ' We cannot close
without saying a word for a means of grace which we prize very
highly, and which may almost be accepted as a distinctive characteristic of our Church, namely, the Class Meeting. There is but one
opinion as to the worth of this institution, considered as a means of
grace. There many of our members have learnt what, perhaps,
they had never known from any other sources, that there are clearly
defined degrees of spiritual life ; that there are temptations common
to all ; and that there are temptations which grow out of peculiarity
of temperament, or are the effects of faulty training in early life.
What many of the old Puritans longed for we have in our Class
Meeting—a place where believers meet face to face for the purpose
of comparing things spiritual with things spiritual, and of exhorting
each other to higher attainments in the Divine life. Do you shrink
from such an exercise? If you do, we would earnestly and affectionately ask you to look into your own heart, and ask yourself why you

MODEL SCHOOLS, ADELAIDE.

are averse to this simple searching, and, as we believe, this Scriptural communion of saints. Such a process of self-examination may be productive of very blessed results; and will, at the least, be one means of responding to the exhortation of Holy Writ, 'Examine yourselves whether ye be in the faith; prove your own selves.' As my full time of three years was up in the Burra Circuit, I was appointed Superintendent of the Port Adelaide Circuit, with the Rev. S. F. Prior as my colleague. The Rev. Samuel Knight succeeded me at the Burra. On the 28th the Minutes were signed, and I returned home the same evening.

Feb. 1st.—We had a Society Tea Meeting, when from one hundred to one hundred and fifty members and communicants were present. It was a glorious meeting, and must do good. On the 7th I presided at the United Monthly Meeting of the classes. The members were in a good state. 'What must we do,' I asked William Taylor, when in Sydney, 'to preserve these new-born souls the Lord has given us as the fruit of your labours?' 'Do?' said he. 'You must feed their emotional nature by fellowship meetings and love-feasts, and keep them in a good state of soul, as well as preach to them from time to time.' This 'winner of souls' was right, as experience has shown me in every Circuit in which I have laboured.

Feb. 13th.—I held a Special Circuit Meeting to consider certain alterations to the old parsonage, or to erect a new one. We agreed that a new parsonage should be built on Limestone Hill, to cost £1,000.

Feb. 21st.—I read the *Melbourne Spectator*, and was much pleased with the Rev. G. Daniel's charge to the newly ordained brethren at the Melbourne Conference. There is an appropriateness of subject, grasp of thought, earnestness, and affection, in its whole form that commanded my admiration. Such a charge should not only be printed, but widely circulated among the rising Ministry of our Church.

March 10th.—I was very unwell this morning, and I had to send for Dr. Brummitt to assist me. He pronounced the inflammation in my foot to be the gout. Alas for me that I should be the first of my family to be afflicted in this manner! The result, doubtless, of exhaustion from the great heat and hard work.

March 27th.—I held the Quarterly Meeting at Mr. Tiver's, Aberdeen. We had a large attendance and a fine meeting. The returns

25

are :—Full members 157, on trial 52, Catechumens 52.   The increase on the quarter was 36 members.   We agreed to purchase a parsonage site, 101 × 211, for £30, on Limestone Hill, Kooringa.   Mr. George Sara, senior Steward, did us good service in this matter.

April 6th.—This day we left our dear friends at the Burra for our new Circuit.   There had been two valedictory meetings at Redruth and Kooringa, when very kind things were said to us by Messrs. Forder, Sara, Tiver, Rabbich, Dunstan (Redruth), and Messrs. T. Drew, Joseph Sleep, Wilkinson, F. W. Holder, Dr. Brummitt, John Lane, and Dr. Stephens, with many others (Kooringa), to which I responded as well as I could.   I had had three happy, laborious years at the Burra, and I felt deeply when the time came to say *Vale.*

I was appointed to the Port Adelaide Circuit at my own request. It is not always safe to choose one's own sphere of labour ; this was the first time I had ventured so to do.   There were good reasons for this departure from the course I had habitually pursued during my forty-three years of itinerancy, which I need not state.   At the Port Station the Rev. S. F. Prior, Mr. Theophilus Hack, and Mr. Jarvis were there to receive us.   At the Parsonage, Dale Street, Mesdames Prior and Shorney were in waiting to give Mrs. Bickford and me a hearty welcome.   The Methodist system of itinerancy would be intolerable were it not that the pain, connected with the severance of friendship in leaving Circuits, is soon compensated by the free and immediate openings to other equally sincere friendships in the new Circuits to which one has to go.   It was certainly so in this case ; for, in a few days, we were quite at home with our new friends, and were hard at our beloved work.   The principle of the itinerancy is in accordance with Apostolic practice.   It recognises the fact, that the ministry is one of the ' gifts' of the Mediatorial Lord to the Church for its preservation and extension in the world. And it seems to be an equitable arrangement for Synods, Conferences, or any other appointing power, to give effect to the principle by distributing equally this 'gift' over the entire vineyard of the Great Husbandman, for its cultivation and help.   This, 'beyond all controversy,' the Methodist Conferences in England, Ireland, America, Australia, the West Indies, and Southern Africa, endeavour to do.   And the system works well wheresoever it is faithfully applied.

I found in my new Circuit that I was committed to a vigorous administration of its affairs. I began by a personal pastoral call upon every family connected with our congregations. I then addressed a note to each treasurer of the Church Trusts, for a copy of the balance sheet as audited and presented at the last Anniversary. My object was to get an exact knowledge of the financial condition of each Trust. I advanced the cash necessary for paying off the Circuit debt (£129 19s. 10d.), so that all interest might be stopped. The way now seemed cleared for an 'onward movement,' and my colleague, Mr. Prior, the local preachers, and other Church officers, braced their energies to the Lord's work. This was a courageous policy of administration, and it answered well. We were, indeed, only following a Divine injunction : ' Cast ye up, cast ye up, prepare the way, take up the stumbling-blocks out of the way of My people.'

April 9th.—I opened my commission, by preaching at the Semaphore in aid of the Sunday School. On the next day Mrs. Bickford, Miss Jarvis, and I, accompanied the teachers, children, and parents to their annual picnic. There was a large gathering, and the enjoyment of all was innocent and stimulating. We had a Sunday School Teachers' tea in the evening, over which I presided. This was a good beginning of active ministerial service.

May 24th.—The Queen is sixty-three years of age to-day. I went to the Governor's *levée* in her honour, as is my invariable custom. I then went to North Adelaide for the annual Conference of the ' South Australia Temperance Society and Band of Hope,' and took my full share in its proceedings. In the evening I went over to Birkenhead, and presided at the Good Templars' Meeting. I returned home at 9 p.m. much tired, but it was not a lost day by any means.

May 29th.—I voted for Messrs. Salom, Madge, Ridgeway, Cotton, Glyde, and Murray, who were candidates for seats in the Legislative Council. I regard the franchise our democratic Constitution gives me as a solemn responsibility, and I always exercise it as I think just and right.

June 7th.—I, also, as an Austral-Englishman, claim the privilege of corresponding with the 'powers that be,' in the old country, on matters affecting distinguished men in the service of the Queen, when I think proper so to do. To-day, with that feeling, I addressed a letter to Mr. Gladstone, Prime Minister, asking that the honour of a K.C.M.G. might be conferred on ——— as one eminently deserving that distinction. It is a strange omission in some quarters that this has not been done long before this.

June 28th.—Nothing like a diligent attendance to the routine work of a Circuit for spending time pleasantly. Here we are already at the end of June, and our Quarterly Meeting has to be held this evening. We accordingly met at Mr. Shorney's, at the Semaphore, and had a large attendance. The income had sprung to £150 9s. 11d., and the expenditure was £150 8s. 11d. The number of members' names on the class-books was one hundred and forty-seven, so that our income was a little over £1 per head, taking for convenience the members as a basis, for the quarter then ending. On the motion of Mr. E. Butler, it was unanimously agreed to invite Dr. Bollen, Messrs. J. Ottaway, J. Rofe, and J. Bray to resume their former positions in the Port Church, and I was requested to conduct this delicate business, which I gladly consented to do.

July 1st.—Our so-called 'White Elephant' (the Northern Territory) is still a practical difficulty with our Government. Just now the Legislature is engaged in discussing a Bill entitled, 'The Indian Immigration Bill,' for the introduction of Coolie labour to work the sugar estates. I secured a copy of the Bill ; and, if I rightly recollect, it is pretty much a transcript of an Act passed many years ago by the Court of Policy in British Guiana for a similar object. I was constrained, in the sorrowful remembrance of the working of that Act, to write a strongly remonstrative letter for publication in the *Register*, in opposition against the Bill now before our Parliament. How can we expect these poor creatures, on their arrival in the Territory, entering into written engagements with white men, and under penalties, too, the meaning of which they cannot understand. But this is only one aspect of the matter.

July 25th.—I interred to-day the remains of the late Mrs. Dr. Mitchell. I found her ill when I came to the Port last April, and now she is gone to the land where sickness is unknown. She was the daughter of Dr. Bollen, and died at the early age of twenty-five. Sweetness itself in her temper, and heavenly in her aspirations, she seems to have been too good to battle with the storms of human life. Her end was eminently peaceful. She 'fell on sleep.'

On the 24th I received a letter from the Hon. G. W. Cotton, M.L.C., approving of my view of the case.

July 28th.—We made an effort for the reduction of the debt on

Alberton Church. The Revs. R. S. Casely and G. E. Rowe did us valuable service. We raised over £100.

Aug. 7th.—I prepared a lengthy article on the Methodist Confer- ences of Ireland, France, and England, for the *Christian Weekly.* So few of our people take the *Watchman,* or *Recorder,* or *Monthly Times,* that I think it one's duty to supply them with such in- formation as my article contains. On the 11th I wrote a letter, for publication in the *Register,* on ' The Egyptian Embroglio and England's Duty.' I gave much care to the preparation of this communication in the hope that it may clear the mistiness away which clouds many minds in regard to the origin of this melancholy outbreak.

Aug. 8th.—I read in Dean Stanley's ' Christian Institutions ' with surpassing satisfaction. The Dean is the kind of ' Churchman ' that I greatly honour. He is faithful to historical traditions, although they may be against the high assumptions of the hierarchs of his own Church. But, in the largeness of his Christian instincts, he cannot help it. ' The love of Christ constrains him.'

Aug. 21st.—I breakfasted at the Rev. J. B. Stephenson's to meet his eminent cousin, the Rev. Dr. Bowman Stephenson, Mrs. Stephenson, and daughter. We arranged a programme for the Doctor's visitation of Circuits while he remains with us. ' The Children's Home' is the burden of his tale, and a good tale it is. South Australia is bound to help this Apostle of Humanity in a substantial manner.

Sept. 27th.—We held the Quarterly Meeting. Samuel Rossiter was recommended as a candidate for our Ministry. It was a really good meeting.

Oct. 3rd.—Dr. Stephenson, in the Port Town Hall, this evening gave his lecture on the ' Children's Home and Orphanage ' in England. He had a sympathizing audience.

Oct. 7th.—Mrs. Bickford and I left for Blackwood, and were welcomed by the Hon. John and Mrs. Carr. We spent an inter- esting evening with the family and friends who were there to meet us. I preached the next day in behalf of the Church Trust.

On Monday evening the tea and public meeting came off. We had a fine attendance, and raised £56.

Oct. 10th.—I rose at 4 a.m., and saw a comet in the east. I have seen many in my time, but this one is a stranger to me. But we shall soon learn what Mr. C. Todd, our learned scientist, has to say of this brilliant visitor.

Oct. 14*th.*—Dr. Bollen and I called on Mrs. Bayertz, a converted Jewess, and a successful evangelist, about the proposed services it is desired she should hold in the Semaphore Church. The interview was very pleasant, and I was impressed with her freedom from all foolish airs. She was natural, intelligent, self-possessed, and eminently religious in her whole bearing. We were much pleased with her.

Oct. 20*th.*— The District Meeting closed to-day. We recommended James Robert Bradbury, William George Clarke, John Charles Hill, and Samuel Rossiter for our work. We were nearly four days in session. The Rev. R. S. Casely presided over our deliberations; and under his guidance we had a happy and successful meeting.

Nov. 6*th.*—Mrs. Bickford and I embarked in the *South Australian* for Geelong *viâ* Melbourne. We were forty passengers, who, soon after starting, disappeared. Poor things !

We reached Geelong on the 8th, my nephew, the Rev. E. S. Bickford, and Allan his son, were at the station to receive us. We went to the annual ' Flower Show ' in the evening, which was very beautiful. Mr. and Mrs. Hitchcock were the presiding genii of the affair. We saw many of our old friends, which was a real pleasure to us.

Nov. 13*th.*—Dr. Stephenson lectured for his great ' charity,' the ' Children's Home.' We had a good attendance, and, at the close, I said a few words in commendation of his object.

Nov. 14*th.*—I called in at the District Meeting, when the brethren welcomed me with much warmth of feeling. The Rev. Henry Bath was in the chair. In the evening I lectured at Newtown in aid of the Trust funds. My subject was ' My Trip to England and Back,' which took me an hour and a half in its delivery.

Nov. 15*th.*—We went to Melbourne, and were the guests of our early and kind friends, Mr. and Mrs. Edward Oakley, at Carlton. In the afternoon I dropped in at the District Meeting, the Rev. W. L. Binks, presiding. It was pleasant to see a few of my former comrades in many a struggle, occasioned by the distractions of the discovery of the Goldfields. But all, even the youngest of the brethren, were warm in their welcome. Blessed be God for the brotherhood of Wesleyan Ministers ! We visited about a great deal, but the weather was too hot for much enjoyment.

Dec. 1*st.* [Diary Jotting]—'On board the *South Australian* on our way to Port Adelaide. Passengers very agreeable, and the weather beautiful. But I am out of sorts somehow. I shall be better, I hope, when again on shore. Mrs. Bickford was much indisposed after the voyage.'

Dec. 10*th.* [Diary Jotting]—'Could not preach to-day, but was confined to the house quite ill.'

Dec. 15*th.* [Diary Jotting]—'Little better, but still unwell. The gout is come into my left foot to distress me still further. This is the second time in my life I have had this terrible evil upon me.'

Dec. 16*th.* [Diary Jotting]—'Given up all thoughts of preaching on Sunday, in obedience to my medical adviser, Dr. Mitchell. Can't put my foot to the floor without the acutest pain. (Is this a messenger of Satan to buffet me?) Mr. President Casely came to see me and Mrs. Bickford, who is also very ill.'

Dec. 20*th.*—We have had the Rev. Mr. Youngman here as missionary deputation but I could not hear him, which was a great deprivation. The Rev. Joseph Nicholson did us good service at the Semaphore.

Dec. 24*th.*—I was able to take my appointments. Blessed be God! 'Though He slay me, yet will I trust Him.'

1883.

Jan. 1*st.* [Diary Jotting]—'In God's good providence I have entered upon the duties and responsibilities of another year. At the "Watch Night Service" I gave myself, "body, spirit, and soul," to my Lord and Saviour. May God accept the surrender, and be with me for good!'

Jan. 6*th.*—Our popular Governor, Sir William Jervois, held a *levée* to-day, prior to his leaving South Australia for New Zealand. I went, of course, to show my respect for the Queen he has represented during his gubernatorial reign over us; but, also, for himself, as one of the best Governors this Colony has ever had. Indeed, for blamelessness of character, and as a vigorous administrator, I class him with Sir Henry Barkly, and that is no small compliment.

Jan. 7*th.* [Diary Jotting]—'Heard Mr. Prior preach an excellent sermon at the Port. In the afternoon I conducted the "Renewal of Covenant Service," and gave the Lord's Supper. I preached at Alberton in the evening; held the "Covenant Service," and gave the Lord's Supper.'

Jan. 8*th.*—For some months I had given a weekly visit to our day school, at Birkenhead, conducted by a Mrs. Jones, a qualified teacher from England, to assist her in giving a Bible Lesson for the attendant children. There was no difficulty in carrying out this exercise to the fullest extent. This pleasing fact led me to consider, whether it would not be possible for some arrangement to be made for giving Bible Lessons to the Port Model School, by ministers of religion, on one or two days in each week, according to the Board's Regulations, or in some other way. I, therefore, sent a circular note to each minister, asking them to meet me in my study to consider the desirableness of our making some attempt to accomplish this object. Accordingly, this forenoon, the Rev. Canon Green, Pastor Bambour, Revs. J. C. Kirby, J. H. Angas, and M. Lloyd, met to talk the matter over. We agreed to try to secure permission from the Board for the use of one of the classrooms, during school hours, for meeting such of the pupils as choose to attend, and Mr. Kirby and I were requested to communicate with the Minister of Education on the subject. This we did, but we failed to get the desired concession; besides which there would be a monetary charge upon us, even if the exercises were held before or after the hours for the daily routine school-work. We saw, therefore, that we could proceed no farther until the Act was so amended as to permit Bible Reading being given within school hours, instead of before or after as the Act provides. And at that point we stopped for the present. We agreed at this meeting to form a branch of the Society for the Promotion of Social Purity, and Canon Green was requested to act as Secretary.

Jan. 11*th.* [Diary Jotting]—‘Mr. T. Hack informed me that the “Site Committee,” which had been appointed by the Quarterly Meeting, had recommended the sale of the property in St. Vincent Street, and the purchase of a new site in Dale Street. So that I am in for work of an anxious kind. I have no doubt but that God will help us through.’

Jan. 16*th.*—I held a Special Trustee Meeting of the Port property in Vincent Street. We agreed to ask the permission of the Conference to sell the property, and erect new premises in Dale Street. All the trustees were of one mind in this proposed action.

Jan. 17*th.*—The Rev. R. S. Casely opened the Annual Conference this (Wednesday) evening, and I was elected as his successor by a majority of twenty-four votes. The probationers were examined the next day, and the stations were read a second time in the Saturday forenoon.

Jan. 21*st.*—I preached the official sermon in Pirie Street Church. Text, Eccles. ii. 26. By invitation, the Revs. Knight, Casely, Lane,

Hunter, myself, and Major Ferguson dined at the Chief Justice's, Montefiore Hill, North Adelaide. His Honour is happy, indeed, in his manner of entertaining his clerical friends. We certainly had a lively, but not a frivolous, time. I heard Mr. ex-President Casely preach a good sermon in the evening.

Jan. 26th. [Diary Jotting]—'I went to Conference, and presided all the day. We had a great debate on "Bible Reading in State Schools during school hours," but a vote was not taken. In the afternoon, Brother Patchell, in a few minutes after he had spoken, was seized with an apoplectic fit, from which he never rallied. He died in one hour and ten minutes from the time he was attacked. We could do no more business; and, after a season of prayer, we met in the evening to make arrangements for the funeral.'

The next day, in the afternoon, the mortal remains of this good and useful man were laid in the silent grave, at the Western Cemetery, in the presence of the bereaved Mrs. Patchell, a large number of friends of the family, and by nearly the whole Conference of Ministers. I felt more than I can describe, whilst reading the service at the grave over the remains of my former colleague in the Pirie Street Circuit.

Jan. 28th.—As President it fell to my lot to preach the funeral sermon for my departed friend the day after the funeral. I was very unwell, but I did the best I could. After the service I went to my friends the Wallaces' for the night. I was much wearied and sorrow-stricken with the painful scenes and labours through which I had passed.

Jan. 30th.—We reached the end of our business. The Minutes were signed at 9 p.m. My old heart thanked God for His merciful aid vouchsafed to me from day to day as I presided over the Sessions of this Conference.

Feb. 4th.—By request of the Conference, I visited Goolwa, to improve the death of their late pastor, Mr. Patchell. I had a large congregation at the evening service, and much feeling was shown by the bereaved church. I met the officials, and arranged for a supply until April next. I left Mrs. Patchell and family, after commending them to the care and love of the Heavenly Father.

Feb. 19th.—I went up to the city to witness the ceremony of the swearing-in of the new Governor, Sir William F. C. Robinson. Several of the brethren were present. Sir William held a *levée* on the 21st, when 600 gentlemen were presented. I read the address, which the Governor nicely responded to.

Feb. 22nd.—I now feel as if a cup of sorrow were about to be administered to me. My dear wife is prostrate in body and mind, from a paralytic attack. It came on early this morning, when her sister, Mrs. Jarvis, perceived that she was unable to articulate her words. We sent at once for Dr. Mitchell, and committed the case to him to do his best.

Feb. 23rd.—We thought Mrs. Bickford would have died in the night, but she has rallied a little this morning. She can speak, but not converse with us. Kind friends keep calling, but the doctor has peremptorily ordered that no visitors must see her. Perfect quiet and nourishment are all that can be done just now. Mrs. Saunday came and sat up with the dear sick one.

Feb. 24th.—I tried to do something for to-morrow (Sunday), but found myself unequal to it. Mrs. Bickford is still very, very ill. Alas! for the cloud of sorrow which has come upon us.

March 12th.—Notwithstanding Mrs. Bickford's precarious condition, I was compelled to leave her and go to Port Augusta, to give evidence in a case of bigamy. The journey was two hundred and eighty-five miles by rail. I arrived in time to speak at the Church Anniversary for a few minutes. The Rev. W. and Mrs. Reed gave me a kind welcome.

March 13th.—I attended the Court, presided over by Chief Justice Way. Johnston, the bigamist, after confronting me, by the advice of his Counsel, 'confessed judgment,' and was sentenced to six months' imprisonment. The Rev. Samuel Knight lectured this evening on his 'Travels in Europe and America,' which was full of fine touches—descriptive and oratorical. It was well received. I moved a vote of thanks to him.

March 14th.—The Rev. S. Knight, Mr. Moncrieff, and I left for Quorn this morning. I had a fine view of the Pichirichi Pass. I preached in the evening, and met afterwards four of the church officers, and heard their grievances. They want, they say, a Methodist Administration of the affairs of the Circuit. Mr. Knight was present. We were in the church until a late hour. We were the guests of Mr. and Mrs. Moncrieff, who showed us all possible kindness.

This is the third time my brethren have elected me to the position of President of Annual Conference. As an expression of their confidence, it is valuable; but the office involves much responsibility.

It is not a sinecure by any means: it confers no financial advantage ; the honour of the office is its only reward. It does not create a higher grade of ministerial 'orders;' but rests upon a previous historical eldership received from Wesley and Coke. For the time being, the President is a veritable Bishop (ἐπίσκοπος), and does the work of visiting the Circuits, and guides the affairs of the Connexion over which he is placed. In addition to the duties of the Presidency, he is generally the Superintendent of a Circuit, and takes his turn with his colleagues in preaching and pastoral labours. An onerous position for any man ; no one covets it ; but, when it comes, it is cheerfully accepted. My visit to Quorn was in virtue of my office as President. But this was only a beginning of such 'journeyings ;' for on the 23rd instant, I had to be in the Laura Circuit on a very difficult errand. The Rev. D. S. Wylie drove me from Gladstone to Yarcowie, where I had to meet the Church officers in their Quarterly Meeting. I heard their 'tale' of troubles ; and, ultimately, by mutual concession and explanations, I succeeded in making 'peace among the brethren.'

I attended the Church Anniversary in the evening, when I gave, extempore, the substance of my lecture on ' My Trip to England and Back.' We had a very fine meeting. We then drove to Laura, and I was kindly entertained by Mr. and Mrs. Close. This has been a trying day in many respects.

March 25th.—I was at Kooringa in the interests of the Sunday School ; and at the beautiful ' Service of Song ' in the afternoon, I read the connective pieces. In the absence of the Rev. Samuel Knight, Superintendent, the next day I held the Quarterly Meeting, which was easily got through. The usual tea and public meeting were held in the evening, and passed off well. I returned home on the 27th, and found Mrs. Bickford, considerably improved, downstairs in the parlour.

March 30th.—I held the Quarterly Meeting at Woodville. We reported 240 members ; income, £170 7s. 1d. ; expenditure, £148 1s. ; balance in hands of Stewards, £22 6s. 1d. It was an excellent meeting, but it always is the case when the balance is on the right side. I had two deputations to-day about the supply for Kangaroo Island, and Woodside in the Mount Barker Circuit.

April 15th.—I was at Yankalilla in the interests of the Church Trust. I preached twice to good congregations. The next morning the Rev. John Watts took me to see some good Wesleyan families—the Heathcotes, Duftys and Faulkners. We went also to see the Gorge on the sea-coast, which is finely romantic. I lectured in the evening: Messrs. Watts and O. Lake were present.

April 17th.—Two young ministers from England came to-day: Messrs. W. A. Potts and G. W. Kendrew. The next day we appointed them to their stations until next Conference. Dr. Kelynack is visiting us upon missionary business. Messrs. Burgess, Stephenson, and I met him in consultation. We shall help him all that we can.

April 25th. [Diary Jotting]—'I went to Prince Alfred College to receive the Governor, Sir W. T. C. Robinson, who was coming to see the Institution. About 400 boys were present. His Excellency was much pleased at what he saw and heard.'

April 27th.—I wrote a letter to the *Register*, *re* the action of the Anglican Synod ignoring our efforts in the Northern Territory. How foolish it is for these clerics to shut their eyes to the presence of the plainest facts! But it can make no difference to us, for we began evangelistic work at Palmerston before the Anglicans, and shall 'hold the fort' against all odds.

May 6th. [Diary Jotting]—'I am this day sixty-seven years of age. May the good Lord forget me not as my strength shall fail; but be merciful to me to the end.—Amen.'

May 10th.—I took tea at Mr. T. Hack's, with several friends, to meet Dr. Kelynack. His lecture came off in the evening. We raised £60 for the missions debt.

May 24th.—I attended the *levée:* Messrs. Casely, Hunter, Stoyell, and I went in together. The Governor was very complaisant and nice. Bishop Kennion and I spoke a few words to him. Introduced the brethren to Sir William.

May 31st.—I was at Port Pirie on very unpleasant business.

June 2nd.—Mrs. Bickford had a second attack of paralysis at 5 o'clock this morning. She is perfectly helpless.

June 8th.—I met thirteen young men, to form 'The Port Adelaide and Alberton Young Men's Christian and Literary Society.' If vigorously carried out, this Society will meet a great want which has long been felt.

June 11th.—I wrote my dear friend, Mrs. Holder, at the Burra, on Mrs. Bickford's dangerous condition, and requested the prayers of my late ' flock ' for her.

June 14th.—I wrote a letter to the *Register* on the subject of Immigration, suggesting that the Government should arrange with the *Orient* line of steamers for conveying them from England to Port Adelaide instead of coming by sailing vessels. I gave good reasons for the change I suggested.

June 18th.—I attended the Bible Christian Church Anniversary. Mr. Mattinson, M.P., in the chair. I gave a guinea for Mrs. Bickford, as an expression of her loving memory of her brother, John Brown Tapp, who, for many years, was an able minister of that body. He died in Canada in 1876.

June 20th.—I went to the Upper Sturt to hold the Quarterly Meeting. The Hon. John Carr, M.P., was with me. I lectured in the evening.

June 29th.—We held the Quarterly Meeting, .The membership had risen to 251; on trial, 35. Income, £196 7s. 10d. Expenditure, £166 7s. 10d. Credit balance, £30.

July 14th.—Bishop Kennion and I travelled from Hamley Bridge to Moonta. As we rushed along, we had much conversation on English Church affairs. In the afternoon he and I addressed the miners in the carpenters' workshop at the mines. It was rather a romantic service. I spent a quiet evening at the Handcocks.' The next day I preached at Moonta in aid of the Trust of Yelta Church. It was cold, and I felt very uncomfortable all the day. I lectured the next evening (Monday) at Moonta, to about 300 persons. The financial result was satisfactory.

Aug. 13th. [Diary Jotting]—' The "Salvation Army" had a great row to-night in Commercial Road. Captain Gibbs and Captain Ross were in deadly opposition ; the former proved the stronger party. It was a disgusting exhibition of ignorance, irreligiousness, and boisterousness.'

Aug. 14th.—I went as usual to visit our Birkenhead day school, and was much pleased with the Bible Lesson: Subject, ' The History of David.' About eighty children are in attendance.

Sept. 26th.—In the absence of the Rev. T. Lloyd, the Superintendent of the Glenelg Circuit, I went thither to hold the Quarterly Meeting. Income, £126 0s. 8d. Expenditure was £91 3s. 9d. Members, 171. I was the guest of Mr. and Mrs. A. A. Scott.

Sept. 28th.—We held the Quarterly Meeting. Members 290. on trial, 68. Income, £197 10s. 1d. Expenditure, £177 12s. 6d. The official returns of our Sunday Schools were :—Teachers, 82 ; Children on the Roll, 815. Meeting in class, 57.

Oct. 9th. [Diary Jotting]—'I held the Monthly Fellowship Meeting of all the classes. There was a fine attendance and a good feeling.'

Oct. 16th.—I left early for the District Meeting. We had two cases of discipline, which were a great pain to us. The Financial Meeting was held the next day. We had an evening sitting and closed the business of the Connexional funds. We sat on the 18th and 19th, considering the cases of candidates, probationers, etc., and finished our work. This was a distressful District Meeting to me, which was only compensated by an unanimous vote of thanks from the brethren for my conduct in the chair.

Oct. 23rd.—I went to Parkside, and purchased a newly erected cottage in Young Street, near to the church now in course of erection. This has been done in the expectation of my becoming a Supernumerary at the next Conference. Mrs. Bickford's enfeebled health, and my physical inability to do the pastoral work of a Circuit, compel me to take this course.

Oct. 28th.—I preached at Mount Barker. In the evening the Institute was quite filled. The next day I attended the tea and public meeting, and spoke fifty minutes with considerable freedom. I was the welcome guest of the Hon. J. and Mrs. Dunn.*

Oct. 30th.—I went over to Woodside, and lectured in the Institute on ' My Trip to England and Back.'

Oct. 31st.—Mr. Wheatley, just from England, preached a good, practical sermon at the Semaphore this evening. I shall have every confidence in sending him to Mitcham, until the Conference, as second preacher in the Unley Circuit.

Nov. 1st.—By invitation I attended the laying of the ' Foundation Stone ' of the Young Men's Christian Association, and attended the banquet in the Town Hall. This good enterprise is launched under high auspices, and I hope and pray it may contribute much to the advantage of those for whose benefit it has been undertaken.

---

* Nothing like the country for a little leisure for reading. To-day, at Mr. Dunn's, I read the Revised Edition of St. Paul's Epistle to the Romans right through in the morning. It was a great treat, and I enjoyed it much.

Nov. 2nd.—I read an article in the *Nineteenth Century* on 'After Death.' Thank God for the Holy Scriptures, which have brought 'Life and Immortality to Light.'

Nov. 3rd.—I went to the Hon. John Colton's to dine. There was a select gathering of friends. I saw the dear old Mrs. Colton, and conversed and prayed with her.

Nov. 5th.—I had the pleasure of attending the stone-laying ceremony in the rising suburb of Parkside. We have probably a hundred families already settled in the neighbourhood, for whom, as a Church, we are only now beginning to provide religious ordinances. The Rev. J. B. Stephenson, Superintendent, and the Pirie Street Trustees, originated this movement in the most generous spirit. The church to be erected will be commodious and elegant; and in every way in keeping with the rising importance and attractiveness of the district. The cost, inclusive of site, will be over £5,000.

Nov. 7th.—We laid the 'Foundation Stone' of the additions to the Semaphore Church, and raised £55. It was an enthusiastic affair.

Nov. 19th.—We laid the 'Stone' at Woodville of a new church, to cost £1,050. Assets, so far, probably £532.

Nov. 27th.—We held the Quarterly Meeting. Income £194 6s. 6d.; expenditure £177 18s. 11d. Dr. Mitchell and Mr. George Shorney were appointed Circuit Stewards, and Mr. Hack as Representative to Conference.

Dec. 31st. [Diary Jotting]—'My mind is much affected this morning with a deep sense of the goodness of God to me and my dear partner. "I will sing of mercy and of judgment; unto Thee, O Lord, will I sing." I conducted the 'Watch Night Service;' Messrs. Hounslow, Ottaway, and Rofe took part. We had a good attendance and a good time. One young man came up to the Communion rails, and weepingly sought salvation.'

During this year I had, as President, several communications with the Rev. John Kilner, of the London Mission House; the Rev. William Lowe, the venerable chairman; and the Hon. George Shenton, M. L. C., Perth (West Australia), on the subject of a steady ministerial supply from home for that sparsely populated but important colony, at the Committee's expense. Under date, February 14th, 1883, the Rev. John Kilner, senior Missionary Secretary, thus wrote Mr. Shenton:—

'We pray that your work may so take root and spread, that you may be able readily not only to meet the comparatively small expense of passage and outfit of the needed reinforcements from England referred to, but to occupy new ground until the land is won for Christ.'

Of this paragraph Mr. Shenton says in a letter to me, May 23rd, 1883—

'I forward Mr. Kilner's letter, and you will take notice that he only refers to " passage and outfit," therefore I do not see how they can ask us for the college expense. I hope you will speedily hear that they are sending us two men.'

Since then, the South Australian Conference has undertaken to supply the Sister Church with ministers, but the District and Circuit claims are to fall entirely upon Western Australia itself. This is an equitable and final arrangement.*

1884.

Jan. 1st. [Diary Jotting]—'I commenced this year on my knees in the Port Church. Possibly, I may stand aside from the itinerancy after the Conference. If so, the wrench, after forty-six years of unremitting service "among my own people," will be severe. But Dr. Mitchell says "that he cannot incur the responsibility of not advising a removal of Mrs. Bickford from the Port." God's will be done. This removal, at the end of two years, seems to involve my becoming a. Supernumerary. But, I shall not be inactive. I will serve Methodism in my comparative retirement.'

Jan. 12th.—The Rev. J. B. Stephenson called to ask me if I would accept Parkside as a station in April next, should the Conference make me a Supernumerary. My duties would be few, and just what my strength permitted. He came in the name of the Circuit Stewards, Messrs. Dungey and Colton, to consult me on the matter. I thanked him for his kindness in thinking of me.

Jan. 16th.—I opened the Conference in Pirie Street Church at 7 p.m., and, after ' supplications and prayers' by two or three of the brethren, I gave a *résumé* of the work of the year. The Rev. Robert

---

* In a letter, dated July 13th, 1883, the Rev. John Kilner, senior Secretary of our Foreign Missions, in reply to letters from me urging the continuance of the Committee's help to Western Australia, says : ' The Committee cannot re-open the question of our relation to the Mission in Western Australia. They cannot do anything towards the maintenance of the work there. This is the unchangeable conviction of the Committee. Be assured that our sympathy for Western Australia, and for other openings within the area of your Conference, is as real and as warm as ever. If we can help you in anything that does not mean money grants we shall be glad to do so.'

FERN WATERFALL, ADELAIDE.

Morris Hunter was elected as my successor—a position he has earned by his fine character, and wise conduct of all the Circuits in which he has travelled. The Rev. W. Lowe, Chairman of the Western Australia District, after many years of highly honourable service in Tasmania, Victoria, South Australia, and Western Australia, was, at his own request, made a Supernumerary Minister.

Jan. 19th.—I examined the four-years' men, Thomas Britton Angwin, M.A., and George Edwards Rowe, both of whom were received for Ordination to the full work of the Christian Ministry. We received six candidates, and two as students in Prince Alfred College.

Jan. 23rd.—At Kent Town Church this evening, I gave the 'charge' to the newly ordained ministers. It was founded upon Acts xx. 17, 28 : 'And from Miletus he sent to Ephesus, and called to him the elders of the Church. And when they were come to him, he said unto them. . . . Take heed unto yourselves, and to all the flock, in which the Holy Ghost hath made you bishops, to feed the Church of God, which He purchased with His own blood' (R.V.) The object of my 'charge' was specially to show the undoubted identity of the 'Elders' and 'Bishops,' as an 'order' of ministry in the Apostolic and Primitive Churches; and, that, if the ministerial* succession, as shown in the earliest reliable ecclesiastical history, be of any value in the argument, then the Branch of the Catholic Church known as the Wesleyan Methodist, has a valid ministry derived from Wesley and Coke, who were presbyters ('elders) of the Church of England. This was the only controversial charge I have given; it was well listened to by a crowded congregation, and the whole Conference of Ministers, with evident satisfaction. It was a great relief to me the next morning when the Hon. John Carr, M.P., moved : 'That the thanks of the Conference be given to the Rev. J. Bickford, the ex-President, for his able, practical, and appropriate charge to the young ministers who have been received into full connexion.' I knew that the ground over which I had travelled was novel, and, perhaps, a little dangerous ;

---

* I designedly disown the misleading phrase, 'Apostolical' succession, and use instead 'Ministerial.' The Apostles, as such, had no successors—no lineage ; in the course of nature, they died as do other men ; and, with their deaths, the 'order' ceased. But not so the ministerial succession ; which lives to day, and must live on, until this dispensation of grace is closed by the Lord Himself, 'when He shall come the second time without sin unto Salvation.'

but, I have had no reason since to regret the course that I adopted. I felt that the time had come for me, as the oldest minister in the South Australia Conference, to try, at least, 'to stop the mouth of every foe' by justifying our position as a Scriptural Church, having a valid ministry beyond all reasonable assailment.

The Conference was pleased to insert in its Minutes the following notice of my retirement from the Methodist Itinerancy:—

'REV. JAMES BICKFORD.

'After forty-six years of active and valued service in the Ministry of our Church, in the West Indies and in these Colonies, the Conference regrets that it now becomes necessary, mainly on the ground of family affliction, to accede to the application of Mr. Bickford to become a Supernumerary. But, in meeting this request, the Conference places on record its high appreciation of Mr. Bickford's labours in every department of our Church work. Mr. Bickford has several times been Chairman of District; and on three occasions has been elected to the Chair of the Conference. He has most faithfully discharged his duties as a pastor, a preacher, and an administrator of Church affairs. He has won a high place in the esteem and affection both of his brethren and of the members and adherents of our Church. The Conference trusts that, in the comparative retirement of his present position, he will have many years granted him, during which he, with his ripe experience, will still be able to continue to render help in the great cause to which he has devoted his life.'

Jan. 28th.—We closed the Conference to day. The Minutes were read and signed: 'So we departed.'

Feb. 3rd.—I was at Willunga in the interests of the Church Trust. The next morning I went to the Slate Quarries in the company of Mr. George Sara, J.P., and soon found that there was a mine of wealth there only waiting to be worked on a larger scale. I lectured in the evening to a good audience. Proceeds between £70 and £80.

Feb. 10th.—I opened for Divine worship the new church at Aldgate. On the Tuesday evening the after meetings were held; the Hon. L. Carr presiding. It was a successful service.

Feb. 18th.—I read, in the *Nineteenth Century*, Earl Grey's article on the 'Condition of Ireland.' I was much disappointed with it.

March 4th.—I went to the stone-laying ceremony of the Dunn Memorial Church at Mount Barker. This church, now in course of erection, is the gift of the Hon. J. Dunn, ex-M.L.C., to the Wesleyan Methodist Connexion. It is a princely benefaction to the Mount Barker District: 'beautiful for situation,' like Zion of old, to which the tribes of our Israel will go up to worship as the centuries roll on.

March 17th.—A valedictory meeting was held at Port Adelaide for the Circuit ministers (Messrs. Bickford and Prior) in anticipation of our departure at the end of the month. It was largely attended, and Dr. Mitchell presided over it with affectionate courtesy. The following address was presented to me ; and, as it is the last of the kind that I could receive as an itinerant Wesleyan minister, it is here given in full :—

· To THE REV. JAMES BICKFORD,—Superintendent of the Port Adelaide and Semaphore Circuit, and ex-President of the Wesleyan Methodist Conference of South Australia.

' DEAR SIR AND BROTHER,—

'It is with no ordinary feelings that we approach the pending change of ministers, blessed as the Circuit has been in having you as Superintendent for the past two years. That we shall regret the departure from us of our experienced and beloved pastor will, we hope, require no assurance here, seeing the appreciation that has ever manifested itself in regard to your earnest, genuine, and faithful ministry amongst us ; and that you will have our earnest prayers and heartfelt sympathy in the unusual circumstances of your departure will, we believe, be as readily understood.

'Having been a minister of the Gospel in various lands for forty-six years, and thrice President of Conference, it is no insignificant and uninteresting fact to us, that your retirement here dates your retirement from that official and active work for God and His Church, which we know has been your delight. Greatly as we regret the loss of our minister, we more deeply regret the Church's loss of your continued eminent services.

'The Lord in His providence, "too wise to err, too good to be unkind," has dictated your retirement in the affliction of your dear wife, but we pray that your joint lives may be spared to enjoy for many years the rest you both deserve and need. Our sympathy will follow you, and may the Great Father amply sustain you to the end of this life, and give you an abundant entrance to a higher sphere beyond it.

'We cannot conclude without referring to the success of this Circuit in connection with your ministry and administration. You have promoted harmony, and re-organized the finances, while the membership has doubled, and important enterprises have been initiated. With earnest for the Divine blessing on your house,—

'On behalf of the Circuit,

'We are, yours very sincerely,

'JAMES T. MITCHELL, } *Circuit Stewards.*
'GEORGE SHORNEY,

' *March 17th,* 1884.'

April 7th.—A mere 'fly on the wheel' surely I am this very day. God works, and I am no more than than the smallest insect in the evolutions of His providence. My last Quarterly Meeting was held on the 26th ult., and on the 6th current, I opened the new church at Woodville. The preachers for the day were, myself, the Rev. G. W. Kendrew, and the Rev. J. Angas. In the evening I preached in the Presbyterian Church, after which I went to the Town Hall, and addressed Mr. Hounslow's nautical congregation So closed my ministry at the Port.

[Diary Jotting]—'We left the Port this morning for Parkside : Mrs. Bickford and Miss Jarvis went on in the waggonette, and I went by rail. Mrs. Harris and Mrs. Jarvis were at " Edmeston Cottage " to receive us. Everything was well arranged—thanks to my friends. Mrs. Bickford stood the journey much better than I expected. Here we shall have a quiet retreat : God grant that we may for some years enjoy it !'

April 12th.—I read two or three Lent addresses by a French Jesuit, which were very fine in some parts. I prepared an outline for to-morrow evening at Archer Street. The quiet of this place is delightful after all the worry of my itinerant life.

May 4th.—We opened the new Church at Parkside to-day. The dedication of the building was begun at 7 o'clock, which was a time of gracious visitation. The 'ark of the covenant' was then brought 'into the House of the Lord.' The Revs. J. B. Stephenson, R. M. Hunter, and J. Bickford preached the sermons. It was a day of great rejoicing to us all.

May 6th. [Diary Jotting]—'I am this day sixty-eight years of age. I am the Lord's by personal consecration, and HIM will I serve with every power I possess.'

I am busily engaged in preparing for the public meetings of this evening. We had large attendances, and, everything included, the result was, say, £220. We had many presents. Mr. and Mrs. A. A. Scott, gave the Communion Service ; Mrs. Catt gave the carpeting for the rostrum and communion ; Mrs. Gully gave the Bible, Hymn, and Service Book; Mrs. Wallace gave the pulpit chair; and the Misses Gully gave the pulpit cushion. Messrs. Pengelly and Knobe promised the Communion Table. It was certainly a glorious beginning of the cause at Parkside.

May 8th.—I read in Bacon's Essays, with Archbishop Whately's Annotations, for two hours, and received some solid instruction.

May 10*th.*—We let 131 sittings in the new church to-day. Thank God for this token of His favour.

May 14*th.*—The first Society class was held to-day. There were present :—James Bickford, Leader ; and Mesdames Norton, Sykes, Patterson, and Shepherd. In the evening the Rev. R. M. Hunter preached, and held the first leader's meeting. There were present. Mr. Hunter in the chair, and the Rev. James Bickford ; also Messrs. W. Gully, B. Norton, G. Viney, and A. A. Scott. On the nomination of the Superintendent, the following appointments were made :— Society Stewards, W. Gully and George Viney ; Poor Stewards, B. Norton and A. A. Scott ; Leaders, B. Norton, J. B. Butler, and T. T. Prisk. I was requested to take charge of the Wednesday afternoon class. The new cause was thus organised, and set to work.

May 16*th.*—I read the Memoir of the late Rev. Frederick Jobson, D.D. It much interested me, as I had known him so intimately, and had received from him many acts of kindness. It is a beautiful work, and might be enlarged with much advantage.

May 17*th.*—I read in ' Mosheim ' and ' Ancient Christianity ' for several hours. I am becoming quite fascinated with this kind of reading.

May 28*th.*—We held the first Sunday School Teachers' Meeting. The necessary officers were appointed, and the school was fully organised. There were 113 children's names taken down last Sunday. Strange to say, two children did not know their names. The Hon. A. Catt, M.P., was appointed senior Superintendent ; and Mr. Gillingham, senior Secretary.

June 17*th.*—I held the leader's meeting, and entered up in the stewards' books the number of members, the contributions in the classes, and the collections, for the Quarter Board. We appointed Mr. E. Alcock as leader, and Mrs. Wallace to meet a ' Young Christians ' class. Mesdames Gully, Norton, Scott, Prisk, Peacock, and Pilben were appointed a visiting committee of the sick and poor. It was a very nice meeting, and all seemed to be in good heart.

June 18*th.*—I attended the Quarterly Meeting as a supernumerary minister attached by special agreement with the Circuit. It was a large and successful meeting. Pleasing references were made by Mr. Colton and other brethren to the success which has attended the Parkside enterprise.

June 20th.—Richard Dunstan and W. A. Millikan, Prince Alfred College students, came for their theological lecture. I like the spirit of the young men very much. Papers from England to-day. The Egyptian question, even from a financial point of view, is terrible. But El-Mahdi is on his way to the north. May God in His providence stop the cruel career of this false and bloody man!

July 31st.—I wrote a letter for the *Register* on the subject of 'Free Education,' which I advocated in the strongest terms I could use. I do hope that the Legislature will grant this boon to the poor children of the country.

Aug. 8th.—I attended the 'Holiness Convention,' in Pirie Street. The addresses of Messrs. Burgess, Nicholson, Davison, and Nock were able and to the point. The day's proceedings were marked by much of the Divine blessing.

Aug. 16th.—I attended the funeral of the Rev. James Way, one of the pioneers of the 'Bible Christian Church' in this colony. The departed minister was held in high respect for his blameless life and useful ministry.

Sept. 3rd.—I read Joseph Chamberlain's speech in answer to Lord Salisbury—'A Roland for an Oliver.'

Sept. 4th.—I read in the *Wentworth Telegraph* and *Murray Advertising News* a cruel and impudent critique on our Chief Secretary, Hon. John Colton, M.P. The man who wrote it cannot know the man of whom he thus writes. But colonial public men have to pay large penalties for their positions.

Sept. 18th.—I wrote two articles for the *Melbourne Spectator*, on 'The Proposed Dismemberment of the Australasian Wesleyan Methodist Connexion' in New Zealand, and on our own Northern Territory Mission.

Sept. 24th.—I attended the Quarterly Meeting. Balance in hand £185 11s. 10d. I was invited to continue in charge for another year at Parkside.

Oct. 4th. [Diary Jotting]—'Telegram from Rev. Robert Kelly: "If you want to see Mr. Hack, sen., come quick." I went at once, and found on my arrival at the Semaphore that he had died at a quarter to 11 a.m. He was nearly eighty years of age. To him the words apply : " Mark the perfect man, and behold the upright : for the end of that man is peace."'

Oct. 7th.—There are circumstances connected with the Churches (not including the Anglican) which are suggestive of the desirableness of a closer union among the ministers, for dealing with questions which often arise of a social, political, and religious kind, which demand consideration and guidance. Acting upon this belief, the Rev. James (Presbyterian) sent out circulars inviting his brethren of other Churches to form a 'Ministerial Association,' for conference and prayer as occasion may arise.

Oct. 12th.—I went, by special request of the family, to the Semaphore, to preach a funeral sermon for the late Mr. J. B. Hack. Text: Job xiv. 20, 21. The congregation was large, and the attention, throughout the delivery of the sermon and the reading of the obituary, was unbroken. A good colonist, a true Christian, and another of my most attached friends has gone home.

Oct. 13th.—I presided this morning at the first meeting of ' Ministerial Association.' After devotion, 'we agreed not to take any united action to prevent the taxation scheme of the Government relative to the inclusion of church sites.' For this negative result, I am very sorry. I was so much dissatisfied at the non-action, that I wrote a strong remonstrative letter to the *Register*, in opposition to the scope of the tax, over the signature of ' *Presbuteros.*'

Oct. 14th.—District Meeting all day.

Oct. 16th.—I examined, at the request of Mr. President Hunter, Alfred Pickford Burgess and Frederick Finch, who were candidates for our Ministry; both were recommended to the Conference. Messrs. Bennett and Wheatley were to be employed as home missionaries for the year ensuing. I also examined William Andrews Bainger and John Goss for full connexion; both passed very well.

The Sessions closed on the evening of the 17th. As the President was leaving for New Zealand to attend the General Conference, I was requested by him to take charge of the Circuit and all presidential business during his absence, which 1 willingly did.

Oct. 23rd.—I read for a couple of hours, Rev. J. Haslam's Life, which is a very wonderful story. It is the severest thing I have seen for some time, on the hollowness of the High Church theories of certain Anglican Clergymen at home, by one of themselves.

Nov. 4th.—I wrote a letter to the *Register*, entitled, ' Dr. Dendy : Wooden Churches and Dissent.' It is in a jocular style, and may serve a purpose. Ridicule sometimes is a more powerful weapon than cogent reasoning.

Nov. 7th.—Mr. G. W. Coombs died this day. The chequered

life of this servant of God is now over.   He has entered into peace.

Nov. 10th.—I went to the Mayor's banquet this evening.   There were 120 gentlemen present.   The speaking had too much political smack in it for a social gathering.

Nov. 20th.—I read an article in the *London Quarterly*, entitled, 'Christian Perfection.'   The best part of it is the last ; the early and middle portions are too diffuse and difficult to be of much use to ordinary readers.

Nov. 23rd.—In Pirie Street Church, this evening, I preached a funeral sermon for the late G. W. Coombs.   It was a trying time to me and drew largely upon my nervous power.   We had a large congregation, and I got through, I suppose, fairly well.

Nov. 27th.—I wrote to the *Register* a long letter under the signature of ' A Practical, but not a Perplexed Churchman,' in reply to ' A Perplexed Churchwoman,' which had just appeared.   It possibly may clear away some mist.

Dec. 1st.—I attended the meeting of the ' Ministerial Association ; this morning.   The Rev. Dr. Paton spoke well on the aspects of ' Modern Infidelity.'   A full conversation followed of an edifying nature.

Dec. 18th.—I met Mr. Joseph Hardy's class for tickets ; eight present.   I had a conversation with the members about a leader to take the place of Mr. Hardy, who is very poorly.   The feeling was in favour of Mr. Alfred Catt taking the position.

Dec. 20th.—I went to North Adelaide to see Sir H. T. Wrenforsley to have a chat with him on missionary work in Fiji.   Mr. Casely accompanied me.   The ex-Judge bore a noble testimony to the character and work of our brethren in those islands.

Dec. 23rd.—I finished my fifty-first budget of Australian news for the *Watchman* and *Recorder*.   This number I have sent to London, for publication, in the interests of the capitalists, merchants, mechanics, and agriculturists in Great Britain and Ireland, as well as for the benefit of Australians themselves.   I commenced these letters in June 1879, and have continued them to this date, without fee or reward.

Dec. 26th.—I have been trying this week to get my strength up again ; for I was much run down with the two months' engagements. The President was away.

Dec. 31st.—I held the 'Watch Night Service;' the first of the kind in Parkside Church. About 120 to 150 persons were present. Mr. E. Alcock gave an address, and Brother Unwin offered prayer. It was a pretty good service, and I pray that it may bear some fruit.

I have just met with a clipping on the 'Temperance' question, which I insert as my closing record for the year :—

'Almost all thinking men in the country—ministers of religion, judges and magistrates, and statesmen—are agreed that that which most hinders the moral and spiritual welfare of the people is the prevalence of drinking habits. The clergy know very well that it is impossible to hope that the truth of God will have free course among the people, and will prevail over sorrow and sin, so long as drink stands in the way. Drunkenness is punished, not only in the person of him who commits it, but in the persons of his wife and children, who are innocent of drink, and only deplore it.'—ARCHBISHOP OF YORK.

1885.

Jan. 1st.—Another year! Blessed be God ! I am hoping that the peacefulness and quietude of this day will be often repeated in my heart and in our humble home this year. Mrs. Bickford's health appears a little stronger, and I am trusting in the Heavenly Father for her in all respects.

Jan. 14th.—I am still reading the Rev. J. R. Gregory's work on 'Conditional Immortality.' What a fine book this is in close reasoning, keen criticism, and strong putting of the salient points of the controversy. The Rev. Edward White, of London, the leader of the new theory of (so-called) ' Life in Christ,' acknowledged to me that he was the only opponent who had successfully attacked his views. He inquired of me who he was, and said that he would much like to be acquainted with him. Mr. White, I thought, appeared to great advantage in this conversation, as a hard-headed but generous opponent.

Jan. 21st.—I wrote H. H. Fowler, M.P., Under Secretary of State for the Home Department, on the unpopularity of the Earl of Derby, Secretary of State for the Colonies, throughout Australia. We blame the noble earl for allowing the eastern portion of New Guinea being annexed by the Germans, thereby creating prospective difficulties to us in those seas lying to the north of Australia. In the event of a war between Germany and Great Britain, our commerce with China and India might be seriously interfered with.

Jan. 21*st.*—The Conference was opened to-day, and the Rev. C. T. Newman was elected President. Mr. ex-President Hunter gave a good address in retiring from the chair.

Jan. 26*th.*—I examined Messrs. Bainger, Blackett, Goss, and Hadley. The ordeal was intentionally thorough, and occupied nearly two hours to get through it. The young men were unanimously received for ordination on the 25th current.

Jan. 30*th.*—At the mixed Conference, Mr. David Nock's motion for making Bible reading in the State schools, during school hours, came on. I moved an amendment, somewhat in the following terms : ' That inasmuch as " Bible reading " was provided for in the Act, and might be had by any two parents of children attending the school requiring it, this Conference recommends to the parents and guardians of State school children to avail themselves of the provision as found in the Act.' The motion was carried. By this Conference, I was officially appointed as Theological Tutor of the ministerial students at Prince Alfred College—a work of love which I cheerfully accepted.

Jan. 31*st.*—The Conference closed to-day.

Feb. 6*th.*—' Khartoum.' I read, this morning, in the telegrams, that El-Mahdi, through treachery, has captured this old city, and massacred two thousand of its inhabitants. The torture of suspense, *re* the fate of General Gordon, is terrible. It may surely be hoped, that, in the absence of the arrival of the relieving party, he has made good his escape from the doomed city, as he has river steamers at his command, and, by going south, may be soon out of the reach of his bloodthirsty enemies.

Feb. 10*th.*—Mr. Hunter brought me the sad intelligence of the murder, in cold blood, of General Gordon on the 26th ult. I am sorely distressed at the death of so good and courageous a man at the hands of a band of savages. But, then, we ought not to be there ! A cordon of defence, along the dividing line between the two countries of Soudan and Upper Egypt, is all that British interests can demand in this inhospitable and deadly climate from the English Government. But the end is not yet.

Feb. 20*th.*—The Rev. Mr. Goodwin (P.M.M.) spent an agreeable hour with me this morning. He and Mrs. Goodwin are going to England for a year's rest. I always liked Mr. Goodwin as a brother minister and servant of Jesus Christ equally with myself. In the course of conversation he told me that he had sat under the ministry of the late Rev. Samuel Coley, at Cheetham Hill, Manchester. He spoke in the highest terms of the character and eminent ability of this soul-saving preacher of the ' Old Body.' I gave him, on leaving, a copy of my work on ' Australasia,' as a momento of our brotherly friendship.

March 6th.—The Rev. Henry Haigh, from India, dined with us to-day. He is a most interesting man, and an able advocate of our Missions. I expressed to him my earnest hope that he would deliver his lecture—'The Two Indies '—in Exeter Hall, London, as it would supply most valuable information for the use of Statesmen, as well as for the Directors of the Missionary Societies, whose representatives are labouring in India. Mr. Haigh, whilst in Adelaide, was the welcome guest of Mr. and Mrs. W. Rhodes, of Kent Town.

March 10th.—I wrote the *Register*, under the signature, 'Εἰρηνοποιοί' (Matt. v. 9.), on ' The Times : how critical ! ' for my contribution to the reading public as a protest against the war spirit, now so ripe in some quarters. My prayer is, ' Give peace in our time, O Lord ! '

March 26th.—I read in the *London Quarterly* an article on old Doctor Johnson. The Toryism of this publication disgusts me very much. The animus of the writer is seen in the abuse it pours upon the brilliant and philanthropic Macaulay, and its glorification of the great lexicographer—Doctor Johnson. But to burn incense to the memory of the latter, did not require in its wretched performance, the author to do injury to one of the greatest literary lights England has yet seen. But prejudice is blind and cruel !

April 3rd. (Good Friday)—I am most anxious that here, in Australia, the Crucifixion of our Lord shall be piously commemorated in our churches, in the form of a full service, as on the Lord's Day. Accordingly, I preached at Parkside at 11 a.m., on John xii. 32, 33. We held in the afternoon a special religious service in Pirie Street. At the request of the President, I offered the opening prayer and read an appropriate lesson. The Revs. C. T. Newman, H. T. Burgess, S. Knight, and R. M. Hunter, severally spoke on the last words of Jesus. The service was repeated in the evening with good effect. This is a new departure, and it is right.

April 8th.—Read in the *Fortnightly* for an hour or two. The article which attracted my attention most, was 'The Seats Bill.' I am astonished at Mr. Courtney's opposition to this Bill. It is endorsed by the principle leaders of the Government, and should have had the approval of the Liskeard Member. Its principle is the 'One-Member Constituency,' which, if established, would secure a 'House of Commons' elected by the majority of the voters in Great Britain and Ireland.

April 27th.—I sent an article to the *Advertiser*, on England and Russia. My object was to show the origin and nature of the disagreement between these two great powers; their comparative military strength, and the duty of the Churches of the 'Prince of Peace' uniting in earnest prayer to Almighty God for the success of the British arms, should a war break out. And wherefore? Because in this instance, Russia is the aggressor—the disturber of peace in the East. She has not learnt the lesson our Lord has left upon record : 'All they that take the sword shall perish with the sword.'

May 24th.—I attended as usual the Governor's *levée*, in honour of our good Queen Victoria. It was well attended by the leading gentlemen of the Colony. In the afternoon, I presided at the annual meeting of the Temperance League at North Adelaide. We held a great meeting in the evening, when we had good speaking and an enthusiastic feeling.

June 8th.—Mr. B. Norton and I went to the Parkside Lunatic Asylum, and saw the buildings which are assigned to the men. Everything was beautifully clean. There were some 250 men wrecked and ruined by various causes, mostly by drink ; to whom the pity of Christian people can now scarcely reach. We came away much affected with what we had seen.

June 16th.—I wrote the Hon. and Rev. S. W. Baker, Premier of Tonga, in the hope of inducing him to use his influence to heal the dreadful schism which has come upon our mission churches in the Friendly Islands. The following is the latter referred to :—

'PARKSIDE, ADELAIDE : *June 10th*, 1885.

'MY DEAR BROTHER BAKER,—Yesterday I received a letter from my nephew, the Rev. E. S. Bickford, now of St. Kilda, in which there is a reference to the Deputation which has returned from Tonga. From the general complexion of the reference, I would infer, that what has happened there has been a source of much concern to you. As my eye dropped upon this statement, I felt that I could no longer defer the fulfilment of a purpose I had often formed of writing you. And now I do so, as one of your oldest friends ; the Rev. Thomas Raston is before me, but not much. I was one of the so-called " Triers," who heard you preach in Brunswick Church in 1859, and spoke and voted for you in the District Meeting which followed. For the good work you did in the Friendly Islands, for several years, I greatly honoured and loved you. And I have not forgotten when you came up to the Colonies the first time, and came as a Deputation to the Geelong Circuit, how nobly you spoke of the dear Tonga king and the Tonga Christians; also, how much I envied you the pure satisfaction you enjoyed at the retrospect of your labours in that glorious field of missionary success. But now, from circumstances which cannot be re-called, but which may be Christianly deplored, nearly all this is changed. And this is what distresses me, and constrains me to write to you. I am now an old man in my seventieth year; and must, in the natural order of things, soon reach the end of my career. And I therefore want to see this dreadful schism healed—for dear King George's sake, for the sake of the Tonga Mission churches, and for your own sake, so that it may be well all round. May God help you to feel, as I feel, at beholding the " rent garment " daily before your eyes. I am deeply impressed that the 'evil should be checked before it becomes more cruelly marked than it is; I am also impressed, and firmly believe, that " in the bowels of Jesus Christ " you can do it, if you will.

' I have had during my long ministerial career some experience in grappling with troublous times and troubling officials. And this I have found—that no good results have ever followed from " fighting out to the bitter end " differences of ministers with each other; or differences as between ministers and laymen. The " more excellent way " is, for Christ's sake, to entirely cease from all further recrimination of each other, and the exercise of mutual forbearance and forgivingness of disposition towards each other. We cannot without inflicting deep injury on the Church—which is " His body," go into civil courts, or into any other arena of strife and accusations for settling our ecclesiastical and spiritual affairs, without displeasing and grieving our Lord Jesus Christ Himself. I would recommend—permit me this great liberty—that on your bended knees before the Crucified One, yourself and the Missionary brethren should pray for forgiveness in " this thing." Dear Brother Baker, I implore you to lay the state of the Church to heart, and, at once, to use your great influence to heal the dreadful schism which has come upon the Tongan Church. It is in your power to save the dear old king from going down to the grave in sorrow, through leaving behind him a divided church and disturbed kingdom. Heal the breach, and stay all further distraction and mischief in King George's dominions.

' Permit me to suggest also that you do not impose upon the Conference, as the price of the renewed loyalty of the king and of yourself, conditions, which, to accept, would possibly be a great injury to their representatives (as ministers) whom they commission and recognise; and humbling to the Conference itself, as the superior court of the body. My meaning and issue are: Forgive and forget the past; be reconciled to each other in Christ; reconsecrate yourselves to the great purposes of the Mission—the salvation of the people's souls. Then leave it with the Conference to do what shall appear necessary in the matter of continuing or discontinuing the present staff; and any other action which the case, in all its surroundings, shall require.

' The Rev. John Watsford's report of the visit to Tonga is not yet published. I need not say what interest I shall feel in its perusal. This much I hope to see—that the persecutions of our people for not attending the State Church (so called) are not founded in fact. I cannot bring myself to believe that you, in your high position as Prime Minister, could permit anything so wicked to be done; neither should any officials under you be allowed to do anything contrary to the principles of religious liberty, and, what is even of more importance, the principle of religious equality. The very idea of a spirit of persecution in Tonga —hitherto, as we have always believed, the very garden of the Lord—is too much for human credulity. If it has been practised, in however small a degree, the Lord will hear the cry of the oppressed, and will come down in providential dispensations, for their deliverance. But I will believe, that so evil and so criminal a thing as persecution for attending the old Tongan Methodist Church, my brother and old friend, Shirley Baker, will never permit. No, it cannot be.

'This letter is in no sense official. It is simply written in the interests of yourself, as it respects your own spiritual comfort, the quiet of the king, the good of the Church, and the power of Methodism. Oh, how my heart warms to you as I indite these hurried lines! How much I wish I could see you and your dear wife, whom I knew so well in her young womanhood, the daughter of the good Brother Powell, whom I loved so much. I suppose you remember that Dr. Waugh, then resident at St. Kilda, and I buried his dear remains, and that I preached his funeral sermon. And Mrs. Powell I love as a "widow indeed," and worthy of all honour.

'You are at liberty to show this letter to Messrs. Moulton and Watkin, if you think well to do so.

'I am, my dear Brother Baker,

'Yours ever truly,

'JAMES BICKFORD.

'The Hon. S. W. Baker, etc., etc.,

'Tonga, Friendly Islands.'

To this communication Mr. Baker has sent no reply. His silence carries with it its own comment.

June 27th.—I wrote, under a deep sense of public duty, a letter to the *Register*, signed 'Sanguineus,' in defence of the Hon. John Howe, Minister of Lands, on the subject of Assisted Emigration. How hard some people, especially political opponents, are to please! 'Strike high,' or 'strike low,' it is all the same with them. It is a repetition of the old enquiry, 'Can any good thing come out of Nazareth?'

July 3rd.—I attended a meeting on the Tongan business. After considerable discussion, we passed a resolution expressive of our abhorrence at the persecutions of the Tongan Christians, who are loyal to us, and of sympathy with them. We recognised also the painstaking labours of the deputation, who had gone to Tonga in the interests of the distracted Wesleyan Church.

July 17*th.*—This evening at the 'Young Men's Literary Society's Meeting,' I spoke on the 'Federation of the Australian Colonies,' after which a good debate ensued. It was carried, by an unanimous vote, that no such federation was practicable or desirable at present.

July 30*th* —I read again Dr. Hatch's great work on the 'Constitution of the Early Church,' and finished it. It is truly a marvellous book of research and logical array of incontestable facts. Alas for the High Church pretensions, which are herein so ruthlessly disposed of by one of their own order! But then, 'facts are stubborn things.'

Aug. 1*st.*—I received a touching letter this morning from my venerable friend, Rev. W. Moister, informing me of the death of Mrs. Moister, at Sedbergh, Yorkshire, in her eighty-first year. She was a second mother to me, when, as her husband's colleague in Trinidad, 1838, she cared for me in my first illness. She was a kind, good lady; besides being a fellow-helper to her husband, in the West Indies, Africa, and in English Circuits. She died honoured and loved.

Aug. 25*th.*—I read in the *London Quarterly* the article, 'George Eliot,' the severest reviewer, I think, she has yet come under. Poor, unfortunate creature, whose creed destroyed her moral sense!

Sept. 8*th.*—My first of a series of Ecclesiastical Lectures for the 'Young Men's Literary Society,' entitled, 'English Christianity,' was finished to-day. It has run to thirty-one closely written pages. I hope it will be as interesting to those for whose special benefit it was prepared as it was to me in composing it.

Sept. th.—I read *Nineteenth Century* article: 'Mr. Gladstone as a Foreign Minister,' by J. Guinness Rogers. I fully endorse every word of this able and just article, and I sincerely thank Mr. Rogers for it.

Sept. 24*th.*—I began a second lecture for the 'Young Men,' on 'Scottish Christianity.' This exercise I find to be profitable to me in every way. It is to be deplored that young ministers have so little relish for such subjects.

Sept. 30*th.*—I attended the Quarterly Meeting in Pirie Street. By resolution it was agreed that a probationer should be obtained for Parkside Church at the next Conference. So let it be!

Oct. 2*nd.*—At the 'Young Men's Society,' the head master of 'Prince Alfred College,' F. Chapple, B.A., B.Sc., gave a most telling lecture on 'Latimer, Bishop of Worcester.' It was crowded with apt quotations from the quaint and learned writings of the martyr-bishop. The founders of the Reformation had their baptism of fire at the stake; they suffered for us. A quotation from his published sermons will show the spirit of this reforming 'Father of the Reformation:'—

'There is God's way, and man's way. I will tell you what a Bishop of this realm said once to me; he sent for me, and marvelled that I would not consent to such traditions as were then set out. I answered him that I would be ruled by God's Book; and rather than I would dissent one jot from it, I would be torn with wild horses. And I chanced in our communication to name the Lord's Supper. "Tush," said the Bishop, "what do you call the Lord's Supper? What new term is that?" There stood by him a dubber, one Doctor Dubber, he *dubbed* him by-and-by, who said that this term was seldom read in the doctors. And I made answer that I would rather follow Paul, in using his terms, than them, though they had all the doctors on their side.'

Oct. 8th.—I do not recollect when students of God's Word, in ordinary reading even, met with so much of exegesis, bristling with controversy and challenging old and accepted tenets, as at the present time. The consequence is, that I cannot make headway in reading now as I could in former years. I take an illustration, I have lying upon my desk the *Quarterly*, in which I find an able article on the 'First Christian Council in Jerusalem, A.D. 50.' The learned writer deals deservedly hard with the 'Revisers of the New Testament,' in forcing a rendering upon Acts xv. 23, which is manifestly incorrect. The Greek *presbuteroi*, in the 'Authorised Version,' is properly rendered 'elders,' and the passage reads, 'The Apostles, and elders, and brethren;' but the revisionists have it, 'The Apostles and the elder brethren,' thereby ignoring the rightful position of this class of ecclesiastics in this the first Council of the Church, and absorbing them in the general designation of 'elder brethren.' It is surely, to put it mildly, an unfortunate and misleading blunder, as the critic (an Anglican clergyman) so severely points out.

Oct. 12th.—I wrote a letter to the *Register* on 'The Depression of the Colony.' The mechanical and farming classes are leaving in great numbers, simply through their inability to make a decent living. To this condition of things the Government appear to be blind, and the Parliament simply looks on. This letter was followed a few days after by another on 'The Public Finances,' but there is not much chance of exciting sympathy in the hearts of the ' governing ' towards the governed. But we shall soon see !

Oct. 20th.—I attended the Annual District Meeting, Mr. President Newman in the chair. We had some disciplinary work before us, and our President acted with much courtesy and firmness in conducting the business to the end. I examined W. A. Potts for full connexion, and he was cordially recommended to the Conference to be received.

Oct. 30th. [Diary Jotting]—'I spent a quiet evening in reading Mr. Joseph Chamberlain's splendid oration at Glasgow. "A coming man," no doubt. Perhaps a successor to the grand old man. Mr. Gladstone, some day.'

Oct. 31st.—I left for Melbourne, per steamer *Victoria*, for the purpose of recruiting my health, and attending to private business. My nephew, the Rev. E. S. Bickford, was at the Wharf, and we went together to St. Kilda. I lost no time in visiting my brother N. M. Bickford, and family at Northcote; my sister, Mrs. Wyatt, and Mr. Wyatt at Carlton; and my brother George and his daughter at Myrtle Creek, near Sandhurst. My nephews and nieces, and former friends, I also called upon. On *Nov. 21st* I reached home once more, and found Mrs. Bickford much the same as when I left her, three weeks ago. My heart was full of gratitude to God for His gracious care over her during the time I had been away in Victoria.

MRS. BICKFORD'S LAST ILLNESS AND DEATH.

There was so evident an improvement in the health of my dear wife that, on the evening of my return from Melbourne, we had a sweet conversation on the hopeful aspects of the next few years. I had arranged all the business matters for which I had gone to the sister colony; and she herself had so far recovered her strength, that we felt warranted in anticipating a quiet and unbroken eventide of life. But our hopes were doomed to miscarry, for a Higher Power had appointed otherwise. Between 4 and 5 o'clock on the morning of the 26th I had hastily to call in Dr. H. Wigg for her. She had been so ill during the night that we feared she would have died before medical aid could be got. The severity of the attack was such that she lost both sight and speech; and the symptoms, otherwise, were most alarming. With various alternations, she lingered on until

27

the afternoon of *Dec. 7th*, when she, 'in sure and certain hope,' yielded up her spirit to God. And thus ended a life which had been 'yoked' with mine, in the Lord's work, in many lands and among many people, for forty-four years. A few jottings from my Diary will pointedly show the experiences of the next few days :—

'*Dec. 8th.*—Sad and solitary this morning. I am looking forward to the scenes of this day with distressful sorrow. May the merciful God help me through them ! The funeral took place this afternoon. We had a short but beautiful service in the house, conducted by the Revs. C. T. Newman (President), H. T. Burgess, Joseph Nicholson, and T. Raston. At the Western Cemetery the Revs. R. M. Hunter, J. T. Simpson, J. B. Stephenson, and S. Knight officiated. There was a large attendance of ministers and friends from neighbouring Circuits, and from the city. We came back and spent a mournful evening with our kindred in chastened conversations and family worship. I learnt from Dr. Wigg that my precious one died from "pneumonia and cystitis, originating in a chill, and accelerated by *mort. cordis*, and a general senile decay." Dear, precious one ! when I remember how great were your sufferings, I could not wish you back again "in this vale of tears." '

'*Dec. 13th.*—At my request, the Rev. J. T. Simpson, who had been an inmate of our Geelong home, in 1866, in the commencement of his ministry, preached the funeral sermon for my late wife, taking as his text, "Thanks be unto God, who giveth us the victory through our Lord Jesus Christ," to a large and sympathising congregation. He read, at the close of his discourse, a memorial sketch of Mrs. Bickford's early life, conversion, marriage, and after life in the West Indies and Australia, which was listened to with breathless attention. The service, from beginning to end, was highly spiritual, and was well calculated to comfort mourning friends, and to impress the general hearers with the safety and great value of earnest service in the Lord's work.'

Dec. 21st.—Shoals of letters of condolence now came to me by every post. Among these I may specially mention one from our oldest missionary friend, the Rev. W. L. Binks, in Victoria ; and another from the Rev. John Watsford, formerly one of our honoured missionaries in Fiji. Mr. Watsford enclosed in his very welcome epistle the following verses :—

'PARTED—SOON TO MEET AGAIN.

'When the tenderest ties are broken,
    Loving hearts asunder torn ;
Farewell words so sadly spoken,
    And the sufferer left to mourn ;
Bright the hopes that yet remain.
Parted—soon to meet again.

THE LATE MRS. BICKFORD.

WOODBURYPRINT, WATERLOW & SONS LIMITED.

' Parted—all the conflict ended,
  One from earth has soared away ;
Gone, by heavenly hosts attended,
  To the land of cloudless day ;
Gone, no more to suffer pain,
Parted—soon to meet again.

' One is left, while one is taken,
  Left to walk his lonely way ;
Left awhile, but not forsaken,
  His a sure and constant Stay ;
Blessed hope will now sustain,
Parted—soon to meet again.'

This bereavement is the great sorrow of my life. But I bow to
the Divine decree, which has torn from me my other self, with all
the submissiveness that I can command. And the new and inspiring
thoughts which have come to me, since my dear one has gone from
my side, of the deathless nature of the human soul, and its living
personality in the heavenly state, is to me a new revelation full of
comfort and strength. My loving and trusty companion is 'not lost,
but gone before.'—' Father ! Thy will be done.'

I moved along quietly to the end of the year, taking all the Sunday
services appointed for me, meeting the Society and Theological classes,
and generally presiding at the weekly meeting of the 'Young Men's
Literary Society.' Indeed, all the work I had engaged to do in
the Circuit I faithfully performed. At the 'Watch Night Service'
Dr. J. R. Stephens preached the accustomed sermon, and I did the
remainder. It was to me a faithfully oppressive winding up of the
public duties of the year.

1885 is gone ! What a year it was to me ! The culminating
incident was the death of my life-long companion and wife, after
an illness of twelve days, following upon two years and nine months
of previous indisposition. Now she has 'all her sufferings passed, and
is entered into rest.' But my poor heart is sad and sorrowful beyond
endurance, only as my Heavenly Father may help me. I tremble as
I contemplate the new year with all its environments, as touching
my health, life, and engagements. Oh, that God may help me ! My
prayer is, 'Now, also, when I am old and grey-headed, O God, forsake
me not, until I have showed Thy strength unto this generation, and
Thy power to every one that is to come.'

1886.

Jan. 19*th.*—Once launched on the new year, the time for holding the Conference soon came on. It was opened this evening, and the Rev. Charles Lane was chosen as President. The next morning I wrote the President, asking to be released from daily attendance at the Sessions. I received a reply, a sympathetic letter, expressive of the hope that I would be present when my health and convenience permitted.

Jan. 25*th.*—I left for the Burra, and spent a few days with my hospitable friends, Mr. and Mrs. Field, at Monavea Farm. The cool air and the daily buggy exercise refreshed me much.

Jan. 29*th.*—I returned to Parkside tired and wearied with the journey. I found the Conference still in session. It was unheroic, and soon got through its ordinary business. It properly recorded the following notice of one of our noblest laymen, who had died at Barnet, near London, during the year :—

'THE LATE T. G. WATERHOUSE, ESQ.

'This Conference records its high esteem of the character and life of the late T. G. Waterhouse, of London, and its sense of loss in his removal. During an absence of eighteen years, Mr. Waterhouse manifested unabated attachment to the Wesleyan Church of this Colony. His generous assistance to the Connexion, his devotion to the interests of Prince Alfred College, and his widespread charity, have greatly endeared Mr. Waterhouse's memory to the Methodist Church of South Australia. The Conference offers its condolence to Mrs. Waterhouse, whose large-hearted sympathy ever associated itself with Mr. Waterhouse's Christian benevolence.'

The Minutes were signed by the President and Secretary on the 30th.

Feb. 1*st.*—Acting under strong personal persuasion, I went to Woodside for the rest of the summer, taking with me my niece, Miss Jarvis, and the servant also. The Rev. G. W. Kendrew, the young minister, the Tembys, the Perkinses, and Mr. and Mrs. Caldwell showed us much courteous attention. I visited the Hutchinses, Mitchells, Haldsteads, and other Christian families, with much pleasure.

Feb. 22*nd.*—I attended the Annual Missionary Meeting at Mount Barker; the dear old John Dunn, J.P., presiding. I was the guest of Mr. and Mrs. Sexton, who were very kind. The next day, the Revs. P. C. Thomas, John Leggo, and I went to see the public school.

There were over two hundred and thirty scholars, and a very competent staff of teachers. A first-class school. In the evening, at Woodville, we held the Missionary Meeting. Mr. Leggo, and his companion, a native Fijian teacher, greatly interested the congregation.

Feb. 27th.—I read of the failure of the Commercial Bank in Adelaide. It is a terrible calamity. The *Lantern*—a facetious paper, an imitation of *Punch*—was cruelly hard upon certain religionists, because of the wreck of this once promising and obliging institution.

March 1st.—I went to Parkside to see my dear friend, Mr. Joseph Hardy. I found him very ill. He bore a beautiful testimony to his personal sense of the infinite mercy of God as shown in the death of Jesus Christ. His experience much reminded me of that of the late Percival Bunting. It was Christ, and only Christ, in whom he trusted. I was much comforted, and left him in the full belief that he was 'ready' for the 'coming' of 'The Master.'

March 2nd.—I found here ten letters of condolence awaiting me. The reading of these caused my tears again to flow, and my deep sorrow was renewed. Shall I ever get over my crushing bereavement? What a change has come upon me! I am no longer the same man! May God help me!

March 10th.—I commenced reading Mr. Gladstone's article 'Proem to Genesis,' in the *Nineteenth Century.* A biblical critic of a high order, as well as a statesman of unrivalled greatness. A match for Huxley, Max Müller, *et hoc genus omne.* Marvellous man, who 'fears God always.'

March 16th.—I have now written fifty theological lectures for our ministerial students, which completes the first year's programme. This has been a real help to me in my sorrowful experiences.

March 17th.—I began reading in Plumptre's 'Spirits in Prison,' and so far I am disappointed with the work. Why does not the author tell us in the beginning of his work what he believes himself?

March 19th.—Busy in preparing for the Young Men's Meeting this evening. The questions is: 'Which is the better statesman, Gladstone or Salisbury, for administering the Government of Great Britain and Ireland at the present time?' I need not say on which side I was. The votes were largely for Mr. Gladstone.

April 4th.—I preached in the Parkside Church this evening a semi-valedictory sermon, as marking the termination of my engagement with the Pirie Street Circuit. Thank God I am now free from all obligatory work, after forty-eight years of pastoral, preaching, official, and administrative labours in the West Indies and Australia. It is only by the ' help of God that I have continued to this day.'

April 9th.—Busy and important day. I attended a great meeting in the Adelaide Town Hall to consider the state of the Colony. We agreed to observe the 18th as a day for special humiliation and prayer. Two other intermediate meetings I attended, which filled me with pain and anxiety. In the evening I heard the Rev. S. Knight lecture on Gladstone. He did his hero ample justice.

April 16th.—I read telegrams this morning, that Hartington and Salisbury are combining to defeat Mr. Gladstone's intention to give ' Home Rule ' to Ireland. We may have therefore to wait a few years before this act of national justice is done, but it will come nevertheless. ' Right,' like truth, prevails in the end.

April 26th.—I read to-day in Rev. Thomas Jones's work, ' The Divine Order.' It is exquisitely written ; besides showing a powerful imagination, and extensive reading. Looking phrenologically at Mr. Jones's picture, it greatly surprises me that the author could produce such a book. But phrenology is not a science, as yet.

May 3rd.—My niece, Miss Jarvis, and I went to see Mrs. Bickford's grave. It is five months ago since she left us for the ' better country.' How much I miss her—every day, every hour— none but myself can know.

May 11th.—The President, Mr. Lane, inaugurated the South Australian Jubilee movement to-night. It was a good beginning of the other services yet to be held. Our Church in this Colony was commenced on May 11th, 1836, when two classes were formed. Since when, there have been expended for churches and parsonages £249,000 ; Prince Alfred College (inclusive of land), £30,000. The present debt is £24,000. The Breakfast Meeting was well attended —seven hundred, at least, being present ; at the afternoon meeting £1,000 was subscribed. We hope, by this movement, to save some £5,000 we are now paying in interest on our church properties.

May 19th.—Joseph Hardy died last night. He was brother-in-law to the Rev. William Linnex, formerly one of our Missionaries in the West Indies, who, with Mrs. Linnex, Mr. Hardy's sister, will deeply feel our friend's death. Mr. Hardy was a good man; one of our leaders in Parkside Church, and a true friend of the ministers. These English (early) emigrants are dying out very rapidly.

May 21*st.*—Dean Russell died from accident last night at the Town Hall. The Anglican Church has thus lost its ablest preacher, Bishop Kennion a wise counsellor, and the Adelaide poor a generous sympathiser.

May 24*th.*—I attended the *levée* in honour of our good Queen. I afterwards presided at the Annual Meeting of the 'Temperance Society and Band of Hope' at North Adelaide. We had a very successful day. I was appointed President for a third year.

June 14*th.*—I wrote Mr. Gladstone on 'Irish Home Rule,' approving of the principle of his bill; at the same time I recommended that the Imperial Parliament should be asked to pass such a measure as would enable the Australian Governments to annex, from time to time, certain islands adjacent to our coasts, in the name and on behalf of the Queen. The passage in the letter is nearly as follows :—

'I may say a word upon the question of the annexation of certain islands in the Pacific, contiguous to Australia and New Zealand. The rumoured action of France, *re* the New Hebrides, is causing a bitter feeling throughout the Australasian group. The one feeling is, that France cannot, and must not, be trusted. And delays are dangerous. It was through the tardiness of Lord Derby that Bismarck appropriated the eastern, the best, and largest portion of New Guinea, New Britain, New Ireland, etc. A sad and terrible blunder, as I fear will yet be seen. And to prevent future complications, it would be well for the Imperial Parliament to pass an "Enabling Act," empowering the Australian and New Zealand Colonies, with the consent of the chiefs, to annex, in the name of the Queen, all those islands respectively contiguous to their Governments, so that they might become integral parts of the British Empire; but to be administered by the authorities out here, standing at the head of each batch, and by the individual Governors appointed for us by the Queen in Council. Such actions, as that which I suggest, would prevent, in the future, all discontent and hard feeling as between the English Colonial Secretaries and the Australasian people. I feel sure that Lord Rosebery, who knows us well, and feels kindly towards us, would heartily approve of such action as that now suggested. And it would, besides, be immensely popular; and be the best thing possible for the natives of the Western Pacific themselves.'

July 9*th.*—I finished my first lecture on 'Scottish Christianity,' for the 'Young Men's Literary Society.' My contention is now fairly proven that, from the earliest authentic accounts, Scottish Christianity has been ruled by an eldership, and not by an episcopacy. And I suppose that it is the only Church in Christendom that can boast of an uninterrupted succession of 'elders,' from the inception of the Gospel in Scotland, down through the succeeding centuries. All attempts of Episcopacy to supersede it by cruel persecutions have miserably failed. Let the Scotland of to-day be proud of its Scriptural inheritance, and hold to it with a grip as strong as death. No middle course will do.

Aug. 19*th.*—The result of Mr. Gladstone's appeal to the electorates of Great Britain and Ireland was telegraphed to us this morning :—Conservatives, 316 ; Unionists, 78 ; Gladstonians, 191. Parnellites, 86. In this historical election (for so it will be regarded as years roll on) 1,388,718 votes were cast for Mr. Gladstone's Irish policy ; and 1,416,472 against it. I sympathise deeply with the defeated Statesman ; but, as his relentless rival, Disraeli, used to say, 'All good things come to those who wait.' So let him wait.

Sept. 6*th.*—My brother, A. M. Bickford, who is on a visit to me from Melbourne, and I went to see the far-famed Adelaide Botanical Gardens. He was much pleased with the beauty and abundance with which he was surrounded. We afterwards went to the Western Cemetery to see Mrs. Bickford's grave. Both of us felt more than we could express. How strange, yet how affectingly true, it is that, out of the five brothers we are, four are widowers.

Sept. 15*th.*—Mrs. Fairweather, a saintly woman, has gone home to her Father in heaven ; and Mrs. Dr. Stephens has also passed to her rest. Two good members whom we could ill spare from our Church.

Sept. 17*th.*—Under the guidance of the Rev. C. T. Newman, we had a Young Men's gathering to-day, when 1,000 were present. It was a grand and impressive sight. The hope of our Church in this land is in such young men as I saw assembled in the great meeting in Pirie Street Church to-night.

Oct. 14*th.*—The Rev. W. L. Binks, my oldest ministerial friend in Australia, called upon me to-day. The next day Mr. Binks, and the Rev. Thomas Williams, from Ballarat, were with us in the District Meeting. At the request of the Chairman I examined Samuel Rossita and J. C. Hill—four-years men—for full connexion. Both were recommended by an unanimous vote to the Conference for ordination.

Nov. 8*th.*—The Rev. T. Williams greatly interested an audience in the Pirie Lecture Hall, by an exhibition of numerous curios which he had collected in Fiji, accompanied by an excellent explanatory speech. Dr. Stephens presided.

Nov. 9th.—The Wesleyan Sunday School Jubilee gathering came off to-day, when—so it is estimated—5,000 children were present.

Dec. 1st.—I went to the Mount Gambier District as a missionary deputation. I visited in succession Border Town, Narracoote, Millicent, Beachport, Glenburne, Kingston, and Mount Gambier. We had good attendances on the Sundays and on the weekdays, and much interest in the cause of our South Seas Mission was shown— I returned to Parkside on the 28th, greatly fatigued. I cannot speak too highly of the kindness of the Rev. John and Mrs. Trevorrow, the Rev. J. H. Hadley and Mrs. Hadley, the Rev. A. D. and Mrs. Bennett, and Revs. G. W. Kendrew and W. H. Hodge, to me during my first tour throughout this vast district. With Mount Gambier I was delighted.

Dec. 29th.—The Rev. J. W. Simpson brought me the sad news of the sudden death of the Rev. R. W. Campbell, at Perth, Western Australia. He was in full work on the Sabbath, and died during the quiet hours of the following night. His work was 'finished.' In his death we have lost a fearless and able preacher of the Gospel of Salvation. With the bereaved widow, her children, and the Church at Perth, and throughout the Western Australian District, the sincerest regret and sorrow will be shared by all good Wesleyans in this colony. It is a mysterious dispensation of Providence, but the Heavenly Father can overrule it for good.

Dec. 31st. [Diary Jotting]—'In the mercy of God, I have lived to see the last day of this year. How much of sorrow I have passed through, God only knows. But I have been helped by His presence and grace. I praise Him; I bless Him; for He is good to me. Dr. Stephens and I conducted the "Watch Night Service." We had a fair attendance, and a solemn time. Oh, that the coming year may be one of blessedness and grace to us in our churches! Amen.'

1887.

Jan. 2nd.—The first Sabbath of a new year. I had a full day, preaching at Pirie Street and Parkside. In the evening, at the Covenant and Sacramental Services, we had about 100 persons present. It was to me an encouraging beginning of another year's work.

Jan. 10*th.*—I was at Woodside. Telegram : Sir Stafford Northcote, my county-man, has been superseded at the Foreign Office, and has resigned his connection with the Salisbury Ministry. His son has also resigned. I am very sorry, for I have always regarded Sir Stafford as a conscientious statesman, and, in his religious instincts, taking rank with Lord Selborne, Mr. Gladstone, Samuel Morley, and Sir William McArthur. Such men are as necessary in the Councils of the Cabinet as in the House of Commons itself. The next day news came of the sudden death of the ex-Minister at the Foreign Office. Dismissal from the service of the Crown followed, within twenty-four hours, by a call from God to the higher service and rest in heaven. It is very tragic and admonitory.

Jan. 18*th.*—I went to Adelaide to be present at the opening of the Conference. The Rev. J. T. Simpson was elected President ; and the Rev. J. Haslam, Secretary. The brethren have shown their wisdom in choosing two able men for the highest offices in the Conference. The Rev. John Leggo, a returned Fijian missionary, by a cordial vote, was received as a member of our Conference. The Rev. J. B. Stephenson was made Supernumerary for one year, and had permission to reside in England. A suitable obituary notice was approved, to be printed in the Minutes, of the character and useful labours of the late brother, R. W. Campbell, at Perth, W. A. I examined the 'five-years men'—for full connexion. They were W. G. Clarke, J. C. Hill, G. W. Kendrew, C. H. Nield, and S. Rossiter, all of whom were unanimously recommended for Ordination. We also received on trial Augustus D. Bennett, Horace Faull, Thomas Trestrail, and Henry Wilkinson.

Jan. 25*th.*—I went again to the Conference and took my full share in the business. The next evening, the Ordination Service was held at Kent Town in the presence of a devout and large congregation. The Rev. Charles Lane, ex-President, gave an excellent charge. This was in every sense a thoroughly business Conference. The Minutes were signed on the 31st.

Feb. 8*th.*—I read to-day the Tongan Report presented by the Rev. E. Crosby to the New South Wales Conference. The brutality to which the Wesleyan subjects of King George are said to be exposed is simply infamous. It reminds me of the state of things in England in the days of the Stuarts, of execrable memory. Who is this wicked Ahithophel at the bottom of such infamous conduct ?

Feb. 15*th.*—1 finished reading to-day 'India for the Indians." Such a book ought to open the eyes of our statesmen to the evils of our present administration of the Government of India, and lead to a radical change. One is constrained to ask, whether a conference of ex-Governors General might not be held for drawing up a sufficient, but safe, form of constitutional Government, in which the British and the upper class of the natives might take an equally responsible part. This 'reform' would be conservative in the highest degree. The administration should be in the hands of a Governor General and of Provincial Governors, with such local Representative Councils, or parliaments, to be created under competent authorities. The present system cannot possibly continue for long.

Feb. 18*th.*—General telegram from 'Tonga :' 'Five men shot for the late attempt on Shirley Baker's life.' The Rev. J. E. Moulton's telegram was : 'The men who shot at Mr. Baker are not Wesleyans, or have anything to do with us.' But this is only a repetition of the conduct of the Maori Wesleyans in the ten years' war in New Zealand :—' No Wesleyan took up arms against the British Government in that disastrous conflict.'

March 9*th.*—I read in Dr. Stokes' 'Celtic Church' for three hours. I am seeking information on 'The Introduction of Christianity' into Ireland for our 'Young Men's Literary Society.'

March 29*th.*—I came from Woodside to be present at the marriage of Miss Thompson, late of Bradford, England, with the Rev. G. W. Kendrew. Many were the good wishes for the long life of the happy pair.

April. 7*th.*—I re-arranged my study, and once more set to work. I feel much stronger after two months' residence at Woodside. The 'hills' and not the 'plains,' for old Englishmen in the summer months, is the proper thing in this Colony.

I read in Sir Charles Gavan Duffy's 'Young Ireland' an account of the wrongs inflicted by English kings, Cromwell, etc., on the poor Irish. In the matter of the supersession of the Irish Parliament and the Legislative Union of Great Britain and Ireland, carried by Pitt, Sir Charles fearlessly says :—

'It was while the people were prostrate and gagged that the Union was carried. Within the Parliament a majority was bought, and paid for ; over a million sterling was spent in secret bribes ; and a million and a quarter openly, in buying the interest which patrons were supposed to possess in the right of boroughs to representation. In the army, in the navy, in the customs, patronage was distributed as bribes. Those, who preferred money down, get a sum of £8,000 for a vote, but an office of £2,000 a year was not considered too high an equivalent. No less than twenty peerages, ten bishoprics, one chief-justiceship, and six puisne judgeships were given to men who voted for the Union. Thus, it will be seen that the Union was obtained by fraud and injustice, whilst the leading men of the nation were powerless to prevent it.'

It is really surprising to find so acute a writer as Duffy lending his name and pen to the perpetuation of the statement of Mosheim, that Ireland is indebted to Rome for its first knowledge of Christianity. He says :—

' The Irish race first felt the contagion of a common purpose, not in war, but in labours of devotion and charity. Lying on the extreme verge of Europe, the last land then known to the adventurous Scandinavian, and beyond which fable had scarcely projected its dreams, it was in the fifth century since the Redemption that Christianity reached them.'

Then follows the story of St. Patrick's Mission, who, says Duffy, was received with extraordinary favour, and before his death nearly the whole island had embraced Christianity.

The late Dean Stanley, and Professor Stokes, D.D., have searched this matter to the bottom. The result is thus briefly given :—

' The origin of Irish Christianity is a vexed question. Whether it came from Rome, or from Asia Minor, one thing is certain, that its form in our earliest knowledge of it is totally different from what it assumed at that time in any country. There were bishops of their own type and beliefs who could be counted by hundreds. In a single monastery one hundred of these were crowded together. . . The peculiarities of this early Church are in diametrical opposition to the usages of Catholicism and Protestantism of later times. . . . " This," says the Dean, " is the old national religion of Ireland." '

Professor Stokes's work has the following passage as the result of his learned and laborious enquiries :—

' Celtic Christianity was older than Irish Christianity, and more extensive ;' adding ' that British Christianity and Gallic also were both Celtic. Gallic Christianity may have come from Galatia, and thus we reach Asia Minor, one of the earliest fields of St. Paul's labours—" the true church of Celtic Ireland," says Stanley, " which until the fifth century had stood alone and apart from every Church in Christendom." '

If Sir Gavan Duffy ever brings out a second edition of ' Young Ireland,' I hope he will be so good as to acknowledge that Christ's Gospel was known in Ireland long before Palladius visited in the year A.D. 423.

April 11th.—Dr. Adam Clarke on Acts xvii. came in the course of my reading this morning. It is wonderfully critical and able. How sorry I am that I have allowed so many years to pass without a consecutive reading of this great Commentary. I once read right through, day after day, the Doctor's annotations on the Book of God, and I can never forget the intensity of desire I felt to know the full meaning and high purpose of this, the world's oldest poem. In the summer months, when I am in the 'Hills,' Dr. R. N. Young's edition of Clarke is my favourite daily reading.

April 17th.—I heard Mr. Prior preach this morning from the text : ' Brethren, pray for us.' It was strong and robust all the way through.

May 12th.—I received a letter from the Rev. Thomas James, this morning, whose beautiful references to my late wife affected me very much, and caused my tears again to course down my cheeks.

May 16th.—I read the Rev. Corbett Cook's ' Apostolic Succession, for three or four hours. What a puzzle the respective advocates make of this ridiculous myth !

May 24th.—I prayed for our dear, good, old Queen this morning. I was unable to be present at the *levée* as usual, having had a previous engagement at the Burra.

June 7th.—I wrote a long letter to the *Register* on ' Ireland and Mr. Goschen, M.P.' It was in condemnation of further ' Coercion Bills ' for Ireland, and recommended instead concession, liberal land laws, and emigration, as remedial measures.

I now quote from my Diary for a few days :—

' *June 13th.*—This afternoon I attended a Committee Meeting of the International Convention, and presided over the deliberations. In walking to and from the tram, I became conscious of a diminution of leg-strength. I was glad to get home and rest.'

' *June 14th.*—I was quite poorly this morning from severe chill. I was glad to keep by the fire and nurse myself. At night, when retiring to rest, I was attacked with shivering, and from 10 to 2 in the morning my hands and feet were cold as ice. My pulse and breath were difficult, and I was very ill. At last, I was relieved by the simple warmth of the bed, and I fell asleep.'

' *June 15th.*—I sent for Dr. Stephens, who ordered me to keep in bed. My pulse was a hundred and two, and I was full of pain. The Rev. S. Knight, Mr. B. Norton, and Dr. Stephens prayed with me after the Home Missionary Meeting. I heard the clock strike eleven, twelve, one, two, three, so wakeful was I. But the temperature has gone down considerably.'

' *June 16th.*—Remained in bed all day. The pulse had fallen twenty-three from the hundred and two beats when the doctor called this morning. He ordered another medicine, and perfect quiet. Slops and no meat is the *régime.*

'*June 17th.*—Better this morning. The pulse is in a normal condition, God be praised! I came into the sitting-room and took a little boiled mutton for dinner. I went into the garden and everthing looked so nice.'

'*June 18th.*—Kept inside the house for fear of cold.

'*June 19th.*—A prisoner all the day (Sabbath). In the evening, my old friend, Mr. James Scott, spent a profitable two hours with me. I read to-day, " John Wesley in Company with High Churchmen." It is amusing to see the ritualistic Anglicans claiming Wesley to be one of themselves.'

'*June 22nd.*—I am regaining my strength very slowly, and am unable to take any preaching work. Read Greville's " Memoirs and English Papers " with much profit and interest.'

'*June 27th.*—I went to Stow Church, and heard Rev. C. Manthorpe lecture on " The Act of Uniformity," passed by the English Parliament in 1662. It was a terrible tale he gave us, and all was done by vile men under the guise of religion. How shocking is the thought! The principal actors were more like incarnate fiends than Christian men.'

Aug. 5th.—I attended an aggregate meeting of leaders in Pirie Street Church, when the Rev. G. E. Rowe and Mr. John Funnell, Circuit Steward, read papers on the Class-meeting question. I think the real point was missed, although the papers were good as far as they went. The question really was: 'What can be done to prevent the cessation of followship in our Church?' But no remedy was suggested by any of the speakers—which was disappointing to me.

Aug. 10th.—The *Register* of this morning was a very fine issue. In it appeared a letter from Bishop Kennion, in which he pleads for certain changes in our Education Act, but the sapient editor is wideawake, and no harm to our popular system of day schools is likely to come about.

Aug. 11th.—I read forty pages of the late Dr. George Smith's excellent work on the ' Pastoral Office,' which I think able, cogent, Scriptural, and highly respectful to the large body of local preachers to which he belonged. It was written at a time of agitation in English Methodism, and effectually deals with Dr. Melson's famous motto: ' One Work; and One Call.' The immediate reason of the publication has passed away; still, there is such a setting forth of the reasons for justifying a separated ministry, as will be always of great value to those Christian readers and thinkers as are found in English Methodism.

Aug. 24th.—I made copious extracts from the July number

of the *London Quarterly* article : 'The Service of Man : Positivist and Christian.' The writer deals smartly with John Morley and James Cotton Morrison. Deluded men, who would rob us of our God and Christianity, and give us instead their miserable husks. May the merciful God ' open their eyes ' that they may see and know better !

Sept. 13*th.*—I presided at the International Temperance Convention, and gave an inaugural address. We had a large attendance of delegates from the neighbouring colonies. Some of them appeared to be very able men. We sat until the 15th, when we closed by a great meeting in the Town Hall. The Hon. James Munro, M.L.A., from Melbourne, presided. For the success of this Convention, we are mainly indebted to Messrs. G. W. Cole and F. W. Wood, the Honorary Secretaries.

Oct. 5*th.*—By invitation of the Chancellor of the Adelaide University, I arranged to hear the Primate of Australia, Bishop Barry, give an address on ' Higher Education.' We had a splendid gathering of the *élite* of the colony present. The Primate spoke only as a great man and ripe scholar could. There was a perfect absence of any attempt at grandiloquence, smartness, ecclesiastical clap-trap. Bishop Kennion introduced me to the Primate, as an ex-President of the Conference, and as the oldest Wesleyan minister in the Colony. Bishop Barry shook hands with me very heartily. Mrs. J. B. Smith, from Victoria, accompanied me to hear the good and learned man.

Oct. 12*th.*—I heard to-night of the death of my earliest Victorian friend, the venerable and Reverend William Butters. From July, 1854, to February, 1879, his friendship with me had never known the slightest diminution. I prepared for the press a sketch of his fine character and eminent labours in Tasmania, Victoria, and South Australia.

Oct. 20*th.*—The District Meeting closed to-day. I was too much engaged with Jubilee visitors to be in attendance on its sessions.

Oct. 31*st.*—I finished my article on Gladstone, for the ' Young Men's Society.' It falls much below what a man of the ex-Premier's calibre and commanding personality merited. But I did my little best. It is, at least, my tribute to the high character and patriotism of England's greatest man.

Nov. 4*th.*—I attended the Committee on ' The Transfer of Property Bill,' for our Church in South Australia. The Attorney General (C. C. Kingston) has made two concessions, but he refuses to insert tho proviso for a separate registry of sales of property by a Court of our own. But we can enlarge the number of trustees at any time, without having recourse to any power outside ourselves. This is something gained.

Nov. 15th.—Sad news of a political nature from London this morning. The Government have created by the *ipse dixit* of Mr. Matthews, Home Secretary, two new offences :—(1) The public airing of their grievances by the thousands of unemployed in London ; (2) The holding of public processions and meetings in Trafalgar Square. For less blunders than these Louis Philippe lost his throne.

Nov. 22nd.—I read in Dr. Cochrane's work, ' Future Punishment,' for some hours. This is a head-splitting production, but I mean to go through with it. I must read such works—if not for myself, but for others. I am, though, rather unfitted for such reading from the weakening effects of my recent illness. I have other works of the same kind in hand just now.

Nov. 28th.—Sir R. D. Ross, Speaker of our House of Assembly, died last evening of heart-disease. He was the son of John Pemberton Ross, Esq., a sugar planter in the island of St. Vincent, West Indies. There were scores of emancipated slaves, who bore his name in several of the plantations when I was there in 1838, and downwards. Sir John was a man of dignified bearing, an able debater, and ruled the Assembly with the discretion of a wise, strong man. His death is a great loss from the ranks of our best public men.

Dec. 31st.—I took part in the ' Watch Night Service ' at Pirie Street : Revs. J. Read, S. Knight, and I conducted it. I founded my address on the words: 'Thou crownest the year with Thy goodness.' I returned to Parkside at about 1 P.M., and was chilled with the cold, strong south wind, which I had to breast all the way. Mr. Samuel Gully drove me home in his buggy. And so the years roll on.

1888.

Jan. 5th.—Being poorly again, I am very much concerned to get away from the great heat on these plains which tries me so severely. To ' The Hills,' for the remainder of the summer is my inexorable duty.

Jan. 6th.—I wrote to day upon ' English and Irish Politics ' for

TOWN HALL, ADELAIDE.

the *City Press.* My heart was moved with deepest sympathy for the Irish people as I thought of their pitiable condition. I transcribe two paragraphs, as follows :

'It is to the cruel policy of "Coercion," *alias* "The Crimes Act," that Lord Salisbury's Government, assisted by Lord Hartington, Mr. Goschen, etc., has committed itself. I often wonder if dead statesmen have any consciousness of the effects of words which they uttered when alive and in high places. Such words, for example, as those which the late Lord Beaconsfield once uttered in earnest tones of warning to the Liberal Government, which he then hated and opposed with cruellest perseverance. "It is not in human nature," he said, "and all history teaches this, that men should be content under a system of legislation and of institutions, such as exist in Ireland. You may pass this Coercion Bill, you may put men in gaol, you may suppress conspiracy, but the moment it is suppressed there will remain the germs of the malady, and from these germs will grow as heretofore another crop of disaffection, another harvest of misfortunes." The probability is that Salisbury, who was then Beaconsfield's *fidus Achates*, was sitting by his side, and heard these words of common sense and prudent forecasting. The dead statesman may be oblivious to them, but the living statesman ought not to be.

'The administration of the Crimes Act is creative of crime, instead of being a cure for it. I wonder again if Lord Salisbury has ever dropped upon the following pregnant sentence:—"Where no freedom of thought could be indulged, where every noble aspiration of a citizen was sternly suppressed, secret societies afforded the only breathing place amid the stifling dungeon-like air surrounding them." The proper safety-valves were fastened down, what wonder if the heated vapours at last burst its bounds, and overthrew thrones, principalities, and powers? Sir, is there, under such sorrowful conditions of Irish life as we have indicated, no helping hand anywhere to be found? I would to God that Englishmen would take a just and merciful look at this sad case. We can do it without injuring ourselves or losing India, as Lord Salisbury has indiscreetly hinted. There is a touch of true nature, and of God-like justice, in the simple yet forcible words of him, whom I used to call, with justifiable pride, honest John Bright—"I believe," he said, "that these Irish people are made as we are ; that they are patient beyond belief, but, at the same time, broken spirited and desperate, living on the verge of starvation in places in which we would not keep our cattle." It is some forty years ago that the old thunderer (the *Times*) wisely insisted "that the rights of property, viewed in the light of nature and common sense, must include some regard to the poor man under God's charter to live and breathe in this the Almighty's world." Let this judgment of God, for it is such to me, have due consideration at the hands of the existing Irish landlords, and of the English landowners and merchant princes of London, and then it may be hoped that such harrowing telegrams as we have received this very week from London, and elsewhere, will be written to us no more.'

'I am fearfully and wonderfully made.' What says the *Christian Commonwealth* just to hand?—'The total number of pores

28

of the body may be about 7,000,000, and the length of the per-spiratory tubing about 1,570,000 inches, or nearly 28 miles.' Did this marvellous machine make itself, or how was it made?

Jan. 14th.—Once more at Woodside, and entered the cottage on the hill. The air was simply delightful—the true elixir of life to me.

Jan. 17th.—Returned to the City for the Conference. The Rev. James Haslam was elected as President, and the Rev. D. S. Wylie as Secretary. We heard to-day of the melancholy death of Mrs. Kendrew, occasioned by her dress catching fire at Strathalbyn yesterday. The Conference was quite broken with grief.

Jan. 19th.—Conference all day. The Rev. E. H. Sugden, B.A., B.Sc., from England, called on his way to Melbourne. He was suitably addressed by the President, to which he replied very nicely. After a little friendly shaking of hands with the brethren, he took his departure for the Head-mastership of Queen's College, Melbourne.

Jan. 24th.—An interesting episode took place in the Mixed Conference this morning, which took me by surprise. Mr. Frederick Chappel, B.A., B.Sc., the Kent Town lay Representative, after a neat speech, moved the following resolution :—

' That this Conference heartily congratulates the Rev. James Bickford on having reached, and nearly completed, the fiftieth year of his ministry. It rejoices with him in his having been spared to toil so long and so honourably in this noble work, and to occupy such important positions in the Methodism of Australia ; including the occupancy of the Chair of the Conference three times. And it desires to place on record its high appreciation of his personal character, and of his labours as a preacher of the Gospel. It glorifies God for the grace that has been vouchsafed to him, and it trusts that it may please God still to spare him to aid and to give counsel to this Conference and to our Church.'

This resolution was seconded by the Rev. Samuel Knight, and after a few remarks from the Revs. T. Lloyd, Raston, and some other members of the Conference, was cordially adopted. I replied as well as I could. In the afternoon session, when the Tongan case was under discussion, I moved, but not with much heartiness, the following resolution :—

' That this Conference, whilst sympathising with the Missionary Committee in all their difficulties in relation to the Tongan Mission Churches, recommends to the General Conference that the Friendly Islands District be constituted a separate Conference, affiliated to the General Conference, as the best means in our judgment of securing peace in Tonga, and of promoting the interests of the Church in these islands.'

This motion was not carried, the Conference feeling that the facts of the whole case were not sufficiently known to it to justify such action.

Jan. 25*th.*—The most striking incident of this day's session was the presentation by the Conference Evangelist, the Rev. D. O. Donnell, of the year's operations. He had preached 222 times, and had given 29 other addresses. There had been 63 Bible readings, and 1,120 had presented themselves as penitents; 613 of these were over sixteen years of age. Towards the support of the work, there had been received from Circuits £137 13*s.* 3*d.*, and donated £107 17*s.* The expenditure up to December 31st had been £224 10*s.* We thanked God for such results.

Jan. 30*th.*—The Conference was closed to-day.

Feb. 6*th.*—METHODIST ADMINISTRATION. The Class-test of member-ship has been for some years a perplexing subject in our Australasian churches. Indeed, it has become the *vexata quæstio* in every ecclesiastical court of Methodism, and what to do with it we cannot tell. I resolved, therefore, in the quietude of Woodside, to think out a few practical steps, for easing down something of the formidableness of this 'giant' in our path of progress. The case can be seen at a glance: (1) We have in our Australasian congregations thousands of persons regularly worshipping with us, who will not join our Church because of the Class-meeting condition of membership. (2) Whilst, of those persons whose names are on our 'roll of membership,' not more than one half of them comply with the rule requiring them to meet in class. (3) We are constantly losing the sons and daughters of Methodist parents because of our test of membership. (4) The ministers in charge of Societies find it impossible to rigidly administer the law relating to membership, without cutting off large numbers of persons who approve of our worship and accept our pastorate. I could not, I confess, find any way out of this condition of things by any new (say) radical, legislation, even if the 'General Conference' had the power, which it has not, under the 'Constitution' which we accepted from the English Conference in 1874. But I contend, nevertheless, that the Annual Conferences, in the exercise of their administrative rights, might so broaden and liberalise our 'rule' as to make it competent to Circuit Superintendents, in part, at least, to lessen, if not completely remove, this incubus to the natural growth of our Church.

In a letter to the *Christian Weekly*, I put forth the following suggestions as helpful in this direction, that is to say :—

1. All persons desiring to become members shall signify by personal application to the minister in charge, or, in his absence, to one of the leaders, their desire to join the Church.

2. At the next Leaders' Meeting thereafter, the presiding minister shall read the names of such applicants, with the view of gaining information respecting their character; when, if it appear there is no objection to the reception 'on trial' of such persons, the minister shall enter their names on the Church-roll. He shall also enter their names in the class-book, for the use of the leaders to whose spiritual supervision they are confided.

3. That in all those instances of persons thus received, when any of them, from various causes, do not attend the weekly fellowship, they shall be required nevertheless, to observe our discipline as provided in the 'General Rules of the Society,' viz :—(1) They shall attend, whensoever practicable, the established means of grace, such as the public worship of God, the Lord's Supper, and meetings for united prayer and Christian fellowship. (2) They shall be visited at suitable times by the minister, for the renewal of tickets and pastoral counsel.

4. An official register shall be kept by the minister in charge of the whole membership of the Church, or Society, in any given locality, and which shall be revised from the class-books at a special Leaders' Meeting, say, to be held ten days before the holding of the Annual District Meeting. This roll, so revised, shall be the official return for the September Quarterly Meeting, the District Meeting, and the Conference.

5. The present law of the Church, *re* the 'recognition of those members' (p. 114, 'Methodist Laws'), should be carried out in whole, or in part, in all our Societies and Circuits, our present practice being too unimpressive: hence the leakage which is so much deplored from year to year.

6. In the Minutes of the English Conference for 1821, on cases of backsliding from the Society, the following regulation was agreed to :—' Let us pay particular attention to backsliders, and endeavour in the spirit of meekness to restore them that have been overtaken in a fault, and by private efforts, as well as by our ministrations, to "recover them out of the snare of the devil." '

7. In the recommendations of the Committee, appointed by the last English Conference to consider the question of ' the class-meeting and membership, are two, especially sustaining the views expressed in sections 3 (1, 2) and 4, in substance, and almost equally in form, in this letter. I, therefore, with the more confidence submit the suggestions herein to my ministerial and lay brethren in our South Australian Connexion. I have relied on our Laws and Usages, as I have known them administered in the earlier years of my official life, with great advantage to the ' flock,' over which the Holy Ghost hath made us overseers.

Feb. 16th.—I read in 'Marcus Aurelius' this evening. It is a marvellous collection of wise and weighty sayings.

Feb. 27th.—I preached at Angaston yesterday. The next morning I went to see my dear father's grave. I felt much as I thought of the dear old man resting in that silent home. He died at North Rhine in 1851. In the afternoon the Rev. T. Angwin, M.A., drove me to see the Hon. J. H. Angas, M.L.C., in his lovely seat. We had an interesting interview, Mr. Angas manifesting concern in the visit I was paying to the district. In the evening, at the Public Meeting, I spoke of incidents which I remembered for the last fifty years. The audience was attentive.

March 1st.—Woodside. I again called on the aged Mrs. Disher, and prayed with and for her. I think she is maturing in soul for the final vision.

I read to-day in Bonwick's 'Romance of the Wool Trade.' It is a book of invaluable information for those who have to do with that great staple of the world's commerce.

March 11th.—I improved the death of William, the late Emperor of Germany. Text: 'Moses My servant is dead.' There were several of the German residents present, who appeared to take much interest in the service.

March 27th.—I wrote to the *Register* on the resolutions of the English Conference *re* the 'Union of the Methodist Bodies.'

The following is a copy of the letter :—

' SIR,—

' First impressions I have often found are not only the safest, but the wisest, among religious men. Hence I hasten to express the profound satisfaction I feel, at the information which has reached us this very day on the crucial question of Methodist Union in England. It is well known in all Methodist and other Christian circles, how persistently I have striven for some years to prevent any hasty action being taken by the Conferences, of which I have been a member, for the purpose of precipitating a course of action for which we and the other bodies concerned were not prepared. But I now think light of the right kind and measure is beginning to dawn upon us. The English Conference Committee have met the representatives of the four union branches of the British Methodist Church, and have passed a resolution in favour of an organic union of the five divisions therein concerned. Sir, all along my strongest objection, indeed I may say my only objection, was in the legal aspect of the relation of the parent body to the offshoot : but it seems that this will be met, and got over, by the third of the resolutions of the united Committee, viz , " that the Conferences be affiliated to the Wesleyan Conference.' This proviso saves the poll-deed of Wesley intact, and projects into the future the fullest legal recognition and ministerial rights for the united Methodism of Great Britain. The first of the resolutions passed by the Committee is simply one of ecclesiastical order and equality ; the second is one of trusts and trustees, and the third avoids all legal difficulty by the affiliation of the minor Churches to the old Body. We shall watch, Sir, with intensest anxiety, the further elucidation of the scheme, and hope and pray for its final unification. Once accomplished in England, Australian Methodism will not be slow to follow the example set before it. At least, so I think.'

April 4*th.*—We returned to Parkside to-day. 'The Hills' had done us much good. Lovely drives, striking scenery, fresh, cool air, and restful nights—what more could we wish ? Everybody was kind, and tried to minister to our comfort.

April 10*th.*—In a dream, early this morning, I had delightful intercourse with that greatest of living men, Mr. Gladstone. It was most real. I want an Abernethy to explain to me the philosophy of this.

May 8*th.*—I wrote the fifty-third lecture for the students; subject, 'Baptism.' I am sure, I made out the case for our custom of baptizing infants and children, to the satisfaction of every un-prejudiced mind.

May 11*th.*—I heard Miss Finkelstein lecture on the 'Homes and Haunts' of Jesus. It was a beautiful lecture, aptly illustrated, and gracefully given. There was a great crowd in the Town Hall to hear this wonderful converted Jewess.

June 4*th.*—I wrote my fifty-fourth lecture for the students; subject, 'The Ministry of the Church.' How the subjects of these lectures widen in my hands ! It does me good to prepare them.

July 10*th.*—I read in the magazine for March Dr. Gregory's reply to Dr. Dallinger. Without being a scientist, I cannot but think that the talented editor has greatly the advantage over the philosopher.

July 16*th.*—I finished reading Drummond's 'Central Africa ;' it is a capital book. The hand of the naturalist and the scientist is apparent in every page of this work.

July 25*th.*—I completed my article on the 'Federation of the Australian Colonies' for the *Young Men's Quarterly.* The drift of the paper is to show that, for such objects as defences, railway gauges, intercolonial trade, and the creation of a final Court of Appeal, etc., such a Federation would be desirable. But no such combination could be permitted as would impair the perfect autonomy of our constitutional Government, as now existent, in each of the Colonies. Neither could we permit any additional burden of taxation to come upon the people for meeting expenses connected with a Federal Parliament. 'Imperial Federation' (so called) is simply a dream as far as the Australian Colonies are concerned. Our wisdom is to be content with the evils we have, rather than to plunge into others of which we do not know.

July 26th.—A valuable budget of English news this morning. I read Mr. Gladstone's criticism on Mrs. Ward's religious novel, 'Robert Elsmere.' It is a deep, searching, and profound criticism. Besides, its ring is worthy of the great statesman. I read also his House of Commons speech on the melancholy death of Frederick III., late Emperor of Germany. No wonder that the House was so deeply moved. Lord Hartington, under the inspiration of the speech, paid a high compliment to the noble-minded ex-Premier.

Aug. 6th.—At the Ministerial Association Meeting this morning, I mentioned the subject of the gambling-machine, yclept, 'the Totalizator,' and suggested that we should petition the Parliament against the re-enactment of the law permitting its use. The Rev. James Lyall, the Rev. F. W. Cox, and I were appointed a sub-committee to look after the matter. The next day Mr. Lyall and I waited upon the Premier (Hon. Thomas Playford), to seek his advice as to how we should proceed. He advised that we should memorialise the Council. The Attorney General (Hon. C. C. Kingston) also advised that course. We therefore ordered the necessary bills, circulars, etc., and essayed to fulfil our mission. Mrs. E. S. Bickford, my niece, and Gerty, my great-niece, left us to-day for Melbourne.

Aug. 15th.—I wrote to the *Press* to-day a strong letter on Sir John Downer's Bill, now before the House, for extending the 'Law of Divorce' in this Colony. I am afraid that if this Bill be passed it will be followed by serious and far-reaching consequences.

Aug. 28th.—I began to-day writing an Autobiography of my life-work in the West Indies and Australia. But I want, at least, twenty years of younger life to do all that is in my heart to do. All my friends tell me that I ought to leave behind me such a record as that now contemplated. So, by God's help, I will try what can be done.

Sept. 13th.—Miss Jarvis and I left by 'express' for Victoria. At

Ballarat, the next morning, Mr. Thomas Wills, a very true and old friend, received us at the station, and we accompanied him to his home. In the course of the forenoon, the Rev. R. C. Flockart came for me to be his guest during my stay in the city. Miss Jarvis remained with my friends, Mr. and Mrs. Wills. On Sunday I preached in the new and beautiful church in Lydiard Street; and, in the evening, at Barkly Street. On Monday I gave my lecture on ' Irish Christianity ' in behalf of the Trust funds. I saw many of my friends, dating back to 1857, and I was greatly pleased with their remembrance of me.

Sept. 18th.—We left for Kew this morning by train. At the Spencer Street Station, Melbourne, I saw my nephew, the Rev. E. S. Bickford in the crowd, with whom we left for his home. We spent a quiet, delightful evening.

Sept. 20th.—We went to the great ' Exhibition.' We were, in all, quite a little party—the Rev. E. S. and Mrs. Bickford, Mrs. J. B. Smith, Mrs. McKensie, Miss McKensie, Miss Jarvis, and myself. This ' Exhibition ' is worthy of our grand Australian history. A marvel of skilful arrangement and uncounted wealth. Such a gathering of peoples, from many lands, at such a time and place, is suggestive of the bounties of God's providence, of the Divine Mission of the Austral-Englishman, and of the inexhaustible character of the material resources of the possessions of the Crown in the Southern World.

Sept. 21st.—I and my nephew, E. S. Bickford, went to Frankston for Home Mission objects. The next day (' Sabbath ') I heard the Rev. R. Osborne Cook preach an excellent sermon on the ' choice of Moses.' There were both originality and force in the construction and delivery of the discourse. At 3 p.m. I addressed the Sunday School, and in the evening I preached. We held the public meeting the next day; Mr. Cook and I were the speakers. I tried to develop the whole scheme of Home Missionary operations in Victoria, so as to induce a sympathetic co-operation of the Circuit with the Society in its widespread efforts. Treby Bickford Moysey, my nephew, whom I had not seen for many years, called upon me in the afternoon. He bids fair to become a rich man, and I pray that he may be a good, Christian man also. I left my hospitable friends, Mr. and Mrs. Cook, on the morning of the 26th, and joined my nephew at the station to call upon the Rev. J. B. and Mrs.

PRINCE'S BRIDGE, MELBOURNE.

Smith at South Brighton. We proceeded from thence to Kew, where we arrived in the evening.

Sept. 28*th.*—We went to Northcote to spend a few days with my brother, N. M. Bickford and Mrs. Bickford. Sunday morning we worshipped once more together in God's house. This was a great pleasure to me. The Rev. Samuel Cuthbert preached to a devout and interested congregation. I occupied the pulpit in the evening. Subject, 'The Pentecostal Church in Jerusalem.'

Oct. 1*st.*—I went to Carlton to see my sister, Mrs. Wyett, Mr. Wyett, and Laura. In the afternoon I called at Queen's College, and saw the Rev. E. H. and Mrs. Sugden, with whom I was much pleased. Here we have a noble Institution, well-manned, well-cared-for, and well patronised. It must be, in every respect, a great blessing to the youth of the Golden Colony.

Oct. 2*nd.*—I had the pleasure of seeing at the Book Room Revs. Symonds, Binks, Quick, Wells, Crisp, Daniels, Rigg, Shaw, and Howard. It was a pleasant surprise to me.

Oct. 4*th.*—A notable day for Melbourne. The new Prince's Bridge was opened to-day for general traffic. It has three spans, each of 120 feet, and a land span of 24 feet, while its measurement from end to end is a fraction over 400 feet, and its width 99 feet; 63 feet being taken up by the carriage-way, and 18 feet on each side of the footpath. David Munroe & Co. were the contractors. It is a glorious structure, and apparently as strong as solid rock.

Oct. 6*th.*—My niece and I went to Geelong, and found Miss Hitchcock at the station awaiting our arrival. I preached in Yarra Street on Sunday morning, and addressed the Sunday School in the afternoon. In the evening I heard the Rev. Thomas Angwin preach. He and I gave the Lord's Supper at the after service. It was a specially good day to me. Blessed be the Lord !

Oct. 8*th.*—My kind hostess, Mrs. Hitchcock, drove us to the Orphan Asylum, Bell-post Hill, etc. It was a most delightful drive. In the evening we took tea at Mr. and Mrs. Thomas Daniels', and spent a most delightful time with them, Mr. and Mrs. W. Thacker. and other friends.

Oct. 9*th.*—We took lunch at Mr. and Mrs. Oldfield's, and called upon many of my former charge. It did my old heart good to see them again.

Oct. 12*th.*—At Kew I gave a lecture to the 'Young Men's Mutual

Improvement Society,' the Rev. P. R. C. Ussher, presiding; subject, 'A Talk on the West Indies.' I was heartily thanked for the address.

Oct. 14th.—I preached at Brighton and South Brighton. We spent a nice time with our dear friends the Smiths. I took services at Clifton Hill, Kew, and St. Kilda, when I had the gratification, always welcome to an old Itinerant, of seeing familiar faces again, and of worshipping our one Father together. And this was my happiness to the full.

Nov. 7th. [Diary Jotting]—'We left our dear kindred at Kew this afternoon for Spencer Street Station. We said good-bye to our old friends, the Rev. John and Mrs. Harcourt, and Mr. James Lowe came along with us to help us with our "traps." My brother Nicholas, Frank, my nephew, Edwin Pascoe, were there to see us off. At Ballarat, my unfailing friends, the Wills, were at the station with tea and other good things to help us on our journey. From Dimboola to Adelaide my niece and I had the carriage to ourselves. We reached the Adelaide Station the next day, and found Mr. William Gully there with his trap to convey us to Parkside. I met my class in the evening.

'What a host of matters I have to attend to from being away eight weeks! Our back garden is smothered with weeds, and looks like a forsaken wilderness. And so will the heart be choked, in the absence of care and cultivation, by the noxious presence of sin and temptation.'

Nov. 15th.—Working hard at the Autobiography. In the evening I read in the *London Quarterly* for a couple of hours; article, 'The Self-revelation of God.' Tough reading, and unadapted for general use.

Nov. 16th.—I went to Norwood to see my friend the Rev. William Jenkins, P.M.M., who is in a dying condition; Rev. Wellington and I prayed with him, and commended his soul to God. He was always a good, earnest man in the Lord's work.

Dec. 10th.—I went to the Ministerial Association Meeting, and heard Dr. Hannay's address. It was, after its way, no doubt, able, but it bristled with points of controversy. But for these we had no time. I moved a vote of thanks. I read in the afternoon in Fish's 'Conferences of the Reformers and Divines of the Early English Church, on the Doctrines of the Oxford Tractarians.' It seems to me to be an admirable summary of potent arguments against the 'High Oxford Party,' and shows them up as in dead opposition to the principles of the English Reformers, who were the founders of the ' Reformed Protestant Church of England.' The motto on the ' Title-page,' chosen by the reverend compiler of the work, is singularly well chosen :—

> ' The peace of the Church, and the unity of her doctrine, is best conceived when it is judged by the proportion to that rule of unity which the Apostles gave ; that is, the creed for articles of mere belief, and the precepts of Jesus Christ, and the practical rules of piety, which are most plain and easy, and, without controversy, set down in the Gospels and writings of the Apostles. But to multiply articles, and adopt them into the family of faith, and to require assent to such articles, which, as St. Paul's phrase, are of doubtful disputation, equal to that assent we give to matters of faith, is to build a tower on the top of a bulrush, and the further the effect of such proceedings does extend, the worse they are."—JEREMY TAYLOR.

Dec. 12th.—I went to Adelaide to meet the President. There were ten brethren present. The President read a letter of resignation from David O'Donnell, caused by the action of the General Conference in appointing him to New Zealand, instead of to the Victoran Conference, which he requested. We agreed that a reply should be sent, suggesting to him to reconsider his action.

Dec. 17th.—I presided at the Pirie Street Missionary Meeting this evening. The Rev. William Reid gave us a very effective speech on Fiji, confirming from his recent observation in the Group the grand successes of our missionary brethren. At all events, there has been brought about the complete cessation of heathen, savage customs; and the archipelago of islands is now a colony of the British Crown.

Dec. 31st.—I buried the mortal remains of poor Mrs. Slater ; 'from sufferings and from woes released.' I baptized the motherless baby on our return from the Cemetery. A dreadful accident occurred last night in ' the Hills,' about two and a half miles from Mitcham, by the overturning of a coach full of picknickers; one young man was killed, and several young persons were seriously injured. If the party had returned by daylight this catastrophe had not happened.

The ' Watch Night Service ' was held by the Rev. H. C. George and myself. We had a good attendance, and a solemn time of heart-searching and of consecration to God. With this service I finish fifty years of Christian work in the Lord's vineyard. And so the story of my Autobiography is ended.   I think the desire to write such an account must have been from God, for I find in my Diary for August 1st, 1888, the following jotting :—

' In the evening, whilst reading the *London Quarterly*, an inspiration came upon me, *re* the West Indies, the anniversary of the freedom of whose slaves, in 1838, we commemorate this day.   Possibly this may be the beginning of an autobiographical record of fifty years' work in the West Indies and Australia. Who can tell ? '

CONCLUSION.

'Australia is in an ocean by herself."—GOLDWIN SMITH.

WE are indebted to the Churches of Christ for building up the Australia of to-day. Yet we are of such modern growth, that this fact is hardly known among the older nations of the world. The ignorance that prevails even in Great Britain of the material and ecclesiastical condition of Australia is extraordinary. Probably, few of English statesmen are seized of the idea that a possession of 1,884,591,920 acres, here in these seas, has been, in the order of Divine Providence, donated to the Anglo-Saxon race; and that already there has sprung up between the five Colonies of Australia and Great Britain, America, etc., a commerce of imports and exports of an annual value of £106,208,599 sterling. But, inclusive of Tasmania and New Zealand, it amounts to £112,862,353 sterling. And, although we are only ' of yesterday,' we have a population of over three millions; whilst, with Tasmania and New Zealand added, we have close upon four million souls. It is estimated that, in twenty years, from fifteen to eighteen millions of people will be settled in Australasia.

The ecclesiastical arrangements are all that Anglo-Australians can reasonably expect. There being no State Church, the most perfect religious equality obtains. With our free and independent parliaments, elected upon the basis of a manhood suffrage, there need be no fear of any legislative meddling with the rights of the people to worship their Creator according to the dictates of their own consciences, and to support such of the Churches as they shall choose. Every denomination stands on its own merits, and all duly appointed ministers are estimated at their real worth as moral reformers and pastors of the people. Our systems of public instruction are intended to carry the benefits of educational training to every child of school-age, and to be had by the payment of a small

fee, or no fee at all.   Ministers of religion, as such, are eligible to
sit on 'Boards of Advice;' but they are never elected to that
position.   In each Colony, excepting perhaps Western Australia, a
Minister of the Crown is the authorised head of 'Public Instruction,'
and is directly responsible to Parliament.

He would be a bold man who attempted to cast the horoscope of
the Australias.   That there is no serious thought of separation from
the Mother Country must be patent to every observant man who
moves much amongst the people; and no such feeling is likely to
arise, as long as the Australian Parliaments are not interfered with
in matters of domestic legislation.   The veto of the Crown must be
sparingly used.   There is, however, no idolatrous reverence for
Imperialism, which can never become a 'fetish' amongst us.   The
trend of political feeling, as far as we can judge, is in favour of a
Republican form of Government, rather than to be under the heel of
the Colonial Office, and subject to interference by the Houses of
Lords and Commons.

An Australian empire, at no distant period, is the cynosure to
which all eyes are looking, as certainly as that the needle points to
the Pole.   But even in that form—if such be the will of Providence—
the great South Empire would not be in antagonism to, but be a
loving and strong ally of, England in any struggles she might have
with Continental powers.   Such a fair and true daughter, as
Australia has proved herself to be, would not forsake her 'Old
Mother' in a time of extremity.   Still, the policy in the main must
ever be: 'Peace' within our own borders, and 'Peace' without,
with all the world.

Printed by Hazell, Watson, & Viney, Ld., London and Aylesbury.

www.ingramcontent.com/pod-product-compliance
Lightning Source LLC
Chambersburg PA
CBHW032008110726

47901CB00004B/1013